Shining Praise For...

Also by Johanna Kingsley

SCENTS
FACES

JOHANNA KINGSLEY

TREASURES

WARNER BOOKS

A Time Warner Company

WARNER BOOKS EDITION

Cover photography by Don Banks
Cover design by Anne Twomey

Warner Books, Inc.
666 Fifth Avenue
New York, N.Y. 10103

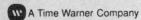 A Time Warner Company

Printed in the United States of America

This book was originally published in hardcover by Warner Books.
First Printed in Paperback: December, 1991

10 9 8 7 6 5 4 3 2 1

For my own irreplaceable diamonds—big and little

TREASURES

Prologue

Pietra D'Angeli lifted her hand again. The room was dim, with only a single bedside lamp burning, but the meager light was pulled into the heart of the diamond on her finger and sent back as beams of fire and color.

She had looked at many diamonds in her life—studied them—yet the one sparkling on her hand meant more than all the rest. Its worth lay not merely in the qualities that jewelers called the four C's: color, clarity, carat weight, and cut proportion.

This stone made solid a man's intention to spend the rest of his life with her.

Was she ready to give herself to him?

Though dressed only in a filmy nightgown, "Pete" D'Angeli pushed out through the doors that led onto the terrace of her penthouse and gazed down at the velvety darkness of Central Park, the streetlamps strung out against it like glittery hailstones. A single hansom cab rolled slowly along the curving road that skirted Fifth Avenue. In New York, even at three o'clock in the morning, the stage was set for lovers.

Why did she still hesitate to accept her own lover? Did she have to follow a pattern that had been set by others—

dictated by another Pietra, her namesake—even before she was born, a search for treasures around which others had built their lives? Did she have to rescue those who had been wounded by the quest? Surely it was time to live for herself. Time to seize the treasures of the heart.

Once more she lifted her finger, to see if the diamond could trap even a moonbeam.

The loud clanging of the alarm bell sounded at that moment, spilling from the open door behind her, shattering the stillness of the night. Pete whirled and ran inside. She was already heading for the phone when her housekeeper, Maddy, burst into the room a moment later.

"My God, Miss! Isn't that from the store?"

Seeing how distressed the housekeeper was, Pete swerved from the phone and went to her. The store had been open more than a year now, but this was the first time the direct alarm tied to the apartment had ever gone off. A shocking sound.

"Yes, somebody must have broken in. But don't worry, Maddy. The police will be there in minutes." Pete gave the woman a reassuring squeeze. "Now hurry and make me some coffee. I'll need something to get my engine running."

Calm now that she had something to do, the housekeeper ran off to the kitchen. Pete turned quickly to the bedside table and pressed a red button on the base of the phone. The alarm stopped as suddenly as it had started. She punched another button, a direct line to the store, but she got only the bleep-bleep of a busy signal. They must be trying to reach her, too. Instead of trying another line, she started hurrying into her clothes.

Her outfit for the next day was already laid out on a chaise: skirt and blouse, underwear beside them, appropriate jewelry in the pockets, shoes and handbag on the floor. She stepped into the alligator pumps as she buttoned the green silk blouse, smoothed the camel-hair skirt as she reached for a hairbrush.

She was gathering her heavy, dark hair into a loose French twist when the phone rang. She secured the hair with two combs of silver and lapis lazuli and picked up the phone.

"Pete, it's Jim Bateman. Just want you to know I'm here already. Cops are on the job, too."

"Good. I'm on my way," Pete told the head of her store security. "How bad is it, Jim?"

"It's a robbery, Pete, that's bad enough. I haven't had a chance yet to check what's missing. From a quick look, though, I can see they left a lot of good stuff."

Pete sighed and hung up. No time for makeup. She grabbed only a lipstick and ran from the room.

Maddy caught her at the elevator with a cup of steaming coffee. Pete drank it down gratefully.

"If there are any calls, Maddy, don't say where I am." The elevator arrived and Pete stepped in. "Could be anybody—newspapers, insurance men. I don't want to start an unnecessary stampede at the store."

"I understand, Miss."

Pete left the housekeeper with the cup and nodded to the elevator man to take her down.

Eight blocks farther down Fifth Avenue, police cars flashed their lights in a circle around the entrance to Tesori–New York, the newest and grandest in the chain of Tesori stores around the world. Begun in Lugano, in the Italian corner of Switzerland—a heritage marked by the company's name, the Italian word for "treasures"—Tesori had spent its first two decades establishing branches in all the capitals of Europe, casting what some called a "jeweled web" over the Continent. More recently it had expanded to Caracas and Rio, to Tokyo, and finally to the United States. The branch in New York, though located on the same stretch of Fifth Avenue as such established jewelers as Harry Winston, Cartier, Bulgari, Tiffany, and Dufort & Ivères, made no attempt to rival the others in size.

Yet there was a flair to the store, as conceived and managed by Pietra D'Angeli, that enabled it to attract as many customers as its bigger rivals—customers with as much of an appetite for the most expensive stones and the most original pieces, especially those designed by Pete herself. In fact, the

New York Tesori was now regarded as the flagship outlet of the entire firm.

Half running, half walking, Pete covered the eight blocks from her apartment to the store in less than five minutes.

"Over here, Pete!"

The call came from Jim Bateman, a barrel-chested man with a thin blond moustache. He was one of a dozen men standing in front of the store, some talking, others writing in notebooks, others looking along the ground like shell hunters at the beach.

Pete hurried toward Bateman in the glare of police flood-lights, her eyes scanning the display windows. The thick armored glass, beveled and faceted so it looked like a jewel itself, was intact. Behind it jewels—gemstones and pearls—tumbled out of silver buckets in profusion. By day the glitter was real, worth millions; at night, cut glass replaced the genuine stones. In fact, Bateman had begged her to remove even the glass rather than bait robbers who wouldn't know the difference.

"Jewel thieves are a sophisticated crowd," Pete had argued. "The type who break armored windows will know good stuff from bad. But leaving a little glass gives the ladies who stroll by at night something to dream about—something they can send their gentlemen in to buy when we open our doors in the morning." Jim Bateman stopped resisting her. Who could say which of Pete's ideas accounted for Tesori having the highest sales per square foot of any top jeweler in the world? You didn't argue with success.

Pete came up to her security chief. "Good morning, Mr. B." She put as much cheer into it as she could, taking it as her job to lift the morale of the troops.

"Not quite so good," Bateman countered.

"You get a better idea of what's missing? You look a lot grimmer than you sounded on the phone."

"Mainly it seems we've got a lot of heavy housekeeping to do. Take a look." With a gentle hand on her arm, he steered her through the main entrance into the store.

Inside was a scene of confusion. Many of the glass counters

had been smashed open, jewelry pulled out and scattered around like rice after a wedding. Diamond rings littered the black granite floor. Emerald bracelets and ruby necklaces were strewn across display cases. A rare opera-length double strand of black pearls snaked across an Art Deco chaise longue supplied for customers, and dangled to the floor.

Faced with this scene of chaos, Pete had to struggle for control against the rage that swelled up inside her, rage at those who could treat so much beauty with such obvious contempt. She reached for a diamond brooch lying on the floor by her feet.

Jim stopped her. "Don't touch anything, Pete. The photographers and fingerprint boys have to cover it first."

She straightened. "Of course. I'd still like to know how much we lost."

"Can't be sure till we sweep up and take inventory, but the estimate so far is very little. Nothing major, anyway."

A wiry man wearing a sport jacket with a loud check came over and stuck his hand out to Pete. "Miss D'Angeli, Captain Dave Petroselli," he announced himself. "I'm with the—"

"I know, Captain," Pete said. Even if she hadn't noted the police I.D. hanging from the handkerchief pocket of his jacket, she would have recognized Petroselli's name. As a specialist in robberies involving jewels, rare artifacts, or valuable paintings, he was something of a legend. "I'm glad you're on the case."

"A place like Tesori's gets hit, that's my beat." He looked around. "At first glance, it seems you got off pretty lucky. Smart jewel thieves usually go after medium-sized pieces they can move fast at a good price, or stuff they can break up and sell as loose stones. Most of the things I see lying around fit that description, but they weren't taken. And Mr. Bateman says the big pieces are here, all tucked away in your safe. So they were after something else."

Bateman nodded a confirmation at Pete. "Even the workroom, where we keep a lot of unset stones, wasn't touched."

Pete shook her head and waved to the mess around her.
"I don't get it. What was all this for if they didn't want
anything?"

"I didn't say they didn't want *anything*," the detective
said. "I think maybe they made the mess as a kind of distraction, to put us off the scent a bit, slow us down from
getting a quick fix on what they really wanted."

"Which was . . . ?"

"You tell me," Petroselli said. "I'm only guessing, but
I think whoever came in here was looking for something very
particular. In fact . . . I think it may have been an inside job.
Someone who knew there was something pretty special hidden away. Do you know of anything like that, Miss D'Angeli?
Something you were keeping, something that maybe only a
few people—"

"Oh God," Pete gasped suddenly, and dashed straight for
the stairs leading to the offices on the mezzanine.

Panting when she reached her own office, she threw open
the door, stumbled in, and switched on the overhead lights.
There it stood—her private safe, the door hanging wide to
reveal its emptiness. The darkness within seemed vast beyond
the confines of a mere metal box, the darkness of a past that
now could never be fully known.

The treasure was gone.

She sank to her knees before the open safe. Tears stung
her eyes, tears of anger, frustration, disappointment. She let
them fall and looked down as they rained onto her lap, where
her hands were knotted into fists.

She saw the diamond on her finger then, and she thought
again about him, about what was important. Must she go on
chasing old dreams, following other people's obsessions? One
treasure was gone, but another of a different kind could take
its place.

No. God help her, she had to have *this* one. Without it the
old mystery could never be unraveled, the old injustice never
put right. The two that were separate could never become
one.

She had to answer the questions of the past before she
could go on to the future.

BOOK
I

~

Settings

Chapter 1

Tuscany—1938

The jewels glittered on the rows of satin pillows on her bed. Necklaces, bracelets, tiaras, rings. Dozens of them. And the pins that had been designed specially for her. It was the first time she had looked at the entire collection in years. She had never really needed to look until now. Laying the jewels out one by one was merely part of the process of making a written inventory. Even now, seeing them was scarcely necessary. There were more than a hundred pieces, but she knew them all by heart.

By heart, exactly. For every one had been the bounty of love, proof of some man's devotion.

Reaching down almost at random into the field of sparkle, she lifted a long necklace of large emeralds set with diamonds, draped it around her neck, and went to a mirror—one of the many placed around the ornate bedroom, for she had never needed to be afraid of mirrors. Even now, in her seventh decade, the reflecting silver showed a woman of great beauty who looked twenty years younger. Kept young, many said, by a very simple sorcery—the magic of being loved, of receiving the passionate attention of so many admirers over so many years . . .

9

Ah, the emeralds. Seeing them on her now, set off by her ivory skin, they threw off memories as easily as they refracted the light. They had been given to her by a prince, in a tryst the night before his arranged marriage to a duchess from another country. Something green, he had said, to complement her sapphire eyes and reflect the inky blackness of her hair.

But that was long ago . . . in a time of princes. In this new age power was in the hands of brutal men with no breeding, men whose dream of conquest was not simply to possess a beautiful woman, but to desecrate nations, their art, their culture . . .

The thought sent her hurrying back to the bed to begin gathering up the jewels, returning them to the separate boxes in which she had stored them over the years. She concealed them again in a special closet behind the panels of the room and then sat down at her dressing table.

In the center lay a box crafted of jade about six inches square—a valuable item itself, but insignificant compared to the single object it contained, the one thing she had omitted from her carefully prepared inventory.

Opening the box, she lifted it from a bed of thick rose silk, the greatest of her treasures, unique in her collection, for it was not to be worn. It was, at first glance, simply a figure of a gowned, bejeweled woman some five inches in height, as intricately wrought as any of the imperial Easter eggs made by Fabergé. The head was made of enameled gold with sapphire eyes, the shoulders formed a single baroque pearl. A heart-shaped ruby formed the bodice of the gown, and diamonds and emeralds covered the skirt in swirled lines that made the figure seem to be twirling in a dance. From beneath the hem poked slippers of gleaming black pearl.

For a moment she admired it, drifting again into a memory of the man who had given it to her. The gift had come as the world was facing the threat of a great war, she remembered—as she feared it was again. Perhaps it was appropriate that the figure should be given into other hands now that the circumstances were so similar.

Given . . . though not quite in the same form. Grasping

the top of the figure with one hand and the lower part with the other, she twisted gently and the figure separated into two halves. The air was suddenly redolent with the leftover fragrance of long-dried perfume rising from the small golden bottle within the figure.

She sat with the two halves, one in each hand, balancing them, pondering the decisions she had reached this day. She recalled the story of King Solomon sitting in judgment over two women both claiming the same child. ''Very well,'' he ruled at last, ''the child shall be cleaved in two, and half given to each.'' When one of the women wailed in protest at the decision, he awarded her the child, alive and intact, knowing that she must be the true mother.

But there was no one to say she should not divide this possession in two—a mere bottle. It represented the end for her, she thought, a kind of death. There were the secrets, too, that she would be forced to divulge.

But what choice was there? Looking at the two pieces of the bottle, she realized that they represented the perfect embodiment of her feelings. For the perfume bottle had been created as an image of her—and she was being torn in half by what the world had become and by the choice she was being forced to make.

Chapter 2

Milan—1938

Il Duce a Milano!

The ink on the hastily printed placards had begun to run like black tears when the rain started, but the message and the face were still discernible in the evening light. Papers and pamphlets left over from the afternoon's rally littered the Piazza del Duomo, plastered to the pavement by the rain.

Stefano D'Angeli stood at the window of his office, staring down at the age-old stones of the cathedral square, empty now but for a few hurrying black umbrellas with legs peeking out from under them. The pink marble statues, gargoyles, and pinnacles of the great Duomo were dripping. He could even see the little gilded *Madonnina* atop the highest spire glistening wetly as though weeping for what she had seen a few hours earlier.

All afternoon the roar of the crowd shouting, *"Viva il Duce!"* had reverberated off the stones. The strains of the "Giovinezza," the Fascist anthem, had echoed in the air, spilling into Stefano's office and making his work as a law apprentice all but impossible. What made it hardest was knowing that somewhere in the mob of chanting fools had been his own brother.

12

Stefano returned to his desk, ran his fingers through his thick jet black hair, and picked up the brief he'd been trying to complete all day. Bad enough he'd been unable to concentrate with all the chanting and cheering outside, the work itself bored him even on the best days. At twenty-four, was his life already mapped out as an endless string of days in offices and courtrooms? He'd rather be under a tree beside a river writing a poem, or reading Dante, or sitting in one of the cafes in the Via Verdi discussing art and literature with his friends.

"You should have left by now," said Carlo Brancusi as he walked into the room.

"I haven't finished this brief."

"It can wait. You have a long drive ahead of you, and with the rain . . ."

Stefano looked up at Brancusi, the firm's senior lawyer. His was a commanding face, the face of a Roman emperor engraved on an ancient coin. The nose, large and long and definitely patrician, ruled the other features. His hair was still mahogany brown, except at the silver-brushed temples, his eyebrows dark and commanding over deep brown eyes. A face that inspired trust.

"Is it really necessary for Vittorio to go with me?" asked Stefano. "After today . . . well, you know how enthusiastic he is. Probably shouted himself hoarse at the front of the rabble out there, and I'll have to listen to his love songs to Il Duce all night in the car. Sometimes I wonder if one of us was switched at birth with some other child. I don't see how we can really be brothers."

Signor Brancusi smiled and laid a hand on the young man's shoulder. "These are certainly times that require patience, Stefano. Even patience with one's brother. There can be no deviation from the instructions given to me by this client. Both you and Vittorio are to make the journey, and she will expect you to arrive no later than midnight."

"I'm not sure I can survive several hours of his company." Stefano laughed as he stood up. "Or his driving. But for you, Carlo, I will take the risk."

"For my client. She's an unusual woman. You won't be sorry you met her."

"All right, Carlo, for her." They walked together to the door, and Brancusi helped Stefano into his overcoat. In farewell, they embraced like father and son, for that was what they were, if not by blood then by the bonds of the heart. Brancusi was not only Stefano's employer, he'd been guardian to both him and his brother since they were infants. Their parents, friends of Brancusi, had been killed in a railroad station by the explosion of an anarchist's bomb—the sort of outrage that Il Duce had promised to eliminate, thus helping bring him and his Blackshirts to power.

It was growing dark and bone-chillingly cold as Stefano stepped into the piazza. He turned up his collar and hunched down inside his coat, his hands pushed into the pockets. Walking across the square, he couldn't avoid the drifts of paper left behind from the Fascist rally. They stuck to his shoes, to the cuffs of his pant legs. They were everywhere.

Pockmarked by rain, the belligerent face of Mussolini stared up at him. "Conqueror of Ethiopia," "Redeemer of Italy," the flyers cried. Ridiculous, Stefano thought as he kicked at the offensive propaganda. He saw no redemption in the scowling heavyset face. He saw only cruelty.

How could his brother follow this man, believe he was—what had Vittorio said in their last argument?—"the new Caesar"? To Stefano, fat Benito would never be anything but a scoundrel who knew how to manipulate his countrymen's love of good theater. Give them a good show and keep them well fed, and they wouldn't stop to think about the cost to their pocket or their conscience. The old Caesars had known the formula, too, Stefano mused— bread and circuses. Now it looked like Il Duce was about to join forces with Der Führer. What a circus that would be. What a pair of clowns! Joining hands in a joint rampage with all Europe as the butt of their deadly jokes. They'd rape the Continent in their lust for power and territory, Stefano was sure. Even *la bella figura* of Italy herself would not be spared.

And Vittorio would gladly help. He was making his way

up through the party hierarchy already, spouting its slogans. He spoke of the new Axis as "a natural joining of two moral leaders" to purge Europe of its "decadent elements." Which to him meant its poetry and culture, imagination, that wonderful inborn Italian *dolce vita*—in short, everything Stefano lived for.

As he approached the arcaded buildings on the north side of the piazza, a voice called softly, "*Caro. Vieni qui, caro.*"

He smiled at the prostitute and called back a good-natured "*Ciao, bella*" before walking on. Milan was full of whores, but at least they were honest whores, working to feed and clothe themselves, to survive. Vittorio was much worse than the woman in the piazza. He willingly prostituted himself in the service of the *Fascisti* merely so he could grow richer and fatter.

Stefano stepped through the triumphal arch that marked the entrance to Milan's glorious shopping arcade, the Galleria. Inside, gray evening light filtered through the high, glass-domed roof and mixed with the warmer glow from ivory incandescent globes, bathing the space in a pearly haze. Once or twice he tipped his hat to an acquaintance as he made his way through the throng, his heels clicking on the mosaic pavement. The Milanese called the Galleria *il salotto*, the living room. Friends greeted friends. Shoppers strolled from store to store. Two matrons on their way to Savini, where Verdi and Puccini had dined, argued the merits of the latest tenor at La Scala. In the window of Biffi, two lovers gazed at each other across a damask-covered table, their *aperitivi* untouched. Stefano walked through the Galleria with a smile on his face. How he loved Milano! But would it survive Il Duce?

Near the end of the long gallery, Stefano turned into the door of his brother's store, one of the most elegant leather and paper goods shops in all Milan. Until recently, it had belonged to a wealthy Jewish merchant—owned by his family for three generations. Now the Jew was gone, "persuaded" to immigrate to South America with nothing but his family and his life. Because of his party connections, Vittorio had been given an opportunity to purchase the shop and all its contents at a fraction of its true value.

Vittorio D'Angeli stood behind a counter, checking over a ledger. He and his brother were like night and day in more than their politics. Where Stefano was lean and moved with a natural grace, Vittorio was large and burly and had a way of moving that suggested he was out of rhythm with the world around him. In contrast to Stefano's black hair, Vittorio's was a pale brown, not quite light enough to be called blond, and his eyes were also a nondescript brown. The shape of his nose and mouth were not unlike Stefano's, but they were balanced differently in his broad face, so that he wasn't nearly as attractive.

He looked up from his ledger as soon as Stefano entered. "I was expecting you at six," he said curtly, pulling out his gold pocket watch. "You're late—as usual."

Stefano went to the counter. "Forgive me, brother," he replied, his pleading tone mockingly exaggerated. "I may have paused a moment to smell the rain or to smile at a pretty girl."

Vittorio closed the ledger with a bang and began walking around the shop, checking that the display cases of beautiful wallets and briefcases were locked, the shelves full of marbleized paper goods neatly arranged, ready for the next day's business. "Probably you've been lounging in a cafe, scribbling some of that drivel you call poetry. There's nothing you like so much as dreaming away your days. If I didn't know better, Stefano, I'd think you'd been born a lazy Roman. But this is Milan. In Milan we work. We get things done. On time."

"Well, any day now your wonderful Benito may find a way to put people on a rigid schedule just like he's done for the trains. But until he does, I intend to enjoy myself."

Vittorio glared at him, and Stefano expected the defense of Il Duce to begin at once. But instead, Vittorio took a different line of attack. "My God, how can I think of going anywhere with you, being seen in your company. Hair un-

cut, hanging in your eyes, your tie crooked, shoes unshined.
You look like a gypsy."

Of course, Vittorio was his brother's opposite in this, too.
Though only four years older than Stefano, he had a much
more substantial air about him. Since he'd come up in the
world, he had taken to dressing in the staid—and
expensive—manner of a banker twice his age. White shirts
made at Truzzi, black shoes mirror-shined from di Ballini.
His gray serge suit was exquisitely hand-tailored, his burgundy silk foulard perfectly knotted.

"But even if I didn't mind being seen with gypsies,"
Vittorio continued, switching off the lights, "I can't see
why I have to be involved in this business of yours."

"It's not mine. It's for Carlo."

"All the same, why should I drive across half of Italy
in the dead of night just to visit one of his fool clients?
You are his apprentice, not me."

"And we are *both* in his debt. Without him we—"

"Yes, yes, we'd have been put in the orphanage. Must
I listen to that sob story again? I'm taking care of myself
now. I need a better reason for doing anything for Brancusi
than just because I should kiss his hands with gratitude every
day of my life." There was only one light left on now, by
the door. Vittorio went to retrieve his coat from a rack. "I
was invited to go to La Scala tonight with the regional party
secretary. There had better be a damn good reason why I
should give that up."

Stefano eyed his brother with amazement. How could he
be so devoid of feeling? Or was that what made Vittorio
the perfect party functionary? Harshly, Stefano said, "If you
need a practical reason, brother, it's because you own a car
and I don't. What's more, the client asked specifically that
we both come."

This made Vittorio pause. "Yes? That's interesting. Who
is he?"

"It's a woman. She's told Carlo she has some valuables
she wants transported."

Vittorio's eyes sparked with interest, as Stefano had

known they would. "Aha, I see. A *contessa*, perhaps? A *principessa*? Well, that explains why she asked to have someone reliable on this mission. She'd hardly want to turn over her valuables to a ragman like you." He smoothed his kid gloves over his large hands, brushed an invisible speck from his hat, set it on his slicked-back hair, and took his umbrella from the rack. "Well, let's go then. You've made us late enough already." Vittorio opened the door and with a gesture swept Stefano outside and locked up behind him.

As they walked the length of the Galleria, a number of female eyes trailed them. But it was not Vittorio with his custom-made suit and highly polished shoes who caught the attention of the Rosas, the Ginas, and the Francescas lounging in the cafes. It was Stefano, with his silky hair, his ocean-blue eyes, his dancer's grace. No matter what clothes he wore, he had a natural elegance, a bearing that spoke of sensitivity and a grin that hinted at fun.

As they stepped out into the piazza, Vittorio pointed with the tip of his umbrella to the far side where his car was parked. Then he raised the umbrella against the persistent drizzle, mixed now with the heavy fog that so often blanketed Milan.

"You should have been at the rally," he said. "Thousands . . . tens of thousands of loyal citizens turned out to welcome Il Duce."

"I heard them. And I can see for myself the mess they left behind. Someone will have to clean all this up." He kicked at a soggy picture of his brother's hero. "I wonder who will clean up his bigger messes."

"Be careful what you say, Stefano. You ought to realize by now that the future of every man in Italy will be determined by where he stands in relation to the party."

"You know where I would like to stand," said Stefano. "Right behind his high-and-mightiness so I could give him a swift kick in his fat ass."

Vittorio stopped, a mixture of alarm and fury twisting his features. "Stefano!" he hissed sotto voce, looking about to make sure no one could hear. "Don't take advantage of my good nature. I won't listen to any more of that talk, and you'd better be careful not to spout off like that to anyone else. It's true I have some influence, and, if things go as I expect, I will soon have more. But there is a limit to how much protection I can offer."

"I don't want your damn protection." Stefano walked on and Vittorio hurried after.

"And I suppose when our tanks begin to roll you will simply say, 'Don't bother me, I am reading a sonnet'?" Vittorio's lips expelled a scoffing puff of air. "I suppose you'll think I'm obliged to defend you anyway because you are my relative."

Stefano smiled wryly at the term. Relative, not brother. Already, it seemed, Vittorio was putting extra distance between them, preparing for the day when it would be impolitic to acknowledge him at all.

"Don't worry, brother," said Stefano, relishing the emphasis he put on the last word. "I won't expect you to defend me. If war comes, you'll be too busy defending yourself."

Vittorio grasped at Stefano's sleeve as though to pull him up short, but Stefano kept striding forward. "Listen to me, Stefano, they are making lists already. Lists of everyone who cannot be trusted, people whose doubts and cynicism can poison our dream of a new empire. I don't want your name taken down."

"For my sake? Or for your own?"

"It wouldn't be good for either of us," Vittorio answered.

"I'll keep that in mind," Stefano said.

They reached Vittorio's small Fiat and climbed in. Within minutes, they were out of the city center, racing south along the road toward Florence.

During the drive they were content to keep their silence. Stefano didn't like arguing with Vittorio, and it seemed that was all they were able to do lately. Better to say nothing. The rain had grown heavier, and the snick-snick of the windshield wipers was hypnotic. Stefano dozed as they drove through Lombardy, but he woke up as soon as they reached the Tuscan hills.

As a child, he'd spent summers in Tuscany at Carlo's summer villa. He had always felt most at home among the ocher and umber hills, as though he belonged here. Now, in the dark and with rain beating steadily against the windshield, he couldn't see the cypresses, the olive groves, the vines quilting the hillsides . . . but he could sense them. Tuscany, sweet as fermenting grapes, pungent as the first-pressed olives yielding their thick, virgin oil. This land had given birth to Dante and Petrarch, to Leonardo and Michelangelo, and the Etruscans before them. Perhaps that was why the land spoke to him.

As they passed a road sign indicating that Florence was ten kilometers ahead, Stefano reached into his coat and took out the envelope Brancusi had given him containing instructions and a hand-drawn map sent by the client. Unfolding the papers, Stefano switched on a map light and studied them.

He passed on the directions to Vittorio—left here, right there, leading to an estate in the hills outside Fiesole. The rain began tapering off, and in another twenty minutes they were approaching a long avenue of cypress guarded by marble pedestals chiseled with the name of the estate. As they made the turn, the headlight beams picked out the engraved letters: *La Tana*. A sweet name, Stefano thought—"The Nest."

Suddenly Vittorio slammed his foot on the brake so hard the car skidded forward through the wet gravel. Stefano had to brace himself against the dashboard to avoid hitting his head on the windshield.

"What the devil—?" Stefano erupted, glaring at Vittorio.

"You didn't tell me we were coming to La Tana," Vittorio complained.

"What of it?"

"Can you be so naive, Stefano? Don't you know who lives here?"

"Carlo said she's an interesting woman, that we'd be glad we met her."

"Glad, indeed! If she decides to do for us what she has done for half the rich men in Europe . . ."

Stefano gave his brother a puzzled look.

"So . . . Carlo didn't tell you about this woman, the mistress of La Tana?"

"No . . ."

"You've never heard anyone speak of La Colomba?"

Stefano's eyes flared with recognition. The Dove. Yes, of course, somewhere he'd heard of La Colomba—or read about her. A legendary woman, perhaps the most famous courtesan of her day. A woman who had made a career of love, never marrying yet linked with some of the greatest men of her time. There had been noblemen, artists, politicians, and famous opera-singers—even King Victor Emanuel himself was reputed to have loved her in his youth. It was said La Colomba was faithful to them all—but only for a year or two at a time—and out of her many liaisons, out of the gifts her lovers had bestowed upon her, she had become a very wealthy woman.

Vittorio threw the gear stick into reverse, and the car lurched backward.

"What are you doing?" Stefano snapped.

"Do you seriously think I am going to call on Europe's most notorious old whore? You may have no reason to care about your reputation, Stefano, but I'm not ruining mine. Not now."

Stefano put his hand over Vittorio's and pulled the shift out of gear. "Don't be an ass. She's a wealthy, intelligent woman. Beautiful too, I hear. A courtesan, perhaps, part of a tradition that's died out; but not a woman to be shunned. It's well known that she has many influential friends."

A mocking sound came from low in Vittorio's throat before he said, "Not for long. This is just the kind of decadence Il Duce will root out and banish completely from Italy. A whore having the ear of ministers and kings! Unpardonable." He peered out through the windows and his voice fell as he added, "I wouldn't be surprised if this place was already being watched."

"I'm not leaving," Stefano declared. "This is a duty I owe to Carlo."

"Yes," Vittorio muttered, "trust Brancusi to have such a client."

Stefano was on the verge of getting out of the car, saying he'd manage on his own and Vittorio could go . . . when the bright moon broke through the clouds. Ahead, on a gentle hill rising above the cypresses, they could see a huge villa bathed in silvery light. It was a magical sight, Stefano thought. Casting a glance across the car, he could see that even Vittorio was impressed.

"She chose the name of her home well," Vittorio said. "La Tana—the lair of foxes, where a vixen entraps her victims."

"La Tana also means 'the nest,' " Stefano said. "Perfect for the home of the Dove."

They gazed at it for another moment, then the clouds closed in again, blotting out the vision. But even that brief glimpse of La Tana had tantalized them both. Abruptly, without any urging from Stefano, Vittorio shifted back into forward gear and drove slowly through the gate and along the avenue of cypresses.

Minutes later, they pulled up before the villa. Built of pink and white marble in the Palladian style, it was fronted by a columned portico from which two long wings extended. The great iron-studded oak doors under the portico swung open even before Stefano could reach for the bell.

"Welcome, gentlemen," said the woman in the doorway. "Welcome to my home."

Stefano had expected a servant—a dozen servants—but this had to be La Colomba herself, the woman who had charmed Europe for nearly half a century. He stared, helpless to stop himself. He had never seen a woman who combined such elegance and beauty in a single form. Her glistening black hair was piled high on her head, pointing up the fineness of her bone structure. A silk gown of dusty rose embroidered with pearls hugged her still slender form and fell in soft folds to the floor. Her face was radiant, made more so by the blaze of diamonds at her neck. Cleopatra, Helen of Troy, Josephine . . . Eve herself . . . no

woman in history could have been more exquisite and alluring than La Colomba.

Stefano felt an unreasonable disappointment when she
turned to his brother first. "You must be Vittorio," she said,
extending a hand.

Stefano held his breath, concerned that Vittorio might
unleash his disapproval in a stream of insults. But after a
hesitation, he took her hand and gave it one swift pump.

She gave him a small smile and turned. "And you are
Stefano . . ."

On an impulse he could not control, he took her hand
and bent to kiss it. Her skin against his lips felt as soft and
smooth as a feather. When he looked up again, her sapphire
eyes held his, and she smiled very slightly, a smile that
brought a radiance to her face. He could understand how
she had made so many men love her.

"Please come in," she said. "I have been waiting for
you both for a very long time."

Vittorio hesitated, and Stefano noticed that his brother
wore a troubled, suspicious expression as he stepped over
the threshold.

As for himself, he already knew that he would do anything for this woman. Anything at all.

Chapter 3

As he stepped into the world of La Colomba, Stefano felt as if he were going back in time. The only sounds were the soft swish of her gown as she led them down a corridor and the resonant ticking of a porcelain-faced pediment clock. Even the rain beyond the heavily draped windows could no longer be heard. Candles burned everywhere—overhead in chandeliers, in wall sconces, in silver candelabra; their flames flickered off the polished surfaces of the countless priceless objects that filled La Tana: porcelain, ormolu statues, buhl tables, silver boxes, paintings in gilt frames.

At the end of the corridor a brighter light glowed, and she led them toward it. She moved with the grace of a girl one-third her age, Stefano thought, and with the confidence of a woman who had been feted on three continents.

When they turned into the sitting room, he sucked in his breath. It was a lovely room of golden accents against rose, pink, pale violet, and mauve. Cherubs cavorted in a painted sky overhead; flowers bloomed on a Savonnerie carpet underfoot. Paintings lined the walls. One, a naked odalisque wearing only a luminous string of pearls, drew Stefano toward it.

"Titian?" he asked reverently.

"Yes." She smiled, obviously pleased that he recognized it. "It's one of my favorites."

"And this," he said of another large canvas, an opulent nude resting her head against the white breast of a swan. "Rubens. Beautiful."

"Decadent," said Vittorio, but in a murmur. He was not unaware of the value of the paintings. In fact, he'd been totting up the price of every object he'd seen since entering the house. Degenerate she might be, but by God the woman was worth a fortune.

"Please sit down," she said and motioned them toward an arrangement of velvet-upholstered chairs and a sofa before a fireplace. As she gestured, the diamonds at her wrist caught the light of the dancing flames, tracing a luminous arc in the air. In front of the sofa, a table was set with a golden coffee pot, translucent china demitasse cups, and damask napkins on a lacquered tray.

Vittorio sat stiffly in one of the chairs, but Stefano moved at once to sit on the sofa beside La Colomba. Ambushed by her magic, he longed to become part of the aura she carried about her. He'd never met a woman who affected him so strongly. Her scent enchanted him; her voice soothed him; and though he'd been in her company only a few moments, he felt as though he knew her, had always known her.

As she picked up the pot to pour the coffee, the rings on her fingers flashed in the firelight. She wore them on every finger but one, Stefano noticed. Only the traditional ring finger of a bride was bare.

"I hope you will forgive me for serving you myself," she said. "I have asked the servants not to attend us. I thought our business better conducted in private." She finished filling the first demitasse and held it out to Vittorio. "I believe you drink yours black, Vittorio . . ."

For a second Vittorio's reaching hand froze and almost drew back as though fearing the coffee was poisoned. But when La Colomba kept offering the cup, her hand steady as a rock in front of him, Vittorio took it. The suspicion did not vanish from his eyes, however.

"And you, Stefano, you prefer yours with a dash of milk, do you not?"

"How do you know, Signora?" Stefano asked quietly as he accepted the cup.

"From Signor Brancusi."

Vittorio leaned forward. "And why does he think you would be interested in such things as the way we drink our coffee?"

Her eyes sparkled. "He knows I care about providing perfect hospitality to my guests, whoever they may be."

Vittorio frowned, clearly unsatisfied by the answer, but he was distracted from pursuing the matter by La Colomba's own question: "And how much do you know about me?"

Their answers came in unison. "Quite enough, Signora," said Vittorio. "Not enough, La Colomba," said Stefano.

She tossed her head back and laughed, a clear, bell-like sound Stefano could easily imagine ringing around a mirrored ballroom or floating up into the damask hangings of a lover's bed.

But her laughter seemed to irritate Vittorio even more. Finishing his coffee in a gulp, he set the cup aside and said briskly, "Signora, we have driven a long way in the rain in the middle of the night to satisfy your whim. Whatever business you have with us, please get on with it so we can be on our way."

Stefano was not only mortified by the tone Vittorio had taken but disappointed at the idea of cutting their visit short. He was about to dissociate himself from his brother's impatient demand, but La Colomba spoke first.

"You do not approve of me at all, do you, Vittorio?" she said in a tone surprisingly gentle and sympathetic.

"What is there to approve of, Madam? Everyone knows what you are . . ."

"Everyone? How very flattering. And you, Stefano, what do you think of me?"

He thought, hoped, he saw something different in her face when she looked at him, as though she was sincerely concerned about having his good opinion. "Your life has been an adventure," Stefano said. "I see nothing bad in that."

Vittorio rolled his eyes conspicuously.

"You are kind to say so," she told Stefano. Her eyes held a lovely softness as they dwelled on his face, but then they clouded and drifted toward the shadows of the room. "Unfortunately, my adventures have resulted in my making enemies as well as friends. And though I live quietly here, wanting nothing now but to be left alone with my gardens and my books, my farmers, and this house I love . . . there are foolish people who think of me as a dangerous woman." Her eyes focused and turned back to the brothers. "The result is that I must turn over something of great value that is no longer safe with me." Vittorio pulled up straighter in his chair. "But you are not to take it back to Carlo Brancusi."

"Not—" Vittorio began.

"It is my gift to you, both of you."

Stefano exchanged a baffled glance with his brother. "Why should you give us a gift?" he asked, though in the back of his mind an astounding possibility had already begun to form.

La Colomba reached for the gold pot on the tray. "Would either of you like more coffee?" she said. "Because to explain properly, I should tell you something of my life . . ."

"Signora, please," Vittorio objected. "I have no doubt your life story is very entertaining, very . . . colorful. But it is late, and I am needed in Milan in the morning."

She turned to him, her eyes flashing. "Oh yes, I know you are a busy man, Vittorio. Punctuality is something of a god with you, isn't it? You always enter your shop at exactly eight twenty-nine, arriving before your employees, unlocking the door with the keys you keep hanging on a gold chain at your waist. At eight thirty, the boy from the cafe brings your espresso, and at precisely nine you open for business. You are never late."

He stared at her. "How do you—?"

But she spoke over him, though her voice softened slightly. "You, Stefano, I'm afraid you are not nearly so efficient. Mornings you like to stay too long in bed—often the bed of a pretty young signorina—until you throw your clothes on in a great rush and run to the office. Your clothes are rarely pressed, and half the time your hair looks as though you combed it with a rake. You spend your lunch hours in the library reading Pirandello and Dante and then have to run to reach your office before you are *too* late. Signor Brancusi would scold you, but he is beginning to understand that perhaps you are not cut out for the law . . .''

Stefano stared at her, feeling stripped bare, reeling with both confusion and enchantment.

Vittorio stared, too, but with malice in his eyes. "You've been spying on us! Do you know I could have you arrested for that alone? I could go to the phone right now and—"

"I know you could," La Colomba broke in. "And I know you won't."

"Oh yes?" Vittorio ran his fingers down the creases of his trousers, as though preparing himself to visit some party superior. "How can you be so damn sure?"

A crack of thunder penetrated the thick walls and invaded the room. The windowpanes rattled from the force of a fresh downpour lashing against them. Ignoring Vittorio's question, La Colomba walked to the window, drew back the heavy drape, and peered out a moment at the rain. "I don't think I should allow you to drive back to Milan in weather like this," she said.

"Allow us?" Vittorio echoed hotly. "You think you can command—"

La Colomba put in quietly, "I meant only that you are welcome to stay the night."

"Impossible! Why, if it should become known that I spent the night in this house, the house of a—"

"Vittorio!" Stefano roared. "You will not speak to her that way. I won't have it."

"Never mind, Stefano," La Colomba said gently. "I have heard far worse, and it's been a long time since it bothered me. I apologize, Vittorio, for putting you in such an awkward position. I understand that your friends in the party would not approve. But no one knows you are here. Nor will they. So why not let me make you comfortable. We can conduct our business at leisure and you can return to Milan in the morning."

"We would be honored to stay," said Stefano.

Vittorio did not give in so easily. "Signora, I have no time for—"

"You must make the time. I assure you it will be in your best interests to do so." For the first time she had raised her voice, and there was such a ring of determination and authority that Vittorio instantly sat back in his chair, signaling acquiescence. Of course, it was not lost on him that she had earlier promised a reward for his investment of time.

"Good," she said. She poured more coffee. "And now we have all night for you to hear the story I have to tell you."

A loud crack of thunder sounded overhead, like the gavel of the gods signaling an end to any argument.

For the next hour the D'Angeli brothers listened. It was, indeed, a colorful story. Stefano was mesmerized by both her voice and her words. Vittorio was drawn in despite himself. "You may know of me as La Colomba," she began, "but my name is Pietra Manzi, and I was born in the Spacca quarter of Naples." Her voice remained neutral as she detailed the story of the death of her entire family in the decade before the turn of the century. "Cholera. Tens of thousands died. It took my sisters first, three little girls, then my mother. A week later my father."

She paused, breathed deeply a moment. "Then Agostino Depretis, the Italian premier in those terrible days, issued his dictum: *Bisogna sventrare Napoli*—'Naples must be disemboweled.' To avoid another disaster, you see, he decided to tear down the slums. Never mind the disaster of sending hundreds of people into the streets with nowhere to go, unable to afford anything else. The whole of the Spacca was razed. Nothing was left, not a wall or a window. I was thirteen."

She told of how she'd lived with an aunt, widowed by the disease, until she was taken in as unpaid help by a shopkeeper.

"The rest is a very old story, a fairy tale you've heard a hundred times. *La Cenerentola*, little Cinderella raised from the ashes by a handsome prince—though he wasn't a prince and I didn't marry him."

Vittorio gave a harsh laugh. "That is hardly a surprise."

She ignored him. "You see, my life was not a fairy tale

at all. There was no magic involved. What I got I worked for. I *made* my wishes come true and achieved all any woman could want—wealth, love, position, power."

"You call that power?" said Vittorio. "To wallow in lust, passed from man to man, selling yourself to the highest bidder."

Glaring at his brother, Stefano rose halfway from his seat, fists clenched. "I apologize for my brother's rudeness, Signora."

"There is no need," she said. "I know what he is. I know what you both are." She closed her eyes and for the first time she looked old, as though she had been keeping the years at bay by the sheer force of her vitality. "When I was in my late thirties, I made a decision. A very ordinary decision, really, one millions of ordinary women had made before me. I decided to have a child." A rustle of laughter lightened her voice, and when she opened her eyes they seemed almost mischievous. "I had been told, you see, that it was the greatest experience a woman could have, and I was never one to pass up a new experience."

She had her audience now. They hung on her every word. "I had no lover in my life at the time. Don't snort, Vittorio. It happened frequently. I was very selective and always faithful to any man I was with. But there was none at this time, and of course a man was necessary for my plan. So I waited eagerly for the moment when he would appear."

She found him in a gentleman who approached her one night at the opera. "A commanding figure, both physically and socially, an impressive man in many respects. He was quite well known but with the kind of bold arrogance that made him unafraid to make his own rules . . . and to be seen publicly with me. I accepted his invitation to dine. Over the Grand Marnier, I decided he would do splendidly."

As with everything La Colomba set her mind to, she succeeded almost at once, though she confessed to having an uncomfortable pregnancy and a difficult birth. "Not the 'transcending' experience I had been led to expect," she said dryly. But the child, a willful little boy with sturdy legs, was the delight of her life.

"Four years later I became pregnant again—not by design that time. The father was a different lover, a man who truly owned my heart. He, too, was an important figure—and married to a woman who was barren but whom the Church forbade him to leave. Nevertheless we were both happy when I conceived, certain we would create a splendid child together. And so we did . . ."

At this point in her story, La Colomba leaned back in the chair, her face a mask of pain as the memories washed over her. "I loved my sons almost desperately, so much so that I knew I had to give them up. My world was no place to raise children. You see, I understood the stigma that would attach to them. They would have no chance for a decent, respectable life. It was like cutting off a limb to part with them, but I knew it was for the best."

So shortly after her second son was born, La Colomba sent her children away. "I had a very dear friend, a lawyer in Milan. I arranged for him to take my sons and raise them. We thought it politic to give them another name," she continued. "Mine was too well known. I always thought my children were precious gifts from the angels. So I named them D'Angeli—Vittorio and Stefano D'Angeli."

Only then did she focus her gaze on them directly, each in turn, her expression a combination of defiance and pleading.

Both men sat stunned, but for different reasons. Stefano felt as if he had been handed the keys to the kingdom. He had a mother, a living mother as beautiful as he had always imagined—yet even better than the woman of his dreams, for she had courage and spirit and magic.

Vittorio was devastated. "Lies!" he cried, jumping from his chair. "My parents were killed by—"

"By an anarchist's bomb?" she said. "That was the story Carlo and I invented to spare him—to spare you—embarrassment."

Still, he refused to yield. "No! You, *my* mother? This is monstrous," he went on, rigidly posed in a fighter's stance. "You have made me into a bastard, the bastard son of a whore." He moved forward, his fingers working as if they might reach out and strangle her.

Stefano leapt up to stand between Vittorio and . . . their mother. "I'm warning you, Vittorio. Never speak to her that way again!"

"Sit down, both of you." She did not shout, but her voice cut through their rage—the voice of a mother sure of the obedience she can command from her children. "I will not have you fighting in my house."

They lowered themselves slowly into their chairs, though Stefano kept a wary eye on his brother. No. His *half*-brother, he realized. It explained so much.

Vittorio looked at the floor, his shoulders slumped in a pose of defeat.

"You are very like your father," La Colomba addressed him. "He would not have been pleased, either, had I told him about you."

Vittorio looked up sharply. "He doesn't know . . ."

La Colomba gave him no chance to pursue the point, but turned instead to Stefano. "You, too, are very like your father. He was brilliant, perhaps a genius. You would have been proud of him." They shared a smile.

"And would I be proud?" Vittorio demanded.

"Oh yes, you would have been proud of your father, Vittorio, and he of you." There was irony in her tone, but Vittorio didn't seem to catch it.

Stefano looked at the beautiful woman glowing in the candlelight, her eyes kind, her diamonds blazing. An hour ago —was it possible? only an hour?—La Colomba had been just a legend to him. Now . . .

In his mind, he tried out the word and the concept: *mother*. He wondered who he would have become had he been allowed to grow up beside her.

"If it should be discovered," Vittorio muttered, almost to himself, his head shaking slowly. "I have pledged myself to a new Italy where people like you will be impossible."

"And you have nearly succeeded," she finished. "That is why it was necessary to call you here tonight."

"I will do anything to help you, Signora," Stefano began,

then he paused and studied her face, a pleading look in his own. "Or may I call you mother?"

"I wish you could know how long I have yearned to hear that word from you, from both of you. I never thought I would. You see, I had no intention of telling you about myself. Not now, not ever. But your black-shirted friends have made it necessary, Vittorio," she went on in a bitter voice. "As you say, I am a perfect example of the 'decadence' that cannot exist in a modern Fascist state. Now it has come to my ears that I may soon be arrested as an anti-Fascist 'collaborator.' One of my dear friends has pledged his vast fortune to opposing Mussolini. Also, he is a Jew, and you, Vittorio, have special reason to know of our Benito's increasingly rigorous anti-Semitism." She smiled sadly, glancing at her hands. "Il Duce is eager to waltz with the German Führer."

Stefano tried to catch her eye, to warn her not to speak too freely in front of Vittorio, but she went on. "La Tana and all its contents may be confiscated at any moment."

"No!" said Stefano.

"You cannot blame the state for wanting to condemn such ill-gotten riches," said Vittorio, though the tone of conviction was curiously lacking.

"I suppose there is nothing ill-gotten about having taken your shop away from a Jew," she countered sharply.

Vittorio was frozen in a blustering pose, unable to defend himself. *Bravo*, Stefano said to himself, admiring his mother more with every second.

"For the moment, the Blackshirts are riding high," she continued. "No one can stop them from doing what they want, no matter how wrong it may be. But I'll be damned if I will stand by and watch everything I own, all that I've earned, vanish into their pockets."

"How can we help?" asked Stefano.

"Be careful, Stefano," Vittorio said. "She admits to being an enemy of the state. If we help her . . ."

La Colomba gave him a tolerant look. "Of course, my son, I would not want you to violate your principles. But before you decide against me, you might wish to see what I have to offer." She walked toward the door. She extended her hand, and her smile beckoned. "Come. I will show you."

Stefano joined her at once. But Vittorio hung back, still concerned that he might be compromised. From what she said, it was indeed possible that the house was under surveillance. Suppose he had been seen entering. Suppose it were known that this woman claimed to be his mother, for he still viewed it as nothing more than a claim, unable to accept it as established fact. True or not, it could damage him, destroy his opportunities . . .

Yet balanced against that risk was her talk of a gift. What might it be, coming from a woman of such wealth? For another moment Vittorio looked around at the masterpiece paintings, the furniture and tapestries, the golden surfaces that caught the firelight. Then he, too, followed her out of the room.

She led them up the curving mahogany staircase. Everywhere were treasures, but they combined to create an atmosphere of opulent comfort rather than the static luxury of a museum. La Colomba did not own a thing unless she loved it—or unless she had loved the man who gave it to her.

At the top of the stairs she turned and walked to a door with a gold handle in the form of a mermaid. Inside, the room was decorated entirely in ivory silk and gold. Heavy ivory satin draped the windows and covered the furniture. The ceiling was embossed with gilded rosettes and angels formed in plaster. Tall rococo mirrors lined the walls above carved paneling. It was an intensely feminine room, the very heart of La Tana.

More candles had been lit here, apparently only moments before they walked in, though no human presence was seen or felt.

"My dressing room," she said, "though I call it my treasury." As she spoke, she passed her hand over the painted oak paneling. With a soft swish, it moved, parted, swung open to reveal a deep recess within the wall. She reached in and pulled out a marble-topped table mounted on well-oiled casters.

On its gold-veined surface sat more than a dozen boxes—

velvet-covered boxes, leather ones, gilded, enameled, and inlaid wood boxes. Opening one, she pulled out a necklace of emeralds and sapphires. It slithered through her fingers like a serpent from the sea, its watery colors slipping sensuously over her hand.

"*Magnifico*," said Stefano as she held it out to him. A sinuous scrolled "C" in diamonds adorned the clasp.

Next she pulled out earrings of perfectly matched pigeon's-blood rubies, so called because they were said to be the exact hue of the first two drops of blood from the nostrils of a freshly shot pigeon. These she gave to Vittorio. He harrumphed softly, but his fingers caressed the cold surface of the rubies as tenderly as if they were the warm flesh of a desirable woman.

She showed them a wheatsheaf brooch with diamond kernels mounted on wires so delicate the sheaves trembled as if in a summer breeze whenever the wearer moved. Another brooch was designed to look like a bunch of raspberries, each juicy kernel a separate ruby. Still other pieces were brought forth. A cuff bracelet of heavy gold set with cameos. A Lalique ring of delicate *plique-à-jour* enamel over gold. A parure of emeralds and diamonds consisting of tiara, necklace, earrings, and bracelet. "It belonged to the Empress Eugenie," she said with more than a touch of arrogance.

Stefano watched, transfixed, as she drew forth jewel after jewel, handling each piece with respect, even reverence. As they glittered in her hands, he knew he would never see anything like this spectacle again. No queen could have a greater collection of treasures than did La Colomba.

"This is one of my favorites," she said, lifting out a brooch fashioned in the shape of a phoenix, the bird rising from its own ashes. Outlined in gold and diamonds, a huge heart-shaped pink diamond, the rarest of all diamond hues, formed its breast; its eyes were of sapphire, and emerald wings spread wide as it rose from a bed of ruby flames. "My personal crest," she said. "It seemed an appropriate symbol of my own magical resurrection from the ashes of a Neapolitan slum."

She studied the faces of her sons. Stefano's reflected awe,

not greed, she was pleased to see, as he touched a string of perfectly matched pearls. Vittorio wore a quite different expression as he ran his fingertips lightly across a waterfall of diamonds in their specially molded, velvet-lined box.

Stefano's eyes came up to meet hers. He shook his head. "So many, so beautiful. How you must have sparkled when you wore them."

She laughed, and laid a hand over her chest. "They made me sparkle in here, even when I didn't wear them. Without them . . ." She trailed off as she reached for a small casket and opened it to reveal a perfect rose-cut diamond, unset. "I always believed they made me what I am."

Stefano could see a memory in her eyes, and he waited for her to continue. But after a second she closed the box with the diamond. "A story for another time," she said quietly.

"Indeed," said Vittorio as he fingered a diamond dog collar choker. "You said we had business to conduct, about the collection."

"So, my jewels are not too decadent for you?" she said with a teasing lilt. Then she added flatly. "That's good. Because they are yours to share. They are your inheritance."

To give them time for the scope of the fortune and the truth of their inheritance to sink in, she lit a cigarette, walked to the window, and stared out at the rain. When she finally spoke, she was all business.

"The jewels must be taken at once from La Tana to a safe place. Vittorio, you will bring them to Switzerland."

Stefano glanced at her with alarm. After all she had seen and said, did she have no doubts about trusting Vittorio?

Perhaps she caught his look, though she didn't openly acknowledge it, because she went on to explain the logic of her choice. "Thanks to your party connections, Vittorio, you have certain privileges that Stefano does not. You can obtain travel permits and cross borders without being extensively searched as he would be. You will take the jewels to Geneva, where I have arranged for them to be kept in a bank under special conditions. Once deposited, the entire collection may be withdrawn only upon the simultaneous presentation of two very particular pieces of identification.''

She moved gracefully to a dressing table, returning with a small box of carved jade. "In here is the key to my life—and to your fortunes.''

She opened the hinged lid. Inside, nestled in a bed of velvet, was the jeweled perfume bottle. The pearl shoulders, the diamond skirt, and ruby bodice flashed and sparkled and glowed in the amber light. But the total beauty of the figure transcended the gems themselves—it was magical, other-worldly.

Vittorio gasped. "A masterpiece. I've never seen anything to match it. Cellini?'' he asked, referring to the greatest of all Renaissance jewelers.

"You have a good eye,'' she said. "It is in his style. But no, it's not a Cellini. It was made in Amsterdam some years ago. A replica of me. My eyes were once as blue as these sapphires.'' She said it almost to herself, one long-nailed finger stroking the deep blue stones. "We loved each other very much.''

The man who had the figure made for her, could it have been his father? Stefano wondered.

He might have asked, but she stopped him by twisting the figure in two then holding it out to them, one piece in each hand. She gave the top to Stefano, the bottom to Vittorio. "These are the two pieces of identification that must be presented to withdraw the jewels from the bank. Without them both, the collection will not be released. When you go to claim it, you must go together.''

Vittorio turned the piece in his hand. "Why take the risk of smuggling them out of the country? Why not simply hide them?''

"War is coming; anyone who does not see it is blind. When it comes Italy will be destroyed.''

Vittorio bristled once again. "Italy will be victorious!''

She shrugged. "Believe what you must. In any case, Europe will soon fall into chaos. I believe, however, that the jewels will be safe in Switzerland.''

"If they get there safely," Vittorio said, in the tone of a dare.

Stefano whirled on Vittorio. "If you can't make sure they get there, I will."

"There is no need to worry," La Colomba said confidently. "You may be a Fascist, Vittorio, but you are also a practical man. We both know it would not be in your best interests if your friends found out about your parentage or your good fortune. I'm sure you will obey my instructions to the letter."

"Which are?"

"The jewels are to be delivered to a Mr. Lindner at the Helvetia Kreditanstalt in Geneva. As soon as he receives the collection and assures himself that it is complete, I will be informed. If I do not hear from him within three days, I shall be forced to report the theft to certain members of the government. And I would not hesitate to tell them that I had entrusted the jewels to you. To my son."

"Three days is cutting it too fine," Vittorio protested.

"The traveling time is less than a day. That leaves you two days to secure the necessary permissions. With your contacts, you should have no trouble cutting through as much red tape as even the *Fascisti* can create."

Vittorio allowed himself a smile. "You truly are a cunning vixen."

"When I need to be," she agreed. "And never have I needed it more than now." She looked at them. "It is not only the safety of the jewels I am hoping to protect, but your safety as well."

"Ours?" said Stefano. "How can you protect us?"

"You know nothing of war, either of you. I know more than I would ever wish to. War does more than turn nation against nation. It can turn brother against brother. What I am doing now is to prevent that. When the war is over, when the time comes to claim the jewels, you will have to be united. I have guaranteed that you will do everything you can to protect each other through the coming slaughter. Protect each other and survive, and you will have a fortune to rebuild when the chaos ends. But without one another, each of you will have nothing."

She rose, her face drained and tired. "And now, I think we must go to bed. The storm should let up during the night. You will be able to leave first thing in the morning. I will have the jewels packed into your car, Vittorio." She slid her hand through Stefano's arm and gestured to her other son. "Come, I will show you to your rooms."

The storm played itself out well before dawn. By the time Stefano threw open the shutters of his opulent bedroom, the sun had cleared the top of the hills to pour like melted butter onto the tawny fields and silvery green olive groves. The world looked reborn. The distant hills were blue and misty, and the air was as fresh, as soft as new white wine.

Autumn plowing had begun, and Stefano watched a pair of oxen plod across the ocher soil of a field not far away. The song of a lark drifted up to meet him. He had never felt more peaceful, more complete in his life. Knowing he had a mother—a woman of such beauty and depth—reinforced his feeling of destiny as a man of sensitivity. A poet.

Voices sounded below and he looked down just as La Colomba rounded a corner of the house. He was surprised to see her awake so early. From what he knew of his mother, she had lived her life at night. Her appearance this morning was also a departure from the image of grandeur she had presented the night before—a flowing skirt and blouse under a wool challis shawl wrapped close against the morning breeze, her hair pinned carelessly back.

She was carrying on an animated conversation with a man dressed in work clothes. "I will speak to the carpenter about it," Stefano heard her say. All he could hear of the peasant's reply was a respectful "Donna Pietra" before he walked away.

When the farmer was gone she looked up, almost as if she sensed her son's presence at the window. "Good morning," she called with a cheery smile. "I hope you slept well."

"Very well," he called back.

"Come join me for breakfast. Just turn right at the bottom of the stairs."

Five minutes later he entered a sunny room with French

doors opening onto the back garden. On a sideboard sat a pot of coffee, platters of cheeses and meats that looked home-cured, a basket of freshly baked rolls, and pots of fresh butter and jam. The doors were open wide to let in the morning air.

Just beyond the doors, La Colomba sat at a wrought-iron table overlooking a garden, its flowerbeds edged with box hedges, a fountain gurgling at its center. Stefano helped himself to a plate of food and a cup of coffee and joined her.

"Do you know," she said, her eyes fastened on the cypress trees atop the hill, looking like swords stuck hilt-down in the earth, "I think I was meant to be a country girl."

"You?" He couldn't keep a chuckle from his voice. The woman whom all the world knew as La Colomba, the most famous courtesan in Europe, the woman who had blazed with jewels a few short hours ago and who was at home in the company of princes and dukes, a country girl?

"Don't laugh," she said with a chuckle of her own. "It's true. Yes, I enjoy Paris and Rome, I appreciate palaces and champagne. I even once counseled a maharajah. But I have never felt more at home than I do at La Tana—puttering in my garden, watching the olives being dumped into the oil press, discussing the harvest. It is so . . . so comfortable."

He sipped his coffee and studied her profile, elegant and clean and still young despite her years. His eyes were drawn to her hands. Their long fingers wrapped around her coffee cup, and he suddenly realized that now she wore not a single jewel. But the hands were no less beautiful. "You are an extraordinary woman. I would like to know you better."

She put down her cup and frowned. "We may not have time."

A surge of anger overtook him, blocking out the sunshine and the glow he'd felt when he awoke. "We could have had the time! We could have had twenty-four years of time!"

She pulled back as if slapped. "You feel I have cheated you."

"Haven't you? Didn't you cheat me of a mother? All these years I thought you were dead. While I wondered what you had looked like, what you cared about, we could have had each other, known each other. Didn't you want to know me? Didn't you care?"

"Oh, Stefanino," she said on a sigh, and he almost broke at the sound of the affectionate name on her lips. "I cared so much, so very much I sometimes thought I would die of it. Can you not understand? I cared enough to send you away. But I kept you always in my heart, and often in my view."

"In your view?"

"I watched you wobble across the piazza on your first bicycle. I saw you win the swimming medal when you were twelve. How it broke my heart not to be able to hug you then." She looked into his eyes, eyes so like her own, and lifted a hand to brush a lock of dark hair from his forehead. "Can you imagine how I have longed to perform such a simple action as this?"

He reached up and grabbed her hand and closed his eyes against the emotions whirling inside him.

She went on lightly, "Do you remember the poem you wrote when you were fifteen, the one that was published in the newspaper? How proud I was! But how embarrassed you were to be interviewed. You fidgeted and mumbled and you were too shy to look the interviewer in the eye."

"How could you know . . . ?" It came to him suddenly. "You? The lady journalist with the white kid gloves and the French veil? And emeralds . . . I think she wore emeralds."

She smiled an answer.

"My God," Stefano sighed, "if only I'd known."

"Perhaps we will be lucky. Perhaps there will be time."

"I . . ." He stopped, feeling closer to tears than he'd been since he was a child. "Mother." He held her hand to his cheek.

That was how Vittorio found them. Actually, he'd been watching them for several minutes. The emotions the sight stirred in him were not only unfamiliar, they were unwelcome. Vittorio did not like feeling jealous of any man. When he spoke, he was even more brusque than usual.

"We've got to get going, Stefano."

La Colomba turned to him and smiled. "And good morning to you, too, Vittorio."

"We have a long drive, Signora."

"You should learn patience, Vittorio. You were very impatient with a customer last year, a rather fussy German lady looking for stationery. She nearly drove you to distraction with her requests for finer rag."

He looked at her with surprise before a hint of a smile betrayed his admiration. "You?"

She bowed a yes and gave him such a coquettish smile he couldn't help laughing. "Have some coffee, Vittorio," she said when he stopped.

"Thank you, Signora, but no. If the jewels are to reach Switzerland within three days, I must start my arrangements at once."

"I suppose that's true," she said. She rose and went inside to the sideboard. She piled several rolls and pastries into a basket and brought them to Vittorio. "At least take these with you in case you get hungry on the road."

"Isn't it a little late to be mothering us?" asked Vittorio, but there was no edge to his voice.

"It may be my only chance."

Vittorio accepted the offering, and she led them through the house and out the front door. At once Vittorio opened the trunk of the car to check that the jewels had been packed. They were there, transferred to several plain cardboard boxes and covered over with a greasy burlap sack.

"I'm worried about you," Stefano said to La Colomba while Vittorio checked their cargo. "You spoke of being in danger . . ."

She smiled. "I said there were people who considered me a dangerous woman. But I have landed on my feet more times than you have fallen down, Stefanino." She took his hand. "I am as slippery as an old eel. And I have had the foresight to keep one or two smaller pieces of jewelry as well as some loose gems easily hidden. They will make tempting 'arguments' if I ever have to buy my way out of difficulties. Don't worry about me."

Vittorio slammed the trunk shut and came back to where they stood. He offered La Colomba his hand.

Instead of taking it, she leaned forward and kissed him

once, quickly, on each cheek. "Good-bye, Vittorio. Though I abhor your politics, I will always wish you well."

He smiled, a tentative smile. After a pause, he said, "And I wish you the same." There was another pause before he added, "Mother."

She turned to Stefano and they looked into each other's eyes for a long moment. "*Arrivederci*, Stefanino," she said, holding his cheeks in her hands. "*Arrivederci*, my son."

"*Arrivederla* . . . Mama," he answered and kissed her cheek. "I will see you again soon. I must."

"We will have hope. Now go."

He ran down the steps and got into the car. Vittorio was already impatiently revving the engine. As they turned into the cypress-bordered road and drove away, Stefano looked back out the rear window. She was still standing on the step, a shrinking figure dressed in a simple skirt and blouse yet looking regal as a queen. He watched until she was hidden by a curve in the road.

There were tears in his eyes when he turned around again, and a swell of emotion unlike any he had known before rose within him. He would see her again. He must. There was so much to learn from her. How had she risen so far from such lowly beginnings? And someday she would tell him about his father, though he wasn't sure it mattered who his father had been. It wasn't that part of his heritage that gave him hope that he might fulfill his dreams for a life of poetry and adventure. It was his mother and what she had given him— the legacy of a great soul.

A man could do worse, much worse, Stefano thought, than to be the son of La Colomba.

Chapter 4

Naples—1886

As she had every morning for the past year, fourteen-year-old Pietra Manzi woke with the nightmares of the dark hours still flying around in her head and the nightmare of another new day about to begin. "Holy Mary, Mother of God," she prayed just before throwing back the covers, "deliver me from this hell."

A year earlier, Pietra had believed nothing more could be taken from her. Everything was already gone—mother, father, sisters all dead from the cholera, her home razed to the ground to check the spread of the disease, friends and neighbors cast to the winds like mere ashes. Nothing remained. When everything is gone, there can be nothing left to lose, she remembered hearing some of the elders say to cheer themselves in the wake of their own losses.

But they were wrong, Pietra had learned. She had her spirit left to lose, her heart and soul . . . and Lena Sacco seemed determined to take even that.

As usual this morning, it didn't take long for Lena to start on her. Pietra had barely risen from her pallet by the stove and washed herself in the icy water she'd brought in from the well the night before, when the curtain dividing the kitchen from the shop was thrown back with a sudden snap.

"Lazy little slut. You haven't even started breakfast yet, and the grate hasn't been cleaned." The frown lines between Lena's dark eyes were gashes in her pointy face. She was a few years shy of forty, but the sour resentment etched into her features made her look a decade older.

"I'm sorry, Signora," Pietra said, the only acceptable answer. Any other earned her a sharp slap with the back of Lena's hand, the one with the coral ring that could cut flesh. Pietra wore only a pair of ragged cotton underpants—all she had to sleep in—and she scrambled for her dress. She hated it when Lena stared at her naked body. It made her feel dirty.

Lena grabbed her before she could cover herself. She gripped the girl's upper arm so hard there was sure to be a bruise. Then she smiled the wolfish smile that looked as if someone had taken a sharp tool and pried her lips back over her rotten teeth.

"The little slut is growing ripe," she said, her eyes sliding over Pietra's body. She knew well enough it was the sort of roundly luscious body men would make fools of themselves over, with all the curves Lena had never had herself. She reached out and ran a hand over the dewy skin of one hip, smooth as alabaster, then squeezed one of the girl's breasts; they had begun to swell and grow rounded in the past few months. "Like a plum ready to fall from the tree, eh?" said Lena. She pinched the nipple, twisting it in her steely fingers, and laughed, an ugly noise. Pietra fought against making a sound. Any show of pain only seemed to encourage her tormentor.

Lena thrust her away. "Cover yourself. My husband will be ready for his breakfast soon. I won't have you flaunting yourself at him."

Finally, she left. Pietra dressed quickly in a frock of thin brown cotton, tied back her heavy black hair with a piece of yarn, and folded away the pallet. Then she scooped the ashes from the stove, added fresh coal, and lit the fire. With her first tasks accomplished, Pietra sent an imploring look to the kitchen Madonna smiling serenely in a niche on the wall. She reached up to lightly touch the ivory rosary hanging at the Madonna's feet.

"Holy Mary, Mother of God . . . ," she chanted softly. Pietra had not given up on prayers, even though they had yet to do any good.

So began another day. With a sigh, she stirred the polenta, took down the salami curled around a nail on the wall, and sliced a half-dozen slabs for Giovanni's breakfast.

For a while after the cholera had orphaned Pietra, her aunt, *zia* Gemma, had taken her in. But seven of them in a dark *basso*, one of the cavelike ground-floor dwellings that filled the slums of Naples—it was impossible. Widowed by the same epidemic, *zia* Gemma barely earned enough doing laundry for the city's wealthy elite to feed her own children. She had tried her best to see that the only surviving child of her dead sister was sheltered and fed. In the run-down waterfront neighborhood where she lived, there were many small shops, and Gemma found a place for her niece with a craftsman named Giovanni Sacco. In return for providing help in his shop, Sacco promised to take care of the girl.

Giovanni Sacco's principal income was derived from carving the coral objects so popular with the Neapolitans. He was a decent man, but his wife was another matter.

After suffering Lena Sacco's abuse for a week, Pietra had run back to her aunt and begged to be allowed to return. Though her heart ached as she said the words, Gemma had told the child there was no choice.

"I know Lena Sacco is a bitter woman," *zia* Gemma said. "Seventeen years married and no baby, not even a sign of one. She feels cursed, so she takes it out on the world. But you can defend yourself against bitterness, Pietra. Against hunger there is no defense, and I cannot feed you. Stay with Sacco—and his wife—or you'll wind up in the streets."

Pietra had seen the waifs who were sold like sheep on the streets of Naples, to be used for pleasure as any man or woman desired. *Zia* Gemma called the fate of the young whores "worse than death."

But sometimes Pietra thought that might be a fate preferable to living with the cruelties of Lena Sacco.

Pietra knew that Lena had done everything possible to conceive a child. An entire wall of her bedroom was a shrine to the Virgin. Fertility charms hung over the bed beside images of female figures great with child. Rosaries were said. Flowers were laid at the feet of the patron saints of fertility.

While Pietra prayed for herself, she also prayed for Lena. If only the woman could bear a child, then perhaps she would learn to be kind, and life with the Saccos would be bearable.

Working in the shop was not itself unpleasant. It was one of dozens along the Santa Lucia waterfront dealing in small items of coral, bone, and tortoiseshell. Some of the larger stores sold beautiful snuffboxes, intricately carved horn and ivory beads, jewelry designed for the wealthy customers who came down from the villas in the surrounding hills.

Sacco's clientele came mostly from the fishermen and boat builders, the junk collectors and washerwomen of the district, men with small purses and big superstitions. He made them horn-shaped *cornuti* and other amulets dear to the hearts of the fearful Neapolitans, talismen to ward off the *jettatura*, the evil eye. Much of it he carved himself. The more intricate pieces he bought from others.

Pietra liked Giovanni Sacco. He wasn't much to look at. A short, squat man, heavy with too much pasta, his skin as dark as a ripening olive and often shiny with oily sweat. But he treated her well, rather like a kindly uncle.

"Put down your broom, little one," he said this morning after Pietra had been sweeping a while. "It's hot today, and the floor is clean enough." He set the combs he'd been dusting back into their tray. "Go and get yourself a cool drink from the kitchen."

She gave him a grateful smile. "And a glass of wine for you?"

"Of course," he said with a grin that lifted the ends of his droopy mustache. Then he winked and added, "But don't tell Lena."

She returned with their drinks then sat on a high stool

behind the counter to sort some horn buttons. This was Pietra's favorite time of day. There were few customers and Lena was always out, on her knees at morning Mass, imploring every saint who might consider giving her a child.

"Pietra," Sacco said after a while, "is there anything in my shop that you would like for yourself?"

She looked up at him and blinked in astonishment. Anything? There was almost nothing she wouldn't like—well, not some of the charms, perhaps—but the combs carved of tortoiseshell and coral, or the mirrors with carved frames, or the little brooches.

Reading her face, he smiled. "Your aunt tells me that the day after tomorrow is your birthday. It's a well-remembered day in Naples for more reasons than that, of course . . . but your birthday is good enough reason to give you a present."

Pietra had almost forgotten about her birthday. And it was so easy to remember, since she had been born on a day when Mount Vesuvius jolted the city with one of its volcanic eruptions. It had not been a major one, and the coincidence with her birth had always been regarded as a good omen in her family. Though she was named for San Pietro, her name had another significance. Pietra, "stone," like those thrown up out of the heart of the volcano on the day she was born. As the oldest child, she had been the rock of her family. Whenever she lost her temper—which was often before everyone died and sadness overwhelmed anger—her father used to tease her and call her Pietrina, "little flint," because of the sparks that shot from her angry blue eyes.

"Take a day to think about what present you would like," Sacco was saying now. "Within reason, of course, not one of the very best pieces I might sell to a passing nobleman. But anything else . . ."

"Oh, Signor Sacco," Pietra cried gratefully. She was on the verge of jumping from her stool to hug him, but it was lucky she didn't, for at that moment Lena reappeared, and Pietra sensed at once that her mood was especially dangerous.

"I need another phallus," she said the moment she walked in the door. Glaring at Pietra, she added, "Since *she* came, one is not enough. She has made my flow dry up."

Giovanni dutifully went to a display case and removed a box that he handed to his wife. She began pawing through the carved charms heaped in the box. "None of those is as big as the one you already have under the mattress," Giovanni observed.

She ignored him and selected the largest and reddest of the miniature phalluses, carved from coral in realistic detail.

"What about the herbs," he asked, "and the oil I rubbed on your stomach last night?"

"Those herbs make my mouth feel like a desert, and the oil is useless." She grasped the little charm in both hands, pulling it close to her chest. "I have done everything, Giovanni. You know how I have gone on my knees to the Virgin until they are bloody, how I have fasted, how many candles I've lit." She was pleading, as though he would give her a baby if only she could convince him. "I haven't missed Mass once since we were married."

"I know, *cara*," he said, patting ineffectually at her shoulder. "But you must be patient."

Lena glared at Pietra, who busied herself rearranging some coral *cornuti*, wishing she could just disappear. "It's her," Lena went on in a spitting voice. "She has cast the evil eye on me."

Giovanni came over to Pietra. "Signora Griselli wants her button box today. Take it to her now, Pietra," he said quietly.

Thankful for the chance of escape, Pietra grabbed up the package, took her shawl from a peg and hurried to the door. But Lena was not so easily satisfied.

"Yes, it's good if you go," she called out shrilly. "But it would be better if you don't come back."

Pietra froze in the doorway, suddenly fearful that to step outside would mean permanent banishment to the streets.

"Lena!" Sacco shouted, rare for him, particularly when talking to his wife. "We need Pietra. She's . . . a good worker."

"Yes, good at working her curses against me."

"For pity's sake. She's a child, with no malice in her. Be kind to her and perhaps the saints will reward you. It's her birthday the day after tomorrow . . ."

"Her birthday?" Lena repeated, her eyes growing wide and wild as she turned toward Pietra. Still grasping the red coral phallus in one hand, she stroked it rhythmically up and down across her breasts as she advanced on the girl. "Tuesday is your birthday?"

"Yes," Pietra said softly, edging away.

"The twenty-sixth of April? And you'll be fifteen?"

Pietra nodded timidly, already sensing that something bad was coming.

"Aieee!" Lena wailed abruptly, clawing crazily at her hair. "I was right! It is a curse! April twenty-sixth, 1871. She was born the day Vesuvius erupted. A day of death and destruction!" She jabbed at the air with the red phallus. Pietra shrank back farther. "Born while ashes turned the land barren. Just as she has turned me barren!"

"Lena," Giovanni said forcefully, trying to calm her. "The girl has done nothing to you."

Her voice rose to a shriek. "I want her out. I will never bear a child while she is here."

Giovanni looked at Pietra, his sad dark eyes apologetic. Afraid to hear what he might say, she spun around and ran. From behind her came the fading sound of Lena Sacco's triumphant cackle.

At a corner, Pietra stopped and caught her breath. Then, with the memory of Lena's condemnation still ringing in her ears, she began to wander along the waterfront, ignoring the catcalls of the sailors, stepping around the rotting garbage of the market without seeing it. "I will be a stone," she said over and over to herself, in the litany that had become her personal rosary. "Stone endures. It is hard; it does not break." She pulled her shawl up over her shoulders and hugged her arms close around her. "I am Pietra; I am stone." Like a stone, she might be cast away, but she would come to rest somewhere else.

Suddenly she became aware that she was still clutching the package in her hand that Giovanni had given her for delivery. Should she take it back or perform the task she had been given? Surely, if she dutifully did as she was asked, Giovanni would keep her. She set off to make the delivery.

Pietra could have made her way blindfolded through the beehive of passageways and courtyards and narrow, winding *vicoli*, shadowy and damp, that made up the poorer sections of Naples. When she was lucky, an errand took her past the grand piazzas, legacy of a time when Naples was the capital of the Kingdom of the Two Sicilies, the home of Spanish viceroys and Bourbon kings who had left behind great palazzos.

One night she had gone past the Teatro San Carlo just as the opera-goers were arriving for the performance. She stood in the shadows, mesmerized by the sight of the ladies in exquisite gowns and jewels, men in flawless black with discreet accents of gold. How must it feel to wear such clothes, to be so beautiful, to be rich enough to have the whole world just waiting for your command?

Today's brief errand took her along the waterfront, pulsing with life, color, and especially noise, the great din and racket that underscored all life in Naples. In the Sacco house, she always felt alone, isolated. But out in the streets of the city, she could almost feel as if once again she was a member of a happy boisterous family.

Lines of laundry hung from every balcony, out every window, across every street, festooning the city like bright flags and flapping noisily in the sea-borne breeze. A young mother leaned out an upper window to take in her sheets. They reflected the sun down into the sunless street, a flash quickly gone. As she worked, she called in a sing-song voice to a neighbor.

At the fish market, Pietra breathed in the smells of fish and salt. Slithering eels, mullet with bright eyes, octopus shining opalescent in the sun begged for inspection.

"*E, bella,*" a fish-monger called to her. "Does the beautiful young lady want a beautiful snapper? We can make a trade. My fish . . . for your cherry." He pushed the fish toward her, but she waved it away and hurried on, past a donkey loaded down with bags of rock salt and a fisherman mending a net.

She arrived soon at Signora Griselli's door. The woman thanked her for her package, then peered at the girl's face and frowned. "You should be careful, my child," she said mysteriously. "The sailors around here will think nothing of pulling you into an alley . . ." The woman crossed herself before closing the door.

Pietra thought about the comment as she headed back to the shop. But a voice cut into her thoughts. "*E, bella*," cried one of the sailors lounging in the doorway of a cafe. When she turned to look at him, he clutched his heart. "*Che bellissima*!" he cried. She might have been flattered by his praise of her beauty, but he spoiled the effect by clutching at the place between his legs and laughing obscenely.

Even at fourteen, there was already an unmistakable aura about Pietra Manzi, a presence that pervaded the very air around her, sending up a shimmer of heat and scent that pulled attention toward her. Already she had experienced the indignity of being followed by the *scugnizzi*, the rowdy Neapolitan street boys, trailing her all the way home like dogs on the scent.

When she had begun to bleed several months ago, she had run back to *zia* Gemma, afraid it might be some belated sign of the disease that had killed the rest of her family. After calming her fears, Gemma had added, "You are a woman now, Pietra, no longer just a girl. Guard the jewel God gave you."

"Jewel? I have none . . ."

"You have your purity—your virginity. You are untouched by any man, and that is a treasure. As a virgin you may be desired by a man who will share all that he has in return for this jewel. But if you lose it too soon to a man who leaves you, then you are no better than the meanest *puttana* in the gutter. So guard your treasure like you would a diamond and give it to no man but your husband." Pietra had sworn an oath to her aunt that she would protect her "jewel," and she was determined to keep that oath.

Reaching the shop after her errand, she entered stealthily. All was quiet. Lena must be out again, picking through the market for the makings of the evening meal.

Pietra peeked into the tiny workroom at the back where Giovanni was busy carving. He looked up.

"You needn't look so frightened, child," he said. "She's calmed down. You can stay."

The thought of staying was almost as frightening as being cast out, but Pietra nodded, then obeyed Giovanni's order to remain in the shop to serve any customers who might come this early. "Call me if it's someone important," he said.

She stood in the shop, her eyes roaming over the shelves —the tortoiseshell combs, the mirrors and picture frames, the dainty coral carvings. Did she still dare to choose a present? Better to have her birthday forgotten.

The shop bell tinkled, and Pietra turned with a guilty start. The woman standing in the doorway was a vision, coolly elegant in a high-necked summer gown of the lightest lawn green sprigged with violets. Deep purple velvet ribbons trimmed the bodice and looped up a pert little bustle in the back. Ruffles spilled over a matching parasol. She looked like something out of a picture book. She even smelled of violets.

"*Buon giorno*, Signora," Pietra said with a respectful curtsy. She felt shame as she looked down at her own drab shapeless cotton. As she raised her eyes again, Pietra noticed the man who had stepped in just behind the woman. As perfectly dressed as his companion in a dove-gray suit, with brushed hat and gold-topped walking stick, he was also one of the most stunning men she had ever seen—thick silver-white hair combed back, eyes the color of a winter sky, a full mouth, and skin so fair it seemed never to have been touched by the sun.

Pietra was hardly aware of the woman as the man stepped forward. "I am the Duc di Monfalco," he announced, and with his stick he pointed to a set of ivory buckles on a shelf. "I would like to see those . . ." He spoke Italian rather than Neapolitan, and Pietra thought it the most musical sound she'd ever heard. Everything about him was amazing. A duke! No one of such high station had ever before visited the shop.

At last she found her voice. "I will get my employer." She started toward the back room.

"No, stay," the man said firmly. "I want you to serve

me." Pietra turned and saw that his gaze was fixed on her.
For a moment she didn't look away—couldn't. His eyes were
like magnets locked on hers. Then she remembered the buckles and went to the shelf to pull them down.

"What do you think of her?" she heard the Duke ask his
companion.

As Pietra returned with the buckles the beautiful woman
took hold of her free hand, positioned her directly in front
of them, and studied her from hair to boots. "*Très belle, très
charmante*," she finally said. "An amusing *entr'acte*," she
added with a throaty laugh. She tossed her head and the
emeralds at her throat flashed green fire. She lifted a kid-
sheathed hand to Pietra's chin and turned her head this way
and that. "Yes, *très delicieuse*."

Pietra couldn't understand, though she knew the woman
was speaking French. She'd heard it on the waterfront whenever a boat from Marseilles docked. But it had never sounded
as lovely as it did coming from this woman's mouth.

"I'll take them," said the Duke, still staring at Pietra. He
hadn't once looked at the box of buckles.

The noise from the shop had alerted Giovanni, and now
he hurried in from his workroom. Instantly, he recognized
the Duke and bowed awkwardly.

"I have just made a purchase," the Duke said quickly to
Giovanni. "Have it delivered tomorrow. At six."

"Of course, Your Grace," Giovanni said, eager as a
puppy. "I will bring them myself."

"No. The girl shall bring them." He turned and walked
out, the woman trailing after him, chuckling.

"Well," said Giovanni. "See how fate rewards you, my
child. You will have a chance to see the Palazzo Monfalco.
They say it is very grand."

"Was that the Duchess?"

He laughed. "Of course not. He would never bring his
wife to a place like this—and she lives mostly in the country,
I hear. That was his mistress, Maria Blanco, the famous opera
singer."

"She is very beautiful. I think she liked me . . ."

He smiled at her youthful eagerness. "Who could not?

Perhaps she will be there when you deliver the buckles to the palace.''

"The palace," Pietra echoed, looking through the door to see a carriage drawn by a matched pair of white horses vanishing up the street. "The palace," she repeated again. The word lingered on her tongue like the taste of a strange, exotic fruit.

Pietra's first look at the Palazzo Monfalco stopped her dead. Set on a cliff in the hills of Posillipo overlooking the Bay of Naples, it was built of pink stucco accented by red brick and a red tile roof. Towers emphasized each corner. Her eyes took in every detail—the trees pruned into animal shapes below a terrace, naked statues atop a wall, bougainvillaea bushes heavy with pink and purple flowers.

At last she made herself move. Giovanni had told her she mustn't use the front door but should go around to the servants' entrance. It took her a while to find it, hiking up and down marble stairs that went all around the outside of the vast building.

"Ah, the girl from the coral shop," said the heavyset woman who opened the door. Pietra was startled by the ordinariness of her Neapolitan dialect. She'd expected something more exotic, as though she'd entered a foreign country. The woman looked Pietra up and down. "The Duke wants you in the music room." She didn't sound like she approved. "Guido!"

A young man, not much older than Pietra, appeared and beckoned her to follow him. They went through a vast kitchen, down a corridor, through too many doors to count, and emerged into a hall with a high vaulted ceiling and a crystal chandelier so large and heavy she was afraid to walk under it. Enormous portraits in gilt frames hung on the walls.

She heard music. It grew louder when Guido opened a pair of double doors, and they stepped into a blazing white room—walls, ceiling, furnishings, everything was white—except the trimmings of gold and a golden harp in one corner. Over the fireplace, the largest mirror Pietra had ever seen reflected it all back to her.

Beside a window with a view of the sea, the Duke sat playing a sweet melody on a white piano. His eyes were closed.

Pietra heard the door click shut behind her and turned to discover the young man had left. She had a moment of panic, but it was soothed away by the music. After a minute she edged closer to the piano, curious to see the Duke's long, slender fingers moving over the ivory keys. The music became faster and louder, and the Duke's head shook as he played, so that his silky silver hair fell over his face. Pietra found herself wondering about his age. He seemed both young and old at the same time.

He pounded a low note that he held for a long moment, then his eyes snapped open, already aimed directly at Pietra. He didn't seem surprised to see her.

"Do you play, Signorina?" he asked. She shook her head. "No, of course you don't. But perhaps someday you would like to learn?"

To sit at such a wonderful instrument in such an exquisite room and make beautiful music . . . yes, she would love to learn. But all she did was curtsy and thrust her package at him. "The buckles, Your Grace."

He took the box and set it aside, and Pietra pulled her hands behind her back. Though she scrubbed them endlessly, her fingernails were still black from cleaning the grate. It was impossible to get them clean, and she couldn't bear to have him see them.

Rising from the piano bench, the Duke went to a table beneath the mirror where a decanter and some crystal goblets stood.

"What is your name, child?" he asked, as he filled the goblets from the decanter with a wine the color of liquid gold.

"Pietra."

"Ah, yes," he said, as though he had heard it before and merely forgotten. "Would you like a glass of wine, Pietra?"

"No, Your Grace. I must return to the shop."

"Please . . ." He held out a glass to her. "Why must you hurry? Your employer knows you are with me, and I am quite certain he is pleased to have my custom. If you visit with me, I may come back to the shop to buy more . . ."

Pietra blinked in confusion. Why should a man so important as the Duke want to keep her for an extra minute? Her errand was done; she should go.

But he was still holding out the wine. "Have you ever had wine before?" he said.

She nodded. Every Neapolitan child, even the poorest, tasted wine practically from birth.

"Of course you have. But this one is very special. It's called Lachryma Christi—Tears of Christ. I thought you might like it especially, because the grapes from which it is made are grown on the slopes of Vesuvius."

Her confusion grew. Was he hinting that he knew about her birthday, the significance of the date? She felt both frightened and excited by the possibility. As if guided by a mind apart from hers, her hand reached out to accept the glass.

She waited until he took a sip from his goblet, then did the same, touching the delicate glass carefully to her lips, afraid it might shatter at any moment. The wine was cool and delicious, nothing like the raw biting stuff regularly given her at the Sacco table. She closed her eyes a second, the better to feel it on her tongue. When she opened them again, the Duke was smiling at her.

"I can see that you know how to taste things, Pietra. You know how to enjoy your senses."

"I . . . I must go," she stammered. Being with the Duke suddenly made her feel as though she were suffocating. She thought of the fish she had seen brought in from the boats, still alive but flopping around on the quays. She couldn't survive here any more than the fish could without water. She didn't belong.

But the Duke went on smiling. "Is it really so terrible here, Pietra, that you cannot wait to leave?"

"Oh no," she said quickly. "It's beautiful."

"And you have seen only a small part. If you stayed here with me, there would be much more to see . . . much more to taste . . . much more to learn."

For a moment she was silent, wondering. Then, as inexplicably as a puff from the mouth of Vesuvius, the question burst forth: "Why? Why should you care what I see or taste or learn?"

Pietra put her hand over her mouth, shocked by her own daring, but the Duke nodded in approval. "Look around you, Pietra. As you say, it is beautiful. In my life, I have always wished to surround myself with things of beauty. But few things can be beautiful without being crafted and cared for. That mirror . . . the glass was once only sand on a beach; the gold of its frame was lost in a pile of dark earth until they were turned into a work of art. I enjoy bringing out beauty. I would like to bring out yours."

"Why?" she couldn't help asking again.

"Because," the Duke said, "I have nothing else to do."

She hesitated another moment and then went for the door. Still a fish out of water, she knew.

But he followed quickly, grabbed her hand and pulled her up short. "I know," he said, "you think it is impossible for you to become anything more than what you are now . . ." Abruptly, he shoved her in front of the mirror and forced her to look at herself. "Can you see what others see? Or is your beauty hidden from your own eyes by the fog of poverty and ignorance and hopelessness? You are exquisite, child. A wonder. I knew the moment I laid eyes on you that in you I could create a masterpiece."

Pietra shook herself loose. In the mirror she saw only her dirty face, her ragged hair. The hand that she wrenched loose from him still had fingernails as black as pitch.

"Please, Your Grace, pity me. Don't fill my head with dreams that can never come true."

"But I mean everything I've said. Look . . ."

Reaching into his pocket, he pulled out a dull gray rock the size of a pigeon's egg. He held it out to her as he had the wine. Only a rock. This time she took it without question, letting him place it in her palm.

"All you can see now," he said, his voice low and soft as silk, "is a plain and unremarkable stone. But hiding within that stone is a miracle, waiting for an artist with the right tools and the right knowledge to bring it out. One day a man will study the stone. He will make precise measurements, apply a knowledge of physics and mathematics and the phenomenon of light. He must have courage and great patience. But when he is done, when all his skills have been brought to bear on the stone, the result will be . . . Well, let me show you.''

Moving quickly, almost dancing it seemed to Pietra, he went to a cabinet between two of the high-curtained windows and took a velvet pouch from a drawer. With the quickness of a magician, he whisked away the dull stone and upended the pouch over her empty palm. Out tumbled a dazzling diamond, brilliant cut, flashing back the fire of the sun that poured through the windows and turning it into rainbows on her face.

Pietra's wide eyes locked on the stone. It drew her into its magic depths, captured her in its web of light. She felt as though it could burn her skin with its brilliance.

''The diamond has but one purpose,'' he went on, his voice a caress. ''To be beautiful, to give pleasure. Does it please you?''

''Oh yes,'' she said as soft as a prayer. ''Yes.''

''You are like the rough diamond, Pietra. I see just such perfection within you. It needs only the proper artist to bring it out and make it shine. I can do it.''

Perplexed, she looked up from the fire of the diamond to the fire of his eyes. ''How?''

''By teaching you . . . about beauty and pleasure. About the pleasure a woman can give to a man—and receive from him in return. It is an art form, perhaps the greatest of all. You were created for love, Pietra. I can see it if you cannot. I can turn you into the greatest artist of love in all Naples, in all Italy.'' He watched her as the words began to sink in. Watched as her eyes went back and forth between him and the diamond. At last he added, ''If you will put yourself in my hands, become my pupil, and let me teach you to love and be loved, the diamond will be yours.''

In her mind, she was thinking about what *zia* Gemma had told her. She had a jewel of her own. Should she trade it for the one offered by the Duke?

The expression on his face frightened her, the intensity of it. Slowly, her hand moved until it was over his, then she poured the diamond back into his palm. Without its brilliance her hand felt cold. When his fingers closed over it, it was as though the light had gone out of the day.

"It is very late," she murmured. "I must go."

"Yes, little one, go. And when you are ready, come back." He dropped the diamond into his pocket. She turned to the door. "And Pietra," he said, stopping her. "When you return to me, you may come to the front door of the palace."

It has been said that Naples is a city of palaces and churches. After leaving the first, Pietra ran to the second, Gesù Nuovo in the Spacca, the church of her childhood. It was shadowy inside, cool and quiet. A mass had recently finished; the air was still heavy with incense. She went straight to a statue of the Virgin, lit a candle, and fell to her knees.

"Holy Mother, Blessed Virgin . . . ," she began, and then stopped, uncertain of her prayer. What did she want? Did she seek the courage to deny the Duke's temptations—or the courage to accept? "Give me a sign," she begged.

She heard a voice, but not the Virgin's. It was the echo of her aunt's words: "Virginity is a jewel . . . more precious. . . ." She tried to picture her virginity, like a shining star. She looked into the flame of the candle and imagined it was the light of her treasure, a jewel meant only for her husband.

But all she could see was the diamond, flashing fire in her mind, brighter than innocence, more piercing than pain, as eternal as the sun. Her own "jewel" seemed dull and lifeless in comparison. She wanted to believe that the Duke could find such beauty within her as the men who found diamonds in dull stone.

Yet even if he could, was it worth losing her soul for?

The wall beside the Virgin was covered with *ex-votos*, small silver arms, legs, eyes, hearts, left in gratitude for the

Virgin's help in healing illness. "For prayers answered," they were inscribed.

"Why do you never answer *my* prayers?" Pietra cried, her fist pounding on the wooden railing.

Her head dropped onto her hands. Slowly, a new thought intruded. Perhaps the Duke's offer *was* the answer to her prayers. To become something more, to learn, to be surrounded by beauty instead of squalor and despair. Perhaps it was a way to *find* her soul.

The candle flickered, the flame grew smaller, nearly extinguished. In the dancing shadows, the Virgin's lips seemed to move. "It is the one thing that is yours, Pietra, more precious than diamonds. Do not give it away lightly."

She sighed. "Thy will be done," she whispered and rose stiffly; her knees hurt. She had decided. She would obey the Virgin and *zia* Gemma. She would not go back to the palazzo.

But as she left the church, she dragged her feet. She felt as if someone had forced her to draw the shutters on a sunny day.

The shop was empty when she entered, but she had no trouble hearing the voices of Lena and Giovanni coming through the planking from their room upstairs. They were having a fierce argument.

"Whoremonger!" shouted gentle Giovanni, who rarely raised his voice. It terrified Pietra to hear him. "You're worse than a whore yourself—doing that sort of business with a man like Hamak!"

Hamak? Of course, Pietra knew about Ruggiero Hamak. Who didn't know the Turk? He had a finger in every filthy business on the waterfront.

"I want to be rid of her!" Lena screamed. "How much better to rid ourselves of a curse and be paid into the bargain."

Santa Maria! They were arguing about her, Pietra realized.

"I won't accept that kind of money!"

"But you'll take the Duke's gold for a buckle! What harm if he pays Hamak for the girl, and Hamak pays me? Let the Duke have her, Giovanni. She's a witch!"

"*You* are the *strega*, you barren old hag," he yelled. "You hate her only because I love her. You live on hate. No wonder you can't bear a child. It would be cursed with such a mother.''

Lena's shriek rang down the stairwell, piercing, sharp as a knife. Footsteps sounded above, heading for the stairs. Pietra ran behind the counter for protection from the woman's madness.

Lena rushed into the room, her face splotched purple with rage. Giovanni followed, arms waving, a bag of coins in his hand. "Tomorrow!" he shouted. "Tomorrow you give the pimp back his money. Pietra is not for sale, not at any price!"

Lena saw Pietra, and her fury erupted with Vesuvian force. She ran into the kitchen and back out again. In her raised hand was a large carving knife.

"Aeiiiii!" she vented one of her terrible screams and charged at the girl. Pietra stood stock-still, frozen with horror.

"No!" yelled Giovanni, lunging to intercept his wife. But he was too late; her momentum was too great to stop, the knife already locked into its downward arc. She plunged it into her husband's heart.

He lurched against Pietra, eyes staring in astonishment. His body jerked like a puppet before he slid to the floor. A gurgling sound came from his throat; blood pumped from his chest.

Pietra fell to her knees beside him. "No," she moaned. "Signor Sacco . . . get up." She put her hands over the spurting wound, trying to stop the blood, but it seeped through her fingers. In seconds she was covered with it.

"Murderer!" Lena cried. Pietra raised confused eyes to see a look filled with hatred. "You've killed him, you've killed my Giovanni." Pietra rose, backing away in horror. Lena lifted her dead husband and began rocking him in her arms. "Murderer! Murderer! She's killed him."

Pietra ran out the door with Lena's cries behind her, stabbing the night.

An hour after Giovanni's murder, she crept back through the streets toward the shop, sneaking around corners. A crowd had gathered, and they were all muttering her name. Soon the *carabinieri* would be looking for her.

She had no friends to appeal to for help. Months ago *zia*

Gemma had gone north with her children in search of work. She couldn't even go into a church; she was covered with Giovanni's congealed blood. There was nowhere.

For three days she hid in the maze of alleys around the waterfront paralyzed by fear, numbed by grief. She slept in the darkest corners, ate scraps she found in the market when everyone was gone. She had to fight the rats for every morsel.

When the first shock of fear wore off, grief replaced it. Giovanni Sacco had been the one person left in Naples who cared for her. Now she had no one. And nowhere to go. "I am Pietra; I am stone," she chanted over and over, but the litany no longer worked its charm. She hurt too much.

Throughout those dark days and darker nights, one image kept coming to Pietra's mind. It was the one thing that kept her sane—the diamond, so brilliant, harder than any stone, pure and flawless as a star in a world that seemed otherwise evil and pitiless. The diamond was the one thing she could believe in.

After dark on the third day, weak with fatigue, dizzy with hunger, she began the long walk toward Posillipo.

She was almost too weak to lift the heavy knocker on the door. A servant answered and led her straight to the room where the Duke sat in a silk robe beside a warming fire. At the sight of her, he held his arms wide.

"You've come," he said as she fell to her knees before him.

Chapter 5

She woke with the standard prayer on her lips, murmured just before she opened her eyes. "Holy Mother, deliver me . . ."

And her prayer was answered. She found herself gazing up wide-eyed at the sky-blue silk canopy of an enormous soft bed. She was in a clean white nightgown, too, on sheets of soft linen.

Then she remembered where she was.

"*Buon giorno*, Signorina."

Pietra sat up as a husky girl with a wide florid face bustled into the room with a tray of food—fruit, cheese, rolls, an egg in a porcelain egg cup. She set the tray across Pietra's lap. "I am Antonia, your maid. You've slept well; it's past noon." She poured chocolate from a silver pot. Its rich aroma filled the room, and Pietra drank it greedily. "The Duke says he will see you this evening. He has gone into the city. When you're finished eating, I will help you into your new clothes."

"New clothes?" Pietra echoed uncertainly.

The maid giggled as she went to a huge armoire and threw open the carved doors. Inside, it bulged with dresses—soft

64

silk, cotton, glowing velvet, gowns of brocade and lace and soft wool challis. Shoes in a rainbow of colors and shelves of lacy underthings.

"You'll wear this one today," said Antonia, pulling out a dress of pin-dotted muslin the fresh green of new spring leaves. A silk rose adorned the waist, and the long skirt draped up behind. It was the most beautiful dress Pietra had ever seen or imagined.

She couldn't imagine putting on such a dress. It would be like changing her skin. She wasn't cut out for such finery.

"I can't wear those," she murmured.

"Then you'll wear nothing," said Antonia, "for the Duke had me burn those old rags you wore when you arrived. Now come, these are here a week already waiting for you."

A week? But how?

And then she remembered the argument that had led to Giovanni's death—the talk of Lena's dealings with Hamak, using the Turk as a middleman with the Duke. Even so, Pietra wondered, how could the Duke have known for certain she would come to him? Or was he so rich he could buy mountains of clothes merely on a hope that his whims would be answered? Well, since he had . . .

She spent the next several hours trying on one dress after another. Pietra couldn't believe how many undergarments had to be worn—a corset and muslin camisole, eyelet-trimmed drawers, a horsehair bustle, embroidered lisle stockings topped by half a dozen petticoats. Without Antonia's help, it would have been impossible to manage it all. No wonder the women who wore these dresses all had maids.

When Antonia brushed her hair, drew it up into a knot, and pushed her in front of the mirror, Pietra could hardly believe the figure looking back from the glass was herself.

"His Lordship will be pleased," said Antonia before she left to help with the other chores in the house.

Alone, Pietra alternated between standing in front of the mirror—or running giddily past it sometimes, to make sure the reflection would keep up with her—and sitting stiffly in a chair, hardly moving so that the dress wouldn't wrinkle.

As the hours passed, she was increasingly anxious that Antonia should be right. She wanted His Lordship to be pleased.

But he still hadn't come when the view from her window showed the sun sinking into the bay and Antonia returned with a large bowl of a delicious fish stew, some bread, and a glass of wine on a tray. Pietra took no time at all consuming her dinner, sitting at a small table while Antonia stood and watched.

As she cleared the napkin from her lap, Pietra suddenly let out a wail and burst into tears.

"What's wrong?" asked Antonia.

Choked with sobs, Pietra could only point to the spatter of stains that had collected on her dress as she hastily gobbled the stew.

Antonia laughed. "Don't worry, dear. You're about to take that dress off, anyway. It's time to get you ready for the Duke."

Pietra was confounded. Hadn't she put on the dress to be ready? What a strange life she'd come to—where such fine dresses were worn only for the purpose of sitting alone in one's room.

She submitted unprotestingly as Antonia helped her out of the dress and into a zinc-lined tub that was pulled in front of the fire and filled with buckets of steaming water. Antonia chattered about her life in the palace as she lathered Pietra's back with violet-scented soap and washed her hair. Then the maid took care of drying and powdering and combing Pietra, rubbing lotion onto her skin and dabbing perfume on her body.

Pietra said almost nothing throughout the whole ritual.

No, she kept thinking, her prayer had not been answered. It was only a dream, and she would surely wake in a cold alleyway to be hunted down and condemned for a murder she had not committed.

Yet the dream went on.

Antonia brushed her hair till it fell down her back in ripples, glowing like polished ebony in the firelight. Then she brought her a robe made of Chinese silk as red as a ripe tomato and embroidered with flowers. "He wishes you to wear this," the maid said. "Nothing else." She drew the curtains, lit some candles, and was gone.

The Duke entered a few minutes later.

Knowing what he would expect, Pietra had lain down on the bed to wait. He walked over and looked down at her; then he laughed lightly, a friendly sound.

"Oh, my dear, the way you look—stretched out as flat as a board! Is that what you think I want to do, simply bang a nail through a plank?"

She raised herself up, curiously disappointed and alarmed. The dream might continue . . . but only if she could please him.

His laughter subsided, and he held out his hand. "Come."

He went to a chair beside the fire and seated her in his lap. Then holding her gently, stroking her hair, he murmured soft words until she began to relax. After a few moments, her arms crept up and around his neck.

"You are like a jewel box, my pet," he whispered in her ear. "Beautiful on the outside, but the contents are more wonderful still." She basked in the glow of his words. The way he held her made her feel so warm, so treasured. So safe.

He slid one hand inside the dressing gown, caressing her silken skin. She tensed.

"Be not afraid, *carissima*," he cajoled. "Your body was given to you by God. He must have loved you very much to make it so beautiful. Be proud of your beauty, Pietrina."

No one had called her that since her father had died. She almost cried, but then his hand slid down to touch one nipple and she gasped instead. Sensation shot through her, making her stomach flutter, shooting all the way to her toes.

He chuckled. "Yes," he said softly. "Feel it. Enjoy it."

She couldn't help feeling it. It was everywhere—the heat, the fluttering within. Could it really be a gift from God? Could it possibly feel so good if it was not?

At last he rose with her still in his arms and carried her to the big carved bed. When he eased her out of the dressing gown, she made a reflex move to cover herself with her hands. "No, Pietra," he said, lifting her hands away. "Never be ashamed of your beauty." He pulled back to look at her and murmured, "More perfect than I could have imagined." He cupped his hand around one breast, flicked his nail lightly across the nipple.

Again that sensation shot through her, centered now in her groin, a sort of pain but one she didn't wish away.

"Pietra," he said, his voice falling almost to a whisper. "Tell me to leave you now and I will. I want you to trust me . . . to desire me."

She looked up into his eyes, almost midnight black in the shadowy light, and she thought of the cold world that was waiting if she disappointed him, of the dresses in the closet, of the comfort of Antonia's help and company . . . and she thought of his gentleness and the bolts of lovely sensation she had already felt.

"Do not leave," she whispered, as though afraid to hear herself say it.

"Then it is time to explore," he said and held up two fingers. "These are my explorers, *cara*." He placed them against her lips. "They are going on a voyage across Italy. Here"—they trailed down to her breasts—"are the beautiful Alps with their glorious peaks"—his fingers slid between them—"and the Val D'Aosta at their base." Her eyes closed as she lost herself in feeling.

"Here"—his hand slid lower—"is the fertile land of Lombardy and here, Tuscany." He caressed her belly, chuckling as the skin jumped beneath his fingers. "This is where the grapes grow, sweet and delicious, bursting with juice, to make a man forget his cares in the wine that flows down, down to the delta, here." He stroked the inside of one thigh, fluttering lightly over her flesh. She began to squirm, her muscles moving beyond her control. The warmth of the sun that ripened the grapes seemed to be coursing through her body.

His fingers moved to her tangled triangle of shiny black hair. "And here," he said reverently, "we come to the Holy City of Rome. A pilgrim is seeking entrance to the holy sepulchre." He licked his finger and slid it deep inside her.

She gasped loud and arched her back. Her eyes flew open.

"Shhh," he said to reassure her. "Shhh, sweet Pietrina." He moved the finger gently inside her. She could feel her muscles tighten around it. She pressed her thighs together, capturing his hand, wanting to hold the feeling inside.

"Wait," he said and removed his hand. He rose and quickly removed his brocade gown. He spread her legs and positioned himself between them. Her eyes widened at the sight of his penis, rising like a beacon, red, eager. "Touch it," he said and guided her hand to it.

It pulsed beneath her fingers. He moaned, and she wondered if she'd hurt him, but his hand wrapped over hers, squeezing the thick shaft and guiding it down. "A pilgrim," he repeated, "a penitent seeking a state of grace, in need of holy baptism."

The enormous thing teased at the lips of her holy place, stroking across it, building the fire within her while it stoked her fear. The thing was so huge; it would never fit. She tried to push him off, her fear too great, but he held one shoulder firmly with his free hand. Then with a sharp thrust he entered her, breaking through her barrier, a small dam bursting.

There was pain, but not much. He lay still and it subsided. Then he began slowly to move, in and out in a rhythm as old as time. She opened her eyes, not minding her tears, and her long legs wrapped around him as though they belonged there.

His tempo increased. The friction was still painful, but she no longer resisted. His face grew darker, his breathing heavy. Sweat popped out on his forehead and upper lip. Then suddenly he tensed, every muscle taut, his face a grimace, the veins in his neck like rope. He groaned through clenched teeth. Deep inside her, she felt him pulsing. He collapsed against her.

After a panting moment, he slowly withdrew. With one hand, he stroked her hair. "*Mia gioia, mi gioiello*," he murmured. "My joy. My jewel."

She was warm and wet. She looked down. Blood was seeping onto the fine cotton sheets, and she was afraid he would become angry.

But he gave her a gentle smile. "A virgin's blood is holy,"

he said softly. Then he rose to his knees and lowered his mouth to lick away the last drops of blood. "Thank you, *cara*. You have given me a great blessing."

The bleeding was quickly over, but the Duke kept licking at where the blood had been. All the pain was gone, but now Pietra felt something else happening—a feeling, a warmth, blossoming inside her. She started to push him away, timid, frightened. But also thrilled. Again, he gently stopped her.

He lapped at her, probing with his tongue till her head snapped back on the pillow. His hands pushed up to her breasts and found her nipples, hard as little diamonds. Her hips rose of their own accord, pushing her closer to his mouth, his tongue. As he squeezed her nipples, the dam burst in her again, but different this time, hot and surging and wonderful, spreading out from her center to fill all of her. Her body bucked and she cried out and shuddered as he drank from her, licking up her juices as she rode on a wave of pure feeling, finally sliding once again into peace.

He held her in his arms while she cried, rocking her like a baby as great sobs of joy shook her whole body.

Afterward, when she was once again aware of him and of herself, when she could feel his heart beating beneath her ear, she didn't feel ashamed. She felt calm and loved. Grief was gone. So was the numbness that had been with her since Giovanni's death.

She felt—no, knew—that a barrier had been crossed and there was no going back. On the other side was her history; on this side was her life.

She woke alone, but such a different waking than she had ever known before. When Antonia appeared with the breakfast tray there was a vase on it holding a single rose. In the center of the rose, like a drop of dew, was the cut diamond the Duke had shown her on her first visit.

She plucked it out, wiped it on her napkin, then jumped from the bed and ran to hold it up to the window so she could see the sun through it. A rainbow of colors flashed across her face, momentarily blinding her. She rolled it between her palms, feeling every facet, then ran her tongue across it. She wanted to taste it. Her diamond. As pure as sunlight.

As she spun in a dance of delight, she saw him standing at the door. A witness to the whole performance, he was laughing.

She ran to him. "It is really mine, isn't it?"

"Did I not promise?" he said.

She pressed it to her heart. "It is the most beautiful thing I shall ever own. I'm so lucky."

The Duke laughed again and took her in his arms. "No luckier than I am to have you, my little dove," he said.

It was the first time she was called *colomba*.

She became the Duke's *concubina*. Though of course not his only one, Pietra was the one he treasured most. He moved her to one of his smaller villas, a *palazzina* high on the Costa Amalfitana overlooking the sea south of Naples, a jewel on the water. He could not keep her in the Palazzo Monfalco. The Duchess of Monfalco would be returning soon from their Sicilian estates.

He visited as often as he could. Always he brought some object of beauty and taught her how to read its value—how to tell silk from cotton and solid gold from gilt, how to match wine to food, how to tell a Titian from a Tiepolo. Sometimes he brought Maria Blanco with him, and she and Pietra became good friends. "There is much she can teach you, Colombina," the Duke said.

The house was beautiful, its rooms awash in the dappled light reflected from the water. Pietra never tired of looking at the sea, a miracle of changing colors, calm beauty . . . and peace. The constant clamor of Naples that had filled her ears since childhood was far behind her. Even the shrieking voice of Lena Sacco had faded from memory. Now the sounds of her day were the soft voices of the servants, the clicking of her shoes on marble floors, the humming of her own voice, and, when she opened a window, the boom and shushing withdrawal of the waves on the rocks below.

Eventually, the quiet seeped into her soul and did its healing work. The specter of men arriving at the door to haul her away to jail ceased to trouble her. Late one hot night, after she and the Duke lay sated from their lovemaking, she confessed her terror of being arrested for a murder of which she was innocent.

"You have nothing to fear," the Duke told her. "You are under my protection." Then he added that the matter had already been cleared up. It was known that Lena had stabbed her husband. She had been put in the madhouse.

Pietra clapped her hands gleefully, but the Duke caught her at the wrists. "No, Colombina, no. Never gloat over such misfortune in the lives of others. The wheel goes round . . ."

Whatever he said, she listened. Sometimes she didn't understand his meaning at first, but she knew she would eventually. He had taught her so much.

Almost from the day she arrived, the string of tutors began—young graduates of the famed University of Naples, where Thomas Aquinas had been a professor in 1272 (one of the first things she was told by her history tutor). They were enchanted by her. She could feel their admiration in the way they looked at her, these young men with wavy hair and laughter in their dark eyes. But she was never tempted to accept an invitation, even if one had been stupid enough to offer. She belonged to the Duke; she knew it and so did they.

Though they were sometimes convenient for practicing her newly developing art of flirtation, what really excited her about these young men was what they could teach her. As information poured from them, she soaked it up like a sponge. First they worked on reading, the basis for everything else. She progressed like a bullet, and they went on to other fields. Literature, history and philosophy, mathematics and music, astronomy and French—she loved them all. Pietra took to knowledge like a barnacle takes to a rock. Long after her tutors had begged for a break, she would still be asking eager questions.

"I am proud of you," the Duke said one cool autumn evening as they dined on the terrace above the sea. "You have been with me nearly six months, and your tutors are ecstatic over your progress. You have more than fulfilled my expectations.''

''I want to be able to talk with you and not bore you,'' she said as she daintily peeled a leaf off an artichoke, dipped it in butter, and brought it to her lips.

''The one thing you will never do, Pietrina, is bore me.'' He fed her the next artichoke leaf, and when the butter dribbled down her chin, he leaned over and licked it off. ''Delicious,'' he purred.

An hour later, he was licking parts of her body the butter had not touched as he gave her one more lesson in the subject he entrusted to no one but himself—the art of sensual pleasure.

These lessons occupied hours. Firelit evenings or long lazy afternoons spent in her bed like a bower, draped in sea-green silk embroidered with flowers. Touch and smell, the music of tender words, build-up and release were all part of her lessons. She learned when to tantalize and when to give wholeheartedly, when to hold back and when to open like a flower in a spring rain. Using exotic texts that came from the Egyptians, the Persians, the Japanese, from men who had explored every dark corner of the earth, the Duke educated her in every nuance of the art of love.

Pietra paid close attention to every detail. She wanted desperately to please him, this man who had plucked her from despair and given her so much. And in pleasing him, she found more and more pleasure for herself. Soon she was laughing at the silly girl who had wept before the Virgin, afraid of losing her soul if she gave herself to the Duke. Nothing that felt so good, she now believed, could possibly be wrong.

She had been in her beautiful little *palazzina* nearly two years when the Duke said during an evening walk around the garden, ''It will be your birthday soon, Colombina. I've planned a special celebration.''

She had forgotten it was to be her birthday—happy to forget because Lena had told her the day was cursed. But now she turned to the Duke with eager surprise. With him there were no curses. Everything, every moment seemed blessed. "Eduardo," she said, "you are too kind . . ."

He smiled, pleased not only by her modesty, but by the manners she had learned so well from his tutors. "In a fortnight, my dear, Il Teatro San Carlo is having a gala . . ."

Pietra swirled around, the force of happiness spinning her like a top. The opera! The vision came to her of a night when she had stood in the chill shadows watching ladies in beautiful gowns being escorted into the glittering opera house. She had longed then to join their company but never dreamed it would be possible. She had never even dared mention the idea to the Duke. Yet now he was taking her. He knew the dearest wishes of her heart without even being told. She looked at him with adoration as he went on.

"Maria will be singing *Rigoletto* with Lancona. It should be a fine performance. Many think Ettore Lancona is the greatest tenor of all time, and Maria, of course, is incomparable. Alberto, your music master, will go over the score with you in advance. You will enjoy it more that way. You'll need a new gown, of course. I will send the dressmaker tomorrow."

She grasped his hands and danced with him around the garden path, making him laugh. "It will be the best birthday ever," she said. "The very best." Then she stopped, overcome with the need to show her gratitude. "Come upstairs with me now, Eduardo. Let me make a gift to you."

In her bedroom, he reached for her at once. "No," she said in a soft voice. "You have been my teacher from the start. Tonight I shall teach you." She pushed him gently into a wing chair near the fire with a glass of wine, then sat at her boudoir and began a performance created out of her conversations with Maria, her studies of great women in books, and a growing comprehension of the allure of women in certain paintings. Of all the sources she drew on, however, the greatest was her own instinct, freed at last from all inhibition.

Slowly she pulled out her tortoiseshell hairpins to let her

lustrous black tresses fall in heavy coils down her back. Occasionally she glanced into the mirror at the Duke, but mostly she closed her eyes, as if lost in her own thoughts. She was having fun.

She hummed a little tune as she unhooked the lace at her throat, unbuttoned her bodice, unfastened her skirt and petticoats until the whole combination dropped to the floor and she could step out of it. With infinite slowness, she untied the satin ribbons of her camisole.

She peeked at him then. His head was tossed back, his eyes mere slits as he watched every movement of the private exhibition while sipping slowly from his wineglass. She moved her eyes to his lap and was pleased to see evidence that her performance was having the desired effect.

Turning around, she offered him her back. "Unlace me," she demanded. He stood behind her and took off all the rest, until the only thing she wore was the pendant he'd given her just last week, an emerald on a gold chain.

As his hands began to rove over her firm silken flesh, she unbuttoned his shirt, twining her fingers in the wiry hair on his chest. Then she pulled him closer, unbuttoned the fly of his trousers, and tenderly pulled out that part of him that so clearly wanted her. For a while, she sucked at him, as though moistening and tasting a delicious fruit. Then she gently prodded him toward a chair, and when he was down, straddled him and ever so slowly lowered herself onto him. For a long moment, she held perfectly still, forcing him to do the same.

Finally, she began to move, gracefully, as in a dance. It was the first time in their lovemaking that she had set the rhythm; she could see that it was driving him higher than ever.

She knew instinctively when it was right for him, as it was for her, too. She watched his face, watched him watching her, matched his breathing, even matched his heartbeat, she felt sure. The heat within them built until, at exactly the same moment, it exploded, rocking the chair.

Later, as he held her and their heartbeats returned to normal, he said, "You are perfect, little dove, more perfect than

I ever dared hope. If I have done nothing else with my life, I have succeeded in creating one masterpiece—you, the perfect woman.''

"But only for you, Eduardo," she said. "You made me, I am yours. I will serve you and love you always."

He was silent a minute, as though to savor her words, before he said, "No, Colombina."

Puzzled by his denial and the sadness she heard in his voice, she raised her face to look at him. He smiled at her, a smile that was full of sadness, too.

"You are still very young, Pietrina. I know more of the world than you. I know that one day you will leave me."

"No, Eduardo. Never!"

"Shhhh." He brushed the hair from her eyes, his fingertips lightly caressing her cheeks. "You will leave me, my love, because you should, you must. Do I dare to create a masterpiece and keep it only for myself? When a day comes—and it will—that you wish to go on to greater promises, to a younger lover, I will not stand in your way."

She tried to protest again, but he put a finger to her lips and continued. "Someone, someday, will offer you more of a future than I can, and you will grab for it with both hands because I have taught you to live life to the fullest. You have given me a very precious gift, my Pietra. Your freedom is my gift to you."

His words frightened her. She couldn't imagine life anymore without him, this man who had become the very center of her world. She snuggled closer into his arms. "Don't speak of the future anymore," she begged. "There is only tonight. Make love to me again . . . and again."

"With very great pleasure, Signorina," he replied, and scooped her up in his arms.

In the two weeks before the opera gala, she nearly drove her dressmaker crazy with her ideas, her fantasies, her changes of mind. After making him sketch up a dozen frothy creations, she decided at last that she must change her look from the innocent dresses with high necks and soft colors that the Duke preferred. For this occasion she wanted to look older than her seventeen years, to appear far wiser than she was. She wanted to look like one of the sophisticated women of the world she had seen that long-ago night when she'd been a street urchin standing outside the theater.

She settled at last on a sleeveless, low-cut gown, almost severely simple, of changeable silk in violet and blue. Silver lace edged the neck and trimmed the bodice, and a swag of deep blue watered silk draped up over the skirt and fell into a train. She practiced walking in it for four solid days until she was sure she wouldn't step on the sweeping skirt and trip down the theater steps to fall flat on her face.

On the night of the opera, the Duke came to pick her up in his large carriage, pulled by a pair of matched white stallions. She came down the wide curving steps of the foyer to meet him, her dress hidden by a Russian sable cape, her arms sheathed in long silk gloves of dove gray, satin slippers that matched her gown on her feet. Antonia had done her hair in an upsweep of curls, with long tendrils that spilled like a fountain from a ring of creamy orange blossoms. In her ears were diamond drops, also his gifts. She carried a painted silk fan, which Maria had taught her to use to great advantage, and she glowed with happiness.

Where the cape was open, a diamond lavaliere could be seen hanging on its chain so that it just kissed at the cleavage of her breasts, teasing, inviting.

The Duke admired her with his eyes, before he said in a hush, "Magnificent." Then he produced from the pocket of his formal black coat a fancily wrapped package tied with silver ribbons. "To mark the occasion," he said.

Her eager fingers tore away the wrappings and opened the velvet-covered box. She gasped when she saw the contents, a jeweled pin in the shape of a bird. Its breast was a rare pink diamond, the flames licking at its feet were made of dozens of rubies. There were over a hundred gems in all encrusting the pin.

"Do you know the story of the phoenix, Pietra?"

She had found it in her studies of the Greeks. "The bird of myth that rose from its own ashes?"

"Tonight you are completing your own flight, rising from

the ashes of that hell in which you were born, to soar as a woman of perfection far above all others. So let this be your symbol. You shall always rise . . . and keep rising." He pinned it to her cape.

"I love you, Eduardo," she said.

"I shall always remember that," he said, and swept her out to the carriage.

She had to force herself not to stand gaping in childish disbelief at her first sight of the interior of the Teatro San Carlo. The finest opera house in all Europe, more famous even than La Scala or Venice's Fenice, glowed with light, sparkled tonight with the fire of a thousand gems, rang with refined chatter and delicate laughter.

It reminded Pietra of a jewel box done entirely in gold and ivory, lined with six tiers of boxes paneled in crimson silk. On the ceiling was a fresco of Apollo and the Muses. The Royal Box, designed for the Bourbon kings of Naples, was sumptuous with golden hangings, gilded angels, and antique mirrors.

"The interior is all wood and stucco," the Duke explained. "Even the marble decor is merely cleverly painted wood. That is why the theater has such perfect acoustics."

As they entered their box, a sea of silver lorgnettes and mother-of-pearl opera glasses swung toward them. The Duke acknowledged one or two friends with a regal nod and totally disregarded all the other curious stares. Well known for his wealth, for his taste, and especially for his beautiful mistresses, he was used to being the center of attention. But he could tell there was more excitement and curiosity than usual in the stares he attracted tonight.

Pietra tried hard to seem as blasé as the Duke, but it was nearly impossible. Whispered questions floated up all around her. "Who *is* she?" came from several directions. "Spanish, do you think?" was another. "Look at that hair, that tiny waist," said a woman in a nearby box. "She *must* be related to the Empress Elizabeth."

As the Duke took her cape, the smile she gave him was so full of adoration that a dozen male hearts in various parts of the Teatro San Carlo broke at that moment.

"I am looking forward to hearing Lancona sing," the Duke said when they were seated, oblivious to the stir they continued to create. "They say he's an anomaly, a tenor who isn't fat. I understand he has some novel theories about how to project his voice without a lot of sheer girth."

Suddenly the lights dimmed, music swelled up from the orchestra, and the painted curtain rose in front of the stage. Pietra's eyes were at once riveted to the scene. She'd never seen or even imagined anything like this enchantment.

The world vanished as she gave herself to the music, humming softly along at the parts Alberto had studied with her. When Ettore Lancona entered and began to sing, Pietra was enchanted by the tall, handsome, swaggering Duke of Mantua, a charming rogue, a seducer, whose only pleasure lay in conquest.

"*La donna è mobile, Qual piuma al vento . . .*," he sang. "Woman is fickle, A feather on the wind." As the notes rose up to meet her, Pietra felt as though her own being were rising out of herself, carried away by the music and by his presence. She became Gilda, the young heroine, daughter of the hunchback Rigoletto. When the tenor looked up at the first tier of boxes and his golden eyes seemed to focus on her, she could imagine Lancona was actually singing to her: "*il sol dell' anima*," love is the sunlight of the soul; "*la vita è amore*," love is life itself. The music was so beautiful and Lancona's voice so pure, as flawless as the diamond that hung around her neck.

During the intermission Pietra refused to leave her seat, unwilling to break the spell. When the last note faded away and the curtain fell to thunderous applause, she merely sat quietly, too stunned to clap or even to move.

It was the Duke's voice that brought her out of her reverie. "Now we must go backstage and congratulate Maria on a fine performance. Perhaps she can be persuaded to introduce us to the great Lancona."

Though Pietra nodded calmly, the prospect of meeting Lancona filled her with a storm of excitement. During the final acts, he had glanced increasingly in her direction—so much that she believed he was truly aware of her.

Backstage, Maria was surrounded by her usual throng of admirers, but they parted like the waters to let the Duc di Monfalco and Pietra pass through.

"Eduardo!" the diva exclaimed. "Tell me how I sang tonight. You are always my best critic."

The Duke bent to kiss the air above her gloved hand. "Always," said the Duke, "because you always enchant me with a voice that is always superlative."

Maria laughed. "And you are always a wonderful liar, too," she said. "Though tonight I know I was good, because I invariably sound angelic when I sing with Ettore. He brings out the best in all his partners." She turned to Pietra. "Look at you! *Who* helped you choose that gown? It is divine." She kissed the girl on both cheeks then pulled back for a more careful appraisal. A small frown marred her perfect forehead. "I knew you'd turn out well, Pietra, and for Eduardo's sake I was glad to help, but I had no idea you'd become *quite* so beautiful *quite* so soon. I think something must be done about this, *toute de suite*."

Pietra laughed, but before she could say anything they were interrupted by the great Lancona himself. "Maria," he said, staring at Pietra, "introduce me at once."

"*Mais oui*," said Maria with a chuckle. As she introduced the tenor to the teenaged girl, their eyes connected as though pulled by a magnetic force. Pietra could not tear her gaze from his. His eyes were light hazel, the gold of sunflowers under the sky of a late autumn afternoon. He was tall, though not as tall as the Duke. His thick black hair was brushed straight back, giving him something of a devilish look. His shoulders were broad, waist narrow, hips slender. Just as the Duke had said, there was nothing of the classically hefty tenor about him. He had the sleek body of a well-muscled cat.

The electricity between them was palpable; Pietra felt it charging through her body as she studied him. As if under the contol of someone else, her hand rose up toward his mouth and he bent to kiss it, not pursing his lips to the air as custom dictated, but pressing them to her glove till she thought she felt a faint burning through the thin silk.

"Eduardo," Maria's voice came from somewhere nearby, "look who's here, the Conte di Brenacia. He has been asking after you." Maria and the Duke faded away.

"Maestro," said Pietra softly to Lancona, "it is an honor."

Lancona kept gazing at her intently. "Do you belong to him?" he asked, bending close to her.

"He is my protector," she replied.

"Why?" Lancona said hotly.

She didn't know how to answer or even whether to speak. She knew she was on dangerous ground, could feel everything that had been solid and reliable for the past two years slipping away. Yet she did nothing to pull herself back to safety. Could do nothing.

"Tell me," Lancona insisted. "How did the Duke manage to win such a prize as you?"

When her hand went to the diamond at her breast, he caught the movement and smiled. "Ah. Is that all? I will give you a hundred diamonds. A thousand."

"He has given me far more than diamonds."

"I will give you more, anything you want, everything. Come away with me."

"It would be wrong," she said, finally pulling her eyes away to look down.

His hand cradled her chin, lifting her face again so she had to look at him. "Signorina Manzi, we are not small people to be ruled by convention, slaves to petty morality. I am meant to fly with the eagles, and I have seen no one until tonight who I believed could fly with me."

Her latest gift from the Duke came to her mind, the phoenix pin, the great bird rising from its ruby flames to fly free. Still, the crazy impulses of her heart remained at war with the lessons in her mind.

"I owe him too much," she said. "I cannot leave him."

"Do you believe in *la forza del destino*? When destiny tells us where our lives must go, we can no longer choose our own path." He leaned closer. "I knew the first time I saw you tonight that you are my destiny and I am yours." He bent closer still, and so softly that only she could hear, he sang a line from one of the evening's arias, a line that had clutched at her stomach as she sat in her box: "*Adunque amiamoci, donna celeste*—Then let us love, celestial lady." He straightened. "I will send my carriage for you in the morning."

She stared at him, at once disbelieving and wholly submissive. If the carriage truly came, she would float into it, she thought, unable to control herself.

Then she felt the Duke's hand on her elbow. "Pietra, we have a long drive. Signor Lancona, a pleasure to meet you. I enjoyed your singing." With a slight but undeniable pressure on her arm, he led Pietra away.

She glanced back over her shoulder at the handsome tenor. His golden eyes burned into hers. And even when she looked away, she could feel their heat on her back until she was out the door.

The Duke was silent for much of the ride home, but as they neared her *palazzina*, he turned from the window and took her hand.

"I will be all right, Colombina," he said. "Even if you go, part of you will always stay with me."

"What are you talking about, Eduardo?"

"Please, my dear." He patted her hand as if she were a child. "Didn't I tell you this day would come? I hoped it wouldn't be so soon, but *c'est la vie*. I have known from the start I could not keep you permanently. You are my work of art, Pietrina, and now the world shall know it. You must go with him."

She looked into his eyes and saw that he meant it. She threw her arms around his neck. "Oh, Eduardo, my dear, dear friend. My heart breaks to think of leaving you . . ."

"But it will mend soon enough, annealed by the heat of a passion greater than you have known before." The carriage pulled up at the steps of her *palazzina*. When he spoke again, his voice was cool and level. "Now dry your eyes, little one, and go upstairs. Antonia will help you pack. I know the look in Lancona's eyes; I've worn it myself often enough, God knows. He will not want to be kept waiting."

They climbed from the carriage. He took her shoulders

and turned her to face him. "But tell him this: If he ever dares hurt you, I will kill him."

She nodded gravely, then gave him a quick kiss, picked up her heavy skirts, and ran up the stairs. He climbed back into the carriage and it rolled away again, but she was already inside the house, calling for Antonia.

As the consort of a celebrated opera star, Pietra's horizons expanded dramatically.

First and foremost, she discovered love, and with it a romantic passion she couldn't have guessed existed. She had been genuinely fond of the Duke and had known physical pleasure in his arms, but with the added element of the ecstatic love she felt for Ettore she soared, she ascended to the peak of perfect sensation, calling out his name as he pushed her over the top and she slid into a space whirling with bright colors and beauty and music, a space full only of him and her and their love.

Lancona adored her; she worshipped him. Wherever he performed—at La Scala, La Fenice, in Rome or Florence—she went with him. He showered her with flowers, with attention, with love. Remembering the Duke's diamond, he also showered her with jewels, as he had promised he would. Not only emeralds and sapphires and rubies, but garnets from Vienna, Milanese chrysoberyl with a gleaming tiger's eye to protect her from harm, pearls from Paris, opals from Madrid. And diamonds, always more diamonds. She kept them in a box of hammered gold he bought from a shop on the Ponte Vecchio when he was singing in Florence.

As much as she loved her jewels for their light, their color, their hope of perfection, she treasured them above all as symbols of Ettore's devotion. But the more he gave her, the less important they became, for in love Pietra believed she had found something more tangible to put her faith in, something as durable as any stone.

Only one shadow blighted their happiness. Years before Ettore had entered into an arranged marriage to the daughter of an affluent merchant. She was a plain young woman with no interest in opera or any desire to travel. Ettore saw her as dull and homely, yet it was the Muses he was really marrying. For he had begun to recognize the gift of his own magical voice and to dream of a career in opera, and he knew that his wealthy father-in-law would provide the money to pay for master classes with the great teachers who lived in Milan and Rome, cities far from his village.

Now Ettore had his career—he was the greatest tenor in Europe; opera houses everywhere clamored to book him, Verdi had written a new opera especially for him. Only one wish remained to be answered. He wanted desperately to marry Pietra. But he and his wife were both Catholics; divorce was an impossibility. Ettore applied to the Pope for an annulment—a foolish hope after so many years of marriage, but his only hope. The petition was denied.

Whenever he bemoaned the impossibility of becoming her husband, Pietra assured him it made no difference. "We are together. We can be no more bound than we are by hearts and souls." If there was ever any doubt that they were united to the very core of their beings, it was dispelled each time they blended into each other's flesh, always rising together to the purest pitch of excitement before the climax that brought them, still together, to the quiet of perfect contentment.

Their idyll could probably have continued regardless of the prevailing social conventions, except that Ettore's wife decided one day to make one of her rare journeys to see her husband perform at La Scala. Of course, she knew he dallied with women outside of his marriage; she also knew he would be hers forever under the law and that none of his *amours* had ever lasted beyond a few months.

But when she made her surprise appearance on the night of the performance, she saw the way he gazed up from the stage at the beautifully gowned and jewel-bedecked young woman who sat in a side box. Signora Lancona saw, too, that the woman in the box was very young and breathtakingly beautiful. This would be no mere dalliance, she realized; she could not take comfort in the certainty that her later years would be spent with Ettore at her side. Whatever the law said, whatever God said, Ettore was married in his heart to this other woman. She resolved, however, that God and the law would have the last word.

Thereafter, in various cities where Lancona was performing, the Signora turned up unpredictably to sit in the audience in a shabby black dress, her forlorn, tear-reddened eyes following her husband around the stage while her rough hands twisted a handkerchief—the picture of the neglected wife.

And every night Signorina Manzi, beautifully gowned and covered in jewels, sat in a box, alone in her splendor—the acknowledged concubine.

At first there were just a few cat-calls at Ettore's performances, nothing serious, hardly worth acknowledging. But the Signora continued her campaign relentlessly, and soon the cat-calls began drowning out the performance. Sopranos started refusing to perform with him.

Finally the worst happened. On the eve of a major gala, La Scala canceled his appearance. Soon the other opera houses of Italy followed suit; his appearance on their stage was "not suitable."

"I will go away," Pietra said the day the final cable arrived, from Rome this time. "They'll ask you back if I'm out of your life."

"No!" he said, storming around their Venice hotel room. "I don't understand it. What do they expect of me? Of course I have a mistress. This is Italy! For a married man to remain forever faithful to his wife would be ridiculous, contemptible even. Look at your Duke. No one censured him because of you or any of his other mistresses."

"His wife never objected. Yours wants you back."

He clung to her. "I won't give you up."

"You must, Ettore. I know what they say of me. They used to laugh and call me your *giocatello*, your plaything. But now they know our love is eternal. That is what they cannot accept. Our sublime happiness."

"Then let them rot!" he stormed around the room. "And let her rot, too, my precious wife! We don't need Italy and its pettiness. We will go where beauty and music are appreciated, where love is appreciated."

"Where, Ettore?" said Pietra. She was deathly afraid of losing him. "Where can we go?"

"To France. We will live in Paris."

The lovers adored Paris and it adored them. They found an apartment on the Île St-Louis with a view of the towers of Notre Dame. They made friends among the artists of Montparnasse and were as much at home over a pernod beneath the crystal chandeliers of Le Procope as they were sipping champagne at Maxim's. They climbed to the top of that latest Wonder of the World, the Eiffel Tower, and strolled hand-in-hand along the banks of the Seine.

Ettore had been right. The opera-goers of Paris couldn't have cared less about his marital status. They loved his voice, his pretty Pietra, his *brio*. Every seat sold out whenever he performed at the Paris Opera. Noblemen paid him huge fees to sing one aria at their private soirées, as often as not making it a condition that he bring along the exquisite Mademoiselle Manzi. Soon, he was richer than ever, buying Pietra more diamonds, rubies, and, to match her eyes, sapphires.

Signora Lancona accepted defeat along with a very large monthly check and returned to her village.

Lancona to Open Opera Season with Pagliacci announced the headline on the cultural pages of *Le Figaro* for April 1892. The part was the greatest challenge for a tenor. Lancona had been rehearsing for weeks. Every newspaper speculated on how high his highest note would be.

Ettore and Pietra were both glowing with happiness and excitement as April 26 approached—the night of his greatest triumph and her twenty-first birthday.

"Wear your white satin dress tonight," he said that afternoon, supremely confident about the evening ahead.

"Of course," she said. It was his favorite.

That night in his dressing room, Ettore pulled a Cartier box from his pocket. "Your birthday present," he said as she opened it with childish delight.

Inside was a magnificent parure—a necklace of sapphires surrounded by diamonds, matching drop earrings, a pair of bracelets. And a ring, the first he'd ever given her. It was a single star sapphire the color of a midnight sky.

As he was clasping the necklace around her neck, there was a knock at the door, a telegram. He tore the flimsy envelope open, scanned the words, and let out a whoop like an Indian.

"The Metropolitan Opera! They want me in New York for next season!" He picked her up by her waist and twirled her around.

"Ettore! I'm not in the ballet. Put me down!"

"America! Do you know what this means, *cara*? It means we can get married. We will have babies, lots of babies. *Bambini Americani*!"

"Wait." She laughed too, struggling for breath. "America is still part of this earth, isn't it, and you are still married."

"Yes. No. It doesn't matter." He flapped his expressive hands in the air. "They are different there. We won't need a church to get married. I'll get a divorce somehow. About this they are very civilized, Americans. Someday you will be Signora Lancona, my heart. And tonight, I sing *Pagliacci* to make the angels weep—just for you and for our *bambini Americani*." He laughed and patted her stomach where his *bambini* would grow one day soon. "Here, put on the rest of your present. I want to know that you are wearing it tonight." He slipped the sapphire ring onto the third finger of her left hand, where she had never worn a ring before. "Wear it and know, my sweet Pietra, that I will never leave you."

The performance was sublime. She had never heard Ettore in better voice. As he sang, his eyes went constantly to her box, just to the right of the stage, and each glance seemed to give his voice yet more power and color and depth.

She closed her eyes, savoring the richness of the sound, remembering the night four years before when she had first heard that glorious voice, seen the clear hazel eyes that had captured her soul. How desperately she loved this man!

The high note rang out pure and clear, but it was cut off by a short, strangled gasp. Her eyes flew open. Ettore was staggering about the stage like someone blind or drunk. As she watched, his legs gave way.

Later, she didn't remember screaming. She didn't remember racing through the maze of corridors, tripping over the train of her satin gown, pushing through the crowd gathered around him.

She remembered only his face when she finally reached him and understood that his eyes would never again lock onto hers, sending out electricity and magic and love. The explosion of a vessel in his brain had taken him from her, taken away the whole of her future.

The last words he had said to her were his oath never to leave her. But the oath had been broken. And where he had gone, she could not follow.

On the day Ettore was buried at Père Lachaise Cemetery, she returned to the apartment they had shared on the Île St-Louis, took off the sapphire ring, and put it in her jewel box, never to be worn again. For a month, she mourned alone in the apartment, refusing all visitors. Finally the tears were done. She would always grieve, but it was time to get on with living. She knew Ettore would approve.

She dressed in black—it made her even more beautiful, if that were possible—and put on a single piece of jewelry, the phoenix pin the Duke had given her. She brushed her fingers across the flames, touched the emerald eye. "It is time to rise again," she said softly. Then she instructed her maid that she was ready to receive visitors.

It didn't take long. The Baron Alain de Valéry, a dashing patron of the opera, was eager to share Mlle. Manzi's grief and to lift some of life's burdens from her round, very white, very smooth young shoulders. He mentioned, oh so casually, his château in the Loire Valley, "a jewel on the water," he added. "You are a connoisseur of jewels, I believe?"

She smiled, amused by the game. "My collection is small."

"Not for long, I trust, Mademoiselle. I hope you will do me the honor of viewing my collection . . . and choosing something from it."

"Perhaps one day, Monsieur le Baron."

"May is a poem in the Loire."

"I am sure you are right. But as you see, I am still in mourning. Black is no color for springtime."

"Summer, too, is beautiful in the country. Green everywhere. You could wear a necklace of emeralds to match . . ." His eyes glittered invitingly.

She folded her hands neatly in her lap, aware that the black silk made her skin look paler, her eyes more blue. "The time will come, of course, to cast off my mourning. But be sure, Monsieur le Baron, that when I do, it will be to make my own choices about how to live my life . . . and with whom. And even"—she eyed him mischievously—"which jewels to wear. You knew Ettore Lancona; you perhaps know something of the Duc di Monfalco as well." He nodded. "Then you know the sort of man to whom I am accustomed— intelligent, wealthy, generous, and extremely . . . vigorous. I will settle for nothing less."

He smiled in admiration at her candor as well as at her beauty. "I think you will not be disappointed," he said.

"That will depend on the man," she said, refusing to surrender so easily. She held out her hand signaling the end to their conversation, and he bowed over it.

By that summer of 1892 she was ensconced in a château in the Loire— while the Baroness de Valéry visited in Rome. Pietra Manzi was set on the path to becoming one of the greatest courtesans of Europe, sought out first for her skills in the bedroom and salon, eventually for her advice and opinion on matters of state.

She was no longer the plaything of a duke, the passion of an opera singer. She had matured into La Colomba, whose influence would be so feared years later by the dictator of her country that she would turn to her sons to save the treasures she had earned for love.

Chapter 6

The Apennines—October 1943

Except for the breeze riffling the leaves and the faint occasional chink of a sheep bell carried down from the higher peaks on the night air, it was quiet. Under the pale bluish light of the half moon, Stefano and his band of *partigiani* were visible as no more than shadowy smudges behind the rocks and shrubs.

Stefano picked up the binoculars again and scanned the ridge. He could make out the line of a road snaking across the spine of the nearest ridge, the backbone of this part of the Apennines, south of the River Po. Farther below lay the fenced outlines of the new Nazi supply depot, and to the right of it lay the main road through the valley.

Tonight, if their intelligence was correct, the first shipment of munitions for the supply depot would arrive by that road. If it was allowed to get through, Stefano knew, the Germans would have the means to mount an offensive that might eliminate the partisans from their mountain stronghold.

Nazi bastards. Their hopes of claiming victory against the partisans would be ended tonight, their damned munitions blasted to the sky, and a fair number of them with it.

But where was the convoy? Daybreak couldn't be far off, and the Germans always planned their arms shipments for darkness, when they had some protection from Allied bombers. The trucks should have passed here hours ago.

God, it was cold. Stefano blew warm air on the fingertips poking from his half-gloves then fumbled for a pack of Milits. Terrible cigarettes, rough and black, yet the best they had. The Italian army issued them to its soldiers, and the soldiers deserted and brought them to the partisans. He hunched down low behind a rock, shielded the match with his body to block the light, and lit one. The harsh smoke filled his lungs, and he fought back a cough. Then his stomach grumbled alarmingly, an alto mewing sound that descended to a baritone complaint. He hadn't eaten all day. He shifted position, aching in every muscle from the long hours of watching. Sharp rocks cut into his knees as he lay in the flinty gully. His toes were nearly frozen.

"If we wait much longer, we'll need sunglasses," came a hoarse whisper to his left. Stefano smiled. Mimmo could always lighten the worst moments. He was the oldest member of the band, with shaggy gray hair, a frosting of stubble on a face as rough-hewn as the mountainside.

"Patience, old man," Stefano whispered. "All things come to those who wait."

"Wait long enough and your balls turn to ice," Mimmo hissed.

"Yours were already stone long ago," Stefano teased. "Now quiet, old chatterbox." He went back to the binoculars, but there was nothing to see. And nothing to hear. Only numbing cold and sore muscles to feel.

Think of something else, he told himself. Think of a hot fire and a warm bed.

Think of Marisa.

Raven-haired, charcoal-eyed Marisa. Marisa with skin the color of olives and soft as silk, who smelled like cinnamon and fresh bread from the bakery where she worked for her father, Marisa with black eyes that looked at him with so much love it made him feel he was melting.

The memory of the morning before filled him, chasing

away awareness of the cold. The smell of fresh hay as they lay together in the loft, the amber eyes of the barn cat watching them, the warm, wet feel of her tightly clinging to him as he poured his love into her.

He'd known from the moment he first saw her that they were meant to be together. He'd been ordered north to take over command of a band of *partigiani* operating near her village. When he arrived, she was standing in the doorway of her father's bakery on the main piazza, her tawny skin polished with sweat by the ovens, her lush black hair spilling around her shoulders, a beguiling pout on her full mouth. The desire he felt for her at that moment was only enhanced by the admiration he felt after they met at the partisan hideout and he learned of her bravery. For months she'd been hiding refugees—partisans, escaped Allied prisoners, Italian boys who refused to rejoin their army units to fight for the Germans. She found them hiding places in closets, under floorboards, and in caves in the woods. She fed them, scrounged clothes for them, and tended to their wounds.

At night, when the work was done, with everyone taken care of for one more day, she fell into Stefano's arms to love and laugh and dream of the children they'd have after *la bruttatura* was finished—the brutal war, with its hunger and deprivation, the terrible risks they were forced to take, and, worst of all, the times when they had to be apart.

The sound of truck engines rumbling far below in the valley snatched Stefano from his reverie. He trained the binoculars on the road below, all his senses alert now. A ripple of expectancy passed through the darkness, leaping from man to man. Metallic clicks rattled along the line as they readied their guns.

"*Piano*," Stefano urged. "*Pianissimo*." This was no time to give themselves away to some Nazi advance party sent to scour the hillsides. Patience . . . quiet . . . they would have their victory.

And Stefano would have his own special triumph. For each mission he took now, each bullet he shot and each German he killed, was also a blow struck in his battle against Vittorio, that greedy, boot-licking traitor.

* * *

For a while at the beginning of the war, the brothers had been able to maintain a tenuous relationship. Vittorio was forced to close his shop; with a war on, there was little market for fine rag paper goods and no leather for exquisite bindings, soft luggage, and wallets. But with the Italians fighting as part of the Axis with the Germans, he moved up quickly within the Fascist hierarchy. Stefano continued working in Brancusi's law office while covertly printing and distributing pamphlets against the Fascists.

La Colomba had not been arrested, but neither had Stefano managed to see her again. He'd had several messages from her, though, assuring him that she was all right and asking for news of him. The knowledge that he had a mother who cared about his welfare inspired a vow to see her again. He would protect her through this war or die trying. And if it meant staying on good terms with his half-brother, he would do that too.

But on an evening in November 1942, returning home from a meeting of a newly formed resistance cell, Stefano found his room had been ransacked. Books were swept from the shelves, drawers pulled out, and their contents scattered, the mattress and chair cushions cut open, and the stuffing pulled out.

Outraged to the point that all sense deserted him, Stefano stormed directly into Vittorio's office at Fascist headquarters.

"You won't find it," he said in a voice barely controlled as he leaned across his brother's wide oak desk. "You'll never find it, so call off your goons."

Vittorio stood up, an impressive sight since he'd been steadily gaining weight as he ate well through the war while others starved. "You have a nerve charging in here like this!"

Emboldened by the belief Vittorio would not hurt him—especially when he had not gotten hold of the missing piece needed to release a fortune in jewels—Stefano advanced around the desk.

"I just want to be sure you understand, my dear brother." He smiled at the wince his loud declaration brought from Vittorio, who raced to close the open door of his office.

"For godssake, Stefano. Don't push me so far I have no choice—"

"You have a choice, a simple one. Leave me alone . . . and believe that my part of the bottle is hidden where you will *never* find it." He pulled back. "And one more thing. You've finally worked yourself up to a position where you can provide some real protection. I've had word through friends that a woman whose welfare we both care about is still free and safe, but she may not be for long."

"I do what I can for her," said Vittorio softly. "I have managed to shield her from arrest for her seditious beliefs."

"Well, see that you continue to do so, because if anything happens to her, Vittorio—*anything*—I'll hunt you down and make you pay for it. *Verstehen*?"

Vittorio came back to the desk, grabbed Stefano by the elbow, and steered him toward the door. "I'll do my best to see that nothing happens. Now go, and don't come here again!"

"Gladly!" said Stefano, yanking his elbow free. "Just remember what I've said, and I'll be happy to stay away from the stench of this place."

But it was only eight months later that Carlo Brancusi was arrested.

That same night Stefano waylaid Vittorio as he left the opera, resplendent in spotless evening clothes, a white silk scarf draped around his abundant neck. On his arm was a young woman with blond hair. When Stefano confronted them, she poured out some excited words, her Italian conspicuously marked by the guttural sounds of a German accent.

"Damn you, Vittorio," Stefano declared. "You let them take Carlo."

"He brought it on himself," Vittorio said, after he'd instructed his *Liebchen* to wait for him at a distance.

"Couldn't you have stopped it? Good God, the man was like a father to you!"

"His politics were not father to mine, however. He was printing pamphlets right there in his office! If I defended him, I'd be put in jail with him. Now clear off. If that girl I'm with gets suspicious about you, I won't be able to help you either."

Making it clear that it was pointless to argue anymore, Vittorio turned and started walking away. But Stefano was not quite through. Darting up behind Vittorio, he gave him a mighty kick in his fat behind and sent him sprawling in his spotless suit into a Milanese gutter.

That night Stefano left Milan and headed to the mountains to join the *partigiani* wherever he could find them.

It was only later that he learned that the blond *Fraulein* he'd seen on his half-brother's arm was named Gretchen Koppveldt, and she was Vittorio's fiancée. The news came through to partisan headquarters in an intelligence report that included one other significant piece of news: Gretchen's father, Rudolf Koppveldt, had just been promoted from a southern garrison commander to *Oberst* and *Kommandant* of Nazi forces in the northern Apennines.

The sound had grown louder, and soon Stefano's trained ears could distinguish its separate parts—the uneven growl of engines running on badly refined gasoline, the syncopated putter of motorcycles pulling sidecars, the peculiar whine of the cross-country tires of German army vehicles rolling over a hard surface.

Despite the long hours of waiting, Stefano and his men were as alert as hunting dogs on the scent. Every gun was cocked. Extra grenades were ready, not the pathetic *diavoli rossi*, the red devils of the Italian army, which had very little stopping power when they worked at all. These were American "pineapples," dropped to them by the Allies two weeks ago. Fingers rested gently in the pins, ready to pull and throw. The hands on the plungers that would trigger the dynamite placed in the road were steady.

The first truck rounded the bend about a hundred yards away. The convoy was so late that there was enough lavender light in the sky to see the silhouettes and make a count— fifteen trucks carrying guns and ammunition, three others overflowing with men. An armored car headed the column and another brought up the rear. As they came closer, Stefano's binoculars were filled with a sight that brought a huge grin to his face, showing his teeth stark white in his charcoal-smeared face. Near the head of the column were two officers in an open Mercedes, and one of them was wearing the red tabs of a general on the lapels of his leather coat. An unexpected bonanza. He'd take that one out personally, Stefano decided.

Stefano let the convoy approach to a point nearly beneath his little band, then gave the signal, a low owl-like hoot. As it died away in the dawn air, the earth erupted. Noise, flashes of blinding light, color, and more noise, deafening, painful in its vibrations.

Stefano pasted himself against the side of a rock for safety as shrapnel whistled around him. The grenades his men launched against the trucks had done their work. Once ignited, the shells carried in the trucks began to detonate, shooting off like holiday fireworks gone mad, taking the whole string of trucks one after another. Huge fireballs rolled up to the sky, billowing black smoke before them.

Even through the sound of the explosions, the screams of dying men could be heard. Looking around the edge of his rock, Stefano saw bleeding bodies lying everywhere, and half-crippled soldiers still charging up the hill behind automatic rifles spouting lead.

"Fire!" Stefano yelled. His men opened up, cutting them down as fast as they came. Peering through the smoke, he looked for the General's Mercedes. Amazingly, it was intact and trying to drive past an overturned motorcycle and a barrier of bodies on the road, searching for the point where it would be able to speed away.

Oh no, you swine, Stefano swore inside himself. And racing down the slope, he pulled a grenade pin with his teeth, took aim, and threw with every bit of strength he had. The brown oval sailed through the air, turning end over end as if in slow motion. It plunked onto an open stretch of the road just as the car drove over it. The Mercedes was lifted into the air, flew several feet, and landed on its side. Beside it lay the man with the red tabs on his lapels. He didn't move.

Stefano let out a whoop of triumph. A bullet raced past his ear and he dove for cover again.

The shooting and the explosions continued for another five minutes, sending down a hellish rain of white-hot metal and severed limbs. Then it was over. Not one German was left alive; not one truck was salvageable.

A silence gripped the battleground. Eerie and complete, so loud in his ears that Stefano couldn't hear his own voice when he rose from behind his rock and called to his men.

Bleeding from scratches and shrapnel wounds but whooping like schoolboys and patting each other on the back, they came and surrounded him. Mimmo came last, wheeling a single survivor of the debacle, a motorcycle he thought surely he could get to run.

They couldn't bring it back to the village; its presence there would condemn them all. So they took it with them a short way, then concealed it in some thick brush before continuing their long trek back through the hills to the village.

By the time they got there it was nearly noon.

They stopped a half mile from the village. There was always the chance that the Germans had already traced them here. While the others waited, Stefano, Mimmo, and Tonio, a tough-as-barbed-wire boy of seventeen, crept over a wall, along a field, through the cemetery. They inched their way up a narrow street past houses with shutters closed against the noon sun. Finally, they peered carefully around a corner into the piazza itself.

Everything looked normal. Beside the statue of Garibaldi, two little boys kicked a soccer ball. Old Signor Pretti and Signor Richelli were playing checkers outside the cafe, sharing a carafe of red wine and slapping the wooden disks onto the board as though they were weapons. Pigeons fluttered in the campanile then took wing as the bell began to strike twelve.

And there was Marisa. She was bent over a pot set on a crude fire in front of the bakery, making soap from kitchen fat, potato peels, and soda. Her flowered blouse was partially unbuttoned against the heat, and she frowned in concentration as she stirred.

For Stefano, the hunger disappeared, all the aches went away, the horrible images of death and destruction faded as he looked at her. She was life and renewal.

As she stood up to brush her heavy hair from her face, she saw him and ran to him, her arms wide.

He grabbed her and held her close. She smelled so good, earthy and real and full of life, not tainted by death. He wanted to bury himself in her and forget everything he'd seen, everything he'd done since leaving her.

"Come," she said and pulled him inside. "I will fix you a bath."

Tonio went to tell the others it was safe to come in.

While Stefano soaked away the pains of the long night, she brought him bread fresh from the oven and ersatz coffee made from roasted almonds. As he climbed from the tub, from high overhead came the dull roar of American Hurricane bombers on their way to drop their bombs on Milan, Turin, and Florence.

At the sound, Stefano seethed with hatred for Mussolini. His beloved Italy was being crushed by the vise of two powers, one that wanted to occupy her and one that supposedly wanted to liberate her. Between them, they seemed determined to see that nothing was left. "See what you have done to her, *stronzo*, bastard!" he shouted.

"Hush," Marisa soothed as she rubbed oil into his shoulders. The sheets were clean and cool, the mattress soft. Her hands were warm and loving. He slept.

When he woke it was dark. Marisa lay naked beside him on the bed, her eyes open, watching him sleep. He pulled her to him and kissed her deeply, as if drinking from her soul.

"You must be hungry," she said when he would let her speak. "You have had nothing since yesterday afternoon."

"Starving," he agreed, "but not for food." He traced the curve of her hips with the cup of his hand, dipping in at her compact waist, brushing down across her belly and up again over her breasts. He took them, one by one, into his mouth and worshipped them with his tongue.

She tasted of salt, the healthy body salt of labor on a hot day and the sweat of the anxiety she had felt for him through the long night. He swallowed her salt taste, and his love for her hardened, making his whole body rigid with desire for her. He wanted to join himself to her now, thrust inside of her, but he forced himself to wait, to hold back, to let her come with him on the journey they'd made so often and always together. Lowering himself over her, his lips brushing along the curves of her body, he flicked his lips between her thighs, entered between the velvet folds and sucked the taste of her until she began to moan, writhing, her hands reaching for him.

She had been a virgin the first time he'd made love to her. She had come to him as naturally as breathing. Now she was as eager as he for their lovemaking, wanting him inside her, loving everything he did to her.

He was throbbing, nearly spilling over as he raised himself on top of her, and her legs jackknifed up to grasp him around the waist, drawing him down, his hard member searching to become part of her.

"Here," she whispered, reaching down to guide him inside. Then they began to rise and fall together, as surely as the waves of the sea in a building storm, until finally her arms wrapped around him and she pleaded hotly, "*Piacere, mi amore*, please, my love, *adesso, adesso*! Now!"

He plunged into her and they took the journey together until they came safely home again.

He slept again, held close in her arms, and this time Marisa slept beside him, dreaming of a lifetime of nights to share their passion and then to sleep together side by side.

She shook him gently awake several hours later. She had been out of bed for some time, fixing a meal, binding up the last scratches of the partisan band, preparing the dough for the next morning's baking. "Stefano, get up. You've had a messenger."

Slowly, he rose to the surface of consciousness. When he moved it seemed he ached in every muscle. She handed him a steaming cup of coffee and he sipped—real coffee, by some miracle, though the grounds had clearly been used many more times than once, then carefully dried and roasted.

"A messenger?" he said curiously.

She handed him an envelope with his name written on the front—heavy blue paper, good quality though it was grimy. From the few similar letters Stefano had received in the past through the underground chain, he recognized the stationery at once and the bold, backward slanting handwriting. He tore open the envelope.

> *Mio Figlio,*
>
> *If this reaches you it means I have finally been arrested. I'm told La Tana will become a German headquarters. I don't know where I shall be taken. Naturally, I trust you will do your best to discover it, but my purpose in writing is not merely to ask for your help. I know I would have that anyway.*
>
> *This may be my last communication to you, my beloved son, and my last chance to tell the most important truth of all. I will always love you, Stefano. And I am very, very proud of you.*
>
> *Your loving mother, La Colomba*

He jumped from the bed and began to dress. "I must go at once." He stuck his arms in his shirtsleeves, jammed his feet into his shoes.

"What is it?" cried Marisa.

"I'm going to get my mother."

He grabbed Marisa around the waist, pulled her to him hard, and gave her one last kiss before he scooped up his carbine and headed for the door. As he raced past, she handed him a salami and a loaf of bread. "Be careful!" he said as he opened the door. "I love you."

"I love you, Stefano." Her voice followed him into the piazza. "*Te amo!*"

His long legs carried him through the town and into the hills at a trot. Thank God he was well rested. He gnawed on the bread and salami as he covered the miles back toward the spot where Mimmo had hidden the motorcycle.

Naturally, the area was crawling with Germans looking for the perpetrators of the ambush, but the motorcycle was some distance from the center of their operations, still undiscovered, thank God. Stefano walked it silently over a hill, out of sight.

It took him an hour of fiddling before it would work. He rocked it back and forth to slosh the gas in the tank. It sounded nearly full, a piece of luck. The Germans might have heard the roar as he fired up the engine, but he was well away before they could investigate.

The main highway to Florence was out of the question. It would be littered with checkpoints. Also, the Allies were strafing anything that moved on the roads. He followed back roads and, when necessary, rode cross-country, bumping over hillocks, nearly being bucked out of his seat more than once.

Many times he spotted German patrols, and he had to pull the motorcycle into bushes or ditches or behind trees, trying not even to breathe until they were gone. But then he was on his way again, miles flying past, thinking of nothing but getting to La Tana, rescuing La Colomba.

It was around midnight when he turned into the cypress lane. From beyond the crest of the hill there was a glow, as if a full moon had just gone down. When Stefano rode over the summit, his eyes widened in horror. The glow was not moonlight but fire, and it was consuming the villa. Flames shot out of windows and through gaps in the roof, sending sparks swirling up into the trees. The front door, that giant slab of oak Stefano had approached for the first time not so many years ago, had been blown out, and the hall visible within looked like the white hot cavity of a blast furnace. The blaze had obviously been raging for some time.

Stefano braked the motorcycle to a stop and stared for a minute at the beautiful home of his mother, dying before his eyes. Still, the memory lived—of that golden evening when she had revealed herself to him . . .

Perhaps she lived, too. The message had said she would be arrested. He would find her. *Free* her! He jumped on the starter pedal, wheeled the motorcycle around, and sped toward Florence.

He had gone only half a mile along a small back road when a squad of armed men jumped out of the shadows in front of him, carbines pointing, sporting the neckerchiefs that clearly proclaimed them as *partigiani*.

Stefano skidded to a halt. "Don't shoot," he called as he threw up his hands. "I'm one of Cadorna's men." General Raffaele Cadorna was in overall command of the partisans in the north.

It took him a while to convince them, but then they were all smiles. The partisan grapevine was fast and accurate, and when he mentioned the attack on the supply depot and convinced them he had led it, they were ecstatic, shaking his hand, slapping him on the back.

"Ah, but we have successes of our own, eh, *ragazzi*?" said one, pointing his carbine over his shoulder toward La Tana. The glow could still be seen in the sky.

"You?" said Stefano.

He nodded. "The Germans took it over as a headquarters only a few days ago. A few of the big brass were meeting there tonight." He chuckled. "Trying to figure out how to deal with us. We dealt with them instead!"

"But La Tana . . ." Stefano began.

"Yes, a terrible loss. But Donna Pietra had passed the word to us long ago. If the Germans arrested her and tried to use the house for themselves, we shouldn't let them. 'Blow it up if you have to,' she said. So we did."

"Do you know where they've taken her?" Stefano asked quickly.

"We've heard she's still in Florence."

"Where?"

The leader shook his head. "Could be the police station —or, by now, the Gestapo."

Stefano was back on his motorcycle in a flash. "*Grazie*. I've got to find La Colomba."

"Why?" one partisan called out as Stefano gunned the engine.

"Because I love her," Stefano said as he rode away, smiling to himself at the false assumptions the men would no doubt make about a young man and the famous courtesan.

Staying to the back roads, he encountered no patrols or checkpoints and reached the outskirts of Florence in less than half an hour. Just when he was ready to ditch the cycle, it began sputtering, hungry for gas. He tossed it down a shallow ravine and walked closer to town before hiding his carbine in some grass near the Arno.

With the great rust-colored Brunelleschi dome of the Duomo as his compass point, he made his way to the center of the city, and soon he was standing across from the central police station. It was early morning; the doors had just opened. Armed officers and policemen streamed in and out. How to get inside, he wondered, or failing that, how to get the information he needed out?

A young woman walked by holding a boy of about six by the hand, both thin as rails except that the little boy had the distended belly of the malnourished.

"Signora," Stefano called on an impulse. She stopped and looked at him with mistrustful eyes. "Signora, the child is hungry . . . ?"

"What of it?" she snapped. "All Italy is hungry."

Stefano pulled the remains of the salami Marisa had given him from his pocket. There was still enough for a meal. The woman's eyes grew wide at the sight of such bounty. "This is yours . . . if you first do something for me."

She sagged, a resigned gesture. "Where do you want it? Can I send the child away first? Paolo, go into the church and wait for me."

Stefano grabbed the child's bony wrist. "I do not want you, Signora. I merely want the child to ask a question for me. In the police station."

"That's all?"

Stefano nodded.

The woman's eyes darkened with distrust. "Will it make them suspicious of him, this question?"

"I don't know," Stefano replied honestly. "From a child, I don't believe so. But whatever answer he gets, I will give you the salami, all of it."

"Paolo," the woman said, shoving the boy toward Stefano. "Do what he wants."

The boy had a dull expression, but he listened carefully, repeated the instructions back to Stefano, then trotted across the square into the station. He was back in a few minutes, his expression unchanged.

"She's dead," he said in his little voice. "She tried to run away last night so they shot her."

The woman snatched the salami from Stefano's nerveless fingers, and mother and child ran away before the crazy man could change his mind.

Stefano didn't move. If the *carabinieri* had come rushing out of the station at that moment to drag him away, he couldn't have run, would have put up no fight at all. He was frozen. She was gone, the mother he'd barely had a chance to know. He made not a sound, but tears began to course down his cheeks.

However long he stayed there, finally he felt a hand on his shoulder. He looked up and saw a priest. Stefano had stopped believing long ago, but when the priest pulled him to his feet and led him into a nearby church, he went like an obedient child. Soon he found himself on his knees, alone, murmuring quiet words.

But not in prayer, even if they were said with all the force of a prayer.

"I will kill you," he repeated over and over. "I will kill you. You let her die. Your own mother. I swear I will kill you."

Chapter 7

As usual, when he returned to the village Stefano approached warily, careful not to put himself in danger or bring any on his friends and comrades. He knew, however, the moment he reached the edge of the village and turned into the first narrow back street that danger had already arrived.

There was no one to be seen, scarcely a sound to be heard except the trickle of water down the cracks in the paving stone, the slight fluttering of curtains hanging at empty windows where no faces appeared. As he inched his way along the street closer to the piazza, looking into doors that stood open on empty rooms, his heart began to pound. It was midmorning, the time when old men should be gossiping in the cafe, when women should be going to draw water from the well in the middle of the square beside Garibaldi's sword. But no one was going anywhere.

Then he heard something, a faint humming.

He edged around the corner, his gun at the ready.

Lined up in neat rows across the piazza, ten rows of twelve each, were the people of the village, all of them. They were lying dead on the stones. Pools of congealed blood lay beneath them, and the air was black with buzzing clouds of flies.

Stefano retched at the sight. And the smell. With no one left to bury them, they must have lain like this since it happened. Two days ago, perhaps. The massacre must have taken place on the same morning that he left . . .

"Marisa!" The cry exploded from his mouth. Sure as he was it would not be heard, still he thought if only he called loudly enough, often enough, he might summon her back to life. He began running around the piazza, looking at one horribly bloated corpse after another. Pretti. Old Richelli. Martini, the mayor. Tonio. Brother Franco, the priest. Little Adela of the big eyes, who had followed Stefano like a puppy. They were all riddled with bullet wounds. The Nazis had obviously stood them up in front of machine guns and mowed them down, more than a hundred lives taken in a matter of minutes.

All the time he searched among the bodies, he howled or sobbed. "Marisa! *Mi amore*!"

At first he saw only the faces of others, the old and the young, the harmless as well as those who had fought with him at night and gone on leading their lives during the day.

When he found Marisa's father, a crucifix still clutched in his hand, Stefano knelt over him, pausing to recover his strength, knowing he would need it in the next minute.

And when he rose and looked nearby, she was there. She was wearing a red sweater, the one he liked so much because it made her skin glow. But now her skin was pale and cold. Her face was untouched and her eyes were open, staring up at Stefano as though begging him to make it untrue.

He knelt and lifted her up by the shoulders, leaning her head against his chest. With one hand, he closed her eyes, but the rigor of death opened them again and they gazed back into his, begging, loving, apologizing for abandoning him.

He didn't cry. He had cried for his mother two days before, but he could not cry for Marisa. The horror was too great.

He picked her up and started carrying her out of the square, determined to bury her properly. As he walked, he passed the church and saw the notice nailed to its door. Standing with his dead love cradled in his arms, he stopped to read:

ACHTUNG! ACHTUNG!
ATTENZIONE! ATTENZIONE!

By order of Oberst Rudolf Koppveldt, reprisals are hereby ordered for the deaths of 73 German soldiers and five officers, including Herr General Heinrich von Badeswirth, at the hands of Italian civilian criminals on the highway at Bresenza. For each German soldier killed, five Italian civilians shall be shot. For each German officer killed, ten Italian civilians shall be shot. As reprisal for the death of Herr General von Badeswirth, twenty Italian civilians shall be shot. These civilians, a total of 435, are to be drawn from the villages of Tocia, Coliba, Faranto, Barasci, and Curza.

Scrawled across the bottom of the order was the signature: Rudolf Koppveldt.

The father of Vittorio D'Angeli's bride-to-be.

The murderous fury, the piercing need for revenge, swept through Stefano with twice the force he had experienced in the wake of La Colomba's death.

He stumbled away from the church, and carried Marisa to her room above the bakery. There he washed away all the dried blood, then dressed her in a plain white cotton shift and wrapped her in a sheet. At last, he brought her to the cemetery.

In the keeper's shed, he found a shovel and dug a grave beside her mother's. He laid her tenderly in the open earth and tucked the sheet around her, pressed his warm lips once more to hers—cold as alabaster—then covered her over.

He walked back to the square, his eyes nearly blinded by tears. What could he do now? There were too many victims to bury them all. Weak and disspirited, he collapsed into a chair at one of the two small cafes in town. Cold cups of coffee and half-empty glasses of wine remained as evidence of the moment when men had been dragged from their leisure to be executed. In the other villages it would have been the same. Their total population would just meet the deadly quota called for by the Nazis. Like Tocia, the others would have ceased to exist by now.

For one dark moment, Stefano considered ending his own life. Marisa was dead. La Colomba was dead. A world in which the Nazis could exist was hell, anyway.

Except that they would lose in the end. The handwriting was on the wall; the Americans had already landed at Anzio and begun smashing their way inland. The enemy would be beaten.

And, Stefano swore, he must be the one who personally declared victory over his damned half-brother.

Fueled by that oath even though his every dream was dead, he was able to walk into the hills, heading toward Milan. Yet his body felt as ravaged by grief as it might by a virulent germ, and after walking half a day he could go no farther.

He was taken in at a farmhouse where he fell into a fevered unconsciousness that lasted several days. When he woke at last, the fever abated, he was terribly weak. In retrospect, he suspected his condition was brought on not only by emotional collapse but by something contracted from the decaying bodies.

"Thought we were going to lose you, my young one," said the old farmer. "You must have a good reason to live."

Do I? wondered Stefano. Then he remembered Vittorio. "Yes," he said, "a very good reason."

By the time he had completely regained his strength, it was the farmer's planting time. He stayed on to work; to clear a field of stones, wheelbarrow after tedious wheelbarrow, to plow, to help with the sowing. When he finally said good-bye to his benefactors and headed south on foot, he was strong and healthy again.

He slept in the fields by day and by night he walked. Often he had to dive into a ditch to avoid an Allied bombing run or a German convoy. The opposing armies were constantly engaged now, and word passed quietly among Italian patriots that Mussolini was finished at last and the Germans would fall soon after.

He reached Milan late on a hot afternoon at the end of June. Stefano was shocked by the sight of this city he loved.

Everywhere slabs of wall stood like markers in a cemetery, holding up nothing but the memories of the people who had once lived behind them, the rest of the buildings gone, pounded into dust by American bombs. Huge potholes pocked the streets. Devastation was everywhere. It was clear that the Allies would enter the rubble-filled streets of the city any day. A rout of *Fascisti* and their sympathizers was underway.

But he felt no pity for Vittorio. It was the stupidity and greed for power of all his kind that had brought Italy to its knees. Making his way through the ruined streets and across lots where the remains of vanished buildings still smoldered, Stefano's will was still fired by the hunger for revenge. Miraculously, the apartment building where Vittorio lived on the edge of the Piazza Mentana was still standing. Even the windows were intact, though the street entrance was open, doors hanging off their hinges as if they had been battered down. Had an angry mob come for Vittorio, Stefano wondered, deprived him of his own sweet retribution?

He ran up the curving marble stairs, taking them two and three at a time. The door to the apartment stood open, too. He raced through the empty rooms. Clothes still hung in the closets, Vittorio's neatly pressed suits and evening wear beside the frilly dresses and fur coat belonging to his wife— The Butcher's daughter. The kitchen cupboards were stocked, and a stew sat in a pot on the stove, the flame turned off beneath it. The table was set, complete with a vase of flowers just past their prime.

The departure had clearly been sudden, but from the absence of disarray Stefano guessed it had not been forced or violent. It was clear that Vittorio and Gretchen had fled.

He began a methodical search of the fashionable apartment from one end to the other, in every corner, under every piece of furniture. He unscrewed wall fixtures, removed drawers, pried up floorboards, removed the stuffing from the furniture, and checked the linings of every piece of clothing.

No matter how quickly Vittorio had taken flight, no matter how lightly he had been forced to travel, he had not left without his key to a share in La Colomba's fortune. His half of the perfume bottle was definitely gone.

Stefano drifted out of the apartment, his mind already roaming the map of Europe. Where could he find Vittorio? Had the collaborator escaped to Germany along with his wife and her father? Or had they all slipped across the border to the neutral safety of Switzerland?

Or had anti-Fascist mobs caught up with them en route and murdered them? Stefano had no way of knowing. But did he *need* to know? If Vittorio was alive, he was not going to forego his share of a fortune. As soon as the war was over, Stefano guessed, maybe even before, Vittorio would come to him so they could unite the bottle and claim the jewels from their safe deposit in Switzerland.

Stefano had no more heart for fighting, and he knew the fight was nearly won, anyway. Instead of rejoining the partisans, he stayed in Milan, working on the clean-up crews that carted away the rubble after the bombing raids.

In April 1945, the last of the Germans and Mussolini were finally dislodged from their stronghold in the Apennines. Caught by partisans while trying to sneak out of Italy dressed as a woman, Il Duce was shot with Carla Petacci, his mistress. Their bodies were brought back to Milan and strung up to be reviled by the mob.

Stefano went to the spot where the grisly carcasses were on display. He wanted to see this man who had ruined a nation and caused so much pain and death and utter despair.

But when he saw the bodies hanging from a gibbet, heads down like dead cattle, he could take no pleasure in the sight. He'd seen enough of death to last him a lifetime. Now, looking at the mutilated corpses, it occurred to Stefano that Il Duce's enemies were acting no less barbarically than he and the Nazis had while they were joined in their pact with the Devil.

As he turned and walked away from the gruesome display, Stefano put his hand into the pocket of the jacket he always wore, the rough wool peasant's jacket that had been made for him by Marisa. He had asked her to sew one especially deep pocket, concealed in a special flap behind the lining. She had never asked why, and he had not told her, thinking he would save the perfume bottle to show her on a special occasion, their wedding night.

Now, through the lining, he gripped the object concealed in the pocket. Throughout the war he had carried his half of La Colomba's bottle with him, wrapped in a protective coating of lamb's wool. He had survived, he believed, because of the power of that lucky charm. By the same superstitious logic, Stefano decided that Vittorio must be alive, too.

Nor did he spare himself the thought that if La Colomba had not given it away, the luck that had blessed her life would not finally have deserted her.

As his finger touched the bottle, Stefano made a silent pledge. No matter how difficult it would be for him, he and Vittorio must claim their legacy together. It was, after all, what their mother had wanted.

The war had been over for a year when Stefano came to realize how foolish he had been—basing his plans on mere superstition. Yes, in wartime it was natural and excusable to cling to illogical notions, anything that kept you going from one day to the next. So he had believed his life was saved by a lucky charm. Believed, too, that Vittorio must be alive and would come to him.

But as time passed and there was no sign of Vittorio, Stefano began to doubt his brother had survived. He searched through Fascist party records as they became available, checked the records of the Allied authorities pertaining to escaped collaborators and war criminals, but he could find no trace of Vittorio D'Angeli—or of Rudolf Koppveldt. The only discovery he did make was that Carlo Brancusi had died in one of Mussolini's prisons in Libya.

As Brancusi's ward, Stefano attained the right to look through whatever papers of his guardian could be located. He found a letter in Brancusi's handwriting stating that the lawyer agreed to take legal responsibility for the sons of Pietra Manzi and, with it, baptismal certificates for himself and Vittorio. There was no clue, however, to who their fathers had been. Someday, Stefano thought, the papers might come in handy, so he tucked them away.

He had lived a solitary life since the war's end, unable to take any pleasure from the company of women, though there were many who sought to reawaken his desire. Unable to find a niche in the everyday world, he took odd jobs, and whenever he accumulated a bit of money, he went to the mountains where his love was buried, haunted the empty houses of the village where her laughter still echoed, and tried to write poetry.

The inspiration never came, however, and always Stefano returned to Milan, hoping that Vittorio would arrive—and that the legacy of La Colomba would save him from mediocrity.

At last, he decided there was no reason to wait any longer.

On a day in September of 1947, Stefano strolled along the rue du Rhone in Geneva savoring the unexpectedly mild weather and the simple pleasure that came from walking down a street in a nation that hadn't suffered the ravages of war. There were no bombed out buildings in Geneva, no street urchins begging chocolate and cigarettes from the GIs who still swarmed over most of Europe, no syphilitic young girls selling themselves on street corners for a few lire to feed their families. The prevailing sense of order and normalcy encouraged a sense of optimism in Stefano.

The day's sunshine seemed a good omen, as did the very name of the city where he felt his luck was about to change: Geneva. Like Genoa, it came from a Ligurian word that meant emerging from the waters. He had been drowning in the despair left by the war, Stefano thought. Now he was ready to emerge.

He expected little trouble in accomplishing his mission. Vittorio had been missing for two and a half years, the war over for nearly as long. The likelihood was that he had perished or else he would have tried to make contact by now.

Stefano came to the Helvetia Kreditanstalt, turned into the vaulted lobby, and walked across the gleaming marble floor to the desk where a clerk sat. Speaking in Italian, he gave his name and asked to see the man with whom La Colomba had made her arrangements. Stefano remembered the name from the one time his mother had mentioned it: Herr Lindner.

"I am sorry, sir," the clerk replied in Italian, "but Mr. Lindner is no longer employed here. Perhaps Mr. Stimmli, his successor, can assist you."

Stefano felt a momentary twinge of panic. It was Herr Lindner with whom La Colomba had arranged to place the jewels. If there were favors to be asked, a variation in the conditions for release of the collection, wouldn't an old associate of La Colomba be most likely to oblige? But then it struck Stefano that Lindner had also been the official on duty when Vittorio had made the original deposit. Perhaps it was best to deal with someone who did not have a prior acquaintance with either of La Colomba's heirs. Yes, Mr. Stimmli would do nicely, Stefano agreed.

The clerk vanished for a minute, then returned to lead him into a paneled office, austerely furnished in the Swiss style.

A tall man with pewter hair plastered tightly to his skull rose from behind a large burlwood desk and offered a soft handshake. As was customary with many Swiss bank officials, he was dressed in the formal morning outfit of striped trousers and a swallowtail coat. He introduced himself before waving Stefano to a facing leather chair.

Stimmli also spoke impeccable Italian. "I am told, Signor D'Angeli, that you asked to see Herr Lindner. I've taken over all of the matters that he was handling."

"This involved something rather unusual—a deposit made before the war and left untouched until now."

Stimmli gave a passive nod. "Nothing unusual in that, Signor. At that time, many people were seeking safe harbor for—"

"It wasn't the timing that was unusual," Stefano broke in impatiently, "but the substance of the deposit: a large collection of jewelry worth many, many millions of lire."

"Yes?" Stimmli managed to look genuinely baffled, as though this were something he ought to have known about, yet didn't.

"The collection belonged to my mother . . . she was known as La Colomba. The point is, I'm here to claim it."

Stimmli gazed back at him, offering nothing but the thinnest of smiles.

And why should he offer more? It was part of the fabled Swiss caution, nowhere as evident as in matters of banking. It was for his protection, too, Stefano reminded himself, so no impostor could steal his legacy.

Yet in spite of his reasoned reminders, Stefano felt the first stirrings of nervousness. Exactly how did he establish his claim? Were there written instructions left with the bank explaining the terms for withdrawal, or had La Colomba relied solely on Herr Lindner?

Before babbling his way through the details, Stefano thought it would be easier to fall back on the man who already knew them. "Can you get in touch with Herr Lindner?" Stefano asked. "He could explain everything."

"I'm sorry, that would be very difficult. He resigned suddenly last year and left the country."

"Suddenly? Left—?"

"Yes. Quite unusual. Picked up and went to America of all places. He was a widower with a daughter, you see. She married an American from the diplomatic service who was stationed here during the war. When the husband was posted back to Washington, Lindner moved abroad to be near her."

Stefano's nerves were increasingly frayed, his imagination playing havoc with his worst suspicions. A bank official entrusted with millions of dollars' worth of jewels had resigned abruptly and sailed across an ocean. He could restrain himself no longer. Reaching into a pocket, he pulled out the roll of lamb's wool and undid it. The top half of the perfume bottle lay naked on the edge of Mr. Stimmli's desk.

The bank officer's eyebrows elevated nearly to his hairline. Speaking rapidly, Stefano explained the significance of the object as a piece of identification, the original conditions that called for his brother to appear as well, and the logic that dictated releasing the jewels in view of the likelihood that his brother was missing and might be assumed dead—and that his half of the bottle had disappeared with him. To bolster his claim, Stefano produced the letter written by Brancusi and his baptismal certificate.

Stimmli pored over the documents for a minute, then spent a bit more time fondling the dazzling jeweled artifact. Abruptly, he rose, leaving the perfume bottle on the desk. "If you will be kind enough to excuse me, Signor D'Angeli, I must confer immediately with a colleague."

The speed of the bank official's departure sent Stefano's thoughts on a new trajectory. Perhaps he had established his claim after all; after a few formalities, the collection would be turned over to him. As for the wild idea that the jewels had been embezzled, why shouldn't a man leave the bank to be with his daughter in America?

Stimmli returned in a few minutes, a leather-bound folder under his arm. There was less spring in his walk as he went to his desk, less starch in his backbone.

"Signor D'Angeli," he began after sitting down, "I have found the file that relates to this matter. A letter written to Mr. Lindner by Signora Pietra Manzi stipulates in no uncertain terms that her collection is to be released only on simultaneous presentation of both halves of the bottle."

"But I am her son, and I've explained—"

"I am in no position to doubt your statements, Signor D'Angeli. What I can tell you is that whether I believe you or not is of absolutely no importance. I am unable to give you the jewels."

"Then let me speak to your superiors, the directors of the bank. My mother certainly didn't intend for these jewels never again to see the light of day, to set here forev—"

"Excuse me, Mr. D'Angeli. I have yet to explain fully. The essential reason it is impossible to release the collection to you is that we no longer have it in our custody."

The terrible premonitions that had nagged at Stefano earlier were now confirmed. He felt suddenly as shaky and hollow as the hundreds of bombed-out buildings he had left behind.

"How . . . ?" he said in a hoarse, trembling voice.

Stimmli opened the file and scanned some of the top papers.

"The records show that Mr. Vittorio D'Angeli appeared in this office before Herr Lindner fourteen months ago. He satisfied in full the conditions for withdrawal of the collection, and it was released to him immediately."

"Satisfied in full?" Stefano sat forward. "Did he come alone?"

"Yes. He produced a valid death certificate, showing you had died in Milan in 1944."

Stefano was stunned for only a second, then he snorted. "He had no trouble getting that, of course. He was a Fascist party official." Stefano grabbed up his half of the bottle from the desk. "But he didn't have *this*!"

Stimmli checked the file again. "But it seems he did. Two halves of the perfume bottle were given to Mr. Lindner and matched against a photograph of the completed bottle in our file." Stimmli picked up a piece of paper and waved it. "This is an affidavit, attesting—"

Stefano bolted to his feet. "He couldn't have had both halves, because I have one." Stefano pointed his at Stimmli, as if brandishing a sword. "Don't you see? It was a forgery!"

Stimmli's *sangfroid* never wavered. "Or is that the forgery in your hand?"

The retort punctured Stefano's rising indignation like a pin stuck into a balloon. Of course. It was too late now to care about the technicalities. Without the actual second half of the bottle, Stefano realized, he would have difficulty proving that his was the genuine one.

Vittorio had used his time in hiding well. He had claimed the collection, then crawled back under a rock.

"May I see the affidavit?" Stefano asked, quietly now, a tone of acceptance and defeat.

Stimmli handed over the paper. The facts of the closing transaction were stated exactly as he had reported. On the line for the supervising officer of the Helvetia Kreditanstalt of Geneva was the signature "Kurt A. Lindner."

"Thank you, Mr. Stimmli," said Stefano.

The bank officer gave an acknowledging nod and stood to see Stefano out. "Signor D'Angeli, you realize, we had no way . . ." His hands circled through the air, a gesture of futile apology.

Stefano walked dumbly out of the office, out into the unfelt, unseen sunshine of Geneva. It wasn't only for himself that he felt cheated and betrayed, but for his mother. La Colomba had been so clever in her life, had amassed so much, and tried to pass it on in fair and equal parts to her sons.

But, just as she hadn't figured on living in a world that could give birth to the Nazis, she hadn't planned on producing a son like Vittorio.

Stefano thought, at first, of giving up. But the memory of her and of that one magical night when the jewels had glittered in her hands and she had told them the careful plans she had made kept him going. Vittorio must not be allowed to violate that memory.

Stefano decided then that the most tangible link to Vittorio was Herr Lindner. Could it be mere coincidence that only a month or two after Vittorio had been allowed to claim the jewels, Lindner had also departed? A sympathetic hearing at the bank certainly would have done no harm to Vittorio's petition. One or two fewer questions, one or two hours less of waiting for the transaction to be processed, surely that would be worth one small baguette from the trove of jewels Vittorio had collected.

Stefano believed he had enough information already to trace the retired Swiss bank officer. His daughter had married an American, a member of the foreign service who'd spent the war years in Geneva. That would narrow down the search.

It took Stefano four months of waiting around the docks in Genoa to find a ship that would take him on as a mate in return for passage to New York. He wasn't sure whether the current laws would permit him to stay, but he had heard that America was good about taking in refugees from the war.

As his boat entered New York Harbor, passing the Statue of Liberty, Stefano reflected that La Colomba's legacy had already brought him one prize—even if he didn't find the collection. He loved Italy, but it would be many years before that ravaged land could be rebuilt. The great opportunities were here.

As they leaned on the rails, looking at the skyline of Manhattan, a shipmate told Stefano that there was a part of the city where many Italians lived. He could find work there even without speaking English. After disembarking, he found his way to Little Italy. For a couple of weeks, he worked in the storefront factory of a man who made brooms, until he had learned a handful of English words and gathered the confidence to buy a train ticket and travel by himself to Washington.

By hit and miss, speaking to anyone who would listen and make an effort to understand him, Stefano found his way to the State Department. A translator was quickly found who agreed to search the files of wartime personnel in the U.S. embassy in Switzerland and see if one had brought back a Swiss bride, maiden name Lindner.

Stefano sat in a hallway for three hours. At the end of that time, he was approached by a sturdy young man in his midthirties wearing glasses with gold metal frames. Speaking limited but serviceable Italian, he introduced himself as James Harrington, who had married Heidi Lindner in Geneva in the summer of 1946.

"Why are you looking for Heidi, Signor D'Angeli?" Harrington asked after they sat down in the hallway chairs.

"It's not your wife I'm seeking," Stefano answered, "but her father. It's about a confidential matter he handled at the bank where he worked in Geneva. I need some information only he can give me."

After a thoughtful moment, Harrington excused himself to make a phone call. He returned quickly and told Stefano that his father-in-law would be pleased to see him. Stefano was so eager that he muttered a quick "thank you" and started to race away. The young American laughed and called him back.

"Signor D'Angeli, I can guess you've come a long way in a short time and that getting around isn't easy. I've arranged for a State Department car to take you to Mr. Lindner's house."

Was it kindness or guile? Stefano wondered for a second. Wouldn't Lindner's son-in-law help in concealing guilt of bribery? Why be so nice as to provide him with a car? Perhaps he would be taken to meet the wrong man . . . or—

Idiot! Stefano chided himself. Had Vittorio's treachery robbed him of all ability to trust anyone? "A thousand thanks,

Signor Harrington. I hope I'll be able somehow to repay your kindness.''

The car brought him to a small apartment house in George-town. Harrington had given Stefano a slip of paper with instructions in Italian. As the paper directed, he went into the lobby, pushed a button next to Mr. Lindner's name, and a voice came through an intercom inviting him to take an elevator to the fourth floor.

Lindner was waiting in a doorway opposite the elevator when Stefano stepped into the hallway. The man that Stefano had often envisioned as Vittorio's accomplice was about sixty, with a tonsure of gray hair around a bald dome with the same deep tan as his face. Dressed in slacks and a car-digan, he seemed instantly relaxed and friendly, quite the opposite of Herr Stimmli.

In excellent Italian, he greeted Stefano, invited him into the apartment, and offered him his choice of refreshment.

Stefano declined all hospitality. Standing in the foyer, he said at once, ''Herr Lindner, the name D'Angeli should mean something to you.''

''It does, of course. That's why I agreed to see you. A man by that name claimed a large collection of jewels from the bank where I worked.''

''That was my brother, Vittorio. I am Stefano D'Angeli.''

''But he proved—''

''That I was dead.'' Stefano smiled bitterly. ''I'm here to prove otherwise.''

Lindner's face began an evolution through a spectrum of expressions—from concern to alarm to comprehension to abject regret.

After exchanging only a few more questions and answers, Stefano had no doubt that Mr. Lindner was a true Swiss bank official right to the marrow, unbribable and incorruptible. Vittorio had presented the necessary ''proof '' to redeem the jewels, and Mr. Lindner had simply fulfilled his responsibility to La Colomba in turning them over.

The Swiss man could not have been more sympathetic to Stefano's loss. ''My son-in-law is with the American State Department, you know. I'm sure he could be of some help in alerting the international police. These jewels have to appear somewhere, sometime . . .''

But Stefano knew that Vittorio would not be easily caught. The collection could be broken up, the separate gems split into smaller stones to keep them from being recognized. Politely, he declined Lindner's offer of help. "I've already let my dream of these jewels pull me halfway around the world,'' he said. "They've made me crazy at times—so crazy I thought you might be the thief." He smiled apologetically at Lindner. "I don't know if I'll be able to let go of the dream, but I think it's time to try.'' Across the rooftops from Lindner's window, it was possible to see the top of the tall pointed spire erected as a memorial to George Washington. With his eyes fixed on the point, Stefano added, "In this country, I think, there are other dreams to chase.''

Herr Lindner nodded and took him to the door. "If ever you need anything, Signor D'Angeli,'' he said, "don't hesitate to ask. I owe you that.''

On the street again in an unknown city, Stefano looked left then right, wondering which way to go. It was fine to say brave words about chasing dreams, but how did he begin? Indeed, would he ever find anything to match the dream La Colomba had offered?

He hadn't felt so frightened since the day of the massacre when he had taken his first steps into that ghostly quiet village, nor so alone since he had found the lifeless body of his dear Marisa.

But he had to start. Stefano turned his face toward the dome of the great Capitol building. Union Station, he knew, was just beyond it. From there, he could catch a train.

He started walking.

BOOK
II

Inclusions

Chapter 1

New York City—1966

Among people in the diamond trade, it was called simply The Street. Forty-seventh Street, between Fifth and Sixth Avenues in New York City. One small block. Yet more than half the diamonds in the world changed hands here. It was a world designed for one business. It flashed. It gleamed. It glittered and sparkled and blazed with the cold fire of diamonds.

Pete loved The Street. She loved everything about it—the polished windows curtaining the spray of light from multi-faceted gems, the office girls on their lunch hours mooning over wares they would save twenty years to buy, the newly engaged couples looking for the perfect ring to seal the deal. She loved the bearded and black-coated men gathered at the curbs doing business, passing merchandise, or just *schmoozing* in half a dozen languages.

Everyone on the street knew Pete (no one but her mother ever called her Pietra). She was as much a fixture as Goldman, the gem setter, or Brailoffsky, the dealer in findings. She'd been coming here after school for most of her fourteen years, scrutinizing the overflowing trays of gems on offer ever since she'd been tall enough to peer into the display windows by standing on tiptoe, studying, too, the people who bought the jewelry, thinking about why they made the choices they did.

Now bearded faces smiled at her as she made her way through the knots of Hasidim, the orthodox Jews who had a virtual monopoly on The Street. Ear-locked heads in wide-brimmed black hats nodded as she passed; discreet Yiddish conversations were stopped to give her a cheerful "Good afternoon."

Appreciative glances followed her, too. At fourteen, Pete was gawky, all arms and legs, sharply angled bones, and hair the blue-black of a raven's wing. But the signs were already unmistakable. Pietra Anneke D'Angeli was going to be a singular beauty before she was done.

Her eyes were large and as blue as lapis, the eyes of the grandmother she'd never known. The finely carved features she'd inherited from her father were pointed up by skin the color of polished ivory brushed with peach. Under her school jumper, white blouse, and knee socks, her body was just beginning to hint at the grace that would soon leave her coltish awkwardness behind.

Pete was already a tall girl and likely to get taller before she stopped. Her legs were long; so were her fingers. "Hands made for wearing diamonds," her grandfather always said. Oh, how she hoped he was right!

On this humid April afternoon, those hands were thrust into the pockets of her wool jumper, and she walked with single-minded determined energy. Any other day she would have stopped to chat with Mr. Hirsch, to buy a hot dog from Manny on the corner, or to look into the Gotham Book Mart in mid-block to ask the aged lady named Frances what she should read next. But not today. Today she was on a mission—a secret, *dangerous* mission. If she did it well, it would be the first of many. She made a secret vow, for herself alone. I will not be afraid, she promised. The very worst thing in the whole world is to be afraid.

She stopped before a nondescript building and darted a glance up and down to see if there were any suspicious characters, anyone who might be following. No one. On the ninth floor, behind a frosted-glass door lettered with chipped gold paint announcing "Shapiro and Sons, Diamond Traders," a burly man in white shirt and black yarmulke was at work behind a grill-protected worktable lit with harsh fluorescent tubes.

"Mr. Zeeman sent me," said Pete.

The man looked up, one eyebrow arched skeptically above the jeweler's loupe he left in place. "You? He sends a child . . . a *girl*?" His tone was harsh, as if he'd been insulted.

"I am not a child!" said Pete, giving a shake of her head that sent a ripple down her long mane of hair.

Mr. Shapiro stared at her a moment. With his loupe still in place, he gave Pete the feeling of being examined under a microscope. At last, the man grabbed the phone and dialed. "You sent her?" he said into the receiver after a moment. He frowned at the response. "You'll guarantee it?" Then he shrugged, muttered ". . . on your head," and hung up.

He swiveled around on his stool, opened a safe, and slid out one of its many drawers. Quickly he flipped through several white packets, the traditional *briefkes* of the diamond trade, sheets of white paper folded five times in an ancient pattern. Pete watched, her eyes even larger than usual. Two flags of excited pink flared in her cheeks. From each of four *briefkes* Mr. Shapiro shook out several whitish, rough stones. He counted them, separating them neatly with a long fingernail, slid them back into their folded papers, and made a notation in a memo book on his desk. Then he pushed the packets through the grill to her.

"You know those stones are worth more than fifty thous—"

"I know," she cut in. "Don't worry." She dropped them into the deep pocket of her pleated jumper.

"Don't worry," he muttered. Turning back to his worktable, he adjusted his jeweler's loupe and bent low again over a diamond. "Don't worry, the child says," Pete heard him mutter again as she pulled the door shut behind her.

Back on the street, she looked carefully at the faces around her before setting out with her determined stride, eyes down, a small, proud smile on her face.

"Hey, pretty thing," said a voice mid-block. She looked

up to see a stranger, a boy a few years older than herself, ogling her. "You got something for me?"

Her eyes widened a moment and her breathing came quicker before she realized he was only making a pass. It was a relatively new occurrence in her young life. She quickly walked away leaving the young man laughing at her blush. He wouldn't be laughing, she thought, if he knew what was in her pocket. Her fingers brushed against the *briefkes* and she smiled again.

Despite her caution and her determination not to be afraid, the cargo of diamonds in her pocket was safer than it would have been with an armed guard. Though her age and sex made her an unusual courier, on The Street it wasn't odd to entrust a small fortune in uncut stones to a mere pocket, without a receipt. The diamond business was run on trust, on handshakes and unspoken guarantees. Fortunes were carried in brown paper bags, enormous transactions carried out without a cent changing hands and nothing more official than a mental note marking the deal.

Five minutes later she pushed open the door of another workroom very like Mr. Shapiro's. The stencil on the frosted glass read "Josef Zeeman, Gem Cutting and Polishing."

"So, Pietje," said the old man behind the counter as soon as she came in. "Were you frightened?"

"No, Opa," she told her grandfather, a transplanted Dutchman with thinning silvery hair and a round, rosy, Rembrandt face. Not tall, but solidly built, Josef Zeeman gave an impression of being solid and dependable, like a sturdy yet unadorned piece of Dutch furniture. "If anyone was frightened," Pete added with a grin, "it was Mr. Shapiro. I'll bet he calls to make sure I got here."

"Shapiro is an old woman."

"An old woman with a beard," she said with a laugh. She pulled the four white *briefkes* from her skirt pocket and held them out to her grandfather, her face wide with pride.

"Well done, *schatje*," he said with the Dutch endearment he so often used for her—little darling. This girl child, this miracle called Pietra, was the light of Josef Zeeman's life.

"What are you working on, Opa?" she asked, leaning over

his grinding wheel. Before he could answer, the phone at one side of his counter rang.

"Yes, yes, she's right here, Jacob," Zeeman said when he answered. With a wink at Pete, he went on, "Of course, she had to fight off a tribe of wild cowboys and Indians to do it."

Pete smothered a laugh.

"Just Indians, Opa," she said after he hung up. "They don't have tribes of cowboys in America."

"Ah, well," he sighed. "You will teach me about America, I will teach you about what I know. Come," he motioned her closer, "you asked what I'm working on. It's Van Dieman's baguette. Have a look." He handed her a jeweler's loupe, which she wedged under her eyebrow with the dexterity of long practice. She took the mushroom-shaped dop stick he handed her, the partially cut diamond stuck to one end with a small glob of solder.

"Ick! What a dirty diamond," she said after studying it only a moment. "Rutile inclusions all over the place and even a carbon speck there, near the top."

Josef beamed. "How would you grade it?"

She looked again, concentrating fiercely. She hated to get it wrong. "P-two?" she ventured.

"Not bad," he answered. "Actually it's a P-one. A P-two would be even dirtier." She wrinkled her nose in disgust and he laughed, a hearty merry Dutchman laugh. "Van Dieman cares more for size than purity. His customers don't care if a stone's as cloudy as Amsterdam in December. They want the biggest rock they can find."

"Then they're stupid," she said, handing back the dop stick and dismissing the inferior stone with a shrug.

Josef set it aside. "What do you think of this one?" he asked, picking up a tiny brilliant cut with a pair of tweezers. Again, she put the loupe to her eye.

He'd been testing her like this for several years, honing her natural abilities, training her eye. When she was only six, he'd begun explaining the intricacies of diamond cutting. He'd made it sound like a fairy story and she'd listened with rapt attention.

One day when she was ten she came in with a handful of carob pods she'd picked up in the park. He'd explained that the word *carat*, the standard weight unit for gems, came from the Arabic word for carob, *qirat*. Carob seeds were so consistent in weight that the Arabs had used them as counterweights in weighing gemstones. She'd spent the whole afternoon shelling the seeds and weighing them on his superaccurate gem scale. Seed after seed came up at exactly 200 milligrams, and she'd laughed with delight.

Later, he taught her the precise formulas devised in 1919 by Marcel Tolkowski, a mathematician and engineer from Antwerp. He explained the correct angles and ratios in which facets were cut to maximize brilliance—"that means the amount of white light reflected back to you when you look at the stone"—and dispersion or fire—"all those pretty colors the light breaks up into."

She'd been a remarkable student. He had to admit it even if she was his granddaughter. She had a natural eye for judging gems and innate taste, a longing for only the best.

Now Pete carefully studied the tiny diamond for today's test. Silently peering down into its depths, her concentration was no less complete than if she had fallen through a hole and found herself in a cave with crystal walls.

"Lovely!" she said at last, adding with confidence, "VS quality, I'll bet."

"Exactly!" he exclaimed, slapping the counter with pride. "You are getting better and better, *schatje*. Now, tell me about the color?"

She took the gem to a table by the window and laid it on the pure white surface in front of the set of master stones, six round-cut, quarter-carat diamonds graded by color to use as standards for comparison. She measured her diamond against several of them, going back and forth, looking, turning it in the pure north light from the window, comparing again.

"I'm not sure, but . . ." She moved it once more back and forth between two of the pregraded stones. Finally, she looked at him. "I say G grade. Wesselton."

"Very good," he said, enormously pleased. "Very close. It's Top Wesselton. F grade."

"Rats!"

"Hush," he soothed, brushing back her heavy, dark hair with one hand. "It takes years, many years, to learn to grade diamonds perfectly."

"But you've been teaching me for years," she said impatiently.

"True," he agreed, "but not for *many* years." He took the diamond and returned it to its opened *briefke*.

"Will I ever learn, Opa? Will I ever be perfect? *Prima*?" she added, using the Dutch word.

He paused to look at her with adoration. "Oh, my dear, you are already *prima*."

She laughed. "Only to you. But, Opa, I want to learn to do it right. I have to!"

"You will, Pietje. *Geduld*."

Pete's nod was accompanied by a frown. She didn't like it that the Dutch word for patience sounded like "get old." She didn't see why she had to get old to learn everything about jewels.

Josef smiled with forbearance. Asking a teenager to be patient was like asking the tide to stop, he knew, but his granddaughter was better than most. Gems never bored her. Diamonds, rubies, emeralds were as much a part of her world as hot dogs, go-go dancing, and Sean Connery as 007. Gemstones seemed to hold more magic and mystery for her than the ambiguities of her teenaged world. Yes, she listened to the Beatles, sometimes humming "Yellow Submarine" as she read, but her book was more likely to picture famous jewels than the rock stars other girls her age swooned over.

"Come," said Josef. "Watch me polish the table of the baguette." He set the cast-iron grinding lap to spinning, spread it with a paste of diamond dust and olive oil, the only abrasive hard enough to affect the hardest of gems, and picked up the dop stick with its attached stone.

Pete watched as though mesmerized. She breathed in the delicious dust, let her ears drink in the soft whirring of the wheel, measured with her eyes each fine, precise movement of her grandfather's experienced hands. She let the magic pull her in.

She was still standing there when Stefano D'Angeli arrived to take his daughter home. He stood for a moment and watched her. She seemed hypnotized by the spinning lap, the emerging brilliance of the diamond. Pietra, named for the mother he'd known so little but loved so completely. Pete, the one thing in his life he knew he'd done right. He loved her with a fierceness he sometimes thought was the only thing that kept him going. He would not let her life be ruined as his had been, seduced by the beguiling glitter of jewels.

Josef was talking softly as he worked, intoning some of Tolkowski's precise rules to enhance light reflection. "The table must be exactly fifty-three percent of the width, the crown angles at thirty-four-point-five degrees, and the pavilion angles at—"

"Forty-point-seven-five degrees," she cut in.

"Precisely," he said, smiling as he bent over the wheel.

"Come on, Pete," Stefano said harshly, his voice pulling his daughter from her reverie.

"Hi, Papa." She looked up with a bright smile. "Come look."

"It's late. Haven't you got homework to do?"

"Papa, it's Friday. I have all weekend to do it."

Josef stopped the wheel and frowned at his son-in-law. "She can come home with me, Steve," he said. Stefano had been known as "Steve" since his earlier days in America.

"No, Joe. I don't want you enchanting her with nonsense about diamonds. Come on, Pete. I have things to do if you don't."

Papa was in a mood, Pete thought. And that meant she'd better just shut up and go quietly. She grabbed her schoolbooks and leaned over the grinding wheel to kiss Josef on his balding forehead. "*Dag*, Opa," she said in Dutch. "See you at home."

"*Dag, schatje*," he answered with a fond smile.

As they waited for the elevator, Stefano frowned. "You spend too much time with your grandfather's diamonds," he said. "You should be thinking about the real world, looking for a productive way to spend your life."

She hugged her books to her chest. "Why do you hate jewels, Papa?" The question had nagged at her for much of her young life. So often she had heard her father disparage what her grandfather did for a living or belittle her own fascination with gems.

"Dreams frozen into dead stone. That's all they are, all they'll ever be. It's wrong to believe too much in their value. A terrible mistake . . ." The elevator arrived and he stepped in quickly, as if eager to escape her questions.

In the elevator, Pete surreptitiously eyed her father, wondering about the source of his bitterness. Was it because of Mama? Did he hold a diamond to blame for what had happened to her?

No, Papa could not be so simple-minded. It had to be something else. Her father sometimes hinted vaguely at a secret in his past—something to do with being caught up in a dream involving jewels. But she could never pin him down about the details. He shielded himself from her questions by projecting such a powerful sense of unhappiness about the subject that she knew it was wrong to pursue it. It was almost as if he had actually fallen under a curse as the characters did in the fairy tales she'd read as a young child. As if he had wandered into a cave full of jewels jealously guarded by evil spirits.

Recently, Pete had been reading one of her grandfather's books about diamonds—descriptions of some of the largest and most valuable stones in history—and there had been a chapter about one huge blue-white stone to which a curse was supposedly attached, the Hope diamond. Everyone who owned it had suffered misfortune or death not long after it came into their possession. Pete was simultaneously thrilled and frightened to think her father might have been touched in some way by such a curse.

They came to the lobby and walked out into the late afternoon sunshine.

"Papa," she asked after a minute. "Did you ever hear about the Hope diamond?"

"No," he said quickly. "And I don't want to."

Stefano was silent as they walked west on Forty-seventh Street. It was Pete's favorite time of day, with the sun leaning toward New Jersey and slanting through the buildings and down the cross streets and the brick buildings glowing rosy pink. As Pete walked home she tried to ignore her father's gloom and lose herself in the beauty of the day.

But nothing could make Hell's Kitchen anything but ugly. It was a place of ugly buildings and desperate lives, a neighborhood of never enough money and never enough beauty, where dignity was a luxury few could afford.

As she crossed Eighth Avenue, Pete looked at the local hookers on the stroll for johns, their heroin-ravaged faces poorly masked by their gallant attempts at makeup. A rat skittered across the sidewalk and disappeared into a crack in a crumbling brick wall. A scream wafted out of a window. They were sights and sounds not fit for a fourteen-year-old's eyes, but Pete, like every other kid in Hell's Kitchen, had grown up with them.

They turned south to Forty-fifth Street. When they reached their building, a wino was passed out on the stoop, not for the first time. Pete stepped over him while her father kicked him awake and yelled at him to move on.

They were home.

Stefano stood in the doorway to the kitchen later that evening and watched Pete glue a piece of cobalt blue glass into place.

What did I do, he asked himself, as he had so many times since Pete's birth, to deserve this enchanted child, this being of such budding beauty that she makes my heart sing and my eyes smart with unmasculine tears? Silently, he blessed his mother, for it was clear at the slightest glance that La Colomba's genes dominated in her granddaughter. The only thing she had clearly inherited from her mother was her porcelain pink skin and willowy height.

She *must* be happy, he thought with a fierceness that actually cramped his stomach. She *will*. And he was certain, absolutely convinced as he had never been of anything else, that a future connected to jewelry could not accomplish this absolutely necessary goal. Jewels led to pain. They led to hate and frustration and heartbreak. He would allow no one and nothing to break his daughter's heart as his had been broken.

"Such a waste of time," he said, "this infatuation with jewelry when you could be doing something important."

Pete looked up, startled. She hadn't heard him come in or she would have put the project away. Pete knew well enough what he thought of her hobby. "I enjoy it, Papa. Is enjoying myself a waste of time?"

"Where will it get you? Do you want to be like your grandfather, tapping away at lifeless stones all day with a hammer and chisel? Or maybe you'd rather have the glory of being a saleslady at a jewelry counter?"

"Why not?" Jewelry counters had been Pete's favorite hang-outs since she was eight. Her greatest treat at age nine was when her grandfather took her to see an exhibit of the work of the great Jean Schlumberger at the Wildenstein Gallery. She knew her way around the sales floors of Tiffany, Cartier, and Harry Winston as well as she did their kitchen at home. After school, before going to her grandfather's workshop, she always walked up Fifth Avenue to gaze at the glittering windows full of treasures there. She could stand in front of a tray of brooches for hours, studying the curve of an enamel butterfly's wing, the shadings of a Lightning Ridge opal set in platinum, the intensity of the "star" in a star sapphire.

"Because you're smarter than that, that's why," Stefano said. "Because you live in a country where you've got a chance at a good education if you'll just grab for it!"

Because I don't want jewels to ruin your life as they did mine, he might have said, though he held it back.

Pete was about to put the project quickly away when her father said, "Never mind. I'm going out now."

Several nights a week he rode the subway downtown to Mulberry Street, the heart of New York's Little Italy, where he could sit over a glass of *vino* with his equally uprooted *compatrioti* and pretend he was still an idealistic young man in Milan or a *partigiano* hero in the Apennines.

As soon as he left the apartment, Pete went back to work. When she stopped again at eleven, her neck hurt. She didn't realize till she looked at the red plastic clock over the stove how long she'd been hunched over the table. Three hours.

When working on a project, she was able to block out everything else. She didn't hear the raised voices of her father and grandfather—arguments over money, over her mother, or over nothing at all, their only outlet for the frustrations of their lost dreams. She didn't think about how much she missed her mother. She forgot about the ugliness of the rubble-strewn lots outside her window, of the violence that waited around its corners and the taunting of the other children.

When she was working, there was only the balance of colors, the way one surface absorbed or reflected light from another, the symmetry of the design. There was only the terrible longing to create something beautiful that would last beyond tomorrow.

She looked at the results of her work: a simple celluloid comb, a boar-bristle brush, and a child's mirror made of shiny unbreakable steel housed in pink plastic—but they had been transformed into a birthday gift for her beautiful mother.

For months she'd been saving the delicate, silk-thin silver foil from sticks of Juicy Fruit chewing gum, begging the wrappers off classmates and even spending precious dimes of her own to buy the sugary stuff she never chewed. With elaborate care, she peeled the foil from its paper backing and smoothed it out. She used it like the silver leaf she couldn't afford, gluing it to the comb and brush and mirror, smoothing out every bubble, until the implements were completely silvered.

With tiny beads and bits of beach glass her grandfather had helped her shape on his grinding lap, she recreated the rose window at Chartres Cathedral in France on the mirror back. She'd found a picture of it in the library, and the richness of the colors, the symmetry of the pattern had seemed both peaceful and vibrant at the same time. It struck Pete as the perfect symbol for the peace and hope she wished her mother could feel. The brush back got a similar design made from opalescent bits of shell. For the comb, she let her fancy run free, running a beach glass vine along its shank ending in a big bunch of white grapes made from imitation pearls with leaves of stiffened lace.

She couldn't wait to give it to her mother the next day.

Pete leaned down and kissed her mother's pale cheek, stroking one hand across her still beautiful silver-gilt hair. "Good-bye, Mama. We'll be back next week."

For Pete, the Saturday ritual was always the same. With her father or grandfather—rarely both but never without one or the other—she made the long, dreary trip to Yonkers, changing from subway to train to bus before finally arriving in front of the grim gray building that squatted on a bluff overlooking the Hudson River. The first time Pete saw it, she thought it looked like a horrendous rotted tooth growing out of the jawbone of a giant. Even as she grew older and other fairy-tale associations faded into memory, this one stayed in her mind. The State Mental Institution at Yonkers was a place of decay that chewed people down to nothing, grinding away their souls and minds with giant jaws that, once clamped shut, never seemed to open again to release their victims.

Pete was never allowed into her mother's room. Instead, Papa or Opa made her wait in the visitors' lounge while they went and got Mama. Sometimes it took a long time before they brought her out. Occasionally, Papa came back alone to where Pete waited on her hard chair and said, "Mama's not feeling well today; we'll see her next week," and Pete knew better than to argue.

Bettina had good days and bad days, and Pete had learned early on how to tell them apart with a single glance. On good days they'd all go outside and walk together on the scraggly lawn laced with crabgrass and peppered with canary-colored dandelions. Or they might sit under an oak watching the swiftly running Hudson, sometimes flowing down to the sea, other times racing upstream with the incoming tide.

On the good days Bettina smiled and even chatted a little. Pete told her about school, about what she was reading, about a new dress or a show she'd seen on television. And when it was time to go, Bettina gave Pete a fierce hug and kissed her good-bye. She seemed almost normal then, and Pete always asked, "Why can't Mama come home, Papa?"

"It's too soon, Pete. She's not well enough yet."

"Will she ever be well?"

Stefano stared out at the river. "I don't know, *bambina*. Maybe one day."

On not-so-good days Bettina withdrew into herself, her face a blank, and she scarcely said a word, as though the jaws of the institution had closed around her mind. On those days she sat quietly on a sofa between her husband or father and her daughter, not seeming to notice that they were holding her hands, while she stared at something no one else could see.

Today had been a good day. Josef had brought Pete to visit, and Bettina had loved her gift. Later they had all stood on the bluff together and watched a single-masted, shallow-draft Hudson River sloop tack across the current, buying the wind with its bellying sail, pushing for Albany a hundred miles upstream. As it disappeared, Bettina recounted a sailing outing at Scheveningen she'd made as a child, her face smiling softly and her eyes aglow with remembered innocence as she said softly, "Remember, Papa?"

"Yes, Tientje," Opa replied in a voice so sad Pete wanted to cry. "I remember."

Pete also fought to remember—to hold on to some of the bright memories she had shared with her mother. To let them all fade away was like losing part of the battle to save Mama's life. She could remember holding her mother's hand and walking in a park by the river while Mama recited the Dutch names of flowers along the path. Daisies were *margrietjes*, she remembered, and marigolds were *goudsbloemen*, gold-flowers. And whenever Pete saw an iris, she could still hear her mother's sing-song laugh, like the glass windchimes Mr. Morris next door hung on his fire escape. *Regenboogen*, she called them. Rainbows!

She remembered walking with Mama on the sand at Jones Beach, watching her delicate skin get all pink in the summer sun. And family trips on the Staten Island Ferry, the poor man's yacht, when they sailed back and forth for hours at a time because Mama was so happy on the water and never wanted to go home.

But it was hard to remember the good. Often her memory was so crowded with darker memories—of Mama sitting in her rocking chair with the lights off, not speaking for days, of the times she made them both hide in the closet "till the bad men go away," of the sound that she knew was Mama crying but sounded more like an animal that had been terribly hurt.

On the train home from Yonkers, a man was sitting across from Pete, holding a newspaper. As he folded back the pages one after another, pictures passed in front of her—another airport melee to greet the Beatles, Civil Rights marchers lined up across a street in Selma, soldiers running across a rice paddy in Vietnam. It struck her then how long it had been since her mother had lived at home. There had been no Beatles then, Vietnam and sit-ins weren't regular subjects in her current events classes. Pete looked over at her grandfather. "Tell me the truth, Opa: Do you think Mama will ever be able to come home again?"

He smiled at her, the way he always did when she asked her perennial question. "I pray so, *schatje*, every night."

"I do, too." Pete wanted so desperately to make her mother all right. And she was so utterly helpless to do it.

Chapter 2

New York—March 1950

Stefano walked into the small stall run by Josef Zeeman in one of the jewelry arcades on Forty-seventh Street. It was his last stop of the day. As a wholesaler of jewelry findings, he called on many of the small dealers and repairers who rented stalls here.

Many, like the Dutchman, were refugees of the war, men like Stefano himself who would have been doing better things if the war in Europe had not thrown their lives so disastrously off course. Josef had been a respected diamond cutter in Rotterdam before the war, but here he repaired broken bracelets, reset inferior stones for secretaries, and put new watchbands on old watches.

Tonight Stefano was delivering some earring backs.

"Let me sell you a nice old watch," Josef said when they concluded their business. "I took it in trade for some work. I could give you a good—"

"I don't need a watch," Stefano said.

"But it's a woman's watch. I thought you might like it for your wife."

"I'm not married." Seeing the persistent gleam in Mr. Zeeman's eye, Stefano added, "And I have no girlfriend."

When he saw that the gleam in Zeeman's eye did not fade, Stefano began to suspect the game. He was not at all surprised when the Dutchman brought up his daughter and suggested they might meet.

"She's a very pretty girl, my Bettina, and smart. You'd enjoy her company."

"Perhaps . . . sometime," Stefano said gruffly. Even if the scar tissue on his heart had healed over from the wound of losing Marisa, he didn't imagine for a second that he could love the daughter of a Dutch watch repairman, a rosy red-cheeked *huisvrouw*, no doubt plump from too much lonely nibbling on her own wonderful cooking.

The Dutchman looked at him sharply a moment. "Wait here," he said. In a moment he'd returned with a bottle of *genever*, Dutch gin, potent stuff. He poured a couple of shots—*borreltjes*, he called them—and they each drank. He began talking about the deep wounds inflicted by the war and about the love and attention his daughter needed to heal them.

"What happened to her?" Stefano asked.

Josef told the story with an energy and immediacy that suggested it was the first time he'd shared the details since coming to America.

For a time after the Nazis occupied Holland the Zeemans had gone on living much as before. Miraculously, their house had been spared in the wholesale bombing of Rotterdam. Josef had his work as a diamond cutter; his wife kept house. Bettina attended school, though she had to ride her bicycle several miles through rubble-strewn streets to reach an un-damaged school building.

Even when stories began circulating that religious Jews were being rounded up and sent to labor camps, Josef wasn't alarmed.

"Of course we felt sympathy for those who were up-rooted," he told Stefano, his voice tinged with irony, "and we were shocked by such cruelty. But we were quiet people, boring people. We were not involved with the Resistance. There was no reason we should be drawn in. No reason at all."

Josef was a Protestant, and though his wife had been born

a Jew, she had stopped practicing the customs when they married. If she still bought her meat at the kosher butcher, her bread from the Jewish baker, why, it was only out of habit. Her mother had always bought there, the cuts were better, the bread fresher.

"Then one Friday afternoon," Josef said, his voice dying a little, "a German army truck rolled into the Nassaustraat. Many shops there were owned by Jews. Women were shopping for the Sabbath dinner. My Anneke was there . . ."

His wife had been one of dozens of women rounded up at gunpoint, herded into trucks, driven away.

"At first I was sure it was a terrible mistake. What else could it be? I went to the authorities. But the Nazis did not make such mistakes. It was then I knew the world had gone mad."

Soon after, Josef heard that Jewish children were being snatched from their schoolrooms. Bettina was in danger. Though she had never set foot in a synagogue, to the Nazis she was as Jewish as her mother. With his wife gone, protecting Bettina became the most important thing in Josef Zeeman's life. So he took her into hiding.

Their refuge was a corner of an attic in the house of a Christian doctor, an old friend. In a space barely eight feet square concealed behind a false wall, with no windows and no water, they waited out the war. "The doctor brought food and took away our waste," Joseph said in a flat voice. "Once a week, at night, we crept silently out to wash. For three and a half years, we lived like that, like rats in a cage."

After hearing the tale, it seemed only natural for Stefano to recount the horrors and losses he had experienced himself. For years, he had bottled up the memory of Marisa, the pain of her brutal killing and the guilt he felt over it. But the *genever* loosened his tongue, and he hoped he might ease the Dutchman's burden, reminding him that however hard the war had been for his daughter, she had survived. She had a life ahead of her.

Throughout the account of Koppveldt's massacre of Marisa's village, Josef shook his head slowly. His eyes watered when Stefano described finding her body. At the end, after another silent shot of Dutch gin, he said, "Some evening, perhaps you might come to my house and meet my Bettina. She . . . she needs someone."

Stefano searched his mind for the most considerate and uncomplicated way to put the Dutchman off. How could he explain that his heart felt dead, that he feared his own need to use any woman only as a medium to soothe the sexual ache he felt in the absence of Marisa?

And how could he explain about the pain and frustration of his fruitless search for a lost treasure? After he had come back from Washington, D.C., that night three years ago, he had almost given up and admitted that Vittorio had won. But as he took out the bottle, all that remained of his legacy, prepared to sell it and at least have the money with which to start a new life, he found he couldn't part with it . . . or the memory of his mother . . . or the dream. He had entered the jewelry business in the hope of picking up a lead. He had sought out anyone who might have had the extraordinary skill to duplicate half of the bottle, followed up any lead that might point him in his brother's direction. Once he read of a ruby bracelet sold at an auction that sounded like one he had seen at his mother's villa. But it was a dead end. They were all dead ends.

Josef's voice intruded on his thoughts.

"Do you ever wonder, my friend, why we were spared when the others died—your Marisa, my Anneke, so many others?"

The force of the unexpected question set off a maelstrom of conflicting desires in Stefano. He wanted to flee, wanted to pour out his heart, wanted to damn Zeeman for tapping into the torture that nagged at him through so many sleepless nights.

"*Naturalmente*," he stammered at last, emotion driving him back to his native tongue. "*Tutti giorni*, every day I wonder . . ."

"And do you have an answer?"

Stefano shook his head.

"Neither do I," said the old man. "Because there is no answer. But I know one thing, *maatje*. I know that we who lived through that hell have a duty to see that they did not die for nothing. We must live the best lives we can, the lives they never had a chance for. You must have the children your Marisa will never have, teach them what she would have taught them. Bettina must keep alive the teachings of her mother, pass them to a new generation. You see? It is the only way to make sense of their deaths, to keep a part of them alive.''

Stefano gripped his glass and quickly downed more of the Dutch gin. At least the man's direct, he thought. And he certainly knew how to go for the gut. Well, he'd earned it. Someone who knows that life can be shattered in an instant —merely by the arrival of a truck outside a butcher shop— must think it foolish, even sinful, to waste time beating around the bush.

Words emerged from his mouth almost before the thought could form in his brain. ''Perhaps you would ask your daughter if she would enjoy seeing a movie with me on the weekend.''

Josef turned to begin clearing away their glasses and the bottle. ''If you wish to see my daughter, Mr. D'Angeli,'' he said quietly, ''you may come over for coffee Sunday afternoon.''

No, not a subtle man, Stefano thought again. But very proud.

Early in the afternoon on a bright, cold Sunday, Stefano found himself standing in a corridor that smelled of garlic and stale cigarette smoke, rapping on a metal door covered in peeling green paint, holding a box of chocolates in one hand and a bottle of Chianti in the other.

Josef opened the door and greeted Stefano eagerly. ''Come in, Steve, come in. It is good to see you.''

The moment he walked into the little apartment, Stefano felt comfortable. It was cramped, the walls were uneven and the floor sagged, but in every other way it was totally at odds with the depressing neighborhood outside. Starched lace curtains hung at the windows. A flowered shawl was draped across an oak sideboard, its scarred wood polished to a gleam.

On the mantel, a porcelain clock gently chimed the hour while the viola of Mozart's *Sinfonia Concertante* played softly on the radio.

Josef gathered up the newspapers spread on a table beside his half glasses—the *New York Times*, *Figaro*, *Het Parool*. His pipe smoldered in an ashtray, sparking in Stefano a memory of the cheroots Carlo Brancusi had always smoked after dinner.

As he handed Josef his coat, he took in the smell. More than anything else, the room smelled of home—dried roses from a bowl of potpourri, the tang of pipe tobacco, the pungent odor of cinnamon. And something else. Ah, real coffee! Its rich, deep aroma filled every corner.

The room welcomed Stefano in a way none of the American homes he visited ever had. It felt . . . yes, European.

Then she walked in, her fingers busy at the knot of her apron.

"Papa, isn't it time you—" Seeing Stefano, she stopped short. "Oh, I . . ." She hesitated, embarrassed at being caught unprepared. "I didn't hear you come in."

Stefano merely stared. Bettina Zeeman was small-boned and delicate, with hair of a color somewhere between platinum and gold, a sort of shimmering silver-gilt. It swept up from her face into soft rolls on either side of her forehead, accenting her high cheekbones and the hollows beneath them. She was simply dressed in a pleated gray skirt and a long-sleeved sweater a shade lighter than the gray-blue of her eyes. Simple clothes, but she wore them with grace and a subtle pride that made them seem rather elegant.

She laid the apron aside as Josef beckoned her closer to be introduced. She was tall, nearly as tall as he was, Stefano realized, and slender, like a bare winter branch waiting for spring to flesh it out with new leaves. Her breasts were high and her legs were long—like Marisa's had been, he couldn't help thinking—long enough to wrap around a man and cling tightly.

Yet as much as he appreciated the long, lovely body, it was the face that dispelled Stefano's last doubt about having come. Mother-of-pearl skin, rose quartz lips, and those eyes the deep gray-blue of an ocean over which storm clouds perpetually hover, eyes that seemed to project a sadness that could never be lifted.

There was, over all, an intensely fragile air about her, like a piece of fine crystal that could be shattered by the sound of a single harsh note. Bettina Zeeman was not merely pretty, Stefano thought. She was exquisitely beautiful. Hauntingly so.

"Good afternoon, Signor D'Angeli," she said with formal solemnity as they shook hands.

Her voice rang like a musical note. Her hand felt tiny and delicate in his, with no strength beneath the almost translucent skin. She didn't merely look at him but fastened her eyes on him, taking him in feature by feature, studying the face as if it were truly the mirror of the soul.

Again he thought of Marisa, of her eyes gazing deep into his as they had lain together that last night . . .

In truth, the two women were nothing at all alike. Marisa had been all brown hair and chocolate eyes and skin the color of polished amber; she had been laughter and earth and the taste of rich Tuscan wine. Bettina Zeeman was pearls and blue crystal and fresh spring water.

Yet Stefano sensed that the two women shared a secret force of energy—explosively visible in Marisa, coursing like a subterranean stream through this Dutch girl—and the perception sent his thoughts reeling back to the parched peaks of the Apennines, back to the nights they had lain in her bed, the smell of fresh bread filling the air. Even now the memory made his blood pulse with desire for her.

His hand trembled as he removed it from Bettina's grasp, and she gave him a curious glance.

"I am enchanted to meet you, Miss Zeeman," he said, making an effort to keep his voice neutral.

Josef beamed. "Tientje, bring our guest some coffee."

"Of course, Papa, but might we at least allow him to sit down first?" The barest hint of a smile reached her eyes, the first Stefano had seen. It banished the sadness, transforming her. When it vanished as quickly as it had come, he longed to bring it back.

Belatedly, he remembered the candy he was holding—
Schrafft's best chocolate-covered peppermints—and offered
her the dainty, satin-covered box.

Her face lit with childlike delight; her long fingers tore at
the cellophane and pulled back the lid. She thrust her nose
into the box, breathed deeply, and laughed, a happy child's
giggle. Then she popped two candies into her mouth at once,
sucking them until they dissolved. She was about to pluck
out another piece when Josef reached for the box. Bettina
frowned and for a moment it seemed she would not give it
up.

"*Schatje*," he said firmly. "*Er is genoeg. De koffie.*"

Instantly she released the box. "Thank you for the candy,
Mr. D'Angeli. Sit please. I will bring the coffee."

She returned at once with a tray and poured coffee from
a Delft pot into delicate flowered cups. It tasted as good as
it smelled, stingingly strong, deeply flavored as fine old wine.
Nothing like the pallid brown imitation that usually went by
the name of coffee in America. Stefano held a second sip in
his mouth a moment, closed his eyes the better to savor it.
"Ah," he sighed.

"Yes," Josef agreed. "They know nothing of coffee,
Americans. Not the real thing, like my Bettina makes it. A
taste of home, *ja*?"

"Yes, home," Stefano agreed.

Home. It meant something to the three people in this room
that no one who hadn't lost everything could truly understand.

"*Tientje*," said Josef, "bring Steve some of your
koekjes." He turned to their guest. "Real Dutch cookies,
with almonds and spice. Bettina is a wonderful cook, you
know. A wonderful housekeeper, in fact. She takes perfect
care of me . . ."

Josef was a fond father to his daughter, Stefano thought,
and a very decent friend. But he was not a subtle man.

Stefano D'Angeli and Bettina Zeeman strolled up the shank
of Fifth Avenue, the crisp March air adding a glow to their
cheeks. Bettina drew glances from every man they passed.
It was their first real date. Stefano had asked her that Sun-

day evening if he could take her to a movie the following Sunday.

There could be no doubt that Josef had dug deep into his pockets to make sure his daughter was well displayed. Her chic navy-and-white checked suit was a faithful copy of the long-skirted "New Look" that had crossed the Atlantic not long ago from the runways of the hot Parisian designer, Christian Dior, causing an uproar among American women indignant at the idea of going back to the corsets and layers of petticoats the style demanded. Bettina's slender body, as insubstantial as swansdown, might have been made to showcase Mr. Dior's genius. The long, round skirt flirted with the air as she walked; the wide navy belt emphasized the narrowness of her waist. She wore it with the flair of a runway mannequin.

Her face was framed by a hat of white chip straw trimmed with a navy ribbon. Stefano thought she looked like a flower and smelled of spring.

They made a striking couple. He was still a handsome man. The war that had stolen his youthful idealism had also given his features new character, and he still wore clothes well—a gray pinstripe suit, crisp white shirt, and a well-brushed trilby. He felt almost as though he had been thrown back to an earlier self—the dashing young man eyeing all the prettiest girls in Milan and making them blush.

"I hope you like Radio City," he said as they walked.

"I've never been," she replied in her soft musical voice.

"Then you have a treat in store. I took myself there the first week I came to New York. It was the most American thing I could think of to do."

"Not the Statue of Liberty?" she said with a teasing lilt.

"That is for immigrants. I wanted to make myself an instant American. So I went to the biggest movie theater I could find. They call it 'a movie palace'—as if movies were the kings here. I couldn't even understand the English words the first time I went, but I loved it just the same. So will you."

"I will try," she said with such solemnity that he half suspected she was teasing him again.

"I'll make sure you do."

She smiled one of her rare smiles. It so completely changed

her, brightening the very air around her, that he made winning more of them from her grave countenance a mission.

At Radio City, he bought popcorn, and she ate it like a hungry child, stuffing it into her mouth until her cheeks bulged, licking the butter from her fingers. There was a certain charm in it, he thought, yet it also struck him as strangely at odds with her restrained ladylike facade.

The film was *Francis*, a silly bit of fluff. The antics of Donald O'Connor and a talking army mule made her laugh out loud, a clear, bell-like sound, almost carefree. The stage show delighted her even more—the lights, the orchestra, costumes flashing sequins made her eyes grow wide and dart from one side of the huge stage to the other. When the Rockettes began their precision routine and the audience broke into cheers, she squeezed his arm.

As they left the theater, Stefano felt like a man who had successfully carried out a mission of some importance.

They walked down Fifth Avenue, Bettina happily peering into the windows of the expensive stores that drew eager shoppers from all over the world.

"That's mink," she said as they stood in front of Best & Company. "And that's white fox next to it. Fox is very warm, but not as warm as sable."

"I know nothing about furs," he admitted.

"Italians never do," she said and he laughed.

Peck and Peck had a whole window full of shoes and she stared and stared, looking lovingly from one pair to another—pumps and sandals, boots and brogues and platforms. It was as if she thought it a miracle that the world held so many shoes.

"Those will be lovely with the new spring suits," she said of a pair of spectators. Of another pair, she said, "Those won't hold up to much walking, but they are pretty." The boots were "rather dowdy, don't you think?" and the sandals "perfect, really perfect."

"I never knew there was so much to say about shoes," he said.

She gave him a self-conscious smile. "Forgive me, I am boring you. But for so long such things were—"

He laid a hand on her slender arm. "I understand."

"Someday I will have shoes to match every dress. And boots for the rain and fur-lined ones for snow and beautiful slippers for home—"

Suddenly Stefano clapped a hand onto her thin wrist and tugged her away from the window.

"What are you doing?" she protested.

"When dreams are so small, why wait to make them come true?"

He urged her through the store's revolving door. In a few minutes they were in the shoe department of Peck and Peck. He persuaded her to try on a pair of snow boots lined with rabbit fur—on end-of-season sale, luckily—and some sheepskin slippers.

She tried them on almost reverently, then turned and walked and turned again, studying them from every side in the angled floor mirrors.

"We will take them both," Stefano announced to the clerk.

"Very good, sir," she replied, and began packing them into their tissue-lined boxes.

"Oh, no," said Bettina. "You must not. I can't—"

"Please," he said. "Let me."

She searched his eyes with hers, as though looking for hidden motives. But after only a second, she broke into a smile that brightened her whole face. "Thank you."

He watched as a week's worth of commissions were whisked away in a pneumatic tube toward the upstairs cashier, but it was a small price for the smile that stayed on her face throughout the trolley ride home, her packages clutched tightly to her chest.

In retrospect, Stefano had to wonder if his gesture had been wise. What for Stefano had been nothing more than a generous whim, Josef, with his rigid Old World customs, would no doubt see as a veritable engagement gift, the first installment on a trousseau!

And yet, all the way back to his own drab room and throughout the next day, it pleased him to think of the smile he had won from that beautiful but unusually solemn face.

Chapter 3

I am definitely not the man for her. Each time he saw Bettina Zeeman, Stefano went home telling himself the same thing. She needs someone less confused, someone more patient—a man not shackled to bad memories. She deserves a man who will love her as I never could.

He promised himself he would explain to her gently why she mustn't look to him to fulfill any dreams larger than a pair of wool-lined slippers. When he called at Josef's booth and the two men talked about Bettina, Stefano always explained that he could never make her a suitable husband.

"Have you someone else?" Josef always asked.

When Stefano confirmed that he hadn't, the old man urged him to give time a chance to do its work. "It is exciting when love comes like the strike of *bliksem*, a bolt from the blue, but lightning burns bright and is gone in a moment. Love that comes slowly can last longer. Do not turn from her yet, Steve. With you, she has a chance to be happy. *You* have a chance . . ."

Each time, Stefano went away touched by the old man's appeal. He was moved, too, by the image of her haunting loveliness. For all the darkness in her soul, when the light broke through it was like a rainbow falling suddenly over a bare, forsaken landscape. The poet in him was not so dead he could resist a rainbow.

So when each weekend came he had arranged to see her again. Like tourists, they took in the sights of the city. They rode the ferry to the Statue of Liberty, huffing their way to the top of the torch. They visited museums, ogled the view from atop the Empire State Building. Often they ate together. Bettina loved the Automat, where a nickel made coffee spout from a metal lion's mouth and a few coins dropped in a slot bought one of the meals displayed behind hundreds of small glass windows.

"When you go hungry week after week," she said, "you think paradise must be a place like this."

The effect of her war experiences, Stefano came to realize, was with Bettina constantly. If happiness came only in flashes, if her eyes were always shadowed by sadness—even fear—it was because some part of her had yet to be liberated from that tiny attic room in Rotterdam.

The desire to bring a smile to her face, to revive for a moment the effervescent wit and gaiety that must have belonged to the girl she was before the war, became a compulsion for Stefano, and the constant effort revived some of the spontaneity and high spirits of the glib young man from Milan. He began to look forward to their meetings more and more.

One warm Saturday at the end of June they went to Coney Island. A week earlier Bettina had begged, "Will you take me to the sea? When I was a little girl, we spent our summers at Scheveningen, near Rotterdam. I miss it so terribly. The beach, the water, the endless space." He could not refuse her.

When they got off the subway, the streets were alive with people and sound, laughter and the music of the carousel, the shrieks of riders as the Cyclone raced over its soaring trestle. But Bettina hardly noticed any of it. She pulled him straight toward the boardwalk.

"Oh, Stefano," she exclaimed, "I can smell it already."

Up on the boardwalk, she took in the broad panorama with

wide eyes, the long strand of beach, the waves rolling in eternally. She pulled the pins from her long silky hair. As it fell, she shook her head so it fanned out around her shoulders, framing her face and billowing in the fresh salty breeze.

Stefano thought he'd grown accustomed to her beauty, but now she took his breath away. He was reminded of a fresco, a Madonna he'd seen in a Sienese church when he had traveled through Tuscany before the war—a time when he'd had the conceit to think himself a poet in search of inspiration. The fresco had been high on a wall, mostly in shadow, but at certain hours of the day sunlight streaked in golden bands through the arched windows, illuminating the Virgin's face. It was the most beautiful work of art he'd ever seen.

As she breathed in the peace of the sea, Bettina Zeeman seemed no less miraculous to Stefano.

He put his hand lightly over hers on the railing, pushing his fingers between hers. She turned to him with a curious expression, a slight frown that seemed almost . . . puzzled.

A second later, she bolted from the boardwalk and ran down the steps to the sand. Though the sun was bright, it was too cold to swim. Still, Bettina pulled off her shoes and ran into the water until it swirled around her ankles, then her calves, and surged up to her knees. The hem of her cotton frock got soaked even though she lifted it to her thighs. From the edge of the surf, Stefano watched as she turned her face to the sun, closed her eyes and flung her arms open to embrace the ocean. For the first time since he'd met her, he read absolute contentment on her face.

While she was happy like this, it was easy to desire her, he realized. The fear that his passion might overwhelm her and destroy something fragile disappeared. He let his eyes feast on her beauty. The breeze and the damp made the lightweight dress cling to her, outlining the soft curves and angles of her body.

Could he love her, Stefano wondered? Did he already? In this moment, it had begun to seem possible.

Reluctantly she walked out of the sea. Her teeth chattered as she wrung water from her hem, but she was glowing. Draping his windbreaker around her shoulders, Stefano steered her to a cafe on the boardwalk where he ordered two large mugs of very hot tea.

They found a window table and wrapped their hands around the steaming mugs. But no sooner had she lifted her cup, smiling at him, than her gaze was riveted to something outside the window. Her naturally pale face drained of all color until her eyes stood out like blue marbles. The cup plummeted from her hand, spilling the scalding tea and dashing the crockery to pieces as it fell to the floor.

Stefano whirled to see what had caused her reaction. In the path of her gaze a tall man with a moustache stood on the boardwalk talking with a petite woman in a flowered dress.

"Bastard!" Bettina hissed. She was shaking, her eyes burning as they pinned themselves on the man outside. "Don't touch her," she seethed. "Leave her alone!"

Stefano reached across the table and grabbed her wrist. "Bettina?" Other customers were staring at them.

Her eyes glazed with fury, and he looked again at their focus. The tall man leaned to kiss his companion on the cheek.

"Run!" Bettina urged. "Run away fast."

"Bettina, what is it?" Stefano persisted.

The couple parted and the man walked away. Bettina's eyes shifted to Stefano, and all at once their fire was extinguished like a candle snuffed out.

"Who was he?" Stefano asked.

Bettina shook her head as though to clear it after a faint.

"That man . . . ?" Stefano prompted, nodding at the retreating figure. "Who—?"

"I was wrong," she said quietly. "It wasn't who I thought."

"Can you tell me about it?" he asked finally.

"There is nothing to tell."

The incident at Coney Island strengthened Stefano's belief that Bettina needed more patience and a more definite commitment than he could ever provide. When he took her home that evening, he meant to make some excuse not to see her for a while.

But when they reached the smelly hallway with the green

metal door, she spoke first. "You are afraid of me, aren't you?"

It took him a second to answer. "No. I am afraid *for* you."

"Is that why you never touch me? I mean . . . as a man touches a woman?"

The brazenness, so at odds with her usual demure reticence, left him speechless. She moved closer, so close he could smell the sea salt on her skin. Her eyes shimmered with the luminescence of moonstones. "You think I would disappoint you? You didn't think so earlier, at the beach. I saw the way you looked at me. You wanted me . . . " The music of her voice was no longer the sweet melody of a lullaby, but low and sinuous—a song of seduction.

"Bettina," he began, totally confused, not sure whether to discourage or invite. Before he could decide, she brought her lips up to meet his. The light flicking touch melted his last restraint, and when he pulled her closer and pressed his mouth to hers, she ignited as though he had set a glowing ember to a dry stack of tinder.

Her mouth opened and her tongue darted out, forcing his lips apart. She put her hands around his neck and twined her fingers in his hair, pulling, twisting. She ground her body into his.

He slid his hands around her waist, up to her small, high breasts, back down to cup her round bottom through the wrinkled cotton of her dress. Her mouth opened wider, as though she would swallow him if she could.

Then, as suddenly as it began, it was over. She pulled away, slightly flushed, and stared up at him. Her eyes seemed darker, as dark as the sky at midnight.

"And now I think I must say good night, Signor D'Angeli," she said. She opened the apartment door. The smell of Josef's tobacco drifted out to them. "You see, dear Stefano," she whispered before disappearing behind the closed door, "there is no reason to be afraid. No reason at all . . ."

He was still afraid. Now, however, he was also inflamed. He wanted to see Bettina Zeeman again as soon as possible, to unlock the mysteries hidden behind her changeable masks. More than anything, he longed to touch her again. All of her.

By the light of the next morning, caution returned. Making his rounds through the day, Stefano kept debating when to see her again—or whether to see her at all. That fiery embrace was so out of keeping with everything he knew of her that he found himself doubting his own memory. Perhaps it had been merely a waking dream of desire inspired by his long pent-up grief for a passionate love. It had been a kiss, after all, nothing more. The ardor of her movements, the shadings of her voice, they must have been colored more by his expectations than her intentions.

At the end of that day he stood before Josef's repair stall, on a hunt for any clues to Bettina's character.

"Ah, Steve," the Dutchman greeted him heartily, rising from his workbench. "Or should I call you Stefano? Bettina tells me she likes that better. More romantic, she says."

"What else has she told you?"

"Well . . . that you had a lovely day at the beach."

"That's all?"

"Don't be coy, my friend. Is there something I should know?"

Looking at his smile of anticipation, Stefano realized the old man was expecting some sort of happy announcement.

"No," he said flatly. "But there was a curious incident at the beach . . ." The Dutchman cocked his head with concern, and Stefano told him about the stranger on the boardwalk. "She acted like he was someone evil, a kind of devil."

Josef's eyes narrowed, and he nodded slowly.

"You know who she mistook him for?" Stefano asked.

Josef lowered his eyes to the floor and shrugged. "No one I could name. But she . . . she has dreams about her mother. She thinks she was taken away by an evil man, not a group of anonymous soldiers." He looked up. "My fault. When her mother didn't come home—Bettina was so young—I couldn't tell her the truth. I said she'd gone off with a friend for a visit. I expected she'd be home in a few days. When she didn't come back, Bettina began asking endless questions about the friend. It was a while before I could bring myself to tell her the truth."

Stefano nodded thoughtfully. The daylight outside was fading. Josef switched off his lamp and took his coat and hat from a peg. "Why not come home with me tonight? Your work must be finished. Bettina will make you dinner. You haven't tasted her cooking yet, have you? Unless, of course, she's been to your—"

"I haven't tasted it," Stefano said.

"Then come with me," Josef said as they stepped together into the twilit street. "Come home."

Stefano hesitated, but that last word had worked its magic.

When he walked in with her father she was all shy surprise. Wearing only a simple wraparound housedress, she was obviously unprepared for company. "Papa . . . how could you? Look at me! And I haven't enough food for—"

"There is always enough, and you look beautiful." Josef silenced her. "Anyway, have you forgotten I am invited to the Dutch Club tonight? Lucky me, I shall have *Goudse kaas* and herring and *paling*—smoked eel—a real Dutch meal," he said. "So I thought it would be nice for you to have company."

Stefano studied the wily old man. Was this all preplanned to get them alone together, with Bettina an accomplice? No, they couldn't have known he would call in at the shop. Yet why did he feel he was being maneuvered into a box that got smaller and smaller? What did the American cowboys call it when they caught a cow for branding? Corraled?

Bettina gave him a shy, apologetic smile. "I am glad you're here," she said, "but if you don't want to stay—"

"Of course I do," he said, remembering once more the sensation of holding her. Even now he could smell her cologne, like gardenias after a spring rain.

Josef picked up his coat again. "Enjoy yourself, Papa," said Bettina, handing him his hat.

He set the fedora at a jaunty angle. "And you two, enjoy yourselves as well."

As the door closed behind him, Bettina turned to Stefano, her moonstone eyes calm. "Will you make love to me now," she asked matter-of-factly, "or after dinner?"

It excited him by its very coolness, this offering herself to him so totally, unquestioningly, on any terms he wished. He answered her by sweeping her to him and putting his mouth over hers.

Leaning into him, her tongue probed his mouth as her hands scanned his chest, unknotting his tie, searching for the buttons of his shirt and opening them so quickly one popped off and skittered across the floor. She slid the shirt down over his shoulders, capturing his arms against him. Her hands twined in the curly dark hairs of his chest; her fingernails dragged across the tender skin, circling the nipples. Then her mouth left his and roamed downward, across his neck and chest to his right nipple. She found it with her teeth and nipped at it, hard.

His reaction was immediate. His penis jolted up inside his pants with an urgency he hadn't known since he was a boy. In seconds it was iron hard and throbbing, the need growing as she nibbled on one nipple while pinching the other with her nails.

Her other hand worked at his belt, freeing the leather from its buckle. She unhooked his pants and slid down the zipper of his fly. He started to undress her, but she pushed his hands away.

"No," she said softly, but with a harsh edge, and pushed him back into the wall so that he couldn't move.

In a moment, she had his penis in her hand, stroking the velvety skin, trailing a fingernail the length of the shaft. The hand slid down to cup his balls, the nail tickling the incredibly sensitive skin at the base. Then she squeezed gently, a tantalizing moment, but with an implied threat. He gasped and thought he heard her exhale a stifled laugh. He'd never felt so helpless, so vulnerable. Or so aroused. He ached, throbbed with it. Where did she learn to handle a man so deftly, he wondered, though at the moment he didn't much care. He just didn't want her to stop.

She eased his trousers down over his buttocks. He still couldn't move, and now he was totally exposed to her. Her slender body slid down his till she was on her knees before him. Her lips slid around his penis, first teasing the tip, circling, flicking, sucking lightly. Then she jammed her mouth all the way down to the base, hard and fast. The end of his penis hit the back of her throat. It seemed she would swallow him completely. She moved her head up and down, her tongue circling the shaft, her teeth nipping at the head until he moaned.

He'd never known anything like it. In one lucid moment, he thought this must be what a butterfly, freshly caught and pinned to a board, still alive, feels like. He couldn't touch her, couldn't move, couldn't get away even if he wanted to. He was completely at her mercy.

The pressure built until he was sure he would explode. Then suddenly she stopped, rose, and stepped away from him. She was smiling, her eyes glittering. Not an expression of mere happiness, Stefano thought, but one of triumph.

Her hands went to the sash of her housedress, and it slid to the floor. Beneath it she was naked. By the light of a single lamp burning across the room, he could see that she was magnificent. Not the voluptuous, fully rounded curves of Marisa, but a perfectly sculpted figure. Her breasts were small and firm, with pale pink areolas around nipples hard as pebbles, her waist tiny, her hips just round enough for womanliness. The soft lamplight made her alabaster skin glow like warm pearls. The triangle of hair between her legs glistened like spun gold.

He had only a moment to enjoy the sight before she pushed him onto the floor. Then she was on him, sliding down over him, hot and moist and tight, so tight, squeezing him with strong muscles. One of her perfect breasts was in his mouth. As she pumped up and down, he sucked hungrily, trying to milk her as she was milking him.

She pulled away from his mouth, sat almost upright and continued to move up and down. His eyes closed as the exquisite agony built, but just before he exploded into her with a shout, he opened them.

Yes, it was triumph on her face. She was smiling like a queen in total command of her subject.

In the quiet aftermath of their lovemaking, he got back into his rumpled clothes while she excused herself to the bedroom. She returned wearing a dark blue shirtwaist dress, as demure and unadorned as a schoolgirl's uniform. Her face was scrubbed, and her hair was pulled off her face with a barrette.

"And now we will eat," she said calmly.

As she went back and forth between the kitchen and the small sitting room, setting the table, bringing plates and silver, fetching bowls of *hutspot*, a crock of butter, and a basket of fresh baked bread, he could only eye her in astonished silence.

The sex had been the most overwhelming he'd ever known. He'd never been so out of control. His orgasm had seemed to come from his very soul. Already he wanted to feel again that intensity so extreme it was excruciating—until it was transmuted into dizzying pleasure at the moment he shot into her. But the craving was not only to feed his own sensation. As a man, he needed the satisfaction of bringing her to the same peak. She hadn't come; she hadn't even been close. She'd given him no chance to bring her to it, almost as if she weren't interested.

What was the truth about Bettina? How had the years spent in confinement turned her into such a bizarre amalgam of innocence and lust, reticence and abandon? Was he wrong to be frightened of the mixture?

When she sat opposite him at the table, he could no longer maintain the quiet pretense that what had happened wasn't unique.

"I have never known anyone like you," he said, cursing his own awkwardness as soon as the words were out.

"Isn't everyone different from everyone else?"

"But . . . the way you changed . . ."

Slowly she buttered a piece of bread then gave him a glance edged with a sparkle of wickedness. "Do you think I am naughty?"

"No. I just wonder why you keep so much of yourself hidden."

"Hiding is how I survive."

"Not anymore."

"If I come out of hiding, I will die."

He shook his head, uncomprehending. "Bettina, this is America. A new country. A free country."

She put her spoon down and fixed him in a direct gaze. "Let me be as I am, Stefano. Let me be . . . and I know I can please you. I will be good for you. Only you will know the hidden part. I will be the perfect wife."

His mouth opened but no words came. Not to speak doubts now would be to yield to her assumption—to accept *her* proposal. But at this moment, he wanted her, wanted not only the promise of passion she embodied, but to help her, to heal her pain and restore her trust. Her moods unnerved him, her changeability kept him on edge, the dark side of her soul frightened him. But if he abandoned her—especially now—he would think for the rest of his life that it was done out of cowardice, out of weakness.

Whatever he had lost of his poet's heart in the war, Stefano longed to believe that there was something left. To take Bettina Zeeman into his life once and for all—to protect her even if he did not love her—was a mission worthy of the man he had been.

And if she showed her secret self only to him, what reason could he ever have to regret that?

Chapter 4

New York—April 1952

"*Moetie! Ik wil moetie!*" Bettina moaned, reverting to her native tongue and calling for the mother who had been dead for a decade even as she shuddered with the pains that would make her a mother herself.

As the taxi bumped toward the hospital, Stefano gripped her hand. Even with the extra weight of pregnancy, her face was gaunt, her cheekbones stretching the porcelain skin.

"We're almost there, Tina, hold on," he reassured her, but he was worried. The baby was early, more than a month, and Bettina seemed so afraid. Her blue-gray eyes alternated between being wide with fear and squeezed tight against the pain. Her fingers clutched his in a death grip as she called for *Moetie*, Momma.

They'd been married just over a year. A good year, on the whole. With Stefano and Josef's incomes combined, they could afford a decent apartment for the three of them—and now for the baby, too—a place on Riverside Drive with a view of the Hudson.

It was a new life for them all, and before long the Old World Stefano had become the new American, Steve. Gradually, the dream represented by La Colomba's perfume bottle faded to the back of his mind. He had a wife now, and within months of their marriage a baby on the way. He had a new future to dream about, a future more real than fantasies of diamonds and gold.

He still couldn't make himself sell the half bottle—its symbol was too potent, the memories too dear—even though he understood what a difference the money would make to his family. Such sentimentality embarrassed him, so he told no one about his treasure. He hid it away until it was all but forgotten.

Once he'd given up the dream, Steve's work options expanded. He was intelligent and well educated, thanks to Carlo Brancusi, and before long a help-wanted ad in *Il Progresso*, the Italian language newspaper, led to work at an Italian language radio station. He wrote scripts for commercials and short radio plays, made the rounds of the city selling air time, translated from American news reports; he even filled in occasionally as a disc jockey. He loved the work, and he knew he was good at it.

He was not disappointed with his marriage. With his expanded income, he bought Bettina an inexpensive rabbit fur and a pair of flirty, sling-back pumps of red silk. He brought home bottles of her favorite gardenia cologne and bags of the chocolates she adored and could never get enough of—and which never seemed to add an ounce to her willowy frame. They walked all over the city together, and her laughter bubbled more and more often.

The erotic promise of that first night was amply fulfilled as well. Bettina was an endlessly innovative lover, full of tricks he'd never even fantasized about. Her cool, Grace Kelly beauty and birdlike fragility were in total contrast to her wantonness in the bedroom, her ability to arouse him to the screaming point, and the more she gave him the more he wanted. He came home every day hungry for her. He might even have called it love.

But he was bothered, even saddened, by her lack of response to him. When he tried to bring her to a passion that met his, she gently pushed his hand away or twisted out of reach. She was always willing, eager even, to make love to

him, to do anything, try anything that would heighten his
response. Her own pleasure, however, she kept firmly below
the surface.

She still fell into sudden darknesses at odd moments, memories washing over her and plunging her into long silences.
But the horrible memories of the war seemed to be receding.
He was confident that with patience the past would finally be
put to rest; the future would reclaim her soul completely.

When he learned Bettina was pregnant, Steve whooped for
joy and swung her into the air. Josef brought out the *genever*
and they all drank a toast to the coming child. Steve promptly
went shopping and brought home a white-painted rocking
chair where Bettina could sit to nurse the baby, an enormous
stuffed panda, and a crib dripping with lace.

Bettina glowed with quiet happiness throughout her pregnancy, but when the labor pains finally came in the hours
before dawn on the night of a thunderstorm, her eyes clouded
with terror.

At the hospital, a pair of starched, unsmiling nurses
whisked her away, leaving Steve and Josef to stare at each
other over endless cigarettes and cups of bad coffee. The
ticking of the clock grew louder by the hour until it pounded
a tattoo in Steve's head. He shivered with fear for her, surprising himself with the depth of his own worry. What if
something happened to Bettina? Could he stand another loss
like the one he had suffered with Marisa?

With the silent question came the realization that Bettina
had in truth begun to fill that empty place in his heart. And
now there would be a child, too!

It was eight hours before a nurse finally came in. She
smiled. "Congratulations, Mr. D'Angeli. You have a daughter."

A daughter. He sat down with a start, flooded with joy.
And with gratitude. "A daughter," he whispered. Suddenly
the name surged up out of memory, out of the fountain of
reclaimed love. "Pietra."

Beside him on the waiting room's orange Naugahyde sofa,
Josef's seamed face glowed. He clapped his son-in-law on
the shoulder. "Yes. Pietra Anneke D'Angeli," he said. The

child would carry the names of her two grandmothers, both of them dead at the hands of the Nazis.

She's so small! That was Steve's first thought when a nurse put his daughter into his arms for the first time. A stragglylooking little thing, barely six pounds, with enormous eyes and the tiniest feet in the world. One of his hands could completely cover her head with its cap of dark, downy hair.

His next discovery was that he had never really loved anyone before. Not like this, with such fierceness, such all-consuming power, with the absolute conviction that he would fight, maim, *kill* anyone or anything that threatened her.

Despite her premature birth and tiny size, Pietra was healthy. It was her mother who had Steve and Josef worried. Bettina refused to feed her baby. Refused to hold her. When the tiny bundle was brought to her hospital room, she turned away, unwilling even to pull back the pink blanket and look at her.

Steve had hoped with all his being that the advent of a child—a new life, a link to the future—would bring Bettina true contentment and rekindle her optimistic view of the world. Just the opposite seemed to be happening.

On the third day, Steve overheard Bettina speaking calmly to the nurse. "They kill the babies, you know," she said matter-of-factly. "They put them in ovens and burn them up."

"She's terrified," a hospital specialist explained. "Afraid if she starts to love Pietra, or even acknowledges her existence, the child will be taken from her as her mother was taken."

"What can we do?" asked Steve, feeling more helpless than he ever had.

"I do have an idea that might work," said the doctor.

While Bettina was sleeping, they laid Pietra beside her on the bed, her blanket pulled back so that her little pink face would be the first thing her mother saw when she woke. All morning, Steve sat in a corner of the room, waiting.

When Bettina's eyes finally opened, he leaned forward, scarcely breathing. She blinked at the bundle beside her on the pillow then quickly turned her head away. Steve waited.

After a few moments, the baby made a mewing sound. Slowly, Bettina turned toward her again. A tiny fist emerged from the pink blanket, waved in the air, then screwed itself into one deep blue eye.

Tentatively, Bettina reached out and stroked the little fist. She leaned over it and licked it. She put her nose to her baby's chest and breathed deeply. At that moment, Bettina fell as hopelessly in love with her daughter as Steve had.

Yet despite that love, her depression did not lift. At home, in fact, it seemed to grow worse. Night after night, Steve returned from work to find Bettina sitting in her rocker with the lights off, clutching the baby. Often Pietra had a dirty diaper or was crying with hunger, and it took all his coaxing to get Bettina to let go of her so he could tend to her needs. She seemed terrified of letting the child out of her arms.

At night, they slept with the crib beside their bed. From the start Pietra was a good baby, sleeping through the night after the first month. But Bettina often awoke screaming, "They're coming! They're at the door!" Then she'd pull the baby from her blankets and scramble under the bed with her.

No matter how he tried, Steve couldn't make her understand that the pounding at the door was nowhere but in her own head, a ghost Gestapo with no power to hurt her or her baby.

Steve was overwhelmed by the enchantment that was his daughter. A child animated by curiosity, her eyes were always moving, roaming about, drawn to anything bright or colorful. As a toddler, she unrolled whole boxes of tin foil just to look at its sparkle, the patterns of light thrown onto the walls and ceilings by its mirror surface. She could amuse herself for hours with a box of shells, moving them around in various patterns. Her first word was "pretty."

Gradually, Bettina's gloom lifted. When Steve came home one night to find her waiting in their bed, her golden hair freshly shampooed and gleaming around her head like a halo, her skin polished and warm, her smile enticing, he dared to hope once more for a normal life.

But on a snowy night in February 1956, Steve arrived home

after work to find the apartment in total darkness. Usually a light was left burning for him in the small entranceway. He remembered that Josef had planned an evening at the Dutch Club. Perhaps he had come home late, too, and turned off the light.

Yet there was an ominous edge to the silence that greeted him. Steve stood for a moment just inside the door, listening, trying to define the intangible quality that disturbed him. No radio, no sound of the kettle in the kitchen where Bettina sometimes waited up for him with a ready cup of coffee.

Slightly alarmed now, he hurried to the bedroom. The bed was empty.

Rushing to the nursery, he discovered that Pete's tiny bed was also empty. Now his heart began to pound. He went from room to room, punching light switches, throwing back doors.

"Pete! Tina!" he howled, unable to imagine that they could have disappeared from his life. He ran out of the apartment into the hall and called again. Perhaps they had gone to a neighbor's; perhaps Pete had hurt herself and they had gone to a hospital.

"Pap—" The cry was instantly cut off, muffled. But it had come from behind him, he realized, from within the apartment. He spun around and raced again through the rooms, looking under beds, pulling open closets, throwing wide the doors of cabinets, peering behind furniture.

"Pete, Papa's here, *bambina*! Where are you?" he called in a frenzy. "Pete!" He pulled linens from the linen closet. He dug into a cupboard, throwing aside luggage and blankets and boxes of tools. He yanked open the double door of Josef's old-fashioned armoire and shoved aside the suits and overcoats and hat boxes.

They were huddled in the corner. Bettina's back was to him as she bent protectively over their daughter, trembling. "Shhh," she whispered into Pete's ear.

But the little girl couldn't hear. To stop her crying out and giving them away, Bettina had clamped one hand over Pete's mouth in a death grip. By now the child had stopped breathing.

Steve pulled them from the armoire, hurling Bettina across the room so he could get to Pete.

"*Mijn kindje!*" she cried "My baby! Don't take her away!" She rushed him, nails poised like claws. When he tried to fend her off, she jumped on his back, pulling hair, scratching, biting, trying to save her child from what she thought was certain death at the hands of Nazi murderers.

Steve had no choice. He had to help Pete. With difficulty, he peeled Bettina from his back, held her in front of him, and struck her a blow that knocked her out. Then he rushed to his daughter. She was still unconscious and not breathing. A faint blue pallor had stolen over her skin.

"Oh God!" Steve begged. "Help me!" He'd recently read something about mouth-to-mouth resuscitation. He was not sure how to do it, but he knew he had to get air into her lungs. Going to his knees, he covered Pete's mouth with his and blew gently.

"Breathe!" he shouted between puffs. "Breathe, dammit!" He kept filling her lungs like a balloon, crying, begging.

Within a minute that seemed like a year, Pete coughed. He shook her by the chin till she opened her eyes.

"Papa?" she said in a small voice, looking dazed and still terrified.

He clasped her to him, rocking on his knees. "*Grazie,*" he whispered, as tears ran down his cheeks. "*Grazie, Santa Maria.*"

Steve had to quit his job to stay with Pete, and the need for money became acute. In an attempt to bring Bettina some peace of mind and insure Pete's safety, they had numerous expensive psychiatric evaluations done on Bettina. They soaked up most of the money Josef brought in. The result was a decision that Bettina's depression was treatable at home as long as she was kept on tranquilizers.

Even with this reassurance, Steve refused to leave Pete alone with Bettina. He couldn't take that chance. If anything were to happen to Pete, he would die. By posting notices on local bulletin boards, he picked up translation jobs now and then—booklets, ads, once a small textbook—and wrote the occasional letter back to the Old Country for immigrants with no American-educated kids to do it for them, tasks he could do sitting at the kitchen table while Pete played at his feet.

For the rest, they scraped by as best they could on Josef's salary. Through a friend in the network of transplanted Dutch refugees, Josef had finally been able to leave his repair stall for a job at the New York branch of DuFort & Ivères, the Parisian jewelers renowned since the time of Napoleon. He did routine polishing and setting and enjoyed the chance to handle once again the gems that had been his life. His starting salary was two hundred dollars a week, a fortune compared to the seventy-five he'd been netting in his own small business. And then, he'd had a raise. Noticing that one of DuFort & Ivères' gem cutters was about to make a costly mistake in cleaving a moderately valuable sapphire, Josef had offered a polite suggestion. The man wasn't too proud to take it or to pass on to his supervisor the word that "Dutch" Zeeman had a good eye. Josef became a gem cutter again, working on the small, routine stones used to complement the more valuable gems in the pieces designed and sold by the firm.

In the summer of 1957 a rumor wafted through the cutting room at DuFort & Ivères. It was said that the French owner of the firm, Claude Ivères, had been entrusted with a remarkable rough diamond, a stone the size of a baby's fist.

Day by day, more details were whispered from one cutter to another as the men worked over their grinding wheels. The diamond was said to be the property of a wealthy Vietnamese who wanted the prestige of Ivères associated with its cutting and setting. Yet the owner was fearful of sending his prized possession to Paris. Only a few years earlier Vietnam had chased the French colonists and their defending army out of the country with a crushing defeat at Dienbienphu. The recently elected premier of France, the great wartime general Charles de Gaulle, was known to be smarting from the blow to French pride by the loss of its colony in Indochina. There was a strong likelihood that if the diamond entered France, the government would order it seized as war reparations. Accordingly, a plan had been formed for Ivères to take possession of the diamond in London, then bring it to New York for cutting. As more news of the stone filtered down through the grapevine, the excitement among the cutters grew. A weight of a hundred and twenty carats was mentioned. Most astonishing of all, it was said to be of River quality.

"That means it's the very best," said Josef to Pete one evening as she sat on his lap with her eyes fixed on his beloved face. She was five years old, and Josef found her an eager listener to all his talk about gems and jewelry. Lately all he could talk about was the mystery diamond. "A River diamond is the purest and whitest of all. The term comes from the time hundreds of years ago when the most beautiful diamonds were found in the Golconda River far away in India. They were so brilliant and full of light that the people who dug them up thought they were magic. And the purest stones, like the one Mr. Ivères has, could only be given to the ruler of Golconda."

Pete sat silently, taking in every detail of the real-life fairy tale he spun for her. "Why do they want to cut it up, Opa? Won't it hurt the magic?"

"Oh no, little one. It will make the magic all the more powerful. Right now this diamond looks like a big chunk of dirty glass. But when it is cut—if the job is done well—it will be as glorious as a frozen sunbeam. And it will cast a spell over everyone who looks at it."

Just as it had already cast its spell over him, Josef thought. From the moment he had heard about this fabulous stone, he had dreamed of making the cut. It was the kind of challenge that could lift him straight to the heights of his profession, forever after linking his name with the stone, as Kaplan's was with the Jonkers, and Asscher's with the Cullinan.

"How is it done?" Pete asked, pulling Josef out of his fantasy.

"Well, a diamond is very complicated, Pete. There are invisible lines that hold it together. If the stone is cleaved right along one of those lines with a special kind of knife, it will break in two. That way, the parts with cracks and other flaws that keep it from being beautiful can be cut away, and you end up with a diamond that is pure all the way through and has a pretty shape. Next it has lots of sides ground into it and they are polished. These sides are called facets.''

"Like faces," Pete put in.

"Yes, *schatje*. Facets are the faces of gems. And when they are done just right, they catch the light and shoot it back to you—the way a smile on your face is like dazzling sunshine to me." He nuzzled her cheek and she giggled. "Remember last year, we went to Coney Island and you went in the House of Mirrors?" She nodded, her eyes not leaving his. "A well-cut diamond is like that. Each facet catches the light from one mirror and shoots it to the others. But each mirror has to be angled just right or it won't shoot the light back—it will swallow it up."

"We must have good diamonds, Opa," Pete said. "Or else the world will be dark."

Josef smiled. "Yes, little love, we must have good diamonds."

"I don't like the dark," Pete murmured, and fell asleep on his shoulder.

On his way to work one morning, Josef noticed a long black limousine pulling up to the corner of Fifty-fourth Street and Fifth Avenue, half a block from Dufort & Ivères' main entrance. A chauffeur held the door, and a man climbed out. He wore a formal black suit, a black homburg on his head, and on his feet gleaming black shoes with dapper yellow cane insets at the tip. No more than a few inches over five feet in height, he still projected the sort of authority that made people describe men of such height as Napoleonic. In the brief glimpse that Josef had of the man's face, he saw that his eyes were almost as black and shiny as his shoes, and he had a moustache as thin as a blade. He carried a gold-topped ebony walking stick, which he used with jaunty authority as he walked briskly along until he got to the row of glittering show windows of Dufort & Ivères. There he paused for a leisurely inspection, then strode into the store, past the uniformed doorman, who actually saluted the man as he entered.

It was no surprise to Josef when he entered the cutting room only minutes later to find it already buzzing with the news that Claude Ivères had arrived. What did surprise—and disappoint—Josef was to learn that the senior cutter, Kurt Louers, a Belgian from Antwerp, had already been called to a meeting in Ivères' office on the floor above. The job Josef dreamed of had evidently been assigned.

Two hours later, Louers returned. The job was not his, not yet, he reported to the other cutters who gathered around him. The time with Ivères had been occupied totally by an interrogation, Ivères questioning him not only about his past work and the way he might cut a large diamond, but about everything else under the sun. Was he happily married? What did he like to eat? How much wine did he drink? Had he been seriously ill at any time in the past few years? Where had he spent the war? Even about how old his parents had lived to be.

"Either he's a madman," Louers said, "or he's very clever. I haven't been asked so many questions since the Gestapo pulled me in back in '43 . . ."

For the rest of the day and into the next, the cutters were called away one by one to spend an hour or two with Claude Ivères. As he waited his turn, Josef began to wonder if he had any hope at all of getting the job. Could he possibly give the "right" answers to so many questions? Should he say that he liked his drop of *genever* when he came home every evening? And if he was asked about family . . . ah, there was the biggest problem: what should he say about Bettina? What might be inferred about his ability to handle stress if too much were known about her?

His turn finally came at the end of the second day, the very last cutter to be interviewed. Whatever eager anticipation he might have mustered was gone now. Cutting this stone, he believed, would remake his life. But now he felt there was almost no chance of being awarded the job.

A secretary showed him through a beautiful walnut door with gold fittings into the office of Claude Ivères, a large wood-paneled room with a grandiose desk set before the tall windows. Josef was stunned to see heavy drapes drawn across the glass, blocking out all but a sliver of daylight. Strange for a man whose business depended on light and its effects to work in such a dim room. Perhaps Ivères was, indeed, a bit mad.

The small man sat behind the immense desk, looking at a file by lamplight.

"Sit down, Zeeman," he said when Josef entered.

And then it began, the litany of questions reported by the other cutters. Birthplace, past history, job experience, and then the personal questions. At first, Josef answered patiently, though he could see no point. No doubt to entrust to a man a diamond that might eventually yield several million it was reasonable to know something of his background. But what point was there in knowing how he spent his leisure time, how often he went to the Dutch Club at night, what books he read?

"What about family?" Ivères asked at last. "You have children?"

"A daughter, Monsieur," Josef answered. "And I have a beautiful grandchild, the light of my life."

Ivères smiled, and in the pause Josef asked quickly, "Why is that important to you?"

Ivères sat forward quickly. Was he annoyed by the impertinence of being questioned himself, Josef wondered.

Yet Ivères answered quietly, "The process of examining this stone, thinking about the cut may—*must*—take many months. It interests me to discover how you will be sustained through the process, whether there are people to see to your needs, to care for you and keep your mind at ease. Also, I'm glad to hear there is this special grandchild—someone you would like to do nice things for, I should imagine. That will give you the incentive to succeed. Does that answer your question?"

Josef nodded and waited anxiously for Ivères to pursue the subject of his family. Instead he asked, "Who is your favorite painter?"

It would have been easy enough to say Vermeer—that was the simple truth—but something in Josef snapped. The man was toying with him, he thought, using his power to tantalize with a hope that could not be fulfilled. "*Genoeg*," he burst out unthinkingly in Dutch. "Enough of this quiz game. Why don't you ask me about the one thing that matters? The stone!—what would I do with the stone?''

The eyes of Claude Ivères widened in a burning glare. "So, Zeeman," he said, "you are a man of short patience."

"No. I have no patience for nonsense. And if that matters, then use someone else. Otherwise let us talk about what is important. The heart and soul of your diamond, not my heart and soul. Ask me questions about the stone, and for that you will find my patience is endless."

Ivères' razor-thin moustache twitched with what might have been a momentary smile. "Zeeman," he said softly, "I have been waiting two days for someone to dare to be bored with me, to dare to question my power over them and the strength of my reasons. Whoever I choose to cleave this stone must be a man of daring, willing to defy the strength of the diamond. You are the first man to tell me to my face that it is a waste of time to talk about anything other than the diamond. I am not at all certain the rest is pointless, but I have no doubt this task cannot be performed by a man without the courage and spirit to take that kind of risk." He rose from his desk and abruptly threw back the drapes. The late afternoon sunlight slammed Josef in the eyes. Ivères picked up a polished wooden box from the windowsill, set it on the desk, and opened it. Inside was the rough diamond.

"You have twenty minutes. Study it. Then tell me what you would do with it."

Josef willed himself not to blink against the sun as he replied, "Twenty minutes is nothing. The Cullinan was studied for nine months before—"

"I don't have nine months. And I am not asking you for a definitive analysis, merely an educated guess. In the end, that's all you can do anyway."

It was unfair, Josef knew. Undoubtedly, exhaustive examination of the stone had already been done. But what did he have to lose at this point?

He reached out and picked up the stone, the size of an apple and nearly twice the weight. Moving it out of the direct sun, he turned it slowly, rolling it in his hand, his thumb brushing against the top. A small window or clear spot had been cut into the stone's grayish skin. Josef took a loupe from his pocket, put it to his eye, and peered into the stone's murky heart. His Rembrandtian face wrinkled up in concentration.

Ivères sat watching throughout. After a while he drew a gold fob watch from his pocket, opened the lid, and set it on the desk in front of him. Josef continued studying the stone. At last Ivères closed the watch with a loud snap. "Well?" he said.

Josef replaced the stone in the box. "Of course, after a lengthy study I might have different ideas—"

"Of course."

"But from what I see now, I believe I'd give it a modified Old Mine cut. The grain is right for it. A cushion cut, probably ninety facets like the Tiffany Yellow, with a few altered to eliminate that feather inclusion I can see. We reduce wastage that way. I'd think we could get at least forty-five carats out of it, maybe fifty. And I'd make the table slightly higher than Tolkowski. We lose a little brilliance but get maximum fire. The stone can carry it."

"You'd go with just one make?" Ivères asked, meaning just one finished diamond from the stone.

"Yes." Josef said it without hesitation. It was a daring approach for this particular rough—an oddly shaped crystal with one flat edge—but he felt sure it would work. It would mean just one cut, one clean cleavage along the grain, before grinding and polishing.

"Louers and DeSmet both thought four."

"They probably think the grain is parallel to that flat spot. I don't believe that." His Dutch-accented voice rang with confidence.

It was what Ivères wanted to hear. His client had demanded the biggest, flashiest stone possible. Zeeman was the only one who had sensed that and who instinctively understood how to achieve it.

Ivères stared at the Dutchman's face a long moment. Zeeman was respected, he knew, but he wasn't in the top ranks

of New York cutters. Word was he'd done a couple of relatively important stones back in Holland, before the war, but
that was years ago. And this stone was crucial. Still, one
stone, forty-five carats, maybe even fifty . . .

He pushed the wooden box across his desk toward Josef.
"The job is yours. Take as long as you need."

Chapter 5

When it comes to cleaving, a diamond is unforgiving. Either it is done perfectly, or the diamond is ruined. There is no middle ground.

Josef began romancing the stone, studying it for hours at a time under his twin-barreled jeweler's microscope in the glare of a Diamondlite. He diagramed his ideas for the final make. He made several solid plaster of paris models and studied them. He constructed other models with taut lines of thread pinned into sticks of balsa to represent the stone's interior crystalline structure. At dinner, he formed balls of soft white bread into an image of the odd, flat-bottomed diamond, rolling them awhile, then chewing on them meditatively. Ivères' diamond became practically a member of the family.

Often, needing to hear himself talk through the problems, Josef confided his thoughts to Pete. Steve didn't interfere, but he watched, frowning, as he saw his beloved child being sucked into the gem's magic field. Was it some sort of D'Angeli destiny, he wondered, a kind of kismet, to be so easily seduced by the glitter and promise of gems?

Bettina, too, felt the stone's magnetic pull. Captured by

its mystery, she found herself listening intently whenever Josef discussed his plans for it. She imagined herself drawing strength from the impregnable hardness of the diamond, clutching its perfection as a symbol that survival was possible after all.

Sometimes Josef just held the stone, pacing the room with it, trying to mine its essence. Before he touched the diamond with his cleaving mallet, he had to know it, know its surface and its heart and its eons-old history as well as he knew his own face in the mirror.

"I must be like a sculptor," he told Pete, and she listened, ready to be enchanted. "I must be able to *see* the finished diamond sleeping inside the rough stone the way a sculptor sees a statue inside a lifeless block of marble."

He enlarged the window on the bottom of the stone to peer deep into its center. Only then could he be sure of where all the inclusions lay. "I must crawl inside it," he told Pete, "walk around in there and see what I can see."

"Like the bear who went over the mountain," she said with a giggle.

"Yes. Exactly like the bear."

It was nine months before Josef was ready to make the cut. Claude Ivères was informed, and he cabled back from Paris that he would fly in to be present. The event was set for a Sunday morning at the end of March. With all the cutters and the management team of the New York branch of Dufort & Ivères invited —indeed, commanded—to be present, the affair took on the trappings of a gala. Cases of champagne were standing by in the cutting room to be uncorked as soon as the stone was cleaved.

It would be a momentous achievement for Josef, and he asked to have his family present. Bettina had been much better lately, allowing them all to hope once more for her complete recovery from whatever terrors her soul still harbored. Josef imagined that the cleaving of the stone, its opening up, might set his daughter free, too. And he wanted Pete there because of her interest in the stone, an interest he had carefully cultivated.

Morning sun sparked the air in the cutting room. The room seemed full of people. The excitement produced an almost audible buzz of electricity. Bettina had dressed six-year-old Pete in her prettiest dress, a bright blue and white cotton print with a taffeta sash. A blue ribbon tied back her thick, unruly black hair, and brand-new black patent leather Mary Janes adorned her feet. She kept looking down to see if she could still see her face in their shiny surface.

Opa sat at his workbench, ready. He had already marked the cleaving lines on the stone with India ink. He had stuck it to its dop with a kind of glue, his own special mixture of shellac, resin, and brick dust. With another sharp-edged diamond, he had made a groove called a "kerf." Then he had set the dop firmly into a hole on his workbench to keep it from jiggling.

They brought a chair for Bettina. Everyone else stood. "Mr. Zeeman," said Claude Ivères, clearing his throat nervously. "Are you ready to begin?"

"Yes," said Josef. He adjusted his head loupe. "If you will all step back a little?"

He picked up a small, rectangular blade made of steel. Slowly, with perfect precision, he positioned it in the kerf on the diamond. He lifted his wooden mallet. Beads of sweat trickled down his forehead. Pete could feel her mother holding her breath beside her.

Josef leaned over the stone. He raised the mallet in a ritual more than five hundred years old and brought it down onto the blade with a firm rap.

The blade snapped.

Nervous laughter rippled through the room. "Perhaps we should have had a doctor and an oxygen tank on stand-by," said one of the men with a chuckle, "like Kaplan did when he cut the Jonkers." Josef didn't seem to hear. Calmly, he picked up another blade and placed it in the kerf, moving it back and forth a bit to test the position. Again he picked up the mallet, raised it, brought it sharply down on the blade.

The diamond shattered into a hundred pieces.

For a moment the crowd of spectators was frozen in stunned silence, as though the room itself and everything in it had turned to stone. On the work table now, lay not one central focus of triumph . . . but a pile of worthless fragments.

Josef had read the stone wrong, disastrously wrong. In an instant, a unique diamond valued at millions of dollars was reduced to nothing.

At last the silence broke, a tide of voices began rolling through the room, rising higher and higher. Pete wasn't sure what all the commotion was about, but she knew it was something bad. Opa was staring at the little pieces of the rock, staring as if he were a statue. Papa's hand on her shoulder clutched hard, hurting her. Mama began crying, silently at first, the tears flowing down her pretty cheeks, but then sobs, too. Louder and louder until she was screaming and Papa had to slap her to make her stop. Mr. Ivères pushed through the crowd, his eyes blazing as he shouted at Opa to get out, get out, and never dream of cutting again for him or anyone else! The room was full of noise and anger, hurt, and the stunned look on Opa's face. Pete wanted to help him, to help them all, to put the little pieces of rock back together again and make it whole. But what could she do?

With the shattering of the diamond, whatever had held the D'Angeli family together also broke apart, splintering into pieces with sharp, piercing edges that drew blood.

Josef lost his job immediately and he knew no comparable job as a cutter would come along for a long time, if ever. Though it was generally acknowledged that any cutter could make the same mistake Dutch Zeeman had made, no one would risk alienating Claude Ivères by hiring the man he'd blacklisted. Josef's shattered confidence in his own judgment surfaced as ill temper, and fierce shouting matches with Steve became frequent. The two men had no one but each other on whom to exercise their anger and resentment.

Bettina seemed no more tangible than a ghost. When the diamond had shattered into rubble, her mind had suffered a blow as severe as the stone. She sank into a depression deeper than any of the past, lying in her bed day and night, never talking.

With Josef unemployed and apparently unemployable,

Steve had to earn a living for all of them. He went reluctantly back to the one thing he knew would bring in some steady income. Hating every minute of it, he returned to the jewelry district, once more making the rounds of the independent stall-holders in the arcades, the repairers and setters and bead-stringers, carrying his case full of cheap goods.

His earnings were not nearly enough to keep them in the comfortable apartment on Riverside Drive. They moved into four small rooms on West Forty-fifth Street near the Hudson River—a neighborhood called Hell's Kitchen, where prostitutes lingered at all hours in doorways, derelicts collected on corners, and gangs of young toughs ruled the streets.

Pete was left to amuse herself. Often, imagining how rich and wonderful their life would be if only Opa had cleaved the diamond in the right way, she would get out her crayons and draw pictures of how the diamond should have looked. She drew magnificent settings for it, rings and brooches with surroundings of emerald or ruby or sapphire.

The best days were when her grandfather took her on walks to the nearby piers on the Hudson River. After walking just a few blocks, they could leave behind the rubble-strewn vacant lots of Hell's Kitchen, the sad-eyed mothers with too many children and no husband, the able-bodied men who sat on the street playing dominoes all day because there was no work for them in all this big city. Pete and Opa could turn their backs on it all, turn their faces to the river, and imagine themselves in another world. Pete liked to count the seagulls and smell the salty air, and watch the huge ocean liners come into port.

"The docks are like Rotterdam," her grandfather told her with a wistful smile. "Like home."

Pete knew about Rotterdam. She knew it was where Mama had been born and where her grandmother Anneke had died, killed by bad men called Nazis. She knew it was all the way across the blue part of the map, a long way away. And she knew Opa missed it. He never said so, but she could tell.

She knew a little bit about her other grandmother—that her name was Pietra, too, and of course she came from Italy, where Papa had been born. Pete wanted to know more, but when she'd asked Papa about her once, a shadow of sadness had filled his eyes, and he hadn't told her very much. "She was a queen, with ebony hair and skin like ivory and thousands of jewels. She lived in a place far away. I didn't know her very well."

"Would she have liked me, Papa?" Pete asked.

"She would have loved you, *bambina*, just like I do." Then he changed the subject, and Pete knew somehow that she shouldn't ask him any more. Maybe not ever. But secretly she always thought of her queenly grandmother as her fairy godmother.

On an evening at the beginning of a new spring, Josef came home feeling terrific. After almost a year of haunting the jewelry district, pestering every old acquaintance and knocking on every door, he'd found a job. A real job, as a gem cutter. Oh, he wouldn't be handling anything like the stone he'd ruined for Ivères. He accepted that no one would ever again trust him that far. But he'd be cutting small, ordinary diamonds and maybe an emerald or a sapphire now and then. And he'd be bringing in money, good money. He could afford to get his beautiful daughter the help she needed.

With a light heart and a light step that belied his sixty years, he bounced up the sidewalk with a bunch of pink roses, Bettina's favorite, in one hand and a bottle of wine in the other. Tonight they would celebrate and Bettina would smile again. He gave a cheery wave to a neighbor taking the air on the stoop and went upstairs.

As soon as he opened the door to their apartment, the smell hit him. Gas. Gas from the kitchen!

He dropped the flowers. The wine bottle shattered on the scratched yellow linoleum. He ran into the kitchen, nearly choking on the acrid smell. Beneath the oil cloth–covered table, Bettina crouched over Pete, holding her down. She had blown out all the pilot lights on the stove and turned on all four burners plus the oven.

Quickly, Josef turned off the gas. He tried to open the kitchen window, but it was stuck fast. Making a fist, he smashed out the panes then ran into the living room, throwing open every window there, too. Then he pulled Bettina and Pete out into the hall, away from the poisonous fumes.

Though they coughed and their eyes teared, he could see they were all right. He sank to the floor beside them.

"Why, Tientje?" he moaned, rocking his grown daughter in his arms like a child. "Why would you do this thing, *schatje*?"

She answered in a whisper, "I won't let them have her, Papa. Not Pietra, not my baby. I'll never let her know what it's like."

"Ah, my poor love, my poor *liefje*."

"Why didn't they kill me, Papa?" she cried, her voice now a keening. "It would have been better if they'd killed me. Why didn't they put me in the gas showers like they did Mama?"

He held her and rocked her and stroked her hair. As tears spilled from his eyes, he whispered to a ghost. "Oh, Anneke, what did those bastards do to our baby?"

Terrified at what Steve might do, Josef was determined to keep Bettina's suicide attempt—and the lethal danger to which she had exposed Pete—a secret from his son-in-law. There was no sign of it by the time Steve came home from work. The windows had been left open for hours to clear out the gas, and the kitchen curtain was pulled across the smashed panes. Bettina was put to bed, sedated with a tranquilizer and a cup of herb tea.

But Pete was old enough now to understand what had happened, even if she couldn't understand the reasons for it. At bedtime when she asked Steve, "Why does Mama hate me?" the whole story came out.

Like a mad bull, Steve charged out of the closet they had turned into a sleeping alcove for Pete. Racing into his own room, where Bettina was asleep, he tore the covers off her.

"How could you do it?" he cried, seizing her by the shoulders and shaking her. "What kind of monster are you to do such a thing to your own child?" If Josef hadn't been home, Steve might have finished the job his wife had started on herself.

Steve's shouting and Bettina's shrieks brought Josef running from his own room. With his big, bearlike arms, he pried Steve off his daughter and pinned him against the wall. "*Genoeg!*" he shouted. "Enough! It is over."

As he looked at his wife, cowering on the floor beside the bed, her delicate hands covering her head in a protective gesture, Steve's fury drained away, replaced by utter determination to protect his daughter. "No, Joe. It can never be over while she is in this house." He turned and left the room.

Pete watched it all from the hall until her father carried her gently back to bed.

Steve and Josef talked all night. Anger was gone, replaced by a terrible sadness, and they were able to discuss the problem rationally. Finally, they reluctantly agreed it was no longer possible to keep Bettina at home. She must be sent someplace where she could get the treatment she needed. She must be sent away so Pete could be safe.

Even with Josef's new job, there was no way they could afford to put Bettina into an expensive private sanitarium. No matter how many times they juggled the numbers, how many cuts they tried to make, the dollars just weren't there. There was only one option.

Bettina was sent to the New York State Mental Institution at Yonkers.

For a long time, Pete didn't understand where her mother had gone or why. When Steve tried to explain that Mama was sick and she had to go to a hospital where they could make her well again, Pete nodded gravely and seemed to accept it. But she often woke up screaming from bad dreams, and whenever Steve or Josef got the least bit sick with a minor cold, or even a headache, she grew nervous and bad-tempered, not at all like herself.

Once, when Bettina had been in the hospital six months, Steve came down with a nasty case of the flu. Pete crawled into his bed even though she'd been warned to stay away from him so as not to catch it.

"Are you going away, too, Papa?"

"What?" he said, confused.

"Opa said you're sick. Are you going away to the hospital like Mama and never coming back?"

"Of course not. It's only the flu, *bambina*. I'm not going anywhere."

"Promise?"

"I promise." And he hugged his daughter close to him and stroked her hair and kissed her forehead, not caring if she caught his damn flu or not.

Pete began to grow up very fast. At school, she was cruelly teased about her "crazy mother" who lived in the "loony bin." Once she came home with a black eye after Tommy Gallagher followed her down the street meowing at her because her mother was a "Krazy Kat." Pete had jumped on top of him with claws out.

From one day to the next, Pete kept her eyes open for some early warning of the next crisis in her life. She was learning to expect the bad. The shattered diamond. The loss of a comfortable home. A mother gone crazy. Whatever small moments of happiness she'd known, they couldn't hope to balance the losses. She had seen with her own eyes how fragile happiness could be, how easily it could be destroyed with one ill-placed blow. If she couldn't keep entirely away from the mallet of fate, Pete realized, then she would have to grow a hard shell, harder even than the diamond had possessed. She needed a suit of armor as impervious as that of any magically protected knight in a fairy tale.

"He's so handsome, Papa, like a movie star."

Eight-year-old Pete squatted in front of the big new Sylvania TV and watched a smiling young man with a grin like a spotlight wave to his supporters in his quest for the presidency of the United States. Steve and Josef watched silently, saying nothing to each other, barely responding to her. Since it was election day, neither man had worked a full day, and Pete knew they had visited her mother that afternoon. Whenever they came home from visiting Mama at the special hospital, they were both grim and untalkative for hours.

Pete begged her father to let her stay up late and watch the election returns until Jack Kennedy was officially declared the winner, but the tally dragged on and on and there was school tomorrow. At ten o'clock, she kissed the two silent men good-night and went off to bed.

Two hours later she was awakened by shouting.

Her grandfather's voice first, so loud and harsh it reminded her of Mr. Ivères the day the diamond had been ruined. "No, Steve, no! I cannot allow you to leave Bettina there any longer! The place is filthy—a snake pit!"

The phrase caught in Pete's mind along with the realization that they were arguing about Mama again, Mama, in a pit of snakes? She had been gone several months, and Pete had never been allowed to visit her. What kind of secret were they keeping from her?

Pete crept out of bed as her father shouted back. "There's no goddamn choice, Joe. What the hell do you imagine we'd do with her? She's dangerous."

Pete crept into the hallway. She could see into the living room, where her father and grandfather stood opposite each other in the middle of the rug. Their fists clenched, the veins in their necks standing out as they glared at each other, they looked like two boxers in a ring.

"They say she can be kept calm with drugs," Josef said.

"It would take too much, and even then it's a gamble, and you know it," Steve said. "Suppose the dosage is wrong. Suppose she . . . tricks us somehow, doesn't take her pills. Are you willing to bet on Pete's life that it would work?"

"But nine months she's been there! Nine months in that hell hole. You've seen what it's like, Steve. She will die there." Steve didn't answer. He looked hopelessly at a wall. "You want her dead, don't you?" Josef shouted. "You want Bettina out of the way for good."

Steve whirled to face Josef again. "Of course not. She's my wife, goddammit! I ache for what she's gone through. But haven't I given up enough of my life to her craziness, Joe? Don't I deserve a chance to live, too?"

"Not if it kills my daughter!"

"Well, I don't want to lose mine!"

Pete couldn't watch any more, couldn't listen. She ran

back to bed and burrowed deep down under the blankets, pulling them over her ears to block out the shouting. "Make them stop," she whispered into her pillow. "Please, please, make it all right again."

She groped in the covers for her most precious possession, "Raffie," a stuffed giraffe her father had bought when she was born. The newly grown-up part of her was embarrassed by her need for such childish reassurance, but she still pulled him to her chin, and squeezed him so tight she heard a seam open with a loud *pop*.

"I'm sorry, Raffie," she whispered to the stuffed animal. "I didn't mean to hurt you." But she couldn't stop squeezing the toy with all her strength.

Eventually the shouting stopped. Pete waited a long time, listening, then slowly emerged from her blanket cocoon. A tiny yellow nightlight burned at the foot of her bed—she couldn't sleep in the dark since the closet incident—and the little alcove was suffused with a soft, buttery glow. Now she could see the torn seam along the belly of the giraffe. She probed it with the tip of her finger. "Maybe I can fix it," she whispered.

Some of the cotton batting had started bulging out through the hole. She poked it back in, and as her finger went inside the animal, her nail hit something hard.

"What did you eat?" she said with a soft giggle. "A rock?" She pulled the batting out again and dug around inside Raffie's tummy until she could extract the small hard object.

It was a sort of miniature doll, she saw. Or a half-doll anyway, because there was no skirt or legs, only the head and shoulders and a pretty red blouse. It wasn't quite like any doll she'd ever seen, and far more beautiful—a beautiful, magical lady like a fairy godmother all made of precious jewels. Like a treasure from Aladdin's cave.

Only half-awake, maybe dreaming still, it seemed to Pete that her silent wish had been answered. Here was the magic lady who would make Papa not be angry, who would make Opa smile and would bring Mama home, the fairy godmother who would make everything all right again.

Tumbling out of bed, she ran into the living room. Her

father was alone in the room now, sitting in one of the two easy chairs. He looked very tired, his eyelids drooping though not quite closed, yet he was still propped upright. A glass sat on the arm of the chair, and a bottle of whiskey was beside him.

"Papa!" she cried out. "Look what I found! Where's Opa? He has to see it, too."

Her father turned very slowly to look at her. The way he squinted made Pete think of the way she had to squinch up her eyes to see through a fog. "What are you doing up, *bambina*?" he asked.

She jumped in his lap, knocking the glass off the chair arm, but she was too excited to care. "I found this!" she explained again. She held the treasure up right in front of his eyes.

For a moment, it was as if he saw nothing. Then his eyes focused. Pete was surprised to see no excitement in his face.

"Isn't it the most beautiful thing in the world, Papa? My fairy godmother gave it to me."

Slowly Steve lifted his hand and plucked the top of the perfume bottle from his daughter's grip. Puzzled, Pete didn't protest.

"How do you know who gave it to you?" Steve asked quietly. He didn't have to ask where she'd found it; he had sewn it into the toy long ago, knowing it would always be with her—safe as long as she was safe—but knowing, too, that he wanted it buried and hidden where it could no longer tantalize him.

"It came out of Raffie just now," Pete said. "I know it must have been put there by the same kind of magic fairy who gave Cinderella a coach made from a pumpkin."

Steve paused and looked down into his palm where the half figure of a woman lay on its back. "Do you know, *bambina*," he said, "there are magic things we are given sometimes not as gifts . . . but to tempt us. Like the big red apple the evil witch gave to Snow White."

"That was poison, Papa. This isn't poison."

"It is made to tempt us, though. And like the apple, it's

best if we don't touch it. Or even speak of it. You should forget you've seen it. And you must never tell Opa. That is important, you must promise.''

"Why, Papa?"

"Because it would hurt him very badly. Now back to bed with you," he said, trying to sound firm. "Go!"

Confused, Pete climbed slowly down from her father's lap. But she didn't go. "Can it really be bad, Papa—something so beautiful?"

"I only know, little one, it was bad for me. Very bad."

"How?"

"It . . . it lured me into going . . . nowhere. If I had never seen this thing, I think my life would have been very different."

"So different you wouldn't have me?"

His face softened, and for the first time it looked to Pete as though he weren't seeing her through a fog. "Oh no, my precious *bambina*," he said, and swept her into an embrace. "For you, for you alone, I am glad that nothing can be changed."

He rose then, picking her up in his arms, and carried her back to bed.

As the blankets were comfortingly tucked around her, Pete asked one more sleepy question. "Papa, if the thing is bad, why did you keep it?"

Steve had no answer. He could only tighten the blankets once more around his little girl, kiss her lightly on her smooth, white forehead, and tell her to go back to sleep. "Sandman's coming," he whispered, hoping to replace one bit of magic with another.

The next morning when Pete reached for Raffie there was no hole in his side, no torn seam. She poked at him. She couldn't feel any lump in his tummy. Papa had told her once, when she had a nightmare about being locked in a cold, black freezer, that dreams could seem awfully real sometimes but they were just pictures in the mind that came in the night and were gone by morning.

But the doll with the pearl shoulders and the blue sapphire eyes—that had been real. Hadn't it?

She was no longer sure but she knew one thing instinctively. She must never ever talk of the thing again. Not to anybody.

Chapter 6

New York—1966

It was a rainy Saturday in late April. Steve was in bed with the flu, and Opa had a rush cutting job for his biggest customer. They had regretfully told Pete she would have to miss her visit with her mother because neither of them could take her. Pete went to the tobacco humidor where the household money was kept, counted out a few dollars, and put it in her pocket. Then she let herself quietly out of the apartment. Less than an hour later she was on a train pulling out of Grand Central Station, heading north.

It was only recently that Pete had learned the whole story of her grandmother's capture and the details of Mama and Opa's hiding place. Josef had tried to protect her from the horror of it. Maybe he even hoped that by never acknowledging it, by refusing to discuss it in any way, he could erase the effect it had had on his daughter, he could make it not have happened.

But when he came home one day and found Pete crying over a book she was reading for school, he knew he owed her the truth. She was old enough now to hear it. The book was *Anne Frank: The Diary of a Young Girl.*

"She was only one year older than me when she died, Opa," said Pete, tear tracks striping her face. "Just fifteen."

"I know. And if she had lived, she would be exactly the same age your mother is today."

"It isn't fair!"

"Fair? Fair! Nothing about the Nazis was fair. They made a world in which 'fair' became a dirty word, a stupid childish hope." His voice rang with the bitterness of a very old hatred he would never allow to die. "Your mother would not be what and where she is today if the Nazis had cared about fair."

He told her about it then, the years spent in hiding. He described their closet-sized attic hiding place in detail, told her about the kind doctor who helped them and how hellish it was to be absolutely silent for hours at a time. He answered all her questions about what they ate, what they read, what schoolbooks Bettina had with her so she could keep up with her studies. How they managed to live without even a glimpse of the sun.

The ending of the story was fuzzy. "But what happened then, Opa?" Pete asked, as though he were reading her a fairy story out of a book.

"Then?"

"Yes. What happened next? How did you get out?"

For one short moment, his face contorted in pain, then he wiped the look away, replacing it with an expressionless mask. "The war ended," he said, and walked quickly out of the room.

Pete was impressed despite the awfulness of her mother's experience. It was just like Anne's story; Mama was just like Anne Frank, even the same age. But unlike Anne, Mama had survived the war, she had lived—if you could call what Mama did in that awful institution where she was now living.

Anne Frank's story, her courage and humor and belief in the world despite the horror she'd seen, made Pete more determined than ever not to let her mother down, to do everything she could to help her, to bring her back to the world and to their home.

* * *

Standing alone on the curved gravel drive, Pete stared up at the hated pile of gray stone where her mother was forced to spend her days. Through the iron-barred windows on an upper floor, blank faces stared back. A horrible thought suddenly seized Pete. What if she went in and somebody decided she was crazy and they put her in a room with bars on the windows and kept her there? How did you convince people you weren't crazy if they said you were? You could argue and scream and fight and cry . . . and that would only make you seem crazier. How much difference was there between some of the people who were outside staring in, and those who had been put up there behind the barred windows?

Why did Mama have to be here?

The scary thoughts held her back for a few minutes, shivering in the sharp cold, but at last she summoned the courage to go inside. She mustn't disappoint Mama. True as it was that there were times when her mother didn't even seem to notice her, Pete hoped and prayed a day would come when being there for her, with her, would make all the difference. It might even be today.

The burly orderly behind the front desk looked at her suspiciously when she walked into the drab tiled lobby, even though Pete knew he recognized her from past visits. "You alone, kid?" he said.

So that was it. Would she be allowed in? "My father is sick. My grandfather is working. Can I see my mother? She'll be waiting . . ."

"Your mother, eh? What's her name again?"

"Bettina D'Angeli."

The orderly lifted a clipboard and checked a list. "Okay. She's not in the violent ward, so you can visit. But you won't be allowed to take her out for a walk, like your father is. You'll probably find her in the day room. Through there and straight down the hall." He pointed to a pair of double doors with large insets of wired glass, but Pete didn't need to be told the way. She had seen her father and Opa go through that door hundreds of times.

Once she passed through the first doors, however, she was in an entirely new world. There was a green-walled vestibule where a second guard sat on a stool beside a steel door with a small barred window. A huge ring of keys was attached to his belt by a chain, and they jangled loudly as he lifted the ring to unlock the steel door. "She's in the day room. You know the way."

As she went through, Pete heard the door close behind her with a dull thud. The keys jangled again, the sound muffled now by the thick steel, as the guard locked her in. She shivered, and for a moment she really wanted to turn around and pound on the door for him to let her out again. But Mama was waiting. She lifted her head and started down the hall.

It was a strange place. She sensed a wildness around her. Animal-like cries washed in from distant places, as in a jungle. Two or three people shuffled past her—patients, she could tell from their gowns and slippered feet—and there was so much pain in their eyes that Pete had to look away. Now she understood why, on all her past visits, she was made to wait by the entrance while Papa or Opa went to see how Mama was. With the ironic awareness of a precocious fourteen-year-old, Pete was mature enough to know she was too young to be here.

At the end of the corridor a small woman in a uniform stood at an open door. "Is this the day room?" Pete asked.

The woman nodded.

Pete looked in timidly. The place was alive with noise—cackling, crying, buzzing, screaming, whispering, laughing. And everywhere there was movement, aimless movement—people roaming about just for the sake of activity, tracing misshapen circles on the linoleum floor, some of them with vacant faces, others with grimaces or expressions of manic glee. Looking at it made Pete feel as if spiders were crawling up her arms. In her wildest imaginings, she had never thought it could be so awful in the place where Mama was made to spend her days.

"Oh God . . . ." A small sigh escaped her lips, an unfinished prayer to free her mother from this hell. Pete started looking around the room, searching through the haze of movement and noise and cigarette smoke, looking for her mother. Finally she realized her mother wasn't there.

She might have asked the guard at the door where to find Mrs. D'Angeli, but what if the woman wouldn't let her go to wherever Mama was? What if she made her leave? Anyway, the guard was busy settling a loud argument between two patients who had been playing cards. So Pete walked out of the day room and found the stairway leading to the upper floors. On past visits, her mother had waved good-bye through the barred window of her room as Pete stood on the gravel below, so Pete knew Bettina lived on the third floor. She closed her eyes and remembered her mother's face at the window, then mentally counted how many windows over from the corner of the building it was. Four, she was pretty sure. Mama was in the fourth room. Or maybe the fifth.

In the deserted third floor corridor, the gray metal doors were all closed, but each was set with a small window like the one in the locked door in the vestibule downstairs. Pete walked along, counting the doors and peering in through each window to be sure she didn't miss her mother's room. Inside, she saw cell-like rooms, each one furnished with a bed, a table, and a single chair. Though small, they didn't seem too awful. The windows were hung with curtains in a flowered fabric, and there were pictures taped up on some of the walls. In one room an old man sat reading in a chair; in another a young woman lay on a bed. Pete felt a little better. At least in the places where the patients lived, life seemed cleaner and quieter, almost normal.

But that comforting thought was erased by her first glimpse through the fourth window. A woman sat on the floor by the bed with her legs splayed out. Her hair was stringy and matted, her shapeless gray dress blotched with dark stains. With her eyes closed, she looked to be in a kind of stupor. But then Pete noticed that her mouth was moving and that both hands were pushed up under her skirt, stroking rapidly between her legs.

Pete recoiled in shock and began to hurry along the corridor.

Then another realization hit, one that had been blocked out by the initial shock.

She stopped dead, facing away from the door, her nerves twisted by conflicting impulses: to run . . . or to go back to the window and look again. To be sure.

As if drawn by a magnet, she was pulled back to the heavy metal door. Her head turned slowly until she could see . . .

Her mother was still on the floor, her hands moving faster now, plunging up inside herself. And her lips weren't just moving soundlessly now, she was talking, loud enough that Pete could hear the lurid chant through the door: "I'll fuck you; I'll fuck you, but you won't fuck me. I'll fuck you; I'll fuck you . . ."

A cry burst from Pete's throat. "Mama!" Her hands grabbed at the knob of the door. She twisted and pulled, but the knob wouldn't turn. The door was locked. She started hammering her fists against the window.

"Mama. Mama!" she called over and over, her voice rising until it was a shriek.

At last, her mother's eyes half opened, and her gaze drifted up to the window until their eyes met. But her hands didn't stop moving, the chanting didn't stop, and she stared at Pete almost defiantly as her body arched up off the floor.

"Mama." It was no longer a shriek, but a soft cry of futility. It was as if her mother were on an ice floe, drifting slowly away on a cold, cold sea, drifting so far Pete would never be able to reach her and bring her back.

And then Pete felt hands gripping her shoulders and pulling her away. She looked around to see a hefty woman guard.

"What are you doing here?" the woman demanded crossly.

"I . . . my mother . . . ," Pete stammered.

The guard's large hand gripped Pete's arm, hard enough to bruise. "You're not allowed—" the woman began, pulling Pete away from the door.

"But she needs me," Pete pleaded. "She needs to be washed, to have her hair combed. She has such pretty hair, if only—"

"You have to go," the guard insisted, pulling harder.

"We've got fifty crazy women here. We can't have kids wandering around, getting in the way."

"No, please!" Pete screamed, resisting, her feet dragging on the hard floor.

Finally, something in the guard's face, her fiercely threatening glare, penetrated Pete's consciousness. She remembered the nightmare vision she'd had of being called crazy, of being locked up like her mother.

All the fight went out of her. She turned back once more to the window, straining to see into the room. Her mother was quiet now, curled up in a ball on the floor, panting slightly.

"I'll be back, Mama," she said softly, but there was steely determination beneath the words. "I swear I'll come back, and take you away from here."

On a muggy July evening, Pete walked home from the library with her usual long-legged stride. Heat radiated from the brick walls and bounced up from the pavement in a relentless attack. In an attempt to fight it off, Pete was wearing shorts, sandals, and a sleeveless T-shirt. Her father had taken her to Coney Island the week before, and her long legs were tanned the color of polished amber.

As an antidote to the heat, someone had opened the fire hydrant. While the younger kids splashed in the cool, gushing water, the older ones leaned against cars and sat on stoops, drinking beer, wisecracking, and passing around a marijuana joint.

Pete had just turned the corner, when Joey Rachetti, a smart-mouthed kid who lived in the tenement on the corner, put his hands over the stream from the hydrant, geysering the water up through his fingers straight at her, drenching her. She screamed and looked down at herself, acutely aware of how clearly her newly budding breasts were now outlined by the sleeveless T-shirt plastered to her body. If embarrassment could kill, she would have died.

Liam O'Shea, a broad-chested, red-headed Irish kid, was perched on a stripped-down Chevy guzzling Budweiser from a can. At eighteen, he was a local gang leader and proud of his reputation as a big shot. Once, Pete overheard some of the older girls refer to him as "O'Shea's Service Station." She didn't know what they meant, but she could tell by the way they laughed that they weren't talking about cars.

Now he didn't join in the laughter at Pete's expense. Instead, he handed off a joint to the girl beside him and gave a long, slow whistle. "Hey, *principessa*," he said, blocking Pete's path as she tried to go past.

It was Joey Rachetti who had given her her nickname. Following her down the street on her return from school one day, mimicking her ladylike walk, he started out by making lewd kissing noises and comments about her anatomy. She didn't answer or pay him any attention at all. Her father had told her never to talk to the tough kids on the street.

"Hey," Joey had called to the other kids. "The *principessa*'s too high and mighty to talk to us peons."

Principessa—little princess. After that the name stuck.

"Hey, *principessa*," Liam repeated.

Too embarrassed to speak, Pete simply tried to step around him.

"Y'know," he said, eyeing her up and down, "this is getting nice. Real nice." He reached out and ran one hand up her long, wet leg to the hem of her shorts. She shivered. "Won't be long before we'll be needing to do something about this."

"About what?" she whispered, staring at the pavement, too embarrassed even to move away.

His hand went up to her wet T-shirt. "Yeah," he said, cupping one small, budding breast. "Won't be long now."

"Forget it, Liam," said Charlene, a girl who'd been sitting beside him sharing his joint. "Princesses don't fuck. Everyone knows that." Then she laughed in a way that made Pete want to knock her off the car.

"This one will," Liam said, and grinned at Pete. "She'll fuck good and she'll love it. I can always tell." As Pete finally managed to squeeze past him, he whispered, "One day I'll fuck you, princess, and I'll bet I can make you fuck me back."

She bolted into her building and ran all the way up the three flights of stairs to her apartment. Curiously, the echo she heard in her ear was not the crude taunt she'd just heard, but another voice from the past—Mama's, that day at the institution. *I'll fuck you, but you won't fuck me!*

The memory of her mother, Pete's desire to understand her illness, crowded aside her anger and shame and what had just happened. Liam O'Shea was a dumb punk, not worth thinking about. Instead, she tried to concentrate on her mother, on understanding. Who had Mama been talking to? Who had she been screaming at with such hatred in her voice and in her eyes?

Pete was determined to learn the secret to her mother's dark terrors. For how else could she make them go away?

As the months rolled on, Pete began spending more and more time at the mental institution. On her Saturday visits, she went earlier and stayed later and went on other days, too, when she could. She never stopped hating it, but she did stop being afraid of it. Her one goal now became to get Mama out of the institution, however long it took.

She worked constantly with her mother—reading the newspapers aloud to her and making her pay attention, telling her about school, asking her advice, doing all the things Bettina's doctor had suggested she do, forcing her mother to be a part of her world once more.

Pete also got to know some of the other patients. When she discovered that the only time fat old Mary was quiet was when she was playing chess, she played game after game with her and let Mary win. She listened to Consuela sing Spanish songs over and over again, humming along and smiling, and she kept an eye on a young woman named Susie, who was both schizophrenic and diabetic and frequently went into insulin shock. Pete had learned to recognize her symptoms and twice saved her from fainting by running for Susie's orange juice in time.

For Pete, who was such an outsider in her own neighborhood, the asylum became a kind of substitute social life. Even the matrons and guards, skeptical at first about the presence of a young girl among so many crazy women, grew used to her presence and finally welcomed it. She had a way of calming some patients they found impossible to handle. The nurses called her "a natural."

Gradually, an idea began to form in Pete's mind, an idea that maybe one day she could help a lot of people like her mother. She thought now that she might become a psychiatrist.

Returning from Yonkers one evening, Pete turned the corner of Forty-fifth Street to see the usual crowd out in front of Gangemmi's, the mom-and-pop grocery on the corner—kids playing catch with stolen apples, grandmothers gossiping and laughing, teenaged girls airing their fatherless babies and flirting with tough young guys in T-shirts and black Levi's with the belt loops cut off.

The boys didn't tease her anymore—she had learned enough street smarts lately to handle them—but they still looked. More than ever, in fact, because there was no denying it: At sixteen, Pete D'Angeli was one of the most beautiful young women they were ever likely to see. Her features had sharpened. Her hair, so unruly in the past, now curled with lavish abandon about her piquant face. Her brows swept up and away over huge eyes the color of the finest Burmese sapphires.

As Pete arrived outside Gangemmi's, the biggest car she had ever seen pulled up at the curb. It was a wine red Caddy limo with smoked glass windows hiding the interior, at least fifteen feet long. One of the rear tires was flat.

As Pete watched, a uniformed chauffeur climbed out of the car, studied the flat, gave it a disgusted kick, and strode off down Eighth Avenue toward a phone booth a block away.

Almost immediately, the car was surrounded by the crowd. A limo was not an everyday occurrence on West Forty-fifth Street. While one or two of the boys checked out the hub caps, others ran their hands over the glistening paintwork, speculating on how many coats it took to get that deep shine and how many horsepower lived under that long, sleek hood. Girls sat on the long, sleek hood, posing with exaggerated elegance, or they cupped their hands around their eyes and tried to peer through the opaque glass, longing for a look at the forbidden luxury inside.

Pete was passing the car when a rear door swung open and a girl stepped out. Pete judged her to be about her own age, perhaps a little younger. She was very small and not particularly pretty, but Pete saw at once that she was expensively dressed—a gored linen skirt in a pale shade of peach, a rust-colored ruffled silk blouse, gold earrings and chain necklaces, beige pumps, and a large Gucci bag over one shoulder. Her brown hair was pulled back and tied with a peach silk print scarf. For all its quality, the outfit was far too old and busy for her. Pete thought she looked like a doll dressed up by an overzealous little girl who had studied the fashion magazines.

After giving the girl a quick, silent appraisal, the crowd sprang back into life. The youngest girls reached up and touched her clothes; the older ones stood aside as if touching her would be a contamination. The young men whistled or made loud kissing noises as she tried to walk through the throng toward the grocery store.

"Excuse me," she said in a feathery little voice. She was very pale.

"Rich bitch," muttered one girl with a sneer.

Liam gave the girl a look that defined the word leer. "Well, well," he said, blocking her path just as he had Pete's that day by the open hydrant. "What we got here? A pretty little rich girl come to provide a treat for the peasants?" He fingered her blond hair, and the girl grew paler still, her eyes like two huge pools of gray water in a field of snow.

"Excuse me," she said again. "I have to—" but Liam wouldn't let her pass.

The girl's face filled with panic. Pete's protective instincts, finely honed through years of Saturdays, sprang to the surface. With the street smarts she'd been forced to learn, Pete finally knew how to handle Liam O'Shea.

"Fuck off, Liam," she said, using the language that worked on Forty-fifth Street. She took the girl's thin arm in one hand and pulled her away from the crowd. "You really should have stayed in the car," she said.

"Please," the girl said. "Sugar . . . I really need some sugar."

Looking at the pale girl's face, Pete thought suddenly of Susie, the diabetic at the asylum. This girl had the same trembling, clammy look. She was, Pete suspected, on the verge of going into diabetic shock.

Steering her quickly into the crowded little grocery store, Pete sat the girl in a wooden chair beside the cash register. "Orange juice!" she called to Mrs. Gangemmi. "Hurry or she may pass out."

The heavy Italian woman glanced at the little trembling creature sitting in her chair and ran to the refrigerator case, returning in seconds with a bottle of juice. Pete twisted off the top and held it to the girl's mouth. "Drink it, quick," she said, and the girl did, spilling some onto her beautiful linen skirt as she gulped it.

After a moment, she stopped shaking and looked a bit less pale and a lot less frightened. "Thank you," she said, her voice still little more than a feather of sound.

Pete smiled. "That was a close one. You should watch your blood sugar better, you know."

"I'm sorry. There's usually 7-Up in the car, but this time . . ." Her voice trailed off.

"Hey," said Pete, laying a hand on her arm. "It's okay. Feel better now?"

The girl smoothed her hands across her linen skirt and sat up straight. Pete thought she could almost hear a voice instructing the girl to "mind your manners" as she held out her hand. "Yes, thank you. I'm Jessica Walsh. Thank you for rescuing me."

Pete shook her hand. "You're welcome." On the verge of giving her own name in reply, Pete hesitated. There was something about this girl from outside the neighborhood that made Pete think she ought to be more formal with her, ought to give her complete name, though she hadn't used anything but Pete for years.

"I'm Pietra D'Angeli," she said.

* * *

The wine red limo showed up on Forty-fifth Street again the next day, this time to deliver a note to the D'Angelis' door. On heavy laid, cream-colored paper, Mr. and Mrs. Jonathan Walsh thanked Miss D'Angeli for her assistance to their daughter and invited her to tea on Sunday, the seventeenth, at four o'clock.

The Walsh home was a revelation to Pete—an elegant brick building on Park Avenue at Seventy-seventh. The entrance hall was floored with apricot-colored marble, the parlor walls were covered with silk, and the furnishings were as beautiful as any she'd seen in the antique shops on Madison Avenue. Flowers were everywhere—fresh flowers in vases, dried flowers in bowls of potpourri, brocaded flowers on the upholstered chairs, and embroidered flowers on the linen napkins. Pete had never been anywhere so beautiful, anywhere that exuded such permanence . . . such security. She wished she could stay here forever.

So this, she thought, as she bit into a thin salmon sandwich with the crusts cut off the bread, is how they live, those people who shop in Fifth Avenue stores instead of in Woolworth's, the people who wear jewelry from Tiffany and Dufort & Ivères. She had wondered, but she had never imagined anyone actually lived amid such beauty and delicacy and grace. Her first glimpse of their world convinced her that she wanted to live in it, too.

She fingered her necklace, an abstract design silver-and-amethyst pendant she'd recently made. She hoped it made her cotton shirtwaist seem less plain, less cheap.

Pete studied her host and hostess. Sally Walsh was a stunning woman, sleek as an Egyptian cat. She was blond, tanned, and model-slim, every movement a natural grace note. A single strand of pearls adorned the neckline of her flowered voile dress, and there were small pearl drops at her ears. Simple jewelry, appropriate for afternoon tea. Pete filed the information away in her mind.

Her husband, chairman of an important downtown bank, was more substantial, exactly the way Pete thought a banker should look. His tailored suit was dark gray, his shirt snowy white, his rep tie subtly striped. Pete noticed that he wore an onyx signet ring on his left hand. They both wore their money and position as easily, as naturally as they wore their skin.

Not so their daughter. Jessica looked like a little brown rabbit in a garden. She was seventeen, though she looked younger, and she wore a cotton voile dress much like her mother's—very expensive, very frilly, very wrong for her. The frills overpowered her small features and did nothing for her rather ruddy coloring.

"Thank God you were there, Pietra," said Sally Walsh as she poured the tea. "It's not like Jessica to let herself be caught unprepared like that. Without your help, she would certainly have ended up in the hospital again."

"Mother. . . ," Jessica began, but her voice faded away as her mother turned to her.

"How did you know what to do?" asked Jonathan Walsh. "I mean the orange juice?"

Pete set down her teacup, concentrating on doing it lightly so as not to break the paper-thin porcelain. "I have a diabetic friend." She didn't add that the friend was schizophrenic and lived, as did her own mother, in a mental institution. Ever since the schoolyard Krazy Kat taunts, Pete never mentioned her mother to anyone outside the family. It wasn't shame, she told herself. It was just easier not to have to explain.

Finally both the tea and the formalities of thanks were finished. Jonathan Walsh was eager to return to his study and his paperwork; Sally Walsh had a tennis game scheduled for five.

"Jessica, why don't you show your friend the garden," she said, rising gracefully from the sofa. "Williams will drive you home whenever you like, Pietra. Thank you for coming, and thank you again for your quick thinking. We're very grateful." She offered her hand, the one with the large pearl on the fourth finger. "You will take a nap this afternoon, won't you darling," she said to her daughter. Without waiting for an answer, she left the room.

As soon as her parents were gone, Jessica seemed to unbend like a shirt with its starch rinsed out. "Thank God," she

said, only half under her breath. "Let's get out of here." In
the entrance hall, she said, "You don't really care about the
garden do you? It's nothing special."

"Not if you don't want to show me," Pete said. "I'll go."

"Oh no! I didn't mean that. It's just that I've got to get
out of here. Let's go to the park, okay?"

Pete saw that Jessica was wearing an almost pleading
expression. "Whatever you say."

They crossed Fifth Avenue and entered Central Park, vivid
green in all its summer majesty. Once she was away from
her parents—and not about to faint from low blood sugar—
Jessica proved to be lively, funny, and ripe for mischief.
"Mother thinks I have to be wrapped up in flannel all the
time, with a hot water bottle at my feet," she explained as
they walked near the bridle path.

"Why? Diabetes is usually a controllable disease."

"I give the doctors a little extra trouble. I'm what they
call a brittle diabetic. No matter what I do, my blood sugar's
all over the place, and I'm likely to keel over just when it
seems I'm fine." Her eyes challenged Pete. "Does that scare
you?"

"Not yet. Should it?"

"It scares a lot of people. Scared the bejezus out of Eddie
Martindale the Third, for one." She laughed gaily. "He was
dancing with me last year at a pre-Deb ball when all of a
sudden he found himself with a Raggedy Ann in his arms. I
just went limp. Eddie Three freaked out." She stopped to
watch a horse canter past on the bridle path. "I haven't been
to a dance since."

"Well, I've never been to one in my life," said Pete.

Jessica turned to stare at her. "Why not?"

"We don't have pre-Deb parties on Forty-fifth Street. Besides, would *you* want to circle the floor in the arms of Liam
O'Shea?"

"Who's that?"

"The big redhead who was so taken with you the other
day."

"God, no."

Pete smiled. "Somehow, I didn't think so." And they laughed together, enjoying what was beginning to feel like friendship.

But Jessica was silent then. Pete sensed she was thinking about a subject they'd left unfinished. "It wouldn't scare me . . . ever," Pete said quietly. "If I'm around, I'll just do whatever I can to help."

Jessica turned to look at her, eyes slightly misty. "Gosh, I wish my folks could be like that. They're so damn scared all the time. They think I'm some sort of porcelain doll to be protected and watched over every minute."

"Understandable, I guess, but I can see how it wouldn't be much fun."

"No kidding. And it doesn't help that they're all so disgustingly healthy. And successful. If you want to know the truth, they're all goddamn perfect."

"How many are there?"

"Three kids besides me, but they're years older than me. I was an afterthought, or maybe a mistake. Definitely the runt of the litter."

"I always wished I had brothers and sisters. What are they like?"

"Oh, you'd love them. Everybody does. There's Robert, my big brother. He's on Wall Street—made his first million already. Runs the marathon in under three hours, has a perfect wife, a perfect dog, two perfect kids. Jack—he was the captain of the football team at Yale—he made Law Review at Harvard last year, and he's gorgeous as sin. He starts at a fancy downtown firm next year. Engaged to a Chesterton— very upper-upper, don't y'know. And then there's sister Melissa, but please call her Muffy. She's the oldest. She worked for a few years as a model, just for pin money of course," she said in perfect imitation of her mother's voice, "but now she's settled down in Westchester with her banker husband —works in Daddy's bank, of course—and a brand-new baby. As you can see, Muffy is the perfect Walsh daughter."

Jessica was a good talker. She also turned out to be a good listener, walking along beside Pete, nodding occasionally, scuffing up drifts of dead blossoms and summer leaves and trash, and sometimes asking a question. Pete found herself telling Jessica things she'd never told another living soul. She told her about Papa and Opa, about their unhappiness and her struggle to keep peace between them. She told her about living in Hell's Kitchen. She told her about running the house pretty much single-handedly. She even told her about Mama. It was a blessed relief to have someone to talk to, at long last.

By the time they were ready to leave the park, both knew they had found in the other a key element that had been missing for too long from their lives—a friend.

As they waited on Fifth Avenue for Pete to catch a bus downtown—Pete didn't want to take the car—they made it official. First, by exchanging phone numbers. Then Jessica said, "Listen, Pietra, your name is beautiful, but I've always thought Jessica makes me sound stuck up. So if we're going to be friends, would you mind calling me Jess?"

Pete shook her head and then started laughing.

Jess looked a little hurt. "What's so funny?"

"Nothing about you. It's me—I was putting on airs. I'm always called Pete."

The bus arrived at the stop. "Bye, Jess," Pete said.

"Bye, Pete."

But after the bus was on its way to the next stop, Jess ran alongside, shouting to catch Pete's attention. "Hey, Pete . . . Pete! Call me tomorrow, huh, or I'll call you."

The sound of the exhaust was too loud to call back. But probably, Pete thought, she would call tonight.

Jess Walsh became a friend, a confidante, a window onto another world and another way of thinking for Pete.

For years, the world of wealth and luxury had been something she looked at in glossy magazines or glimpsed through the glass barriers of elegant store windows. The people who lived in that world had been fairy creatures, on a par in Pete's mind with the magical grandmother, draped in jewels, whom she'd never known. She certainly never thought of them as people who got colds and headaches like everybody else, people who had to get up even when they didn't want to, who had to study before exams and were sometimes afraid in the dark hours of the night.

Through Jess she learned different. She didn't become a member of that glossy world, but she was at least an invited guest. All through July, Pete traveled back and forth during the week between Hell's Kitchen and Park Avenue where she would sit in Jess's lavender and green bedroom with its plush carpet, collection of dolls, and huge color TV and gossip and gripe and try on nail polish and talk about the bother of menstrual cramps and imagine which movie stars would be best in bed. Knowing Jess made Pete wish she could go back and be twelve again, only do it with her.

On the first weekend in August, Jess telephoned Pete to invite her for the weekend to a house her family owned in Montauk.

"Where's that?"

"The beach."

Pete sighed. She loved the beach, but aside from a couple of trips with her father to Coney Island, she hadn't spent much time there. Nor had she ever agreed to spend weekend time with Jess before. Saturdays were for Mama. Always.

"I'm sorry, Jess," Pete said after a second. "You know I can't."

"Listen, Pete," Jess said, "Maybe it would be good for your mother if you could treat her a little more the way you treat me. I mean, you're good for me because you're the one person who lets me forget I'm breakable. So . . . write your mother a letter, or call and say you'll be away for a weekend, or explain the next time you see her. But give *her* a chance to be someone, like any mother, who might want you to have a chance to grow up and have a life of your own."

Pete was silent for so long that Jess wasn't sure the connection hadn't been lost. "Pete, you there?"

Pete was so full of emotion, it had just taken her a moment to find her voice. "I'm just so damn lucky I met you, Jess."

She wrote a nice letter to her mother, the kind she would have written if Mama had not been in an asylum, telling a

lot about her new friend and how nice it was to be invited
to go lovely places.

The weekend at the Walshes' beautiful house overlooking
the ocean turned out to be the best two days of her life. And
it gave her the idea for the mermaid.

Chapter 7

New York—December 1968

It was the best Christmas present Pete could have asked for. She'd felt it coming, like a tingle in the blood. She had even embarrassed herself by praying for it, though she wasn't at all sure she believed in God. But she'd been afraid to actually go so far as to hope.

Bettina was coming home.

All through the last two years, she had been getting better. Pete could see it so clearly. Better tranquilizers meant the daytime anxieties and nighttime terrors could be kept at bay without turning Mama into some sort of lifeless zombie. She seldom burst into tears for no apparent cause. She laughed at jokes and frowned at stupidity and even scolded Pete for letting her hair get straggly or wearing too much lipstick.

By 1968, Pete's proven ability at handling her mother convinced Bettina's doctor to try a weekend pass to visit her family. When no major problems developed, the decision was made. Bettina would be permanently released in time for Christmas.

On a freezing December day the whole family drove to Yonkers in the aged Chevy Steve had borrowed from a friend.

"Now remember," Pete explained as they drove up the circular driveway, "she'll be nervous. This place may be awful, but it's been her home for nine years. It represents safety to Mama."

"Yes, Doctor," Steve teased with a grin. "We will remember."

"And we will give her a new safety," said Josef with determination, but he was also smiling hugely.

Pete grinned back at them both. "Come on then," she cried and, grabbing their hands in hers and tugging them after her, she ran through the crunchy snow toward the big gray edifice.

Bringing Bettina back to Manhattan, the three of them chattered so much at her in the car that she had no time to feel her fear of this leap into freedom. She just gazed out the window at sights she'd not laid eyes on in nearly a decade and smiled at the family that surrounded her like a cocoon. When they got home, she laughed softly at the holiday decorations—holly on the mantel, a Christmas tree dripping with paper chains and popcorn strings and other handmade ornaments, and a bright green and white "Welcome Home!" banner strung from wall to wall across the living room.

After a celebratory glass of champagne, Bettina was tired and went to lay down for a nap. Pete sat in her mother's rocking chair beside the bed, watching her sleep, filled with a warm sense of thankfulness as the snow softly blanketed the city's ugliness beyond the window.

That night, in the privacy of their bedroom, Steve and Bettina faced each other. Neither was sure exactly how to act. Steve had grown so used to his life without her that he had mixed feelings about her return. During her one weekend pass, he hadn't touched her except for innocent kisses on the cheek and the occasional hug. Now that she was home for good, he wasn't sure he wanted more than that. He watched as she brushed her still beautiful hair with the hairbrush Pete had made her two years earlier.

"You have done a wonderful job with our daughter, Stefano," she said, gazing at him in the mirror. He smiled at the name. No one but Bettina had called him Stefano in many years. "I'm sorry I had to leave so much of her upbringing to you."

"You had no choice, Tina. And Josef had as much to do with raising Pete as I did."

"Yes." Her voice faded as her mind wrapped around the miracle of being finally at home, able to watch her daughter, to listen to her father, to gaze at her still handsome husband for as long as she wanted. She felt like someone newly awakened from a long nightmare. But she had awakened, and she was going to stay awake. She would put the institution in a little box in her mind marked "history," right alongside everything else she wanted never to think of or remember, and she would never take it out again. "I wish I could have given you a half dozen more like Pietra."

"I don't need them. Pete is enough."

Bettina put down the brush and walked to the bed where he was stretched out, wearing only some striped cotton pajama bottoms and smoking a cigarette. "You don't have to be afraid of me," she said, and smiled a slow smile he remembered only too well. "I told you that once before. Do you remember?" He did. She slid off her robe. She was wearing only a thin nylon nightgown, almost transparent, a welcome home gift from Pete. She lay down beside him. "I am not made of crystal, Stefano. I don't break."

She laid her hand softly, almost tentatively, on his bare chest and let it simply stay there awhile before she began sliding it slowly across his skin. He grabbed it to stop its roaming, but before long he released it again and let it do its work.

He'd had many women during the years Bettina was away. He had never really expected to have Bettina in his bed again. He certainly didn't expect ever to want her again. Yet in minutes she had aroused him to a pitch of desire no one but Marisa had ever brought him near. In all those years she'd been locked away, she hadn't forgotten how to touch him, tantalize him, make him crazy with wanting her. Her lips and fingers, her slithery tongue and long, entwining limbs had lost none of their magic, their ability to beguile his senses until he was lost in her. She made him forget that he was now more than half a century old.

Perhaps it would be all right after all, Steve thought. Perhaps they could have a real marriage at last.

It was that rarest of all holiday joys in New York, a spotlessly white Christmas, and Pete awoke tingling with anticipation.

She wasn't the only one affected; the very air in the D'Angeli/Zeeman household crackled with expectation. A neat pile of gifts lay under the small but pretty tree. The air was pungent with the scent of almond and cinnamon as Bettina baked the special Dutch spice cake called *gevulde speculaas*. As soon as it was set out and the coffee was poured, the gaily wrapped packages were attacked with gusto.

Pete watched as her father and grandfather first opened Bettina's presents. Steve exclaimed over the muffler and proclaimed the book "exactly right." Josef put the gloves on at once but had to take them off again to remove the wrappings from the record album.

"*Uitstekend!*" he cried when he saw what it was. "I must play it at once." He put it on the stereo, and soon the room filled with Mahler's rousing, joyful chords, a perfect accompaniment to the morning.

There was a bottle of cologne and a soft blue challis blouse for Bettina, a new pipe for Josef, a coin purse full of subway tokens for Steve, because he never had a token when he wanted it.

The largest pile of packages was for Pete—a book bag and a pale pink lipstick and a daringly short miniskirt her mother had made her. "I know, I know," Bettina said when Steve started to protest, "I don't like them either, but they are the fashion, Stefano. It's important for a girl to be in fashion, to fit in. And Pietra does have the legs for it." He kept frowning at the minuscule square of skirt, but he shut up about it.

Each member of her family had given Pete something to read, and she had to laugh when she saw them: a biography of Freud from Steve, an oversized book full of beautiful color photographs of famous jewels from Josef, and from Bettina a subscription to *Seventeen*. "Well, no one can accuse this family of excess subtlety," she said with a giggle as she gave each of them a hug.

Pete had saved her present to her mother for last, and now she pulled it out with an eager smile. It was small, square, and beautifully wrapped in silver paper with dark red and silver ribbons spilling over its top. Pride and nervousness made her fingers tremble as she handed it to Bettina.

She had been working on the gift for months, beginning with earning the money for the materials. She had been working after school and some weekends in the jewelry district, typing orders, answering phones, delivering goods, whatever needed doing. She had managed to save nearly a hundred dollars for her mother's gift, knowing she would need all of it. She could no longer be content with trifles made from beach glass and chewing gum wrappers, no matter how inventively used. For this very special Christmas she needed a very special gift—the real thing.

Bettina smiled at her daughter as her fingers worked at the ribbons and pulled away the silver paper. She grinned with anticipation as she opened the blue velvet box. Then she gasped. "Oh, Pietra, how beautiful!" she exclaimed.

Nestled on a bed of white satin was a large brooch in the shape of a mermaid. Pete's growing knowledge of the craft of jewelry making, combined with her grandfather's professional contacts, had produced a work of true beauty.

The mermaid's entire torso was carved from a piece of abalone shell, pearlescent and gleaming. For the head, arms, and sinuous fish tale, Pete had first modeled the shapes in wax then paid Chaim Grossman, a silversmith who had his workroom in the same building as Josef, to cast them in sterling. The creature's graceful arms curved forward to cup a freshwater pearl like an offering. Her face and hair were cloisonné enamel, the eyes formed by two tiny deep blue sapphires Pete had managed to get at cost.

Somehow, the top half of the figure had been simple. From the start, she had seen it clearly in her mind's eye. But the tail had nearly stumped her. The shape finally emerged, but she couldn't think how to create scales. Then one day, walking through one of the arcades on Forty-seventh Street, she'd watched Manny Lieberman slicing opals for inexpensive settings. She bought three dozen of the tiny iridescent pink-blue slabs and set them onto the sterling tail, overlapping them like scales. At the end of the tail, she set a small purple amethyst into each fin, like the eye of a peacock's feather. The total effect was dazzling.

After her initial praise of the pin, Bettina grew pensive. She lifted the jewel from its snowy bed and held it in her hand.

"It's really me, isn't it?" she said after studying the mermaid pin a moment.

"You? What do you mean, Mama?"

"Well, she looks human, even beautiful," Bettina went on, "human enough to fool anyone who doesn't look at what's below the surface."

"What is below the surface, Mama?" Pete asked in a soft, gentle voice.

"The trap."

Pete gazed back at her, puzzled.

Bettina stroked one finger across the mermaid's opal-scaled tail. "Look. She's trapped in her own special world because she doesn't have the necessary equipment to survive in the real one."

Steve looked nervously at his wife. "You're not trapped, Tina. You're—"

Josef cut him off, as always eager to divert attention from Bettina's peculiarities. "This is wonderful work, Pete!" he exclaimed. "Really inspired." He'd known for months that something was in the works even though Pete had carefully kept him uninformed, but he'd had no idea how ambitious the piece was. He marveled at its craftsmanship.

Despite his son-in-law's objections, Josef hadn't given up his dream that Pete would one day follow him in some aspect of the jewelry trade. She was so gifted at it, with such a natural eye. At sixteen, she could judge diamonds as well as—no, better than—he could. Just a week ago a customer had brought in a very good diamond for appraisal. After studying it for fifteen minutes solid, he'd still not been one hundred percent certain how to grade the color. He asked the customer to leave it until his "associate" returned. Then he had Pete grade it. Her answer was swifter and surer than his—and she'd been right.

Now he gazed with admiration approaching awe at his granddaughter's creation. "Such originality! Such technique! I *knew* you had what it takes, Pete. This proves it. If you work hard and develop your talent you could be a great jeweler."

"Joe—" Steve began, but Josef cut him off.

"I know what you're thinking, Steve, you want her to be a doctor, but the child has an amazing natural talent. Just look at this. And there's no shame in being an artist such as Cellini or Fabergé or Cartier."

Steve stared at the pin, a frown etching two small parallel lines between his eyebrows.

"What do you think, Papa?" Pete asked timidly, clearly eager for his approval of her work.

He didn't answer right away, staring instead at the pin. Josef, not wanting Pete to feel hurt, jumped in again. "Whatever gave you the idea for this, Pete? In all my years in the business I've never seen anything quite like it."

As her father's eyes locked on hers, a memory inched into Pete's mind. To focus it more clearly she began to talk, her voice soft, her memory groping for the details to reconstruct the scene. "I remember once when I was very young. I found a beautiful jeweled lady. It was buried inside Raffie." She chuckled at the memory. "Remember Raffie, Mama, my stuffed giraffe? The jeweled lady had shoulders made from a pearl, an enameled head, and sapphire eyes. She sparkled like a fairy princess."

Steve stared, as if he could stop her speaking, even stop her remembering with the intensity of his gaze. Then he smiled. "A jewel in a stuffed giraffe?" His tone said it was preposterous.

"Don't you remember, Papa? I showed it to you, and you told me it was evil and took it away. You said I should forget about it so I did. Maybe I thought it was just a dream. But when I began sketching ideas for Mama's pin, it must have been there, waiting in my mind. The mermaid just poured out of my pencil.''

''Pete,'' Steve began, ''I don't think—''

Josef hunched forward in his chair. ''When did this happen, Pete?''

''When?'' she asked. ''I don't know. I . . . wait, I remember. Kennedy had just been elected so it had to be . . . 1960. I would have been eight.'' She turned to her father. ''Why did you say it was evil, Papa?''

''Because it was.''

Josef's head snapped up. ''Was? You mean it was real? What was this magical charm?''

Pete spoke. ''It was like a doll, but small, and only the top half. It was covered with gems, diamonds, and rubies—real ones I think.''

''If you were eight,'' Josef said, thinking out loud, ''you were old enough to know if they were real or not. I had already taught you a lot about diamonds by then.''

''It wasn't a dream, was it, Papa?''

Steve slumped forward, his elbows on his knees, his head hanging, his whole body spelling defeat. He didn't answer.

Josef's eyes changed from confusion to icy hardness. ''What is Pietra telling us?'' he asked in a tight voice.

Bettina had been watching silently as the confusion and tension built in the room. She turned wide, frightened eyes to her husband. ''Stefano? What was it?''

His daughter's voice made something snap in Josef, and he exploded out of his chair and lunged at Steve, grabbing the lapels of his corduroy jacket and yanking him to his feet. ''Tell me!''

''All right!'' Steve shouted. ''Yes! She's right! It was real. The diamonds on it were real—worth a fortune.''

Josef's rage exploded. ''In 1960! You had a fortune in your hand in 1960 while your wife was rotting in that snake pit because there was no money to pay for better?'' He was shaking Steve by the lapels.

"Opa!" cried Pete, "Stop!"

But Josef was not to be stopped. "You let my daughter break apart like an egg when you could have paid twenty doctors to keep her together?"

"Yes! All right!" Steve cried, his voice anguished. "Perhaps it was wrong, but I—"

Josef kept shaking him, roaring Dutch insults. "*Rotvent*! *Sodemieter*! Bastard. Stinking, rotten, *fucking* bastard!"

"Don't," cried Pete, grabbing Josef's arm and trying to pull him away. "Please!"

"Look at her," Josef shouted, pointing to Bettina, who was now cringing in her chair, her eyes scanning from face to face. "Look at what that place has created—what *you* have created!"

"Opa!" cried Pete again. "Let him explain." She turned huge, begging eyes on her father. "You can explain it, can't you, Papa? Tell us."

"Yes, Steve," said Josef. "Tell us. Tell your daughter why she had to live without a mother all these years because you were too goddamned selfish to pay for the private hospital that would have made her well."

"It wasn't like that," Steve cried, with a sound like the cry of a wounded animal.

"What was it like, then? Just exactly what was it like to damn your own wife to hell while you hid away a fortune in jewels? What was it like to sit around waiting for her to die or disappear so you could enjoy alone what you would not share? *What was it like, you bastard?*"

Softly, Steve answered. "It was hell. It's still hell."

"Still?" said Josef. "You mean you still have it? Where is it? Where the hell is it?" He grabbed Steve's lapels again, but Steve scissored his arms up and away, sending Josef sprawling onto the floor.

"Stop!" cried Bettina, sinking lower into her chair, her hands crossed over her head as if to shield herself from their anger. "Pietra, make them stop."

Pete ran to her mother, bending over her protectively. "It's okay, Mama, it's all right." She whirled on the two men.

"Look what you're doing to her. Stop it, both of you. Now!"

It became absolutely silent except for Josef's breathing, coming in gulps, and Bettina's sobs, and the final chords of Mahler's First Symphony resonating from the stereo.

Steve stared at his wife, at his father-in-law, at his daughter. His whole body slumped. What could he tell them? How could he explain to them what he didn't understand himself—that he had a fortune in jewels he couldn't force himself to sell, but that he didn't have the guts to use it to find his lost legacy? Guilt, anger, shame, resentment, frustration, embarrassment—they all welled up to create a stew of rage and loathing in him for himself and everyone else.

They were all looking at him, waiting, hoping for an explanation, but he didn't have one. Suddenly, he couldn't breathe in this room. He couldn't stay here. He had to get out. He grabbed a coat and went charging out of the apartment.

"Stefano," Bettina whimpered as the door slammed behind him with a sound like thunder. "Papa? Where's he going, Papa?"

"To hell, I hope," Josef said. "But don't worry, *Tientje*, we'll take care of you. We don't need him anymore."

But she didn't seem to hear him. "Stefano," she sobbed. "Pietra. Papa." Her voice rose with each name. "*Moetie. Ik wil Moetie*. Pietra, my baby. Where's my baby? I want my baby. *I want my baby!*" It was a primal wail, a keening, the howling of a wolf. Pete would have preferred to put her hands over her ears and bury her head in the sofa cushions. But instead, she sternly instructed her grandfather to get Bettina's medication, grasped her hysterical mother's hands, and told her over and over, "I'm here, Mama. It's Pietra, I'm here. I'm all right. I'm your baby, Mama. I'm fine, we're both fine."

It was an hour before they had Bettina finally asleep in her bed, heavily sedated. Pete surveyed the pile of discarded wrappings on the rug, the pumpkin pie that had burned unheeded in the oven. The mermaid pin lay on the floor among the ribbons where it had fallen from Bettina's fingers. Pete kneeled to pick it up, holding it gently, stroking the creature's jeweled head.

There, on her knees, she surveyed the ruins of their "perfect" Christmas.

Chapter 8

Steve didn't come back. One of his drinking buddies from Little Italy showed up a few days after Christmas with a sheepish request for Stefano's clothes and a few other necessities. He left the address of the furnished room Steve had rented downtown, but he needn't have bothered. Josef was far too angry to contact him, and Pete was too hurt.

Her despair was made worse by anger at her father, a rage stoked daily by Josef's bitter rantings against Steve, and a passion made stronger by the depth of her love for him. She struggled to understand why he had allowed her mother to suffer as she had when he could have prevented it. She strained to comprehend why he had abandoned them instead of explaining. She tried to make sense of the jeweled lady. What was it? Where had it come from? Why did her father have it, and why had he kept it hidden away all these years and called it evil?

She had no answers, and finally the questions themselves became too painful so she pushed them away. And soon she had more than her father to worry about.

The day after Christmas, she found her mother methodically pulling the filigreed wings off a Christmas angel. "You look so sweet," she said in a vicious voice as she destroyed the little figure, "but I know you. I know you're a whore, a filthy little whore." When the wings were gone, she started shredding the silk gown, gouging the papier-mâché with her nails. "Whore, whore, whore," she chanted dully, finally smashing the angel on the floor.

Pete blinked hard and breathed back a sob. Having learned young that it always made her mother's condition worse when she cried, she had banished tears. But the hopelessness that overwhelmed Pete as she watched her mother slipping away and into the darkness once again was almost unbearable.

"Mama?" she said gently, and reached out to touch her shoulder.

Bettina reacted as if she'd been burned. She jumped up from the floor and whirled to face Pete. "No! I won't, not anymore. Get away. Don't touch me."

Pete backed off instantly. "It's okay, Mama. No one's going to touch you; no one's going to hurt you."

Bettina crouched, her eyes flying around the little room, searching for danger in every corner. "No, no, no," she muttered.

"Shhh, Mama," Pete soothed. "Come to bed. It's safe in the bedroom. They won't follow you there." She held out her hand. After a moment, Bettina let Pete take her hand, lead her into the bedroom, and obeyed when Pete told her to get into bed. She swallowed the pill Pete brought her, and soon she was asleep.

Only then did Pete give way to tears, convulsed in a chair and aching with the despair she had hoped was over forever.

Bettina seemed to have slid once more into her own abyss.

Pete spoke every day with Bettina's doctor in Yonkers. When she described her mother's condition, he didn't sound hopeful. Pete's own hope was as thin as the tinsel on the rapidly dying Christmas tree, but she refused to stop trying to pull her back.

Jess, home from Bryn Mawr for the holidays, was an invaluable ally for Pete, a support propping her up, and for the first time Pete fully realized what she'd been missing in

a lifetime without true friendship. She could talk to Jess—
in long phone conversations or hours walking the wind-
whipped streets while Bettina slept. She could rage at her
father for his absence. She could worry about her grandfather,
who seemed paralyzed by his own despair. Pete learned that
a friend was someone who listened without judging, who
offered advice when appropriate. Someone who cared.

A week after Christmas, Pete felt safe in going out for an
hour to take Jess the Christmas present she'd made her—a
pair of delicate earrings of twisted silver wire. Bettina was
asleep when she left, and she knew her grandfather would
be home soon.

But when Josef returned, he discovered the apartment filled
with dozens of lighted candles—on tables and windowsills,
on the TV, on the floor, everywhere. One had burned all the
way down to the rug beneath it; another was dangerously
near the curtains. In the middle of them all, Bettina, on her
knees, was chanting: "*Yis-ka-dal v' yis-ka-dash*. . . ." It was
the Kaddish, the Jewish prayer for the dead. Josef didn't even
know his daughter knew it. He'd heard it himself only once,
when his father-in-law died.

Bettina's precariously balanced equilibrium had disintegrated, and Josef suspected, with a dread heavy as a Dutch
oven in his gut, that it would now never be restored. The
doctor agreed. Before the New Year was a week old, he
urged that Bettina be returned to Yonkers.

The Hell's Kitchen apartment took on the feeling of a tomb.
Josef seemed to have aged ten years overnight. He ate, he
slept, he worked. That was all. He stopped going to the Dutch
Club to meet his cronies. He didn't read; he no longer played
his records. He even gave up smoking his pipe. It was as
though he no longer believed he deserved the smallest pleasure in his life while his daughter suffered so horribly.

Jess had gone reluctantly back to school. She had tried to
convince her mother to let her stay in New York; Pete needed
her, she explained. When Sally refused, Jess even considered
faking a diabetic attack, but Pete wouldn't hear of it. So Jess
got on a train, and Pete was left alone.

She surrounded herself with work and activity so she

wouldn't have to think anymore. When she wasn't in school or studying, she worked in Josef's workroom, losing herself in her attempts to create beauty, honing her craft.

Steve called regularly. But when Josef answered, he would slam down the phone. If Pete answered, she would hang up more gently, but the result was the same. She refused to talk to her father. The emotions were too raw, too close to the surface still, and too confused. Finally Steve stopped calling, though a check arrived every two weeks, made out in Pete's name, with his familiar signature scrawled across the bottom. She thought of tearing it up, but the practical side of her nature forced her not to.

As usual, it was Jess who made Pete rethink her position about her father.

"You're not being fair to him, you know," she said as they wandered through Bloomingdale's one afternoon. It was late May and Jess was just home from her first year at Bryn Mawr. Pete hadn't seen or spoken to her father in five months.

"I don't want to be fair," Pete said, but there was no conviction in her voice. The anger had faded, and she missed him terribly. "What do you think of this scarf? A leopard print would be perfect with that black jersey dress you bought."

Jess yanked the scarf from her fingers and dropped it back on the counter. "Screw the scarf. Damn you, Pete. You don't even see what you've got and you're willing to throw it away. I'd kill to have a father who cared about me the way yours cares about you, someone who was always there to hold me when I was sick and tell me happy fairy stories when I was afraid of dying, instead of someone who just called the doctor and the florist and paid the bills on time."

"He left me," Pete said softly.

"He was scared and confused. Maybe he's not anymore. Don't you owe it to him, and to yourself, to find out?"

Suddenly Pete wanted more than anything in the world to feel her father's arms around her. Her mouth turned up in an ironic smile. "Damn you, Walsh. Why do you always have to be right? Buy the damn scarf and let's get out of here. I've got a phone call to make."

Steve answered on the second ring, and when he heard her voice his relief was so palpable she could feel it flooding through the phone line.

"Oh, *bambina*, I'm so glad you called. I've missed you."

Tears pricked her eyes at the sound of the beloved nickname. "Me, too, Papa. Me, too."

"Can we talk? I have so many things to tell you."

"I have things to tell you too, Papa."

They arranged to meet the next day.

The restaurant was in a neighborhood Pete had never been to, an area of century-old cast-iron buildings designed to be warehouses and factories, with high ceilings and oversized windows to let in the light and keep down electricity costs. Now the factories were mostly gone and artists had started moving in, taking advantage of the huge loft spaces that fit their work and the low rents that fit their pocketbooks. Since it was south of Houston Street, the artists had started calling it SoHo.

Steve sat at the bar near the door, one hand wrapped around a beer, his eyes in a magnet-lock on the door, when Pete came in. Before she was three feet inside, he caught her up in a bear hug and squeezed her so hard she gasped. When he put her down she was laughing, even though tears glistened at the corners of her eyes.

"*Che bella*," he teased. "You look beautiful."

"And you look very handsome." He really did look great, she thought, relaxed and fit and . . . happy.

"Come, eat. The hamburgers here are great."

In a wooden booth in the back, they made small talk about the weather, about school, about her graduation coming up in two weeks. They talked about SoHo.

"You live nearby?" she asked as she bit into an enormous hamburger. What a bizarre question, she thought. How many girls had to ask their fathers where they lived? "I thought you had a room in Little Italy."

"I moved. I . . . ." He picked up his beer and took a long, slow swig. "Pete, I don't live alone."

"You have a roommate?"

"Sort of. An artist, a sculptor." He paused and something in his voice made her eyes lock on his. "Her name's Anna. I met her at the laundromat."

The hamburger fell from Pete's fingers. "Anna? You're living with a woman?"

"Yes."

The simple answer slapped her in the face. When she spoke, her voice was hardly above a whisper, shaking with emotion she had no idea how to control. "Papa, how could you do that?"

"I fell in love with her, Pete. You're old enough to understand that."

Though sunshine was pouring through the window, dancing past the hanging ferns, the room seemed icy cold to Pete. She felt betrayed. How long, she wondered, had he known this woman, loved her? Could he have started the fight with Opa deliberately so he could leave and be with her? Was it possible he pushed Mama over the edge on purpose so he wouldn't have to live with her anymore? Pete wouldn't, *couldn't* believe that of him, even now. But what was the truth then? Her mind groped blindly for an explanation.

"How long?" she whispered.

"Three months. I met her in February."

"February. It didn't take you long, did it?" She hated sounding bitter, but the pain was almost overwhelming.

"What do you mean?"

"I mean you walked out on us—on Mama and Opa and me—and the first chance you had, you forgot us and found someone else."

"I *never* left you, Pete. I never will." He reached out and took her hand, which lay limply on the polished wood of the table. "You're my daughter, and I love you."

"What about your wife? You must have loved her once."

"I did. And I tried . . . you saw that, Pete. I tried to live with your mother, to help her."

"Maybe you didn't try hard enough."

"You're smarter than that. I tried as hard as I could—tried until I knew my own soul would die if I didn't . . .

come up for air. Your mother may be a mermaid, not quite of this world. But I'm just a man."

"So you sent her back to that place."

"Your mother is sick. She's been sick a long time. I don't know why, and I don't know if she'll ever get well. I hope so, but I can't live my whole life on hopes and dreams that may never come true. Not anymore."

It was as though she hadn't heard. "How can you be so selfish? Why didn't you sell that perfume bottle so you could pay for better treatment?"

The flat of his hand slapped down on the table. "It's not selfishness, goddammit!" He reached for her hand, but she snatched it away. "Pete, please. I know you're angry and hurt—I don't blame you—but try to understand."

"Then explain it so I can!"

"I'll try." He paused thoughtfully. "It goes back to your grandmother, really. To things that happened then—to the things I lost because of your Uncle Vittorio."

"My Uncle—?" The word surprised her like a splash of cold water.

"I need some air," Steve said. "Let's walk, and I'll tell you." He threw some money on the table and led her out the door.

As they walked through the streets of SoHo, their strides perfectly matched, oblivious to the late spring sunshine and the bustle around them, he told her the whole story, from the beginning. Pete listened spellbound, wrapped up in a history she never knew she had. He told her about Vittorio, about Carlo Brancusi, and about the one and only time he had met his mother. She could tell from the way the words lingered on his tongue and the extra lilt his accent took on that every moment of that time thirty years ago was still totally alive in his memory. The shadows of the beautiful villa near Florence, the smell of candles burning in silver candelabra, the fire of the diamonds around the neck of a magnificently beautiful woman, a woman of mystery and romance and magic—he brought it all to life.

"La Colomba," Pete repeated the name. Her grandmother.

He stopped, took out his wallet, and handed her an old newspaper photo—faded and grainy—it was a woman, one of the most beautiful women she'd ever seen. She was drinking champagne and smiling straight into the camera.

"Can I keep this?"

"I've been saving it for you."

Then he told her about the perfume bottle and the legacy it represented, a legacy lost because of the treachery of his half-brother. The dazzling memory of the bottle was as clear now in Pete's mind's eye as the night she'd seen it when she was eight.

"I did everything I could think of to track Vittorio down," he said as she stared at the photo, willing her grandmother to speak to her over the years. "I kept an eye on the auction news, read all the reports of jewelry sales. I always hoped something from my mother's collection would turn up, something I'd recognize. But nothing ever has. Perhaps it's all gone now, broken up for the stones, sold, maybe even recut. It was my search for Vittorio that got me involved in the jewelry business here. That's how I met your grandfather."

"Then if you hadn't come to America to find your half-brother, I would never have been born?"

He smiled, the old, beguiling Stefano smile, and saluted the sky. "Thank you, Vittorio."

They walked a while in silence while she digested the story she'd just heard. It explained so much. Not everything, but a lot. But it didn't explain why he had given up.

"Why did you stop looking for him, Papa? Why don't you start again? I could help. We could find him. I know we could."

"It's been thirty years since that bottle was given to me. Once I let it set the course of my life, and it nearly ruined it. I have to let go."

"But Papa—"

"No, Pete. Look what the bottle has done to us, to me, to your mother. I think I was right when I called it evil. It took away the life I should have had. If I can give up once and for all the idea that someday I might find the jewels, maybe I can find myself again."

"Papa, where is it now? Where's the perfume bottle?"

He hesitated. "If I tell you, what will you do?"

"I don't know. But I have to see it again. It was my inspiration for the best piece of work I've ever done, remember? I need to see it as much as you need to let it go."

"Maybe it is time to put the bottle to some use at last. Sell it. Use the money to help your mother. Or pay for your education. I should have done it years ago."

"I don't know, Papa," she said, and he nearly cried. "I think I understand now why you couldn't let it go, even when we needed the money so bad for Mama. It was your mother's, the only thing you had of hers. But if you're ready to do it now . . ."

"It's where it's been for the last nine years, where I put it the night you pulled it out of Raffie—in the purple pillow your mother embroidered, on our bed at home. Take it, Pete, and do what you must with it. It's yours now, your legacy." He gave a soft, sad laugh. "Certainly the only legacy you'll ever get from me."

"Oh no, Papa. You've given me so much more."

The rift was healed, and the love flowing between them would have lit up the sky in a blackout.

"Come home with me, Pete," Steve said suddenly. "It's just around the corner. Come and meet Anna."

"No." The mood cracked. It wasn't shattered completely, but it would fall apart at a touch.

"Please. You'd like her."

She gave him a small smile. "If she loves you, then I probably would. But I can't meet her, Papa. Not yet."

He nodded his understanding. Don't push it, *paesano*, he counseled himself. One step at a time.

"I'll call you, Papa," Pete said, and swung off alone into the artsy streets of SoHo, her bag slung over her shoulder and her long strides carrying her off.

Steve stood on the corner and watched his golden child, whom he loved so much it made him ache, walking away from him. But not disappearing. She had said she would call.

He had won his daughter back.

* * *

Alone in the room that had been her parents' and now was hers, Pete sat staring at the beautiful perfume bottle retrieved from the pillow. The image of her grandmother, the buried fortune of her father. She could no more solve the puzzle of what to do with it than her father had been able to do. Should she sell it as he suggested? She knew enough about jewelry to guess pretty accurately at the astronomical sum it would bring. She hated to think of it cut apart, its stones prised out to be sold one by one. It was not only a treasure, it was a work of art and her heritage.

Would the money make any real difference to Mama now? Sadly, Pete knew it would not. The course of Mama's illness was set and nothing was going to change it. Also, recent changes in the state's mental health system had wrought dramatic improvements in conditions at the institution in Yonkers. Bettina was comfortable there. She almost seemed happy to be back "home."

What, then, of Pete's own future? The bottle would buy her a first-class education, but her scholarship would pay for that. It would get them a better place to live, but with Papa gone, their apartment was fine for her and Opa. He had made friends in the neighborhood. It was only a five-minute walk from his work.

Should she keep the bottle then? Should she save it until she could use it to help chase her father's dream? With her grandmother's jeweled likeness in one hand and her photo in the other, Pete felt the strong pull of this woman's life on her own. She had even been named after her.

"Well, Grandmother," she said to the two objects, her new talisman, "what do you think? You wanted Papa to have the jewels, or half of them, anyway. Shall I find them for him? It might take a very long time. Years maybe. I don't know enough even to start yet."

A shaft of sunlight lancing through the window hit the bottle. It seemed like an omen. "All right," Pete said quietly.

She put the bottle back into the embroidered pillow where it had rested untouched for nine years and sewed up the seam again. She would keep it safe until she was in a position to take up her father's dream, to track down her Uncle Vittorio and reclaim her heritage. She wouldn't tell her grandfather.

I'm sorry, Opa, she thought. I'm sorry to lie to you, to let you think Papa is just being selfish. But this is something I have to do. You might not understand, but my grandmother would. My grandmother Pietra.

bits of text, a dream lived out in her Uncle's Volvo and Eleanor's bed too. She wasn't idiot but performers. I wish I cards the thought I whenever they would tell you that I want to be a great being a doctor. She didn't wish to be interesting, but to understand while the information flows.

Chapter 9

New York—1970

"Want to get a bite to eat?" the young man asked as Pete was packing her book bag. A delicious-looking blond hunk named Larry Carver, he was her lab partner in Anatomy 101 at NYU. Keen to become a doctor—to go and take care of the troops in Vietnam, he said—Larry was an ace student in the course and had spent the last hour with Pete huddled over a chart of the human body, as they drilled each other for an upcoming final exam on terms like *olecranon process* and *innominate artery*.

"Thanks for the invitation, Larry," Pete said, scooping up her bag, "but I've got to get home."

As she reached the door, he placed his not insubstantial bulk squarely in front of it. "What is it about me, Pete? Have I got dandruff? Bad breath? You hate my jokes? I've been trying to get you to go out with me for six months, and it's always 'Thanks, Lar, but . . .' "

Pete sighed. She'd felt this coming for a while, but she still wasn't eager to play out the scene. As she often had before, she took the easy way out. "As a matter of fact, I can't have dinner with you because I already have a date . . . with a man I care about very much."

He nodded in resigned acceptance. "Might have known. All the best ladies are taken." He picked up his notes and looked her up and down, smiling his appreciation of the view. "Lucky guy."

She laughed. "See you Wednesday," she said and swept out the door and down the hall.

She hadn't lied, she told herself as she bounced down the steps, hit Washington Square, and headed downtown. This time she really did have a dinner date—with her father. But if she hadn't, she would have found some other excuse not to go out with Larry Carver. He was too confident, too good-looking, the kind of guy who would expect more than she was willing to give.

Pete had no intention of getting seriously involved with any man. With the shambles of her parents' marriage as her only guide, she saw no point in putting her faith in a romantic commitment. She didn't need it; she didn't want it. Her life was full enough without it. She had her studies; she had the part-time job in the jewelry district that provided her spending money. Whenever Jess could manage a weekend in the city, they spent every hour they could together.

Admittedly, she did wonder now and then about sex. She was eighteen. A lot of the girls she knew from classes—and practically all the ones from her neighborhood—had given up their virginity long ago. Even sheltered Jess had taken the plunge last year, with a Sigma Chi from Princeton, no less. It was, after all, a great new era—the seventies had begun. The Sexual Revolution was revving up. There must be something to it all, some point that she wasn't getting.

But whenever Pete thought of finding some perfectly nice, good-looking, willing boy—someone like Larry—and satisfying her curiosity, her whole being recoiled and the intentionally fuzzed memory of her mother masturbating on the floor of her sanatorium room crystallized in her mind's eye. If that was where sex could lead, she could easily put it off.

She shook her head to clear away the thought. The breeze picked up her heavy black mane and spooned it out away from her face. It was a perfect spring day, the best time to be in New York, and she was glad of the walk to SoHo. She needed the time and exercise to clear her thoughts and get herself ready for the coming encounter. Finally, after more than a year of refusing, Pete had agreed to go to the loft her father shared with Anna Janowski and meet the woman he said he loved.

Pete had long since given up her anger at her father for his betrayal of her mother. Bettina couldn't be a wife to him and hadn't been for a long time. Still, Pete had avoided the idea of meeting Anna, of actually facing this "other woman" who made such pangs of jealousy slice through her on her mother's behalf.

It was something she'd come across in one of her psychology texts that changed her mind. There it was, right on the page, reluctant though she was to admit it, and once she'd seen it she couldn't pretend she hadn't. It was not Bettina she was jealous for; it was herself. *She* was jealous of Anna. For so long, Pete had had her father's exclusive love. She had been the center of his world. The truth was, she just didn't want to share him.

Once that knowledge was allowed in, she had to act on it. Pete was a perfectionist, and jealousy was an imperfection she would not tolerate any more than she would tolerate fear. She would meet Anna and accept her, even if she couldn't like her.

Her long, Levi-clad legs pumped steadily, carrying her down the avenue like a pair of scissors trimming the blocks off a map.

She crossed Houston and swung down West Broadway, stopping to study the window displays in the trendy boutiques, especially the jewelry stores. Despite her college load and her resolution to become a psychiatrist, Pete had never given up her intense interest in everything having to do with jewelry. She still spent much of her free time in her grandfather's workroom, absorbing everything she could, experimenting with ideas, learning new techniques. As often as not, when she should have been conjugating French verbs, she was poring over the scientific writings of Tolkowski and other gemologists. Instead of solving problems in calculus, she'd be lost in the seventeenth-century classic *The Six Voyages of*

Jean Baptiste Tavernier, the memoirs of Louis XIV's gem merchant detailing each of his three-year voyages to trade in precious stones in the bustling markets of ancient Kabul and Delhi, Ceylon and Golconda. The stories fired her imagination and fueled the fantasy that she might some day be part of that world, even if the gem markets were now reached by jet plane rather than brigantine.

In a store near Spring Street, she stopped short. In the window, pieces of jewelry were half-buried in sand or draped across Greek statues or hanging from invisible wires, shimmering as if floating in midair. They were astonishing pieces, sculptural and boldly original. The place was as much a gallery as a store. Jewelry as art.

One piece in particular caught her attention—a wide necklace of hammered gold, thick in places, almost tissue thin in others, studded here and there with translucent cabochons in different sizes—garnet, carnelian, moonstone—patterns that seemed abstract one minute then evoked animal faces or flowers the next.

Pete gazed at the piece with astonished reverence. She imagined the artist bending over his worktable, making sketch after sketch until he knew the design was perfect, hammering the gold to shape it, using a delicate pair of tweezers to position the stones. She imagined his feeling of satisfaction as he sat back to look at the finished piece and said, yes, it will do.

I want to be able to do that, she thought with a desperate hunger. I want to know how to create something that perfect, that beautiful. That lasting.

The woman's handshake was firm and warm, and it drew Pete into the room with an undeniable welcome.

"Pete," Steve said in a voice both eager and nervous, "this is Anna."

"Hello, Pete," said the round-faced woman with brown hair and smiling eyes as she held out her hand. "I am so very glad you finally meet me."

Her accent was charming, lilting and sexy, Pete thought as she looked at the thirty-six-year-old émigré. Pete wasn't sure what she'd expected, but Anna Janowski was not it. She wasn't especially pretty, Pete thought, certainly not a beauty like Mama. Her hair was a neutral brown, long and pulled back with a rubber band at the nape of her neck. Deep-set eyes, broad cheekbones, and a firm mouth announced her Slavic heritage.

Pete wondered for a moment if her father's choice was a reaction against Bettina. After being married to such a beautiful woman and finding her unstable, perhaps he needed to try something else. Anna might not be beautiful, but she looked solid and dependable. Not that she was unappealing. Pete recognized the natural sexuality she exuded, a sense of being comfortable with herself, with being a woman.

Somewhere Pete had heard it said that a man who left one woman often ended up with another one very similar. But in her father's case that clearly wasn't true. Where Mama was reticent, quiet, and closed off, Anna had a warm, open smile that filled her whole face, and her eyes sizzled with enthusiasm for living. Where Mama was frail and small, Anna was a big woman, as tall as Steve. Anna was also, Pete estimated, about ten pounds heavier than she should be, but she carried it well. Anna Janowski had presence.

The loft was like nothing Pete had ever seen, certainly no place she'd ever imagined anyone living. The single, open room must have been nearly thirty by fifty feet. Two walls were solid windows; the sunset was bleeding through them, turning everything rose and salmon and soft, soft yellow. A row of cast-iron pillars thick as oak trees marched down the center of the room, supporting the fifteen-foot ceiling.

"Dinner is ready in fifteen minutes," Anna said.

"If you can call it that," Steve teased as he draped an arm around her shoulders. "Tell Pete your idea of the perfect meal."

Anna laughed, a comfortable sound, totally lacking in self-consciousness. "One I do not have to make," she said. "I hate to cook—such a waste of time and talent."

"So, we're eating deli," Steve said.

"Yes," Anna agreed, "but what deli! I shall tell you I spent two hours shopping for best smoked kielbasa, finest pickled herring. We have cabbage salad and pickles and roasted peppers and, and . . .'' She dug into a bag sitting on a table near the door and began pulling items out. ''. . . and potato chips, and fresh mozzarella, grapes, Hershey Bars, and . . . '' With a flourish, she produced two bottles of wine, one white, one red. ''And vino! Now do you dare tell me, Stefan, I do not work as hard on this meal as a master chef?''

''Never, *mia cara*,'' said Steve and kissed her head. ''Now off to the kitchen, woman, and finish the job. You can at least slice the sausage and put the rest on proper plates.''

''Yes, yes. I make it so very beautiful. Like you,'' she said, and kissed him back.

Pete watched her father in amazement. She couldn't remember ever seeing him so relaxed around her mother, so happy and smiling, so easy. With Anna he had a relationship that seemed to be built on both loving and *liking*. They obviously had fun together.

Pete had noticed changes in her father in the year he'd been living with Anna. He looked younger, laughed more than he had in years, and he had given up smoking. Also, he'd found a job he loved, working as an editor and reporter in the New York bureau of a major Italian newspaper.

Pete was happy for him, for the fact that after so many unhappy years he'd finally put together a life that seemed to give him some satisfaction. Didn't he deserve it?

''Stefan, why you don't take Pete away to be comfortable?'' asked Anna. ''While I am in kitchen.''

''Because I have some translation to finish before dinner,'' said Steve. ''Pete, go help Anna, will you? She's about as likely to slice a finger as she is the kielbasa. The woman needs constant supervision in a kitchen.''

An onion sailed over his head from the direction of the kitchen area and hit Pete on the shoulder.

''Bull's-eye!'' Steve cried, and threw it back. Then he disappeared around a partition.

Pete went to the kitchen corner of the huge room, divided from the rest by a butcher-block counter, glad of the chance to get to know Anna better. The space was filled with gleaming copper-bottomed pots that looked as if they'd never been used. Dried herbs and flowers hung in upside-down bunches from an overhead eave.

"It is pretty, no?" said Anna. "A friend helped me buy all these things. She thought I should try to fool people, I think." She gave Pete a conspiratorial smile. "I fooled your father. For one week. He thought I make the potato salad and borscht myself." She laughed her hearty laugh.

"He doesn't look like he's going hungry," said Pete, reaching for a knife and grabbing a ripe tomato.

"No, no. I feed him all the time. That is the Polish way."

"Have you been here long, in this country?"

"Five years. I know I sound more like five months. English is a strange language."

"You do very well. Why did you leave?"

"I am an artist. To be an artist in Poland, it is very difficult, especially if you do not want to make 'party art.' It is not possible to breathe there. To be an artist, the soul and mind and heart must be free—free to soar like giant birds, or to do a bellyflop onto your face." She laughed again, and Pete thought it was the freest, most joyous sound she'd heard in ages.

"It must be wonderful to be an artist," she said, thinking again of the beautiful piece of jewelry art she'd seen on her way here. "To create something of beauty, for others to appreciate, and to know that they see the same beauty in it you do."

"Yes! That is it, Pete. That is what I mean when I work in my studio. To share my idea of what is beautiful." She gestured with enthusiasm as she spoke, the butcher knife in her hand drawing great arcs in the air. "It is the best ever when someone you do not know, who has no reason to love you or lie to you, tells you the work is good, the work is beautiful, that it has meaning for them, too. That is when I know why I am an artist."

"I'd like to see your work some time."

"Good. You will come to my studio. I show you."

They worked then in silence. Just before they carried the

overflowing platters to the table, Anna turned to Pete again. "May I tell you something?"

"Of course."

"I love Stefano, and I know he loves me too. We are good for each other. But I do not try to take the place of your mother, Pete. Never."

"I know that now."

"But I hope we will be friends, Pete. It is good to be friends, no?"

"Yes. I would like that, too."

"Good." Then she surprised Pete by putting down the knife and enveloping her in a great, warm hug. It felt wonderful.

"The feast is ready," Anna called out from the kitchen, and they all headed for the table.

It was a gay, lively, funny meal. Pete was struck again and again by how right her father and Anna seemed together, how good for each other.

"You are finished?" asked Anna when Pete had finished only a single heaping plate of food. She sighed. "I wish I had your little appetite. But always my head is saying *mangiolo, Anna, mangiolo.*"

Pete giggled and Steve guffawed. "I have been trying to teach her Italian. It doesn't seem to be working."

"For that insult," said Anna, "you must make the coffee."

"I always make the coffee. If I didn't, you would have poisoned us both by now."

He went to the kitchen and Pete sat back, studying the woman her father loved. Anna was unlike any woman Pete had ever known. She'd never met anyone so full of life and warmth, laughter spilling out of her pores, smiles filling the air around her. She was a woman comfortable in her own skin. It occurred to Pete that she would like to bring Jess here to meet Anna—someone who was not a classical beauty but who had developed her own kind of beauty, a sort of inner glow that warmed everyone around her.

She realized how much she enjoyed being here, and kicked herself for putting it off so long. It was nice to be a part of the glowing circle of love these two people had created. Papa deserved that much, and she was glad for him.

But how sad that Mama had never been able to have this kind of comfortable love in her life.

It was late when Pete got home that night, mellow from the good food, fine wine, and excellent company. The last vestige of anger at her father was gone.

Josef was still up when she came in, nodding over a book and trying to stay awake. He always tried to stay up for her, though he didn't always manage it.

"Where have you been so late, *schatje*?" he asked, standing to stretch.

"Just out, Opa," she said, not wanting a scene. Then she changed her mind. It was time he faced the fact that she had a father, that she loved him, and that she was going to see him. "I've been having dinner with Papa. And Anna."

Josef snapped to attention, all sleepiness gone. He sputtered, and within seconds his face was cherry red. "You . . . you've been with that bastard? Pete, why . . . why would you do that? How could you be such a traitor to your mother?"

"Sit down, Opa."

"No. I—"

"Please. Sit down and let me tell you."

Even after all this time, Josef's anger at Steve was still raw. But his love for his granddaughter far outweighed it, and he saw something in her face he'd never seen before. Determination. So he agreed to sit and listen, rather than alienate the one person he had left to love.

Pete told him then about Anna, about how happy her father seemed to be, and especially about how happy she was for him. "He deserves this, Opa, and it isn't hurting Mama, not really. She's beyond that now."

"I know," he sighed. "If we can't help her, neither can we hurt her very much anymore."

"We can only love her, Opa, and we will never stop doing that."

"No. Never."

Seeing that he was no longer about to explode at the mention of Steve's name, Pete decided to take the next step. She went to her bedroom and retrieved the perfume bottle.

At the first sight of it, Josef looked as if he might grab it and throw it out the window. "Look at it," he sneered. "You know what it could have meant to you mother."

"But that is past, Opa. It can't help her now."

"Perhaps not, but—"

"No buts, Opa. I understand now why Papa couldn't bring himself to sell it. I'm not going to sell it, either." Now she told him the full story of La Colomba and the legacy of priceless jewels that was stolen by her uncle, of the quest that had brought Stefano D'Angeli to America and turned him into Steve, of the years of lost hope and the dreams deferred.

"Papa said I could sell it. But I can't, Opa. Don't you see? It gives me something I've never had before—a past, a heritage. And maybe even a future."

Josef was a man who had spent his life helping to create beautiful jewelry, and he couldn't help but be caught up in the romance and mystery of the tale. And the bottle . . . He took it in his large, old, competent hands, turned it over as tenderly as a mistress, lovingly stroked the gems and the gold. "It is a marvel," he said, "one of the finest pieces I have ever seen. But like this, broken, incomplete, it cries out to be reunited with the rest."

"That is what I intend to do one day, Opa. Exactly that."

That night, Pete sat up very late, perched on her bed, the bottle in her hands. She thought about what Anna had said about art—to share your idea of beauty, to make someone feel as you felt at the moment of creation. She remembered how she had felt when she was creating Mama's mermaid pin—it had been the most exciting time in her life, a period when she felt fired with creativity and energy and could hardly wait to get up every morning, knowing she would get to work on her creation.

She had never felt more alive . . . or more right.

"Okay," Pete said softly to the perfume bottle, the image of La Colomba. "You win, Grandmother." She smiled into the darkness of the night outside her window.

The decision was made. She was not going to continue with college. She was not going to graduate, go to medical school, become a psychiatrist. Others would have to take on the burden of helping people like Mama.

Pete was going to design jewelry.

Now all she had to do was tell her father.

Anna's studio was a white skylit room on Greene Street. It was huge and messy and smelled of sawdust and lacquer and linseed oil. Pete loved it from the minute she walked in.

The sculptures were big and bold, done mostly in wood that was shaped, sanded, and oiled till it gleamed with a life of its own.

"This one," said Anna, pointing to a sinuous piece of sandalwood that undulated upward like a vertical wave and shone like honey, "is a picture of your father's accent when he is trying to get something out of me." She grinned, and Pete smiled back.

"Seriously?"

"Well, it might be. I do not always know what I am making, only how I want it should feel. I wanted this one to feel like satin and velvet and honey."

"It does," Pete said, thinking Anna had caught the feeling exactly. "Why do you work in wood?"

"Because it is alive." Anna ran her long, capable fingers across the grain of a piece carved from ebony. "I like to look inside it and find the heart, to discover the shape the wood wants to be. Then I release it."

A memory, sharp as an icicle, flew into Pete's mind—her grandfather, romancing the diamond, trying to mine the heart of it and release the luster of the gem. And the diamond flying apart in shards and splinters, cutting lives, drawing blood.

"What happens when you're wrong? Do you ever make a mistake and ruin the wood?"

Anna laughed. "Always. So then I make it into something else. Sometimes a something more beautiful than what I planned in the first place." She moved to a large flattened oval shape with a small wooden ball resting in the hollow. "Like this one. It is meant to be the eye of the universe, but

Stefan he tells me it looks like a squashed bagel with a loose raisin floating in it.'' She laughed loudly. ''For a poet, I sometime think your father has no soul.''

''You are good for him, Anna. You make him laugh.''

''He is good for me, Pete. He makes me care—about myself, not just my work. He reminds me that I am woman as well as artist.''

''But how do you do it? How do you make it work?''

''We are friends,'' Anna replied simply. ''That is the key, you know, Pete. The very best lover in the world is a man who is your best friend.''

Applying the word *lover* to her father was an uncomfortable notion for Pete, but she could see clearly what Anna meant. The love that flowed between them was obvious, but so was the friendship, the genuine liking.

''You must come to our party next week,'' said Anna with infectious eagerness. ''There will be many interesting people there.''

As the party roared around her, Pete leaned on the kitchen counter and watched the dark young man stuff the two dozenth Ritz cracker with cheese into his mouth. Anna and Steve's loft was bulging with people and talk and music, the sort of gathering Pete had never been exposed to, and she was fascinated. For the most part, they were people who made their living by creating—artists, musicians, a couple of writers, a dancer. There were journalists Steve had met through his new job, and a photographer who sometimes worked with him on stories.

She hadn't talked to any of them at length. To tell the truth, they intimidated the hell out of her. She was eighteen; she'd never done much of anything but go to school. And her social skills weren't rusty because she'd never had many to rust. Still, she was enjoying the party, and she was determined to have at least one real conversation before the evening was through.

The hungry young man at the food table was tall and skinny, mid-twenties she guessed, though she wasn't much good at judging age. Boyish, definitely boyish, with straight dark hair that badly needed trimming and kept falling in his face so he was always having to reach up and brush it away like a pesky fly. He picked up another piece of cream cheese–stuffed celery.

"Would you like me to make you a sandwich?" Pete asked. "You look like you need something more substantial than rabbit food."

"What have you got?" he said around a mouthful of carrot stick.

"I think there's some roast beef in the fridge."

"Rare?"

"I don't know. Is the beggar being a chooser?"

"Sure. Life's not worth living if you have to compromise."

She grinned at him. "I'll find you a rare piece."

She rummaged around in the refrigerator till she came up with several slices of bright red roast beef, muenster cheese, lettuce, a ripe tomato, mayo, mustard, crisp dill pickles.

"God, beautiful and she can cook, too."

"Making a sandwich is not cooking. Veal Cordon Bleu and chicken cacciatore, that's cooking."

"Same difference." He plunged into the finished creation and polished it off in half a dozen bites. "I'm Charlie Barron," he said as a belated introduction.

"Pete D'Angeli." They shook hands and smiled at each other.

"What do you do when you're not eating, Charlie Barron?" Pete asked.

"Make art." She'd never heard that phrase before tonight, and tonight she'd heard it a dozen times. Making art. It's what Anna and her friends did. It was what Pete wanted to learn to do with her jewelry.

"What kind?" Pete asked.

"Pop," Charlie said a little defensively. "Listen, Warhol's making it work. Why shouldn't I?"

"I don't know. Why shouldn't you?"

"Because no one understands what I'm trying to do."

"Maybe I will. Why don't you tell me about it?"

And so he did, at length. When the refrigerator was empty and there were only a few scraps left on the food table, they moved to a comfortable sofa draped with Navaho weavings. Mostly Charlie talked and Pete listened. He told her about the huge old printing plant he rented for a song—"off-key at that," he joked—and about the art he was making with found objects—rusty metal, torn bedsheets, tin cans, cardboard, garbage, "the detritus of human life that can really be beautiful if you just look at it with a fresh eye," he explained.

They were still sitting there, sipping red wine and talking earnestly, when the last guest left. "Good-night, Charlie," said Anna, standing in front of him and bending down to talk into his ear, or he wouldn't have heard.

He looked up and around the room, surprised to find it empty. "Party over?"

"Yes, Charlie," said Steve behind Anna. "The party is over."

"Oh." Pete thought he sounded disappointed. She rose and stretched and walked him to the door. "Want to come by my place and see my stuff?" he asked. "Tomorrow?"

She'd been trying to imagine his work all evening. She really wanted to see it for real. And she surprised herself to realize she wouldn't mind seeing him again. "I'd like that."

"Great. I'll come by here and get you at six." He opened the door and turned to say good-night. "You know. You're really beautiful," he said. Then he turned and left.

Charlie's work was certainly unique. His canvases were enormous, covered with plastic drinking straws and McDonald's hamburger boxes, bleach bottles, and flattened boxes of Tide. Others were made up of eggshells and coffee grounds and orange peels, uncooked spaghetti, and crushed candy canes, all arranged in fanciful mosaic-like patterns and coated with clear acrylic.

The "garbage walls," as he called them, were whimsical or dramatic, but they always seemed to work, Pete thought. The final result made you feel something when you looked at it. They reminded her of her mother's dresser set, the set she had covered with bits of shell and ribbon and beach glass, trying to recreate a window at Chartres.

She found herself telling him about that window, about how hard she had tried to reinvent its beauty on the back of a cheap plastic hairbrush.

"Show me," he demanded, and handed her a pencil and a sketch pad.

"What?"

"Show me what you did. Draw it."

She did, as best she could remember it.

"Not bad," he said, "not bad. You starting at the League next week?"

She had told him of her plans to go to the Art Students' League to study jewelry design. "Next month."

"Start next week. You need to work on your drawing." He looked up from the pad. "What did you bring us to eat?"

"How the hell do I tell him I'm not going back to school?" Pete asked Jess during what had become their regular Saturday morning Village brunch. Going away to college had been a major turning point for Jess, because once she was on her own there was no going back. She'd slipped her leash for good. She made it clear to her parents and doctors that there would be no more watchdogs—not Williams, the chauffeur; not Mary, her maid; not her parents. She knew how to take care of herself.

But her newfound freedom had done nothing to lessen her devotion to Pete. They spent as much time together as they could, even though they were both working—Pete in the jewelry district, and Jess as a part-time clerk in a bookstore, handling the things she loved most—books.

"Well, he's got to be told," she pointed out now. "In another month it will be September. He's likely to notice that you are not weighted down with biology texts or running off for some lecture or other."

"I know. But he's going to be so hurt. To him, jewels mean pain and loss. They always have." She scooped up a bite of eggs Benedict. "Eat your spinach salad. It's good for you."

"Look, you've just been telling me you're not going to be a doctor, so can it. I hate spinach salad. I don't know why

I ordered it.'' She moved a leaf or two around in the bowl. ''Maybe Anna can help. She's great with your father, and she understands about art and the need to be creative.''

''She sure does—better than anyone I know.''

''So? Give her a try. And order me an omelette. Jelly.''

''I'll order you one plain. And okay, I'll talk to Anna.''

Anna's advice was, ''Come to dinner. You tell him over the pastrami and leave the rest to me.''

''Are you sure?'' asked Pete.

''On this you must trust me.''

So they were sitting in the loft, which had become something of a second home to Pete, when she told him.

''I'm leaving school, Papa,'' she said suddenly.

He frowned in confusion, as though she'd spoken in Russian. ''What does that mean, leaving?''

''It means I'm not going back next month.''

''And what do you plan to do instead?'' he asked, though he was afraid he already knew the answer.

''I am going to be my grandmother's granddaughter,'' she said and laughed.

''Not completely, I hope,'' said Anna with a laugh. ''You are very beautiful, our Pete, but I do not see a courtesan.''

''No, not that,'' Pete agreed. Steve was still silent. ''But I want to work with jewels.''

''In what way?'' Steve asked. Already Pete heard an edge of disapproval in his voice.

''Not the technical side, not like Opa. I want to . . . to add more beauty to the world, as a designer. I know it doesn't sound important to you. But it's something I feel I can do well. Better than anyone, maybe.''

He slumped a little. Was it a genetic defect, he wondered, some inherited disease, this infectious attachment to the lure of gems that seemed destined to rule the lives of his family? ''Pete, you don't know—''

''Yes, she does know, Stefan,'' said Anna. ''Who can know better than Pete what is right for her life? You? Me? I do not think so.'' Then she got up and left the table, leaving Pete feeling abandoned in her moment of need.

But it seemed Anna knew what she was doing.

"Well, thank God for Anna, eh?" said Steve. "I suppose she is right, and I must admit it. You know, for so long, because of Mama's illness, I had to make decisions about you without having anybody else's advice. So I got used to thinking I was always right." He put his arm around her. "But I guess you know best for yourself, Pete. I wish to God you didn't want to do this, but I will support you one hundred percent."

Her eyes were stinging with happy tears. "Thank you, Papa. I want to make you proud."

"You have already done that, *bambina*."

Friendship is wonderful, thought Pete. First there had been Jess. Then Anna. And now Charlie Barron. His big printing-plant loft became yet another haven for Pete. Pete liked the oily ink smell that clung to the brick walls of the old printing plant. She liked the black industrial rubber floor that Charlie had covered with sisal matting that massaged your feet when you walked on it barefoot and the flat light that came through the frosted glass skylight, gray-white by day, amber-pink from the streetlights at night. She loved the quiet, cut only by the bluegrass music Charlie always had on the stereo. She even liked Renaldo, Charlie's neurotic cat. Best of all, she liked having the sort of friendship she had never known could exist between a man and a woman.

When she discovered that the usual contents of Charlie's refrigerator consisted of a jar of mustard, a bottle of vinegar, three half-used cans of cat food, some leftover Chinese take-out (usually grown moldy), and all his spare cash, she started making it a point to stock it. A couple of evenings a week when she knew he'd been working all day, she showed up with all the ingredients for a veal marsala or the traditional Dutch stew called *hutspot*.

She cooked; he worked. Over dinner they talked about anything, everything. Later she sat and sketched ideas for jewelry pieces at Charlie's drafting table while he went back to work at his oversized easel.

Now and then as she sketched, Charlie came to look over

her shoulder, sometimes adding a single pencil stroke that made all the difference in bringing an idea into focus.

Pete was loving her classes in sketching and jewelry making at the Art Students' League. By day she spent hours with a jeweler's hammer in her hand, shaping gold and silver and copper. She modeled wax for casting. She wheedled her grandfather out of tiny chips of diamonds, rubies, and the other stones he was cutting. She made sketch after sketch of ideas for jewelry—shaping, refining, trying again. Most of them ended up in the trash can, but slowly a portfolio of designs worth keeping began to collect.

Gradually, Pete was learning her craft.

Josef was overjoyed with Pete's decision to give up college and devote herself full-time to jewelry. He praised every sketch, applauded every finished piece.

"So," said Jess as she walked with Pete up Madison Avenue toward her house. "Are you and Charlie Barron friends?"

"What a dumb question. You know we are."

"But I mean *friends*. Like Anna and your father are friends. Remember what she said?"

"Yes, I remember, and no, we are not." Pete had repeated every word of Anna's conversation about friends making the best lovers to Jess. "Charlie and I are not lovers."

"Why not?"

Pete tossed her head, a sure sign she was embarrassed. "I don't know. It just never came up."

Jess trilled a laugh bright as a copper penny. "Never?"

Pete covered her eyes in embarrassment and burst out laughing. "You have a really dirty mind, you know that? That is not what I meant! What I mean is, we're . . . we're just good friends."

"So?"

"Jess!"

"Oh, all right. I'll drop it. But you just better let me know when it happens, Pete, or I'll stop being your friend for all time."

"You'll be the third to know."

* * *

"So," said Anna as they were sweeping up in her studio together later that day. "You and Charlie are becoming friends?"

"Not you, too! I know what you mean, and I don't think Papa would be pleased with this conversation."

Anna dismissed Steve's concerns with an airy wave. "Fathers never want little girls to grow up. They certainly do not ever want to think of them in bed with a man. Does that mean their little girls don't end up there just the same?" She set down her broom and brushed her heavy hair off her face. "Now listen to me, Pete, because this is important. I do not mean to be rushing you. When it is right for you—the time and the man—it will happen and it will be good. But you must not let what happened to your mother or your parents' marriage be standing in your way." She touched Pete's forehead. "This is *your* head." Then she touched her shoulder. "And your body. *You* decide what is right for them."

Pete let the words soak in like balm. "Thanks, Anna. I will."

"And when you do decide it's time, Pete . . ."

"Yes?"

Anna grinned. "Enjoy the hell out of it."

"My God," Pete said when Charlie let her into the loft. Her eyes scanned the cartons on the table. "I don't believe you actually remembered food."

"I get hungry, too, you know."

"I noticed." She started opening the white Chinese take-out cartons. "What've you got?"

"Noodles with sesame sauce, beef with broccoli, chicken with cashews and ginger, brown rice."

"A feast! What's this?" She started to pull the top off another carton.

"Hot and sour—" The lid flew off and about a quart of steaming soup geysered into the air toward Pete. ". . . soup," he finished lamely before he burst into laughter at the sight of her.

"Stop it. Stop laughing," she commanded, sputtering between her own laughter. "This is not funny."

"No," he choked out. "It's hilarious. You look like a drowned Chinaman."

The soup clung to her cotton plaid shirt, plastered her hair to her head, dribbled down onto her bluejeans. A lump of tofu perched on the end of her nose and a beansprout snaked down one cheek. "Are you hurt?" Charlie finally thought to ask. The soup had been hot.

"I don't think so. But I'd like to wash this off."

"Go take a shower," he said. "Toss out your clothes and I'll throw them in the washer. You can put on my bathrobe. It's hanging inside the bathroom door."

The hot water repaired the damage to her hair and body. She had to hope a washing machine would do the same for her clothes. She emerged from the shower with his red terry robe wrapped around her. One hand fluffed her hair with a towel; the other held the robe shut. It didn't seem to have a belt. He had taken off his t-shirt, which had also been soup-sprayed, and was cleaning up the mess from the table and floor.

"What do you use to hold this thing shut?" she asked.

"When I need to tie it, I use my tie."

"A necktie?"

"Well, I never wear it on my neck. I may as well use it for something. And it's red. It almost matches."

"Where is it?"

"I think I lost it." He stood up. He was looking at her oddly, in a way he'd never looked at her before.

"Well, get me something," she said with growing impatience. "I can't stand here clutching at it all day."

"Then let it go," he said, his voice a caress and a tease. He walked to where she stood, her head cocked, one hand frozen in midair where she'd been drying her hair. When he touched her other hand, the one that held the robe closed, her fingers loosened. The terrycloth slipped from her fingers. The robe gaped open.

She smelled of Ivory soap and herbal shampoo, and her

skin glowed shell pink from the rubbing of the coarse terry towel. Her hair hung damp and limp down her back and straggled around her face. Charlie thought he'd never seen anything so beautiful.

His skin glistened with a light sweat sheen. He smelled of linseed oil and lacquer and, just slightly, of hot-and-sour soup. There was Prussian blue paint under the crescents of his fingernails and flecks of gesso in his dark, unruly hair. Pete thought he had never looked more appealing.

Charlie sucked in his breath and let it out again in a slow whistle. Pete held hers.

This was it, she thought. She hadn't planned any of it. But she was ready to let it happen. It was time. She didn't know if she loved Charlie. But she did like him—oh, she liked him very much. And didn't Anna say the best lover was a man who was your friend? Charlie was just about the best friend Pete had ever had.

Yes, it was time and past. Was she not the granddaughter of La Colomba, perhaps the greatest courtesan Europe had ever known? She had inherited her grandmother's love of jewels. Wasn't it time to find out if she'd inherited anything else?

Charlie's dreamy, little-boy eyes were fastened to the foot-wide gap in the crimson robe with a grown-up boy's appetite. He hadn't touched her except for her hand, though he stood very close. She reached up, eased the robe back over her shoulders, and let it fall to the floor.

"Damn!" he exclaimed. It was not a curse but an accolade. He leaned back against the table and crossed his arms over his chest. "I always knew you were beautiful, but I gotta tell you, Pete, you make a man wish he was trying to be Botticelli instead of Andy Warhol."

She giggled but stopped right away. "Please don't make me laugh, Charlie. I don't think I can do this if you make me laugh."

"Shows what you know," he said and stood up. "Sweetheart, laughing is the best way there is." He wrapped his arms around her and murmured into her damp hair, "And I'm going to make you laugh until you think you're dying."

The touch of damp on damp skin was like a chilly current of power shooting through Pete. He kissed her, lightly at first, a flicking at the corners of her lips, then exploring further.

"Relax," he said against her mouth. "Relax your lips. You can't laugh properly unless you relax your lips." She let go of the tension there and found her mouth moving under his as if it were powered by its own battery. His hands slid down from her shoulders, down the center of her bare back, lightly tickling every knot of her spine, his thumbs brushing quickly along her ribs, his palms settling at her waist.

Tentatively, she drew a finger along his collarbone, letting it slip into the little hollow where his pulse beat. It jumped under her finger.

He took her by the hand and led her to the bed. "We are going to do this right," he said as he laid her on the madras-covered mattress. "For Pete, everything should always be right." She watched as he kicked off his moccasins, undid his buckle, slid his jeans down over skin that was whiter than she'd expected. She had never seen an erect penis. His was so beautiful, she wanted to make it into a jewel.

He lay down beside her. His hands were sure and friendly and comfortable, roaming slowly over her body as if they already knew the territory. But he murmured questions as they moved. "Are you ticklish here?" he asked, running a finger along the crease at the bottom of one breast. "Does that make you giggle?"

She wasn't able to answer. The sensations were too new, too powerful and even frightening to say anything.

"Here?" he murmured as his finger snaked up and circled the coffee-brown areola of a nipple. "Here?" The hand slid down across her stomach, caressing the damp crease where her leg met her hip, sliding toward the center, brushing lightly across the top of her curly hair. "Does that tickle? Are you starting to want to chuckle just a bit?" he whispered in her ear.

She made a sound. It wasn't a chuckle, but he seemed to like it just the same and rewarded her with a slight bite on one suddenly swollen nipple. The room was warm, so warm, she wondered the dampness on her body didn't turn to steam.

Her hands began to move across his skin as his were across hers. His back felt like velvet.

But when his hand split open the brush of pubic hair and slid inside the crease, an image pounded into Pete's mind—her mother with her hand under her skirt, plunging, plunging, screaming. She tensed, cried out, pulled away.

He stopped his hand and kissed her again, then breathed into her mouth, "It's okay, love. It's me, Charlie. I'll never hurt you."

It's Charlie, she repeated to herself. It's my friend. Friends make the best lovers. She let out her breath.

His hand started slowly moving again, flicking, teasing, caressing.

Charlies make the best lovers. The thought made her chuckle.

"That's my girl," he said, and slid the finger farther, up into her, while his thumb sought and found the source of endless mirth.

He began kissing her nipples while his hand kept working and she felt something—laughter?—building inside her. Building. Building. He stroked and kissed and in between kisses he urged her on.

"Laugh for me, Pete. Come on, love. I need your laugh."

She felt her knees pressing down, her pelvis arching up, wanting more of his laughing hand up inside her, more of his laughing mouth on her breasts. "Please," she begged, but she didn't know please what.

Then suddenly a great billow of joy burst from her, and she cried out, a gasping, roaring explosion of joy . . . and she was laughing, laughing.

"Yes!" Charlie cried. "Yes, Pete! Laugh for me all the way," and he kept her laughing a long, long time, bubbling it up and out of her in waves.

When she finally stopped and lay back panting and grinning up at him like an idiot, he grinned back just as stupidly. He reached into a drawer beside the bed and took a small foil packet. "For you, Pete, no chances," he said as he slid the condom over his rearing cock. "Not ever."

He raised himself over her, smiling down at her with the

sweetest expression she'd ever seen. She chuckled low in her throat.

"Yeah," he said. "That was just the teaser. Now we get to hear the punch line." Then he plunged into her and it started all over again.

Pete had never guessed life could feel so full, so complete. Her studying, her work, her family—complete with Anna now—her dearest friend Jess, and now a lover.

Papa had finally wholeheartedly accepted Pete's ambition to be the greatest jewelry designer the world had ever known. He took an interest in her classes and looked at whatever she was currently working on. And he told her about La Colomba—everything he could remember. He described every jewel he had seen at La Tana as well as he could remember it. And he described the atmosphere La Colomba created, the magic spell she seemed to weave all about her. It seemed tied up in Pete's mind with the magic of jewelry, and she thought somehow it might be the key she needed to someday find her own style.

"Now that you have decided what you wish to do," he said to Pete one day, "what is the next step? Where do you start?"

"Where else, Papa, but at the beginning?"

Chapter 10

At least the room was air-conditioned, thought Pete. Thank God for small favors. Or could you call air conditioning merely a small favor on a day like this in New York City? For the whole of this mid-July week the temperature had hovered between 95 and 99 degrees. Today was the eighth time in three weeks she'd been told to wait in the reception salon of Dufort & Ivères on the chance it might lead to the interview she sought. Pete looked on the bright side, however. Even if she was being made to sit for endless hours in the reception salon of Dufort & Ivères, at least it was better than being outside, or home. Here she was "cooling her heels" in more ways than one.

Pete glanced around the salon, a large room with huge mirrors and beige walls outlined in gold-leafed moldings. The mansion on Fifth Avenue occupied by the jewelry house had once been owned by a robber baron. In 1910, the eye of the owner's wife had happened to fall on a magnificent necklace of natural black pearls on display at the jeweler's, which then had only a street-level store farther downtown. She simply had to have those pearls, said the wife of the robber baron. Pierre Dufort had agreed to swap the necklace for the mansion.

A pleasant place to sit, Pete thought. But still the velvet upholstery of the elegant Louis XVI sofa beneath her, softly plush though it was, was starting to feel like concrete. She had chosen the straw-colored linen suit she was wearing because the way it hung made her look older than her twenty years, more serious somehow and—as she thought of it—more employable. But it was too heavy for the weather and by now it felt more like armor than cloth. She had read every one of the art and antique magazines on the inlaid fruitwood table three times.

The first time she had come she was told no jobs were available at the moment, did she have a résumé she could leave in case something came up? No? Sorry. She went home and wrote one.

On her next visit she got a raised eyebrow and a cool, "You have no portfolio, no work to show?" Sorry. She went home and spent the next week shooting full-color photos of her best pieces. She developed and printed them herself on the theory that if you wanted something done right you did it yourself. She mounted and matted them, and organized them in a beautiful wine red eelskin portfolio. It had cost the earth, but the portfolio had won her a chance to see a woman one step up from the first receptionist—the private secretary to a Private Secretary.

But there were still "no jobs available, Miss D'Angeli." The secretary pronounced it "Dan-*Jelly*."

After a glance at the name plaque on the woman's desk, Pete had pressed on. "Miss Harrison, don't you think that room should always be made for real talent? When a born jeweler comes along, a job should be found. Or created."

"And you're a born jeweler?" the woman said, making no effort to hide the sarcasm in her tone.

Pete simply nodded and stared her down.

But a stare was no match for Miss Harrison's authority, minor as it might be. Sorry again.

A week later, Pete asked to see Monsieur Ivères personally,

only to be told he was out of town, in Paris, not expected to return for a week or two. At least.

Each time she went home thinking of what she could say or do to get herself, finally and irrevocably, into the inner sanctum. She was sure if she could just see Claude Ivères, show him what she could do, she could make him hire her. She had to.

Not that there weren't opportunities elsewhere. Before coming here she had made the rounds of the other jewelry houses. Cartier, Winston, Van Cleef, Tiffany. There were possibilities. Nothing important, not to start. But as jobs were mentioned, even offered, and she found herself turning them down, she came to a realization. Her refusals of work were not a matter of being offered too meager a salary or being denied sufficient responsibility. In fact, Dufort & Ivères was the only place she wanted to work. It was simply a point of honor, of setting right some balance that had been disturbed years ago—on the day when Opa had been condemned for bravely taking a risk and simply having the bad luck to lose. Whatever other forces had worked to forge Pete's passion for jewelry and her talent and ambition, it was that one moment that had shown her what a profound effect gems could have on people's lives. That moment when the diamond shattered, humiliating her beloved grandfather, cracking her mother's fragile shell, breaking her family into pieces.

So she persisted. She'd be damned if she'd give up until she was finally interviewed for a job by none other than Claude Ivères himself. It was *necessary* that Ivères give her the chance. It would be the first step in setting right so many old wrongs. Though of course Pete had no intention of telling him who she was. Her last name should be enough to mask her connection to Josef Zeeman.

At the beginning of this week, she had finally won a small victory. The frosty and superior Miss Harrison, worn down by Pete's persistence, appeared near the end of the day and led her to the office of an assistant manager in the design department. He was impressed enough to take her down the hall to his boss.

"I will admit your work shows promise, Miss D'Angeli,"

the design manager said. "You have an original eye and a fresh vision. Come in again Friday morning. Mr. Ivères is expected in from Paris the day before. Perhaps we'll find a moment when he can look at your work."

Now here she sat. It was late afternoon, and she had not seen Claude Ivères pass by on his way in or out. It had been fourteen years since she had seen him, and she had been only six at the time, but she had no doubt that she would know his face when she saw it. Perhaps he had not returned from Paris, after all. Should she dare the insolence of asking if she had been brought here on a wild goose chase?

Pete was turning the pages of her portfolio, wondering what she might do to improve her designs, when a voice called her to attention. "Miss D'Angeli . . ."

She looked up to see a slim handsome young man standing in the doorway that led to the inner offices. He had pronounced her name perfectly, giving it the Continental twist.

"Will you come with me?" he said. The voice was deeply masculine and enhanced by a heavy French accent.

She had hoped he might be leading her to see Claude Ivères, but when he took her down the thickly carpeted corridor, he stopped to motion her through a door into a sunny room decorated more like a sitting room than an office. Before turning in, Pete noticed the end of the corridor, where there was a set of impressive double doors with a brass plaque engraved with the name Claude Ivères. So she had failed again, Pete thought. This young man was only another link in the Maginot Line of assistants, clerks, and managers whose role was to defend Claude Ivères from unwanted intruders. Well, if she had to get past him, too, she would. Meanwhile he was not hard to take. About twenty-five or twenty-six, she judged, tanned and smooth, dressed in a dark gray blazer perfectly cut to set off his well-formed body, and a way of moving—with a natural grace—that made her wonder what it would be like to dance with him.

"Please sit, Miss D'Angeli." He motioned her to a Queen Anne wing chair before a fireplace full of summer flowers and sat down opposite her.

"Thank you, Monsieur . . . ?"

"Why don't you just call me Marcel. I'm trying to get used to American informality. It is a bit difficult for us French."

He smiled and she smiled back. His teeth, she mused, were as perfectly lined up as pearls in a necklace. "Okay. Marcel. And you can call me Pietra." Somehow her true name seemed older than Pete.

"Pietra," he echoed. Again the perfect Continental pronunciation. "In Italian, I believe, that means stone."

"Yes. It was my grandmother's name." Too late she wondered if it was a mistake to mention anything personal.

"I can't say if it suited your grandmother," he said, a sparkle in his eyes, "but you certainly don't look like cold, gray stone to me."

It occurred to her to retort that the association of the name ought to be with gemstones, but to encourage any more flirting would certainly detract from her professional purpose.

A woman came in carrying a tray, and while she poured them both coffee in bone china cups, Marcel asked Pete to let him look through her portfolio. He took a minute after the woman left to continue turning the pages. As she sipped at the delicious coffee, Pete watched him over the rim of her cup. Several times she saw his eyebrows arch in a seeming show of approval.

At last he closed the portfolio and laid it aside. "How old are you, Pietra?" he asked.

"Twenty-two," she said without hesitation. She'd been rehearsing the lie for weeks so she could say it with a straight face. And really, how much difference could two little extra years make?

He sat back, his perfectly manicured hands tented beneath his chin. "I shall be honest with you, Pietra, because you are clearly very talented . . . as well as persistent. We have some of the greatest jewelry artisans in the world working for us—here, in Paris, in Milan—men with years of experience as well as talent. You are very young."

"So are you," she said, though she smiled so he wouldn't think her rude or impertinent.

"*Touché.*" He returned the smile. "But it is you we are

discussing. At our level, a great deal of judgment and expense are part of our jewelry designs—the purchase and selection of stones and precious metals, negotiating with traders, vying with dealers. We don't expect our designers to operate in an ivory tower. You must know all phases of the business, and it can get very demanding, more than a little . . . what is your American phrase? . . . rough and tumble. I think it would be difficult for you. As I said, you are very young."

Young and *female* is what you mean, she thought, but she bit down hard on her tongue so the words wouldn't come out. She was sure he was thinking that a woman couldn't be as tough as a man.

He went on. "So, for the foreseeable future, I can't see that you'd fit in here . . . unless you're willing to do something rather routine—a clerk, a salesgirl. That would be a shameful waste of your obvious talent. My advice would be to go to a smaller firm—one of the wholesale houses would be best."

Pete hesitated before speaking. She wasn't sure whether this young man Marcel was offering "advice" as a favor or exercising his authority to tell her she wasn't wanted or needed. She still refused to be dismissed by anyone but Ivères.

"If you think I'm good, why can't *you* give me a chance. Let me show my things to—"

"You need experience, Pietra, and I'm advising you to make it useful experience. Then, perhaps in seven or eight years, you can—"

"Seven years? I don't have that much time!"

"No, of course you do not. I understand that. You are a beautiful young woman. In seven years you will have moved on to other things. Marriage, children . . ."

"No, Marcel. You understand nothing." She carefully put down the delicate coffee cup, afraid her intensity might shatter it. "My passion for this business is not going to be pushed aside. It is my life. I'd start in *any* position you could offer . . . because I know I'll advance quickly. But I need to make a start. And I need to work *here*."

"Need?"

"It's just . . . well, something personal," she said, trying to brush off the intensity with which she had just spoken. "Please, Marcel. If you think I'm good, don't lock me out yet. Let me show my work to Monsieur Ivères. Let him decide."

"Let *him*?" He pulled up, startled.

Oh God, Pete thought, now I've blown it. Underlings on their way up do not like having their authority undercut, and she'd just asked this one if she could go over his head straight to the top man.

But after a moment, his attitude relaxed. He even gave her a slight but pleasant smile. "Let me think about it," he said. "Leave your portfolio with me. Is there a number where I can reach you, Pietra?"

"Oh thank you, Marcel, thank you so much." She scribbled her number on the paper he handed her and thrust it back at him and rose to go.

At the door she turned and flashed him a smile that dazzled like a hundred carats. "And Marcel . . . I'm not a stone. So call me Pete."

An agonized two weeks dragged by. One moment Pete was sure Marcel would get her an appointment with Claude Ivères. He had liked her, she was sure. He thought her attractive, had even called her beautiful. He was on her side.

But when another day passed without a call, her hopes plummeted. Polite he might be on the surface, but he must have thought her silly and young and naive. He'd never pass her name on to Ivères. It might even be as much as his job was worth.

As she mooned around the house, her grandfather noticed that she was distracted and asked once or twice if she wasn't feeling well. She did her best to reassure him without confiding her concern. God forbid he should learn that she was longing to meet Claude Ivères.

The only one she dared to talk to about it was her mother. On her Saturday visits, she gave a full account of her efforts and of the meeting with a young Frenchman named Marcel. But her mother had nothing to say in return. She never did.

By the time the phone call came, Pete was in such a state

she was sure she'd heard wrong when he gave his name, and doubly sure when he asked if she was available to have dinner with Monsieur Ivères that very evening.

"Dinner? Marcel, it's a job I want. What has dinner got to do with it?" She was on the point of saying it didn't seem proper, but she feared an alternative might not be offered.

"*Bien sûr*, Mademoiselle Pete," his voice came back, "it is a job at issue. But Monsieur Ivères is a man who enjoys discussing such things in relaxed surroundings, away from the distractions of the office, the ringing telephone. He knows that where jewelry is concerned doing things hastily can lead to expensive mistakes."

Expensive mistakes, she thought. Like a badly judged diamond. Even after studying a stone for nine months, her grandfather had made an expensive and irreparable mistake.

"Has Monsieur Ivères seen my portfolio?"

"*Mais oui*. He was very impressed."

"Very well. Please tell him I accept the invitation. To discuss business," she added quickly.

She heard a brief good-natured chuckle at the other end of the line. "*Très bon*. Can you be at La Grenouille at eight?"

Oh God, she thought. She had read about the restaurant in *Vogue*—"the Frog Pond" the insiders called it, and Jackie O and Henry Kissinger and everyone else of any importance was always there. What on earth did she have to wear to one of the most expensive, most fashionable restaurants in New York?

"Of course," she replied, hoping the panic didn't come through. "Eight o'clock will be perfectly fine."

She spent the afternoon frantically altering an old evening gown of her mother's—a float of sapphire silk from the days when money had not been so stubbornly elusive in their lives—before Opa shattered the diamond. By removing several layers of stitched-in petticoat, lowering the neckline, and chopping several inches off the bottom of the full-cut skirt and turning them into a sash, she was able to make a gown that was the height of fashion in 1953 look fresh and very today. She thought its clean lines made her look almost the twenty-two she had claimed to be.

"And where is it you are going that you need to steal your mother's evening dress?" Josef asked as she sat carefully making up her face.

"To La Grenouille. It's about a job, Opa," was all she would say.

"A job? Who takes a beautiful woman to a fancy restaurant to give her a job?" His voice rang with suspicion. He did not like his sensible girl acting in ways he didn't understand. And he wasn't at all sure he liked her looking so beautiful or so excited. The blue gown set off her sapphire eyes until they glowed with deep fire. Her hair shone. Her cheeks gleamed with high color.

The look of worry on his face caught Pete's eye as she was picking up her mother's old silver evening compact to sail out the door. She stopped in front of him. "Do you trust me, Opa?" she asked.

He looked deeply into her eyes. "My trust for you and my love," he said, "are the only great jewels I shall ever own."

"Then don't worry." She kissed him lightly on the tip of his nose and sailed out the door.

Yes, yes, he thought after she'd gone, he trusted her completely.

But she was so beautiful—more even than Bettina. So he worried all the same.

It was precisely eight when Pete climbed out of a cab in front of La Grenouille. She'd had the driver circle the block three times to keep from being early. Still, when she was shown to a table, Claude Ivères had not yet arrived. She settled onto the lipstick-red velvet banquette and looked around the room.

She'd heard that La Grenouille was one of the prettiest dining rooms in New York, and now she knew the reports were true. Pale green walls were hung with glinting mirrors and floral paintings in gilded frames. The lighting was soft, a warm ivory glow from sconces on the walls. And the flowers! Pete leaned forward to draw in the heady fragrance of the perfectly chosen blossoms arranged in a snifter on the table. In the corners of the room, extravagant bouquets spilled over pedestals. It was like being in a bower.

The table was set for two with beautiful china and what seemed like a dozen crystal goblets of varying sizes. And, most intriguing of all, sitting at her place was a small package, exquisitely wrapped in shiny black paper with purple and silver ribbons, the Dufort & Ivères' colors. The package alarmed her slightly, reminding her that the dinner had seemed irregular in the first place as a way to discuss a job. Was Claude Ivères going to ply her with food and diamonds and then . . . ? She pushed the package aside at the same time she tried to push the ugly thoughts out of her mind. And yet . . . what kind of man was Claude Ivères?

Perhaps she ought to leave now . . .

A waiter came to the table. "Can I get Madame a drink?" The question thrilled her, since it meant the waiter believed she was over twenty-one. That was worth savoring for a while. She gave up thoughts of leaving and ordered a Kir Royale.

She was sipping it thoughtfully, enjoying the mix of the sweet cassis with the soft bite of champagne, when the table was pulled back by the maître d'hôtel. Pete looked up to see . . . Marcel! He was more handsome than she remembered, and for an instant she was pleased. For *just* an instant. Then the fury swept in. He had tricked her! Played on her hopes and ambitions to lure her out to dinner. But why? Didn't he know she would have accepted a date with him anyway?

"*Bon soir*, Mademoiselle Pete," he said as he took his chair opposite her. He turned to the maître d'. "*C'est parfait, le table. Merci, Henri*," he said and discreetly slid the man a bank note.

"*Merci mille fois*, Monsieur Ivères." Henri walked away.

"Monsieur Ivères?" said Pete. "But you said—"

"Marcel Ivères, at your service," he said with a nod. "I'm sorry, Pete, but you know in your eagerness you never really gave me a chance to explain. Claude Ivères is my father. He spends all his time at our Paris headquarters now. When we met, he had just sent me to take over the management of the New York branch."

"You could have told me instead of letting me make a fool of myself," she said indignantly.

"I was afraid to," he admitted. "Afraid you would be so angry at me for not giving you a job that you would, in turn, deny me what I wanted most."

"Which was?"

"To see you again."

"Then why did it take you two weeks to call me?" She surprised herself with the bluntness of the question, but she was angry. She did not like being manipulated.

"I was called back to Paris right after I saw you. My father wanted a report on my first impressions of the business. He's a demanding man. I just got back this morning."

"Did you have so many first impressions to report?" Not sure whether or not to believe him, she gave the question a tart edge.

He hesitated and leaned closer across the table. "Only one that mattered," he said. "And that one I didn't even mention to him."

His eyes held hers for a moment, until she felt the heat rise in her cheeks and she looked down.

"I called you as soon as I got in from the airport," he said.

She raised her eyes again. Be careful, she told herself as she studied him. He was so much more worldly . . . and a Frenchman. Did she dare to believe a word he said? He was devil-handsome in his flawlessly tailored black silk suit, his shirt almost painfully white and a sky blue shantung tie setting off to perfection. He had dark hair, wavy, and eyes like bittersweet chocolate.

"Well, I'm here," she said finally. "But my interest is still in getting a job with Dufort and Ivères. And you told me this would be a business dinner. If you still plan to refuse—"

"*Certainement, non.* I have given much thought to your application while I was away. Though my first impression was that you were too young for anything more than clerical work—and far too beautiful not be snatched away into marriage by some rich man who passes through our store—it has now occurred to me that I may have been too harsh. As you rightly pointed out, I am young myself. So I came to a decision. You should be given a chance.''

A smile started to break across her face. A chance was all she wanted. But then he went on:

"I have a test for you, Pete."

"A test?"

"This is the chance. To see if you have the necessary skills to work for me. Open the box."

Puzzled, she reached for the beautiful package she had pushed aside earlier and forgotten until Marcel pointed at it. Tearing away the wrapping, she found a velvet pouch inside. After another suspicious glance at Marcel, she undid the silk drawstring to open the pouch and turned it over onto the table. Eight diamonds tumbled out onto the snowy linen tablecloth. At first glance, she judged they were about four or five carats each. As they rolled onto the cloth, a waiter who was about to set a glass of water at her place froze, staring at the icelike stones.

"Well, well, put the water down and go," Marcel said impatiently to the gaping waiter. "And ask Henri to hold the rest of the meal until I tell him otherwise."

"*Oui, Monsieur.*"

"This is your test, Pete," he said when they were alone again. "If you pass, I will give you a starting position at Dufort and Ivères. If not . . ." He gave an irrepressibly Gallic shrug. "But win or lose, you must agree to stay and dine with me after the test is finished. With no hard feelings."

"Feelings are not like jewels, Marcel. They can't be cut to shape. All I can say is if you're fair with me, I'll be fair with you. And I will dine with you." After a moment, she smiled. "And I will probably enjoy it, because I believe I can pass the test."

"Even before you know what it is?"

"If it is about diamonds, I don't believe I'll fail. And if I do, you are probably right. I'm not ready . . . yet."

"Very well."

He set her plate aside and swept the diamonds together in the center of her place. "Among the stones in front of you now there is one—just one—of River quality, a perfect blue-white, completely flawless. In fact, this stone was actually taken from the waters of Golconda a few hundred years ago. We acquired it last year from one of those maharajahs in need of money. The other stones on the table are good—very good—but not from the Golconda, not nearly the same quality.'' He sat back and crossed his arms. ''Show me the River gem and the job is yours.''

Pulling a 10× loupe from his pocket, he handed it to her, then signaled to a waiter who immediately set up a tiny Diamondlite, perfectly calibrated to duplicate northern light. With fierce, single-minded concentration, Pete began to examine the stones.

As Pete held stone after stone up to her eye, peering at it in the pure white light, other customers in the restaurant began casting curious glances toward their table. But neither Pete nor Marcel was aware of them. He kept his eyes on her, and for her there was nothing but the diamonds.

Oh, Opa, help me, she prayed silently. If ever you taught me anything, let me remember it now. All the hours spent testing me with the master stones, all the days explaining the different types of inclusions. Don't fail me now, Opa.

They were fine stones, every one. He was certainly right about that. First quality. But . . . Wasn't there the slightest breath of yellow in this one, the tiniest feather·inclusion in that one, hiding just under the crown? On another, a faceting pattern was just a touch too modern for such an old stone. She went through every stone, and nothing struck the chord of incomparable brilliance.

''You give me your word it's here?'' she asked Marcel.

''My solemn oath. The River stone is there before your eyes.''

She bent back to her concentrated study. The waiter came back and was waved off. The sommelier was waved off. Henri was waved off. Pete kept studying the diamonds, one after another. For nearly an hour.

Finally she was certain—well, ninety-nine percent certain. None of the eight stones was River quality.

She took out the loupe and looked Marcel straight in the

eyes. Could he have lied to her? Was it all just a cruel trick to avoid giving her a job?

Or was Marcel himself perhaps the victim of a deception? Perhaps someone had peddled *him* a lesser stone he'd failed to spot? Or maybe she'd gotten caught in the middle, in a test Marcel's demanding father was giving his son?

Yet as she looked into his eyes, she saw the quality of the man as surely as looking into a diamond revealed its value. He was not a liar. She felt sure of it. Nor was he stupid. He had been raised with diamonds, just as she had.

And what had he said? The River was right in front of her. Her eyes shifted to look back to the table. At everything in front of her eyes.

And suddenly, as if someone had flipped on another Diamondlite, comprehension switched on in her brain. She could barely repress a smile as she thought of the little theatrical scene he had staged with the waiter just as the test was about to begin. Grabbing a large soup spoon, she scooped the eight diamonds into it and reached across to the glass of water Marcel was about to sip from.

"That water looks a little warm," she said, as she ladled the diamonds into his glass. "I think it needs some ice." She picked up her own water glass. "And what would you say if I drink this down?"

He was speechless for a moment. "I'd say you'd have a very bad case of indigestion."

She laughed as she set the glass back down, then dipped her fingers into the water and fished out the Golconda diamond.

The admiration in his face was as clear as the depths of the brilliant jewel on the table. "But how? I . . . I thought you would be stumped."

"I was . . . until I found the key to your test."

"What key?"

"Ah," she cooed, "that's *my* secret. But let's move on to the rest of our deal. I'm starving. Do they have any food in this joint?"

His smile was one of a man enchanted. "I think they could probably . . . what is the word? . . . rustle up something."

"We will have you talking like a real American in no time. Maybe even like a New Yawker."

He shook his head in amazement once more, then raised his hand to summon Henri.

The meal was superb. Over hors d'oeuvres of perfectly fresh, perfectly velvety foie gras, celeriac rémoulade, and tender asparagus as thin as a swizzle stick, Marcel asked Pete questions about herself, her upbringing, the source of her interest in jewelry. Deftly, she diverted them with no answers given, saying she was eager to learn more about him. Soon she had Marcel talking about himself, about growing up in France as the scion of a wealthy family.

"We are not *nouveau riche*," he said, "but neither are we *ancien*. We do have a very nice small château in the Loire Valley. And of course a *hôtel* in Paris."

"Of course," she said, trying to sound unimpressed.

For a main course, Marcel recommended the herbed, garlicky frogs' legs. "You cannot come to a place called *grenouille* and not eat one," he said to convince her, but she opted for the Dover sole in a sharp mustard sauce and a change in the conversation.

"Do you like New York?"

"More and more," he said, his eyes as warm as melted chocolate as he looked at her. "Now, Pete, you must tell me: How does it happen that you know so much about diamonds?"

So he was not going to be satisfied without an answer. But she couldn't tell him the truth—that her grandfather had once been a cutter for his father and had been blackballed for a mistake that any good cutter might have made. "My grandmother collected gems," she said. "I suppose I inherited her passion for them. I've been studying them since I was a child."

"Self-taught?"

"I've had some help now and then."

He paused as though he might want more details, but then he nodded and gestured to the waiter for a dessert menu.

After Pete had enjoyed a remarkably fragile Grand Marnier soufflé and Marcel had worked his way through a Mont Blanc of crunchy ground chestnuts topped with whipped cream, he called for the bill.

"Do you like to dance, Pete?" he asked. "Perhaps we could go from here to—"

She broke in. "No thank you, Marcel. This was a business dinner, remember. And our business is concluded." She remembered wondering what it would be like to dance with him. And yet, if she spent too long in his company, how could she keep evading his questions?

"As you wish," he said. "But I'll see you home."

No, she was not about to have this dashing young Frenchman drive her to the door of a shabby walk-up apartment in Hell's Kitchen, even if he was only château rich. For other reasons, too, it was better he didn't know where she lived, which could lead to making other connections. In any case, it wouldn't hurt at all to be kept wondering about her. An air of mystery never did a woman any harm. That was one of the few true lessons her mother had taught her.

As though deflated by her lack of interest in extending the evening, Marcel paid the bill in silence, then escorted her out to the sidewalk.

"Good-night, Marcel," she said. "I enjoyed it all, the meal . . . and my test. Thank you. I'll make you glad that I got the job, too."

He gave a slight gentlemanly bow. "I'm glad now."

One in a line of waiting taxis pulled up to the door, and Pete moved toward it.

"Just a moment," he said abruptly, and grabbed her arm. For a moment, she thought he was going to kiss her. "I must know—the key to solving my puzzle, what was it?"

"It was very simple, really. All I had to do was trust you completely. You said the stone was in front of me, before my eyes. Once I believed that you wouldn't lie to me, I knew I simply had to look more carefully. When I thought of how elaborately you had had the table prearranged and I remembered that little moment with the waiter who brought the water, it was obvious."

"It was that simple—you trusted me?"

"That made the *looking* simple," she said as he opened

the cab door and she climbed in. Peering up at him from the seat, she added, "Trusting you was the hard part."

He closed the door for her and the cab pulled away.

Marcel stood and watched the taillights disappear up the street until they were lost in the stream of traffic. It was all he could do to stop himself from jumping in the next taxi and shouting to the driver, "Follow that cab," like Cary Grant in some Alfred Hitchcock film. She was lovely, perfectly lovely, this girl with hair that shone like darkest obsidian and eyes like the finest sapphires his father had ever sold.

But he was, after all, a Frenchman, with the proper image of aristocratic aloofness to uphold. Returning to the restaurant, he stepped into a phone booth and began to dial one of the many models who regularly warmed his bed.

Before the connection had been made, however, he hung up the receiver. Tonight he didn't want to be with another woman. He was as happy—happier—to be with merely the memory of a woman.

Chapter 11

The interior of the sleek Rolls-Royce hummed like a softly purring cat. The view of Geneva's Lac Léman outside the window was soothing. But Marcel Ivères was confused.

"I still do not understand why we are going to see this man, Père. You know the sort of businessman he is. I have heard you say often enough that he is not our kind."

Claude Ivères sat back on the deeply cushioned navy leather seat. "Because I wish to hear what he has to say. He says he has a proposition for us."

"Does it involve the New York store? If not, I don't see why I had to fly all the way to Geneva to meet with someone who can be of no use to me."

It had been only a few weeks since Marcel had taken over the management of the Dufort & Ivères' New York store, and he was still uneasy with the job. He couldn't help but wonder why the decision to give him that store had been now—and so suddenly. One day he had been skiing in Chamonix; the next his father was telling him to get on a plane to New York because he was taking over.

And now, just as suddenly, he had been summoned to Geneva.

"Père—"

"Marcel," said his father, "if you are to succeed in this sometimes strange business of ours, you must learn patience. Things are not always what they seem, my son. For now, your job is merely to sit and listen and wait until you are told what is true and what is not."

God, how he hated it when his father talked in riddles. And he'd been doing a lot of that lately, too. And acting in riddles as well.

He didn't want to think about it now. What he really wanted to think about was Pete D'Angeli, the young woman he'd recently hired for the New York store. He didn't know how long she'd stay, but he hoped she wouldn't leave anytime soon. He was intrigued by this beautiful American girl with the boyish name who seemed to know at least as much about diamonds as he did himself. He wanted to get to know her better—much better.

He would call her as soon as he got back to New York. Perhaps another dinner . . . maybe Lutèce this time.

The Rolls swung into the rue du Rhone, the glossiest shopping street in Geneva, and pulled up before the newest and glossiest store in the street—Tesori, it said in gold letters scrolled over the door. As the two men emerged, Marcel looked at his father with fond exasperation. He saw a man impeccably tailored, barbered, and manicured. An aura of prosperity and confidence hung about him like a cloud.

The heavy-handed opulence of Tesori was in total contrast to the understated elegance of the Dufort & Ivères stores. Instead of a few very fine pieces displayed against black velvet, with others brought out for viewing on request, jewels seemed to be piled and hung and displayed everywhere—diamonds hanging from bare miniature branches, rubies sitting in a crystal bowl, pearls coiled into snakes and slithering across counters.

Jewelry as theater, thought Marcel with a snicker.

They were met at the door of the store by the owner himself, Antonio Scappa, an Italian-speaking Swiss in a well-cut, pearl gray suit that minimized his bulk and maximized his air of authority.

"Welcome, gentlemen!" He greeted them with hearty handshakes. "Welcome to Tesori. I am eager to show you what we have created here. I believe you will be impressed."

"That is why we have come, Signor Scappa," said Claude Ivères with dignity.

Scappa was rightfully proud of what he had created. Brass and gold-veined marble, plush red carpets and mirrors set off the gold, pearls, diamonds, and other treasures so lavishly displayed. Hundreds of people were busily at work creating and selling the jewelry that was making Signor Scappa into a rich man. The store was big, showy and, above all, successful. And who can argue with that, Marcel wondered.

They were shown over the entire store—salerooms and workrooms, design studios and private salons. It was as they were coming out of the design studio that a young woman approached them —a tall, ripe-figured blonde in a dramatic red jersey dress.

Mon dieu, thought Marcel, taking in the entirety of her. She was luscious, he thought. There was no other word for it. Thick cascades of honey blond hair, tawny cat's eyes under dark fly away brows, a body Sophia Loren might envy. The dress, the hair, and especially the lawless glint in the amber catlike eyes hit him like a punch to the gut.

"Ah, Andrea," said Antonio Scappa as she approached. "Gentlemen, may I present my daughter, Andrea Scappa."

"*Enchanté, Mademoiselle*," said each of the men in turn, but Claude's was ripe with his usual dignity and grace, while Marcel's twinkled like a naughty boy ripe for trouble. "*Très enchanté*," he repeated and kissed her hand.

The look she returned him was at least as naughty as his own, but there was something more than mere flirtation behind it. She wanted something from him—whether his charming, sexy self or some other, more useful self he was not yet sure. Intriguing. He would find out exactly what she wanted. As for himself, he knew perfectly well what he wanted from her. He wanted to pick her like a ripe peach, bite into her, and let the juice run down his chin.

"Andrea," said Scappa, "bring us coffee in my office, please."

"Of course, Papa," she said and glided off, her beautifully rounded bottom swaying deliciously in its case of red jersey.

In Scappa's mirror-walled office, they were seated in an oversized burgundy Chesterfield sofa.

Scappa sat back, arms on the chair arms, feet squarely on the floor, and surveyed his guests. A satisfied, almost smug smile lifted his fleshy lips. "Well, gentlemen. As you can see, Tesori has become a force to be reckoned with in the jewelry world."

"Unquestionably," said Claude.

"Of course, we are not yet in the same family as Dufort and Ivères."

"That is also true," said Claude.

Scappa frowned, but before he could comment, Andrea entered with a heavy silver coffee service on a tray.

With a smile as enticing as the rest of her, she poured the coffee, then moved to one of the wing chairs opposite the sofa. But she did not sit. She turned to her father, and Marcel thought the look on her face was almost one of pleading.

Antonio frowned at her, looked at Claude Ivères, then looked at Marcel. Embarrassed to be staring at the man's daughter like a dog with its tongue hanging out, Marcel made a show of drinking some of the coffee, burning his tongue for his troubles.

"Father . . . ?"

"Please stay, Andrea," he said, his eyes never leaving Marcel. "Perhaps you will have something to add to our discussion." His tone sounded more like a warning than an invitation to Marcel, a cleverly cloaked way of telling her to shut up and look beautiful. And she looked astonished at being given permission to remain. There was something about their relationship—how did New Yorkers put it?—something "not quite kosher." As though they were rivals rather than father and daughter.

"Gentlemen," Scappa began, "the time has come for Tesori to expand beyond our present Swiss and German bases, to reach out to some of that lovely money out there just waiting to be spent on self-adornment. That is why I wish to buy Dufort and Ivères."

Marcel was so stunned he momentarily forgot Andrea Scappa was in the room. Surely his father was not—would never—consider selling the business, and particularly not to a man with Scappa's obvious lack of taste and gentility.

But Claude had made no acknowledgment of the explosive statement and Scappa went on as if the whole discussion were a mere formality. "Frankly, gentlemen, I need what you have. I need your prime outlets in Rome, New York, and Paris, and the patina of old established quality that attaches to your name. And you, gentlemen, need to sell."

"What makes you think—" Marcel began, but his father stopped him with a hand and a look.

Scappa went on. "We all know how difficult it is to keep a secret in this business. Impossible, I should say. Rumors, whispers, they circulate like fire in a drought-stricken forest. Regrettably, the usual high standards of the entire string of Dufort and Ivères stores have slipped. Very little, of course, but enough to be worrisome for you, I am sure. Your sales are down. In our business, where expensive inventories must be maintained, that is a serious problem."

"We have had difficult periods in the past," said Claude, "but we have always weathered them."

"And very well, too. You have made money when many other companies did not. But now there are other worrisome signs as well. You have given your son full responsibility for your lucrative New York operation, even though at twenty-six he is as yet relatively inexperienced."

Andrea spoke for the first time, her voice low and husky, as though she had just crawled out of bed, thought Marcel. "Father, I am sure Monsieur Marcel was asked to manage the New York store because of his abilities, which I am certain are remarkable, whatever his age." She was speaking to her father, but she looked straight at Marcel, and her eyes said much more than her lips.

"Undoubtedly," said Scappa, frowning at his daughter as though surprised that she had dared to open her mouth.

"I understand, Monsieur," Scappa said, seeming to change tack, "that this is not your first visit to Switzerland this year. I am told you recently took advantage of the excellent facilities of the Gervais Clinic in Davos. They are known for their unique approaches to treating cancers considered impossible, are they not?'' Claude did not answer. He merely tilted his head and continued to listen.

"Father, what is he—?" Marcel said, but again his father stopped him with a stern look and a softly spoken, "*Silence, mon fils.*"

"Then, too," Scappa continued, "there is the evidence of one's own eyes. Many in this business have attributed the great success of Dufort and Ivères to your active, personal management, Monsieur, requiring you to move about constantly among your stores. But lately it has been noticed that you travel very little. In short, Monsieur, it is generally understood that you are ill, that you are grooming your son to take your place, and that you may not have time to complete the task. It would seem that the time is right for you to make a decision that would be to our mutual benefit."

Marcel stood up and leaned over the enormous glossy black desk where Scappa sat. "What the devil makes you think my father is ill? Or that we would entertain such an offer from you?"

"Marcel!" exclaimed Claude.

Scappa was unperturbed by the outbursts. He merely leaned forward in his chair, the picture of confidence touched with ambition. "For sole ownership of Dufort and Ivères, I am prepared to offer . . ." He named a price in the millions, many millions. It was a substantial fortune by any man's reckoning, and Marcel gasped at the amount. He turned to look at Andrea and saw her amber eyes glittering brightly. Was it triumph? Anger? Perhaps a warning? "I am also willing, eager even, to have your son remain in charge of the New York branch. I have never been to America and have no desire whatever to go. I do not understand Americans. Also, it would be wise if an Ivères is seen to be still actively involved in the business. You must admit, Monsieur, it is a very fair offer."

Finally it was Claude Ivères' turn to speak. He walked to the window and gazed out a moment at the lovely view of Lac Léman. The *brume matinale*, the misty morning fog that so often enveloped Geneva, had burned off, and the lake sparkled in the afternoon sun. "You are correct, Signor Scappa," he said with calm dignity. "I am dying."

"Father, no!" Marcel exclaimed. Claude turned and faced his son, and against the brilliant screen of sky and water, he looked suddenly gaunt.

"I am sorry to have you learn like this, Marcel, but it is true. I have a rare form of blood cancer. My doctors tell me it is always fatal." He turned to Scappa. "It is also true that my company has felt the effects of my illness and that sales have been adversely affected. I have been racing the calendar to groom my eldest son to take over when I am gone. I deny none of that, and I came here today because I felt I could not simply ignore a serious offer."

"Excellent," Scappa said and started to rise.

"However," Claude continued, "having seen your operation here, I cannot think Tesori a good match for Dufort and Ivères."

"Not a good match? But—"

"Our styles, Signore, our very reasons for being in this business, are markedly different. Your style obviously works for you, as you have so kindly shown us today. I do not believe it is right for us. I am afraid we must decline your generous offer." He moved stiffly to his son's side and extended his hand to Scappa. "We are sorry to have taken your time, Signore. Mademoiselle," he added, sketching a slight bow in Andrea's direction. The glitter had faded from her eyes, replaced by something that might have been disappointment or might have been sadness and sympathy. Marcel did not know which, and at the moment he was too stunned to try to decide.

"You are making a mistake, Monsieur," said Scappa. "Tesori will continue to grow, with or without you. If you refuse to join us, you will eventually be buried by us."

"Perhaps," Claude acknowledged. "It is a chance we must take. Good day." Then he led Marcel from the room.

A half hour later, both Ivèreses sat in the sunshine on the lakeside terrace of the Perle du Lac, picking listlessly at a lunch of *fondue savoyarde*, fresh lake perch, and Alpine berries washed down with Fendant, the crisp dry white wine from the Valais region, without really tasting any of it. Sunlight glistened on the distant snow-capped peaks of Mont Blanc and the Aiguille du Midi while the Jet d'Eau shot diamonds of water four hundred feet into the air from the otherwise calm surface of the lake.

For a while they avoided speaking of the one thing that crowded both their minds. The sore was too raw to touch just yet.

Finally, when the *ristretto* coffee was served, Marcel looked at his father. "You should have told me," he said, stirring his spoon around and around and around in his cup.

"Probably," his father agreed.

"How . . . how long?" His voice caught on the words.

"A year, they say. Perhaps a bit less."

"*Mon dieu.*" A shiver went through Marcel. Though he'd always been intimidated by his all-powerful father, he loved him even more. Grief and anger welled up together inside him like the pressurized water just before it shot from the Jet d'Eau. "All this time, you let me believe I was given the management of New York purely because you had faith in my abilities."

"As I do."

"But it wouldn't have happened so soon if you were not ill. Would it?"

"Perhaps not. But I did turn down Scappa's offer. Would I have done so if I did not believe you would be capable of taking over when the time came? Was I too hasty in that decision?"

Marcel stared out over the steel blue waters of the lake. He watched a heron take off, wide wings flapping awkwardly until it was airborne and gliding like a cloud. "I don't know!" he cried. He'd been so pleased to be sent to New York, so exhilarated by the challenge, proud of his father's confidence in his abilities. But he had to admit he often felt frustrated by his own lack of experience and overwhelmed by the responsibility of his job. He often wished he had more time just to play, to experiment with life, to enjoy being handsome and rich and only twenty-six.

His father's voice cut into his thoughts like a fresh-honed knife. "Can you do it, my son? Can you take over for me entirely in less than a year? I regret having to push you for a decision, but if you do not want the responsibility, if you think it will be too much for you, you *must* tell me now. We must begin at once to look elsewhere for an offer as good as Scappa's."

"Why bother?" Marcel asked. "Why not simply take his?"

Claude shook his head. "The miracle of gems—the secret of their appeal to us destructible mortals—is that these seemingly hard, everlasting substances are also mysteriously endowed with life, pulsing at the heart with fire and color. This man Scappa, he is just the opposite. Whatever life he seems to have on the surface, at heart he is cold, a lifeless stone. I could not bear to see such a man take over what I have worked so long to build."

"But, Father, Scappa is a legend in this business. No one has been so successful so quickly. He's probably right to hint that Tesori will bury us all. Look how far he's come in only twenty-two years."

"Not far enough to deserve Dufort and Ivères."

The customers were all gone, the huge steel gates had been locked over the main entrance of Tesori. Antonio Scappa sat at his oversized black desk doodling figures on a pad, his back turned to the huge window and the magnificent view of the lake darkening to the color of slate as night came on.

He was angry. He had been counting on Ivères jumping at his offer. He had spent a lot of time and money looking for and finding the one weak spot he was sure he could exploit to force the man to accept his terms.

Tesori needed an alliance with an old-line, established firm like Dufort & Ivères. Scappa had done extremely well since opening his business. Using the energy of Europe's postwar recovery, he had been able to build it up by being aggressive and innovative, by using wholesale methods and modern selling techniques, by buying old collections in places where the once wealthy elite were now in need of ready cash—places like India, where he'd bought dozens of treasures from maharajahs stripped of their vast estates. Sometimes he sold the pieces as is, sometimes he recut them for even greater profit.

But it was not enough, not when there was so much new money in the world, big money, and there would be even more in the next decade. He could feel it. Antonio Scappa wanted his share of it.

After today's meeting he knew there was no chance of doing it with Dufort & Ivères. He knew men well enough to read the absolute finality of Claude Ivères' refusal. Damn the man, he thought, pushing down on the paper until the point of his pencil snapped.

Andrea Scappa walked into her father's office.

"Well?" she asked. "What happens now?"

His answer was brusque. "Nothing happens now. I cannot force them to sell."

"No, I don't suppose you can. I'm sorry." He couldn't know how true that statement was. Although it was her looks that people noticed and remembered about Andrea Scappa, she was also intelligent and ambitious, with a good business head and an innate talent for the jewelry trade. She knew she could be a real help in her father's business if only he would give her the chance. The trouble was, he saw no place for her in it. When he did occasionally let her work for him, it was as a purely decorative social lure, blatantly using her as he had done today, telling her in advance to wear the red dress, reminding her how helpful it would be if Marcel Ivères were enchanted by her. It was the one area in which he freely acknowledged her talent.

But he had never once given Andrea anything to do that tested her intelligence or abilities in the slightest.

When she complained, his answer was always the same. "You want to help me, marry one of the wealthy men who come in here making eyes at you. Then you can become one of my best customers, and I'll have a banker handy when I need a loan for expansion."

Worse still, he actively encouraged her brother Franco to take more of an interest in the business, prompting him to take on the jobs Andrea begged for and was denied. And

Franco, God love his irresistible soul, could hardly have cared less. At twenty-one, he wanted nothing more than to become an international playboy and champion polo player.

Now she leaned over his shining desk, her eyes shining just as brightly. "You don't need them, Papa. Together we could build Tesori into the most successful jewelry chain in the world. Why won't you let me help you, Papa? I could do it. I—"

"Enough, Andrea," he cut her short. "Business is not a place for women, not even you. It is not your role. When the time comes for someone to take over from me, Franco will be ready. I will see to that. Now why don't you take that extremely attractive dress you are wearing someplace where it will do us some good. It is wasted here."

She grew rigid with anger. "One day, Father," she said, her voice trembling with suppressed rage, "I might take *all* my pretty dresses, plus my formidable charm and intelligence and talent, and put them to use in my own business just to prove to you I can do it. I'll give you such a run for your money, you'll kick yourself from here to Paris for not having used me yourself."

She had hoped that in buying Dufort & Ivères, Tesori would expand so fast that her father would have to use her. Now that was not to be.

But perhaps there was another way. . . .

Marcel was asleep, dreaming a convoluted dream of Pete D'Angeli as Lady Godiva on a white horse covered with diamonds riding past a cliff from which his father had just jumped. Marcel tried to catch him, but he was knocked aside instead, landing under the hooves of Pete's horse. As the horse whinnied and reared, the phone shrilled, assaulting him awake.

"*Oui*," he muttered into the mouthpiece.

"Monsieur Ivères," said a woman's voice. "I hope I did not wake you."

"*Non*," he muttered, struggling to wake up enough to place the voice that tickled at a very recent memory.

She chuckled, and the sound sent a tingling through Marcel. Now he realized who it was. "Mademoiselle Scappa," he said in a semblance of his normal voice.

"I did wake you, didn't I? I'm sorry. But I have something important to discuss with you—a proposition to make."

He was fully awake now, sitting on the edge of the bed with his strong bare legs hanging over the side. A proposition? Just what he'd had in mind ever since seeing her.

"I am always open to propositions from beautiful ladies."

"I thought you might be. Shall we say fifteen minutes, in the lobby bar?"

"Let us say ten minutes, Mademoiselle."

The phone clicked softly in his ear.

Sitting in a black velvet tub chair in the lobby, she looked to Marcel almost like a jewel showcased in a gigantic box as he walked toward her from the elevator. She had changed out of the spectacular red dress to one less flamboyant but no less alluring. In fact, in the soft fall of peach silk—exactly the color of her skin, he noticed—she was even lovelier, if that was possible. And he wanted her more than ever.

She rose to greet him, reaching up with one hand to touch his cheek, a curiously intimate gesture. "I don't really want a drink, do you? What I want is to walk with you in the cold night air."

He smiled a smile a hundred women had loved. "When a woman looks as you do right now, cold air is one of the only two possible alternatives." He took her hand, tucked it into the crook of his arm, and led her out the front door.

It was not very cold, but she wasn't wearing a wrap. He offered his jacket, but she refused. "No, I want to feel it," she said. "I love feeling things on my skin." She turned her face to the slight breeze off the lake and let it lift her hair.

They walked a few minutes in silence, comfortable with each other in a way that oddly surprised neither. They'd gone only about a hundred yards when they reached a pier where one of the lake steamers was about to cast off for a midnight cruise.

"You said you had a proposition," said Marcel. "I always think propositions are better on the water, don't you?"

"Many things are better on the water," she agreed, and they sauntered up the gangplank.

As Geneva drifted away behind them, Marcel and Andrea strolled the steamer's deck. They found a table where they ate a dozen oysters each and washed them down with champagne. In the lounge, a small combo was playing dance music, the kind of slow, sexy dance music suitable to a romantic midnight cruise.

By the time they moved onto the dance floor and Marcel pulled her close, he was in an agony of wanting her. With her body hard against his, he could feel that she wore no bra. Her breasts pushed softly, lushly against his chest. Whatever the music, they merely swayed in a semblance of the rhythm. By this time neither could bear to break the contact of body on body.

Nor did they speak. The silence itself became part of the foreplay, part of their intuitive sensing of the other's desire. Marcel didn't doubt that Andrea had come with him wanting to make some sort of proposal other than the sexual one, nor did he doubt that it would, in the end, be made.

But that was for afterward.

When the steamer pulled up to its dock at last, they were the first ones off the boat. They almost ran down the gangplank, Andrea running with difficulty in her high-heeled sandals, Marcel half carrying her. The distance to his hotel seemed miles, too many miles. The lobby they had to cross felt as big as a dozen soccer fields. They couldn't move fast enough.

They reached the elevator, and the doors closed around them.

"Thank God for automatic elevators," said Marcel, and they were the last words he said before he fell on her with hand and mouth, taking her lips into his, his hands roaming frantically over the gloriously round curves under the peach silk. His hand slid up one silk-covered thigh till it reached bare flesh, then higher still until a moment of discovery.

He moaned. Under her garter belt, she wore no underpants, and the springy hair was as wet as a dripping ripe peach. He reached inside her and stroked that peach into even greater juiciness.

"I couldn't wait for you to touch me," she whispered.

"I'll touch you," he said as he did just that. "I'll touch every single part of you."

His room was on the top floor. He couldn't stand to wait. He leaned on the emergency stop button. The elevator shuddered to a stop between floors as he pushed her against the wall, kneading her, needing her.

Her need was just as great, just as urgent. Her fingers fumbled at his fly, unable to open the zipper fast enough. When at last it was down, she worked at the fabric until his cock sprang free, huge and red and glorious in its wanting.

He pushed up her skirt, exposing the dripping blond curls. He grasped her hips and raised her slightly, tilting her forward till she was open and inviting, beckoning him.

"Now," she said. "I want it now!"

The tip of his penis poised at the opening one breathless second, then he plunged into her. They began moving furiously, grinding into each other, pounding their bodies together. The elevator swayed as if a hurricane were blowing along the shaft.

"My God," Marcel said to her in a hush. "You are—"

But he didn't finish. He was seized at that moment by a paroxysm of pleasure that seemed to hit with the force of a thousand volts.

And at precisely the same time she reached her own orgasmic high, everything tightening around him, her hands clawing so hard at his back that he felt he was being carried up to the sky in the talons of an eagle. Nothing mattered but the flight, however, as he rose higher and higher, until the eagle came swooping down again and left him standing, breathless and sweating, in the arms of this woman he hardly knew.

"I think," she said as she adjusted her clothes, "it might be fun to try this again in your room."

Naked, in his bed, they brought each other to orgasm three more times. With all the beautiful women Marcel had known, he had never met anyone as uninhibited and purely animalistic as Andrea Scappa. He could not say when he might tire of her, but right now he knew he wanted more.

It was past three in the morning, and Marcel was half dozing, sated, when Andrea said, "You can use me."

Marcel chuckled sleepily.

She jabbed him painfully in the ribs with one of her sharp red fingernails. His eyes popped open. "No, *chéri*, I'm not talking about sex now," she said. "This is business. Remember why I came here . . ."

"Ah yes. The proposition."

"The fucking was only a part of it."

"Aha. So it *is* a part."

"Why not? I like you, Marcel. I thought you'd make a good lover and you are. I thought you'd like me, too. *Et voilà*, that's one reason we might belong together."

Marcel's eyes narrowed. It made him nervous whenever a woman spoke to him in words suggesting any kind of ownership. Yet he wanted more of this woman, much more. "And what are the reasons?"

"I can help you with your business. Your father is sick, you are likely to suddenly find yourself in over your head. I was raised in the jewelry trade, I've watched my father operate. He won't give me a chance to show what I can do, so I'm offering myself to you."

Marcel recognized at once the virtues of her argument. He was going to need help when his father died—he knew that with certainty—and why not have the advice of someone he could consult even in the middle of the night—between magnificent orgasms.

Unfortunately, the New York office, where he was located, was already fully staffed by competent people.

"I couldn't afford to pay you very much," he said cagily.

Andrea reared back, causing her chest to extend so that Marcel could not resist leaning forward to kiss one of her breasts. She smacked him on top of the head.

"Business first!" she reminded him. "On the subject of pay . . . I want nothing."

"Nothing?"

"Absolutely. For the first six months. Thereafter, if I prove myself of value, you will give me a good salary at an executive level as well as percentages on whatever sales I make or business I bring in."

Marcel could not refuse. "Done!"

"Good," she said. "Now fuck me again to seal the deal." He raised himself over her.

"If only all contracts could be so much fun," he said.

Back in the rue du Rhone, the office of Antonio Scappa was quiet. Blue smoke from a good Havana cigar curled up from a heavy crystal ashtray beside one of the wing chairs. Antonio Scappa was thinking, and he did that best alone. He was a private man, a man for whom secrets were important.

He wanted Dufort & Ivères; he needed it. Why the devil wouldn't the old man sell it to him? He was dying, for God's sake, he couldn't have more than a year . . .

Antonio took a puff of his cigar. Well, he would have to wait the old man out. It was clear that the son was not up to the task of running such a large, old-line establishment as Dufort & Ivères by himself. In no time at all, he would be desperate to get out at any cost before the responsibilities and his own inability to handle them sucked him under.

He could wait. Antonio Scappa was not by nature a patient man, but circumstances had fostered an ability to wait, to watch, and to take his chances when they came. And look how far those lessons had brought him already.

He rose and stubbed out the cigar. He walked to the floor-to-ceiling windows and looked at the moonstruck lake a moment before pulling the curtains closed. There was no one to see in at that level, but he didn't like to take chances.

He went to the door to the outer office, opened it, looked out to assure himself that he was alone, then closed and locked it.

Only then, secure in his privacy, did Scappa go to the wall safe behind a large abstract painting on one wall. Quickly he twirled the dial, his fingers trembling. With surprising gentleness in a man so large, he reached into the safe and lifted out his most important treasure, the one that had started it all and the one that could just as easily end it all.

It glittered in his hand, the eyes beckoning, the diamond and ruby skirt swirling, the pearl shoulders glowing. He held it a moment in his hand, then set it back into the depths of the safe.

As the steel door closed again on La Colomba's perfume bottle—half real, half cleverly forged—he smiled.

"Thank you, Mother," he said softly, "you old whore."

BOOK

III

Facets

Chapter 1

New York City—Autumn 1975

They do wonders for the complexion, too," Pete said, as she stood at the shoulder of Lady Margaret Packenham, who sat facing a mirrored wall, her small eyes critically focused on the four-stranded choker of perfectly matched pink pearls around her neck.

"Yes, yes," Lady Margaret said in the snappish tone she normally used. "I've heard that one. The ancients used to grind them up and drink them in wine, didn't they? But I'd hardly call that a selling point." The straight-backed elderly woman emitted the muffled snort she used in place of a laugh. "Because if I do buy these pearls, my dear child, you won't catch me grinding them up in my wine—my complexion be damned!"

Pete smiled. Lady Margaret Packenham had been a regular customer at Dufort & Ivères for the past half-century. For the last two of those years she had always asked to be waited on by Pietra D'Angeli, who had gradually learned to be affectionately tolerant of Lady Margaret's haughty patronizing tone and her habit of leaping to false assumptions with absolute conviction.

"But you can get the same benefit just from wearing

them," Pete said. "Haven't you noticed the way their color, the pink, lends a glow to your skin? You look absolutely radiant."

Lady Margaret studied herself intently in the mirror. "Hmmm. Well, yes . . . now that you mention it."

They were in one of the small private salons on the second floor of Dufort & Ivères designed specially for the purpose of selling expensive pieces to the most demanding customers. In each one, a Louis XVI dressing table and chair was set to face a full mirrored wall. The other walls were painted a dark plum. The glass of the mirror was tinted a delicate amber shade, and the lighting was carefully angled and its intensity chosen to bring out the glow and sparkle of gems without any harshness. In effect, the room was a small theater in which the customer played the part of a queen trying on her jewels by candlelight.

Pete took a couple of steps back into the shadowed area behind Lady Margaret's chair and for a minute let silence and vanity do their work. Now over eighty, the titled *grande dame* had been a young Ziegfeld girl from North Carolina fifty-seven years ago when she had met a middle-aged English baronet on one of his trips to "the colonies." On a subsequent trip back to America after the war, Lord Packenham had died abruptly and his wealthy widow had thereafter resumed living in her native country. Lady Margaret had a habit of strolling down Fifth Avenue to drop in at Dufort & Ivères the way some women went grocery shopping at Gristedes. She didn't always buy when she came in, but often enough so that Pete took each occasion seriously.

Pete spoke again, softly. "I've always thought that pearls are the most romantic of all the precious things made by nature. Not mined out of earth and stone, but out of something living. Perhaps you've heard the legend of the ancient Persians?"

"I don't think so," Lady Margaret said.

"They believed that oysters rose to the surface of the sea on clear nights and were fertilized by drops of dew that turned into pearls when they trapped the rays of the moon."

"Lovely," Lady Margaret said, shifting to study herself from a new angle.

Pete still hadn't seen the glimmer of uncertainty in Lady Margaret's eyes replaced by the bright fire of decision. "Of course, there's a practical side, too. These pearls are triple-A quality, graded five white-pink, and five for lustre. That's the very highest rating for pearls. And since the supply of top-grade natural seeds is diminishing, a few years from now I'd expect these will have doubled in value."

Lady Margaret raised a hand to her throat and ran a finger over the four strands as if playing a harp. "Oh dear. I do like them, but I already have a couple of nice long opera strands of the whites."

Time for the clincher, Pete thought. "I would think, Lady Margaret, that with your name you couldn't have too many pearls—as long as they're the best."

Lady Margaret wrenched her eyes from the mirror and turned to Pete. "What's my name got to do with it?"

"Didn't you know? Margaret comes from the Greek word for pearl—*margaron.*"

"Goodness. I always thought Margaret meant daisy. And I hated being a daisy. Such a common flower."

"Well, you see. You're as rare as a pearl."

The old woman beamed as she turned again to the mirror. The fire of possession was in her eyes. "How much did you say they were?"

In fact, Pete hadn't said. She never mentioned a price until it was asked, because she knew it was the last thing Lady Margaret cared about.

"Twenty-seven thousand dollars."

Lady Margaret nodded and preened for herself once more. "They'll go nicely with the black dress I bought from Yves . . . and they do a rather nice job of hiding my neck. Lately, I'm afraid, I've begun to look slightly old."

"You, Lady Margaret? Never."

"Oh, Pietra, you are a wicked flatterer." The old woman inclined her neck, indicating she was ready to have the choker removed.

As Pete undid the diamond clasp, she asked, "Do you want to wait for them now?"

Lady Margaret stood. "No, it's late. My chauffeur can pick them up in the morning."

Lady Margaret went to the door of the salon, then turned. "While you're young, my dear," she said, "while you're young and beautiful—that's the time you can make them love you, have anything you want. Where would I be now if I hadn't married Packy? Dead for a start, I can tell you, because there's nothing like money for keeping one alive to a ripe old age. But life wouldn't have been such a bed of roses right down the line . . ."

Pete gave her a neutral smile. She couldn't agree with the kind of choices Lady Margaret had made as a young showgirl, but she didn't want to judge them by voicing her own differences.

Waiting outside the door was a young man wearing a smart short-jacketed uniform and white gloves. Pete gave him the choker, told him to return it to the vault overnight, and instructed him to have it wrapped and ready in the morning. Then she and Lady Margaret continued toward the elevator.

"It isn't that I want to meddle, dear Pietra," Lady Margaret picked up her theme. "But I've grown fond of you in our dealings, and I regard you as an exceptionally lovely and intelligent young woman. You ought to know that you don't have to spend the rest of your life as a shopgirl, any more than I had to spend another year strutting around a stage in those silly hats that Flo made us wear."

Pete pushed the button as they reached the elevator. "I agree with you about doing something more exciting with the rest of my life, Lady Margaret. But I've got my own plans about how to achieve it."

"Very well, my dear. But just remember, if you hit a snag, there's nothing like marrying into a fortune to tide you over."

Pete laughed. "I'll keep that in mind."

The elevator doors opened. Pete started to step through behind Lady Margaret—the best customers were always accompanied to the street door. But Lady Margaret said, "Don't bother about seeing me out, Pietra. It's almost closing time, and I know you've got that sale to register."

Pete seized on the extra minutes she would save, since she had a date at six fifteen. Charlie had called last night and she had agreed to meet him at Rockefeller Center. "Thank you, Lady Margaret. I've enjoyed seeing you."

"Indeed, my child," the old woman replied brightly. "Why the hell wouldn't you?"

The doors closed between them. Pete gave a bemused shake of her head and went to the stairs that would take her up to the third floor clerical offices. The sale of all expensive pieces was logged not only for billing and inventory purposes, but so that the huge insurance charges paid by the store could be quickly adjusted. As she climbed, Pete's mind echoed with the ambitious statement she had just delivered with such bravado. Yes, she planned to do more with her life than work in sales—had planned to do more from the day she went to work here. She wanted to be a designer, wanted to create images of beauty with color and light—she had made that clear to Marcel right at the start. But after three years at Dufort & Ivères, she had moved no closer to achieving her goal.

Starting out at one of the retail counters on the ground floor, she had been told, was simply to give her a necessary grounding in the most elementary aspects of the business. She had endured nearly a year of selling pendants on simple gold chains to teen-agers and baby lockets to doting grandmothers before she had been elevated to fine jewelry. There she had quickly made a mark as one of the most productive salespeople. Her knowledge of gems and her innate good taste linked to a psychological insight gained through the experience of her mother's illness made for a formidable combination. Pete had a talent for reading her customers, sensing not only what would look best on each one, but what would make each *feel* best; she knew how to persuade and encourage, how to flatter or to dare each woman, as personality dictated, into buying the pieces that suited them. Soon she was selling exclusively to the store's wealthiest and most important customers. In addition to salary, she received a commission on each piece over ten thousand dollars. Small as the percentage was, by now the commissions made up the bulk of her income.

By some yardsticks, at twenty-four she was already a success. But that success, Pete knew, had only moved her real desires farther out of reach. The store would never willingly shift her out of sales while she was responsible for putting so much black ink on the balance sheet. And there were ways, she had to admit, in which she had sabotaged her own ambitions.

With her new income, she was finally able to liberate her mother from the hated state mental hospital. Two years ago, she had arranged for Bettina to be transferred to a small private institution in Nyack, an hour from New York on the Hudson River. It was not ideal, not as clean as Pete would have liked, and the doctor who dealt with her mother struck Pete as hard and uncompassionate. But it was a vast improvement on Yonkers and, at the time, the best Pete could afford. If Mama could not come home, Pete was determined that she should at least live in nice surroundings and be treated with kindness and understanding.

She had also moved herself and Opa out of Hell's Kitchen to an apartment on East Twenty-second Street, four high-ceilinged rooms on the second floor of a brownstone just around the corner from Gramercy Park. It was far from lavish, but it was comfortable and charming, with a working fireplace in the living room that delighted Josef as a reminder of the home he'd had in Holland before the war. Even though seven-hundred-fifty-dollar rent was five times what they had paid for the old apartment, Pete considered it a bargain.

Yet with the rent and new furnishings, and paying for Bettina, and buying the kind of clothes she needed to properly deal with her wealthy customers, Pete's income was stretched to the limit. The extras came from what Josef could provide, and for the past year that hadn't been much. He admitted to Pete that his eyes were weakening. He maintained his workshop, but there were more and more days lately when he didn't bother to go in.

Fortunately, Pete's commissions continued to increase. But as soon as any extra money came in, there always seemed to be a waiting need. Five months ago, just when Pete had felt she might finally be getting ahead, she discovered the Cole-Haffner Clinic. Situated on the northern section of the Connecticut shore, it was an old estate that had been donated by its wealthy owners as a care facility for the mentally ill, especially those patients who were nonviolent and judged capable of recovery if given prolonged treatment. During a slow week in midsummer, Pete had taken a day off from work to drive her mother to the clinic to be assessed by the staff doctors. When Dr. Haffner, the head of the clinic, had told Pete her mother would be accepted, she had been overcome with joy and gratitude—not only because the clinic and its grounds were so lovely, but because acceptance implied belief that her mother could be made well again. Expensive as the clinic was, the price seemed small compared with the prize to be gained. With her father's agreement to contribute to the cost, Pete installed her mother there at once, but it made it impossible for her to move into becoming a designer. In the design department at Dufort & Ivères, she would have to start as a low-paid apprentice, and now she couldn't sacrifice any of her earnings.

Even so, she had never stopped preparing herself, learning her craft. Soon after coming to work at D & I, she had started visiting the design rooms on lunch hours and had developed a friendship with a portly fiftyish Frenchman named Philippe Michon. Whenever she had spare time, she would go and sit with Philippe as he created the settings for precious gems. Sometimes she stayed late in the evenings, and the kindly craftsman would instruct her in using the flame and the delicate sets of tools required to mold silver and gold and platinum, in the art of setting gems so that they would be securely held by delicate fingers of metal. Seeing the pleasure she took from it, Michon had offered several times to arrange for Pete to work with him. But she always said no. Sometimes it seemed to Pete that her best chance had already come and gone.

As she pushed through the door from the stairs into the third floor corridor, she was feeling the surge of anger that always rose inside her when she remembered the opportunity she was supposed to have had at Dufort & Ivères—to have *won* for herself. Hadn't she proven her ability to Marcel? That night with him at La Grenouille was so crystal clear in her mind, looking back at the memory was like looking into a diamond. Though here, too, there was obviously a flaw she had failed to see. For she had trusted Marcel, and he had let her dreams die. How blind she had been! She had parted from him that night believing that there was an attraction between them, a special feeling that might grow into something else if they worked together. She realized now that her hopes had merely been a schoolgirl's wishful thinking. For Marcel had gone abroad right after that dinner—and returned from that trip bringing the woman who was now his mistress and his right hand in running the store.

Stop thinking about it, she told herself. *What's done is done.* She turned off the corridor into an office with four desks. Three of the desks were unoccupied, the secretaries already gone home, but at one a plump gray-haired matronly woman was still at work.

"Lottie, will you log in a sale for me?"

"Another one?" Pete had sold a ring for five thousand dollars that morning.

"Lady Margaret came in. She bought the Deladier pearls."

The secretary nodded knowingly. "What does she do with it all? She must have enough stuff already to sink the *Titanic*."

"Buying jewelry just makes her feel good. Isn't that reason enough?"

"I suppose it's better than taking an aspirin—as long as she can afford it." The secretary went over to a table and picked up a ledger, then brought it back to her desk. Pete sat down in an extra chair and dictated the details of the sale— price, name of buyer, description of the piece, inventory number. The practice of keeping such records had been started with the very first sale of a valuable piece by Dufort & Ivères more than a century ago. Since some jewelry was sold and resold or repurchased by dealers at auction, it was possible to trace back its provenance by checking the records. The pearls Lady Packenham had bought were still known by the name of the man who had commissioned them as a gift for his wife nearly a hundred years before. The intrinsic worth of the gems could be enhanced by such historical value.

Lottie was on the point of finishing, when another woman hurried into the office and straight to her desk. "*Merde*, are you the only one still here? I need to dictate a letter and have it sent out tonight."

"It's already past six, and I have to get home," said Lottie. "I'll do it first thing in the morning, Miss Scappa."

At the name, Pete glanced up.

Andrea stood glaring at the secretary, holding a lush silver fox jacket bunched under one arm. "I guess you didn't hear me: I said I need it *tonight*."

Pete stared. She had been aware of Andrea Scappa from the latter's first day in the store and since then had seen her many times. Yet they had never spoken and had crossed paths only at moments when both were on the move, occupied with their separate tasks. On the few occasions Marcel had spoken briefly with Pete—to tell her of a raise or pay a compliment for an especially big sale—Andrea had never been around. There was no occasion to meet otherwise. In her twin positions as Personal Assistant to Monsieur Ivères and, more recently, Advertising Director, Andrea had no cause to deal directly with the sales staff.

So in three years this was the first time that Pete had been able to observe this Swiss woman closely. Today Andrea was wearing a shantung dress of luminous blue with exaggerated shoulders and a wide flaring skirt, her small waist cinched in by a cobraskin belt dyed scarlet. Half a dozen ropes of rock crystal and jade beads were draped around her neck, and several gold and jade bangles climbed up one arm. Her blond hair had been worn short since the summer and arranged to curl around one side of her face like waves breaking over a smooth white beach. Her large amber eyes were dramatically highlighted by gold eye shadow, and her mouth and long nails were a shade seemingly chosen to match the dyed cobra.

Everything about Andrea Scappa was striking—Pete

couldn't deny it. Forced to the point of total honesty, she would have to acknowledge that Andrea was not just cheap and flashy, as Pete had wanted to believe. She was daring and flamboyant and unafraid to be totally herself. She was also sexy as hell.

And apparently as mean as the reptile that had been skinned to make her belt. "Listen," Andrea declared, "I'm not going to argue over an extra half hour of your time. You'll be paid for it, but you'll damn well stay."

The secretary stared back, the muscles in her round fleshy face working visibly as she fought for control. "I can't stay tonight, Miss Scappa. It's important for me to be home."

"Goddammit," Andrea commanded shrilly, "you'll stay or you can clean out your desk here and now."

Pete glanced with alarm at Lottie, who had worked at D & I for almost twenty years and was always the last to leave. If she was making an issue over half an hour's extra work, obviously there had to be a good reason.

Pete stood up. "This doesn't have to be a problem. I'll do the letter."

Andrea turned flashing eyes in her direction. "Stay out of this, Pete. It isn't just a matter of work anymore, but of loyalty, commitment . . . and knowing how to take orders."

Pete stared back, stunned less by Andrea's crass manner than by the use of her name in familiar terms—an unexpected indication that Andrea was fully aware of her, had perhaps discussed her with Marcel.

Lottie had moved to a rack and was slipping into her coat. Andrea swung her attention back to the secretary. "I said you can clean out your desk if you're not—"

"In Monsieur Claude's time," the secretary interrupted with quiet force, "a woman like you wouldn't have been allowed to work here. But I worked for him, as I work now for his son. If I'm going to be fired, I'll need to hear it from Monsieur Marcel. I don't doubt you can get him to do what you tell him, but until then I'll be here every morning at nine thirty. Good-night, Miss Scappa. Good-night, Pete."

It was all Pete could do to keep from applauding as Lottie's small plump frame vanished through the door.

Pete started to walk around the desk, preparing to sit down and take dictation.

"Never mind," Andrea said. "I suppose it can wait."

"If you're sure . . ."

"I'm usually sure about everything."

Pete came from behind the desk. As she did, she was aware of Andrea's eyes following her like gunsights trained on a target.

"In fact, one of the very few things I'm not sure about," Andrea added, "is you."

Pete gave her a questioning glance, but said nothing. Andrea awed and frightened her. On top of everything else, the Swiss woman was no doubt smart as a whip. In three years she had learned to speak English with every colloquial nuance, and she was doing a very good job for the store.

Andrea met Pete's gaze with an enigmatic smile. "Are you on your way out?" she said. "We can ride down in the elevator together."

Pete was torn between wanting to escape from Andrea and wanting clarification of her puzzling remark. "I have to get my coat."

"I'll wait." Andrea fell in alongside Pete as they walked down the corridor to the sales employees' locker room, where Pete hurriedly retrieved her coat. When she emerged, Andrea had slipped into the silver fox. Pete caught the smug appraisal that passed judgment on the cloth copy of a Courrèges she had bought at Ohrbach's. Chic but cheap, was the pronouncement conveyed by Andrea's expression.

"Marcel left earlier for a cocktail party," she said as though making idle conversation. "I'm supposed to meet him there after I change. We'll be going on to an opera benefit . . ."

Attending parties and gala evening events that drew from a wealthy crowd could be an important part of a jeweler's work, making contacts with customers in the very milieu where they liked to bedeck themselves in gems. Occasionally, after work, Pete saw Marcel and Andrea climbing into his limousine together, already in tuxedo and gown, prepared for an evening out. Whenever it happened, she would fantasize what it might have been like if she and Marcel had gone beyond that one dinner . . . if she had agreed to go dancing with him that night, instead of confidently playing the coquette.

How deeply could Andrea see into her secrets, Pete wondered, that she would taunt her by mentioning this part of her life with Marcel? Or was it only Andrea's nature to flaunt what she had before any woman?

They arrived at the elevator, and Andrea speared the button with one of her red talons. There was an awkward silence.

Pete could no longer resist asking. "What did you mean —you're not sure about me?"

"Whether you've given up or not . . ."

The elevator doors slid open. Andrea stepped in and Pete followed. She still couldn't make sense of what Andrea was saying. "Given up on what?"

Andrea faced Pete squarely. "On Marcel. On trying to take him back."

'Back?" Pete's lips mouthed the word, but hardly a sound emerged. Then she found her voice. "I have no personal interest in Marcel."

"Perhaps not," Andrea allowed, as though the facts were beside the point. "But I asked him once a couple of years ago about how he happened to hire you. I was curious about it, I guess, because you were beautiful—and obviously such a cut above the rest of the sales staff. He told me then about the time he'd taken you to dinner at Lutèce—"

"It was La Grenouille," Pete corrected. Only then, by the twinkle in Andrea's eyes, did Pete realize that she'd taken the bait. It was a way of gauging how important the details were to her, how much she might care to remember.

"And of course he told me about that delightful trick with the diamond, how very clever he thought you were to figure it out. You should have been there when he told it, Pete. It would have been plain to anyone who heard it how much that evening meant to him. How much you impressed him."

The elevator opened onto the ground floor, and Andrea strode forward. Pete kept pace. "I don't know exactly what you're trying to insinuate," she said, "but I repeat that there's nothing between Marcel and me—and never was."

"That's right," Andrea said. "Nothing that really matters. But I thought I'd better let you know that I intend to keep it that way."

They had reached the entrance, where the uniformed doorman was still on duty. He tipped his cap to both women, then unlocked the door and pushed it open to let them out. Just outside, Andrea stopped once more. "The truth is, Pete, if you weren't so damn good at what you do here, I'd have tried harder to get rid of you long ago. As it is, I ought to warn you that I'm determined to keep you right where you are, where you're just the hired help."

Without a good-night, she whirled toward the curb where Marcel's Rolls was waiting, the chauffeur holding the door open. With a few steps, she had vanished into the car.

Pete stood in a daze watching the car disappear in traffic. At last she started ambling disconsolately downtown toward Rockefeller Center.

Pete arrived ten minutes late in front of the statue of Atlas, where she had agreed to meet Charlie. The November evening had a bite in the air, and Charlie was evidently feeling it through his clothes, a denim jacket over a tie-dyed turtleneck, topped off with a cowboy-style Stetson. He stood clapping his hands together and rocking from one foot to the other, generating warmth as he waited. As soon as he spotted Pete, his heavy eyebrows lowered with concern.

"You okay? You look worried."

"Nothing serious," she replied. "Only, all things considered, right now I wouldn't mind changing places with him." She pointed up at Atlas, bent low under the burden of a world carried on his shoulders.

"Something about your mother?" Charlie asked as they started walking toward the skating rink.

Pete shook her head.

He took the hint that she preferred not to be pressed further. "Well, let old Uncle Charlie fix you up. A couple of drinks, dinner, and maybe then—"

"Charlie, I'm sorry. I know we planned to spend an evening together. But I'm feeling rotten, and all I really want to do is go home, have a hot soak, and crawl in bed with the electric blanket over my head."

"Gee, hon, sounds to me like you shouldn't be alone. Everything else you mentioned is a good idea, but you need someone to take care of you. Come to my place and you can still do all those things—take the bath and then climb into my—"

"No, Charlie," Pete said firmly.

The last thing she needed was to deal with fending off Charlie's persistent efforts to rekindle their romance. It had been more than a year since she had slept with him, and she didn't believe she ever would again. She cared deeply for Charlie, but only as a dear friend. When she'd come to the realization that she didn't love him and never would, having sex with him had begun to feel wrong to her. Not morally wrong, just not joyous, not the innocent sensuous romp it had been at first.

She was glad they had been able to remain close. She knew that he valued their friendship, too, because she was an anchor to a time when he could be sure he was appreciated purely for himself. In the past two years, Charlie's life had changed drastically. His "detritus" canvases had begun to sell, and he had taken the advice of his gallery's owner: to keep the prices rising, he must make his name known in every way possible.

"Visible artists make for vendible art," Charlie had said to Pete, quoting the gallery owner, a woman named Luisa Raines. So he had dutifully become a downtown social butterfly, showing up at all the right parties, all the hottest clubs. He got himself written up in gossip columns, featured on TV magazine programs, picked up the hangers-on who flocked to celebrities like moths to flame, and he spent time with other rising names—young models, writers, movie actresses. Luisa's advice appeared to work. The prices for Charlie's work continued to rise—lately to above twenty thousand dollars for a single piece. To Pete, however, Charlie had confided that his life was, as he put it, "a bargain with the devil."

His work was in demand because he was a commodity himself, a happening, a media event. The art almost didn't matter.

Whenever he talked like this, Pete advised him to trust his talent more, believe in the work he did, and give up the social whirl. He hadn't yet, but Pete knew that he depended on her encouragement to sustain a belief that he could abandon the flashy empty chase for celebrity whenever he wanted.

Pete sugested they walk awhile. She took his arm as they continued down Fifth Avenue. As they strolled, she noticed several passers-by giving Charlie second glances, recognizing him from a news photo or TV clip.

"Want to talk about it?" he asked at last.

"I guess what it comes down to," she said, "is realizing I may have to make my own bargain with the devil. I'm still not doing what I want, Charlie-O. Today I started to wonder if I ever would."

"You will, kiddo. You've got the stuff, we both know that. You just need a start."

"I thought I'd already made one." Andrea's mean words echoed again in Pete's mind, bringing a fresh awareness of how her career had been derailed.

Until today, she had thought of Andrea Scappa as a clever woman whom Marcel had found to be a help in business and a satisfying adornment to the rest of his life. His choice of Andrea had actually helped Pete to overcome the initial disappointment after the dinner with Marcel led nowhere romantically. He was obviously a man whose taste and desires Pete could never have fulfilled. The negative judgment was confirmed by the failure to keep his professional promises.

But suddenly Pete had a different angle on everything. Andrea was—had always been—a sworn enemy, jealous and afraid, dedicated to putting up roadblocks between Pete and her ambitions. Knowing now exactly what she was up against, could she think of staying at Dufort & Ivères? Perhaps it had been foolish all along to think that working there was a necessary step in setting right some old wrongs, putting all the damage of Josef's mistake behind her.

"Trust me, Pete." Charlie's voice interrupted her thoughts. "Your time is at hand. I can feel it in my bones."

"I think that's just the shivers, Charlie. You never did dress warmly enough."

He smiled briefly, but then he stopped to grasp her by the arms and fix her in a serious gaze. "I'd bet my life on it, Pete. You'll make your mark."

"But maybe I have to make myself famous first . . . like you did."

He eyed her, uncertain whether she was serious or chiding him. "A little publicity never hurt, kid. But it won't matter as much for you."

"Why not?"

"Because my art is just canvas and paint and junk. Ten bucks'll buy everything it takes to put together one of my pieces. The difference is all in the hype. But your art is going to have jewels in it, Pete. All you have to do is get it made, and right away it'll be worth a fortune."

She couldn't help laughing at his logic, though somehow it did make her feel better. She kissed him lightly on the lips. "Thanks, Chaz. It really helps that you believe in me."

"You help me, too."

As they gazed at each other, Pete felt the kind of affection and need for warmth that came dangerously close to making her ready to go home with him after all. She was sure, though, that it wouldn't work out. When she saw an empty cab passing in the street, she removed temptation by breaking to the curb and hailing it, explaining in a rush to Charlie that she would happily see herself home and leave him free to stalk the night's excitement.

When Pete got home, Josef was sitting before a fire in the living room, reading *Het Parool* and sipping a *genever*.

"*Dag, liefje*," he greeted her with a fond smile. "I thought you had a date with your Charlie."

"I've told you a hundred times, Opa, he's not my Charlie." She offered nothing more before kicking off her shoes and flopping into an easy chair.

The old Dutchman studied his granddaughter. He knew her very well, and tonight what he saw troubled him. "What is wrong, *liefje*? You look so *gedrukt* . . . so dejected."

"I'm just tired, Opa." She leaned her head back and closed her eyes.

"A girl your age should never be too tired to let a handsome young man buy her a good dinner." He tapped the cold ashes from his pipe and began refilling it from a humidor on the table beside him. Every movement was slow, deliberate, careful. When the pipe was filled, tamped, and lit, its sweet cherry-scented smoke filling the room, Josef turned again to Pete. "Are you going to tell me what is bothering you?"

She laughed tiredly. "I can't believe there is anything the least bit wrong with your eyes, Opa. You see entirely too much."

"It is that place, isn't it? I knew you would never be happy there."

Josef hadn't bothered to hide his sense of betrayal when he first learned that Pete was working at Dufort & Ivères, the scene of his greatest humiliation. She had tried to explain her motives, but he had never understood. He had come to accept it, however, particularly after his own nemesis, Claude Ivères, had died and his son had taken over.

"It's not the place, Opa," Pete said. "It's just the work."

"But you should be proud of what you've done, Pete. Look how far you've come, at all you've accomplished." He waved his pipe at the pleasant apartment and its furnishings. "Look at what you've been able to do for me . . . and especially for your mother."

At the mention of Bettina, Pete's true feelings burst forth. "But I have no choices anymore, Opa, don't you see? We need everything I earn, so I have to go on selling. It's not what I want, but I'm not free. I'm trapped."

"No, Pete, you are not trapped. You don't know what it means to be trapped." Josef's skin had suddenly taken on a pallor, and his eyes had a hollow, stricken look.

Pete made no apology for her choice of words. "How different is it really, Opa? I'm a prisoner to other people's needs and plans all the time that I long to be doing something else. It's like being hungry—yes, you know what it means to be hungry day after day. Well, that's how I feel. I want to make beautiful things. I want to sell *my* jewelry, *my* ideas.

I want people to wonder what Pietra D'Angeli will dream up next, to think of me when they find a wonderful stone and need the perfect setting. And it's never going to happen.''

"It will, Pete," he insisted. "It will happen."

Yes, that was what Charlie had said. But tomorrow and the next day and the day after she could not imagine anything changing. Pete eased back in her chair and closed her eyes again. The aroma of her grandfather's pipe smoke drifted around her, a smell redolent of his contentment, his pleasure in all the improvements in his life after so many hard years. If anything was going to change, Pete knew, it would only be because she made it happen.

But how? Oh God, how?

Chapter 2

The colors of the leaves were a week or two past their peak, more golden and russet now than bright yellow and scarlet, but the drive to the southern shore of Connecticut in crisp autumn sunshine was still beautiful.

Pete had made the trip several times in the months since she'd moved her mother to the Cole-Haffner Clinic. It was a long drive, yet she kept up the effort to go every Sunday as well as holidays. Only on those rare Saturdays when the store was closed could she make the trip then and have a delicious Sunday for herself. The regular visits had become such a ritual that whenever Pete missed going, she suffered pangs of guilt, imagining the lapse might occasion a crucial setback for her mother.

Seeing the clinic made it easy to be optimistic about the results that might come from treatment here. Set on more than four hundred acres along the Connecticut shore, it consisted of a limestone mansion hardly less elaborate than the "summer cottages" built by the robber barons in Newport, along with numerous outbuildings—stables, garages, servants' cottages—converted to use as offices or dormitories. Other buildings had been added since the establishment of the clinic, but all were designed to preserve the illusion that this remained a splendid private home. The well-tended grounds were covered with specimen trees and benches set in the shade and laced with flower-bordered paths. There was nothing at all depressing about these surroundings.

In a brochure that gave the history of the clinic, Pete had read that the estate had originally been the property of Elias Cole, a shipping magnate. He had bequeathed it to his only daughter, who had lived there alone after her banker husband divorced her. Herself a clinical depressive, she had died eight years ago by slashing her wrists, and her surviving children donated the property in her memory to be used to help other troubled souls. The philanthropy also included a generous endowment to cover basic upkeep and insure the salary of the well-known psychiatrist brought in to head the clinic, Dr. George Haffner.

Pete left her car along the wide circular drive that swept past the mansion and went to sign in at the unobtrusive desk just inside the main entrance. A sturdy young woman with a pleasant face sat behind the desk. Though dressed in ordinary street clothes, Pete knew she was a psychiatric nurse equipped to handle any emergency.

"Miss D'Angeli," said the nurse as Pete wrote her name, "Dr. Haffner asked for you to stop in at his office before going up to your mother's room."

Pete's stomach tightened. "Nothing wrong, is there?"

The nurse smiled a quick reassurance. "No. Your mother's been doing very well. The doctor just wants to give you a progress report."

Haffner's office was a large room at the rear of one wing that had been a library in its former incarnation. There were wood-paneled walls, floor-to-ceiling bookcases, a fireplace with a polished oak mantel, and a view through french windows across the broad lawn that ended at a knoll overlooking the ocean beyond. Except when he was in private conversation or treating a patient, Dr. Haffner kept himself accessible, the door to his office always open.

Pete found him sitting alone in a chair by a low fire, studying a dossier of papers. The image, reminiscent of her grandfather, was comforting, though the doctor and Opa were totally dissimilar. Haffner looked as if he could have been a flyweight prizefighter in his youth. He was a very trim, short man, with steel gray curly hair cropped close to his head, and a narrow face that conveyed an impression of sensitivity. Wide blue eyes that reflected kindness and concern were often masked by black-frame spectacles that reminded Pete of those she had seen worn by Harold Lloyd in his silent comedies.

He stood when she entered the doorway and set his papers aside. "Miss D'Angeli. Please come in." When they were both settled on chairs on either side of the fire, he said amiably, "Don't look so nervous, this won't be bad at all. First, I want you to know how important I believe it is that you've kept up such a regular schedule of visits for so many years. I'm sure it's not easy for a young woman like yourself. It must mean making sacrifices . . . ." He paused, checking her face for any hint of confirmation. He seemed to see it. "It's rare for families of these patients to go on giving so much. After a time, many fall away, content to let mentally sick relatives be taken care of by others, to let them be warehoused. But whether or not your mother has shown it yet, I know that it makes a vast difference that you stand by her."

Pete smiled even as her eyes misted. She needed so much to hear this.

"She's making great progress—that's the point. She's begun talking openly for the first time about what happened during the war, her feelings about it . . ."

"All that time in hiding," Pete put in. "It must have been so terrible."

The doctor snapped a nod. "Yes," he said simply.

Pete got the message that to ask for any more detail would be trespassing on patient-doctor confidences.

Haffner resumed. "I think it's going to be possible for you to take her off the grounds now and then. I don't know if it's a good idea today, but I want to prepare you. Plan on coming up here for Thanksgiving and taking her somewhere for a nice turkey dinner."

"Really, doctor? That would be wonderful."

He smiled. "Really." He rose and Pete stood with him. "Since we're dealing with realities, by the way, I'd suggest making a reservation soon if you want to eat at the best restaurant around here—the Seven Sisters Inn. They do a marvelous Thanksgiving, quite a production. I'll arrange a table for you, if you like."

She thanked him and they went to the door. Before going out, she yielded to an impulse to give him a quick kiss on the cheek. "Thank you, Dr. Haffner. You've made such a difference."

He smiled and patted the place where she'd kissed him. "My pleasure."

She was humming as she climbed the broad staircase from the main hall to the mansion's third floor, where her mother's room was located. She knocked at the door.

"Come in."

That was a change by itself. Many times over the years Pete would receive no response at all when she arrived—not even during a visit.

The room was lovely, walls painted a pale green with cream woodwork, furnished with a comfortable chair upholstered in a pastel flowered polished cotton that matched the bedspread. The window faced the sea and was hung with sheer curtains that let the sunshine pour in.

Bettina sat at a mirrored dressing table, brushing her hair. Pete was struck by how well her mother looked. Despite her persisting love of sweets, she had never gained weight, her skin was remarkably unlined, and her hair was still the shining silver-gilt of her youth. At forty-five, she could pass for ten years younger. The toll taken by living in a dream world was not always visible on the surface.

"You look well, Mama," Pete said.

"I feel well." She turned from the mirror and asked eagerly, "Can we take our walk on the beach now?"

With proper supervision, more than half of the clinic's one hundred fifty patients were allowed onto a long, fenced-in stretch of white sand just below the low cliff where the main house was set. Of course, it was what Bettina loved best about the place, being near the sights and smells of the ocean, and she was thrilled with the beach privileges she had been given two months earlier.

At the fence a guard dressed in ordinary work clothes unlocked a sturdy gate to let them through. For a while, they strolled along the edge of the dune grass without speaking. Once the silences had seemed oppressive to Pete—back when her mother never spoke at all. Now, because Pete knew Mama would choose her own moment to say something, she found them easier to take. While Bettina found a place to sit on the sand and gaze out at the sun-dappled ocean, Pete picked up shells and rounded beach rocks and examined pearly gray shards of driftwood, aware that nature was one of the greatest teachers of good design. At last she went and sat down beside her mother. The salt-scented November wind whipped their hair and pinkened their cheeks. The silence was broken only by the whisper of the surf.

Finally Bettina said, ''I like Dr. Haffner very much. He listens to me.'' She put her head back and looked at the clear blue sky. ''Sometimes I even think he believes me.''

''Why shouldn't he believe you?''

Slowly Bettina turned and looked at her daughter. Over the years, it had been very rare for her to meet anyone else's gaze directly. She usually avoided eye contact, choosing to stare at floors or ceilings, at sea or sky—or at her own image in a mirror. The look she returned now was a kind of deep, visceral human communication Pete could barely remember sharing with her mother in the past, not since she'd been a small child.

''Some things,'' she said, ''are impossible to believe. I don't even believe them myself.''

What things, Mama? Pete wanted to ask, but her mother had turned away again, and Pete sensed that pressing too much would be a mistake. She was making progress, the doctor had said, but things were evidently at a delicate stage.

For a quarter of an hour they sat in renewed silence. Then Bettina stood, dusted off her skirt, and began walking, meandering along the flat sand above the surf line. Pete stayed with her mother, steering her away from the lapping water to keep their shoes dry.

Her eyes down, engaged in looking at the shells and rocks, Pete was caught by surprise when she looked up to see two men walking straight toward them, only a few feet away. They were both tall, but one was blond, slender and narrow-hipped, the other was more filled out and looked more unruly, his thick brown hair wildly whipped around by the sea breeze. Both were in their mid-twenties and quite attractive, but there seemed something angry and forbidding about the expression in the face of the larger man. Pete guessed that he was a patient taking a walk with a friend or relative, and she had her doubts about whether he would observe the polite rule of giving a woman right-of-way. She reached for her mother to steer her wide of the two men, but Bettina moved forcefully ahead, almost as if to challenge them. Fortunately, the two men parted to let her through.

Pete smiled at them appreciatively. The slender one smiled back, but the larger man gave her a long, intense look that smacked of suspicion. As she passed closer to him before moving away, she took in the day's growth of stubble that, along with his clothes—a thick wool turtleneck under a khaki jacket with some military insignias sewn on—accentuated his rugged image. The U.S. military effort in Vietnam had collapsed only recently, with some of the last troops airlifted off the American embassy roof in Saigon as the Viet Cong entered the city, but Pete had already read about veterans returning with symptoms of extreme mental distress. The angry-looking man, she guessed, was a vet recovering at the clinic from the effects of the war. She paused, tempted to express regret at the way many returning veterans were being treated as pariahs. But it seemed hopeless to think any quick remark could make a difference, and she ran to catch up with her mother.

Where the clinic's beach property ended at a fence, Bettina turned and walked back. For a few more minutes, they were silent. The beach was empty again, the two men gone.

At last, looking straight ahead, Bettina said, "You are unhappy, too, Pietra. What's wrong?"

"Nothing, Mama. I'm fine."

"I am getting better, my dear, stronger. You don't have to protect me so much."

"But, Mama—"

"I can see sadness in your eyes, a look of being slightly lost. You cannot hide it from me, Pietra. I see it . . . the way a fisherman can look at a sky and see a distant storm. It's a little bit of what I see every day when I look in the mirror."

Pete was slightly shocked. Were they truly so alike? Certainly her mother had been able to peer accurately beneath the surface. But what did that mean for her own future? Since the night her father had told Pete about her grandmother who had loved jewels, Pete had always liked to think that La Colomba's passion and talent was in her blood, shaped her destiny. But how much of her destiny might be determined by the blood of her mother? It was one reason she longed so desperately to see her mother well again.

Would it help now, Pete wondered, if she spoke honestly about her own troubles? She thought of what Jess had said years ago—that it would probably be good for Bettina to have a taste of being relied on as a mother, not always to be treated as so easily breakable.

Pete was afraid to take the step. She could not go back to being the child again, could not lean on her mother. In her precarious state, Mama needed all her strength for herself.

"I'm all right," Pete said. "Little problems, but who doesn't have those?"

Just before the gate, Bettina stopped and once more looked directly at her daughter. "You are so beautiful," she said. "If only you weren't so beautiful, I'd know you'd be safe."

Like so much of what Bettina said, it was a mystery Pete was reluctant to probe.

And then the chance was gone. "Come," her mother said. "There will be tea in the lounge. And if I am very good and look my best, they may even have a piece of cake for me."

As she drove back to New York at dusk, Pete thought over and over about the moment in which her mother, perceiving her unhappiness, had offered consolation. Had it been a mistake to hold back, to think she must go on hiding her own worries and disappointments? Perhaps a chance to make a breakthrough had been lost.

No. If only Mama kept improving, they would be able to talk together, to really talk. Pete fantasized about it, having someone who could advise her, listen to her troubles, comfort her. How sweet it would be to have a mother again.

Chapter 3

Marcel Ivères arrived for work on Monday morning to find a cable waiting on his desk from the D & I store on the Place Vendôme in Paris. The cable informed him that the store's manager, dealing directly with the estate of a recently deceased collector, had succeeded in buying ten rare pieces designed by René Lalique, the renowned jeweler whose Art Nouveau designs had been the rage in Paris at the turn of the century.

Marcel had been advised previously that the pieces were for sale and had authorized the manager to pursue them. Yet he was dismayed now to see how high a price had been paid. Belatedly, he realized that he should never have given his representative *carte blanche*, that he should have stated a limit on what could be spent. That was how his father would have handled it. No, on second thought, his father would never have delegated such an important transaction to anyone else. He would have handled all the dealings by himself.

And how, Marcel wondered, would his father have answered the questions posed by the manager in his cable? Did Monsieur Ivères want the jewels held for sale at the Paris store, or did he think they should be transferred to New York, where the prices fetched might be significantly higher? Or would it be best to put the pieces in the vault for a while and see how much the market in Art Nouveau appreciated?

Marcel pondered. Place Vendôme had long been considered the main store, and Parisians had a special appreciation for Lalique. But now sales in New York were greater.

What would *Father* have done?

The past three years had been a torment for Marcel. First there had been the shock of learning his father's life was ebbing, followed by the race to learn as much as he could while there was still time, then the struggle to take over the many functions Claude Ivères had managed to perform on his own. Keeping a personal eye on branches in Paris, London, and New York; traveling farther afield to get a jump on buying the best stones from suppliers—visiting ruby mines in Thailand, talking with the diamond cartel in Johannesburg, buying from Indian maharajahs who had lost some of their vast wealth when their country became a democracy and were thus selling off gems that were centuries old. Marcel could barely sustain the pace his father had set. In trying, he discovered that Claude Ivères had "carried his office in his hat." His personal contacts in the world of gem mining and trading and jewel auctions had been such a vast secret network that there had been no time to pass it all on to his son. Nor could he simply hand on his wiliness, the shrewd cunning that was increasingly necessary in the current situation. The supply of top-quality gems had dwindled. The best "old mine" stones—rubies from India, emeralds from Colombia's ancient Muzo mine, sapphires from Burma—had been depleted long ago. The newer mines were all too often located in areas subject to guerrilla insurgencies and war, especially in Southeast Asia.

Demand was also at a low. The recently ended conflict in Vietnam had depressed the American economy with international repercussions, putting a damper on luxury buying. Marcel doubted that the Georgian peanut farmer who had just won the American presidential election would turn things around very quickly. Of course, nothing would stop the very rich from spending, yet even they spent more freely when a carefree, devil-may-care mood was everywhere around them. The balance sheets of Dufort & Ivères were still showing a profit, but it was not by the healthy, constantly growing margin that had prevailed when Claude was alive.

Many times lately Marcel regretted his father's decision not to sell out to Antonio Scappa, though he still felt honor-bound to abide by it. In any case, Marcel was sure the opportunity was dead. Scappa had written his daughter a single letter shortly after she'd arrived in New York, which Andrea had shown to Marcel. In Italian she laughingly translated, Antonio wrote that he would never forgive his daughter for "going over to the enemy like a camp-following whore." Since then there had been no communication between them. Meanwhile, the Tesori chain had been growing by leaps, with new stores in Rio, Hong Kong, Caracas, West Berlin—almost as though Scappa was driven to show his daughter what a mistake she had made. He had yet to open a competing store in New York, but Marcel guessed it would happen eventually. Tesori no longer needed to absorb Dufort & Ivères.

Of course, Marcel was aware that the feud motivated Andrea, too. Hadn't her affair with him been rooted in a need to escape the way her abilities were being ignored at home? Not that he minded terribly. She was still the most exciting woman he had ever taken to bed, a completely uninhibited animal. He never bothered to ask himself if he actually loved her—so far that seemed immaterial.

Without Andrea, furthermore, Dufort & Ivères would probably have lost even more business. She was a tireless worker both in the store and on the social circuit. Her advertising campaigns and publicity ideas were excellent. She had a certain dramatic flair that no doubt his father wouldn't have approved, but Marcel was reasonably sure it was right for the times. The sale of a valuable jewel should be as carefully produced as a play in a theater, she had said when persuading Marcel to install and decorate several small private salons reserved for the best customers.

The other notably bright spot for Dufort & Ivères was the record compiled in the past six months by one salesperson

—Pietra D'Angeli. Among the seven people in the fine jewelry department, she accounted singlehandedly for nearly a third of sales volume.

Marcel leaned back from his desk as the recollection swept away everything else in his mind: that one night . . . the way she had looked, her lovely face concentrated on solving the mystery of the diamond. He remembered the mood between them, the way he had lain awake thinking about her that night, wondering if she was too young, imagining what his father would say if he brought her back to the château in France . . .

A chance come and gone, Marcel reflected. He was in thrall to Andrea now; he had no doubt that the way his relationship with Pete had been abruptly redefined had angered her, even hurt her.

Fortunately, she hadn't been so angry as to recant her desire to work for D & I. She had more than proven her value to the firm. The few exchanges they'd had over the past few years had been cool but cordial. Evidently she could separate business from personal matters.

Marcel got up from his desk and went to a corner table in his large office, where the layout for Andrea's newest ad campaign was spread out. A beautiful model in a raincoat—buttoned loosely to make it obvious she wore nothing else—had been photographed against D & I's recognizable Fifth Avenue façade. Her smiling face was tilted up, reveling in the rain—except the shower of shiny drops slanting down were all diamonds. The one-line caption read: "A girl needs something for a rainy day."

As Andrea explained it, the ad was meant to break through the store's stuffy image and bring in a younger clientele. Traditional diamond ads showed a man and a woman together, played up the jewel as an everlasting bond between them. But more and more, attractive, successful young career women were alone, not waiting for engagement rings. The message of the ad was that they should spend their own money on a diamond—or use sex to get one with no strings attached.

Marcel had no doubt the ad would win a lot of attention for the store. But he couldn't decide if it was time to totally

leave behind the image of staid quality on which Dufort &
Ivères had built its reputation.

In general, he thought, Andrea moved too impulsively, as
in the little tempest she had stirred up with his best secretary,
trying to fire her. Marcel had refused, and then had managed
to smooth Andrea's ruffled feathers. But there were many
more important things in which he yielded to Andrea. Perhaps
he ought to follow her advice about the ad . . .

What would Father have done?

The door to the office swung open, and Andrea swept in
on a cloud of Joy and a swirl of coral-colored silk by Valentino. She barged in so often just at the moment he was
thinking about her that Marcel suspected Andrea possessed
some sort of mental radar. Or was it merely that she was so
often on his mind?

She came to stand next to him as he looked at the ad copy.

"What's your decision?" she coaxed. "Or are you still
worrying about what your dear departed *père* would have
done?"

Marcel's glance at her mingled amazement with reproach.
She knew him too well, he thought, had him too much in
her control. Yet at the same time he was excited to see her.
They hadn't been together last night. Right from the beginning, Andrea had insisted on maintaining her own apartment,
a statement of independence. She said it would also keep sex
fresher if they spent nights apart, broke their routine. Time
had convinced him she was right.

"It's quite brilliant, *chérie*," said Marcel. "But I don't
want to move impulsively."

"It's already too late for the January issues of *Vogue* and
Bazaar. Delay another week and they'll have closed their
pages for February. How long are you going to wait, Marcel?"

"Until I am sure the image of the store will not—"

"To hell with the fucking image," Andrea broke in. "I
can read our financial reports as well as you, *mon amour*.
We're doing less volume all the time, while Tiffany and
Cartier are going down-market and broadening their clientele.
Have you walked across the street to Tiffany lately? They're

moving loads of junk like those little silver squiggles of Paloma's, or gold tic-tac-toe pins. They realize—in a way that you don't—that the kids who buy cheap stuff today may marry millionaires tomorrow . . . or make their own fortune, then come back to buy big. The world is moving faster and faster, while we go on selling to a bunch of old ladies who are slowing down on their way to the graveyard.''

''I'm not against bringing in new customers. But there should be a way to do it without making ourselves look . . . cheap.'' He moved to his desk and picked up the cable from Paris. ''Here, look at this.''

Andrea took the cable and read. ''So? Is this anything new? You've bought some nice estate pieces. Sooner or later you'll find rich people to buy them and give you a profit. But that's hardly going to turn things around for the store.''

''You're smart, *chérie*. Can't you think of a way to make a campaign out of it? These Lalique designs are rare, unique. Why don't we photograph them for an ad—identify ourselves with having the unusual?''

Andrea moved thoughtfully to the window. As long as a way could be found to build sales volume, she wasn't against keeping an image of class and quality. That was one area in which her father wouldn't know how to compete. Across Fifth Avenue, Andrea could see Cartier. How did they do it?

Abruptly she turned back to Marcel. ''What would you say to making copies?''

''Copies?'' Marcel repeated, mystified. The word suggested the very opposite of what he had in mind.

Andrea spoke quickly, excited. ''We'll create a line based on the Lalique things, but within reach of people with only a thousand or two to spend. Look at what Cartier has done with these things they call *Les Mustes*. We can do something similar, call ours . . .'' She paced, her fingers moving nervously as though actually trying to pluck ideas out of the air. ''*Les Objets*!'' she erupted triumphantly. ''Perfect, no? A phrase the cultured can associate with *objets d'art* and even those who don't speak French can recognize as objects, things . . .''

Andrea stopped and looked at him, her hands on her hips. "You asked for an idea. There it is!"

Marcel smiled slightly. He was remembering how his father had ridiculed Cartier for overcommercializing. "Next thing you know," Claude had said after seeing their new promotion for cheaper items, "they'll be giving the shit away in cereal boxes!"

Andrea moved closer. "Well," she demanded, "what do you think?"

Marcel had seen her like this before, so hopped up by an idea that she was like a predatory animal on the scent of blood. Refusing her would be difficult, perhaps pointless. Maybe this was the moment to take a new direction.

"I'm not sure," he said. "Let me think about it."

"Think, think, think!" Andrea sneered, stepping right up in front of him. "Could you have fucked me if you said, 'Let me think about it' when the chance came? You run this business too much with your precious brain, my love. Why don't you *act*, for godsake? Run things with your *balls*!" To emphasize her point, her hand went straight to his genitals, cupped them with teasing pressure.

He stared her down. "Those work well enough in some situations. My brain works better in others."

Her hand tightened as she pressed her body against him and her voice sank to a throaty murmur. "And which kind of situation is this? Can you tell?"

He was fully aroused. His eyes flicked toward the office door, wanting to lock it.

She caught the glance. "No. Stop thinking, *chéri*. Show me you can act." Her mouth went to his ear as she whispered hotly, "Show me. Forget consequence, forget everything. Forget your goddamn image. Show me." She had unzipped his fly, was beginning to stroke him.

The dare, tied to the accusation that he was too timid in business, simultaneously angered and thrilled him. With a sudden rough move, he put both hands to her thighs, pushed up the hem of her skirt, and yanked down her panties. She laughed as she brought his penis into the open, and threw her legs along his hips to let him enter her. He leaned back against the edge of the desk for support.

"Yes, *mon brave*, yes. Show me . . . show me . . ."

As he rammed himself into the warm wetness of her, his hands wound into her short blond hair, pulling her mouth against his in a hard kiss that bruised their lips together, tongues writhing over each other. Hanging on to him, she pumped with him, harder and faster.

"And I'll show you, too," she said in a hiss, broken by her rhythmic exhalations. She tossed her head back as the power built within her. "I'll . . . show . . . you . . . ," she was saying as the explosion mushroomed up from deep inside her and spread to join with his.

As they came down from the peak, pounding hearts quieting, they looked at each other. Slowly they smiled. In the quick, fierce coming together, they both seemed to recognize that the primal force that had united them from the first had lost none of its power.

Andrea eased away from him. They neatened themselves, leaving no outward sign of their tryst.

Clinging to his pride, Marcel said, "So what does this prove? When it comes to fucking you, I can act quickly. What did you 'show me'?"

"That no one will ever do for you what I can," she said defiantly. "You don't want to lose me."

Marcel gave her a sidelong glance. "That has the unpleasant tinge of a threat."

"Does it?" she said flatly.

He knew what was bothering her—the same spark that had ignited their explosion. "In business, I must still do what I think is right. Not what you *tell* me to do."

Andrea gave an exaggerated shrug and crossed to the door. With her hand on the knob, she said, "But isn't it more exciting to take chances? After all, I told you not to lock us in."

She pulled back the door and left it standing wide open as she walked out.

* * *

At forty-three minutes past five o'clock, Pete entered the St. Regis Hotel, two blocks down Fifth Avenue from the store.

She had made a point of arriving late. If anyone was going to sit and wait this time, she thought, let it be Marcel. If he got annoyed and walked out, well, so much the better. She still wasn't convinced it hadn't been a stupid mistake to agree to meet like this, outside the store. She might have refused if she'd had time to think, but she had been summoned to the store phone while in the middle of closing the sale of a sapphire parure to an elderly real estate tycoon—a birthday present for his insatiably acquisitive wife.

There had been time for only one question: "Why don't I just come to your office?"

"It's too hectic here," he'd said. "But don't worry, Pete. This is strictly business, like before."

Like before? His way of trying to smooth over hurt feelings, she guessed, pretending no romantic undertone had ever existed. But that was no more true than his excuse for an outside rendezvous. Pete was fairly sure he didn't want Andrea to know about it.

She stopped at the door of the hotel's King Cole Bar and a maître d'hôtel approached.

"I'm meeting Monsieur Ivères," she said.

The maître d' nodded and led her to a table with two facing chairs where Marcel sat, his face hidden behind a *Wall Street Journal* until the stir around him alerted him to Pete's arrival. He stood as she was seated, then took his chair again. The waiter hovered.

"I wouldn't mind champagne," Marcel said and glanced at Pete to see if she'd second him.

"I like champagne for special occasions," she said coolly. "As I understand it, this is an ordinary business meeting." She looked to the waiter. "Campari and soda, please."

Marcel gave a distinctly gallic shrug and ordered himself a Glenlivet straight up.

"I can't help feeling, anyway, that this is a slightly special event," he said as soon as the waiter had gone. "It's the first time we've sat down together informally since—"

Pete look down as she interrupted. "Marcel, if you're going to talk any more about that night at . . . the time we had dinner, then I'm going to get up right now and walk straight out of here." She looked up, her eyes flashing. "I mean it. You told me this would be business, and I came on that condition because I have my own agenda to discuss with you. Do you understand?"

It was only with an effort that she kept her voice steady. Seeing his lean handsome face across the table, being with him in the dim intimate recesses of the bar, stirred up dreams that she thought were dead and forgotten.

"I understand," he said quietly. "Forgive me for being so insensitive."

She accepted the apology with a curt nod as the waiter put their drinks on the table. They each took sips.

Then Marcel said, "Are you familiar with the work of René Lalique?"

"Of course. He's probably my favorite Art Nouveau designer." Pete had seen only a few of Lalique's pieces firsthand, and then only by attending some of the presale showings of estate jewels to be auctioned at the Parke-Bernet Gallery. These few examples, however, were enough to illustrate the special vision of this master jeweler who had worked at the turn of the century. His settings weren't merely plain precious metals. He also used glass and steel and rock crystal, and was a genius at diaphanous plique-à-jour, the translucent enamel through which light could pass.

"What makes him your favorite?" Marcel asked.

"Each tiny part of his designs is an essential part of the whole." As Pete answered, she visualized the few examples she had seen. "Too many jewelers merely focus on the stones and let everything else be nothing more than a frame. One setting seems interchangeable with another. Not Lalique's. He deliberately contrasted the soft quality of light transmitted by the delicately shaded plique-à-jour with the brilliant light passing through deep-colored stones. No one else made the stone and the setting complement each other that way."

Marcel was staring at her, she noticed. Was it the glazed look of a man who'd ceased listening to a prattling woman? She grabbed up her drink.

"Lalique was also my father's favorite," Marcel said. "He admired this very thing, the blending of different kinds of light. My father knew Lalique personally—he didn't die until 1945, you know. He knew that this control of light went beyond mere design to a statement of philosophy."

"In what way?" Pete asked. She hadn't been boring him at all, she realized.

"The contradiction of light," Marcel said, "hard versus soft—a glinting sparkle contrasted with a soft translucent glow—was meant to represent the central paradox of beauty." He paused and leaned closer across the table before clarifying: "That which is most beautiful is often short-lived—nothing more than a momentary flash."

Her eyes locked with his. It was hard not to map the meaning of his words about beauty onto the best memory they shared—short-lived, a momentary flash.

She shifted in her chair, breaking the spell. "What's all this got to do with business?"

He retreated to his own high ground. "I've just acquired ten Lalique originals."

"How wonderful!" Pete exclaimed.

"They're in Paris now, but I thought of bringing them here. When they come, I want to put them in your hands."

"To sell . . ." Pete said. The edge on her enthusiasm was already fading. They'd been talking about the importance of design, and suddenly she was back to being a salesperson.

"It's clear from the way you talk about Lalique that you can do a better job than anyone else. There's more involved than finding the right buyer. You'll set the prices, think up a special promotion to justify them, publicize our affiliation with Lalique to build up sales of other things, emphasize our commitment to quality."

Pete glanced away, fighting down her irritation. His initial approach had drawn on her very passion for design, then he had squelched it. It was time to raise her own agenda. "Marcel, I don't want to go on selling. There's nothing wrong with it. Selling is honorable work. But it isn't what I long to do. You've known right from the start I was desperate to design, and you haven't given me a chance.''

"But if I put you into design now, you'd lose money for yourself. This is a great opportunity.''

"Not the kind I want. Give *me* what I deserve, what I've earned.'' Even as she spoke, she was reprimanding herself. It was crazy to turn him down. The Lalique sales would bring high commissions, money she needed . . .

Marcel shook his head, evidently stunned. Then he reached across the table. "Pete,'' he appealed, his voice softening.

She folded her arms, putting a wall between herself and his attempts at charm.

Marcel sat back and studied her. Then he gave a sly smile. "I'm impressed with your sympathy for Lalique. I can't think of anyone better to be involved with this. But I have an idea, and I'd like your reaction. It could involve you with making some jewelry . . .''

The wall came down. Pete's eyes met his again.

"We'll use the Lalique,'' he went on, "to inspire a series of less expensive pieces that are similar.''

"Copies?'' Pete asked.

"Not necessarily. They might use the same techniques, but with slight variations. We could make a limited edition of each, but still in quantity, and sell them less expensively than the original. I could pay you a royalty, too, on each sale.''

"No,'' Pete snapped without a moment's hesitation, "I'll have nothing to do with that. Do you know why Lalique stopped designing jewelry in 1908?''

He looked nonplussed. "I have no idea.''

"Because it made him sick, physically ill, to see his transcendent and delicate designs being copied, vulgarized, by all the me-too jewelers who wanted to cash in on his genius and the market he helped create. I'm not a me-too jeweler, Marcel. I won't do that to him, and I won't do it to me. I intend to create, not copy, to be daring, not make some scaled-down rip-off of a masterpiece.'' She pushed her chair back from the table, preparing to leave. "This was a mistake, Marcel, for both of us. It's probably been a mistake for me to go on working for you, but frankly I'm very much in need of what I earn. So I'm not quitting, and I hope I won't be fired. But I'll be perfectly honest: I'm going to keep looking for a way to do what I love."

As soon as she whirled away from the table and strode toward the door, she regretted her stand. It made no sense at all. He'd offered her *two* good opportunities, and she'd turned them down. One out of petulance and one out of principle.

Only as she came down the steps of the hotel into the cool November air did Pete realize what feelings had actually been driving her. She simply hadn't been able to sit with him and keep a cool head. She was afraid of getting too caught up, afraid that she might become a pawn in a game of hearts played between Marcel and Andrea.

In a defiant burst of extravagance, she let the hotel doorman lead her to a cab.

As it sped downtown past the glittering windows of Fifth Avenue, Pete was in turmoil. Would she be fired now? No, she was still too valuable in sales. But perhaps she should quit.

And where would that get her?

If only her mother were better, she could take some risks. Soon perhaps. Thanksgiving was coming, and that might be the turning point.

In the dimly lit bar, Marcel sat finishing his drink. Consulting his star salesperson on what to do with the Lalique pieces was an idea he had *acted* on, he thought—appreciating the irony, since Andrea would undoubtedly hate what he had done. The hints that she disliked Pete—or at least disliked his association with her—hadn't been lost on Marcel—the little digs, remarks that belittled her remarkable sales record. But Andrea couldn't be allowed to control the choices he made, either in or out of the store.

He smiled quite contentedly. There was still a chance, he thought, that Pete might change her mind about selling the

Lalique. But she would never cooperate in making copies. Without knowing it this time, she had passed another test. She had also helped him reach a decision.

And this one, Marcel was sure, was exactly what *Père* would have done.

Chapter 4

When she arrived at the SoHo loft of her father and Anna the Thursday before Thanksgiving, Pete was in a bitter mood. A day after meeting with Dr. Haffner, she had called her father to tell him the encouraging news and had asked him to join them for Thanksgiving. Steve had said first that he wasn't sure his work schedule would allow him the full day off, a lame excuse. Several times since, Pete had raised the subject and each time he had resisted. "I haven't seen her in so long," he had said on the phone two nights before, "it would be too much of a shock for her." Pete had tried reasoning with her father, and he had promised to reconsider.

Yesterday Anna had phoned Pete at the store to invite her for this evening. Being at work, she had accepted without getting into any discussion. She realized, however, that the purpose of the evening was to clear the air.

They all made it halfway through the meal Stefano had cooked remarking on how good the pasta was, how cold the weather was getting, making small talk about their work.

At last Pete could stand it no longer. She put down her fork. "Papa, I don't see why you can't come with me."

In the midst of raising his wineglass for a sip, Steve froze for a second. Then he glanced at Anna, who hastily made an excuse about starting to clear the table. Picking up a few dishes, she went into the kitchen area of the large open loft.

"Don't you know how much this would mean to Mama?" Pete continued. "This is the first time she'll have been outside in six years. If you're there with Opa and me, it will let her feel we all still care as a family, will help build up her confidence and give her hope."

"Hope for what? That things can be the way they were?" Steve leaned closer across the table. "Listen, Pete, I do care about your mother getting well . . . very much. I'm very glad to hear she is improving. But I don't want to give her hope for the wrong things. My life is with Anna now. I'll spend Thanksgiving with her and our friends."

Pete's anger was rising within her, but she fought to control it. "Papa, you have so many other days to be with Anna, to do everything you want. It's just not fair not to give this one day to Mama—just one. You've never been to see her at all since she moved to Connecticut. She's still your *wife*."

"Only on paper," Steve shot back. His resistance was hardening, too. "I didn't see any point in adding to her problems by trying to change that. But perhaps I should have."

Pete glared fiercely at her father.

Quickly, he reached out to her and his tone became imploring. "Pete, believe me, if I thought it would make an important difference I would go. But if you want to help your mother deal with reality, then you have to accept it, too. We can't be a family again. Not the way we were. I'm not part of your mother's life, and I can't be in the future. As long as you and Opa are there, she'll be content."

Pete bolted up, rage burning even more hotly in her eyes. "You just don't care!" she screamed. "That's the reality. You're selfish . . . and cruel. You don't even care if she gets better or not, because it suits you to—"

Steve had risen so quickly that his chair was thrown back onto the floor. With two strides he was around the table, his strong grip locked onto her arm. "No, Pete. I care. But it's you that has to give up on some dreams."

He was hurting her, but she looked back defiantly, unwilling to let him know. In a moment, his hold loosened slightly, but he didn't let go of her. He seemed to think that if he did, she would run.

"Pete, do you remember when I told you about your grandmother, your namesake? She gave me a magical sparkling dream, and for years afterward I chased it. But if I hadn't let go, I couldn't have discovered any other happiness. I'd still be looking for those jewels . . . instead of having you, or Anna, or finding a good, simple, satisfying life. Don't you see? You can't dream about your mother and me being together again . . . and I don't want her to dream about it." His hand slipped away.

Pete stood still. "If I dreamed about having you together again for a day," she asked quietly, "was that so bad? Maybe I hoped for more, I don't know. But I'm not like you, Papa. You're telling me that you had to give up a dream to find happiness. I think fulfilling dreams and being happy can go together. So I'll go on chasing my own . . ." She started to get her coat, then saw Anna watching from the kitchen, her eyes moist. Pete went and embraced her. As she let go and faced her father again, another thought occurred to her.

"Do you ever wonder, Papa, what would have happened if you hadn't given up your dream, if you'd gone on looking for La Colomba's jewels? You might have found them— sooner rather than later, while the trail was warm. And then so many things would have been different . . ."

"I never think about it," Steve said in a gruff, stubborn tone.

It was clear to Pete that he could not let himself think about it. But she was not in a mood to be gentle with him now. Stopping at the door, she said, "Well, I think you gave up much too soon, Papa. In fact, one of these days I'm going to take on your dream as well as my own."

He started toward her as if to add something, but she didn't want to hear him discourage her any more. Before he could speak, she was out the door, going down the steps of the loft building.

On the way home she thought about it. What could be

more wonderful than finding La Colomba's jewels, going on
a hunt for lost treasure? She had said it in a moment of
bravado, not only as a declaration of independence from her
father, but as a way of rebuking him for the way he had
failed Mama. But now the idea teased her. Couldn't she pick
up the trail? Could so much that was beautiful really disappear
forever?

Perhaps Papa wasn't completely wrong, she decided. She
must be careful not to sacrifice everything to a fantasy. There
were more attainable dreams to fulfill. But she wouldn't give
up completely on finding that long lost glittering piece of her
heritage. A time would come someday when she would continue the hunt. Someday . . .

Josef saw no reason to regret Steve's decision. He could
not forgive his son-in-law for failing to rescue Bettina from
madness, nor for deserting her to go to another woman.

"We don't need him," Josef told Pete. "We will have an
even better time, just the three of us."

The atmosphere at home bubbled with a Christmas Eve
sort of excitement that Wednesday evening. It had even begun
to snow, a light, early-season dusting that lent even more to
the holiday air of expectation. Josef had had his best suit
pressed.

After dinner, Pete washed her hair. She had just come out
of the bathroom when Josef suddenly jumped up from his
chair. "Ach! I forgot the chocolate, Bettina's chocolate. She
loves it so, I must bring some. Droste, the best Dutch chocolate." He went toward the coat closet.

"Opa, you're not going now? It's past eight . . . and it's
snowing."

"They sell it at that place around the corner on Lexington
Avenue."

"Then we can get it in the morning, on our way."

"No, they'll be closed tomorrow for the holiday." He had
taken his coat from the closet and was putting it on. "It's
only a block. I'll be back in ten minutes."

She didn't know why, but she felt a terrible anxiety about
his last-minute errand. "Opa, let me go."

"No, no, your hair is still wet. You will catch cold." He was at the door.

She hurried after him with the muffler she'd grabbed from the closet. "You forgot this," she said, and wrapped it around him.

"Thank you, *moedertje*," he said, and went out.

Pete smiled. He always called her "little mother" when she got so protective. She shrugged off her worry. But when he wasn't back in twenty minutes, she began to worry again. She gave herself excuses—he had run into someone he knew—but after more than half an hour her nerves were raw. She started to dress, to go out and look for him.

Then the phone rang. It was a nurse calling from the emergency room at Bellevue Hospital. *Why hadn't she trusted her intuition?* Pete was asking herself even before she heard another word. But then the rest of what the nurse was saying came through. Josef had slipped on the icy sidewalk and broken his leg.

Pete managed to get a cab almost at once, and was at Bellevue in ten minutes.

"I'm sorry, *schatje*," Josef said as soon as she entered his room. He was propped up in bed, his leg already set and hoisted up by a traction unit.

"Does it hurt very much?" she asked.

He smiled. "Only when I dance." And they both laughed.

Pete was torn about what to do the next day. She felt she should stay in the city to sit with her grandfather, but Josef insisted she must go to Connecticut tomorrow as they'd planned.

"Your mother is expecting you. Me she only wants to see, you she needs."

Pete conferred with the doctor, who assured her that, despite Josef's age, he was in excellent physical condition and the leg should heal easily. He would have to remain in the hospital a couple of weeks before being released on crutches, but there was no reason for her either to worry or to sit by his bedside.

"*Schatje*," Josef called to her after she kissed him goodbye and was halfway out the door. "Don't forget your mother's chocolate." And he handed her the largest box of Dutch milk chocolates ever made by Droste Chocolade-fabriek.

The Seven Sisters Inn occupied a gabled, white Victorian house overlooking a small harbor a few miles up the Connecticut shore from the Cole-Haffner Clinic. The snow had stopped last night, allowing the roads to be cleared for easy driving, but enough had fallen so that trees and rooftops were picturesquely frosted with white. Smoke from the inn's several chimneys curled up into a sky of crystalline blue.

As they walked across the parking lot and climbed the steps to the porch, Pete finally began to relax. She had been nervous, at first, concerned about how her mother would respond to each new experience—being allowed off the clinic grounds, driving in the car, being brought to a strange place—and to the last-minute disappointment of Josef failing to make the trip. But Mama seemed to be taking everything pretty much in stride. In the car, she had expressed some anxiety when Pete told her about Josef's broken leg, but no more or less than anyone would. Except for the few nervous glances she flicked to her left or right, as if reassuring herself that no malevolent enemy lay in ambush, she appeared reasonably calm and self-possessed.

Inside, the restaurant had a light, airy atmosphere, all the more pleasing and surprising because of the heavy Victorian structure around it. The walls were papered with floral prints, the windows curtained with matching fabric swagged and tied with big bows. Large arrangements of autumn leaves and dried glasses and seed pods were set about, and each of the several connecting dining rooms had a fireplace lending a welcoming warmth with a blaze of crackling logs. Drifting from one of the rear rooms came the music of a pianist playing the old show tunes of Gershwin, Berlin, Rodgers, and Porter.

As they waited in a foyer to be seated after checking their coats, Pete noted the way the new blue cashmere suit she had bought her mother for the occasion showed off Bettina's delicate beauty to perfection. It wasn't difficult to see how Stefano D'Angeli could have once found her irresistible. Indeed, Pete could see how—when Mama was well again—a new man might yet fall in love with her. That made it easier for Pete to think of forgiving her father for what she had first viewed as his desertion.

"I can't get over how well that suit fits you," Pete said, always ready to fill any lull with some remark meant to build her mother's confidence.

Bettina smiled. "You were very kind to send it, Pietra. It is a very long time since I had anything so beautiful. I don't deserve it."

"Of course you do, Mama. That and more."

Bettina reached out to brush back her daughter's thick dark hair and appraise her tailored black-and-white-checked wool suit. "And you look very pretty, too, though perhaps a little too serious. We are here to have a party, yes . . . ?"

Pete smiled. "Yes, Mama. Thanksgiving is sort of a party."

They were shown to a table set for two in the curve of a bay window looking out toward the harbor, no doubt one of the nicest in the restaurant. Pete suspected that Dr. Haffner had made a point of asking for it.

As they waited for service, Pete noticed the way her mother was appreciating every detail of the table setting, running her fingertips over the surface of the pale pink tablecloth, her eyes glittering at the polished crystal wineglasses.

"It's lovely, isn't it?" Pete said.

"They had linen like this, and silver," Bettina replied.

"Who, Mama?"

Bettina looked up at her, then gave a quick shake of her head as though dismissing the subject.

A young waitress in the costume of a Pilgrim woman appeared at their table with menu cards and wine list, poured them each a glass of cranberry juice, and smiled herself off again.

"Look, Mama," Pete said, scanning the menu written on heavy vellum in fine copperplate style, "it's a set menu, all the decisions have been made for us. It's like eating at home." Her eyes went down the card. "Whew! They're going to have to roll me out of here on a cart."

Bettina's eyes widened as she studied the list of dishes to

be served with the traditional turkey. "It's so much," she said softly. "Too much."

Pete caught the hint of uneasiness. Lightly, she said, "There's always too much at Thanksgiving, Mama. It's a celebration of abundance. But you don't have to eat anything more than what you want."

The glance Bettina threw at Pete seemed curiously skeptical. "We will see," she said.

Pete felt another flicker of concern. The reply carried an odd undertone of feeling threatened. Yet Mama had always made strange remarks, Pete reminded herself. On the whole, she seemed to be enjoying herself, that was the important thing. Hearing her mother begin to hum along faintly with the piano music, Pete felt better. To divert herself from keeping such an anxious watch on her mother, she looked around the room.

Almost at once her gaze landed on a table beside the fireplace where two men were sitting—the same two she had seen a couple of weeks ago on the beach, one fair and slight, the other one built more solidly, with dark brown hair. Today they were both dressed up in slacks, blazers, and neckties, but Pete remembered the faded army battle jacket the larger man had worn on the beach. The one with the more delicate features and blond hair was facing in her direction and their eyes met. He gave Pete a very broad, warm smile, which caused the second man to turn in her direction. As she smiled back, Pete was struck again by the rugged handsomeness of the second man, but his greeting was much more restrained than his companion's, a mere ghost of a smile and a polite nod, not unfriendly yet extremely reserved. He was a veteran, Pete recalled; it would be understandable if he had developed a protective shell.

In a moment he turned away from her, engaging the blond man in conversation, breaking the brief contact.

Pete's attention returned to her mother. Bettina was staring fixedly at the view outside, and Pete noticed that she had shifted her chair slightly to face more toward the window, as if intimidated by seeing so many people in the room around her.

Pete searched for some reassuring words, but before she'd said anything, the pianist in the neighboring room swung into a lively version of "Shall We Dance," and Bettina brightened at once.

"Ah, that song. It reminds me of your father."

Pete smiled. "How, Mama?"

"He took me to see *The King and I* on Broadway the first time it was done—so long ago. When we came home, he was still full of the music. He started singing that song, dancing me around the living room like he was the King of Siam." She gave Pete a twinkling glance. "That was just about nine months before you were born."

The recollection, the playful innuendo—no different, Pete thought, than any woman might have at a moment like this. If Mama could face her memories, she would surely be all right.

"Your father was so good to me once," Bettina said now. "It's too bad he couldn't come today."

Pete was going to make excuses for him, but before she could speak her mother went on.

"I don't blame him, of course. He knows I'm filth."

Pete was struck dumb, her mind racing. How could she respond? Looking across the table, she saw her mother still placid, smiling slightly as she gazed out the window. For a second, Pete doubted she'd heard correctly.

"But I'm so hungry," Bettina murmured. "If only I can eat, I'll do whatever they want."

Pete reached across the table. "Mama, are you . . . okay? If you're not comfortable here, we can go."

Bettina faced her again. Her eyes seemed unnaturally bright. "Of course I must stay. I'm just so hungry. All the time."

Pete thought she knew what was happening now. Thanksgiving, with its promise of abundance, was a mirror of that time her mother had been forced to exist on rations and scraps. She could only hope that, as quickly as Bettina had been captured by the dark fantasy, she might snap out of it. Certainly it wouldn't help to whisk her away, deprive her of the feast.

Only a moment later, the piano music changed to the stately rhythms of a traditional Thanksgiving hymn, and a chorus of singing voices began to drift through the rooms.

"We gather together to ask the Lord's blessing . . . "

Then a procession appeared, waiters and waitresses all costumed in Puritan black and white, carrying beautifully arranged trays of food. On a silver platter at the head of the procession was an especially large turkey, its golden breast glistening, upthrust legs decorated with white paper frills. It was carried aloft by a young waiter dressed in Pilgrim garb —wide black pants, black frock coat buttoned high, a starched white linen stock.

The diners at the tables all applauded as the procession wound its way around the tables, the waiters singing the hymn.

" . . . he hastens and chastens His will to make known . . . the wicked oppressing shall cease from distressing . . . "

Pete heard her mother singing along softly in Dutch. From Thanksgiving holidays years ago, before the illness, Pete remembered being told that that melody was based on an old Dutch tune, one that Bettina had heard a thousand times throughout her childhood, played on the church bells not far from their house in Rotterdam.

Bettina had been watching the winding column of black-garbed waiters and waitresses intently. As the procession neared their table, Pete was aware of her mother's posture changing, growing rigid. She had only a second to register the sudden flaring of panic in her mother's eyes, before the waiter with the large turkey was passing their table.

And then it happened: In an instant, Bettina's hard-won hold on reality disintegrated. She fell to her knees on the floor before the young waiter, kissed his buckled shoes, then raised her head, wide blue eyes locked on the astonished waiter's, and began to rant in Dutch.

The singing stopped. Everyone in the room was frozen with shock. Pete looked around at them, momentarily paralyzed herself at the sight of her mother on the floor, her arms clutching submissively at the waiter's legs as she jabbered in Dutch. No, Pete realized then, she had heard enough Dutch over the years to know this was something different: German. But she had never heard her mother speak it before. Where had she—?

Any question was blown out of Pete's mind, as her mother changed position. Releasing her grip on the waiter, she reared back on her haunches, reached under her skirt and began to pull at her underwear as if to undress.

"Mama, no!" Pete cried, throwing herself out of her chair, hooking her arms under her mother's, and lifting her onto her feet. "Come, Mama, come with me." Pete began to lead her mother from the room, casting glances of abject apology at the gawking diners around them.

Suddenly her mother tore loose from her grasp. "Let them fuck me?" she said in a throaty growl, and turned to the waiters. "Fuck the Jew whore. Just let me eat. Please, I'm so hungry . . ."

She lunged at a tray of vegetables being held by one of the waitresses. Terrified, the young woman thrust the tray down onto a table. Bettina dived at it, scooping up roasted potatoes and onions with her hands, stuffing them into her mouth as fast as she could.

Pete moved to her quickly. Crying now from shock and confusion, she touched her mother gently on the shoulder. "Mama, please. We have to go."

Bettina looked around with blazing eyes that showed no recognition. Then she reached for another handful of food.

Pete grabbed her mother's wrist. "Stop it, Mama," she said in the most commanding tone she could muster. "Stop right now."

Spinning around, Bettina lashed out with her free hand. Powered by the abnormal strength of the hysteric, the blow that caught Pete on the side of the head stunned her, sent her reeling backward until she crashed against the table. Startled gasps rose in unison from the spectators. Bettina bent again over the tray of food and went on eating like a scavenging animal. Pete steadied herself and began to advance again toward her mother. Then she felt a hand slip into the curve of her elbow and hold her back.

"It might be better if you let me," said a man's voice.

Pete turned. It was one of the two men she'd recognized from the beach—the veteran. His appeal was reinforced by a look of genuine concern in his gray eyes. She didn't have time to think about whether or not accepting his help was a good idea before he'd moved past her.

He walked up next to Bettina and stood beside her until, in a few seconds, she became aware of him and looked up fearfully.

"You can have the food," he said firmly, "all of it. But you must come with me."

Her eyes narrowed suspiciously. But when he picked up the tray very slowly, careful to make it clear that he was not snatching it away, she followed silently alongside as he walked out of the room.

Pete followed and was joined by the blond man who'd been sharing the veteran's table. When she went into the foyer, Pete found her mother standing mutely, looking down at the tray of food still held by the veteran but not eating.

Then the manager of the restaurant hurried in. Before Pete could react, the veteran asked the blond man to hold the tray and pulled the manager aside to converse in low tones. The manager left, and the veteran rejoined Pete.

"If he wanted to be paid for the dinners—" Pete began.

"He just wanted to be sure we had things under control."

It was obvious he had answered in the affirmative.

Pete wondered fleetingly whether his judgment could be trusted, then reminded herself that he had so far handled everything very effectively. "Thank you," she said. "I think I can manage now. I ought to take her back to the clinic."

"I'll get my car," he said.

"No," Pete protested. "I don't want to spoil your day out." Only as the words emerged did Pete realize she was still thinking of him as another patient. But could he be?

"It's really best if you have some help." He looked to the blond. "Robby, do you mind waiting here while I go for the car?"

The other man shook his head, and the veteran went out. There was an awkward silence. Bettina appeared bewildered still unable to recognize her daughter. Pete didn't know what to say to her. She turned instead to the blond man called Robby.

"Thanks for your kindness."

"Don't thank me. Thank my brother. He always knows what to do."

Obviously she'd read him wrong. Perhaps he was a doctor. "Is he . . . involved with the clinic?" she asked diplomatically.

Robby smiled. "Not really. But Luke's involved with me. I guess that's helped teach him how to handle an emergency."

It dawned on Pete then. Robby was the patient; his brother, Luke, just a constant visitor—a concerned relative, like herself.

Pete redeemed their coats from the checkroom, and her mother submitted meekly to being helped into hers.

The front door opened. The veteran put his head in. "Car's right outside."

A somewhat battered Volkswagen mini-bus was waiting at the bottom of the steps, the rear door standing open. Pete helped settle her mother in the back seat and got in beside her. Robby got into the front passenger seat, and Luke behind the wheel.

"Lock your door," he said to Pete. "You, too, Robby." Pete listened, regarding the veteran with a steadily growing appreciation of his steadiness and competence.

All the way back to the clinic, she held her mother's hand while uttering empty little reassurances—"You're safe now, Mama . . . you're all right." Bettina was so placid now, her eyes so vacant that Pete doubted she was even aware of being comforted.

When they pulled up in front of the clinic, there were already a couple of husky male orderlies waiting in the drive, evidently alerted by a call from the restaurant manager. Pete's heart sank when she saw that one was holding a straitjacket.

Before getting out, Luke leaned out of his window and spoke to the orderlies. "We won't need that. You guys disappear, and just send out a nurse."

"Listen, Mr. Sanford, we were told this woman was uncontrollable. Dr. Haffner knows about this, and he's coming, and if we don't—"

"She's okay now," he broke in. "Restraining her would be unnecessary, and might make it worse. Please . . . "

"Okay, Mr. Sanford," said one of the orderlies, and they went inside.

The exchange spiked Pete's curiosity about Luke Sanford. He might be no more than the relative of a patient, yet he had done something to win the respect of the orderlies.

One of the reception nurses came out as Pete helped Bettina from the van. "I'll take your mother now, Miss D'Angeli."

For a moment, Pete clung even more tightly to Bettina's arm. Releasing her hold, she felt suddenly, was to relinquish her hold on the dream that the illness would pass. It hadn't really hit until this moment how big a setback Bettina had suffered. So big that Pete suspected her mother might never be well enough to leave the clinic again, certainly not to come home. She felt lost herself, unable to move, until there was a light touch on her shoulder. She looked around to see it came from Luke Sanford.

"Your mother should get some rest," he said quietly.

The perfect words somehow, they allowed her to feel that letting go didn't have to mean she was consigning her mother forever to the institution. Pete unlocked her grip.

"Good-bye, Mama," she said.

Led by the nurse, Bettina shuffled inside without a word or backward glance. As Pete watched, tears sprang to her eyes, the brave front she had tried to maintain starting to crumble.

Luke Sanford put an arm around her shoulder and steered her inside. "This has been hard on you, too," he said. "You ought to sit down . . . "

In the clinic's high-ceilinged entrance hall, she took a chair. Then she looked at the two brothers who were lingering with her. "You've been so kind, but I don't want to spoil your holiday completely. Go back to the inn, please. I'll be fine." But her voice was quavering as she spoke.

"We'll wait with you until Dr. Haffner comes," Luke said. He checked his brother with a glance. "Okay, Robby?"

"Sure."

It did feel better not to be alone. "Thank you," Pete said to Luke. "You were so good with her—the way you calmed her down at the restaurant."

He gave a modest shrug. "All I did was listen. She said she wanted the food. I figured if she knew it wouldn't be taken away, she might behave."

"Do either of you happen to speak German?" Pete asked.

Both brothers shook their heads.

"I never heard her speak it before," Pete explained. "I keep wondering what she was saying."

Dr. Haffner bustled in from a side corridor, a muffler still around his neck. Pete knew he had a house on the grounds where he lived with his wife and the youngest of their three children, who was not yet in college. No doubt he had been called away from their own Thanksgiving dinner.

Pete stood. "I'm sorry, Dr. Haffner—"

"You? I'm the one who has to apologize. My God, if I'd dreamed she couldn't handle it. But I never imagined the associations she might make . . ."

"What do you mean?" Pete asked. "What associations?"

He paused. "Let's go to my office, Miss D'Angeli." Then he looked to the brothers. "If you'll excuse us, gentlemen."

As Pete followed the doctor, she looked back once at Luke Sanford. His face was as solemn as the first time she had seen him. Yet the expression she had once taken as hard and forbidding seemed now to be only a reflection of his sensitivity, an armor against the inevitable cruelties of an unkind world. What she saw there now was compassion and the pain of a shared tragedy.

Chapter 5

There was no warming fire waiting this afternoon in the doctor's office. The late afternoon sky outside the window had grown dark, and the room felt as bleak to Pete as her revised vision of the future. She felt herself shivering as she sat down, a reaction to shock more than the cold, and she kept her coat on, wrapped tight around her.

Haffner sat in the chair opposite. "I hope you understand, Miss D'Angeli, there was no way to predict this kind of breakdown. Your mother truly seemed to be getting better, accepting reality instead of fighting against it. But in a case like hers, we always have to be ready for the mind to be jolted back into the nightmare, making some connection we could never anticipate."

"What connection, Doctor, what associations? You mentioned the same thing before."

"I suppose the ceremony of the occasion had something to do with it," Haffner said grimly. "It's been several years since I was at the inn for Thanksgiving, but do I remember correctly that the food was brought in with a lot of . . . fanfare?"

Pete gave a puzzled nod and provided a brief description

of the procession—the waiters all costumed as Pilgrims, the trays and bowls of food carried aloft. "But how would that affect my mother?" she asked.

"The Pilgrim men would have been wearing black suits in a severe cut," Haffner observed. "In your mother's mind, those could have been transformed into SS uniforms. And seeing the food held high, she might have remembered the way the officers at the concentration camp delighted in torturing the starving prisoners, holding the food just out of reach . . ."

"Concentration camp?" Pete echoed. "What camp?" *Remembered*, he had said, her mother might have *remembered*. But her mother had never been in a concentration camp.

Haffner gazed at her for a long silent moment. "Miss D'Angeli," he said, in a gentle but somber tone indicating he knew the full impact of his words, "your mother spent a year at Auschwitz."

Pete shook her head. "No. That's not possible! I . . . I would have known. It would have been mentioned . . . sometime . . ."

Haffner's voice became even gentler. "It's the truth, Miss D'Angeli. A terrible truth, one that your mother hasn't wanted to accept."

Pete fought harder against the revelation. "My grandfather has told me everything," she insisted. "They lived in an attic. They hid throughout the war. That was bad enough, that's what broke Mama. He's told me . . ." She felt her own hold on reality slipping. Opa? Could he have lied to her?

No. Easier to believe it was her mother's delusion.

And then she remembered a conversation she'd had with her mother's doctor at Yonkers. He had mentioned Bettina's delusions of having been in a camp. She had asked him then if there was any chance it was the truth rather than Bettina's imagination. He said there was absolutely no chance, and now she remembered exactly why.

"She doesn't have a number," Pete said decisively. "There's no number tattooed on her arm. That must prove she wasn't there."

"That threw me off the track, too, at first. I assumed she

was imagining the stories she told me about the camp, reacting to guilt over escaping the fate that took her mother and so many others. But the more she told me about what happened to her, the detail . . . and the horror, the more difficult it became to believe she could be making it up. It simply rang too true to be psychotic ravings.

"I did some checking. I learned that certain prisoners at Auschwitz—some of the most beautiful young girls, the ones who looked most Aryan—were chosen directly from the transports and never became part of the general camp population. These girls were never numbered, never tattooed." He looked directly at Pete. "Because, you see, the group of officers for whom they were intended didn't want the girls to be . . . marked."

Pete's stomach sank as comprehension began seeping into her brain. "What did they do to her?" she asked, her voice low, tentative.

"Are you sure you really want to know, Miss D'Angeli?"

Did she? It had been a secret for so many years. But the secret had led her whole family deeper into the shadows. How could they find their way back to the light?

"Yes, I want to know," she said. "I have to know."

Almost as though she were blind, Pete moved with a slow uncertain gait as she emerged from the clinic into the driveway. It had begun to snow again, and she closed her eyes and lifted her face to let the flakes drift down onto her cheeks, needing their faint sting to remind her she was awake, that she had not dreamed her mother's nightmare.

Dr. Haffner had tried to tell her in a way that would not be too shocking, but, after all, there was no way. Although he had tried hard to keep a close rein on his own emotions, as he passed along what he had heard from Bettina—what he had come to realize was the traumatic truth—Haffner's face and eyes and the changing timbre of his voice betrayed every bit of his own pity and disgust and sorrow and rage.

Bettina had not spent the whole of the war in safe concealment. A year before the war's end, some damn quisling in the neighborhood had noticed that the Zeemans' protector seemed to be buying more food than necessary—not much more, but in wartime the constant flow of extra rations did not go unnoticed. The Gestapo had been alerted, and the hiding place had been found. Josef had been sent to forced labor, Bettina to Auschwitz.

That by itself should have been a sentence of death. But among the SS officers assigned to oversee the unloading of the railroad cars on the day Bettina arrived, there was a captain whose eye was drawn to her. It was not uncommon for officers to single out the more attractive young women and, before they had become too wasted from work and hunger and illness, use them for a time for their own pleasure. Bettina was taken at once to the quarters occupied by the SS captain. She was not tattooed with a number because the captain wanted her unmarked, virginal in every way.

At first he had used brute force to make her submit to his every sexual whim. But it wasn't long before Bettina learned to barter herself—to give a masterful performance as a willing, seductive love slave in return for other favors: an extra turnip, a taste of milk. The officer would even give her honey and melted chocolate, as long as she licked it from his penis or his anus or wherever he chose to make her grovel. Because she was so young and innocent and beautiful, because she had been pure, the SS captain derived an extra thrill from defiling her.

Yet, in the treacherous pathology of sex, he also enslaved himself, because, within a few weeks, he came to want Bettina and no other woman. For the remainder of the war, she was locked into her bargain with the devil. As long as she could continue to enchant and thrill her protector, she would remain alive. It required constant sexual innovation, the abandonment of any shred of self-respect, yet she had chosen survival over all.

"Oh, Mama," Pete cried softly as she stood in the driveway shivering, not from the cold, but the recurrent horror of the newly learned truth. There was no need to wonder it had been kept buried—out of shame, a need for denial. Opa had collaborated all along in keeping the secret, had encouraged his daughter to deny reality, too proud to admit her life had been bought at the cost of her corruption.

The sound of a car door opening and closing startled Pete. She brushed the snow from her face and looked along the driveway. It was almost evening, but through the gloom she saw the battered mini-van parked at the edge of the drive and the man who'd driven her from the restaurant walking toward her. He'd changed out of his dress-up blazer into an old sheepskin jacket. It took Pete a moment to clear her mind and remember his name.

"Mr. Sanford . . . I hope you didn't wait for me." Her voice was shaky and sounded strange to her. She made an effort to seem stable, in control. "You and your brother should have gone back to the inn."

"Robby was too upset by what happened to think of going back to a celebration," he said as he came up to her.

"I'm sorry."

"Don't be. That's one of the signs that he's getting better —he cares about the other patients, about people outside himself. He insisted I wait to help you."

"I don't need any help," Pete replied impulsively. She could hear how ungracious it sounded, but she rebelled against the notion that anything had happened to compromise her independence.

"How about just a lift back to the inn," he said mildly, "to pick up your car."

"Of course," she said, mortified. "That would make things a lot easier." He gestured to the van and they began to walk. Quietly she added, "Forgive me if I was rude, Mr. Sanford. I'm not thinking straight right now."

"No need to apologize. But I would prefer that you call me Luke."

They had reached the van. "All right, Luke," she said, putting out her hand. "And I'm Pete D'Angeli."

He took her hand. "I know. I asked Robby if he knew your name when I saw you on the beach."

At any other time the admission of interest would have flattered her. But with her nerves still raw, she felt suspicious, vulnerable. Should she be glad that this man had asked her name? Was he someone she could trust?

As he opened the passenger door and helped her in, Pete gave his face a close, searching look. Gray eyes with white squint lines in the weathered skin around them, prominent cheekbones, a strong chin, and a nose that wasn't quite straight. It added up to a more than attractive whole. But more important, she thought, there was something about the combination of features that conveyed dependability.

While he walked around to take his place at the wheel, Pete smiled faintly at the memory that the first time she'd seen Luke Sanford, she had thought he was one of the clinic's patients.

They drove several miles in silence. Once or twice Pete thought of making conversation, to be polite to this man who was showing such kindness. But then the sound of Dr. Haffner's voice telling its pitiless tale would echo again in her mind, and she wouldn't be able to see any point in politeness. Hadn't the beasts who'd destroyed her mother been polite, too, even used politeness as part of their savagery?

As the horror of it engulfed her again, Pete turned her face away to the window at her side so Luke wouldn't see her cry. Through her tears, she saw the snow swirling down outside, but even that didn't look clean to her. Nothing was clean.

"Bastards, unholy bastards." The words broke from her lips spontaneously. Then she was sobbing.

She wasn't sure how much longer he kept driving, but she was glad that he didn't stop too quickly and try to comfort her. It felt good to release the pent-up grief—the mourning for her mother's murdered innocence—that had been building since Haffner had told her the truth

Finally she felt the car swing off the road and come to a halt. Then his voice:

"You okay?"

She felt drained of tears. As she looked over at him and nodded, Pete became aware that they were stopped in the parking lot of an old-fashioned roadhouse, a long low building with neon beer advertisements in the windows, and another

flickering orange sign above the entrance that read
"DOOLEY'S—STEAK AND CHOPS."

"I thought a drink might help," he explained. "And maybe
something to eat—as long as it's not turkey."

She smiled, but was about to decline when she realized
how hollow and tense she felt. "It sounds just right," she
said.

Inside the roadhouse it was pleasantly dark, with a line of
booths along the windows, each one lit by a candle in a red
glass holder. A jukebox by a bar was playing a country-and-
western ballad. Several booths were occupied, and some men
at the bar were joking with each other. In mood and decor,
the place couldn't have been more unlike the Seven Sisters
Inn. Because the difference helped to dampen her memory
of the pathetic scene that had unfolded at the inn, Pete felt
at once it was exactly what she needed.

While Luke Sanford went to a booth, Pete excused herself
to go and wash her face. In the ladies' room, looking at
herself in the mirror, she suddenly felt uncertain about her
decision. She needed to be alone, to think, not having a drink
with an attractive man.

When she went back to the table, he had taken off his
sheepskin and was sitting with a beer. A small snifter of
brandy was waiting at her place. His presumption annoyed
her.

"I'm not sure that's what I want," she said as she slid
into the place across from him.

"Then please don't have it. But I thought . . . you were
so upset in the car, a little strong medicine might be better
than a cold beer."

Her perceptions turned upside down again. He'd meant to
be thoughtful, she'd taken it as thoughtless. But how could
she trust any of her judgments again? All her life she'd believed she knew who to trust, knew her mother and her grandfather, knew truth from lie. And she'd been wrong about all
of it.

She took a sip of the brandy, appreciating the warming fire
that settled deep within her. The shivery feeling began to
recede, and she slipped out of her coat.

"Luke, I'm the worst possible company tonight. One drink and we ought to go."

"Whatever you say. I'm here to listen only if you want to talk."

She nodded gratefully, but it seemed unthinkable to share her mother's terrible secrets with a stranger. Better to keep it light, she thought.

"Tell you something funny," she said. "First time I saw you and your brother on the beach, I thought you were the patient."

He smiled thinly. "No reason I couldn't be. There's not all that much that separates me and Robby. A couple of different breaks, a different turn along the path, and it could be the other way around."

"Were your breaks so good?" Pete said. "Weren't you in Vietnam?"

"Yeah, I went. So did a lot of guys. I was lucky enough to be able to handle it. Lucky, too, that I was up in the air flying a chopper while the others were slogging through the mud down below."

Pete had read about the war; she knew that plenty of helicopter pilots got shot out of the air. "So you were lucky," she said drily. "What happened to Robby?"

"I guess he's a casualty from another battleground—America in the sixties. He had too much freedom to do his own thing while he was too young, got into a crowd that was using a lot of dope, and had some real bad LSD trips. It pushed him over the edge into real psychotic behavior. Maybe he could've licked it then if there'd been anyone to help, but my father had walked out on us; my mother . . . she died around that time; and I was in grad school until I was drafted."

He drank from his mug of beer while Pete took another sip of brandy, studying him over the rim of the snifter. The hands wrapped around his mug were strong, the fingers squared off, neat and capable. The index finger lightly traced a path in the moisture on the mug.

It was cold, and he'd put his drab army jacket back on over his tweed blazer. It looked very good on him, but it wasn't fancy and thinking about the battered van he drove, Pete guessed that he had as much trouble making ends meet and keeping a relative at the clinic as she did, maybe more.

"How long has Robby been at Cole-Haffner?" she asked.

"Since the beginning. But he's going to be leaving soon, I'm sure of it. I'm looking for a way to put him to work for me."

"What do you do?"

"I'm an inventor."

Pete broke into a smile. In all the constant exchanges over careers that went on in New York conversation, she'd never heard that one before.

"Like Edison?"

"Nobody's like Edison," he replied.

"Well, what do you invent?"

"Mostly I noodle around with electronic things." He tossed off a little shrug that Pete took as a hint that he didn't want to get any deeper into the subject. Maybe he was protecting some unpatented secrets, she thought, or maybe there was really nothing to talk about.

"What's your work?" he asked, confirming his eagerness to shift the focus.

She had to think a second. Did she want to say simply that she sold things? The more she talked with Luke Sanford, the more he interested her—and the more she wanted to seem interesting to him.

"I haven't done what I want yet," she said.

"And what's that?"

"To be a special kind of designer."

"What kind?"

"A jewelry designer."

"Jewelry," he echoed. "Why are you attracted to that?"

His tone bothered her. It seemed flat, even a bit disparaging. Or was her judgment off again? He had no reason to be critical.

"It runs in the family," she said. "My maternal grandfather is a gem cutter. And my father's mother, so he's told me, adored jewelry and had one of the most fabulous collections in Europe."

"So you never thought of doing anything else?"

Pete gave him a sideways glance. She wasn't imagining it; he was challenging her choice, subtly suggesting there were more worthwhile occupations.

"As a matter of fact," she said with an edge, "I considered psychiatry. I guess I had a dream of curing my mother . . . and all the other crazy people in the world. But then I decided I could go crazy myself if I tried to be a saint instead of simply trying to do something I loved. Does that sound so wrong?"

He looked back at her squarely, evidently weighing his answer. Would he stick to his guns, admit that he thought her work was trivial? Pete wondered. Or would he retreat into some polite, empty pleasantry. Either way, she realized, she would be disappointed.

"I think it's good to do what you love," he said finally. "But I think it's a shame you couldn't love doing something that could have helped a lot of people—maybe including your mother—instead of just adding a little sparkle to a privileged few."

She stared back. In the wake of learning that her own grandfather had concealed so much from her, she found Luke Sanford's frankness admirable—maybe even refreshing in the same way as a mint that was so damn strong it took your breath away.

"Well," she said at last. "I asked, didn't I?"

He had second thoughts then. "Look, I didn't mean to—"

"Yes, you did," she cut in. "You meant exactly what you said. Don't spoil it by watering it down. In your high and mighty opinion, I'm wasting my time."

"That's not what I said."

"It comes close enough. But you really don't have to worry, Mr. Sanford. Because when I talked about my career, I was gilding the lily—and I don't mean as a piece of jewelry. I haven't really done what I want, and after today I can't see how I ever will." She downed the rest of her brandy. "And now we can go. I said one drink was my limit."

He opened his mouth as if to add something, then changed

his mind. With a shake of his head, he slid out of the booth, walked to the bar, and paid the bill. She got up and waited for him by the door.

They were frozen in silence for the rest of the drive back to the inn.

Damn! Pete stewed as she sat with her face half buried in the collar of her coat, why did it have to end like this? He'd been so perfectly considerate in every other way, she'd thought he was so special . . . someone who understood the particular strains of having mental illness in a family . . . someone she'd hoped might stay in her life. She would have liked to have a shoulder to cry on about Mama, about her own stalled ambitions. He'd said he was ready to listen and, given a little more time, she might have taken the opportunity.

But then this damn stupid argument had blown up from nowhere. Her fault or his? Pete wasn't sure. The only thing she did know was that it had destroyed any chance for friendship right at the start. He thought her idea of work was foolish; she thought he was narrow-minded and self-satisfied, incapable of seeing that the creation of beauty was, in its own way, a noble occupation.

In the parking lot of the inn, they stood beside her rented car, both uncomfortably searching for a good ending.

"Thank you," Pete said. "You made a difficult situation a lot easier."

"And an easy situation difficult," he said.

She shrugged.

There was a silence, and then she turned toward her car. "Pete . . ."

She looked back at him.

"I have to be away for a while. But when I come back . . . I'd like to see your designs. I'll bet they're good . . ."

"They will be when I get the chance. Right now, almost all of them are up here." She tapped her head, and he smiled.

She could see him in the rearview mirror, still standing and watching as she drove away.

What could she have said? What had she wanted him to say? Her fault or his? She thought about it all the way back to the city.

* * *

But in the morning all thoughts of Luke Sanford were crowded out of her mind by the rage and disillusionment she felt with her grandfather.

He would be expecting her at the hospital, of course, looking forward to news of the Thanksgiving outing, full of questions: Did Bettina like her chocolates?

And what, Pete wondered, had the Nazis given her mother as treats when she performed well for them?

She put off going to the hospital until late in the morning, but at last Pete knew it couldn't be avoided forever.

He was propped up in the big hospital bed when she came in, looking small and old, his leg high and huge in its plaster casing. His face lit with delight when he saw her.

"*Schatje*, you must tell me everything about your wonderful Thanksgiving. How is my girl?"

"You should have told me," she said, all her anger of the previous day rushing back. Her hands gripped the tubular railing at the foot of the bed. "You should have told me the truth about my mother, Opa. I had a right to know."

"What are you talking about? What great truth is this?" His voice was full of indignation, but a note of fear gave him away.

"About the war. About Auschwitz. About what those Nazi bastards did to her."

He sat up as straight as his leg allowed, as though to defend himself, saw that it was useless, and conceded defeat, sagging deeply into the pillows, looking even smaller than before. "How do you tell a young girl that her mother was a whore?"

"She wasn't a whore! Don't you ever call her that! She was a victim. She was a helpless young woman who lived through hell. And she's been wishing ever since that she hadn't."

His eyes closed, his face looked sunken and gray. "I tried to make it up to her," he said, his voice small and faraway. "I thought if we put it away and never, ever talked about it, if I just loved her enough, if Steve loved her enough, she would forget it in time. Maybe I thought I could make it never have happened."

"But it did happen, Opa, and you never gave her a chanc
to face it, to grieve for what she had lost, to feel her ange
and pain so she could let it go."

He gave her a wan smile. "You should have stayed i
school, Pietje. You would have made a good psychiatrist.'

"And you didn't give me a chance to understand," sh
said, still too angry to be moved by his pain. "I might hav
been able to help her if I'd known."

"Maybe I was wrong."

"You were, Opa, dead wrong, so wrong I'm not sure
can forgive you."

His eyes squeezed shut, and she saw tears seep out an
run in rivers down his deeply lined cheeks. "Please, Pietje,'
he whispered. "I've lost my wife. I've lost my daughter.
can't lose you, too."

Her anger wasn't proof against his tears. She came aroun
and sat in the chair beside his bed, took the hand that lay s
limply on the crisp white sheet. "Tell me now, Opa
everything—how you were caught, what happened to you
how you found Mama after the war. Maybe it's too late t
help her, but you can still help me."

His voice tired and old and shaky at the horror of th
memories, he began. They never knew who'd given awa
their hiding place, but the Gestapo came in July 1944, brok
into the secret attic, and dragged them away. Since he wasn'
a Jew, Josef was sent to a forced labor camp in Germany
Bettina went to Westerbork, the processing center for Dutc
Jews. In September, she was put on the last shipment of Jew
to leave Holland.

"The same transport that took Anne Frank and her famil
to Auschwitz," he said, and Pete shuddered. "It was a freig
train, seventy-five people to a car, with one small, barre
window. The trip took three days."

He told her what he knew of Bettina's time in the camp
learned not from Bettina but from a friend who had been wit
her. It was the same story she'd heard the day before, and
was no less horrible in repetition.

"I didn't know where she was or even if she was alive,"
he said. "I was sent to dig coal in the Saar. I was there unt

the Allies liberated us. Then I was in a displaced persons camp for several months. I tried everything I could think of to find Bettina and Anneke, your grandmother. Finally, I got confirmation that my wife had gone to the gas chambers at Auschwitz. It wasn't until late forty-five that I learned your mother was alive. I found her in a hospital in Marseilles.''

At first she didn't recognize him. Whenever he touched her or spoke to her, she started removing her clothes, fell to her knees, and repeated the scene Pete had witnessed with such horror the day before. But finally the reality that it was over, that she was safe, began to sink in and she began to heal. Josef took her home.

''But Rotterdam held too many harsh memories for both of us. I thought Bettina would forget faster in a totally new place, and there was no place newer than America, so we came.''

''And you met Papa. And you never told him either.''

''Do you think he would have married her if he'd known?''

''I don't know. He might have liked the choice.''

''I thought I was doing a good thing when I brought them together. Your father had lost someone, too, someone he loved. You never knew that, did you?''

''No,'' she said softly, overwhelmed with how much her life had been dominated by secrets she'd never known.

''I thought they could help each other. It didn't work.'' He squeezed her hand. ''Still, I'm not sorry. They gave me you.''

They were both crying now, and she leaned over and gave him a hug made clumsy by the traction wires and pulleys.

''Am I forgiven, *schatje*? I'm not sure I could stand it if I weren't.''

''Yes, Opa, because I could never stay angry at you very long, not even for this. But you have to promise me something.''

''What?''

''No more secrets. Not ever.''

''*Ik beloof*,'' he said. ''I promise.''

Chapter 6

Pete was still more than a block from the store when the rain started to splash down on Fifth Avenue.

Perfect, she thought, as she dashed across the street and along the sidewalk—April showers! It had been a mild sunny morning when she'd started the walk to work, wearing new Italian shoes no less, purchased in her first shopping splurge in months. Now if she didn't hurry she'd be drenched.

Approaching the entrance of Dufort & Ivères, she saw that a couple of maintenance men were already putting up the long purple pennant imprinted in silver with the words "HERE'S THAT RAINY DAY." Another of Andrea's ideas. The "shower of diamonds" ads that had been appearing in the fashion magazines since February had provoked so much comment that Andrea had conceived the pennants to be put up every time it rained. Pete didn't know how much the campaign had actually boosted sales, but a lot more young single women were coming into the store, to browse if not to buy. Andrea Scappa was certainly putting the stamp of her own style on Dufort & Ivères. As she became more important, would she feel less threatened? Or did she remain an enemy, and was the day coming, Pete wondered, when Andrea would have the power to make Marcel get rid of her?

The doorman, Frank, spotted Pete and immediately ran to intercept her with his umbrella. "Morning, Miss D'Angeli," he said cheerfully as he accompanied her to the revolving door.

"Don't know about good, but it sure is wet."

"Don't forget what they say about April showers," Frank offered. "They bring the flowers that bloom in May . . ."

A nice sentiment for a song, Pete thought. She didn't think her own future looked so bright. Lately, Pete felt, not very much had worked out right for her. It had been that way, really, since Mama's relapse months ago.

The prospect of her mother's extended institutionalization had killed any dream of taking risks with her work. When Marcel had brought over the Lalique pieces just after New Year's, she had dutifully applied herself to a special sales promotion—helping to prepare a brochure on the pieces, sorting through customer lists to pick out names of those worth inviting to a gala private showing at the store. The pieces had sold at record prices, and she had been rewarded with high commissions.

But the money gave her little satisfaction. It simply covered the bills. Though her grandfather's leg had healed, he hardly worked at all. As she earned more, Pete also stopped asking her father to contribute to the costs of the clinic. It wasn't only because she knew he earned less than she did. The bigger reason was Pete's feeling that Steve had been cheated into marrying Bettina by the way Josef had withheld the true story of her wartime experience. Would he have married her anyway if he'd known the full truth? Maybe. But the choice had been stolen from him. Pete felt she was making it up to him in some way by no longer requiring him to share the cost of her mother's illness.

Despite this much sympathy, she had remained distant from her father since their argument at Thanksgiving. What kept her away was the decision not to reveal to him what she had learned about her mother. Pete feared the fury it might rouse in Steve once he knew that Josef had hidden so much from him. As it was, the two men had not been on good terms for years. Yet if she saw her father and said nothing, Pete felt she would be an accomplice to the terrible lie. For now, it was easier to stay away.

The morning passed slowly. Pete had no appointments with special customers, so she spent her time dealing with walk-in traffic on the open mezzanine where the display cases of the fine jewelry department were located. The continuing downpour kept the volume light. She spent an hour each with two customers who decided not to buy. Shortly before noon, she was called to a phone.

"Well, what did you think of him?" a voice asked eagerly.

It was Jess.

"Yours or mine?" Pete replied.

They had been out the night before on an old-fashioned double date, seats to *A Chorus Line*, still a hot ticket though it had been running a couple of years, then dinner. Jess had wanted Pete's opinion of a man she'd begun dating regularly. The pretext for giving Pete a chance to look him over was for Jess to have her date bring along a friend for Pete. Though she didn't like blind dates generally, Pete couldn't refuse. Jess knew she hadn't been dating anyone for a long time, and was only trying to do her a favor while tapping into her advice.

"I don't have to ask what you thought of yours," Jess said. "I'd have had to be blindfolded in a total eclipse not to see how you felt."

Pete laughed. The stockbroker who'd been her date had talked only about how much money he was making, and at the theater she'd had to keep removing his hand from her thigh, until exasperation had impelled her at last to plant a spiked heel firmly in one of his wing-tips.

"But what about Fernando?" Jess persisted.

"He seems lovely," Pete said.

"Really?" Jess said. "You really liked him?"

"Hey, don't sound so surprised. He's obviously a man of taste and intelligence if he's stuck on you. What's more, he's gorgeous, fun to be with, and I can see he treats you beautifully. Why wouldn't I like him?''

There was a pause. ''Well, you didn't care for his friend.''

''Maybe it takes a woman to keep a man away from bad company. That'll be your job, Jess, if you stay with this guy.''

''I hope I can.'' Her voice fell. ''He says he loves me, Pete, says he wants to marry me. Can you imagine? It's . . . it's a little scary, because you know I've never had anyone before, and Fernando seems . . . like a dream come true. I'd feel so awful if it just . . . ended.''

''Relax, Jess,'' Pete urged. ''It's not going to end.'' She reeled off some more encouraging words before telling Jess it was time to get back on the job. They agreed to meet for lunch at the end of the week.

Through her lunch hour and the early afternoon, Pete couldn't get the short conversation out of her mind. She had lied to her best friend, and she couldn't decide if it was right or wrong. The truth was that she hadn't liked Fernando de Moratin one bit. He was handsome and dapper, yes, and constantly sweet and attentive to Jess, and outwardly charming, with a ready stream of amusing stories and gossip. But there was something bogus about him, Pete felt. He was too smooth, too ready to please, not at all the down-to-earth sort that Pete imagined would be the right kind of man for Jess. In fact, Pete could not suppress a lurking suspicion that Fernando might be interested in Jess because of her money.

But was there any way to tell these things to Jess? Or would it even be fair? After all, it was only her opinion. And Jess was so happy, so in need of feeling loved by a man.

Where did kindness cross the line into hypocrisy?

As Pete pondered the particular dilemma of when to speak the truth and when to hold back, her encounter with Luke Sanford came to mind. He hadn't held back. He had been honest with her, and she had rejected him for it. This was far from the first time she had thought it over, and with the passing of time she regretted increasingly that she hadn't been able to shrug off his criticism. There was so much she'd liked about him; he had been so thoughtful and sensible in the way he'd helped with her mother. Yet she had nipped a chance at friendship—and perhaps something more—in the bud because he spoke his mind to her. True, he had dismissed as unimportant the very thing that was at the core of her ambition; perhaps that would always have been a sore point between them. But there was a lot to be said for a man who told the whole truth and nothing but.

Not long before, Pete had decided to find out where Luke had gone and to write him a letter. But on a visit to the clinic, intending to ask Robby for Luke's whereabouts, she had learned that Robby Sanford had been released early in March and had joined his brother. The people at the clinic were willing to reveal that the brothers were in California, but they wouldn't provide the exact address, not even the city.

"We'll be glad to forward mail for you, Miss D'Angeli," Dr. Haffner explained. "If Robby answers you directly, that's his choice. But our policy is to keep all records of every patient absolutely confidential, down to the last detail. You should be able to sympathize."

Small as the obstacle was, it gave Pete second thoughts. After years in the institution, Robby Sanford was beginning a new life. Maybe he wanted no ties of any kind to the clinic, no reminders. For that matter, why should Luke Sanford care at this late date if she let him know she shouldn't have taken offense at his opinions? He was in California, thousands of miles away.

If there had been a chance to know him better, Pete realized, it was lost now. Along with her other chances.

The afternoon was even slower than the morning. The serious jewelry buyers, Pete mused, were probably out of town, avoiding the April showers in New York to spend a chic April in Paris.

Half an hour before closing, her doldrums were blown away by a deep, robust voice rising up to the mezzanine from the ground floor:

"My good man," a loud, rich voice intoned. "Kindly step aside and allow me to drip on your floor at my leisure."

Pete went to the balcony that overlooked the entrance.

Frank, the burly doorman, who had been chosen for his job as much for his physique as for his impeccable manners and cheerful disposition, was stolidly blocking the way. "If you could state your business, sir?" he said, his voice all steel draped in politeness.

The man seeking entrance was tall and slender, almost rangy, with dark blond hair lank now from the rain. He wore sunglasses despite the grayness of the day, a soaked Burberry ineffectually draped over his shoulders, and a bandage knotted around his head and across one eye, giving him something of the air of a dissolute boy pirate. He was also clearly the worse for drink.

Pete couldn't blame Frank for wanting to keep him out. But she suspected it might mean the loss of a sizable sale. She hurried down the broad marble stairs.

"My business, good sir," the man at the door enunciated in deliberate pear-shaped tones, "is none of your fucking business. Now, unless you remove your corporeal bulk from my path, I may have to take strong measures."

Frank seemed on the brink of grabbing the unruly intruder by the scruff of the neck to eject him when Pete intervened.

"Thank you, Frank," she said. "I'll take over. Come with me, Mr. MacKinnon." Slipping a hand through his arm, Pete began to guide him up the stairs, steering toward one of the private salons. In his condition, whatever he wanted, it was better served, both for him and for Dufort & Ivères, in private, away from the prying eyes of curious customers.

It was, of course, the voice that had done it. She had recognized its distinctive richness the second it reached her ears. Douglas MacKinnon had been known twenty years earlier as one of the greatest young actors of the English stage. Trained at London's Royal Academy of Dramatic Arts, a long-standing member of the Royal Shakespeare Company, he had begun broadening his public through British movies ten years ago. Then Hollywood had called, casting him in a spate of costume dramas that had led in the past year to his being cast opposite Lyla Weaver, Hollywood's highest-paid woman star, in a lavish film about Napoleon and Josephine. Though both were married—Weaver to her *fifth* husband—

the two stars had begun an affair that had become every bit as celebrated as the one they were portraying. Though neither was yet divorced, the affair was still ongoing. Paparazzi with long lenses followed Weaver and MacKinnon everywhere, and pictures of them lying together, in various stages of undress, on beaches from Mexico to the Mediterranean, appeared almost weekly in the tabloids.

It was not from newsstands and supermarket check-out counters, however, that Pete had recognized Douglas MacKinnon. She had seen some of the early films in which he had played Richard the Lionhearted and General Montgomery—even a daring portrayal of Oscar Wilde in a flowing cape and black slouch hat. No actor was as thrilling to watch and listen to, Pete had always thought, as Douglas MacKinnon.

"Thank you for taking me in hand, my dear," he said as they arrived on the mezzanine. "I would've hated having to hurt that fellow. I shall hope to return the favor someday . . . and take you in hand." He gave her a mischievous glance.

Pete had read enough of the gossip to know that, long before Lyla Weaver, MacKinnon had acquired a reputation as a seducer of heroic proportions. She thought she knew how to handle him, though. "If you've come to DuFort and Ivères," she said wryly, "I would've thought you're interested in buying jewelry, not just showing off your . . . own family jewels."

MacKinnon stopped to look at her and then roared with laughter. "Methinks the lady has a blade for a tongue. *Touché*."

Pete gestured toward the private salons. "Why don't we go in here and you can tell me—"

"We don't have to go anywhere. Just take me to Lyla."

"Lyla? Miss Weaver isn't here."

MacKinnon erupted. "Damn the bloody woman. Never where she's supposed to be. We agreed to meet at five o'clock. I'm a fucking half hour late myself, and she's *still* not here!"

"I'm sure she'll be here any minute," Pete said in her most soothing professional voice. To herself she thought, *wild horses couldn't keep Weaver away.* Pete had reason to feel confident. She had waited on Lyla Weaver several times in the past few years. The star was famous for an almost pathological love of expensive jewels, the bigger the better. She was known to insist her lovers prove their affection with gifts of precious gems. The woman intrigued Pete, echoing as she did the legend of La Colomba and her fabulous jewel collection, tribute from a lifetime of lovers.

Pete gestured again to one of the private salons. "Come and sit down. Let me get you a cup of coffee while you wait."

"What you can get me," MacKinnon said as he went into the salon, "is a nice tall twenty-year-old . . . Scotch." He tossed his wet raincoat on the marble vanity and settled himself on one of the petit point–covered chairs.

"I don't think you need any more—"

"For Christ's bloody sake," MacKinnon exploded in his stentorian voice, "don't start mothering me."

Pete hesitated another second, then lifted a phone from the polished ebony table, spoke into it a moment, and sat down across from him. At forty-five, he was still a compelling man, with eyes of startling blue and deep seams in his weathered face that only made him more handsome. Despite the liquor he'd already consumed, he looked at Pete with such directness and power that she pulled back involuntarily.

"You are a fine-looking wench," he said in his rich, sonorous tones.

She had to laugh. "You are absolutely the first man who has ever called me a wench."

"Yes, well, it's part of the image, don't you see?"

"I think I'm flattered."

He looked around the room, noticing the total privacy it afforded. "Don't suppose you'd care to have a quick tumble while we wait for Lyla bloody Weaver, would you? She probably won't trot in here for another half hour at least, and we seem to have the place to ourselves."

Again, Pete laughed. She'd had more than one man proposition her in Dufort & Ivères' private salons, but none of them with quite as much charm or lack of guile. Or so unconvincingly. "No, I don't suppose I would, but thank you for asking."

"Didn't think so, but it seemed worth a try."

MacKinnon's drink arrived along with coffee for Pete. For a moment, the tinkle of ice in the glass in his hand and the pelting of rain on a skylight overhead were the only sounds in the room. He took a long swallow of the fine whiskey and a long look at Pete.

"What is your name, my dear? As the bard said, one should always know the name of the woman one is trying to screw. It is the minimum of good manners."

Pete laughed. "Shakespeare never said that."

"Oh no? Well, don't let that keep you from telling me your name."

"Pete D'Angeli."

"Pete? Pete?" MacKinnon echoed with rising incredulity. "What sort of a name is that for a beautiful wench?"

"Actually, it's Pietra."

"Ah yes. Much more wenchlike," he said, and rolled the name across his tongue like a fine vintage wine. "Pi-e-traaaaa. Lovely. Yes, it suits you." He sipped at his drink and studied himself in the large mirrors lining the wall across from him. "I look like a bloody pirate with this bandage on."

"What happened? I hope it's not serious?"

"Only to my pride, my dear. My Richard doesn't seem to be quite as light on his feet as he once was. Or as handy with a sword. Today's rehearsal was somewhat bloodier than usual. But it's only a flesh wound. I will recover, have no fear, though my speed may not and my pride definitely won't."

Pete remembered then. MacKinnon was in New York to appear on stage in a special limited run of *Richard III*. Charlie had already asked her to go with him—if it ever opened. According to Charlie's inside sources, there had been some trouble at rehearsals because of MacKinnon's drinking.

"I'm looking forward to seeing you on stage," Pete said. "I've heard you're one of the best Shakespearean actors, and *Richard* is my favorite of all the plays."

"What? Poor knavish Richard? Deform'd, unfinish'd, sent before his time into this breathing world? Good, then we shall be great friends. And you shall have house seats, any night you wish."

Pete was genuinely thrilled. A trip to the theater was always a rare treat, but a chance to see Douglas MacKinnon, and in the best seats in the house, would be heaven. "I don't know how to thank you, Mr. MacKinnon."

"Think, my child, think. It may come to you." He gave her another of his devilish grins, somehow beguiling despite its leering message. "Meanwhile, let us pray that opening night does indeed come to pass." He chugged half his drink, and Pete snuck a look at her watch. Nearly six. She was due to go home shortly, but Douglas MacKinnon didn't look like leaving anytime soon. On the contrary, he seemed to have settled in for the duration.

"She doesn't really believe I love her, you know," he said suddenly. Despite the abrupt change of topic, Pete knew he must be talking about Lyla Weaver. "Says she won't divorce Billy-boy because she's not sure I love her enough to stay with her."

"And do you?" Pete asked, genuinely curious.

"Do I?" the actor said with loud indignation. The rest of the scotch slid down his throat in a single swig, and the glass hit the table with a gentle crash. "I'll show everybody how much I love her." He pulled a crumpled brown paper bag from his pocket. "With this."

From inside the bag, he pulled an even more crumpled tissue, unrolled it, and laid on the table the most perfect, most beautiful star sapphire Pete had ever seen. Her trained eye judged it to be at least ninety carats, and it was the intense, rich blue, unchangeable in sunlight or artificial light, found only in the best Kashmir sapphires. The exact blue of a peacock's neck feathers.

She reached out and touched the stone almost gingerly, brushing it lightly with one finger. "It's magnificent."

"So I should think. One does not pay slightly short of a quarter of a million U.S. dollars for—as you Americans say—chopped liver."

"Where did you get it?"

"From a private dealer in Singapore. Do you think Lyla will like it?" His voice was suddenly filled with a little-boy eagerness.

Like it? thought Pete. For this stone, Lyla Weaver would kill if necessary. "From what I know of Miss Weaver, I'm sure she will be very pleased with your sapphire," Pete said.

"Do you know *Two Gentlemen*?"

"Which two gentlemen?" she asked, puzzled.

"*Two Gentlemen of Verona*. Valentine, Act Three, Scene One: 'Win her with gifts, if she respect not words. Dumb jewels often in their silent kind more than quick words do move a woman's mind.'"

"Believe me, Mr. MacKinnon, her mind will be moved," Pete said, touching the stone again. "May I have a closer look?" He waved his permission, and she picked up the stone, took a jeweler's loupe from her pocket, and peered deep into its heart. The depth of the blue color was astonishing—no trace of green, gray, or violet; this was the pure blue shade treasured by the ancients as symbolizing heaven. She could clearly see the crossed rutile needles that created the six-pointed "star," and the stone had the velvety, hazy quality so characteristic of Kashmir sapphires. "Beautiful," she breathed as she handed it back to him.

"That's all well and good," said MacKinnon, "but where the devil is Lyla? I was going to give it to her today, you see. Thought we'd ask your people to design a setting for it. Something flashy and original; she'll like that. Something that will make her promise to finally get on with the divorce and marry me." He rolled the stone through his fingers like a Greek worry bead. "I need her, you see."

He was growing maudlin; Pete wondered if it was the Scotch talking. "Mr. MacKinnon, I'm sure—"

"She's not coming. I know it." Certainty echoed in his words. "Her bloody husband's offered a reconciliation. She promised me she wasn't even considering it, but I know my girl. If Billy-boy comes through with a diamond pendant or an emerald bracelet, she'll bloody well consider it. What it comes down to, lovely Pietra, is whose rocks she wants more—his or mine.''

From a shelf, a small gold clock with an onyx face gently chimed six times.

"Mr. MacKinnon," Pete said, "I'm afraid we're closing."

"Yes. Right," he said, scooping up the enormous sapphire and wrapping it up once more in its tissue. "She doesn't deserve it. Doesn't deserve me. I'll give it to someone else."

He dropped the stone into the crumpled brown paper bag and jammed it into the pocket of his sodden raincoat. Then he rose and made Pete a respectable though slightly tentative bow. He left the private salon and made his way quickly if unevenly across the main floor of the store, now empty of customers. Pete followed him.

Nearing the door, his steps faltered, not quite a stagger, but definitely a wobble. "I seem to be in need of some fresh air," he declaimed, "I shall walk to my hotel." He threw his Burberry with its precious cargo over his shoulders, shrugging it into position.

Pete scurried after him. The thought of a man in his condition walking out into the streets of Manhattan with a two-hundred-fifty-thousand-dollar sapphire lying loose in his pocket was more than she could bear.

"Mr. MacKinnon," Pete said, "wouldn't you like me to put the sapphire in our vault for you? That way, it will be here when you come back with Miss Weaver."

"Not necessary, my dear," he said, waving away her concern.

"But it isn't safe."

"Ah yes, thieves and vagabonds might set upon me," he said. "And wouldn't the beautiful Miss Weaver be sorry then?" He took Pete's hand, kissed it with great gallantry, and pushed through the door into the rain that was still sluicing down.

Pete watched him meander away from the entrance. If she was a betting woman, she'd put down money that his next stop would be the nearest bar. And after a couple more Scotches, he'd be showing the sapphire to all his new mates. His next stop after that could well be a very dark alley.

Grabbing up the large umbrella Frank kept by the door, Pete ran out after Douglas MacKinnon. The least she could do was get him into a taxi and get the sapphire safely home.

The umbrella blew inside out the minute Pete hit the pavement. By the time she caught up with MacKinnon's long legs, he'd gone nearly two blocks and she was soaked.

Miraculously, a free taxi cruised by just as she reached him. She stuck out her hand and it skidded to a splashy stop beside them, drenching any part of her that wasn't already soaked through.

Pete opened the door, but MacKinnon resisted, saying he preferred to walk.

"Look," said Pete, wiping streams of water from her eyes, "if my boss finds out I knew about that rock in your pocket and I let you go out into the streets of Manhattan without putting it in the store vault . . . well, my ass is grass, as the saying goes."

"Quaint, that. You Americans have so many quaint expressions."

"Right, but could we discuss linguistics and etymology someplace Noah would be less at home, and where that stone would be safe?"

"With pleasure, my dear. Someplace where you can have dinner with me."

She shook her head. "Mr. MacKinnon—"

"Douglas, and don't refuse or you shall be placing me and my precious cargo in the most dire peril."

She laughed in spite of herself. He was a charmer. He was a star. And she did want to be sure the sapphire was secure. To top it off, the impatient cabdriver chimed in: "What's the big deal? Have dinner with him or let me go pick up another fare."

"All right, dinner," she said, and they climbed into the cab.

MacKinnon told the driver to take them around to the Plaza, only a few blocks away.

"I can't go there," Pete protested. "Look at me. I'm a mess."

"You, dear girl, are absolutely exquisite, and we shall see

that you are fit to dine with princes." He leaned toward her. "What did you say your name was?"

She laughed again as she told him and wondered if he'd remember it for longer than ten minutes. Oh, Jess, she thought, wait till I tell you *this* one.

At the Plaza, MacKinnon worked his relentless charm to persuade Pete to change into dry clothes—a red backless Valentino shift that he selected personally from one of the lobby boutiques. To overcome Pete's resistance, he explained that it wasn't a gift, only a loan; the hotel was happy to make such accommodations for stars.

Taking the dress to the ladies' room, Pete changed, then ran a towel quickly over her wet hair, pulled it back, and tied it with a paisley patterned silk scarf from her purse. After freshening her makeup, she felt ready to face the world. Rather than looking like the bedraggled waif who had come in, she emerged looking glorious. The severe hairstyle pointed up the fineness of her bone structure, making her look like a cosmetics model. And the blue eyes flashed with an unaccustomed sense of adventure.

That evening Pete saw a world she knew existed but had never glimpsed at first hand. When they left the Plaza after dinner in the Oak Room, a limousine was waiting. MacKinnon took her for dessert and coffee at Regine's, and after-dinner drinks at Elaine's. At each stop she told herself the evening ought to end, but then she let MacKinnon lead her on to the next. How could she refuse? Not only were they hitting all the hot spots she'd never been to, but she was there on the arm of a man guaranteed to get her more than her fair share of attention. Douglas MacKinnon seemed to know ninety percent of the patrons everyplace they went, and they all seemed genuinely pleased to meet her. Before the night was half done, Pete realized she'd probably show up in a dozen gossip columns the next day as "Douglas MacKinnon's new mystery lady."

It was nearly one o'clock when Pete was whisked through the door of Studio 54 past the ogling line of those not deemed worthy of admission. For Pete it was like arriving in Oz, a place beyond the narrow limits that had held her within the poverty of Hell's Kitchen, then the proper conformism of her job. Above the packed dance floor, a huge crescent moon with a neon coke spoon in its center flashed over the heads of Beautiful People gyrating to a deafening rock beat that pushed up through Pete's shoes and made her blood pulse with it. She laughed freely as MacKinnon pulled her onto the dance floor again and yelled, "Soar, Pietra, soar!"

But as heady as the evening was, Pete tried not to forget to keep a close eye on the raincoat. Whenever it wasn't in a guarded checkroom, she insisted on keeping it with her.

By two A.M. Pete's head was definitely buzzing, and MacKinnon and Mick Jagger had involved most of the people at Studio 54 in a boisterous rendition of "Knees Up, Mother Brown."

"I really do have to go home, Douglas," she said at last, only a little reluctantly.

"Bugger that. We are going downtown, Pietra. Magnificent new place there, I hear."

"Sorry, it's really carriage-into-pumpkin time for me." She yawned. "I'm probably the only person in this room who has to get up and go to work tomorrow morning."

They got the precious coat from the checkroom and went out to the sidewalk. The limousine pulled up and MacKinnon started to tell the driver to take Pete wherever she wanted to go. She realized then that he would be going off on his own—with the sapphire.

"Douglas," she said, doing her best to mimic the high-handed tone she'd heard him using all night. "I have no intention of mothering you. But I am equally determined not to let you be a damn fool. If you're not going home to bed, then give me what you've got in that pocket for safe-keeping." She pointed to the right side of his Burberry.

He frowned thoughtfully, then pulled out the paper bag. "I s'pose that would be wise," he said. And with a deft move he plucked the sapphire from the bag and tossed it to her through the air in a high arc.

Pete threw up her hands and managed to catch it. A breath of relief whistled through her lips before she said, "Your sapphire will be in the vault at Dufort and Ivères tomorrow morning, waiting for you and Miss Weaver." She got into the limousine.

MacKinnon stooped to speak through the door being held by the chauffeur. "Can't make it tomorrow, luv. Have to spend a couple of days in California. Got to see some bugger about a film. Isn't sure I'm right for the part—can you imagine? But I'll be back on Friday, and I'll round up Lyla. We'll want to speak to your designers about a special setting for the stone—something spectacular. Pass the word along." He blew her a kiss and stepped back so the chauffeur could close the door.

On the ride home, Pete leaned her head back and let her eyes shut, but her mind kept working. She thought about Lyla Weaver and her jewel collection—both equally famous, constant generators of publicity—and she thought of what Charlie had said about the importance of publicity in getting one's work recognized, if not appreciated.

Then, in the dark behind her closed eyelids, the image of the stone began to burn. The deep blue, the glittering white of its star, grew until they filled her mind completely.

By the time Pete arrived home, she knew she wasn't going to be sleeping at all that night.

Chapter 7

Thank God he was asleep, Pete thought as she entered the apartment. Often she came home late to find her grandfather nervously awake, full of questions about where she had been. Pete tolerated it because she realized the sad history that haunted him—a wife who had disappeared, a daughter who had been inhumanly brutalized.

But tonight she had no time for his questions. Her future hung in the balance, and there wasn't a moment to waste. Douglas MacKinnon wanted a setting to match the magnificence of the sapphire he had bought for Lyla Weaver. Why turn the job over to the workrooms of Dufort & Ivères? She could do it herself! Would she ever get a better shot at making the move from behind a sales counter to a place at the drawing boards?

She'd have to work fast, though. MacKinnon had said he'd come to the store Friday to discuss a setting. That gave her two days—about fifty hours to come up with the drawings to impress him, finished drawings of the most brilliant and important design of her life.

Suddenly Pete was no longer sleepy, no longer thinking fuzzily from the wine and other drinks she'd had throughout the evening. Her head was as clear as if she'd been inhaling lungfuls of pure oxygen.

She set up a "study station" in her bedroom. An old black velvet skirt from one of her mother's trunks was spread flat across the surface of her desk, a gooseneck lamp positioned to shine down on the center. In the middle of the arena of light, Pete laid the star sapphire.

She gazed at it, mesmerized by its beauty. The first task, in fact, was to shed this awe of the stone and its magic transformation of light. To work with it, she had to become its equal, a partner in creating the final effect.

She studied it intently. All sense of time passing slipped away. Every so often she reached out and rotated the gem a quarter turn one way or the other to see what effect it had on the milky white star bursting from its center. Other times she pushed it a little to the right or left, nearer to or farther from the light. She stood and walked past it, backed away from it then came forward again and sat down. It gleamed at the center of her universe. She was a space traveler flying over a planet that was the jewel. She was an atom that could drift down into the chasms between its molecules and search within.

The personality of the huge star sapphire began to reveal itself to her. There was no denying that the gem was an arrogant stone, showy and brazen and totally confident in its brashness. That's why it was so perfect for Lyla Weaver. It needed a bold, arrogant setting that could stand up to it. Nothing merely pretty or purely ornamental. A statement.

Reaching back into the shadows of memory, Pete recalled the months when her grandfather had been studying the diamond entrusted to him by Claude Ivères. That was the first time she had heard the phrase used by gem cutters—"romancing the stone." Even now, when it wasn't a matter of cutting, Pete thought the words captured the activity perfectly. The purpose of being alone with the stone was to know it as no one else ever could, to penetrate to an understanding of its heart. It was indeed like love.

But hers would be no failed romance, as her grandfather's had been. It mustn't be. This was a chance to leap at one step into the ranks of important jewelry designers. She had to get it right.

Finally, Pete picked up her pencil and drawing pad and started roughing out some ideas for the setting. A flower of platinum petals with the jewel at the core. A harvest moon with radiating beams of diamonds set in white gold. A peacock with the giant sapphire as its breast and smaller faceted sapphires and emeralds set into silver mesh feathers for its tail. Nice. Pretty. Clever. But none struck the right balance of boldness and elegance with simplicity. Where was the brilliant idea she had felt so sure, only hours ago, she was destined to find? Her confidence was fading.

She thought back to a past moment of inspiration—the mermaid she had made for Mama. If only all ideas would come so easily. And then she remembered the source . . .

Bolting across the room, she burrowed into a corner of her closet and pulled out an old cloth book bag unused for years. Stuffed inside, covered over with an assortment of faded old scarves and worn-out stockings, was the embroidered pillow.

It had been a long time since she had looked at the treasure—her father's half of the perfume bottle. She tried to keep it out of mind, as she kept it out of sight, rather than confront its power. Perhaps because she had seen it first as a child, had been warned by her father about the spell it cast over him, she had never completely shed the idea that it was invested with magic. But the magic could have a dangerous side. Pete remembered from the last time she'd looked at the exquisite object how it made her long to take up the search her father had abandoned, to reunite the bottle with the missing half, to find out what had happened to her uncle . . . and to all the rest of La Colomba's jewels. So she had put it away, almost pretending that it did not exist, while she built her life on more realistic ambitions.

But now her need to see it could not be denied. She cut open the pillow at the seam and extracted the small jeweled figure from the stuffing.

God, it was magnificent. The spirit of her grandmother was somehow embodied in the working of ruby and sapphire and pearl and gold. Seeing it reassured Pete that something of magical beauty could be conjured out of her own imagination. The idea for MacKinnon's sapphire was just waiting to be found . . .

And the jewels, too. Someday . . .

The sound of movement gave her a start. Glancing toward the window, Pete saw a pale lavender sky above the rooftops outside. Dawn, and Opa was up and about. He usually woke early and made himself a cup of chocolate.

Gripped by a sudden panic that he might look in, Pete thrust the jeweled bottle back into the pillow, stowed it in her closet, then started whisking away the evidence of the night's work. If he saw what she was doing, there would be far too much explaining to do. Probably he'd insist that she hurry the sapphire straight back to the vault at Dufort & Ivères. And she needed to keep it, to go on working with it.

Then, however, Pete heard the faint noise of her grandfather shuffling back into his bedroom, the door closing. She considered climbing into bed for an hour or two of sleep, realized it was pointless. Her mind was still racing. But where could she work with total concentration, without having to justify what she was doing?

The answer came. Pete packed a small overnight case, wrote a note to her grandfather, and tiptoed out of the apartment.

Anna opened the door of the loft, still tying the belt of a robe she'd thrown on. It wasn't yet seven o'clock. Pete had called from a corner phone booth only a minute ago to ask if she could come up. Luckily Anna had answered, not Steve. Pete had no idea what she would have said to her father, though that wouldn't have stopped her from coming.

"Pete . . . is something wrong?" Anna asked, pulling her into the loft.

Pete dumped her valise and purse by the door and followed Anna toward the kitchen. She could smell coffee brewing. "Nothing's wrong, Anna. But I need help with a design project, and I couldn't think of a better person to ask than you."

Anna laughed gently. "At seven in the morning! Are you

designing jewelry . . . or atomic submarines? I've never heard of such an emergency to make a bracelet or a—''

"This *is* an emergency."

Anna's smile faded. She poured coffee and listened intently as Pete explained: She was keeping in her possession—without authorization—an extremely precious stone that she had promised to put into the vault at Dufort & Ivères.

"Just for a day or two," Pete added. "But it's the only way I can get the jump on the staff designers."

"And what if someone finds out?"

Pete froze at the voice from behind. Her father's. She turned. He was dressed, his thick graying hair neatly combed. Of course, she couldn't have expected to avoid seeing him, hadn't really wanted to. He'd obviously been listening.

"Don't worry, Papa. Please, I don't want you to worry . . ."

They looked at each other across the distance of ten feet, then each moved at the same moment and they came together in an embrace. "Pietrina," he whispered as he held her. "I've missed you. I'm sorry I let you down about your mother, sorry it—"

"No, Papa, no." She pushed back to see his face. "You have nothing to be sorry about." *Less than you even know*, she thought to herself.

He gave her a puzzled look, evidently wondering why she had stayed away for so long if she was so ready to forgive. But then he smiled faintly and said, "So. It seems nothing can get this disease of our family out of your blood. Here you are, letting a jewel run your life, whipping you into a fever . . ."

"I have such a terrific chance, Papa." Unable to contain herself, she grabbed up her purse, took out the makeup pouch, and dumped the sapphire into her palm. As Anna gasped and Steve stared, she rattled off the story of how it had come into her possession.

"In two days," she concluded, "I know I can think of something that would get me the commission. Meanwhile, I'll call in, say I'm sick. The sapphire won't be missed. I'm the only one who knows MacKinnon had it, what he planned to do with it . . .''

There was a silence. Anna looked sympathetically at Pete, but turned then to Steve, waiting for him to speak.

"How can we help?" he asked.

"Anna's mentioned that little cabin she owns in the mountains where she works sometimes, where you both go to get away from everything. I need to concentrate on this. If I could—"

Anna didn't wait to hear the question. "Of course you can use it." She ran to a telephone table and came back with spare keys to the cabin and her Toyota, and a road map. In a couple of minutes, Pete was all set with directions to the cabin on a fringe of the Berkshire Mountains on the New York–Massachusetts border.

At the door, Steve said, "Don't stay away so long."

"I have to be back in two days."

"But after that . . ."

She shook her head. "It won't happen again, Papa."

It was the middle of the afternoon when Douglas Mac-Kinnon appeared again at the entrance to Dufort & Ivères. Today Frank, the doorman, stepped back smartly to admit him, though not merely because he had been vouched for on a previous evening by Pietra D'Angeli or because he stepped out of a white stretch limousine.

Dressed for a brisk but sunny April day, MacKinnon looked every bit the international star of stage and screen. He was wearing a tweed jacket tailored on Savile Row, a Turnbull & Asser shirt of ivory silk open at the neck, and handmade shoes from Trickers of Jermyn Street. The head-wrapping of gauze over his dueling wound had also been replaced by a less obtrusive—and actually rather rakish—adhesive plaster and an eyepatch.

And one more adornment affirmed beyond any other his status near the top of the celebrity ladder: the woman on his arm—none other than Lyla Weaver.

At thirty-six, Lyla Weaver was at the height of her ex-

traordinary beauty. Her trademark river of hair was the color
of deeply polished teak, and it flowed down her back and
spilled around her shoulders in lavish abundance. The features
in her oval face were not uniquely remarkable taken one-by-
one—a high forehead, rounded cheeks, a chin that came to
a slight point. Yet together they formed an ensemble generally
regarded as perfect. And her eyes . . . it was her eyes that
had first made Lyla Weaver famous. They were huge—
thickly lashed and shaped like almonds. The color changed
with her mood and clothing from the pale spring green of a
grasshopper to the deep, rich kelly of the finest Colombian
emeralds. Tiny gold flecks caught the light and made them
seem to dance with delight, and a natural black ring around
the outer edge gave them the mystery of a cat.

Combined with her perfect figure, the full bosom that she
liked to display in evening wear cut to the limits—and sometimes even beyond—Lyla Weaver was acknowledged as one
of the ten most beautiful women in the world, and closer to
the top of the list than the bottom.

As they made the short trip across the sidewalk from their
car to the store they literally stopped traffic. Pedestrians stood
and gawked, audible cries of ''MacKinnon and Weaver'' rose
from the gathering crowd, cars passing on Fifth Avenue were
slowed to a crawl by rubbernecking drivers.

Like royalty, the two stars paused on the sidewalk to reward
spectators with a few autographs. Douglas MacKinnon usually had no patience for the fawning ritual of celebrity hounds,
but today he couldn't have been nicer. He had every reason
to be in a most excellent mood. The beastly hangover that
had plagued him upon waking was gone, chased by a little
''hair of the dog'' at lunch. Also, his agent had called to tell
him the trip to California wouldn't be necessary—the part
had been clinched on the basis of the agent's promise that
MacKinnon wouldn't touch a drop of booze once shooting
began. And best of all, Lyla had reappeared at his hotel suite
to say that yesterday's meeting with her husband to hear his
reconciliation proposal had been a disaster. Indeed, admitted
Lyla, she had only agreed to the meeting to make MacKinnon
jealous.

"I just hate it when you take me for granted, darling," she had said before going down on her knees before him and unzipping his fly.

Now, as they entered Dufort & Ivères, MacKinnon was glowing with the anticipation of showing Lyla how little he took her for granted.

Ten minutes later, however, the two stars were in the office of Marcel Ivères. MacKinnon's mood had plunged, and Lyla Weaver's famous emerald eyes were sending out beams of fury as searing as a laser's.

Seated behind his desk, Marcel was desperate to calm the two stars facing him. What would Father have said? he asked himself. How could he keep the situation from becoming an incident that would bring an avalanche of negative publicity on the store? Everything that happened to MacKinnon and Weaver was widely reported; it would definitely not look good if it were known that a gift meant to cement their love had been treated carelessly by Dufort & Ivères.

Marcel spread his hands in a gesture of apology. "Monsieur MacKinnon . . . Mademoiselle Weaver . . . you have every right to be upset. But we have a reasonable explanation. As Monsieur MacKinnon said himself, he told Miss D'Angeli he didn't expect to be coming in today. So when she felt it necessary to call in sick—"

"I gave her an irreplaceable sapphire to make sure it was safe in your vault," MacKinnon broke in. "I don't bloody care if she came down with the Black Plague, she should've gotten here first thing this morning."

Lyla Weaver spoke up. "And if she didn't because she believed she had two days when no one would know, that only makes the whole thing smell fishier to me."

"Fishy?" Marcel said wide-eyed. "Miss D'Angeli may have shown bad judgment, but she is completely trustworthy. You must have thought so yourself, Mr. MacKinnon, or you wouldn't have entrusted her with the stone."

MacKinnon gave a tentative nod as if to cede the point, but Lyla took up the slack.

"If I know my Dougie," she said, laying a hand that glittered with a gigantic ruby ring on her lover's arm, "he was busy romancing this little tart until she probably got the idea that he'd *given* her the damn stone!"

"*S'il vous plaît*, Mademoiselle Weaver, I would appreciate it if you did not refer in such terms to any of my employees. Miss D'Angeli is a fine young woman of good family . . ."

"Sure, no offense meant," Lyla replied. "But I've been known to behave like a tart myself when I'm trying to get my hands on a beautiful rock. And frankly, I'd like this one. Dougie's giving it to me. So where is it?"

Marcel smiled reassuringly. "It should be here within the next fifteen minutes. As soon as I learned that Miss D'Angeli had called in sick, I dispatched the head of our store security to go directly to her home and bring it back here."

MacKinnon and Weaver were silent. The prospect of such a quick solution had neutralized their attack.

The silence was broken by the ring of the telephone on Marcel's desk. He answered and listened for a minute to the voice of Paul Jamison, his head of security. As the color drained from his face, Marcel was aware of MacKinnon and Weaver watching him like hawks.

"What's wrong?" they asked almost in unison as Marcel cradled the phone.

Even before he could answer, Andrea Scappa entered briskly. Her eyes flew from Marcel, to the two famous faces, and back to Marcel.

"Well, speak up, man!" MacKinnon insisted. "What's happened?"

"Are you going to tell them or should I?" Andrea said.

Ever the gentleman, Marcel's first impulse was to make an introduction. "Miss Scappa is our executive Vice President in charge of advertising . . ."

MacKinnon and Weaver nodded at her.

Andrea simply delivered the news. "When our head of security went to pick up your stone, Mr. MacKinnon, he didn't find Pete D'Angeli sick at home. The only person in the apartment was an old man named Josef Zeeman who also lives there, her grandfather. He didn't know any more about his granddaughter's whereabouts than we do. He showed our man the note Pete had left him—a couple of lines saying she had to be away for a couple of days and not to worry.''

Lyla Weaver jumped to her feet. ''What did I tell you? The bitch has run off with my sapphire.'' She leveled a finger at Marcel. ''Call the police.''

''Mademoiselle, calm yourself. We don't know all the circumstances.''

MacKinnon also rose and leaned over the desk. ''She could be in bloody Brazil before we know all the fucking circumstances. Damn it, I liked the girl. But they say Lizzie Borden could be a charmer, too.''

Marcel was forced to his feet by the need to confront the two clamoring stars. ''Please. I know this woman. Believe me: She's not a thief.''

Andrea joined the line facing Marcel. Her expression was grim and purposeful; she didn't like hearing Marcel defend Pete D'Angeli. ''Marcel,'' she said pointedly, ''do you really know her so well?''

Marcel paused to stare at her, reacting to Andrea's jealousy as much as to her logic.

Andrea went on, ''I believe we want all our customers to feel the store will vigorously pursue any of their missing property without delay.''

Marcel looked at Andrea bleakly. He hated to launch steps that could lead to criminal prosecution, hated to think he could have been so wrong about Pete. ''Andrea, let's take a little more time to see if we can clear this up quietly.'' He turned to Lyla Weaver and forced an accommodating smile. ''Mademoiselle Weaver, your insurance company would certainly be grateful if you didn't use the news media to inform all the cat burglars of the world that you have acquired yet another piece of desirable jewelry. This publicity would be unpleasant for all of us.''

Lyla smiled back coyly. ''Marcel baby, as far as I'm concerned, there's no such thing as unpleasant publicity.''

Marcel's shoulders slumped, and he made no further effort to protest as Andrea went into action. ''Miss Weaver, Mr. MacKinnon, if you'll come with me, I'll help you make the necessary phone calls.'' She guided them from the office.

Alone, Marcel turned to the window and stared out at the tide of people flowing along Fifth Avenue four floors below. Did he really know Pietra D'Angeli any better than he knew all those passing nonentities? They had come close for a single moment, shared a brief romantic fantasy. But in fact she was really a stranger. He'd never even heard until today that she lived with her grandfather . . .

Then something else that had gone by unnoticed in the heat of the crisis surfaced again in his mind. The name of the old man—Zeeman. Josef Zeeman. For some reason it struck a chord in his memory.

The memory came from his own father, Marcel realized. But what had his father said about the man?

Perhaps, Marcel thought, he was long overdue to look more closely into the background of Pietra D'Angeli.

The moment she saw the cabin, Pete knew it was the perfect place to work. Situated on a hillside at the end of a long dirt road, it was a compact log-sided rectangle divided into a bedroom at one end, a small kitchen at the back with a wood-burning stove that provided heat as well as cooking surfaces, and the majority of the space doubling as a studio and living room. There was no electricity or plumbing or telephone line. Coleman lamps provided light at night, in daytime the studio area was kept more than bright enough by a large skylight. Clear, cold spring water came from a hand pump, and the lavatory was an outhouse.

Anna had spoken candidly to Pete of buying the land many years ago for only a few thousand dollars and putting up the cabin herself with the help of handy friends and one past lover who had been a carpenter. As rudimentary as it was, she'd told Pete, owning this house was a dream come true. In Poland, she said, there were many people who had such houses in the countryside. But there they were worth nothing because even when the people were inside their houses they could not feel they owned *themselves*; the state owned them. If they were ever free, said Anna, only then would her countrymen truly know how even a simple hut could be a man's—or a woman's—castle. "To me," Anna said, "my cabin is most beautiful place on earth . . . because there I am most free."

Pete had stopped in Hillsdale, the nearest town, to buy eggs, milk, coffee, and fruit, enough to hold her over while she was working. She had brought all her drawing supplies with her.

She arrived at mid-morning, made coffee, and set to work. She still needed to find the basic concept. Simple but elegant. In fact she wanted a design that was nothing less than . . . inevitable: the one perfect framework for this particular stone.

Again the quick sketches came . . . and went. A scarab, with ruby eyes and legs accented by baguette diamonds. A blue egg in a nest of spun yellow gold. A planet with moons of pearl held by delicate filaments of white gold.

Obvious. Ordinary. Overblown. She was getting stale, rather than finding her way closer to an answer.

She stopped work for a while and took a walk through the woods. She had hoped to be refreshed, but as she passed through the cool shadows Pete began to feel guilty about holding on to the sapphire instead of putting it in the store's vault, as she'd promised. Suppose she couldn't come up with the magical design that proved she alone deserved the job? She was suddenly astonished at her own audacity for running off with property that was not hers worth nearly a quarter of a million dollars.

Yet she was here now. No point in giving up—no need —until Friday. She walked back to the cabin with the thought that, for at least another day, she had nothing to lose by trying again and again to find the inevitable idea.

As she came again to the clearing where the cabin stood, Pete smiled with the memory of Anna's pride and pleasure in what she called the most beautiful place on earth. Looking at the plain rustic cabin, Pete was reminded of the old adage that beauty was in the eye of the beholder.

The phrase was still rooted in her thoughts when she sat down again at her sketchpad, and at once she began to draw a design that she knew was the one. The inevitable.

* * *

It was Thursday morning when Pete heard the crunch of car tires rolling over the surface of the dirt road. Odd, she thought. Being at the end of the road, there was no passing traffic. She stood and stretched. Though she had given herself four hours' sleep during some portion of last night, for all the time before and after she had been developing the design, then making a perfectly detailed fine-line pencil drawing— at four times actual size—that she filled in with water colors painstakingly mixed to duplicate the actual hues and convey an illusion of translucency.

When she looked out the window, Pete saw a New York State Police patrol car stopped right outside. A pair of policemen were already out of the car and heading for the door.

Even before she heard the sharp rap of knuckles and her name called out, Pete knew she was in a lot of trouble.

At the Midtown South precinct, Pete was ushered past a counter-height desk, down a hall, up some stairs, and into a squad room. There was a big wire mesh cage in the corner of the room, and for one panicky moment she thought they were going to lock her up inside it, but she was taken down another hall and put into a small room furnished with only a table and a few chairs. An ashtray overflowing with old cigarettes sat on the table, and the room was suffused with the odor of stale smoke. The uniformed policeman escorting her told her to sit down, then left, closing the door. Before sitting, Pete went to the grimy window and tried to open it and let in some air, but it was either stuck or sealed shut.

She had been placed under arrest by the state police, operating under a warrant issued by the New York City police department. Though the state policemen paid no attention to her explanations once she had freely surrendered the sapphire, they were at least kind enough to let her pack her clothes and, more important, her work. Then they had driven her back to their headquarters in Taconic, New York, where a NYPD squad car was waiting. They turned Pete, the sapphire, and her belongings over to the two city policemen who were waiting with the squad car. These two also refused to spend much time listening to Pete's story.

"You'll tell it to the detectives," they explained, as they put her in a back seat separated from the front by thick glass and a wire screen and bordered by doors without inside handles.

Tired from lack of sleep, frightened and confused by the sudden reversal, Pete went through the rest in a daze.

The door of the small room opened. The man who entered was dressed in slacks and gray plaid sport jacket and had a narrow face and lank straight gray hair. In one hand he held a manila folder, which he opened as he sat down across from her.

"Greetings, Miss D'Angeli," he said in the slightly hoarse voice of an inveterate smoker. "I'm Detective Sergeant Latanzi." He scanned a paper in the file, then looked up. "Well, I hear you got a story you're anxious to tell about why you walked off with this big blue rock."

She spilled it out in a rush. Meeting MacKinnon at the store, their evening together, the opportunity she had seen . . . and seized upon.

The detective's only reaction through it all was to light up a cigarette. The rest of the time he listened with his eyes narrowed in a squint that made him appear skeptical.

When she was finished, he stamped out his cigarette. "So, you didn't steal the sapphire, you borrowed it. That what you're saying?"

"Yes." Pete breathed a sigh of relief. He understood.

"Makes a nice story," Latanzi said then.

"It's not a story!"

"Look at it from the other side, Miss. You take this hunk of stuff worth quarter of a million bucks and disappear. You go off to the middle of nowhere. How do we know what you were planning to do after that? Meet some fence, take a hundred grand for your end, then fly away to Monte Carlo."

Pete didn't know whether to laugh or cry. "Sergeant, I wouldn't do that."

"Oh, you wouldn't. Well, now, maybe I should let you

go home—because you say you're a good girl. The problem is that some other people say you're a bad girl, and if we stack up what you've done against what you say, the other side looks like it's got a case.''

''Where's Mr. MacKinnon? If I can talk to him—show him the work I did—this can be easily cleared up.''

''I don't know how easily, Miss. It's MacKinnon who made the complaint against you. He thinks you took him for a ride.'' The detective stood up. ''I don't think MacKinnon's gonna get here. He'll just send down his lawyer to swear out a complaint. Before then, maybe you want to think about your story. If you cooperate, tell us everything, the charges could be lighter.''

Charges? Pete's hopes plunged. She was beginning to comprehend that her own intentions were much less important than how they were interpreted. Looking back to their night together, MacKinnon must have thought she'd taken advantage of his drunken state.

''Sergeant,'' she asked urgently as the detective went to the door, ''what have you done with all the things I had with me at the cabin?''

''Any personal property will be returned to you, Miss. The rest is evidence.''

Evidence. The word conjured visions of a trial. Before Pete could find her voice again, Latanzi went out.

She took a few deep breaths and told herself to stay calm. But then she was overtaken by her imagination. Suppose she couldn't make anyone understand. Suppose she was given no chance to see Douglas MacKinnon, to change his mind.

A moment from her childhood came back, the day she had stood outside the institution in Yonkers, struck by the terrible fantasy that she could mistakenly be assumed crazy, locked away. The nightmare seemed to be coming true.

She didn't know how long she'd been alone when the door opened again.

''Princess,'' a voice said in a sort of comic stage whisper.

Pete whirled to see a red-thatched head above the blue uniform.

"Yep, it's the *principessa*, all right." The cop came in and closed the door.

"Good God!" Pete gave a sidewise glance to the face, not sure her eyes weren't playing tricks. But no matter what angle she saw him from, the cop still had the face of Liam O'Shea. Brawny, ruddy-faced Liam O'Shea, the terror of the old neighborhood.

"Liam," Pete gasped, "you can't be a cop."

Liam O'Shea grinned at her—the famous grin that had helped earn him the nickname of "O'Shea's Service Station" with the neighborhood girls. Pete couldn't help grinning back, the absurdity of the moment even overwhelming her fear and fatigue.

"Life sure plays a devil of a trick now and then, doesn't it, Principessa? Me a cop? Ain't that the limit? And you . . . ? I couldn't believe my eyes when I spotted you being pushed through the squad room. The *principessa*? And then I hear the charges are grand larceny! Now, that's about a tenth as likely as me bein' a cop. But here we are . . ."

His tone was sprightly and cheerful, but Pete couldn't keep her despair from welling to the surface. "Oh, Liam. It's such a terrible mistake."

"Would we be talkin' about what I've become—or you?" He gave her the famous grin again to let her know he was pulling her leg. Then he leaned over, his face marked by concern. "Tell me, Princess, how the hell did you get in this mess?"

"Oh, Liam, it's a long story."

"I just got off duty. Take your time."

His concern touched her. So she started with the most important part—her ambition to design jewelry, something she would have never dared trying to explain to the old Liam O'Shea who'd stood around on the corners of Hell's Kitchen.

When she was done, he said, "Seems to me you need this guy MacKinnon to get you off the hook. Think you can reason with the English s.o.b.?"

She smiled. The Irish fight against Cromwell and the English was still very much alive in Hell's Kitchen. "It won't be easy," she said. "But if I show him the drawing I did . . ."

Liam nodded. "Where do you think he is right now?"

"Maybe rehearsing. He's got a play opening in a few weeks."

"Oh yeah, *Richard III*—another damn Englishman. Well, sit tight, Princess, I'll have him here in no time."

Without doubt he was going to be doing something beyond the bounds of his authority. "Liam, I can't let—"

But before she could add another word to her protest, he was—bless him—out the door and gone.

"Princess . . . ?"

Pete had put her head down onto her folded arms on the table and fallen asleep. When Liam's voice woke her, she had trouble focusing for a minute. "Douglas?"

Still dressed in his rehearsal clothes, he stood stiffly along-side Liam O'Shea. Slightly behind both men was a scowling Detective Latanzi. It appeared that he was giving one of his patrolmen a certain amount of rope—whether to prove himself or hang himself remained to be seen.

MacKinnon arched one of his thick eyebrows. "I didn't take you for a common thief, Pietra. In fact, I wouldn't have thought you'd be a common anything, but then I am a notoriously bad judge of character. I am, after all, in love with Lyla Weaver."

He didn't sound angry, she thought. More . . . disappointed. "Douglas, I can explain."

"It had better be good."

Before she could begin, Liam stepped forward and thrust out the sketchpad he had been holding under one arm.

Pete gave him a grateful smile, then turned back to MacKinnon. She was about to make some introductory remark when she decided against it. Let her work speak, she thought. If he was going to understand, to forgive, the picture of what she had wanted to do would be worth more than a thousand words. She flipped open the pad to the water-colored picture of her setting for the gigantic star sapphire and turned it toward MacKinnon.

He stared at it a moment, then grabbed the pad out of her hand and walked to the window by the light. Abruptly, he tossed back his head and laughed in a short, loud burst. Turning to Pete again, he said, "Would you like to know how I got my first acting job?"

Mystified, she nodded. The policemen looked on mutely.

MacKinnon played to his rapt audience. "They were doing *Julius Caesar* at the Bristol Theatre. I went around to audition and they turned me down. So when the play opened, I snuck onstage in a crowd scene. Nobody noticed, so I did it again the next night . . . and the next. By then it was getting a bit routine. So finally, one night when everyone else yelled out, 'Hail, Caesar,' I shouted, '*Ave!*'" He shrugged and smiled. "It got me noticed." He walked over to Pete. "And that's what you did, lovely Pietra. You got yourself noticed. *Ave.*"

Detective Latanzi moved forward. "So what's the verdict, Mr. MacKinnon? You gonna sign the complaint or what?"

MacKinnon looked to Pete. "Pietra, I think Lyla will love your design. I'd like to surprise her with it on my opening night in four weeks. Can you have it ready?"

Pete suppressed a smile. "That depends," she said, "on whether or not I'll have to work in jail."

With a wink at the policemen, MacKinnon said, "The choice is yours, my dear. But I thought you preferred being locked away with peace and quiet for getting your work done." He turned to the policemen. "Let the wench go." He swept out.

There was a silence. Latanzi scowled again at O'Shea. "You lucked out, Patrolman. You were on a hell of a limb." He left.

Alone with Liam O'Shea, Pete suddenly found herself hugging him, then being held aloft and being turned around and around in a dizzying whirl.

Chapter 8

Pete used Josef's small space in the jewelry district for her workshop. The tools she needed were all there, and a bench with gas lines so she could work the molten metal; the telephone and electric were paid up.

She worked every day, including weekends, often late into the night, existing on sandwiches or cans of soup warmed over the bunsen burner normally used to heat the gold and silver. Except for an occasional call from Steve or Anna or Josef to ask how she was doing and give moral support, she was undisturbed. She called out only to place orders for material and, a couple of times, to call Philippe Michon at night and ask his suggestion for how to handle a technical problem.

As for her job, she simply didn't go back. Pete was too angry at Marcel to believe she owed him even the courtesy of a trip to the store to quit in person. In talking further to Douglas MacKinnon—who had sent flowers and sweetly called the evening after her release to apologize for putting her through the ordeal of an arrest, Pete had learned that some of the heat generated by her disappearance came from both Lyla and Andrea putting pressure on Marcel.

"The poor lad said a word or two in your favor, but the ladies won the day," MacKinnon explained. Sheepishly, he added, "Of course, I didn't much help matters."

Pete had little difficulty in imagining the scene. Knowing that Marcel had said "a word or two" on her behalf did nothing to soften her attitude. The issue for Pete was that, *in spite of* knowing that she was incapable of committing a crime, Marcel had yielded to Andrea.

Late on a Friday, at the end of her first full week of working on her own, Pete answered a ring of the telephone to hear Marcel's voice. He had barely begun to speak before she hung up. For the next half hour she muttered to herself, but eventually she recovered her concentration.

On Saturday, he called again—twice. She hung up once and told him the second time they had nothing to say to each other.

On Monday afternoon, when she was expecting a delivery of gold wire, there was a knock on the metal security door. Pete opened it to find Marcel outside. Smartly dressed in a maroon cashmere overcoat with a tie-belt, he looked quite out of place in the elevator hallway of the dingy building filled with wholesale dealers.

"It's no use slamming the door in my face," he said. "I won't go away."

Her anger was burned out anyway. She invited him in and closed the door. For an awkward moment they stood looking at each other, she in her work smock, he with his dark hair blown loose by an April breeze so it hung over his brow.

He spoke first. "What did you want from me?"

"I told you what I wanted: to be a designer. You never gave me the chance."

"Was that really all you wanted, Pete? Or does it please you to have made a little storm? To see the store's reputation suffer a little—to cause publicity that makes people think we do not protect our customers, cannot provide them with the creative services they expect."

Pete reared back, shocked and affronted. "Marcel, I didn't want to damage you. In fact, if you'd trusted me, waited a day, let me come back to the store with the design to show

MacKinnon . . . I would have done it in your workrooms, let it go out as the product of D and I."

Marcel studied her. A thin rueful smile crept across his lips. "Trust. I remember—that was *your* secret. All you had to do was believe me and you could find the diamond." He put a hand on her arm, and she didn't shy away because it wasn't threatening; somehow it was more platonic than romantic. "But it is not so easy for me to trust you. I'm still not sure what you wanted from me."

His tone was curious, Pete thought. Sad rather than angry.

"But I did tell—"

He cut her off quietly. "Not everything. You didn't tell me you were the granddaughter of the man who ruined the greatest diamond my father ever saw."

Pete felt suddenly hollow. She guessed it must have come to light because of her arrest. "If I had, would you have given me a chance? Your father blacklisted my grandfather."

"And was that why the chance meant so much? Were you waiting for a day to come when you could get even?"

She shook her head. "Funny you should think so. My real hope was that somehow, by working for you, I could redeem the damage of the past."

Marcel brought up his other hand so he was holding both her arms. "Then perhaps you can still do it. MacKinnon's told me what you're planning for his sapphire. It sounds wonderful. Suppose you come back and do it for me, the firm. You'll have space in our workroom, we'll pay for all your materials, and you'll be given a salary of—"

"No, Marcel. It's too late. This is for me now. I've paid my debt to you. In more ways than one, I think."

He was silent a moment, but she could see the muscles in his jaw working.

"It's not quite enough," he said then. And before she could make a move to resist, his arms contracted, pulling her against him in one abrupt move as his lips came down against hers, firmly but not too hard.

For one second, the last flicker of a dead dream warmed her enough to want to taste him. Then her rage exploded;

she braced her arms between them and catapulted him backward in one move.

"Get out!" she screamed. "Leave me alone!"

"Forgive me," he said in a hush. "But I . . ." His voice trailed off, he bowed his head and shook it abjectly. A moment later, he was gone.

It was hours before she was able to concentrate again on her work.

Sardi's was full of people and flowers, booze and noise. Every celebrity in town wanted to share the moment of Douglas MacKinnon's triumph. His performance tonight in *Richard III* had ended in a tumultuous ovation that kept him on stage an extra twenty minutes. All that remained now was to hear the verdict of the critics, who could write sometimes as if they had been to see a completely different play on a different night.

A champagne cork popped loudly somewhere as Pete was swept in with the crowd. A minute later someone put a glass in her hand. The air of the room seemed to sparkle with almost as much golden fizz as the chilled champagne she drank down thirstily. She felt a tinge of regret at not being able to share the occasion with someone—even Charlie or Opa, in the absence of a special man in her life. But MacKinnon had particularly asked that she attend alone. He wanted to top off the evening by giving the jewel to Lyla, and that would be a most private moment, he said, with no one present but himself and Lyla and Pete.

"I think it should be even more private," Pete suggested. "No reason for me to be there."

"Every reason, dear girl. You are the creator. When I perform, I must see the faces of those I try to please. Why shouldn't you?"

Of course she was eager to see Lyla's first response, but she could understand, too, how Douglas might want to make the gift at the most intimate of moments. Pete didn't see how satisfying her wish at the same time would quite work out, though she felt in no position to argue.

Only a few minutes after Pete arrived at Sardi's the guest of honor walked in, no longer "deform'd, unfinish'd," but resplendent in the stark black and white of his tuxedo. His blond hair glistened, and his blue eyes glittered with excitement. A long, slender cigar was clamped in his hugely smiling mouth. He looked gorgeous, Pete thought.

But even more heart-stopping, she had to admit, was Lyla Weaver. A rare sable the color of a lion's mane was draped loosely over her shoulders, giving a glimpse of a red velvet gown, low-cut to expose her long neck and perfect milk-white bust. Dangling just above the cleavage was the relic of some former marriage or love affair—a pear-shaped emerald to match her eyes.

Between them MacKinnon and Weaver knew everything there was to know about making an entrance. His arm swept the room in a dramatic gesture, and he produced his most ingenuous humble-servant smile. "Friends," he said simply, the word reverberating with more pure theater than a dozen whole seasons of summer stock productions. Beside him, Lyla raised her arms in a gesture reminiscent of a boxer's claim of championship, which caused the sable to slide from her shoulders. She let it fall, assuming, correctly, that someone would be there to catch it.

Pete watched their performance with admiration, sipping a second glass of champagne she grabbed from a passing tray.

"Weaver is something, isn't she," a male voice murmured in a group near Pete, and she could hear the naked longing in it. Weaver's was the sort of beauty people wanted to devour, to take into themselves in hopes of retaining a little of its glow.

But Lyla's own passions were seemingly directed entirely toward the man at her side. As flashbulbs popped and voices cried out her name, she looked up at MacKinnon as though they were alone on a moonlit peak instead of at the center of a roomful of clamoring well-wishers. Then they kissed, not a properly demure public kiss, but long and sensuous, a complete joining, deep, open-mouthed and probing. The whole room seemed to hold its breath. A stab of envy went through Pete, a yearning to know for herself the kind of emotion that crackled between these two magnetic people. She'd never known, never experienced, that kind of passion. She wanted a taste of it in her own life, yet she had begun to despair of ever finding it.

At last Weaver and MacKinnon leaned away from each other, though they stayed close, eyes locked, conveying to each other a message of lust that was visible to the whole room. Only when they turned again to smile at the crowd did everyone resume breathing. The loud babble of voices rose again, people began laughing and shoving and milling. Everywhere Pete looked she saw famous faces from Broadway and Hollywood. Warren Beatty pushed past, smiled at her winningly, but then moved on when she could give back only a tight, flustered grin. *Loosen up*, she told herself, and grabbed another glass of champagne.

"Pieeeeetra!" MacKinnon's loud bellow rose suddenly above the babble. Looking around, she saw him motioning her to swim upstream to meet him.

When she reached his side, he leaned down and asked with quiet eagerness, "Have you got it?"

From her sequined shoulder bag, Pete pulled out a small antique silver box MacKinnon had sent for the purpose, tied with a ribbon of blue silk as dark as the sapphire within.

MacKinnon put a hand lightly on her wrist, pushing the package away. "Be an angel and keep it for now. I want to give it to Lyla at a quiet moment, and I can't see one cropping up among these rabble."

Leonard Bernstein materialized to embrace MacKinnon and tugged him straight off by the arm to another group of friends.

Pete did as she was told. She dropped the package back in her purse and kept it held tight against her body.

Shortly after midnight, the producer of the play stood on a table to read a review from the *Times*. Such was the rare power of MacKinnon's acting, the review climaxed, that "for every single moment he was on stage, there was never a thought of the modern-day publicity that surrounds his name and person. He was none other than Richard III incarnate, keeping the audience hypnotized with the belief that they were not only in the court, but in the body and mind of England's twisted king.'' Along with the rest of the crowd, Pete joined in the boisterous cheering that went up for the rave review.

The revelry went on, the pitch of merriment raised to a new level. Pete had more champagne and began to feel at ease, even when she found herself engaged in conversations about the play or life in New York with Andy Warhol and Bianca Jagger and a couple of people whose faces she recognized but couldn't connect to names.

Still, two concerns plagued her and kept her mainly on the fringes of the party. One was merely the matter of security, making sure the precious package didn't go astray. The other was a curious feeling of being outside the whole event, seeing it as if through a glass wall. She could trace it from the moment she had seen Weaver and MacKinnon embrace. What they felt for each other clearly went beyond love. Was it theirs alone . . . or was it a kind of emotion known to others in a world of glamour, where beautiful people loved beautiful people, and fame and money made smaller cares seem insignificant so that it was possible to concentrate on the cares of the heart?

Whatever its roots, she was hungry to know it, feel it. It had been so long since she'd had any release for her longings.

Could it all be changed by tonight? Could a genie who granted all her wishes be released when the small package she was guarding was finally opened?

Hours had passed, and she had lost count of how many glasses of champagne she'd consumed, when MacKinnon's distinctly resonant voice murmured close beside her ear:

''We're leaving, luv. Grab your coat and meet us outside.''

Pete obliged at once, then found herself waiting on the street for ten minutes as the two stars extracted themselves from their friends and signed a few autographs.

At last they ducked into their waiting limousine, followed by Pete, who sat in one of the jump seats that faced the rear. As they got under way, Pete was acutely aware of Lyla Weaver eyeing her. Except for the brief occasions when Pete had waited on her at D & I, this was the first time they had met.

"You're right, Douglas," Lyla said. "She is a beauty. I guess I never took a very good look at anything but the gems when I was her customer." Her tone became a shade harder. "But what's really important is whether she's *made* something beautiful. Have you, Miss D'Angeli?"

Pete quoted the very line that had provided the first spark of inspiration for her design. "Beauty, Miss Weaver, is in the eye of the beholder. When you look at what I've done, only then—and only you—can answer the question you've asked."

Lyla smiled and purred kittenishly into the lush collar of her sable. "Mmmm. And you're a clever boots, too. Well then, let me see . . ."

"No, no," MacKinnon interjected at once. "This is a ceremony. It can't be done in the back seat of a cold machine."

Lyla gave a throaty laugh and started nuzzling MacKinnon's cheek. "Dougie, you know as well as I do that anything can be done in the back seat of a car."

"Is that a dare?" MacKinnon asked coyly.

Again the look of desire passed between them like lightning leaping from sky to earth. In the next second, they were entwined, their hands roaming over each other's bodies.

Pete looked on, strangely unembarrassed. Perhaps it was only because all the champagne had dulled her usual sense of social propriety. Yet she suspected another cause. MacKinnon and Weaver were two people who made their own rules, and within their aura the same rules applied to everyone. If they felt unrestrained by any taboos, then Pete also felt free of pretense and narrow conventions. She felt more curious than anxious at the thought that the lovebirds might actually soon wind up before her *in flagrante delicto*. But before that could happen, the limousine pulled up in front of the Plaza.

As they marched through the lobby, Lyla slipped her arm through Pete's so that they were walking in a phalanx of three.

Pete appreciated the gesture; it put her at ease, made her feel included.

In his suite, MacKinnon popped a bottle of Dom Perignon that had been ordered earlier and poured glasses all around —not that Pete needed any more; she was floating already.

"To new beginnings," he declaimed, raising his glass in a toast. After they had each drained off half a glass, he moved to put his arm around Lyla. "Very well, Pietra. It's time . . ." He extended his hand.

She got the silver box from her purse and crossed the room to set it on his outstretched palm.

MacKinnon looked at Lyla like a young groom before the altar with his bride. "How do I love thee?" he said seriously, as if prepared to launch into Elizabeth Barret Browning's famous sonnet. But then he added waggishly, "Never mind counting all the bloody ways. Just have a look at this." He pressed the box into Weaver's hands.

She was a woman who had received many gifts, had become accustomed to them. When she took this one, she gave a slow smile as if it were no more than her due. She gave away a hint of her underlying excitement, however, in the way her hands hastily plucked away the ribbon.

The moment she raised the lid of the box, her face was transfigured by sheer enchantment.

Pete's creation held the gaze of those famous emerald eyes with a truly hypnotic power—for it was itself an eye. The star sapphire formed the huge blue iris. Pete had set it into a platinum socket, exotically shaped, with a hint of the Orient about it, and a line of tiny onyx stones set along the edge of the lid as though it were outlined in kohl. Eyelashes of long, narrow baguette-cut dark green emeralds were mounted on platinum wire just thin enough so that they barely trembled with any movement. The final touch came from a number of perfect round diamonds scattered among the lashes to represent glistening tears.

The eye, made to be worn as a pin or a pendant, had an undeniable power. To look at it was somehow to see both outward to its tangible beauty and inward to the spiritual mystery of how this piece of mere stone could be made somehow to seem no less alive than those who looked upon it. Thinking of the eye as the medium through which beauty was seen had made the form seem inevitable to Pete. What better frame for a jewel to be given to a beautiful woman by the man who loved her?

Lyla stared for so long at the sapphire eye in speechless wonder—a condition unknown for her—that MacKinnon finally had to prompt: "Well, lass, do you like it?"

"Like it? Oh my, Douglas," she answered on a sigh, "it's the most perfectly exquisite thing I've ever owned. I love it. I love you." She put a hand to his cheek and caressed it, nothing so passionate or sexy as she had bestowed on him earlier, yet no less sincere an expression of feeling.

Having seen what she'd come for, Pete edged backward, preparing to say good-night. But Lyla stopped her.

"Miss D'Angeli—lady of the angels—you are a great artist. But you ought to stay to finish painting the picture."

Pete looked at her quizzically.

Lyla sashayed toward her. "The jewel's meant to be worn, isn't it? I think you should pin it on for me."

Pete hesitated, not certain what kind of game the star was playing but sensing it wasn't purely innocent. Yet the excitement of being alone with two glamorous stars outweighed any uneasiness. When MacKinnon gave her an encouraging nod, Pete moved toward Lyla. As she came close, Lyla took her hand and pulled her so near that Pete could feel the warmth of her breath as she spoke.

"Where should I wear it, would you say? Here?" Lyla put the pin on the shoulder of her gown. "Or here?" She put it right under her cleavage.

"There," Pete said. She took the jewel now and pinned it on. Lyla took her hand again.

"Special jewels often have a name, don't they?" she asked softly. "Like the Hope Diamond or the Mandalay Ruby. Don't you think my jewel should have a name?"

"The Weaver Star," MacKinnon called out from a sideboard where he was getting himself a whiskey.

"Oh no, darling. How terribly dull. No, I cannot possibly allow a jewel so dramatic to have such a mundane name as that.'' She turned again to Pete, whose hand she was still holding. ''Do you have a name in mind?''

''From the beginning, I've thought of it as the Eye of Love.''

''The Eye of Love.'' Lyla murmured it a couple more times, trying it out. ''Perfect. The columnists will pick right up on that. We'll all get lots and lots of lovely publicity. Play your cards right, lady of the angels, and you can go straight to the top. You can be there right beside Dougie and me.'' She winked at Pete and glanced to MacKinnon. ''Would we like that, Dougie—would we like our brilliant lady of the angels right beside us?''

MacKinnon came to them wearing a bemused expression.

''I don't think it's up to me, darling. Not if our lovely Pietra wants to go home.''

''Go, Dougie? But she's part of what made my beautiful treasure. I want her to be part of everything tonight.'' Lyla raised a hand to Pete's cheek. ''Stay with us, lady of the angels, stay all night.''

Suddenly Pete knew where it had all been leading from the moment that Lyla had asked her to ''finish painting the picture''—no, even before, when MacKinnon had insisted she come alone tonight. She had a moment of shock and then it faded as quickly as a firefly's light. More than anything, she felt curious. She remembered watching Weaver and MacKinnon kiss each other in front of a roomful of people, making their own rules. She remembered longing to ascend into a rarified realm of special passions and feelings. Was this the way?

Her hesitation was all the encouragement Lyla needed. She took Pete's hand once again and began pulling her toward the bedroom of the suite. ''Come,'' she coaxed.

Panic rose up in Pete. A lifetime of staying within the boundaries of convention held her in a grip that couldn't be broken.

Or wasn't it just a matter of will? Why not give herself to the pleasure of the moment? Ascend.

As if he detected the hitch in her step, MacKinnon leaned

close and quoted Falstaff in a whisper: "They say there is divinity in odd numbers."

Pete let herself be led into the darkened bedroom.

"You are an artist, Pietra," Lyla whispered. "You're like us . . . you need to explore."

"You can still go, Pietra," MacKinnon assured her once more.

Slowly, Pete shook her head. She felt slightly dizzy, high on success and her hopes for tomorrow as well as on champagne, but not out of control. She wanted to *feel*—to explore, as Lyla had said. She stood motionless as MacKinnon moved in front of her and closed her eyes when he lowered his lips onto hers in a light feathery kiss, so light that for a moment she thought it had ended. Then his mouth returned, but more insistent now, his tongue forcing itself through her lips. Warmth flooded through her, warmer and softer than the warmth of the champagne, and she gave herself fully to the sensation.

As it trailed off, Pete opened her eyes. Douglas MacKinnon was off to one side, smiling like a saint. And Lyla Weaver's mouth was hovering over hers.

Abruptly, Douglas scooped her up in his arms and carried her to the bed. Lyla had slipped quickly out of her shoes and stockings, and now she began trailing the sheer silk slowly down the length of Pete's long legs. The slither of the smooth sheer fabric was incredibly sensuous. Pete arched up by reflex as MacKinnon slid the thin spaghetti straps of her tube of a dress off her shoulders and inched the smooth satin down, exposing her braless breasts, covering her flesh with kisses as he did so, burning her skin.

She was being attacked by sensation from all sides—Lyla licking her toes, Douglas grasping her hips, stroking the curves of her back, and licking lightly at the areolas of her breasts.

She was attacked, too, from the inside, where a war kept raging. No, the voice of habit cried. Stop! This is wrong. But a louder, more insistent voice drowned out the first and urged her on. She needed to feel, needed to know what it

was like to make her own rules, to become completely un-
bound from rules.

She felt a hand slide up her now bare leg, brushing up her
thigh, pushing her legs apart, snaking under the elastic of her
briefs. She couldn't tell whose hand it was, but by the time
it gently parted her and found the center of sensation, she
didn't care. As thrills flashed through her, she gasped, and
Douglas caught her breath in his mouth in a consuming kiss.

Everything began to happen very fast then. They lay naked
on the bed, all three, Pete being held from behind by Lyla,
and Douglas in front. He kissed her, then leaned over her
shoulder and kissed Lyla even while his massive hard penis
began to probe and push. Lyla ran her mouth along Pete's
waist and hips in a trail of kisses, until she was licking at her
between her legs.

Pete groaned with pleasure as Lyla took her hand, guiding
it until she could feel her hand on the throbbing tube of muscle
that was MacKinnon. "Feel it," Lyla urged her. "Feel how
much he wants you." By the time Douglas finally pushed
her onto her back and reared up to plunge himself deep inside
her, with Lyla biting sharply at her nipples, Pete was so
excited she came at once, engulfed in waves of excruciating
pleasure.

The waves had barely begun to subside when Douglas,
still buried deep inside her, rolled her over so she was astride
him. Lyla climbed on, too, positioning herself in front of
Pete and directly over her lover's smiling face. With his hands
on Pete's waist, he guided her up and down his penis while
his mouth satisfied Lyla. Lyla took Pete's face in her hands
and kissed her hard.

For a brief second she was warring within herself again,
but then it resumed—the heat, the pressure, the pleasure that
felt so good, so goddamn good. He had no need to guide her
now. She couldn't stop the insistent rhythm if she wanted to.
His hands slid up to her breasts, kneading, circling, lightly
squeezing. Lyla slid a hand down, just to the point where
Pete and Douglas joined, using one finger to increase the
sensation to an unbearable pitch.

As he lapped at her, Lyla rocked, her voice a guttural

moan, and Pete found it incredibly exciting to hear that famous voice crying, "More, more, more, damn you! Yes, yes! *Yes!*"

At the same moment that Lyla screamed out her orgasm, Pete felt Douglas explode inside her with a gritted "Fuck!" and a second orgasm of her own, more gripping and powerful than the first—explosive, shattering, gut-wrenching—shook through her from the very core to the tips of every nerve and limb, pulling from her throat a shouted "God!"

Then they all collapsed against each other, panting, sweating, hearts pounding.

After a minute, Lyla cooed softly, "You were wonderful, lady of the angels. Wasn't she, Dougie? One of the best ever . . ."

As if her mind and soul were a landscape that had been shaken by an earthquake that left it rent by great canyons, Pete could hear the echo of Lyla's words rising from the darkness. Overcome with confusion, a feeling that she had corrupted what might have been the best night of her life instead of enhancing it, she bolted from the bed and began hastily gathering clothes strewn on the floor, getting dressed.

"Pietra," MacKinnon said in a sleepy murmur. "You mustn't. No regrets, please . . ."

She looked at the two shadowy figures on the bed, wanting to speak, yet bereft of words. She couldn't blame them—if, indeed, there was anything to blame them for. It was their world, their rules, natural for them. But not for her.

"Let her go, Dougie," Lyla said. "We still have each other." She gave a throaty laugh before adding, ". . . and the Eye of Love."

She retreated to the living room of the suite as she finished dressing, and was soon in the corridor, running to the elevator.

The wine and all the sensation had worn off, and her confusion kept mounting. Why had she let them use her? Out of gratitude for the opportunity she'd been given with the jewel? Had she merely been dazzled by the chance for a once-in-a-lifetime debauch with two of the most famous people on the planet?

She knew herself better. There was something more, a need with a much more powerful hold over her psyche.

Emerging into the bright lobby, she hurried out into the cool night air. Across from the hotel, separated from a broad sidewalk by a long stone wall, Pete saw the tall silhouettes of trees in Central Park, leaves just beginning to sprout from branches that had been bare all winter. In the darkness, the snakey limbs reminded her of trails of smoke rising into the air. The wall, the looming shapes, struck her as oddly frightening, a vision from a nightmare . . .

Suddenly she realized it was her mother's nightmare, not her own. She was thinking of the walls around the camp, of the tall chimneys that had belched smoke from the crematoria . . .

She began then to suspect the impulses that had been driving her when she had put the experience of new sensations —forced herself to submit to the lust of others—ahead of everything else. It was exactly what her mother had forced herself to do to stay alive.

Perhaps it had been a way of joining herself to her mother's psyche, to understand how Mama felt. Or perhaps, on the night of her greatest success, it was a kind of penance she'd had to do before allowing herself to accept the blessings that success would bring.

Pete brushed the tears from her face, pulled herself erect, and walked toward Fifth Avenue to get herself a taxi home. The shame and confusion were gone. But not the longing. She needed a man she could love and be loved by. If she'd had that man with her tonight, she believed, she wouldn't have lost her true bearings, not even for a moment.

A messenger arrived at the apartment late the next morning with three dozen pale peach roses. An envelope nested among the thorny stalks, inside of which was a check signed by Douglas MacKinnon. Pete had already agreed with MacKinnon that he would pay for materials and the stone she had bought on account to execute the Eye of Love, a total of twenty-five thousand dollars. She had planned to discuss the fee later, and was hoping that he would agree to ten thousand dollars. But the check was for a total of fifty thousand dollars.

The accompanying note was in Lyla Weaver's hand.

> *Dearest Pete,*
>
> *Thank you for the precious gift you gave us last night, and forgive us for anything we did to hurt you. We want to give you a gift in return, something that only people in our position can bestow.*
>
> *You have seen our love, and though you may not believe it, I am old-fashioned enough to want to be married to any man I love as much as I love Douglas. We've set a date for next month. To announce it to the press, we have called a press conference for this afternoon at three, at the Plaza, at which time "the Eye of Love" will also be unveiled to the public. It is destined to become famous as the jewel that won my heart. You will become famous with it, dear Pete, deservedly so. I think I can honestly say that from here on out, sweetheart, the world is your oyster.*
>
> *With love and gratitude,*
>
> > *Lyla*

Pete stared again at the check, then breathed in the heady fragrance of the flowers. Whatever mistakes she had made before today, they no longer seemed important. She was on her way now. Her genie had been released from the box.

If only he could grant just one more wish.

Chapter 9

"If it were me," said Jess, "I'd be right there in the thick of it, saying yes to everything and everyone."

"I got myself into enough trouble already by saying yes to everything," Pete replied pointedly. Last night, after arriving at the Montauk beach house of Jess's parents, she had poured out the full story of what had happened between her and Weaver and MacKinnon. Jess had encouraged her not to feel any guilt or regret. It was the kind of experience, she said, that she fantasized about herself all the time. There was no harm in making a fantasy come true.

Now she and Jess were lying on a towel on the sandy beach in front of the massive shingled house. It was warm for early May, and they were slathered with tanning oil except where they still wore the pants of their bikinis, their eyes shielded from the sun by large straw hats. Since Fernando was away visiting his parents in Madrid, Jess had invited Pete to the beach for a few days in the middle of the week. Pete had leaped at a chance to get out of the city with her friend. The last two weeks had been the most dizzyingly hectic of her life.

In the picture of Weaver and MacKinnon that had appeared

on the front pages of the tabloids and an inside page of the
New York Times after the stars announced their marriage
plans, Pietra D'Angeli's jeweled creation had been promi-
nently displayed. Lyla had worn, for once, a demure high-
necked black dress, which provided the most dramatic back-
drop for the jewel pinned near her throat. She had generously
focused even more attention on her precious gift by speaking
of the importance of the Eye of Love in "opening my own
eyes" to the depth of her love for MacKinnon. Pietra had
received credit in print as the designer.

For days afterward, at both the apartment and workshop,
the phone didn't stop ringing. The *Times* wanted to do a
feature for the Wednesday Living Section. Other papers and
magazines sought interviews. Walter Hoving from Tiffany
called to ask if Pete might contract to design exclusively for
the store. Corporations and their advertising agencies wanted
to discuss ideas for special campaigns in which she might
participate, perhaps by making jeweled versions of their trade-
marks and logos.

She kept a list of calls and promised to deal with each
matter after she'd had a chance to stand back and make a
sensible appraisal.

In the second week after the jewel was publicly shown, a
favored gossip columnist carried the news that *Vogue* had
borrowed the jewel from Lyla for a model to wear on a future
cover. Lyla was also quoted as saying she'd received offers
already to buy the Eye of Love—the highest so far being for
an amount "between one and two million." More than the
beauty of the object appealed to people, she speculated; it
had been endowed with totemic power. To wear it as she
did, people seemed to believe, might also enhance beauty
and bring a deeper understanding of love.

Finally, just yesterday, the latest issue of *New York* magazine had carried a close-up of the Eye of Love on the cover,
with a story inside about its inception, including even the
most embarrassing details—Pete's unauthorized "borrow-
ing" of the sapphire, her arrest, and the release that followed
MacKinnon's approval of the design. Pete guessed first that
the details had come from Lyla or Douglas, thinking to do

her a favor since they believed there was no such thing as bad publicity. Then it occurred to her it might be a subtle smear by Marcel or Andrea. She didn't bother checking into it, however. She just wanted to leave the hubbub behind.

As the sun sank toward the horizon, Jess and Pete picked up their blankets and headed for the house. "You're so cool about everything that's happening, Pete," Jess remarked as they walked. "Aren't you thrilled?"

"Sure, I am. I just wish there was someone special to share it with. As for being cool, I know it's important not to make a wrong step. I don't want to be a flash in a golden pan. I want to be around for a long time and reach the top. That means I have to protect my name—not let myself get spread too thin doing gimmicky commercial things for a quick buck."

Jess gave her an admiring glance and said nothing more until they climbed the steps up to the broad stone patio that faced the ocean. Then she blurted, "I need your advice, Pete. Or I may end up being a flash in the pan myself—with Fernando."

Pete sat down at a patio table. "Shoot."

Jess lowered herself into a chair. "Should I get pregnant? I mean, try to make it happen . . . ?"

"Before you get married?"

"That's the point. I know Fernando wants to marry me, but my father is putting up all kinds of obstacles—telling us we have to wait, making Fernando show that he's got a certain level of income. It could be years if we try to satisfy Daddy, and I'm afraid Nando won't wait. No matter how much he loves me, he may get worn down—or insulted."

Pete thought about it. She hadn't completely shed her own doubts about Fernando, yet she was impressed by the way he had behaved, tirelessly trying to satisfy the demands made on him.

"Jess, I can't tell you what's right. That's different for everyone. But I think I can tell you the risks." She paused, assembling her words in the way that would be easiest for Jess to take. "Your parents want the best for you, I'm sure. They've always protected you too much—we both know that—and maybe they're doing it now. But they're probably worried that Fernando is marrying you for . . . the wrong reasons.''

"My money," Jess said. "He's welcome to it."

''Your folks will feel that way, too, once they're sure he loves you. But you're not going to make them sure by getting pregnant. Even if it is your idea, it'll be Fernando who takes the blame. Your father and mother will think he did it just to—how would they put it?—clinch the deal.''

Jess nodded thoughtfully. "You're right. I just hope Daddy gives us his blessing soon. 'Cause otherwise I won't be able to stop myself from having the baptism first.''

One of the maids who had come along from the city to open the house for the season emerged from french doors onto the patio. "There's a call for Miss D'Angeli."

"Oh God, even here," Pete sighed. She'd left the number with Opa in case of an emergency with him or Mama and guessed he'd been careless about giving it out, despite her instructions.

"Tell them," Jess said, "that Miss D'Angeli is taking a few days off from being an overnight sensation.''

Pete smiled. "Please take a number, and say I'll return the call next Monday."

The maid started to go, then stopped. "The gentleman was very insistent. He said it was personal . . . a Mister Sanford.''

It had been so long that the name didn't register instantly. When Pete didn't respond, the maid continued into the house.

"Wait!" Pete suddenly shouted with the urgency of a demolitions expert warning someone away from a bomb. "Don't touch that phone!" She went charging into the house past the astonished maid.

He spoke as soon as she was on the line. "Is it too late to eat my words?"

"We never did get to have dinner together," she answered. "That'd be a good dish to start with . . ."

He laughed. "I saw a picture of that doodad you made for the movie star. It made me feel like such a damn fool for the way I—"

"Never mind. Where are you? How's Robby? What've you invented lately? Can we get together?" She was amazed at the stream of questions pouring off her tongue, amazed by how much she cared to know the answers, even more amazed by the questions bubbling in her mind that she didn't ask. *Have you thought of me as often as I've thought of you? Have you loved any women since we met? Does it excite you to hear my voice the way it thrills me to hear yours?*

She had questions for herself, too: How could she feel so close to a man she hadn't seen in so long? Was she just so hungry to be loved by *someone*?

Wearing jeans—the only pants she'd packed for the beach—and a blue-and-white-striped gondolier shirt she'd borrowed from Jess, Pete stood on the edge of the small landing field outside Montauk and watched the single-engine Cessna fly over once then circle around and glide down smoothly onto the runway. Her dark hair was tied back with a rubber band, and she wore a minimum of makeup. After agonizing for hours over what to wear and how to look, she had decided to keep it as simple as possible. From the little she knew about Luke Sanford—his own choice of clothes, the battered car he drove, and his reaction to jewelry—she sensed he liked things plain, not fancy.

The plane taxied off the runway toward the small hut that served as a terminal. Pete was waiting alone. She'd asked Jess to leave, not sure what sort of fool she'd make of herself when Luke arrived.

He had asked to see her on Saturday, and when she reminded him that her mother was still at Cole-Haffner and that was her usual day to visit, he had suggested picking her up at the airfield and flying her to Connecticut in his plane. The mention of a plane surprised Pete; that was a rich man's toy, she thought. But when she saw the plane, she revised her ideas. It wasn't only small but appeared somewhat makeshift. Pieces of the rudder assembly were painted different colors, and in places the fuselage wasn't painted at all but showed patches of bare aluminum. Pete was sorry she'd agreed to fly with Luke—until the plane stopped and he emerged from the cockpit.

Wearing a short leather jacket, khaki pants, and aviator glasses, he looked every inch the barnstormer as he jumped down from the wing and walked over to her. They appraised each other silently for a moment. He looked the same, she thought. The same tangle of wavy brown hair, the same slightly too solemn expression. The same solidity. She was so glad to see him, to have a second chance, but she was afraid it would sound gushy to say it.

Instead she looked past him to the plane. "Where do you fly that thing? In circuses?"

"It may not look beautiful, but I used it to hop here all the way from California, and it'll get us where we want to go."

"So would a car."

He smiled as he took her bag and led her out to the plane. It might not look sleek and expensive, he assured her, but it was perfectly safe. "I don't see why anybody goes out and buys a new one, when you can take the good parts off a few old heaps and put together something even better than new."

Better? Pete looked at Luke skeptically, but she climbed in when he opened the passenger door and in a couple of minutes they were smoothly airborne. The way he handled the controls quickly won Pete's confidence.

As they soared higher, she scanned the landscape through the side window. The earth was a jewel, too, she thought, set in space. She stole a glance at Luke. She loved being up here, loved being with him.

On the trip to Connecticut, he explained his fondness for flying. "I became a pilot in the army, flying observation planes, then helicopters. I guess I wanted to come out of 'Nam with something I could feel glad about, so I've kept it up."

He also answered some of the questions she'd asked on the phone. Robby was in California. He'd recovered enough to help run a company that Luke had founded to sell a few things he'd invented—electronic devices with medical applications, including a tiny heart-monitoring device and a hand-held machine that could do some basic blood analysis.

Then he answered her unspoken questions. "I've thought about you so much, Pete. I felt . . . I really blew it with you. I wanted to know you better, wanted you to know me. But then I let some of my stupid crazy prejudices get in the way."

Prejudice was an odd word to use, she thought. "You told me there were more useful things to do in the world than designing jewelry. I suppose that's true. I should have appreciated your honesty instead of getting up on my high horse."

He nodded. "And I should've listened a little harder and heard how much passion you have for this work. You've proven it's the right thing for you to be doing."

Was that all it took to put the issue behind them? Pete still wondered why he had spoken of "crazy prejudices" to explain the way he'd reacted against her choice of profession.

But she didn't dwell on it. The last thing she wanted was another argument to flare up from nowhere and split them apart. "Tell me more about yourself," she said.

He glanced at her, then out a side window. "I can show you as well as tell you. Give you an aerial autobiography." He pushed the wheel forward and the planed nosed down and banked toward land. "So happens I'm Connecticut born and bred, and we're starting to pass right over Sanford territory. Straight down below is where I sailed a boat when I was a kid . . . over there is Stamford, where I grew up . . . and if you look up the coast a little you'll see New Haven, home of my dear old alma mater, Yale."

"What did you study in college?" she asked. "They don't give a course in inventing."

"I couldn't decide what to do when I was there. I was always good with electronics, but my father put pressure on me to study things I could use to make money. He didn't want to pay the tuition unless I followed his plan. I got tired of arguing with him, dropped out, and joined the army."

Pete caught a tinge of the bitter tone she'd heard once in the past before he changed the subject, prompting her to tell more about her own background.

As the earth rolled by beneath them, she talked effortlessly and unselfconsciously about the past. Something made her hesitate to tell him about her grandmother and the jewels. She sensed he might not be sympathetic. But she told him everything else—starting with the story of how her father had come to the United States, the way her parents had met, the shattered diamond and all the incident's destructive effects on her family. Luke's occasional interruptions to ask for more details told Pete that he was deeply sympathetic. Yet she was aware, too, that he had skipped very lightly over his own history, and the more he kept her talking the less chance she had to learn.

They were flying over the eastern portion of the coast near the clinic by the time she was able to steer the conversation back to him. "I've told you almost everything that went into making me who I am. What about you? What makes a person become an inventor?"

"Inventing," he replied, "is making something new, something that didn't exist before. Maybe that's what I wanted to do because . . . there was so much I didn't like about the way I was brought up, the way my parents lived, what it did to them. I wanted to invent a new life for myself, that's where it started."

"Were things really so bad, Luke? You talked about having a boat to sail, and when we flew over Stamford, it looked pretty nice."

The little smile he gave her only made him look sadder. "I grew up with lots of toys, Pete, and in more than one very nice place. Stamford was where I lived before my mother and father got divorced. After that I lived with my mother until she died."

"Where?"

He hesitated, then maneuvered the plane into another gently banked descent. "Right down there," he said quietly as he looked through the windshield.

A thousand feet below, Pete saw a beautiful limestone mansion set behind a long rolling lawn that was edged by a beach. Around it were scattered numerous other buildings.

As often as she had seen it from the ground, the perspective from above was so different that it was a very long moment before Pete realized she was looking at the Cole-Haffner Clinic.

He had called ahead and a taxi was waiting at an airfield twenty minutes from the clinic.

During the ride, Luke filled in most of the blank spaces. Sanford was his father's family name, Cole his mother's. She had never been a very happy person, Luke said, but he wondered sometimes whether the worst part of her condition wasn't simply a lack of courage. She had become depressed by letting herself remain trapped within the conventions of her class, burdened with empty obligations imposed by wealth—owning several houses and running them, being a hostess to her husband's associates in the banking and investment business.

"Was there something else she wanted to do?" Pete asked.

"She never thought about it," Luke replied. "Or if she did, she never told anyone. She just . . . went through the motions of being rich, being waited on, never lifting a finger even to trim a hedge or pull a weed. When she killed herself, everyone else said it was because she was mentally disturbed. But sometimes I think maybe she was just bored to death."

After her suicide, it had been Luke's idea to donate the house and grounds as a treatment facility, along with an endowment fund. "I was in 'Nam then, I didn't need or want a big white elephant to live in. And Robby was already off the rails, in need of care himself. I thought it would be the best kind of memorial to my mother—something useful. I've never been sorry."

She understood now what he meant by his "crazy prejudices" coming between them. He distrusted wealth and the luxuries it could buy—like jewels.

When the taxi left them at the entrance, Luke grabbed her hand before she could walk in. He pulled her close so she could feel the warm length of him. With his mouth pressed against her ear, he said, "The last time we were together, Pete, you were in the middle of a crisis with your own mother. I never saw the right moment to tell you my problems; instead,

I said something that drove you away. That was nuts, because I've wanted you from the moment I first saw you. Remember . . . ?'' He nodded in the direction of the shore.

"I remember," she said softly, leaning against his wide shoulder. "When I thought you were the patient."

He smiled and pulled away to look down into her eyes. "Sometimes I think I should be. Right now it feels crazy that I waited so long to call you again. But I've been afraid . . ."

"Afraid?"

"Think of how we met—here, brought together because we're both children of women who lost touch with reality. I've worried at times that maybe it runs in my blood, and I wouldn't want someone I love to have to deal with it. I never doubted I'd fall in love with you; I just doubted that I could make you as happy as another man. That's why I kept away, until finally I couldn't bear it anymore. And seeing your Eye of Love got to me somehow because all your passion came through, even in a photograph."

His eyes, she thought as she looked up at him, were the luminous gray of clouds when a storm is passing and the sun is beginning to break through. Their storm was certainly over, and she felt at this moment they belonged with each other, to each other.

Luke glanced through the door of the clinic. "Want me to come in with you?" he asked.

She shook her head. Her mother had been in an uncommunicative phase for the past several weeks. She saw no reason to subject Luke to it.

He told her there was a former gardener's cottage on the edge of the grounds to which he'd retained ownership. "I'll meet you there later," he said, pointing out the path she should take.

The cottage was a picturebook white frame colonial in miniature, no more than a few rooms on one floor, with roses growing thickly over a surrounding fence and trailing up the corners of the house to overhang the low eaves.

The door was open when Pete arrived at the end of the afternoon. Entering, she found the floor of a central living room covered with cartons, all half filled with books and papers. Searching for Luke, she poked her head through a couple of doors. One led to a small bedroom, beautifully done in rustic fabrics and early American furniture, another to a rear kitchen.

Luke appeared through the only other door on the far side of the living room, his arms cradling a stack of files.

"Packing up?" she asked, trying to sound casual. It was alarming to believe that, on the brink of finding each other, he was already pulling up more roots.

"Dr. Haffner told me a while ago the clinic needed more space. I don't want to let this place go completely, but I said they could borrow it. I don't get here much anymore."

She was reminded that he'd come from California. But she shoved aside the thought of any difficulties in being together.

He was here now.

"How'd it go with your mother?" he asked as he put the files into a box.

"She seemed a little better. Sometimes I wonder, though . . ." She shook her head and left the thought unfinished.

Luke said it for her. "You wonder if she'll ever leave here." He turned to her and dusted off his hands.

Her tears came then. She had wanted so many times to cry after being with Mama, yet there had been no one to comfort her, so the tears remained unshed. Today there was Luke.

And he did not disappoint her. He walked over and wrapped his arms around her. "Let it come," he whispered. "I know just how it feels."

For a minute she leaned against him, and he held her. Yes, he could understand all her old hurts as no one else could.

At last the tears ebbed, but the desire to be comforted was replaced by a different desire. She lifted her face, and he looked down and smiled. She pressed herself into him and his mouth descended to hers, his tongue traced a tingling line along her lips. For a moment, she enjoyed the gentle sensations, but then suddenly, with a force and urgency she had never experienced before, she felt an explosion of need.

"Take me, Luke," she whispered.

He answered her instantly, but without a word. His mouth pressed down harder on hers as he swept her up in his arms and carried her to the bedroom. Clinging together all the while, they wrestled each other out of their clothes. She had never known such absolute, consuming hunger for a man, and she could tell from the way he matched her pace that he felt the same. The golden light of late afternoon filtered through the trees outside and crept through the curtains, making it seem as if the room was aglow with their heat.

Naked at last, the thrill of his skin against hers made her moan with pleasure even before he lowered his mouth to her nipples and then began to kiss the place between her breasts, down across her stomach, her thighs, until he was tasting her and she wasn't sure how much longer she could wait.

Reaching down, she slipped her hands under his arms and pulled, letting him know she wanted him over her, inside her. A moment later he was sliding into the center of her, touching her to the core.

She cried out joyously as she felt his ultimate plunge and came along with him in a meteoric torrent of thrills that went rippling through her like an impossible mix of fire and cool water rushing over a series of rapids.

It was, she felt, the first time that a man had really made love to her.

They came together again and dozed and made love again until long after nightfall.

"Pietra," he whispered in the darkness as he caressed her. The way he intoned her name made her feel somehow that he was appreciating her uniqueness and wanted to know all the mysteries of her origins.

They went for a meal finally. Dining on excellent steaks at the same roadhouse they'd left in angry haste half a year before was a ritual both felt might ward off future idiotic arguments. At dinner, he asked about her name, and she began to tell the story of La Colomba.

"So you were named after one of the great courtesans of Europe," Luke said with a lilt of bemusement.

"Does my pedigree bother you?"

"Why the hell should it? My ancestors were robber barons. I'd like to think, though, that we're both an improvement on past generations."

Pete believed he was sincere. Yet she felt suddenly a little odd about the admiration in which she held her grandmother, and she didn't speak of her any more, leaving the tale of the jewels untold.

Under a starry sky, they flew back to the city, landing this time at the terminal for small planes near LaGuardia Airport. Pete climbed into a taxi with Luke and rode into the city to an address he gave the driver. She didn't ask where they were going. The biggest question seemed answered; they loved each other. She waited to see what else would unfold.

The taxi stopped in front of a Federal house on Grove Street in Greenwich Village, red brick with green shutters. It belonged to him, he explained, as they mounted the stoop, though he'd been renting it to a friend for the past few months. "I wasn't sure whether or not I'd stay in California—not until today."

Inside it was furnished with an eclectic collection of charming clutter. Mission oak furniture sat beside tables made from old winery vats. Navaho weavings hung on the wall beside New England weathervanes. In a front parlor, a sofa upholstered in deep burgundy leather sat before a fireplace. In front of it sat a coffee table made from a slab of glass over a piece of found driftwood. Books were stacked everywhere. It was a house, Pete thought happily, that simultaneously reflected the presence of a man of individual taste and the absence of a woman to organize and decorate.

"Think you could feel at home here?" Luke asked.

"I do already."

"Good. Because I'm officially asking you to move in."

She hesitated momentarily. "Do you think we're taking this too fast, Luke?"

He put his arms around her. "I'll go at any speed you want, Pete. But I'd say I've been moving pretty slow. I fell in love with you months ago, even if I was crazy enough to keep it a secret."

She laid her hand on his cheek. "Nothing crazy about either of us," she said.

"Okay. So I was dumb. But now I want to make up for lost time. Will you live here?"

"I think I have to," she said. "Because anywhere else, I'd only be half alive."

Chapter 10

Pete began to worry toward the end of summer. How long could perfection last? And for months now, throughout the spring and summer—since meeting Luke—everything had seemed too easy, too perfect. Living with him seemed to bring the whole of her life into balance.

As soon as she had assured Josef that she would go on paying rent on the apartment, he had adjusted immediately to her desire to move out. He was obviously pleased that his beautiful granddaughter was going to be sheltered and cared for by a man, though somewhat less thrilled about the nature of her new living arrangements.

"If you love him and he loves you, *schatje*, then why don't you want to be *getrouwd*?"

"That sounds like it might be fun, Opa," she teased, "but I can't do it, if I don't even know what it—"

"Married! You should become man and *vrouw*."

He surrendered quickly, however, when Pete patiently explained the modern realities. She wanted to go on working, not have children; there was no reason to be married. "Anyway," she said, with her tongue deliberately planted in her cheek, "how can I marry this man? I hardly know him!"

Which, in strict practical terms, was true. Yet she and Luke fit together so easily, hand in glove. They quickly discovered that they enjoyed doing almost everything together —cooking in the large kitchen at Grove Street, spending quiet evenings, taking off for weekend jaunts in his plane. During the summer, they flew to Cape Cod and Maine and to Nova Scotia. They loved traveling together, and Luke spoke of taking her to Europe when both were free, perhaps in late autumn. Pete had already gotten her passport. But for the summer, Luke said one night, his vacation plan was simply to make love to Pete all up and down the eastern seaboard.

"Just make love to me all up and down, period," she told him.

Another dimension of their life that she enjoyed was meeting all his friends. Luke welcomed a wide circle of people to the house on Grove Street—old war buddies, college classmates he'd kept in touch with, even some couples that included former girlfriends and men they'd married. When Pete invited Charlie and Jess to the house, they fit right in. Altogether, they formed a diverse and lively group—among them a civil rights lawyer, a gym teacher at a high school in New Jersey, a woman writer, an actor who had begun to make a name on the stage. They came to the house to talk, to have meals, or occasionally to play poker. The one shared characteristic among the people Luke collected around him was that they were all people who didn't care a lot about money. Not that they were unsuccessful. Some, she learned from Luke, were even wealthy. But they didn't flaunt it. They all put in a full day's work, lived simply, and didn't drive flashy cars. The women dressed casually and—Pete noticed particularly—wore very little jewelry.

Luke never raised the issue of her work again, and she was always able to assure herself that creating beauty was a worthy cause in itself. Each day she went off to her workshop fired with enthusiasm for her current project.

After sorting through all the offers in the wake of the Eye publicity, she had decided—not least because it gave her more time with Luke—to stay away from commercial assignments or any exclusive store affiliation, and to accept only the most choice personal commissions. A Saudi prince sent an emissary with a diamond he wished to have fashioned into a gift for one of his several wives; a number of Hollywood personalities promised Pete carte blanche if she would do a piece that could outshine Lyla's; the wives of multi-millionaires called, took her to lunch at Le Cirque and Côte Basque, and dumped fabulous gems onto tablecloths for Pete's inspection.

She took the jobs that she expected would be fun, gravitated to the people who had strong tastes of their own and yet weren't afraid to trust hers. As her confidence grew, she began employing Josef, using him to seek out good stones to accent the major jewels that some customers brought to her. She also had a secretary to take care of correspondence, billing, and fielding phone calls. In fact, she'd hired Lottie, who had grown increasingly unhappy at D & I under Andrea's yoke and had called Pete to ask about a job.

Aside from her secretarial duties, Lottie had taken on one other task—to research the life of La Colomba. The mystery of what had happened to the fabulous collection was never completely out of Pete's thoughts. She kept the bottle now in a safe at her office along with the gems she was using in her designs, and she brought it out frequently to examine it and daydream over it. Lottie had seen it one day and Pete told her the story. Lottie had volunteered to see what she could learn. Numerous letters sent abroad to foreign newspapers and libraries, turned up nothing more than copies of a few faded newspaper photographs taken fifty and sixty years earlier. But they showed La Colomba at the height of her beauty, and always decked out in some of her jewels—fabulous pendant earrings, necklaces dripping with stones, brooches, a tiara, all sparkling brilliantly with the reflection of the cameraman's flashbulbs.

So caught up was she in the magic and glamour of her grandmother's life, that she poured the story out to Luke one night as they lay in bed. His reaction was not what she hoped for. He was frankly disgusted that someone would sell her body for such useless luxuries, such vain and gaudy goods as a handful of jewels.

He was so vehement in his disgust of the whole situation that Pete never brought it up again, but she didn't give up her own search for information. Unfortunately, the faded black-and-white photos she'd managed to find gave no hint of whether the darker stones were red or green or blue, and the designs were not so distinctive that they could be traced purely on description. There was a chance, Pete thought, that she might recognize one if ever she came across it—if the pieces hadn't been broken up long ago. Only a small chance, but Pete told Lottie to continue her research. Someday a stronger link might turn up.

While Pete went off to her workshop, Luke puttered in the basement at Grove Street, where he had set up an electronics laboratory. She had learned that the major part of his work was in developing micro-electronic circuitry with applications in health care. The California company based on his inventions that Robby was now overseeing was evidently successful. At least a week out of every month, Luke was required to jet out to the West Coast to deal with business.

She missed him more each time he went. In October he returned one Friday evening from a trip that had kept him a few days longer than originally planned. When they made love that night, she couldn't get enough of him. Holding him inside her, arousing him again and again with every offering of herself she could possibly make.

"I'm beginning to think you missed me," he said finally in the small hours when they were both drained and sated.

"It's worse than that," she said. "I missed your cooking." He laughed, and she nestled close to him. "I don't want to be apart anymore, Luke. Can't you move your company here?"

He had once explained the choice of California for his business—there was access to many other companies working in allied systems, and that was a help in the development stage. Now that the business was established, however, she didn't see why it couldn't be located anywhere. His customers, after all, were all over the world.

Her suggestion was met with a long silence. "Suppose I asked you to do the same. You've only got to shift a workbench and a pouchful of jewels. Would you consider it?'' Before she could even raise the objections, he anticipated them. ''There are places for your mother out there, too, and your grandfather might like it.''

''They may not be willing to make a change.''

''They'll want to be where you are.''

''I don't know,'' Pete said. ''I feel so at home here. Don't you?''

He smiled and nodded. ''But I don't like being away from you, either. So let's try something else. You'll travel with me. You've never even come for a look—''

''I've been up to my ears—''

''In earrings,'' he supplied. ''But next time you'll come. You might decide you could feel at home out there, too. Have we got a date?''

''Just show me once more,'' she purred, pressing the length of her naked body against his, ''how much you like coming home.''

Luke's next trip west was planned for the first week in November. Pete organized her own schedule to be free. Settling the matter of how to end their constant separations would be just a prologue to planning the rest of her future with Luke. For all the defenses she had made to her grandfather of the casual modern customs, Pete daydreamed now and then about marriage and starting a family.

She was in the workshop on the Friday afternoon before she was to go home and pack for a night jet to California when the phone rang. Lottie was at lunch, and Pete left the bench to answer.

''Miss D'Angeli, please,'' said a voice with a clipped British accent.

''This is Pietra D'Angeli.''

''Miss D'Angeli, my name is John Utter. I'm calling from Paris. I am personal secretary to Her Highness, the Duchess of Windsor.''

Pete paused for a breath. The Duchess was well known to be one of the most avid acquirers of fine jewelry in the world.

Utter continued: ''Her Royal Highness has become aware

of your work and would be interested in meeting you to discuss creating a piece especially for her. Would it be possible for you to come to Paris?''

Pete had to restrain the impulse to let out a whoop. ''I'm sure I could arrange it. When did you have in mind?''

''Day after tomorrow.''

Pete was silent, looking for the right words. She didn't want to change her plans with Luke, but how did one negotiate delaying a command performance with a duchess—*the* Duchess? Before she could speak, however, Utter went on:

''I'm afraid, Miss D'Angeli, that time is rather of the essence. I can't explain everything now, but if you are interested in the assignment, you would have to come within the next two or three days.''

''Of course, then,'' Pete said at once. ''Day after tomorrow.''

''Good. May we expect you at noon?''

Pete said yes, and she was given directions to the Duchess's house in the Bois de Boulogne.

For a moment after the call ended, she was swept up in a vision of the days to come. Paris for the first time! A meeting with a legendary woman. A mysterious necessity to act quickly. She paced the workshop full of nervous energy.

And then she stopped. How much would Luke mind the change in their plans?

Of course, he would understand, she told herself. In her chosen field, a job like this would be the very pinnacle of achievement.

She went down to the basement as soon as she got home. It was a maze of metal cabinets containing high-speed computing equipment, electronic monitoring devices, even a compact laser device for etching the tiny printed circuits that Luke conceived to suit his needs. Whenever she came down here, Pete was struck by how little she understood of his work. The realization frightened her a little. How close could they be if neither understood each other's most basic interests?

She found him in front of a computer terminal and stood silently watching as his fingers tapped at the keyboard, pro-

ducing a complicated line drawing on the screen that rotated
in a three-dimensional simulation.

"Hi, babe," he said at last, his eyes still on the screen.
"I'll be through with this in a minute. We ought to pack."

"Luke, I can't go."

He gave her a startled look, then pushed back from the
computer and folded his arms, a silent demand for an explanation.

She told him about the call she'd received a few hours
earlier.

"And that's more important than coming with me?" he
said tightly when she had finished.

"It isn't more important," she objected. "But I have the
opportunity now. You'll be going to California next month,
and the month after. I can go with you then. Or, if this is
really about being together, you can come with me. I'd rather
be in Paris with you than—"

"I have my own obligations," Luke cut in. He rose from
his chair and came to her. "Look, this isn't just about being
together for a week. It's about planning our lives. I didn't
think there was anything more important than that."

"There isn't."

"But you don't mind if it waits."

"For a few days!" she cried out. "Luke, why do you have
to make this so hard?" Even as she asked the question, she
realized the shaky ground toward which it headed them.

"Because," he shouted back, "I don't see how in hell you
can put this ahead of anything to do with *us*. Damn it, Pete,
does it matter at all if the goddamn Duchess of Windsor gets
one more shiny object to put beside all the others in her jewel
box? I don't care who she is, how rich or famous. What she
buys with all her money is good for nothing more than a few
moments of selfish pleasure."

"Then perhaps it doesn't matter if anyone paints the Mona
Lisa or carves the Venus de Milo out of a block of marble.
Is that *useful*? Luke, if you can't ever accept the value of
what I do, then you're rejecting *me* with it."

He grasped her arms. "No, I'm not, Pete. I love you."

"And what's love by your definition?" she said bitterly. "Anything more than a few moments of selfish pleasure?"

They stared at each other another second, then Pete broke from his grasp and went upstairs to pack—for Paris in the fall.

Arriving in Paris late Saturday morning after a night flight from New York, she went straight to the charming Left Bank hotel Jess had recommended. In fact, calling Jess to gossip about her "secret mission"—and cry on her shoulder about the argument with Luke—had proven valuable to Pete in more ways than one.

"I can tell you a few things about Her Royal Hotstuff," Jess said, "that might help you. I've seen her in action."

"You have?"

"She and my parents have mutual friends with a house in the Caribbean. We were all houseguests together eight or nine years ago. Once you've met Wally, you don't forget her."

Jess had reeled off a number of ways to make points with the Duchess. She was a vain woman who couldn't be flattered too much. She liked people who treated her dogs well, since she regarded them as her children. She appreciated people calling her "Highness" and curtsying when they were introduced—particularly because she was not entitled to such protocols. She wouldn't handle paper money unless it was new and crisp—or one of her maids had ironed it.

"You're kidding!" Pete hooted.

"Believe me," Jess assured her, "you don't have to make up outrageous stories when you're talking about the Duchess of Windsor."

Pete didn't think she'd have any occasion to offer the Duchess money, but it certainly wouldn't hurt to know the woman's idiosyncracies and avoid any that could disrupt easy communication.

On the way to the airport, Pete had grabbed a couple of biographies out of bookstores, and she spent most of her first day in Paris reading them. Her only time away from the hotel was used to visit the original Cartier store, where the Duke was known to have ordered special gifts for his wife's birth-days and their anniversaries, and to browse at the Paris branch of Dufort & Ivères out of sentimental curiosity.

She had no appetite for sightseeing. Glimpses of the Eiffel Tower and the Seine and Notre Dame that were impossible to avoid as she traveled across the city by taxi only made her blue. Paris was a city for lovers, all the songs and poems said so. She should have been here for the first time with Luke.

Though he had apologized to her when she called from Kennedy just before boarding the Paris flight, Pete knew the problem wasn't buried forever. Luke would never be able to completely overcome his resentment of a certain kind of wealth and its destructive aspects. In his own mind, it had killed his mother. He wasn't so foolish as to impoverish himself in retaliation, but most of the money he had would always be used for public-spirited work or philanthropy, not luxuries. So what might come between them, in the end, was not only a difference in values and viewpoints, but some of the very things she loved about him—his integrity, his honesty with her, his straightforward commitment to an unselfish life.

On Sunday morning, Pete dressed in a proper black suit —nothing that stood a chance of outshining the Duchess— and pulled back her hair to look prim rather than flamboyant. *Ready*, she assured herself with a last look in the mirror as she marched out, chanting a little reminder to herself under her breath: "Curtsy, dogs, flattery . . . curtsy, dogs, flattery."

Half an hour later, the taxi turned through high wrought-iron gates on the edge of the Bois de Boulogne, and Pete got out in the front courtyard of a large block-shaped house with a stone balustrade around the roof line.

The door was opened by the white-haired Georges Sanegre, the Duchess's Spanish butler of many years. Tall and straight in striped morning pants and tail coat, he showed Pete in as soon as she announced her name.

She was accosted almost at once by a trio of yappy, dirty beige pugs with gray and black faces who came barreling through from an open doorway and skidded on the marble floor. They were decked out with diamond-studded mink collars and reeked of Dior perfume.

The butler pointed to a book on a marble side table. "If you will sign the guest book please, Miss, I will show you to the salon." Next to the book, Pete noticed as she signed, lay a red leather box embossed with gold letters reading THE KING. A shiver passed through her at even this second-hand glimpse into the history of a vanished era.

She was led from the grand entrance hall with its sweeping staircase and fancifully painted ceiling into an exquisite silver-blue room full of pale, watery sunlight. Mirrors with candelabra set into their centers reflected fine French furniture, and portraits of Queen Mary, Queen Alexandra, and the Duke—in full regalia as Edward, Prince of Wales—hung in silver frames studded with gems.

Tables of every size and shape filled the room, and on every surface treasures gleamed—jeweled daggers, porcelain sweet dishes, Fabergé boxes crusted with diamonds, silver candlesticks, snuffboxes, clocks, tiny lamps, even a Maori battle club.

Flowers were everywhere—sprays of calla lilies, towers of cabbage-sized white peonies, bunches of forced narcissus giving off their heady scent, and huge bouquets of the Duchess's favorite white chrysanthemums.

While she waited, Pete moved to look more closely at the portraits. She was in front of Queen Mary, posed regally in Garter robes, when a voice behind her said flatly, "My mother-in-law. She never saw fit to recognize me."

Pete turned as the Duchess came forward, smiling very slightly, and offered her hand. Taking it, Pete went into the traditional curtsy to royalty she had practiced before the mirror last night. The Duchess smiled more broadly as she gestured to a chair.

"Please sit down, Miss D'Angeli."

At the tail end of her seventies, the Duchess was frail and yet still a striking figure, dressed in ink blue Givenchy, her ebony hair styled that morning by Alexandre as it had been every morning for nearly thirty years. Her reported three face-

lifts seemed to be holding up remarkably well. Her jaw line
was firm, her high cheekbones prominent, but a deep frown
line cleaved her forehead, and her high, arched eyebrows
gave her a slightly surprised look.

The dogs had followed her into the room, snuffling about
her ankles, then running over to sniff at Pete's shoes. The
Duchess watched approvingly as Pete leaned over to scratch
their heads and say, "Hello there." As she lowered herself
onto a settee, the Duchess made a little clucking noise and
the dogs padded away to settle on cushions at her feet.

Curtsy, dogs, and flattery, Pete reminded herself. "This
is a lovely room, Ma'am," she said. "Did you decorate it
yourself?" Pete knew very well she had.

"Yes. I've personally decorated all my houses. It was a
particular joy of mine, and the Duke liked my taste." She
looked around the room. "It's exactly the way it was when
I lost him."

Pete followed her gaze and saw that a box of the Duke's
favorite cigars still sat on a console. His pipes were still in
their rack beside a chair. "I always hoped he would die first.
He gave up so much for me, you know. It's very hard without
him."

"I'm sure it is, Ma'am," Pete said, "but it must have
been wonderful to be loved like that."

The Duchess's deep blue eyes twinkled. "It had its com-
pensations." She idly scratched one of the dogs that had
climbed onto her lap. "Not, of course, that it was ever easy.
Have you seen this?" She held out her bird-thin wrist and
jiggled a bracelet, a single row of diamonds with nine gem-
set Latin crosses hanging from it. Pete knew she had worn
it on her wedding day. "I always thought it represented the
crosses I've had to bear."

"And borne with great style, Your Highness."

The Duchess nodded in full agreement. "Style may be my
greatest asset, Miss D'Angeli. Someday, indeed, it may be
all that I am remembered for. All the more reason for me to
keep it up, even with David gone." Her eyes went to a picture
of the Duke that sat in a frame on an end table. He had been

dead for several years, but Pete could see from the cast of his widow's gaze that she was still in mourning.

"While he was here," she went on, "he always bought my jewelry. It was an act of love, and on each of our anniversaries I have continued the tradition. Every year I hesitate and wonder if it's time to stop. Then sentiment takes over. He loved so much to give me beautiful things. I can't help believing that some of his spirit comes to me through the shine and sparkle of rare gems. Does that sound mad, my dear?"

"Only if enduring love is a form of madness," Pete said.

The Duchess appeared touched. "I'm aware of the very beautiful designs you've created. I'd like you to do something for me."

"It would be a privilege, Ma'am," Pete said. "Do you have any notion about the sort of design—"

Experienced at commanding attention, the Duchess had only to make a slight movement of her hand and Pete fell silent. "In this case, it's not simply a matter of design," she explained. "I want you first to act as my agent."

"Agent," Pete repeated. The word reverberated with intrigue.

The Duchess reached over to a low pile of books on a coffee table. She took the top volume and handed it to Pete. It was a beautifully printed, color-illustrated catalog for an auction to be run by Christie's at the Hotel Beau Rivage in Geneva. On the cover was a picture of an exquisite ruby and diamond necklace. The caption beneath identified the piece as part of "the estate of Dorothy Fisk Haines." The date given for the auction was Tuesday morning: the day after tomorrow.

"I knew Dotty Haines," the Duchess said, "and I know her collection. There is one particular item I have always wanted for myself. I tried to buy it when she was alive, but she wouldn't sell. Yet she never did anything with it. I've marked the picture . . ."

Pete noticed a crisp new—or perhaps freshly ironed—one hundred franc note protruding from the catalog. Turning to the mark, she saw a color photograph of a huge unset cushion-cut ruby. A few lines beneath the picture described it as a century-old stone mined in upper Burma, source of the world's finest rubies, its color pure enough to be called "pigeon blood"—a designation earned by less than one in twenty thousand rubies. Its weight, given as twenty-eight and a half carats, made it doubly rare.

"I'd like you to acquire that stone for me, Miss D'Angeli, and create something as spectacular as the Eye of Love—a design that David would have liked. The gift to end all gifts, one might say. Can you do it?"

It would be mere bravado to make any promises in reply to such expectations. Pete shrewdly stuck to the practical demands. "Acquiring the stone is the first problem. It's bound to bring a high price."

"Yes, and all the more if it were known that I wanted it. But you shall act for me, and you are authorized to pay as much as you think it's worth. I shall rely on your judgment."

"In the seventeenth century," Pete observed, "the greatest jewel fancier of the time, Bernard Tavernier, wrote that 'When a ruby exceeds six carats and is perfect, it is sold for whatever is asked.' This ruby, Ma'am, is almost five times six carats."

The Duchess nodded. "No doubt it will be sought after. But I have a feeling that you will not disappoint me." Briskly, offhandedly, she dispensed with a mere mention of practical matters. A check to cover expenses would be delivered to her hotel later in the day. All other business details, such as her fee and payment for the ruby should be taken up with Mr. Utter, whose phone number and address would accompany the check.

"When the ruby is mine," the Duchess concluded as she stood up, "bring it to me and we'll talk a bit more about what to do with it."

The audience was clearly over. They walked out to the entrance hall together, where the Duchess told Pete she would be driven back to her hotel, and then shook hands.

Pete was disappointed. She had hoped she might be invited to see first-hand the famous collection of jewelry that had been bestowed on Wallis Simpson by her adoring abdicated king. She had seen pictures often enough to know a great deal of the inventory, but there were things that could be learned from a close look at the pieces.

She thought of asking but decided to let it wait. She could do it, Pete thought, when she came back.

Chapter 11

At the end of a busy Monday, the main branch of Tesori on Geneva's rue du Rhone was about to close for the day. With half the important jewelry dealers and jewelry lovers in the world in town for the Haines auction, there had been more than the usual amount of traffic through the store, and even those who were expected to indulge themselves at tomorrow's auction had not resisted temptation upon seeing something at Tesori that struck their fancy. For the very rich, thought Tesori's owner, Antonio Scappa, buying jewels could be described in the same terms as eating peanuts was for the poor: It was impossible to stop after just one.

Antonio should have been content with the day's results, but at the close of business he toured his domain as usual, scowling at salespeople, admonishing gem cutters, haranguing designers. At his best, he ran his business more by the whip than by the glove, and today he was in an especially foul mood.

In fact, Antonio was not merely discontented. He was frightened.

With the last of the store's employees finally gone, the door locked behind them, he retreated to his office at the rear of the store and sat down at his desk. He stared bleakly at the glossy catalog that lay in front of him. This auction tomorrow, it could mean real trouble for him, the first serious threat to his security in twenty-five years.

It could mean the unwanted resurrection and unmasking of Vittorio D'Angeli. Turning to one of the interior pages of the catalog, Antonio gazed at the picture of a magnificent emerald and sapphire necklace, his mind racing back to a time thirty years ago.

At the end of the war, chaos had reigned throughout Europe. Records had been destroyed; no one was where they were supposed to be, and anything could be had for a price. Sometimes it seemed half the people of Europe were on the run from the other half, and most of them did it with false papers.

Vittorio D'Angeli was no exception. As a high-ranking *Fascista*, he was on everyone's list. Running hard from the wrath of the Italian *partigiani*, he had crossed the mountainous Italian border into Lugano, in Switzerland. His wife, Gretchen, was already there, hiding with her father, who had been branded a Nazi war criminal *in absentia*. The group of Nazi sympathizers who were busy day and night turning out forged identity papers for the hundreds of Hitler loyalists trying to escape to South America or establish new, blameless identities in Europe added the D'Angelis and Rudolf Koppveldt to their list.

The hiding was difficult, the waiting nerve-wracking, but before long, Vittorio D'Angeli had ceased to exist, replaced by Antonio Scappa, a respectable Italian-speaking Swiss burgher. While her father moved on to join other fugitive Nazis in South America, Gretchen became Lisel Bamberg, a German-speaking Swiss citizen from Zurich. For the sake of their cover story, Antonio and Lisel arranged to "meet" in Lugano, carried on a highly visible courtship, and married under Swiss law.

Vittorio had managed to escape from Italy with Swiss francs hoarded before the war's end, but the money didn't last long. And no matter how much he managed to earn at whatever jobs he could muster, it paled into insignificance when he thought of the fortune just sitting in a vault only a few miles away. La Colomba's jewels. *His* jewels. He deserved them, and he intended to have them.

He still had the bottom half of La Colomba's perfume bottle, the skirt made of gold and covered in diamonds. Shortly after the war, he took it to the Helvetia Kreditanstalt in an attempt to retrieve the jewel collection he had deposited there seven years earlier. But it was no good. Without both halves of the bottle, the bank authorities would not consider releasing the jewels.

The "Scappas" had their first child, a daughter, and named her Andrea. Now more than ever "Antonio" thought about the enormous wealth that ought to be his inheritance. The knowledge of the jewels' existence gnawed at him like decay at a tooth, the pain growing daily until he could think of little else.

It was his wife who came up with the answer. "We have become someone else with forged papers. When the plastic surgery we plan is complete, we will have forged faces. Why, then, should we not benefit from one more forgery? Find someone who can recreate your brother's half of the bottle."

It took a long time to find the man with both the essential skills and the necessary lack of scruples to forge the bottle. It had to be done entirely from memory of a figure Vittorio had seen once, briefly, many years earlier. But the image was burned into his mind as clearly as identification numbers were tattooed onto the forearms of concentration camp survivors.

He found his artist in Amsterdam—a jeweler named Boersma who had been a collaborator during the war and had subsequently been ruined.

"Difficult," he said when Vittorio approached him with the idea. "Difficult. But not impossible. For a price."

"I can't pay until the bottle is finished and I've collected the jewels," Vittorio said.

"Ah," said the Dutchman. "In that case, it will be twice as expensive." He set to work at once.

It took nearly two years for the work to be completed to

everyone's satisfaction, but finally it was done. Vittorio and Boersma headed for Geneva and the Helvetia Kreditanstalt.

The ruse worked perfectly. The bank's Herr Lindner had no reason to suspect that the two halves of the perfume bottle, exactly as they had been described to him and made to fit so perfectly together, were not entirely genuine. Within the hour, Vittorio walked out of the bank carrying a large strongbox full of his mother's jewels and cast off his true name for the last time.

Boersma was eager to be paid, too eager to wait for Antonio Scappa to quietly sell some of the jewels. When he insisted on choosing several pieces from the collection as payment, Antonio was in no position to refuse.

"But you *must* break the pieces up and recut the stones," he insisted. "If they were ever to be identified as part of La Colomba's collection, I'd be dead. And so would you."

"Yes, yes, of course. Give me credit, *mijnheer*, for knowing my business." He chose a brooch of rare pigeon's-blood rubies, a necklace with at least three dozen easily disguised diamonds, and a pair of very fine "kelly" emerald earrings, the richest, brightest green stones. Lastly, he took a necklace made of hundreds of small emeralds and sapphires he could sell individually at a good price.

Two other pieces from the collection—a wheatsheaf pin and a diamond bangle bracelet—had to be sold at once to pay for Rudolf Koppveldt's resettlement in South America and the plastic surgery that would guarantee Antonio and Lisel's safety.

With new faces as well as new names, the "Scappas" returned to Lugano. They were afraid to sell any more of La Colomba's jewels. Most of the pieces had been made specially for her, and her taste had been distinctive. There was too much risk of them being identified. He broke one or two pieces up and sold the stones, but even that made him nervous. As it turned out, the collection's true value was found as collateral. The banks of Lugano were spilling over with money left on deposit by fleeing Nazis. Once "Antonio Scappa" showed a skeptical loan officer the collection of jewels on which he intended to found a jewelry business, he had no trouble arranging a substantial loan.

With money and safety, he had the leisure to decide what he wanted to do with the rest of his life. The time spent working with Boersma had given him a taste for the jewelry business as well as a pretty clear idea of the huge amounts of money to be made in it. In 1952, Tesori was born.

It was a success almost from the first. Antonio's experience running his confiscated shop in Milan had served him well. Within four years, there were stores in Geneva and Zurich. Soon after, as the "economic miracle" took hold in Germany, he felt safe enough to send Lisel to Munich and Berlin to oversee opening branches there. Through her father's contacts, she had an inside track to the best real estate locations and bank financing.

They had built a good life, a secure life. Until now.

Antonio had been shocked to his bones when, thumbing through the catalog of the upcoming Haines sale, he had come upon the full color photo of a magnificent necklace that looked like a stream of water rushing through dappled shade on a sunny day. It was a distinctive design with rows of invisibly set calibre-cut sapphires set diagonally so that the solid necklace was totally flexible. There were more than five hundred sapphires in the piece, and the whole thing was outlined by nearly two hundred emeralds. It was an exquisite piece, truly one of a kind, and to Antonio it was inescapably familiar.

He had seen it twice before in his life—once slithering through the long fingers of La Colomba in a candlelit villa in the hills above Florence, then again when he gave it to Dirk Boersma on the assurance that it would be broken apart at once.

Stupid fool, he railed at the long-absent Boersma, *stupid greedy fool*! Now he'd have to buy the necklace back. Could he take the chance that someone someday might recognize it as coming from the legendary collection of La Colomba? His mother had been famous, photographed and written about. Her jewels had been no less renowned. From time to time, questions still circulated about whatever became of them.

Something like this could start a firestorm of gossip that might be impossible to put out.

Yet it was such a terrible waste of capital. Once he acquired the necklace, he could do nothing with it but lock it up in sealed boxes within his vault along with the rest of the collection. Did he dare to take a chance of letting it continue to circulate? Mrs. Haines, after all, had worn it rarely and otherwise kept it locked away. Another collector might do the same.

No. He had to buy it. Indeed, though Antonio normally stayed away from public crowds, he thought it might be a good idea to go to the hotel tonight. A last showing of the jewels was being held in conjunction with a gala charity ball. It would be a chance to study the opposition—to reconnoiter his enemy in the battle to kill Vittorio d'Angeli once and for all.

Pete arrived at the desk of the Beau Rîvage on Monday evening to check into the suite reserved for her by John Utter. She had taken the train from Paris, feeling no need to rush from one place to the next. Geneva would be another new experience—and yet just another place where she would miss being with Luke.

As she rode the train, looking out at the spectacular scenery of the Alps, she found herself questioning what she would do if it ever came down to choosing between him . . . and her work. Perhaps it never would; certainly it never *ought* to. Yet Pete realized that there was an irrational edge to the depth of resentment Luke expressed for luxuries that could be afforded by only a few. Not that there was no sense at all in his position. She couldn't blame him for feeling the way he did, though it was ironic that the objection to her work should come from a wealthy man rather than a poor one. But how much room did that leave for her to go on serving the tastes of the rich?

Eager as she was to hear his voice, each time Pete was tempted to call Luke, she was afraid the argument would surface again. The confrontation could wait until she got home.

In the five-story skylighted lobby of the hotel, Pete recognized a number of faces of dealers and collectors who had been involved in the jewelry market for decades. She had been told that there was a gala showing of the Haines collection tonight, and people were pouring through the entrance or out of elevators in formal dress. There was Harry Winston in his tuxedo, heading for the ballroom; Sophia Loren in pale pink Givenchy chic; Elizabeth Taylor in a black and white gown with the immense diamond Richard Burton had given her on a lavalier. No doubt Lyla would be showing up, too, to give Taylor a run for her money. And perhaps Marcel.

Pete barely minded that she had brought nothing formal to wear. She would have a chance to see the jewels on display before the auction started at eleven tomorrow morning.

She had left the desk and was about to be taken up to her suite when she heard herself addressed from near the elevators. "Signorina D'Angeli . . . ?"

Pete turned to see a stranger, heavyset, with thinning brown hair going to gray. "Yes?" she said, studying his face. There was a faint shadowy familiarity about him, as though she might have glimpsed him for a moment many years ago— perhaps standing in the fringes of the crowd that had gathered one day to watch her grandfather cleave a fabulous diamond.

His eyes glittered as he came nearer and held out his hand. "I recognized you from pictures I've seen along with interviews in the fashion magazines. Allow me to introduce myself. I am Antonio Scappa; I own a number of jewelry stores."

"Tesori's," Pete said, "I know." She knew, too, that Andrea was his daughter, and had heard that there was no love lost between them since Andrea had aligned herself with Marcel Ivères.

What Pete did not know was that Antonio Scappa's terror of the past had escalated the moment he'd spotted her across the lobby. Antonio had suspected the first time he'd seen Pietra D'Angeli's name in print that she must be related, probably the child of his brother. The joining of the family name to Pietra was obviously no coincidence; that could only be Stefano's homage to their whore mother.

Much as he had known this, however, Antonio had never before felt a pressing need to determine the truth. But seeing Pietra now in the flesh, he had an instantaneous visceral certainty that this was his niece. Were all the chickens coming home to roost? Was it possible that Stefano had dispatched her to buy the necklace and pick up the trail to the entire collection? Though it meant taking a risk, Antonio decided he had to speak to her and determine how much she knew.

He was reassured by the expression he read in Pietra D'Angeli's face as she accepted his hand. If she had known his secret, he guessed, she would be attempting to hide the knowledge, treating him as a total stranger. Instead, she eyed him with frank curiosity.

"I have a feeling we've met before," she remarked.

"Have you been to my store?"

Pete shook her head. "I've never been to Geneva before —or to Europe, for that matter."

"Then we couldn't have met. I rarely travel myself. I've never been to the United States."

There was a silence. Pete fidgeted slightly as Scappa examined her. Why had he stopped her?

"Well," he said, "I just wanted to tell you how much I've admired your creations. Perhaps at some point in the future you might consider—"

Scappa's voice caught abruptly, and he glared past Pete's shoulder. A couple of words in Italian escaped his lips in a seething hiss.

Turning to follow his gaze, Pete saw Marcel and Andrea emerging from one of the elevators. Andrea's lush figure was draped to perfection in a tomato red Fortuny gown that was slit up to mid-thigh in front and left most of her golden-tanned back bare. Marcel's tuxedo was accented by a silver-gray pleated shirt set off with large diamond studs.

Pete thought for a moment about trying to make a quick escape. She didn't mind trying to maintain cordial relations with Marcel, but she feared the scene that might erupt out of Andrea's senseless jealousy. The explosive potential of the encounter was escalated even further by the hostility between Andrea and her father.

There was no room to maneuver, however, before their paths intersected.

Marcel had barely begun to greet Pete when Antonio Scappa erupted. "I suppose you've come," he accused Andrea, "to goad your boyfriend into bidding up the price on anything I'd hope to buy."

Marcel tried to intervene. "Signor Scappa, don't make a scene, please. Surely you and your daughter can reconcile your—"

"I have no daughter. She's a traitor," Scappa growled at Marcel. "You would have had to sell to me after Claude died if you didn't have her help to turn things around."

It was a backhanded compliment, but more praise than Andrea had ever received from her father before. "I could have done just as good a job for you if you'd have let me."

"I don't need your help," Antonio snapped.

"But perhaps you need *hers*?" Andrea said, flicking a glance at Pete.

Antonio said nothing but looked at Pete with raised eyebrows, as though an idea had just been planted.

Pete spoke quickly to extract herself from the middle. "I'm not interested in working for anyone but myself."

Antonio's glance bounced maliciously from Pete to Andrea and back again. "Perhaps someday you'll change your mind." He swept one more glance over Andrea and Marcel. "We have nothing more to say to each other."

"Perhaps we'll settle our arguments in the morning," Andrea suggested, "with numbers as our weapons."

Antonio reddened visibly and marched away, out of the hotel without another word. Pete saw that Andrea was struggling to retain her composure.

Marcel put his arm around her. "Are you all right, *chérie?*"

"He's my father," Andrea said stoically, "but he's a total bastard. I should have gotten used to it by now." Then she forced a smile at Marcel.

It struck Pete that they actually looked happy together— which they were, having just commemorated their original

meeting at the same hotel with hours in bed that had settled
for both of them that they belonged together. For now.

Andrea turned to her. "So you're spreading your wings a
little, Pete. Are you here for yourself? Or are you buying for
someone?"

"*Chérie*," Marcel admonished her, "you know such questions are bad manners."

"That's all right," Pete said evenly. "I'd ask you the
same—if I thought there was any chance of getting an answer."

Andrea smiled. "Why don't you join us at the ball, Pete?
I'll introduce you around."

Perhaps there was a little edge to the remark, Pete thought,
Andrea showing off that the connections were *hers*. Yet it
seemed a surprising step forward in their relationship that
Andrea should even seek her company. Now that they were
no longer confined under the same roof every day and she
had consolidated her hold on Marcel, perhaps Andrea was
able to relax, to regard her with professional respect.

Still, Pete shook her head. "I don't think I'd have much
fun."

They said good-night. As she stood by the elevator watching them join the stream of others heading for the ballroom,
Pete was surprised to feel a rush of sympathy for Andrea.
Being raised by a man like Antonio Scappa had obviously
given her a rough road to follow for the first part of her life.
Yet Andrea had risen above it, had proven her abilities, had
become an indispensable mate to the man whom—in her own
way—she loved.

It occurred to Pete that it wasn't impossible she and Andrea
might someday be friends. Even now, perhaps because of the
way they had both risen above the adversity of difficult child-
hoods, she felt a strange kinship with her.

Dorothy Fisk Haines—Dotty to her friends—had started
her career as a young boomtown whore during the 1889 silver
rush in Creede, Colorado. By the age of fifteen, her friends
included Calamity Jane, Bat Masterson, even a couple of the

James gang. The day before she turned sixteen, one of her best customers hit the mother lode and carried Dotty off to the preacher. But gold inspired men to be lawless, and at seventeen young Dorothy was a millionaire widow on the train to New York.

When she arrived, Madison Fisk had just made his second million in railroads and, though he was building a Fifth Avenue mansion, he wasn't yet too respectable to be bowled over by the rich young widow who looked like an angel and talked like a miner. During their long marriage, their fortunes increased, and by the time Mr. Fisk died in 1955, Dotty had more money than she could ever hope to count and more jewels than she had boxes for. It was said that emerald necklaces used to lay around in shoeboxes, rubies reposed in ashtrays, and a pearl choker she had tired of was used as a collar for her dog.

The lusty Mrs. Fisk Haines had retired to Monte Carlo, where she lived to the age of ninety-eight, gambling huge sums nightly in the Casino while dripping with gems, and daily keeping the world's jewelers content with her constant purchases. She knew everybody and feared no one.

The one thing Dotty never had was a child. Without an heir, every piece of jewelry she ever owned would be up for grabs this morning in the ballroom of the Beau Rîvage. The collection would bring a fortune, and the fact that it was all going to charity—a children's hospital in Colorado and a battered women's shelter in New York—was likely to push prices even higher.

At fifteen minutes before eleven A.M. on a sunny Tuesday, the ballroom of the hotel was already jammed to overflowing. Well-known corporate raiders, the scions of old banking families, and European aristocrats sat beside equally rich but anonymous businessmen, Arab sheiks in flowing robes, representatives of royalty who couldn't bring themselves to appear in person, and all the major dealers from New York, Paris, and London.

Across the front of the room, near the auctioneer's podium, attractive young men and women in plain black suits waited by a double bank of phones where serious bidders who couldn't make it to Geneva would place their bids. High on the front wall a screen waited to display color slides of each lot as it came up for bid. A large board beside it would record the bids in six currencies.

Arriving an hour earlier, Pete registered and was given a numbered paddle for bidding, then toured the bulletproof glass display cases that lined the edges of the room. Each case was watched over by an armed guard in uniform, though Pete assumed this was only the visible part of a much larger security force.

As she viewed the incredible variety of jeweled pieces and the few enormous stones that Dotty Haines had never had the time or inclination to have put into settings, Pete found herself wondering about her grandmother, about the jewels of La Colomba. As fabulous as the Haines collection was, her grandmother's was reputed to have been greater. Was it possible that the jewels from one trove could have found their way to the other? The wealth of Dotty Haines had cast a wide net when it came to buying jewelry.

Pete went back and looked at each piece a second time, searching for a similarity to any of the pieces she had seen in the old newspaper photos of La Colomba. But nothing rang a bell.

At last she took a seat, choosing a place at the end of a row of chairs toward the rear of the room. The ruby she had come to bid on was one of the earlier lots, and once it had been knocked down, she thought it was possible she would want to leave the auction. Despite the electric atmosphere of the room, she felt vaguely impatient, a gnawing sense that she would rather be somewhere else. Was this what Luke had done to her? Had he taken some of the joy out of what should have been a high point?

No, there was something else mixed in—a half-formed idea that she wanted to be doing something far more active and exciting than sitting here to buy a jewel or even bending over a workbench. She wanted to be engaged on a hunt for lost treasure. After years of sporadic dreaming about the jewels of La Colomba, she felt a gathering impulse to begin the hunt in earnest.

She was distracted from the thought, however, by seeing
Andrea and Marcel arrive, then Antonio Scappa soon after.
They took seats on opposite sides of the room, but Pete could
see the furious glances that went back and forth between them.

A few more last-minute arrivals pushed into the room and
were given places of honor. Paloma Picasso, the jewelry
designer whom Pete had met in New York, caught her eye
and waved, and Lyla—appearing without Douglas (who was
no doubt sleeping off the previous night's carousing)—
shouted a greeting as she went toward the front of the room.
At precisely eleven, the auctioneer mounted his pulpit-like
podium, the overhead screen flashed into life, and the room
hushed. "Lot number one," he intoned, "a pair of gold and
briolette diamond chandelier earrings. I'll start at fourteen
thousand dollars. Fourteen . . . now I have sixteen on the
phone . . . I have sixteen, and now eighteen at the
back. . . ."

The first lot was knocked down for eight-two thousand
dollars in less than two minutes. For the most part, the room
was quiet except for the rustle of catalogs, the scribble of
gold pencils, and the murmur of voices speaking softly into
the telephones, urging money in New York and London to
be spent in Geneva. Diamonds, emeralds, jade, pearls, even
the occasional opal or aquamarine flashed across the screen.
Numbers whirled on the currency board. A few bidders raised
paddles to signal their bids, but most preferred a scratch of
the nose, a subtle wave of a pen, even the raise of an eyebrow.

With notations in her catalog, Pete kept track of the
amounts paid for each item and, whenever possible, the identity of the buyer. It helped her put her finger on the pulse of
the sale—to see if the prices exceeded the printed presale
estimate, to know if dealers were predominating over private
buyers. Pete observed that, from the first sale, pieces were
being sold for two and even three times as much as Christie's
had expected. Among the dealers who had bought several
pieces was Marcel Ivères, with Andrea visibly urging him
on with a whisper or a nudge. Though some of his purchases
might have been for store inventory, from the premium prices

he was willing to pay Pete guessed that he was, like her, functioning as an agent for various clients.

Antonio Scappa, on the other hand, had bought nothing— had not even bid.

"Lot number forty-seven," the auctioneer said at last, "a rare pigeon-blood ruby of Burmese origins weighing almost twenty-nine carats. The bidding will start at one hundred thousand dollars . . ."

The opening bid was not Pete's, and she didn't see where it came from, but the price leaped upward in increments of ten thousand to double the opening amount before Pete had raised her paddle. She had decided there would be no harm in bidding openly, since it would be assumed, in any case, that she was operating on behalf of a client. She entered the fray finally with a bid at two hundred twenty thousand dollars.

"I have two-twenty . . . and now two-thirty . . ."

Pete saw the auctioneer nod directly at Marcel. There were other bidders, but as the price spiraled they fell away and it became a contest between herself and Marcel, with Andrea prodding him to continue.

When Marcel topped Pete's bid of four hundred thousand with another ten, she did not answer. She had reached the amount she thought it reasonable to pay for the jewel. As the auctioneer knocked down the sale with a rap of his gavel, Marcel looked over his shoulder and gave Pete an apologetic shrug. All's fair, it seemed to say, *c'est la guerre*. In another time she might have wondered whether the element of competition between them had been driven by something other than business. But she believed that was behind them now.

Without the ruby, of course, there could be no commission for the Duchess of Windsor, no jump to a higher plateau of international renown as a designer. But Pete found that she wasn't feeling terribly disappointed. Using her best judgment, she had decided that the stone had become too expensive. And returning empty-handed from her trip might make it easier to smooth over the argument with Luke.

She sat through several more items, her mind not really on what was happening, no longer making notations. Then she rose from her seat and started making her way toward the rear exit. At the door, she stopped for a last look back at the colorful and exciting scene. Had she lost the will to function in this arena? Was it even possible that she had surrendered the ruby for the sake of love?

As her eyes swept the room, she became aware that Antonio Scappa was holding up his paddle, bidding at last.

And Marcel was among those in spirited bidding against him. Pete could see Andrea leaning close to him, urging him on. Her glance went to the screen, where the picture of a sapphire and emerald necklace was projected. Pete recalled it from her tour of the display, certainly one of the most beautiful pieces in the collection, its myriad stones invisibly set to make a dazzling streak of blue bisecting the special green of the "old mine" emeralds from South American sources that had been depleted decades ago. She checked her catalog. The published estimate, made in the cool perspective that preceded the sale, had been sixty thousand dollars. In the prevailing atmosphere, Pete guessed it might easily bring twice as much.

Scappa's paddle shot up in answer to a bid from Marcel.

"I have seventy thousand dollars," the auctioneer announced.

The bid at seventy-five was Lyla's. An Arab in a burnoose with gold head-wrappings kicked the bidding up the next five thousand, and Elizabeth Taylor made a voice bid of "eighty-five."

Antonio abandoned his own sedate gesturing to bid aloud. "One hundred thousand," he shouted. There was a faint frantic note in his voice, Pete thought, and as soon as she heard it she knew what would happen next.

"One hundred and ten!" The voice was Andrea's, too impatient to go on bidding through Marcel. This would be her way of settling the score with her father, the weapon of numbers she had threatened him with last night.

"One-twenty!" Scappa came back at once.

One or two other bidders were in up to one hundred fifty thousand, but they dropped out as they perceived that they were caught in something more than a contest for an object

—an apparent grudge match that had already carried the price to the outer limit of the necklace's current value.

Andrea was not deterred, however. The bid at one hundred sixty thousand was hers, and she made it in a bold, confident voice.

The war continued, with Antonio doubling his bid to twenty thousand to preempt the call of two hundred thousand. Surely Andrea would not dare push him any farther . . .

But she came back with a twenty-thousand-dollar raise herself.

Antonio felt his blood boiling. Already because of no one but his traitorous daughter he was being forced to pay far beyond what the necklace was worth. Thirty years ago, when it had been sold by Boersma, it could not have brought more than twenty-five or thirty thousand dollars.

But he could not afford to lose this one. "Two hundred and forty thousand!" Antonio roared, his voice carrying to the edge of the room, a veritable battle cry.

"I have two-forty," the auctioner intoned calmly. His gaze went to Andrea.

She was glaring across the room at her father. Her body tensed and she leaned forward as if to call out, but Marcel put his hand firmly on her arm and pulled her back.

"All done at two-forty?" queried the auctioneer, his eyes holding steady on Andrea. "All through? Going down at two hundred forty thousand." He raised his gavel.

At that moment Antonio allowed a smile to tilt the corners of his mouth.

It was too much for Andrea. "Two hundred and fifty," she cried out. Her voice and her fierce gaze at Antonio left no doubt that this was a challenge, a dare to which she was totally committed. As far as he went, she would go farther.

Even the auctioneer, who had previously remained so blasé, seemed just the tiniest bit affected as he looked again to Antonio. "To you, sir. We're at a quarter of a million." The auctioneer paused.

Antonio was flushed, beads of sweat glistening in the lights overhead. It was Andrea's turn to smile.

"It's going down, sir," the auctioneer said, his quiet,

almost sympathetic tone magnified by the microphone in front of him.

From looking at him, Pete guessed that Antonio would not have an answer. However hard a pill it was to swallow, he had gauged that Andrea's determination to defeat him—backed by Marcel's resources—would outlast any effort he could make.

"Going once, twice . . . Sold at two hundred fifty thousand dollars."

The room broke into applause. A moment later, the picture of a diamond tiara filled the screen.

Antonio Scappa bolted up and pushed roughly through the crowd to the exit. He passed Pete without giving her so much as a glance. As she studied his profile, rigidly set in a resentful frown, she was possessed again by the feeling that she had seen him somewhere in her past.

She felt, too, that there was some reason he'd spoken to her last night beyond a simple desire to pay a compliment. He was obviously not the sort of man to concern himself with such amenities. But then why?

Perhaps it was all her imagination. Scappa was clearly an eccentric character, a bundle of contradictions. He had acquired a reputation for being among the shrewdest dealers, yet he had allowed himself to be drawn into a senseless duel that had pushed up the price of the necklace far beyond what his reasoned appraisal as a dealer should have told him to pay. Of course, if he put it in his vault and left it largely unseen for ten years, as Dorothy Fisk Haines had done, its value would appreciate. But dealers had to sell, not stockpile.

As she retreated from the room, however, Pete put all thoughts of the auction behind her. She was anxious to pack, to get home to the man she loved.

A smile touched her lips as she crossed the lobby. In a way her failure to deliver for the Duchess felt curiously like a success.

Chapter 12

New York—February 1978

St. Thomas' Episcopal Church on Fifth Avenue glowed with the light of a hundred candles—at the altar, highlighting the ends of the pews, in sconces along the walls. The soft amber gave the sanctuary a cozy glow, and illuminated the glow of expectation on the faces of the people inside.

Winter had always been Jessica Walsh's favorite time of year, so when it came time to plan her wedding, she had staunchly held out against her mother's desire to pretend it was spring instead of the middle of February. There wasn't a spring blossom or a summer flower in sight. Instead, the altar was flanked by winter-bare branches arched into a canopy overhead and twinkling with hundreds of tiny white lights. Pine boughs and bunches of holly swagged with burgundy velvet ribbon draped the altar and the pew ends.

The piercingly sweet sound of a single viola rose into the vaulted ceiling as the mother of the bride, regal as a queen mother in a midnight blue velvet Chanel and diamonds, was ushered down the aisle.

"God, how many people are out there?" asked Jess, peeking into the sanctuary from where she waited in the foyer.

"Don't worry," said Pete. "Once you start down the aisle,

you won't see anyone but Fernando at the altar, waiting for you.''

"Is this the voice of experience talking?'' asked Jess.

"I have my sources. Now hold still a minute. Your hat's crooked.'' As she reached up to resettle the tiny velvet pillbox perched on her best friend's head, to smooth out the veil behind, Pete thought Jess had never looked prettier. She glowed with that special beauty reserved for brides on their wedding day, a beauty compounded of equal parts of fussing attention and the happiness of love. Kenneth had softly waved her brown hair around her face, Way Bandy's makeup job was perfection, the dress by Oscar de la Renta was a work of art. The sparkle in her eyes was all her own.

"There,'' said Pete, giving the veil a final tweak.

"Do I look all right, Daddy?'' asked Jess, turning to her father beside her. He looked impossibly comfortable in his tuxedo, as though he'd been born in black wool and starched linen.

"Perfect, darling,'' he said, though he hardly looked at her.

For perhaps the first time in Jess's life, her father's coldness didn't bother her. She was simply too happy. And she knew she looked beautiful without having him tell her so. The de la Renta dress Pete had helped her choose was perfect. It had taken a certain strength of character to fend off the clouds of Alençon lace, miles of *peau de soie* ruffles, and yards of petticoat her mother kept thrusting at her, but finally Pete's simpler, more elegant taste had carried the day.

The dress was a simple gown of ivory deep-pile velvet, rich and sensuous to the touch, cut in a princess line that fell straight to the floor. Its low sweetheart neckline showed off Jess's pale skin, almost exactly the color of the dress. The neck, the trained hemline, and the wide-hanging outer sleeves were edged with white fur; tightly buttoned inner sleeves came right down over her knuckles. It looked like a dress out of a medieval tapestry, and its simplicity was perfect for Jess. Around her throat she wore a wide velvet ribbon with an exquisite jeweled snowflake, fashioned by Pete from seed-

pearls and tiny diamonds, pinned just off center. A feather-
light gossamer veil of silk tulle fell from her pillbox hat,
spilling down her back to the floor. She looked like the Snow
Queen in a fairy tale.

The attendants' dresses were cut on the same lines as the
bride's. Jess's sisters were in wine red velvet. Pete, the maid-
of-honor, wore velvet of a forest green so rich it shimmered
in the candlelight like leaves in a summer storm. Her dark
hair was piled high on her head, baring the curve of her neck
and the roundness of her shoulders, and her blue eyes glowed
with happiness for her friend.

"Hey, look out for that weapon you're carrying," she
exclaimed as Jess turned to give her fur-edged train a final
flick. Instead of a traditional bouquet, she carried a bunch of
shiny green holly dotted with brilliant red berries and inter-
spersed with sprays of baby's breath like clouds of snow
swirling about the glossy leaves.

Jess laughed, lightly touching one of the holly's spikes.
"It's going to be my shield when all the aunts and uncles
and second cousins twice removed feel the imperative to give
the bride a post-nuptial kiss."

"Just as long as Fernando gives you lots of them, who
cares?" said Pete. She peered down the long, white-carpeted
aisle and saw Fernando de Moratin and his attendants step
toward the altar. There was no denying the Spaniard was a
dashingly handsome man, complete to the flashing white buc-
caneer's smile and the matador's swagger. Pete saw him lean
toward his best man and speak a few words. They both
laughed. As long as he made Jess happy, Pete thought, his
fondness for living well needn't be held against him.

The viola music crescendoed, hung on the air a moment,
and trailed off. The buzz of voices dropped to a sibilant ripple
of sound, and the organ began to play.

"Ladies," said Mr. Walsh, switching on a megawatt smile
and offering Jess his arm, "I believe they're playing our
song."

"Then let's go get me married," said Jess.

The first bridesmaid started down the aisle.

* * *

An hour later, a river of shiny limos pulled away from the church and headed uptown toward the Metropolitan Museum. Thanks to Sally Walsh's seat on the board and Jonathan Walsh's sizable annual contribution, they'd had little trouble getting permission to hold their daughter's wedding reception in the museum.

It was a perfect, crackling winter night, and though a fresh coating of snow frosted the ground, the last cloud had now blown away and the air shimmered with clarity; the stars like icy diamonds, the moon a luminous slice of opal. The majestic columns of the museum's facade gleamed in the floodlights, the water of the fountains sparkled silver as the parade of the cream of New York society drove up to the broad steps. The strobes of society photographers popped and flashed as the elite pulled their furs close and swept past with patronizing smiles.

Inside, the Great Hall glowed, the soaring arches and ceiling domes lighted in softest rose-amber. Here guests mingled, chatted, showed off their gowns and latest jewels, and picked up glasses of champagne before moving on to the Medieval Court, where the newly minted Mr. and Mrs. Fernando de Moratin greeted their guests in front of the soaring wrought-iron gates. A string quartet played in the background. Later, dinner would be served in the warmly welcoming Blumenthal Patio, chosen specially by Jess because it had been transported from Spain. She thought it would remind Fernando of home.

"Worse even than I thought," Luke muttered as Pete steered him toward the bride and groom.

"You can stand one evening of opulence and luxury, can't you?" she said in a teasing tone. "Especially when you look so completely the part," she added, giving his black silk bow tie a twitch. She thought he looked even more impossibly handsome in a tuxedo than he did in blue jeans and leather.

"I guess I'll survive," he said. He gave her a grin, but she knew him well enough now to know it was forced. Spending his time in the midst of such luxury was a trial for him. They had managed to put a lid on the issue of wasted wealth since her return from Paris, but it always seemed to be bubbling under the surface. Though Pete was still getting commissions, she didn't talk about her work at home. In fact, the demand for her designs had been tailing off lately, perhaps because she was letting the business slide.

They'd reached the head of the receiving line and Luke gave Jess a warm hug and a kiss on the cheek. "You look good enough to eat, Jessie lass," he said.

"So do you, cowboy," Jess answered with a chuckle. "In that unaccustomed rig you look almost as good as my husband." Then she laughed again. "God, that's the first time I've actually said the words out loud. *My husband!* Now ain't that just the best couple of words you ever did hear? Do me a favor, Pete. If I'm dreaming, don't wake me up, okay?"

"Wouldn't dream of it," said Pete, hugging her friend.

Luke turned to Fernando, and his smile evaporated. "Take good care of her," he said. The words sounded more like a warning than the jocular teasing proper to the occasion.

But Fernando de Moratin merely smiled, his teeth showing very white in his richly tanned face. He tightened his arm around Jess's waist and pulled her close. "We will take care of each other, eh *querida*?"

"*Si, mi esposo*," she agreed with a glowing smile.

When Pete and Luke had moved away from the receiving line, she turned to him. "You weren't very gracious to Fernando."

"You know I can't stand him, and so does he. I'm not going to be a hypocrite and throw my arms around him."

"You like Jess. For her sake you could—"

"It's for Jess's sake that I dislike him. C'mon, Pete, the guy's a card-carrying fortune-hunter! I'll bet he started looking for a rich wife the day he let go of his mother's tit."

Oh God, she thought, this was worse than usual. He seemed to be itching for a fight. Even though she had her own doubts about Fernando, Pete leapt to his defense. To do otherwise seemed too much of a betrayal of Jess on her wedding day.

"Is it so impossible for you to believe that Fernando might love Jess? Do you find her so unattractive as to be convinced she could never catch such a man on her own merits?"

"Don't be stupid. You know I love Jess. That's exactly

why I'm so pissed off at her blindness, marrying someone who's not fit to wash her car.''

His cynical sniping was getting to her, and she didn't want to fight with him, not tonight. "Well, they are married, and this is a stupid conversation. Can we just drop it, relax, and enjoy the party, please?''

"Okay. At least the food is bound to be good.'' He reached out and grabbed a couple of wineglasses from a passing tray. "And the champagne is Veuve-Clicquot.'' He handed her a glass. "Here's to love and money. In the world of these people here tonight, you don't get one without the other.''

Pete looked up at him, the man she loved even when he was being so impossible. "Why must you dislike it so, this world?''

"For the same reason I dislike watching dancing bears and tigers jumping through flaming hoops at the circus.'' He swigged his champagne and set down the delicate crystal flute. "Look at them.'' His hand swept the room, indicating the glittering crowd. "They're all trying so hard to impress, to score a point, make a contact, to gain an edge on each other or hold on to the one they've got.''

"That's cruel, Luke. They're here to celebrate, to wish Jess and Fernando well.''

"You're not that naive, Pete, even if you are blinded by their money. You know as well as I do that most of these men are Jonathan Walsh's clients and squash partners, the fellows who sit opposite him in the leather chairs at the Union Club to discuss and decide the fate of the world. The women are mostly Sally Walsh's society friends. They'd be hard pressed to remember Jess's name if it hadn't been engraved on the invitation.''

"You're being needlessly cynical.''

"Am I? Have you read Veblen? *The Theory of the Leisure Class*?'' She shook her head no. "He coined the term for all this—conspicuous consumption. One must not only be rich; one must be *seen* to be rich, demonstrating, in Veblen's words, 'an ability to sustain large pecuniary damage without impairing one's superior opulence.' And that is exactly what Jonathan Walsh is doing tonight, flexing his financial muscles in public. This party cost him a fortune, you know, enough to feed a few families for a year."

"I know," she said, softly, thinking how true it was that Jess's father had always been willing to spend enormous sums on her yet could barely bring himself to touch her.

Another waiter passed and Luke grabbed another glass. "Shouldn't you be working the room? Lot of potential customers here. These folks do like their baubles, don't they? The dazzle might just blind me."

"Yes, I should," she snapped. "I should also be enjoying myself, which I am definitely not doing at this moment." She swept away, her heels clicking on the marble floor.

Pete did "work the room" for the next hour. These were the sort of people she needed to know, the princes and princesses of the New York aristocracy. Sally Walsh introduced her to several people, many of whom complimented her profusely on the necklace she'd designed for Jess, as well as on the mother-of-pearl and emerald flower brooch she wore on a velvet ribbon around her own neck. A few asked for her card, which she retrieved from the supply she'd stashed in her tiny silver-mesh evening bag.

Luke rejoined her when it was time to sit down to dinner, and his mood seemed to have improved—or at least he was trying. He laughed and teased throughout the meal and impressed the other guests at their table with his charm and smooth manners. If Pete ever forgot that he had, indeed, been born into this very world, she had only to see him operate within it to be reminded.

They feasted on paper-thin slices of smoked salmon, mission figs with prosciutto, creamy leek soup, *pintadeau*, the tiny guinea hens perfectly roasted and set on saffron rice, and individual artichoke soufflés. For dessert, poached pears in spun sugar cages. It was questionable that anyone would have room for a piece of the six-foot-high wedding cake.

Toasts were drunk. Fernando made a rather flowery but charming speech about his good fortune in becoming part of such a family. "No kidding," Luke muttered half under his breath, but Pete shot him a quick frown and he said no more. At ten the string quartet disappeared, to be replaced by the

Peter Duchin Band so the dancing could begin. Jess and Fernando led off the first dance to a burst of applause.

Looking at the glow on Jess's face, Pete felt a little lurch inside her. To be that much in love and that sure of the rightness of your choice, to be able to give yourself up completely to the man you loved, no doubts, no holding a piece of yourself separate—how Pete envied her that.

She felt Luke's warm hand close on her arm. "May I?" he asked and pulled her into his arms. He was a wonderful dancer.

"I'm sorry about earlier," he said, and sounded as though he meant it. "I'm never at my best in this sort of crowd."

"I noticed." She laid her head on his shoulder. "But even at your worst, you ain't too bad."

They danced a few moments without speaking. "God, you feel good," he said finally. "I'd forgotten how much I like to dance with you. You're such a perfect fit."

"Ummmm," she said, and let herself enjoy the feel of his arms around her, seeming so much more solid than the slender Fernando or any other man in the room. The music ended. They smiled at each other.

Luke brushed a trailing curl from her forehead. "I love you, Pete D'Angeli," he said softly.

Then the mood was broken as a short, gray-haired gentleman with a handlebar mustache tapped Pete on the shoulder.

"My dance, Miss D'Angeli. You promised."

She turned and looked down at him. "Of course, Mr. Cates. I didn't forget."

"I'll be back," Luke said into her ear as she passed him, and she smiled her agreement over Mr. Cates' head as they began a spirited fox-trot. Luke headed toward the bar.

Pete danced a number of times, including once with Fernando, who held her a little closer than she liked and murmured flowery Spanish compliments into her ear. She laughed them off with a joke about Latin lovers.

She sat for a while with Jess, who had collapsed onto a settee. "God, how did Cinderella manage to last until midnight?" Jess said, kicking off her diamond-buckled velvet slippers.

"Cinderella didn't have to spend two hours in a receiving line," said Pete. "Where's Prince Charming gone?"

"He's over by the bar, dipping into some very old, very fine Spanish sherry Daddy promised to lay on for him."

"He has expensive tastes," Pete said casually, then glanced at Jess.

"Yeah, isn't it great? No wonder Daddy likes him. Finally, I brought home someone who could appreciate the only things Mother and Daddy have to offer."

Suddenly, ringing above the buzz of the crowd, Pete heard Luke's deep, distinctive voice bellowing across the open space.

"You two-bit son of a bitch!" he yelled. More shouting erupted, the crash of breaking glass echoed up into the vaulted ceiling. A woman screamed. Both Pete and Jess were on their feet at once, running to see what was happening.

Fernando de Moratin, in all his bridegroomly splendor, was sprawled on the floor, blood seeping from a cut at the side of his mouth. Luke stood over him, fists still clenched, a couple of men holding him by the arms. Jess hovered at Fernando's side, looking hurt and confused and concerned, her eyes darting between her husband and the lover of her best friend.

Pete took in the scene quickly, not wanting to believe what she saw. She hurried to Luke, took his arm, turned him toward the door, and pushed him out into the Great Hall, nearly deserted now, shadowy under the pink lights. She was livid, so angry her whole body shook with it.

"I don't know what the hell that was all about," she said through clenched teeth, her voice quivering with her rage, "but we're getting out of here. I'm not letting you ruin Jess's wedding any more than you already have."

"Do you know what that son-of-a-bitch said?"

"It's his wedding," Pete shot back crossly. "He ought to be able to say whatever he damn well pleases. Get my cape. I'm going back to try apologizing to Jess, though I'm not sure it's possible. Then we're leaving. Now." She stalked back into the patio room before he could say anything else.

She made what excuses she could to Jess, pleading drunkenness on Luke's part, the pressures of his work, anything she could think of, though it all sounded lame even in her own ears. She was relieved to see that Fernando was back on his feet. The blood had been wiped from his mouth, and he was slurping champagne, laughing and talking with exaggerated bluster while Jess clung to his arm.

"How dare you!" she said when she returned to Luke in the Hall. Though her voice was low, almost hissing, the sound seemed to swell up to the high ceiling. "How *dare* you get drunk and ruin Jess's wedding party?"

"Unfortunately, I'm not drunk."

"Did it give you a lot of pleasure to wipe the smile of happiness from the bride's face, Luke?"

"Of course not. But when I see ugliness, I can't close my eyes to it; when my nose gets close to something rotten, it recoils from the stench. And Fernando de Moratin stinks to heaven. You should hear what he said . . ."

"I don't want to hear," Pete replied stubbornly. She swirled into her wine red velvet evening cape and stepped out onto the wide steps facing Fifth Avenue. A breeze blew snow devils along the sidewalk. "You just had no right to do that," she said, pulling her coat close around her. "Not anywhere, ever, but especially not here, not tonight."

"He as much as admitted he only married Jess for her money."

"I don't believe you," she said, her arms clasped close about her against the chill.

"Do you want his exact words?"

"No." She started down the steps toward the long line of waiting limos. It wasn't because she didn't believe him that Pete wanted to avoid Luke now; it was because she did and had no idea what could be done about it.

Luke grabbed her elbow and stopped her, swinging her around to face him. "You're going to hear whether you like it or not. '*Padrrre*,'—that's what he calls his new father-in-law, complete with beautifully rolled 'r'—'*Padrrre* is worth two hundred million, give or take a million. Dollars, not pesetas, and that is very many dollars in any language, certainly more than he can spend. No reason some of those needless dollars should not be given to his devoted son-in-law. I have thought so from the first. He will fork up nicely to keep Baby Jessie happy and healthy.' ''

"He was joking."

"You didn't see his eyes when he said it."

"Then he was drunk."

"If he was, then he's one of those men who only tell the truth when they're drunk."

"You still had no right to make such an ugly scene, Luke. Sally Walsh worked so hard to make tonight perfect. Everything was so beautifully done. And Jess looked so happy, radiant even. But you had to ruin that, you had to make ugliness out of beauty and cause pain to someone I love. I think I could hate you for that, Luke. I really think I could."

She headed for the car again, and this time he fell into step beside her. The driver of the car Jonathan Walsh had hired for them for the night opened the door, Luke gave him the address, and they settled into the limousine's warm softness.

As they headed downtown, past the darkly silhouetted bare trees of the park on one side and the high-rises of the rich and famous on the other, Pete sat silently, looking at but not seeing the wintry world outside.

"You're right," Luke said at 59th Street. "I shouldn't have hit the bastard, especially at his own wedding. I'm sorry for that. But I didn't make ugliness out of beauty, as you put it. Because it wasn't at all beautiful from where I sat, Pete, and unlike you I can't pretend everything is pretty and perfect when it's not. I'm not good at pretense, and you've always known that."

He poured himself a Scotch from the crystal decanter in front of the seat, took a long swallow, and set down the glass. "You want to drape the world in flowers and spruce it up with gems so you can pretend it's not rotten underneath the glitter. I can't do that. When I see ugliness, I try to change it, not cover it up with money."

"Money." She almost spat the word. "You know, I've just about had it with your hang-ups about money. Coming from someone who's never had to go without a meal, someone who was born with mountains of the stuff and now has the luxury of giving away as much as he wants, I find your cavalier attitude toward it a bit hard to take. You play at doing without. You drive an old beat-up van and eat hamburgers because it suits your down-home image of yourself. But if you should happen to change your mind one day, you can just as easily order a pound of Sevruga caviar at the Russian Tea Room or run out to the local Mercedes dealer and drive home a new 280 XL, all paid for, thank you very much.''

"That's unfair, and you know it. I am perfectly willing to spend my money on things I consider worthwhile, but I refuse to play into those people's game where the purpose of spending money is to display, on as grand a scale as possible, the ability to spend money.''

"Such as by buying good jewelry, I suppose.''

"You said it, not me.'' He took another swallow of his Scotch. "Those people, what they do with their money, and even more what it does to them, it's ugly.''

She spun toward him on the leather seat. "What the hell do you know about real ugliness? Tell me, Luke. What do you know about growing up in a neighborhood where you step over the winos to get to your front door and the kids are on a first-name basis with every hooker on the block, but it's the only neighborhood you can afford? What can you tell me about arriving in this country with no money and no family, like my father, then having to give up every dream you ever dreamed because you had a kid to raise and no money to do it with? What do you know about seeing your own mother locked up in a state-run snake pit, where she's left to sit in her own vomit or scratch herself bloody because there's no money to pay for better care? There are no Cole-Haffner Clinics for the people who live in Hell's Kitchen, Luke. And what do you know about dreams that feel like they'll never be anything more than that because there's no money to make them real?''

She felt tears prick at her eyes, and that made her even angrier. She dashed them away with a gloved hand. "Money, Luke. Money *can* buy beauty. It can buy a nice apartment, a warm coat, Veuve Clicquot champagne. It can buy the Cole-

Haffner Clinic.'' She turned her head and stared out the window as the car turned past the arch at Washington Square Park. It had started snowing again. ''Money can buy beauty,'' she repeated. ''And the people who have it can buy me the freedom to create beauty.''

''Then do, but in some way that is real. Even I can see that you're talented. You have a wonderful eye. Why not paint? Or become a sculptor, like Anna. Express your talent. Create something beautiful, but make it something with real value, not just a dollar value.''

''I'm not a painter. I barely know scarlet lake from alizarin crimson. I have no feeling for clay. I know nothing about types of wood. But I know just about everything there is to know about judging a diamond or making the most of a sapphire. I can look at an emerald and see a peacock's eye or a spring leaf. I can run my finger over a ruby and know the best way to set it into a ring. That's what I do.''

The car pulled up in front of the Grove Street house, but they didn't get out. She turned to look at him, his beautiful face serious in the yellow glow of a streetlight. ''You said a while ago you loved me,'' she said. ''But my work is me, Luke. It's who I am. How can you love me if you hate the essence of what I am?''

''I do love you. But what you create is part of a world I hate, full of people I despise. I care too much to see you turn into one of them.''

''Then maybe you shouldn't stick around to watch.''

The words were said, and she didn't know if she wished them back or not. They sat in the luxurious car, the snow falling softly outside the smoked glass windows, looking at each other with the saddest faces Pete could ever have imagined.

The chauffeur opened the door.

''Come on. It's late.''

''No, Luke. I can't. I can't pretend this is ever going to work out. I can't keep trying to make you understand, and I can't try to become something I'm not for you.'' In the streetlight's glow, her eyes were fierce with both pain and determination. He reached out and closed the door again.

"The things I want to achieve aren't going to change. I've wanted them for too long . . . and there's nothing wrong with wanting them. I'm not like you, Luke. I grew up in the middle of ugliness, so now I want to surround myself with beauty. I want to create it for others, too. And I want to find some that's been lost—that's another dream I've got that might not make sense to you: to go hunting for the treasures that were stolen from my father."

"Surely you can't mean you want to go chasing off after that fantasy of your grandmother's jewels."

"It isn't a fantasy, Luke, it's my birthright. I wish to God you could understand—that you could want to share it all. But maybe I've got to accept the fact that you can't and never will. And if I'm going to succeed, I'd better start concentrating every bit of my energy on doing what I want. I can't afford to spend it fighting with you over whether I should even be trying."

"What are you saying?" he asked, his voice quiet, his eyes steady, unblinking.

"I'm saying that I need to be away from you for a while, maybe a long while."

"Pete—"

"Maybe forever."

There was a silence. He stared at her. "You mean it, don't you?"

She just nodded.

He closed his eyes a moment, and when he opened them again, his face had hardened into granite crevasses. "I'll be out all day Saturday. You can come and get your things then." He opened the door and got out of the car.

"Luke . . . ," she began, not knowing what she wanted to say. He didn't stop or turn around. A minute later he disappeared into the house.

The limo door was closed with a thud. She wanted to cry, but she didn't seem to be able to. The driver would want to know where to take her. Steve and Anna would be sleeping, but they wouldn't mind being wakened. She would always be welcome there.

She leaned forward as the chauffeur opened the partition between them. "Soho, please," she said. "Prince and Wooster." Then she leaned back in the huge, beautiful, empty car.

She finally cried the next day as she sat across the round oak table from Anna and told her what had happened.

"Shit!" Anna exclaimed, perfectly expressing Pete's opinion on the matter. "How can someone so sensitive and intelligent be so very stupid?"

"Who, me or Luke?"

"Luke, of course." She poured them both more coffee, spooning four big spoonfuls of sugar into her own mug.

Pete wrapped her hands around her mug. She felt so cold. She hadn't felt warm since she'd watched Luke disappear into his house. "What would you do if Papa wanted you to give up sculpting?"

"I would do the same thing to any man who thinks I'm good for nothing but to live in his shadow, have his babies, and spend all my time washing diapers and cooking his dinner. I would throw him out—as I did to my husband."

Pete had never heard Anna speak of a husband before, only lovers. "I didn't know you were married."

"It was for so short, I should not count. We met in art school. He knew how important it was to me that I am an artist. I thought that was why he falls in love with me, because we share the same dream. But his dream was only to have an adoring audience and sometimes a clever critic to support him in *his* work. Mine was not important, certainly not enough important to take the place of husband and children." She sipped the syrupy coffee. "Stupid Pole."

Pete held her mug to her cheek, feeling the warmth against her skin. Tears slid over the smooth surface of the heavy china. "Can I stay here a few days? Just until I sort out a new place to live?"

"You stay forever if you want."

Pete smiled. "Thanks, but a week or so should be enough. Do you think Papa would go over there with me tomorrow and help me pack my things?"

"It will make him unhappy to do so—he likes Luke very much, you know—but of course he will. Now drink your coffee. You need to warm the inside, too."

It was snowing hard the next day, covering over the city's grime and giving New York one of those rare days when it really does look like a scene on a Christmas card. Despite the weather, Luke's house was warm as Pete and Steve packed her things into cardboard boxes.

She was piling sweaters and scarves and shoes into suitcases, her mouth pulled down and her eyes flat in her effort not to cry. She loved this house of Luke's. She loved the person she had been here with him. But she knew she couldn't stay.

Steve sat on the floor, arranging books in cardboard boxes. Unfortunately, for every two books he packed, he found another he needed immediately to explore further.

"Pete, look at this," he cried, holding up a guidebook to Italy. "The Galleria in Milano. It was the most elegant shopping spot in town. It's right across from La Scala. I used to go there with my friends after the opera." Then he remembered that his brother Vittorio had had his stolen paper goods shop in the Galleria, and a shadow darkened his face. He flipped a couple of pages. "Ah, the *Madonnina*." He showed her a photograph of Milan's Duomo, with the little statue on top that he had loved as a boy. "And Carlo's office was right here," he said, pointing again. "This window, here. *Dio*, how many times I stood at that window looking out at freedom, wishing I could run away from the law office and sit at a cafe writing poetry."

"Were you a good poet, Papa?"

He shrugged. "Who knows? Maybe I would have become good." He gave her a sweet, rather embarrassed smile. "I . . . I have been writing a little bit lately."

"Papa! You mean poetry? That's great!"

"Just a couple of sonnets and some blank verse."

"I want to read it."

He grinned. "It's in Italian."

"So I'll read it with a dictionary in hand."

"We'll see," he said, and they went back to their packing, working silently side-by-side for the next half hour.

Finally the last piece of clothing was packed. Pete rummaged among the boxes they'd brought for one small enough for her cosmetics, hair dryer, and toiletries. When she found it, she looked at Steve. He sat motionless, staring at a photograph in a large book.

She sat beside him on the sofa. "That's the catalog from that auction in Geneva last year—the Haines collection." She reached for the catalog. "Let me show you the ruby Marcel bought. The one the Duchess wanted . . ."

He didn't give her the book. In fact, when she tried to take it, he wouldn't let it go for a moment.

"Papa?" she said, studying his face. It seemed very pale. "Are you all right?"

"What?" he said, snapping his head up. His eyes flew back to the picture, a necklace of invisibly set sapphires and emeralds with the letter "C" scrolled out in diamonds on the clasp. He read the brief copy describing the piece, noted the estimated price. "Who bought this?"

"Marcel Ivères, though he didn't actually do the bidding. There was quite a fight over that piece." Pete thought back to the contest between Andrea and Antonio Scappa, though she didn't think her father would be interested in the details. After all, he didn't know the people. She looked over his shoulder at the picture. "It's beautiful, isn't it—though it went for more than it's worth."

Steve looked up. "I suppose everything did," he said. He closed the catalog and tossed it into the box. "Is it quitting time yet?"

"No, master. Not yet." She laughed, picked up an empty carton, and disappeared into the bathroom.

When she was gone, Steve stared at the box a moment, then could not resist reaching again for the catalog and opening it to the picture of the necklace.

Even after nearly forty years, Stefano D'Angeli recognized the sapphire and emerald necklace at once. He ran his finger over the scrolled "C." C for La Colomba. The last time he'd seen it, it had been entwined in his mother's graceful fingers.

Quickly, he thumbed through the rest of the catalog. Maybe he would recognize something else, some other piece that had belonged to his mother. But there was nothing. The rest was only in his memories.

"Vittorio," he said in a choked whisper, suddenly overwhelmed by all the emotion of those last horrible days of the war. For just a moment it felt as though only minutes had passed since he'd learned of his mother's death, of his brother's treachery.

"No," he muttered to himself. "It's history." He closed the catalog. "History," he repeated, and placed the book at the bottom of the box under several others. "Let it stay buried."

BOOK
IV
Luster

Chapter 1

New York—Autumn 1984

"Hold it right there, Miss D'Angeli . . ."

As Pete worked her way through the maze of tables where the elite of New York's fashion world sat waiting for the Coty Awards ceremony to begin, she was stopped again by one of the news photographers wanting a picture.

"That's great," said the man from the *Times*. "Just one more, please . . ."

For all the glamour and style that filled the auditorium of the Fashion Institute of Technology tonight, it was Pietra D'Angeli who was seen to shine the brightest. Not that the body-hugging silver-white Kamali gown she'd bought for the occasion was any more spectacular than gowns worn by some of the other women. What set Pete apart was the sparkle of jewelry of her own design, large abstract diamond snowflakes linked and overlapped to make necklace and earrings, and matching ornaments were scattered in the luxuriant black curls of her upswept hair.

Her preference, usually, was to avoid being showy. She made her jewelry for others to wear, not herself. But Jess had persuaded her to be more daring on this occasion. "Go for broke, kiddo," she'd said. "Don't hide your diamonds under a bushel." After all, she was attending the Cotys this year because a special award for jewelry design was being given. If she was lucky enough to win, she wanted to stand proudly before her peers and dazzle them with some of the best examples of her work.

The strobe light flashed again, and Pete moved on to the table where Steve and Anna were seated with a number of writers from the fashion press. There were several chairs left empty as writers worked the room, and after giving Anna a kiss, Pete was able to sit beside her father.

"Enjoying yourselves?" she asked them.

Anna smiled. "It's a lovely occasion."

Steve gave Pete a mock scowl. "Of course, we will have had a terrible time if you lose."

"Papa, whether or not I go home with something to put on my mantle, I'm not losing. It's still a tremendous honor to be nominated. The thing I'd most like tonight is to share that honor with you, to be together . . ."

Steve's expression tightened and he looked down, a signal that he guessed at the appeal she was about to make and didn't want to hear it.

Pete had hoped the evening would provide the opportunity for her father and grandfather to end their feud. When she had told Steve about the awards, he had agreed to attend only on the condition that he would not have to sit near Josef or speak to him. He'd been in a cold rage ever since learning that the old man had concealed the truth of Bettina's wartime experience. Now, years later, feeling he had been duped into a doomed marriage, he remained bitterly unforgiving. Josef, meanwhile, still nursed a grudge at Steve for deserting Bettina and for long ago failing to provide money for better care and treatment for her.

The anger that emanated from the two people who were closest to her was all but spoiling the night for Pete. At her own table sat Josef, Charlie, Lottie, and Jess and Fernando. There were also two empty places Pete had arranged for Steve and Anna in the hope she'd be able to use the night for a reconciliation. She had to try once more.

"Please, Papa," Pete said, "I'm begging you. The ceremony will begin in a few minutes, and I'd like you at my side. Let bygones be bygones. You and Anna come and join—''

"Pete," he broke in harshly. "I have a right to my feelings. I have a right to think I was used, betrayed by a man I trusted, even loved. You're simply asking too much."

Pete glanced to Anna, silently pleading with her to add an appeal of her own. But Anna gave a slight shake of her head.

Yes, it was too much, Pete accepted. From the words Steve used to defend himself, she suddenly perceived that his feelings of betrayal went deeper than those aroused by Josef. For he had been betrayed another time—by his brother.

"All right, Papa, I'll give up on this one. But there's something else I don't think you have a right to refuse. Mama's asked several times lately if you'd come and visit. I've made excuses, but now I think—''

Again Steve cut her off impatiently. "Pietra, must we discuss this now?"

"I can't help thinking about Mama . . . because she's *not* here."

"That's neither your fault nor mine. Now, please, save all this for another day. Tonight is supposed to be a party, isn't it?"

"Supposed to be," she echoed ironically.

"Then stop trying to make it a peace conference."

She nodded and stood up. "I just wanted something to celebrate tonight—whether I win or lose."

"You'll have something," Steve said. He smiled. "I know you'll win."

She forced an answering smile, went back to her own table, and took her place between Jess and Charlie and across from Opa. Each gave her a word of encouragement, mistaking her look of upset for anxiety about the award.

In fact, Pete didn't feel she needed an award to certify reaching a pinnacle in her own field. Eight years after walking out of Dufort & Ivères, she was part of a very select coterie of artists whose names were known far beyond the boundaries of the fashion world. She had only to glance around the room to certify how far she had risen. Ralph Lauren, with his perpetual tan, his thick silvery hair, and his searchlight smile, sat at a table to her right. Grace Mirabella of *Vogue* was to her left, keeping company with Diana Vreeland. Liz Claiborne, Mary MacFadden, Geoffrey Beene, Calvin Klein—these people were no longer just names in *Women's Wear Daily*. Elsa Peretti, Paloma Picasso, and Angela Cummings were no longer merely star jewelry designers she envied. In the past few years many of the people in this room had become colleagues, even friends.

The separation from Luke, painful as it had been, had marked the beginning of a stage that carried Pete far beyond the flash of notoriety she had received for the Eye of Love. As an antidote to her loneliness, Pete had stopped waiting for the work to come to her and had plunged into more aggressively seeking and promoting her talent. On Charlie's advice, she had hired a publicist who knew how to play up every commission she received from a celebrity or a society queen, placing Pete's name in the columns, making sure she was invited to all the charity events and openings and society balls that guaranteed her high visibility. Pete became a full participant in a style of life Luke could never have endured, and that she had willingly avoided while they were together. Being without him, no doubt, had played a part in her climb. She had gone from being a respected but little-known and almost broke designer to a celebrated, much admired fashion personage, almost a celebrity in her own right. A jewelry design by Pietra D'Angeli was always noticed, often photographed, and frequently mentioned in the columns. One design in particular had thrown her back into the spotlight in the months right after her split from Luke. She had been visited at her studio by the new wife of a Texas billionaire, a woman who instructed Pete to be daring and create something that guaranteed attention. The necklace Pete delivered took the form of a spider's web, as delicate and airy as the real thing, covering the whole neck and throat with woven gold wire lined with the tiniest seed pearls and sprinkled with diamond "dewdrops." Just where it hit the collarbone a spider perched, its legs made of gold, its body formed from twin rubies set to form an hourglass on the back of a large garnet o dark it was nearly black. The "Black Widow Necklace" ad been famous from its first appearance.

For another client she'd fashioned a choker of butterflies, et wing to wing, made of lacy platinum set with more than a thousand diamonds. Soon she was known for her inspired use of abstracted natural forms—leaves and snowflakes, eathers and fins. Commissions poured in, more than she could handle, so that clients were kept waiting months. Some women complained, the wealthiest or most famous were sometimes offended, but no one ever withdrew an order or was displeased with the final result.

The ceremony began, the parade of fashion notables marching to and from the microphones, waving their Coty medallions in triumph and thanking mothers and wives and lovers as they were rewarded for their creativity and innovative daring.

At last it was time to announce the winner of the special award for jewelry design.

Beside her, Charlie put his hand over hers and gave a reassuring squeeze. Their friendship had grown stronger with the years, and he had served often as her escort. There had been other men at times, a handful of romantic attachments that had lasted weeks, sometimes months. They were always attractive and successful, able to satisfy her in bed and make her laugh and keep her company on rainy days. Pete entered each affair with the belief that there was no reason it shouldn't last. Yet the fires died quickly, and she found each time that the only way to be true to herself was to go back to being alone. In her heart, she felt there was a lasting love she was destined to know, but only Luke had ever come close to providing it.

It seemed she didn't even hear her name announced before there was a wave of applause, and then Charlie was prodding her to get up. Pete opened her eyes to see everyone at the table beaming at her, the roomful of people clapping.

Rising to her feet, she made her way to the podium, smiling at people who reached out to pat her shoulders as she passed. She accepted the award and managed to get out her list of thank-yous without, she hoped, sounding like an utter fool.

To suppliers, to craftsmen who'd worked for her, to faithful clients, even a magnanimous mention of her first employer, Marcel Ivères . . .

"And finally, I'd like to thank my grandfather, Mr. Josef Zeeman, who put in my hand the first diamond I ever touched and taught me to love its beauty. *Dank U wel*, Opa."

Josef nodded to her, his pride and joy, and dabbed away the moisture that had gathered at the corners of his old eyes.

Clutching the engraved plaque, Pete scanned the room. This was the cream, the elite, the top of the heap.

And she was one of them.

When the ceremony ended, there were still clusters of people gathered around Pete to add their personal congratulations or request a future meeting to discuss business. Representatives from the same manufacturers who had made million-dollar licensing arrangements with Klein and Blass and Perry Ellis came over to suggest that many of her designs might be adapted to adorn fabrics and linens and housewares; an agent for the largest maker of Japanese wristwatches sought her agreement to create a new line exclusively for them. No doubt her phone would be ringing off the hook with other offers on Monday morning. Pete referred tonight's suitors to Lottie and ducked away to say good-night to Steve and Anna before they left.

It struck her only as she approached her father that she had left him out of her speech while making such a fuss over Josef—hardly a step in the direction of smoothing over their differences. She started to apologize: "Papa, I'm sorry I didn't mention you in all the excitement."

"Me?" He shrugged. "To be fair, I really don't think I deserve any thanks. I always scolded you for playing with jewels, remember? It was your grandfather who gave you encouragement. I may be furious with the old faker, but I'll give credit where it's due." He pulled Pete into a congratulatory embrace, then added, "I suppose I'll have to make up with him someday. Because if he hadn't told his lies, I would never have had you."

"Tonight, Papa," Pete urged, glancing to where Josef sat,

finishing his glass of champagne while he waited for Pete to see him home. "Talk to him now."

Steve looked across the room at the old man. "Not yet," he said quietly. "I'm sorry."

Anna had waited for the right moment to speak on Pete's behalf. "If you're really so proud of your daughter, it might be time to tell her mother, too . . ."

Steve frowned at Anna, but then nodded slowly and turned to Pete. "Yes, I will visit Bettina. A night like this makes me realize how much I owe to her."

After kissing her father and Anna good-bye, Pete practically skipped back across the auditorium, feeling even lighter and happier than when she had accepted the award. There was no longer any hope of fulfilling the wish to see her parents reunited that she had harbored in the early years of her mother's illness. Nevertheless, she was sure that bringing them face to face, even if only for a brief time, would begin the healing of some old wounds.

Preoccupied by the thought as she hurried between now abandoned tables and chairs, Pete almost collided with the tall man in a tuxedo who stepped abruptly in front of her.

"I didn't want the night to end without adding my personal congratulations."

Only then did she realize it was Marcel. He looked dashing in his tuxedo, if just the slightest bit disheveled, a lock of his dark hair hanging straight down over his blue eyes.

"You were very kind to include me in your speech," he went on.

"It wasn't kindness, just the truth. You gave me my first job."

He gazed at her fixedly. "How much more I should have given you. I wonder sometimes if there's still a chance . . ." He raised a hand to her bare arm, stroked his fingers down its length, and let them fall away.

Pete looked back passively. She was sufficiently in control not to feel she had to scold him. "Maybe you ought to ask Andrea about that," she said tartly.

"We're not together anymore," he said flatly.

Pete's eyes widened in surprise. She hadn't kept close tabs

on them, but only five or six weeks ago she'd seen them dancing together at a charity event. "What happened?" she asked.

"Pressures of business more than anything else," Marcel replied. "She became more and more critical of the way I was running things. She thought I ought to make *her* president of the company and step aside. Can you imagine?"

Pete had to laugh. "I can indeed."

Marcel gave her a sideways glance. "I detect a sisterly note of sympathy."

"Whatever problems I may have had with Andrea, I always thought she was a fabulous asset to Dufort and Ivères."

Marcel nodded. "So did I. That's why I'll be sending her to negotiate the lease for a new store in Beverly Hills. I need to keep her in the business—even if we've been arguing too damn much to go on living together."

Pete smiled and started to excuse herself. Charlie and Opa were standing by the table, among the last guests lingering in the room.

Marcel grasped her arm again. "Pete . . . since I've been by myself . . . there have been so many times I wondered . . ."

He didn't have to say the rest.

She stared at him, accutely conscious of his touch yet unable to will herself to pull away. On a night when she had been acclaimed by all her peers, when her professional future was assured, she still had to contemplate falling asleep alone—perhaps being alone for months or years to come, looking in vain for a man who would excite her, share her enthusiasms.

And the spark of attraction she had felt to Marcel so long ago had never been completely extinguished. The question had always lurked in a corner of her mind: What if she had been more daring on that distant night when he had taken her to dinner? What would they have found together on the road not taken?

As the breathless silence lasted between them, Marcel's eyes flared with recognition of Pete's susceptibility.

"Where are you going now?" he asked.

"Home."

"This is a night to celebrate. Let me take you for a drink. Or dancing—we never did get to dance together."

If she thought sensibly about it, she would have refused. But she had been sensible with him once long ago, and she wasn't sure now if she regretted it.

She glanced over at Charlie. She could ask him to take Opa home. He would understand. "All right," she told Marcel. "Just give me a minute to say good-night to my guests."

She had second thoughts almost as soon as she'd moved away from him, left his magnetic field. Yet she begged off with Charlie, kissed Opa good-bye, and returned to Marcel.

She didn't want to be alone on her pinnacle. And Marcel had been there right at the beginning of her climb.

He took her to Regine's, where they drank a bottle of Dom Perignon and he entertained her with lively stories about his father's experiences in the business forty and fifty years ago, when there were fewer jewelers and the ones at the top put their hands to everything, even going into the mines to select stones as they came out of the ground. She danced with him, too, but not the way they would have danced ten years earlier. The gyrations of hot disco steps were not what Pete had had in mind.

When they came out of Regine's and stepped into his Rolls, Marcel told the driver to take them downtown. "We'll go to some of the new clubs in Tribeca," he proclaimed energetically, fueled by the champagne.

"I'm ready to go home," Pete said.

"But you'll enjoy the scene," Marcel persisted. "Andrea loves it down there . . ."

With simply a cool look, Pete communicated that it didn't matter what Andrea liked.

As the Rolls headed uptown to Pete's apartment, Marcel said, "I'm sorry, Pete. It was stupid of me to raise that ghost. You're the one I want to please. Andrea doesn't matter."

She smiled at him understandingly. "Are you sure, Marcel? She's still an important part of your life."

"But only in business." He took her hand. "There are other things . . ."

In the dim light within the car, Pete studied his handsome face. The debate within her was still unsettled. Could they discover a destiny that had merely been postponed?

As if intending to provide the answer, Marcel leaned toward her and, when she did nothing to stop him, placed his lips gently over hers. When he felt her respond, he pulled her closer and the kiss grew more passionate.

It had been a while since Pete had felt the ardor of a man, and her body responded instantly. She answered the probing touch of his tongue with her own and arched herself against him. She released herself from the constraints of conscience and propriety, blotted out the consciousness of time, and imagined that this was the way it would have been if she had given herself to him the first time . . .

Marcel put a hand on her leg and stroked upward, pushing back the silvery fabric of her gown. His mouth roamed down over her neck to her breasts. "Now, *chérie*?" he whispered to her impatiently. "Would you like me to fuck you right here?"

It was not her style. "Not here," Pete whispered in reply. "Wait . . ."

But Marcel was too aroused to stop. He pushed his hand farther up between her legs.

"No," Pete murmured. "Come home with me."

"I will, we'll have all night. But let me fuck you now."

She felt the tingle of her own desire suddenly recede as an inner voice took over. She didn't just want to be "fucked," she realized; she wanted to be loved. For Marcel, perhaps, there was no distinction to be made. But it made all the difference to Pete.

He felt the change come over her, and when she eased him away, he didn't resist.

He was puzzled, however, when the car pulled up in front

of of her apartment building and Pete waved away the doorman who came to open the door of the Rolls.

"Aren't we going in?" he said.

"I am. Not you."

"But—"

"Forgive me, Marcel. I didn't mean to lead you on. I
thought we might be able to go back and rediscover a lost
adventure."

"*Mais, oui.* I thought the same."

"We were both wrong. I think we made the right choice
the first time we walked away from each other."

"How can you know?"

"Call it a woman's intuition."

"Pete . . . Pietra . . . a minute ago you were in my arms,
and you wanted me. You can't deny that. I think it's your
inhibition—not intuition—that is spoiling the adventure."
He reached for her. "Let us have at least tonight to find
out . . ."

She smiled at his charm, but it didn't persuade her. She
pushed his hands away, picked up her Coty Award from the
corner of the seat, and reached for the door handle. Then she
paused. "There's another thing my intuition tells me. The
woman you should be with tonight is the one you've had
from the start."

"Andrea? But I told you, it's over."

Pete shook her head. "Your pride may have thrown up a
temporary roadblock, but if you can get past it, you'll never
find anyone better for you than she is."

Marcel's expression darkened, his brow furrowed. Pete
couldn't tell if he was annoyed or seriously pondering her
advice.

"Call her," Pete said as she opened the door of the Rolls.
"You could take her downtown to one of those clubs she
loves, and on the way home . . . I'll bet she'd want you to
have her right on the back seat."

For another instant, Marcel's face held his grave thoughtful expression. Then he burst into laughter. "Cars, elevators, desks, the floor—it's true, Andrea would rather

fuck anyplace but in a bed. I always did like that about
her.''

"So . . . what are you waiting for. It'll be good for business, too.'' Pete got out of the car and closed the door.

Marcel opened the window. "Pete," he called out, "thank
you.''

She saw that his eyes were bright with eager anticipation.
No doubt, he'd drive straight downtown to find Andrea. If
she was in bed with another man, he might not even let that
stop him.

"Last piece of advice," she said. "For once, try making
love to her.''

Marcel laughed. "If I can remember how," he said as the
Rolls drove off.

Pete let herself into the apartment, where a single lamp
glowed in the entrance hall. She always left it on when she
went out, rather than return to absolute darkness.

The apartment was four rooms in a prewar building on
upper Fifth Avenue, just a block from the spiraling modernity
of the Guggenheim Museum. She had taken it soon after
leaving Luke, because it was a rental, a way station that she
could leave behind easily after her life changed. But there
had been little change, nothing that called for a new lifestyle.
She was comfortable in the red brick building with its high
ceilings, its courtly doormen, and the mix of tenants who had
lived there twenty and thirty years. Over time, she had furnished it with Early American furniture carefully chosen for
good value, with softening touches like the large pillows by
the fireplace.

But tonight it occurred to her that she ought to move soon.
She ought to have a place where she could entertain in the
style her position was beginning to demand.

Or was the idea merely a symptom of a restless desire for
other changes?

She moved to the windows that faced Fifth Avenue. Down
below, cars moved along the street. Looking far to the south
she watched the red glow of taillights shrinking to imper-

eptible dots. One of those vanishing cars was Marcel's. He could have been here with her . . .

A shiver of loneliness went through her. She shifted her eyes to look in a different direction, across the dark expanse of Central Park, facing west. In that direction, she realized, far beyond the horizon, a piece of her heart had gone and remained there still.

Where was Luke tonight? she wondered.

Chapter 2

Pete looked up from the file of correspondence she'd brought with her, pulled her windblown hair out of her eyes, and scanned the beach.

She spotted them about fifty yards away, standing just out of reach of the gentle surf, half turned toward each other . . . her mother listening, while her father talked, his arms folded. It was a sunny day, uncommonly warm for early March, and they had opened their coats. How comfortable they looked with each other, Pete thought, like any man and woman of gracious middle age enjoying a stroll on the beach. For a moment, a surge of sorrow and anger went through her. Why couldn't they be what they seemed? Why couldn't they have had a life together?

Because there was evil in the world, and her mother had been one of its victims. There was no other answer.

As Pete watched, she was pleased—and not a little amazed—to see her mother smile very broadly, then toss her head back slightly and join Steve in a moment of laughter.

If for nothing else, that one laugh assured Pete that she had been right to insist on bringing her mother and father together again. Even after the promise she'd wrung from

488

Steve, he had delayed and delayed, week after week; Pete had been forced to cajole and beg and finally embarrass him, accusing him of being a man who couldn't keep his word, before he had surrendered at last to what he confessed was an ordeal he had hoped to avoid forever.

"What can I possibly say to her?" he had asked Pete with anguish in the car as they drove to the clinic. "If she asks about my life, shall I tell her I'm happy? I can't talk about Anna, can I? I can't tell your mother that even if she gets well someday there's no place for her with me."

"Papa, she knows that. I've had a lot of time to prepare Mama for seeing you . . . and she knows there isn't any hope of your getting back together."

"Then what's the point of today?" Steve snapped at Pete. "What does she expect from me? What do *you* expect?"

"Simply that you don't run away from this part of the truth," Pete replied firmly. "It's been so many years since you saw her, and all that time she's been struggling to face reality because what happened to her when she was young was so horrible. I think—and Mama's doctor thinks—it will help her sort things out to see you in the flesh, to be sure that you were real. Because you were something good in her life: the only decent man who ever made love to her . . ."

Watching them on the beach, Pete reflected that the medicine seemed to have worked. Both her mother and father appeared at ease, glad to be together.

The mood continued when they all went back to the clinic and had coffee in the lounge. They reminisced about the good times and steered clear of the bad. At one point, Bettina recalled the mermaid pin Pete had given her. "My most precious possession," she said. "I keep it in a box under my pillow." Then she turned to Steve. "Did you imagine when our little girl made that pin for me that someday she would be making beautiful things for some of the most famous women in the world?"

"If I had," Steve answered lightly, "then I wouldn't have been so stupid as to keep telling her that playing with jewels was a waste of time."

Bettina smiled, looked fondly at Pete, then back to Steve. "I have no regrets," she said quietly.

It was the kind of remark that, in the past, Pete had taken as not quite relevant, coming from interior thoughts that Bettina didn't share. But today Pete understood. Whatever had happened, Mama was saying, she didn't blame Steve—she was glad for as much as they'd had.

At the end of the afternoon, Bettina walked with them to the car. With the setting of the sun, the chill of winter returned, as though the weather was a reflection of the cooling mood of departure. There was an awkward moment when it seemed that Steve and Bettina didn't quite know how to say good-bye, but then he pulled her into a gentle embrace and touched his lips to her silky hair. Pete held her breath, afraid her mother might cling too hard, refuse to let go. But they released each other easily, like old friends unafraid of good-byes because they expected to see each other again.

"I'm glad you came," Bettina said, her eyes glistening.

"I am, too," Steve said.

Then he got in the passenger seat, and Pete got behind the wheel. They drove away with Bettina still standing in the drive, a smile on her face as she waved.

On the trip back to the city, Steve was pensive. Pete tuned the radio to some light pop music and didn't force conversation. She realized he needed a chance to absorb the experience of seeing her mother again after so many years apart.

As twilight settled over the road, Steve said, "She looks so well. It's amazing how little she's changed."

"Mama was always a beautiful woman, and the way she's lived is like being in a time machine. Nothing changes from one day to the next."

Steve nodded thoughtfully and looked off through the side window. But this time, Pete didn't let her father retreat into silence.

"You're not sorry you came, are you? You meant it when you said you were glad . . . ?"

"I'm glad because, as you said, it had to be done. But I worry that it hurt your mother more than helped her."

"Hurt?" Pete echoed in astonishment. "Papa, I saw her

augh today. You made her laugh, and that's very rare. What
did you say to her?''

"I reminded her of the first time I took her out. She saw
a window full of shoes and she wanted them all. Of course,
n those days there wasn't much I could afford. But we went
ight into that store and I bought her a pair of fur-lined boots
and slippers. Today I told her—for the first time—that it
cost me all the money I had. I suppose," he added after a
second, his voice heavy with sadness, "I must already have
loved her."

"Why do you think the visit hurt? She seemed so
happy . . .''

"You told me I didn't have to hide the truth from her,
Pete . . . so I didn't. But I'm afraid she may not have been
as ready for it as you think. She mentioned hearing about
Anna from you, and she said that she understood—that of
course during all the years without her she couldn't have
expected me to remain alone."

"Sounds to me like she's accepted it."

"But that wasn't all," Steve said heavily. "She also talked
about how wonderful it would be when we were together
again . . . how she hoped the other woman would be just as
understanding when I had to leave her to return to my wife.''

"Oh no," Pete sighed in a whisper.

"I had to tell her then, you see? I had to say we would
never be together again—that I hoped she'd get well, and I
would always be her friend . . . but that she couldn't hope
. . .'' Choked with emotion, Steve's voice failed for a moment. "Was I right?" he asked then in a pleading tone. "Was
it right to tell her the truth? Or should I have lied to her, let
her go on making impossible plans?''

Suddenly Pete found it almost impossible to concentrate
on the road in front of her. She pulled the car over to a
shoulder of the road, braked to a halt, and turned off the
ignition. Covering the steering wheel with her arms, she
dropped her head onto them.

"Pietrina?" Steve said softly, concerned.

She lifted her head after a minute. "I've gone on believing
that someday she'd be well again. I had to believe that . . .

or it would be the same as losing her, giving her up almost as if she'd died. But listening to you, it finally hit me that she'll probably never be well. She can manage in the safe little world that protects her now. But if she ever has to face the challenge of making a new life, she'll come apart again.''

After a moment, Steve asked again, ''Should I have lied?''

Pete turned to him and took his hands. ''I don't think so, Papa. It's hard to be sure, but I think the best chance we all have is to trust each other, not to keep secrets. Maybe everything would have turned out better if we'd lived by that rule from the beginning. If Opa hadn't kept what happened to Mama a secret from you . . . if you hadn't kept your treasure a secret from them. I'm to blame, too. What if we'd sold our part of the perfume bottle instead of hiding it away—used the money to care for Mama and be more comfortable. Maybe that would have made a difference . . .'' She let go of him and turned back to the wheel. ''But it's too late now, too late even to think about it.''

She started the car and steered back onto the road.

Night had fallen, and a thoughtful silence filled the darkened car. Pete turned on the radio again, and they traveled mile after mile without speaking.

The lights of New York were already visible ahead when Steve abruptly reached to shut off the music. ''I've kept something else from you,'' he said, ''because I've always been afraid the knowledge would only lead you to pain and frustration, as it did to me. But I've been thinking about what you said a while ago . . . and I've decided you're right, dear Pietra. It's time there were no more secrets.''

Mrs. Hubert Crozier, Caroline to her acquaintances and ''Caro'' to her most intimate friends—and society gossip columnists—lived in a building on Eighty-sixth Street and Fifth Avenue in a duplex just above the apartment occupied by Jacqueline Onassis. On a morning ten days after their drive to Connecticut, Pete and her father were admitted to the Crozier duplex by a proper English butler who guided them straight into a living room with a sweeping view of

Central Park, opulently furnished with a blend of priceless specimen French and English antiques.

"Madame Crozier will be with you in a minute," the butler said, and left the room.

While Pete took a place on a settee upholstered in gold brocade, Steve paced to the window and looked out. He was obviously nervous.

Was he having second thoughts, Pete wondered, sorry he had launched her on the search? Or was he worried already that this might only be another blind alley? Perhaps his memory was faulty and the necklace he'd seen in a photograph five years ago was not the same one he had seen held in his mother's hands on a night four decades earlier.

No such doubts had kept her from moving quickly, however, as soon as Steve revealed that he believed a necklace pictured in the catalog for the Haines auction had come originally from the collection of La Colomba. As he described the piece vividly, Pete realized it was the one that had provoked a fierce bidding war between Andrea and her father. With the passage of time, other details of the auction were hazy, and Pete couldn't remember whether it was Andrea or her father who had prevailed in the end. But when she dug the catalog out of her shelves, she found the margins scribbled with notations she'd made during the auction to remind her of the buyers and prices. On the page where the lot number of the necklace appeared, the pencil marks read "D & I— 250,000." It came back to her then. Of course, Andrea— backed by Marcel's money—had been the buyer.

Immediately, Pete telephoned Marcel to find out what had been done with the necklace. He was cagey at first, treating her strictly like a business rival who might make competitive use of any information he divulged. But at last he relented.

"I will tell you, Pete," he said. "Because I believe you are my friend. The last time we were together, you gave me good advice."

"I've never tried to do anything else," she said. "The best I ever gave you was the night we met . . . and I told you to hire me."

Through the phone, she heard him chuckle. "Yes. It took me a while, though, to start listening to you." He told Pete then that he and Andrea were back together.

"That's wonderful, Marcel. This time you ought to make it for keeps and marry her."

"Ah, Pete," Marcel said with mock disappointment. "I thought you only gave good advice."

Pete had been perfectly serious, but she didn't press the point. She was more concerned with learning what had happened to the emerald and sapphire necklace.

The buyer, Marcel told her, had been the international banker Hubert Crozier, since deceased. Pete called the banker's widow right away only to be told that she would be out of touch for a couple of weeks, cruising on a friend's yacht. As soon as Mrs. Crozier returned, Pete made contact and explained what she wanted. With some reluctance, Caroline Crozier had finally been persuaded to agree to today's meeting.

Steve and Pete had been waiting for ten minutes when Caroline Crozier came striding into her living room. A statuesque woman with carefully coiffed gray hair, she projected at once an air of *noblesse oblige*, a willingness to spare some time for this meeting despite having many more important things to do. Pete was pleased to see her carrying a green velvet box.

"The request you made on the phone is slightly unusual," Mrs. Crozier said after the introductions were made and she was seated opposite Steve and Pete. "It's the sort of story jewel thieves might dream up to worm their way in here for a robbery."

"Mrs. Crozier," Pete said, "I can assure you—"

"Oh, I know who you are, Miss D'Angeli. If I hadn't, I would never have agreed to this request. I'm not in the custom of giving private showings of my most valuable possessions. But I've wanted to meet you anyway, and discuss having you design something for me."

"Whenever you wish," Pete said, hoping they wouldn't be sidetracked now by a design conference.

Mrs. Crozier smiled appreciatively. "Well," she said, "this is what you asked to see . . ." She handed Pete the green velvet box.

With nervous fingers, Pete lifted the lid. Inside, nestled in a bed of ivory watered silk, the necklace lay circled around a molded form. The sapphires and emeralds, their myriad facets reflecting the bright morning light from the window, showered the room with intersecting beams of brilliant blue and green. So thick was the colored light that it felt to Pete almost as if the entire room had been plunged under water.

She passed the box to her father. "Is this it, Papa?"

Steve stared down at the necklace. Then, tentatively, as though his fingers might be burned, he reached out and touched the diamond "C" scrolled across the clasp. "Colomba," he murmured as he traced the curve of the letter. He looked up at Pete, his eyes glistening. "Yes," he said. "I am sure."

Pete turned again to the owner of the necklace. "Mrs. Crozier, this is the only link my father and I have been able to find to a missing collection of jewels once owned by my grandmother—"

"Look, I acquired it perfectly legally," Mrs. Crozier cut in.

"I'm not contesting that," Pete said. "But if there's anything else you know about the necklace—anything you can think of . . ."

"I'm sorry, Miss D'Angeli. All I know is that it came from the estate of Dorothy Fisk Haines via Marcel Ivères, who sold it to me—for a very handsome price, I might add. It's been one of my most admired pieces whenever I've worn it. I've been asked by a number of people over the years if I'd like to sell it."

Pete took a breath. "Then let me ask, too. Would you consider selling the necklace to me?"

Steve spun to stare at her in disbelief.

As soon as the words were out, Pete had to wonder herself what had possessed her. No doubt, Marcel had sold the necklace at a substantial profit, and in the years since then the market for fine jewelry had reached new highs. The current price of the piece might be as much as eight hundred thousand dollars.

Yet Pete would have mortgaged everything to retrieve the only known link to her stolen past. She would have designed a dozen pieces for Caroline Crozier and given them to her free in exchange.

Still, she felt as much relief as regret when the woman slowly shook her head. "It's the last gift my husband gave me before he died. I'll keep it always."

Before leaving, Pete was able to prevail on Mrs. Crozier to allow the necklace to be photographed. Pete had brought along a compact 35mm camera fitted with a special lens, and she took several extreme close-ups showing the workmanship of the settings, the face as well as the back, and of the clasp. Though highly improbable, it was not altogether impossible that someday she would show the pictures to someone, somewhere, who could provide another link.

When they left the apartment building, Pete and her father walked across the street into Central Park. Despite the failure of their mission to yield any significant result, Pete felt curiously optimistic. Perhaps it was just the effect of spring, seeing the first faint mist of green beginning to brush the winter-bare trees.

"I had my heart in my mouth when you offered to buy it," Steve said as they strolled. "My God, what if she had agreed."

"I would have found a way."

Steve studied her. "I imagine you would. But this is what I'm afraid of, Pete—that you'll chase the dream too far, beyond reason."

Pete smiled. "I've got a long way to go before I get there, Papa."

"The way this turned out, there doesn't seem to be a next step. That necklace was my mother's, there's no doubt. But the trail is broken . . ."

"Only in one direction," Pete said.

"What do you mean?"

"I've tried looking forward and that didn't work." She let er eyes run over the treetops, the skyline beyond, the blue April sky. "Now I'm going to look backward."

In the weeks that followed, Pete devoted every moment away from her work to picking up a thread that might somehow connect the necklace to the man who must have put it back into circulation—Vittorio D'Angeli. If only her father had told her years ago, when he had first spotted the piece in the auction catalog, her work might have been easier. The executors of the estate of Dorothy Fisk Haines, who had consigned her jewels to Christie's auction house, might have been able to provide information about the provenance of her collection. But Dorothy Haines had died without heirs, and her estate had been thoroughly liquidated. The paper trail of records had grown cold.

Nevertheless, Pete copied the photographs she had made and sent a set to the Fine Jewelry Department at Christie's in London with a letter referring back to the sale, explaining her interest in the necklace and asking for the names and addresses of the persons responsible for consignment of the Haines collection. Pete made other sets and sent them out to the older, more established buyers on her personal mailing list, men and women who had an abiding interest in jewelry and might remember being offered the necklace at some time in the past before it had been acquired by Dorothy Haines. She sent similar requests for information to dealers around the world. Remembering that Antonio Scappa had shown a particular appreciation for the piece, and realizing that the volume of his ever expanding business brought him in contact with an especially wide assortment of European artisans, dealers, and collectors, Pete also sent him pictures of the necklace and a personal appeal to show them around—especially among the older generation—on the chance that some connection might be made.

Her efforts yielded no results at first. Polite responses came from people who said they would be glad to help but had no information to provide. Many on her list seemed to understand

that her plea was a hopeless stab in the dark and didn't even
bother to send regrets. From Scappa, she got a pleasant but
unhelpful reply.

> *My dear Signorina D'Angeli,*
>
> *Until your photographs arrived, I had forgotten
> about the Haines necklace. From the story you tell,
> it seems that so many years have passed since the
> piece was on the open market that I don't imagine
> you will have much success in finding the owner
> prior to Mrs. Haines. However, I understand your
> sentimental interest, and if I have the opportunity I
> will ask some questions on your behalf.*

It was curious, Pete thought, that he should claim not to
recall the necklace. Could he have forgotten something over
which he'd fought so bitterly with his own daughter? Or was
that exactly why he had blotted it out?

For the same reason, Pete guessed, Scappa would probably
do nothing to help her. As mild as his note seemed on the
surface, Pete detected an underlying coldness. Perhaps since
she had once worked for Marcel, whom Scappa hated for
making an alliance with his daughter, he also regarded her
as an enemy. Well, it was too bad, but it certainly wouldn't
hold her back.

In the middle of May, she got the first break in her private
investigation. A letter from Christie's came to the office in
the morning mail informing Pete that a search through their
files had turned up the name of Roger Perkins Enfield, Esquire, as the lawyer who had been the primary executor of
the Haines estate. An address and phone number in London
were provided.

Pete handed the letter over to Lottie and told her to place
a transatlantic call at once.

"It's five hours later there, Pete. Mr. Enfield Esquire will
probably be out to lunch . . ."

"Then find out where he eats and call him *there*. I don't

want to wait a another minute on this, Lottie. I'm already five years late."

When the intercom on her desk buzzed a few minutes later to indicate the secretary was putting through a call, Pete grabbed the phone eagerly. Told to track down the lawyer at his lunch, reliable Lottie had probably done exactly that.

But the voice she heard on the line after her own "Hello" didn't have an English accent, and it wasn't a stranger's. She recognized it at once as Dr. Haffner's.

"Hello, Pete," he said. He paused then, and Pete felt a chill go through her even before he said his next words: "Are you sitting down?"

Even before he broke the news, Pete had guessed. She had dreamed once that it might end another way for her mother, yet now this ending seemed inevitable.

She listened passively as Haffner explained that Bettina had taken her own life just after dawn; he had waited until now to call both to satisfy necessary police procedures and because he didn't want to wake her with such terrible news.

"How did it happen?" Pete asked at last.

"She dressed and went down to the beach. There's no one on duty at that hour. The fence has always been security enough. But your mother climbed over . . . and just walked out into the ocean. I'm sorry, Pete. We should have done more to keep her safe."

"It's all right, doctor," Pete said quietly. "She's safe now." After a brief discussion of funeral arrangements, Pete cradled the phone.

Sitting at her desk, she had a vision of her mother walking slowly into the cool blue water. For Bettina, she remembered, the ocean had always been a symbol of happiness, a reminder of good times before the war.

As the tears began to run down her cheeks, a vision formed in Pete's mind, and it seemed no less clear and right than if she were there now on the beach. She could see her mother walking slowly toward the water sparked with the sun's first slanted rays, beautifully dressed, her hair perfectly combed —and wearing the mermaid pin.

Chapter 3

The cemetery was not far from the clinic, a few acres of neatly tended graves climbing a gentle tree-studded hillside that faced toward the sparkling waters of Long Island Sound. Clouds sailed across the sun, turning the day alternately light and dark. A breeze rustled the leaves and bent the grass, carrying with it the faint briny scent of the ocean.

It was the right place for Mama to rest, Pete thought, as she listened to the Twenty-third Psalm being intoned over the coffin in the language of her mother's native land. Josef had asked a retired pastor in the Dutch Reformed Church, a fellow member of the Dutch Club, to come to Connecticut and conduct the ceremony.

Gathered at the graveside aside from Josef and Pete and Steve were Dr. Haffner, a couple of staff people from the clinic, and a handful of patients who had become Bettina's special friends and were judged stable enough to attend. Jess would have come, Pete knew, but she and Fernando had left two weeks ago on a photo safari to Kenya, and Pete wouldn't have dreamed of summoning her back. As great as the personal loss was for Pete, she couldn't fail to perceive a more mundane truth when she looked around at the small group of mourners. Today marked the end of a life in which very little had been achieved, the farewell to a woman who had made few ripples in the world as she passed through it. After the coffin was lowered, it took only a couple of minutes for the mourners to line up and toss down their ritual handfuls of earth, then shake Pete's hand and drift away down the hill to their cars.

"Don't ever blame yourself," Haffner said when he paused in front of Pete. "She'd just gone too far into hell to come all the way back. But no one could have done more over the years than you did. You were the best part of her life."

She gave him a kiss, as she had the first time she'd met him, and he walked away down the hill.

Though Steve and Josef remained with Pete after the others had gone, they stood on opposite sides of the grave, and when they looked up from the rectangular well of darkness and their eyes met, they glared at each other with unforgiving ferocity. They had arrived in separate cars and had said not a word of condolence to each other, even though they were never more than a few feet apart.

As the two men turned and started to walk away, Pete raised her voice, stopping them. "You're all I have left of a family," she said, "*both* of you. During all the years Mama's been sick, you've blamed each other, hated each other. You could have given each other support—and, together, given it to me—but you never did. In a way, Mama and I were left alone. But now she's gone. Now there's just me . . . and I want a family again. So this damn little war you've been fighting has got to end." Steve and Josef had stopped walking away, though their backs were still turned. "And I need you," Pete added, her voice breaking, "both of you." She stretched out her hands, one to each.

They hesitated, then both moved back to her, clasping her hands and embracing her. As they let go, they gave each other a hard look.

The older man spoke first. "She's right, Steve. Can you find it in your heart to forgive me for not telling you everything?"

It was only a moment before Steve bowed his head and nodded. "It was only because you loved her," he said.

"And because I believed you would make her happy."

"I wish to God I could have," Steve said.

The two men studied each other. The fire of resentment and hatred had faded from their eyes.

"Give me a minute alone now," Pete said. She watched with satisfaction as they walked down the hill together, then she turned back to the grave to spend a minute saying her last good-bye.

Mama, she cried silently to the departing spirit, *was there anything I could have done differently, anything that would have saved you?*

Almost as if the spirit were replying to her questions, Pete knew the answer and was at peace with it. Finally, she turned to walk down the hill.

At the sight of the figure standing in the shade of the nearest tree, Pete froze and her heart skipped a beat as if a ghost had actually risen out of the ground.

"My plane got in late," he said. "I'm sorry I missed so much, but I hope you don't mind that I came."

Pete opened her mouth to speak, but her voice caught and all she could do was shake her head. *Mind?* She had never been so glad to see anyone as she was to see him.

Luke moved toward her, out of the shade. It was the first time Pete had ever seen him wearing a plain dark suit. "Dr. Haffner called me. He knew this would be pretty rough for you and it would help to have an old friend around."

His words echoed again in her thoughts. *Old friend.* Oh yes, he was that, she realized . . . and so much more. At any other time and place, she would have erupted with questions. Where had he come from? How long could he stay? Had he come alone . . . and was someone going to be waiting impatiently for his return?

But she merely smiled and said simply, "I'm very glad you're here."

As he came forward, Pete noticed the changes brought by the past few years—the deepening of lines in his face and across his brow, the first frosting of gray in the tips of his brown hair. Yet he didn't really look older, she thought, only more solid.

Reaching her, he bent to kiss her softly on the cheek. At the soft touch of his lips, she had to restrain herself from putting her arms around him and pulling him closer. Yet, she reminded herself, there were still too many unanswered questions.

After the kiss, he took her arm and slipped it through his own and started guiding her back down the hillside to the waiting cars. It seemed the most natural thing in the world to be walking quietly at his side. Pete could hardly believe that any time had passed since the last time they'd been together—certainly not several years.

He apologized again for arriving late. "They had us stacked up over Kennedy. I'd have gotten here quicker if I'd flown myself."

"You still have your plane?" The memories flooded back—soaring in the sky with him, weekend adventures. How could they have thrown it away?

"I stepped up to a twin-engine a couple of years ago," he said. "Longer range. Don't use it much for pleasure, though, just business." He gave her a wry glance. "Like being all dressed up with no place to go."

Was he telling her there was still nobody else? she wondered.

They were nearing the roadway where the two limousines Pete had hired for the day were waiting. She and Josef had arrived in one; the other was for Steve. Pete saw her father and grandfather still talking together.

They broke off to greet Luke. Then Josef said to Pete, "Steve tells me you've located a piece of jewelry that belonged to his mother. You should let me see the pictures, too, and keep me informed about the search. There might be some way I can help."

"Of course, Opa." As casually as she answered, Pete was thrilled. Though she didn't expect that Josef had the crucial knowledge to lead to any breakthroughs, his offer of help was the surest sign that he was indeed ready to forgive the mistakes of the past. Her grandfather had always resented

Steve's decision to keep the perfume bottle, and until now
he had always refused to hear any more about it. At the
moment, however, there was nothing more to tell him. The
attempt to contact the executor of the Haines estate had led
to another dead end. The lawyer, a bachelor, had closed his
London practice a couple of years ago and retired to a sunnier
place than England. Lottie was still trying to locate him.

Pete was nevertheless sufficiently encouraged by the spirit
of Josef's offer to make a suggestion to him and Steve. "Why
don't you two go in one car? I haven't seen Luke for a long
time, and I'd like to spend some time alone with him."

Josef and Steve eyed each other warily, then both nodded
and climbed into one limousine for the long ride back to the
city.

As she settled next to Luke in the back seat of the other
car, Pete was overwhelmed by the accumulated tensions of
the previous few days of making funeral arrangements, the
nights in which her fitful sleep had been disturbed by dreams
of her mother floating under water. She had kept up a strong
facade so that she would not put any more strain on her
grandfather, and would have liked to maintain the impression
of strength now, to hold herself together and be able to talk
with Luke. But as the car turned out through the cemetery
gates, she found herself weeping, giving in to the despair she
felt at the cruelty of her mother's life.

Luke put his arm around her, gave her his handkerchief
and pulled her close. She couldn't imagine wanting any other
shoulder to cry on.

Drained of tears after half an hour, she sat up and for a
while they exchanged small talk about her business and his,
and news of Robby, who had married a California girl and
just fathered his second child.

"Pete," Luke said finally, "there couldn't be a worse way
to get thrown together again, so please don't misunderstand
. . . but seeing you again is like healing a wound. I've wanted
a hundred times to pick up the phone and hear your voice or
just fly in to see you the way I did today."

"Why didn't you?"

He gave her a smile. "Never had the guts. You were the

one who sent me packing, after all, and after so much time apart, I never knew what I'd find. You might be married or about to be . . . or even working on your third set of twins. I couldn't take the risk.''

''You mean, if this hadn't happened, you wouldn't have come?''

''Oh, I'd have come anyway to pay my respects. But it would have been a lot harder if I didn't think there was still a chance to put something back together with you.''

''How did you know there was? Except for the absence of twins,'' she added lightly, ''how much can you tell just by looking at me?''

Luke gave an embarrassed shrug. ''If you'd had someone else to lean on, Haffner wouldn't have called me. But I asked him a few questions, too. He told me you still visited on most weekends, hadn't ever brought a man to meet Bettina . . . and that she'd never boasted to anyone about any new son-in-law on the horizon. It was enough to give me courage.''

Pete was touched by his confession. Yet she was wary of stripping away all her defenses. She cared for him still, and his words left no doubt that he cared for her. Yet if they belonged together, why had they been apart so long? She couldn't forget that he lived by a strict set of rules and that he had judged her—judged, at least, the work she cared about—as trivial, even wasteful.

For a moment, though, she wanted to avoid any confrontation. Being near him, having him hold her, was like being given a drink of water after a long journey across a parched land. She let herself relax, blocked out any concern for what tomorrow might bring. Soon she had fallen asleep with her head on his shoulder.

When she awoke they were in the city, only a couple of blocks from her apartment.

''Can I buy you dinner?'' Luke said as she sat up and stretched out the kinks.

''Thanks, but I don't have any appetite.'' She paused only a moment before suggesting the alternative. ''Come home with me. We'll have something there . . .''

As soon as they were through the door of her apartment,

she started bustling about nervously, collecting mail and newspapers and dishes she'd left lying around during the past couple of days. She filled an ice bucket, asked him what he'd like to drink, then without waiting for his answer, began rummaging in the refrigerator for the makings of a decent snack.

He came into the kitchen, pushed the door of the refrigerator shut, and pulled her around to face him. "I'm not hungry either," he said. "Or thirsty. So why don't you stop running around—or should I say running away?"

She surrendered to the impulse she had denied earlier. Her arms slipped around him, and her mouth sought his. The recent days in which death had dictated her mood made her all the more desperate for the affirmation of life embodied in her rush of sexual need. The hunger to be touched by him was suddenly all consuming, and she didn't hide it. Wrapping herself around him, she moved her hands to help him slip out of his jacket. He answered each move, starting to undress her, too, his mouth roaming down her neck to the mound of her breasts. She moaned impatiently and started to open his belt, then pushed her hand down inside his pants, skimming over his flat hard stomach to take hold of him. She had never felt so aroused, so unwilling to wait—

When the phone started to ring, she tried to ignore it. She kept urging him on and would simply have pulled the receiver off the hook—pulled the phone off the wall—if she could have reached it.

But she couldn't, and the shrill insistent reminder of the world beyond them would not go away. It occurred to her that it might be an emergency—Opa taken ill in the aftermath of the stressful day . . .

She released Luke and picked up the phone. She couldn't completely disguise her breathlessness as she answered.

"Pete . . . are you all right?" It was Lottie.

Her eyes stayed locked on Luke's as she spoke, the message of desire still flashing between them. "Fine, Lottie. But this isn't a good time—"

"I'll only keep you a second. I just wanted you to know I've located your Mr. Enfield."

"You have!" Her concentration switched completely to the voice on the phone. She tugged at her clothes, pulling herself together as she grabbed a pencil she kept with a pad near the phone. "Give me the details."

She wrote down what Lottie told her, then briskly instructed her to make a plane reservation. "No, not tonight," she said with a glance toward Luke. "But first thing tomorrow . . ."

When she hung up and turned back to Luke, she saw him tucking his shirt back into his pants.

"Went crazy there for a minute," he said, "didn't we?"

Her eyes clouded with confusion. "Is that all it takes to bring you down to earth—a short interruption?" She moved to him. "Luke, I still—"

He broke in, his voice rising. "You're still ready to slam the door on everything else to put business first."

"That wasn't business," she shot back. "You heard my grandfather mention the link I've found to my grandmother's jewel collection. Well, I've got a chance to track it down, Luke. I can't let that go . . ."

"No," he said quietly, "I know you can't."

"But it doesn't have to affect us."

"It just did. I'm here now . . . ready to think about making a life with you, trying to pick up right where we left off. Where the hell does that leave me if you'd rather go off on some goddamn treasure hunt for a trunkful of jewels?"

"It's more than that, damn it." Pete couldn't rein in her own temper. "Those things were stolen from my father. This isn't about the jewels. It's about making things right, making a connection to the past, finding justice and truth . . ."

"And for that you'd sacrifice love?"

"No!" she cried. "Why do I have to make a choice?"

Luke said nothing for a moment. "Where are you going tomorrow?" he asked then.

Pete glanced at the pencil notes she'd made during Lottie's call. "Monte Carlo."

"Who do you have to see?"

Pete explained the significance of Roger Perkins Enfield as a possible source of information.

Luke continued his interrogation. "You can't be sure, though, that Mr. Enfield will be able to tell you what you need to know."

"No, I can't."

"So you'll go hunting for the next clue . . . and the next. And whenever you have a hot lead, you'll drop everything else to follow it."

"You could come with me," she said.

Luke picked up his jacket and put it on. "I'm not interested in a treasure hunt, Pete. I came here looking for something more real and important."

She looked away. "I can't tell you this search isn't just as important to me. But it won't be like that forever. I'll either find what I'm looking for . . . or give up."

"How long before that happens?"

"I don't know."

Luke gave her a faint rueful smile. "Well," he said, "whenever it does, that's when I want to be around. Because I don't want loving you to be something I can only do in your spare time."

He gazed at her as if hoping she would make the pledge now, tell him that he would come first from this moment on.

Part of her longed to cry out whatever words were needed to hold him. But another, more deeply rooted strain in her will could not relinquish the quest, a glittering dream that went back to her childhood and even to before she was born.

"Some things may stay lost," Luke said very softly, "but you know where to find me." A moment later he was gone.

From the terrace of the villa on one of the highest points in Monte Carlo, Pete looked down at the harbor where rows of enormous white-hulled luxury yachts bobbed at anchor. Off to one side she could see the roof of the Société des Bains de Mer, the enormous gambling casino that had been the nucleus and main attraction of this sun-washed speck of a country long before Princess Grace arrived or there were income taxes to be avoided. The ghost of a smile touched her lips as she thought back to last night, offering Luke the option of joining her on the trip. Of course, it was much

etter that she had come alone. There were probably few
laces Luke would have despised more than this haven for
ne idle rich.

Glancing back to the open French doors, Pete could see
nat Roger Perkins Enfield was still hunched over the ormolu
ible in his living room, a phone pressed to his ear as he
nade calls to former associates and insurance companies in
n attempt to find out when and where his one-time client,
Dorothy Haines, had acquired the sapphire and emerald neck-
ice in the photographs Pete had brought along. He had already been at it for nearly an hour.

With no reason to delay, Pete had taken the overnight flight
o Nice after all, and had arrived in time to get down the
coast to the principality of Monaco just as Roger Enfield was
nishing his breakfast. Despite the Englishman's surpise at
nding a woman who had arrived straight from New York
n his doorstep, he received her graciously, gave her a Con-
nental breakfast, and went right to work on fulfilling her
request.

Pete sat down again in a garden chair. Perhaps she'd been
foolish to jump right on a plane instead of calling ahead to
ne lawyer, yet she was driven by a lurking fear that the slim
chain of connections would evaporate if she didn't seize each
nk quickly and completely as it appeared. Could she be sure
nat Vittorio D'Angeli hadn't paid lavish bribes to cover his
racks? If he was still alive, how far did his influence reach?
There were still people in Europe with sympathy for wartime
collaborators. Pete didn't want to alert anyone in advance
nat she was on Vittorio's trail.

Roger Perkins Enfield reappeared on the terrace at last. A
all Englishman, thin to the point of gauntness, he sported a
nick white mustache in the style of colonial officers from
ne great days of the empire. The formal image was mod-
rated, however, by his white flannel pants and cricket
sweater.

"Got it," he exclaimed in a robust voice, as he brandished
a sheaf of papers. "Wonderful thing, technology. Between
nsurance company computers and this fax thingamajig I've
nst put in, I've got a print-out on the whole damn collection."

Pete couldn't contain her excitement. "May I see?"

"Certainly, my dear." He handed over the papers.

Pete flipped through the long print-out. Several doze
pieces of jewelry were listed, each with a detailed descriptio
along with the source from which it had been acquired, th
date of purchase, and the price paid.

Halfway through the list, she found the necklace, describe
right down to the exact number of stones, the weight, an
the initial "C" on the clasp. The print-out showed that it ha
been bought for Mrs. Haines in October 1963 at l'Hôte
Drouot, the old auction house in Paris. An additional not
quoted the catalog for the auction as saying that the iter
offered for sale was "the property of a gentleman." Pet
knew that anonymous phrase—or "property of a lady"—
was customary in auction catalogs, yet she was disappointe
to see no other reference to previous ownership.

"These records don't give a name for the former owner,"
she observed.

"I don't think we ever knew who it was. But you migh
be able to get the information from Drouot."

Pete sighed. More than twenty years had lapsed since Mrs
Haines had bought the necklace. Would the auction house b
able to excavate the records? Her eye rested again on th
words that gave her the only remaining clue: "property of
gentleman." Could it be Vittorio himself who had consigne
the necklace?

No, she couldn't imagine he would have been so careless
Especially since the piece was initialed, he would have an
ticipated it might be traced.

"Thank you for helping, Mr. Enfield," she said.

"Anytime. Retirement's getting to be a bit of a bore. Liv
ens things up to do a little detective work. Heading up t
Paris next, are you, to have a word with Drouot?"

She nodded.

"Don't suppose you'd like some company. Great town
Paris. We could do it up together, have a few goo
meals . . ."

Pete smiled at the Englishman's rakish invitation. "N

is trip,'' she said, and excused herself as quickly as pos-
ible.

Water jetted over shiny black and white granite in the
ountain in front of the jarringly modern building that housed
e Hôtel Drouot, the central auction house of Paris in the
arrow rue Drouot.

The flight from Nice, even with long taxi rides at each end
f the trip, had gotten Pete to Paris by mid-afternoon. The
uction house was still going full tilt. People streamed through
e doors, going to or coming from one of the two thousand
ales held there each year, offering everything from chipped
rockery and chairs with missing legs to Renoirs and Gau-
uins and priceless furniture salvaged from the time of
rance's vanished monarchy.

Pete flowed in with the crowd and looked around the lobby,
ying to get her bearings. A bank, a bookshop, an appraisal
ffice all faced onto the huge space. Television monitors
uspended from the ceiling listed the day's exhibitions and
ales; well-thumbed catalogs lay in a heap on a reception
ounter. A harried young woman behind the counter listened
 Pete's question and directed her upstairs to the office of
ne of the directors, Monsieur René Vaugillande.

While she sat waiting to be received, Pete flipped through
 copy of *La Gazette de l'Hôtel Drouot*, the publication that
sted all upcoming sales and had been published every Friday
ince 1891. An auction of estate jewelry was listed for the
eginning of June, a few weeks away. Pete wondered if she
ught to attend—indeed, if she ought to begin canvassing all
e auction houses—then decided there would be far too much
round to cover. In any case, she doubted that Vittorio would
xpose himself to discovery by exploiting such a public
ethod of selling the jewelry. The fact that the necklace had
ppeared at auction years ago seemed to indicate that it was
 one-time fluke, a single instance of carelessness that Vittorio
ad been wise enough not to repeat.

''*Monsieur Vaugillande vous attends, Mademoiselle*,'' said
e secretary, motioning Pete into the inner office.

She was greeted effusively by a dapper middle-aged man who motioned her to a chair beside his desk, then raised his eyebrows in conspicuous appreciation of her beauty. He gave no quarter, however, when it came to meeting her need.

"You must understand, Mademoiselle D'Angeli," he said with a Gallic shrug. "To locate records going back so far would be extremely difficult."

"But you haven't said it's impossible," Pete remarked.

"Mademoiselle, the Hôtel Drouot has been in business for one hundred thirty-two years. Somewhere in our archives we probably have records dating from our first day. But to find such documents could take months, years."

"I didn't ask you to go back to the beginning," Pete persisted. "Only twenty-five years. And I can give you a head start." She produced the print-out given her by Roger Enfield. "I know the exact date on which the auction was held."

Monsieur Vaugillande reached across his desk and took the print-out from Pete. He glanced at the entry around which she had penciled a circle. "But, Mademoiselle," the Frenchman said quickly, "I can see from the information already provided that even if the records are located I would be unable to oblige your request."

"Why?"

"The necklace was listed in our catalog as having been formerly the property of a gentleman. If the owner had wished to have his name known, we would have published it in the catalog. The kind of listing we gave him indicates that he expressed a desire for anonymity. Even with the passage of time, we would not depart from an agreement to keep his confidence."

"Monsieur Vaugillande," Pete pleaded. "If you knew that by keeping that confidence you might be protecting a thief —even a war criminal—would you still deny me the information?"

"Are you saying that such people were involved in this transaction?"

"No. At least, I can't be sure . . ."

The Frenchman hesitated, but then his shoulders twitched

gain with a shrug. "*Alors*, Mademoiselle, the house of Drouot must abide by its pledge to the client."

Still, Pete didn't give up. She cajoled, coaxed, and flirted, playing the coquette for all she was worth until at last René Vaugillande promised to discover the name of the seller of the necklace, contact him personally, and ask if he was willing to have his name released.

Pete wasn't certain whether the promise represented a step forward or backward. If the mysterious seller happened to be Vittorio himself, he would be warned of the hunt, would know just how close Pete was getting, and he might take measures to go deeper underground.

But there was no other choice.

"When can I expect to hear from you?" she asked just before leaving the office of Monsieur Vaugillande.

Once more he shrugged. "Your guess, Mademoiselle, would be as good as mine."

As she left the auction house and started walking through the streets of Paris, Pete felt the ache of loss—not because she had failed to find an answer, but because she had gained so little while leaving behind so much. If she had stayed with Luke it would have made no difference to her quest, none at all.

And yet she was far from certain that she would make a different choice next time.

She flew back to New York that same night, too dispirited to stay and enjoy the romantic beauty of the City of Light.

Chapter 4

"Where is he?" Antonio Scappa bellowed as he stood in the offices of the Geneva Tesori, glaring at the Assistant Manager.

"I don't know, Signor Scappa. Your son didn't come in at all today."

"Well then, find out in which lady's bed he slept last night. Make some phone calls." With a snap of his hand, Antonio dismissed his cowering employee.

Alone in his office, Scappa angrily snatched the black Borsalino from his head and hurled the hat into a corner. He had just walked in after a two-day trip to Barcelona to find that the payroll to be dispensed the next morning hadn't been prepared, phone calls from some of his most lucrative clients had gone unanswered, and several other important matters had been left undone. Given a full week, Antonio mused bitterly, his dear son Franco could probably cut the store's profits by half! Why couldn't the young man show an aptitude for anything but racing fast cars and screwing fast women?

The Tesori chain was still growing at a rapid pace—the trip Antonio had made to Barcelona was to check on the first week's operations of the newest store. Antonio felt he could overtake every one of his competitors if only he didn't have to go on running the business by himself. While a good part of the world starved, there was still another part that seemed awash with money for people to spend on lavish homes and antiques and art and yachts . . . and jewels. Only two weeks ago, he had been invited to bring a sampling of his best pieces to the palace of a German baroness, the young wife of an old man who already owned so many jewels that they filled separate drawers rising from floor to ceiling in one wall of a huge walk-in closet. The baroness had purchased most of everything Antonio brought to show her. He was now thinking that, to make such lucrative "house calls," he might start traveling more. He had avoided leaving Switzerland for the first ten years after his identity change because he didn't want to be put to the test of having his passport constantly inspected. With the passage of time, however, he felt increasingly secure. He was even beginning to think he might expand his boundaries beyond Europe.

Having reached his seventies, Antonio had yet to make any concessions to age. He remained as vigorous and capable as he had been when, as Vittorio D'Angeli, he had fled Italy under a cloud and established his new life. Precisely because there had been from the beginning a sense of achieving it all on borrowed time, Antonio derived a special satisfaction from his success. He never stopped building his business, taking over a larger and larger share of the European retail jewelry market, getting richer. If he hadn't been clever, he would have had none of it, he often reminded himself; he would have ended as a bloody pulp swinging by his heels like that poor fool Mussolini.

Lately, though, Antonio had begun to wonder what point there was in building an empire if there was no successor to whom he could pass it on. That damn wastrel Franco would obviously let it all slip right through his fingers. The outlook for the future so distressed Antonio that he even worried sometimes that it had been a terrible mistake to let his daughter go. But he always ended by reassuring himself that he'd had no choice. The way she had run straight to Ivères proved that she was a traitor and a whore, infested with the worst traits of her grandmother's personality.

With a dyspeptic grunt, Antonio removed the painting that concealed his office safe. He twirled the knob of the combination lock back and forth and swung open the heavy door. He was about to reach for a stack of Swiss francs to use for his employee payroll when his eye fell instead on the envelope he had pushed into a far corner along with some business documents. He had been able to forget its contents for a while, but now he grabbed it up as he had so many times over the past few months. Standing at the open safe, he lifted the flap of the envelope and took out the letter and the color photographs inside.

Pictures of the necklace. What a joke that his niece, unknowing of his identity and their kinship, had sent the pictures to *him*, asking for help in tracing the history of buyers and sellers.

It was not a joke Antonio could laugh at, however. Though Pietra D'Angeli's letter assured him she hadn't been able to pick up the trail, he could no longer rule out the possibility that someday she might. Months ago he had calmly dismissed the likelihood that her search would ever lead back to the rest of La Colomba's collection. But as the days and weeks passed, doubt burrowed deeper into his conscience. Suppose she never gave up . . . suppose she was clever enough or lucky enough to follow the chain of connections all the way back to him. True, the odds were against it. Yet when he had let the necklace get away from him at auction, hadn't he calmed himself then with the thought that it would disappear again into somebody's jewelry box, only to be worn for an hour or two on rare occasions?

If he had done nothing more than send a polite reply to Pietra D'Angeli's letter, it was because he didn't know how else to proceed. To seek information from her, try to find out how much she knew, might only end by arousing her suspicions. She had already witnessed his avid interest in the necklace at the Haines auction.

But Antonio could not shake the fear that eventually he

might be exposed—that he could lose everything, be sent to jail. He longed to know if Pietra had learned anything more . . or if she had given up. But how could he find that out without making her suspicious?

Suddenly, an idea occurred to him. It solved so many of his concerns that he cursed himself for not thinking of it sooner. As he put the envelope back in his safe, Antonio congratulated himself on his cleverness: This notion would not only protect his forty-year masquerade, it might even provide some amusement and, best of all, increase his profits.

Pete sat at her drawing board, staring by turns at the blank paper and the drizzling rain of a May afternoon outside her office window.

For many weeks, it had been a struggle to create anything that pleased her. She made drawings, then tore them up or reworked them so many times that the lines on the paper became a blur. She had a dozen commissions lined up, and as many inquiries about new work. The line of jeweled wristwatches she had done for the Japanese manufacturer had become instant classics, and she was being asked to do another, for which her royalty payment would be doubled. But fresh ideas wouldn't come.

Lottie had watched Pete falling farther and farther behind in her commitments and had taken it on herself for the first time to turn away some inquiries about new work and discouraged potential customers by saying the wait might be more than a year.

"You've been going nonstop for too long," Lottie told Pete. "Close up shop for a month, go somewhere and lie in the sun. Recharge your batteries . . ."

Pete hadn't listened. She kept trying to work through whatever was blocking her. She could imagine nothing but emptiness and boredom if she put aside her work. What else had sustained her through every other loss and tragedy? She suspected, too, that Lottie's suggestion was really a spinster's code for telling Pete to go somewhere and find a man, have a fling.

If she were to go anywhere in the sun, Pete thought, it

would have to be California. She knew Luke was still there
and—the last time they had talked, at least—unattached. He
called every so often simply to say he'd been thinking about
her. At the first sound of his voice she would always be
tempted to pour out her heart, to declare that she was ready
to fly to him the next day if he would only ask. But he would
ask instead whether she was still hoping to find La Colomba's
collection and how many gorgeous pieces of jewelry she was
creating for her rich clients, and before long they would be
arguing again.

"I can't be the kind of woman who gives up *everything*
for a man," she would proclaim.

"That was never what I wanted," he would reply. "I just
thought love ought to come first every time—not be put on
hold for the sake of anything else."

It didn't sound unreasonable the way he said it. But Pete
remembered how he had forced her to choose between him
and pursuing her ambitions. She couldn't foresee any end to
their conflict until she was content to abandon her work completely . . . and give up the search for La Colomba's jewels.

But perhaps the time had come to yield to him. Her work
felt stale, and she had given up hope of making any more
connections to the necklace. The request she had made to
Drouot for further information about the piece Mrs. Fisk
Haines had purchased in 1963 had resulted only in an apologetic letter from Monsieur Vaugillande to say that the auction house could not oblige her, after all. "Upon looking
further into the matter," he wrote, "we have determined that
the pledge of anonymity we gave to the seller must stand."
She had written back with an appeal, reiterating the circumstances, explaining that the man who had offered the necklace
at auction might have come by it illegally, might even be a
wartime Fascist collaborator. Vaugillande's reply gave only
the tiniest additional information. "While we remain committed to preserving our client's anonymity, I can assure you
he is the most respectable of men who could not possibly
have been involved with Fascists."

Pete was infuriated at being stonewalled, but she didn't
see what could be done about it. She had no right to force

he auction house to turn over their records, no proof the
ecklace was stolen goods. Even if she had, the problem of
ighting a transatlantic legal battle was too daunting.

Pete stopped staring absently at the gray rain washing over
he city and looked back at the blank paper on her drawing
oard. What if she never dreamed up another piece of jew-
lry? What if she did stop right here and now and go to
uke . . . ?

There was a soft knocking at the closed door. When Pete
vas designing she turned off the phone and told Lottie not
o disturb her unless there was an emergency.

After the knock, Lottie put her head in. She shot a glance
t the blank drawing paper before she said, "I didn't want
o bother you, but the call's from Switzerland, and he shouted
t me when I tried to put him off and swore that you'd be
hrilled to hear what he has to say. You can see where his
aughter gets her manners."

"His daughter? Who is it?"

"Antonio Scappa."

Pete thought back to their brief correspondence. Scappa
adn't been encouraging, but he had said he would make
nquiries on her behalf. Had he learned something?

"Put him through," Pete said quickly.

The call lasted less than five minutes, and Scappa refused
o tell Pete over the phone exactly why he had called. When
he asked specifically if it was to give her information, he
edged. "I'm willing to answer all your questions," he said.
'But to do it properly, I would like to meet with you." He
dded that he would pay all her expenses to fly to Europe
mmediately.

In her mood of ennui, Pete saw no reason not to agree.
he had been contemplating abandoning her work in any case.

"I can be in Geneva by tomorrow evening," she said.

"No," he replied. "Not Geneva. Come to Barcelona."

By the clocks of the lively capital of Spain's Catalonia, it
vas nearly ten P.M. on the following evening when Pete
hecked into the city's most luxurious hotel, the Ritz on the
ran Via. Though her internal clock was still at five o'clock

in the afternoon, New York time, the journey had been tiring, and at the airport she had looked forward to settling into her room. Yet the lively atmosphere of Barcelona sparked her with renewed energy. On the ride from the airport through the sprawling port by the Mediterranean, she saw throngs of people strolling under the trees that lined the broad avenues, the lights of restaurants where the first dinner guests were just arriving.

At the hotel she was shown to the suite reserved for her by Antonio Scappa, an opulent living room and bedroom and a bath of Roman proportions complete with sunken marble tub. On a leather-topped console table in the living room stood a huge arrangement of yellow roses and white irises. Propped against the vase was a card from Scappa: *"I look forward to tomorrow morning."* He had told her they would have breakfast in the Ritz dining room at ten o'clock.

Taking in the lavish suite and the flowers, Pete realized that Scappa wouldn't be wooing her with expense-paid luxury if he had brought her across an ocean merely to provide information. He had a business proposition and wanted to soften her up. Probably he wanted to offer her a chance to become a house designer for Tesori, as Paloma and Elsa were for Tiffany.

Pete doubted that she could accept working for Scappa, though the reason was not, as in the past, because she preferred to remain independent. Thinking back over the previous weeks in which she had struggled to recapture the creative drive that had once come so easily, Pete simply didn't feel capable of delivering the stream of fresh ideas that such a job would require. If only Scappa had been willing to spell out what he had in mind on the phone, she could have saved him the expense—and herself the time—of the journey.

Now that she was here, however, she wondered if the answer to her loss of enthusiasm wasn't to strike out in a new direction. After all the time she'd given to honing her knowledge of gems, building her reputation, was she really ready to walk away from her career?

And was Luke ready to take the gift of an undivided heart if she offered it?

Seeking distraction from questions tumbling through her mind, Pete shook off her fatigue and left the hotel for a stroll through the city. In the hours just before midnight, Spaniards were just beginning their evening, sitting down to the pre-dinner delicacies in the *tapas* bars, women browsing open flower stalls, men—who seemed to take particular pride in their shoes—getting shines from the hundreds of *limpiabotas* who lined the sidewalks.

How much more she could have enjoyed the scene with Luke. But the dream of recovering what they had lost might prove to be only an empty fantasy if ever it was tested. Perhaps it was too late for them.

Though why should it be? If the Spanish could eat supper at midnight, then love could certainly be revived at any hour.

Wandering aimlessly, Pete found herself in front of a strange soaring structure with twin spires that looked like titanic inverted icicles. A plaque written for tourists in several languages identified the site as the Church of the Sagrada Familia. She remembered reading some years ago about its architect, Antonio Gaudi, whose genius expressed itself in the adaptation of such natural forms as waves, icicles, sta-actites, and stalagmites into this unfinished cathedral and some apartment houses in Catalonian metropolis. Pete spent a long time standing in the darkened plaza around the strange church, memorizing the images—the concrete snails and liz-ards crawling across the facade of seemingly molten stone, the tiled spires twisting into the night sky.

When she got back to her room at the hotel, she stayed up for several hours making the sketches for new pieces that had been inspired by Gaudi's architecture. She could see a new collection beginning to take shape.

As soon as she entered the Ritz restaurant, Pete spotted Antonio Scappa across the sea of starched white linen table-cloths. She recalled how angry he had looked the last time she'd seen him—leaving the auction after Andrea had outbid him for the Colomba necklace—a stark contrast to the broad welcoming smile that dressed his face when he saw the maître d' leading her to his table. Yes, he was all charm, angling

for something. But Pete was already half-decided that it wa
something she couldn't give. On arising this morning, she
had made reservations to fly home this afternoon, thinking
she must try to work things out with Luke.

Scappa stood to greet her. "My dear Signorina D'Angeli,
I cannot express how very glad I am that you agreed to
come." He put out his hand in the old-fashioned Continental
manner, palm upward. Pete placed hers in it, knowing he
would lift her hand to kiss it.

As he bent slightly and touched his lips to her skin, she
studied his face. Again, as she had when they'd met a few
years earlier in Geneva, she had the odd sensation of knowing
him from some other time and place, a sense that he had
played a part in her life that went far back. But she shrugged
it off as the meaningless mental illusion of *déjà vu*.

"You don't have to thank me for coming, Signor Scappa,"
Pete said as they took their seats. "I needed a break from
my routine. You're kind to provide it."

An eager waiter stood by to take their order before they
could continue the conversation. While Pete was content with
fruit and *cafe con leche*, she listened to Scappa ask for steak
and an omelet and an assortment of sweet rolls. He was
apparently a man with large appetites in everything—and an
iron constitution. He still looked surprisingly strong and no
older than his mid-fifties, though she knew he was older.
Pete guessed that Signor Scappa, a man of evident vanity,
must have invested in cosmetic surgery.

"Well, I've come a long way to find out what's on your
mind," she said as soon as the waiter had gone. "How long
will you keep me in suspense?"

"Long enough to bestow some well-earned praise,"
Scappa replied. "I've been watching your career for a number
of years, Miss D'Angeli. I regard you as the very best in
your specialized field of endeavor, and when I see the best
I'm always attracted to it. That's the reason I've done so well
in my business. I find the best locations for my stores, I hire
the best artisans and give them the best materials to make
my wares . . . and then I sell at the best price I can get. I
want the best of everything."

Pete nodded politely. There seemed no doubt now that Scappa was going to ask her to design exclusively for Tesori.

"I have plans," he went on, "for a bold new endeavor. But I don't believe I can make it succeed without some help. In fact, I don't think I can make it succeed unless I have *your* help. I want to join your unique talents to mine."

Though Pete smiled at Scappa's shameless flattery, it only made her wary. She could see as never before that he was an unsubtle man, plainly ready to do anything or say anything that advanced his own interests. Given her own desire for honesty, she imagined there might be terrible clashes between them.

"Signor Scappa," she said, "I appreciate your compliments. But my talents aren't unique. There are other designers who can create pieces that will attract as much business as mine would . . ."

Scappa nodded agreeably and leaned forward as though to impart a secret. "I don't want you to design for me, my dear Signorina D'Angeli."

Pete gazed at him in astonishment. "You don't? Then what—"

"I want you," Scappa said, "to be my partner."

Confounded, Pete sat back, regarding him dubiously. A man didn't build an enormously successful enterprise only to give half of it away.

"I don't mean in the entire chain," he continued, as if he had read her thoughts. "Just for a new phase of the business—something I wouldn't have thought of launching until it occurred to me that you were the perfect person to take charge."

"What is it?" she asked quickly, snared by curiosity.

"Another Tesori—the store I want to open next year in New York. It will be the grandest of them all, a worthy rival for those ancient weak sisters in our business—Cartier, Tiffany, Dufort. I intend to spare no expense to make Tesori the leader. And you are my choice to be in charge of the New York operation. If you agree, you will make every decision from this day on. You will pick the location, design the store, fill it with your ideas—and, if you have the time,

design the most exclusive and beautiful pieces on sale.
should add that, as an exquisitely beautiful woman yourself
you would be a natural promotional asset, an incomparable
showcase for what we are selling.''

For a second, Pete was bowled over. Scappa was offering
her the chance to go, in a single leap, from being involved
in one specialized phase of the jewelry business to having
complete authority over a high-profile outlet in one of the
primary fashion centers in the world. She would be a major
force, perhaps no less important than Claude Ivères had been
in his prime.

But she didn't understand exactly why he should want her
''It's an intriguing offer,'' she said, working to sound coo
and businesslike. ''But as you must know, Signor Scappa
I've had no experience in the selling end. Marketing, advertising, negotiating leases—none of that has played any par
in my work . . . while there are merchandisers who can do
that part of the business in their sleep. As far as promotion
you can hire models to wear your jewels. So why would you
want me?''

The question hung in the air while the waiter came and
laid out their orders. When he had gone, Scappa resumed.

''I told you I want the best. Does that include people who
have done something so many times that they can sleepwalk
through a job? Wasn't it your President Kennedy who said
never trust experts?'' Scappa filled his mouth with a portion
of his omelet, swallowed it down in a gulp, and continued
''It doesn't frighten me that you may have to learn some part
of the job. I can help you with that; we can hire others who
deal with nuts and bolts. What's most important, Signorina
D'Angeli, is that you clearly possess qualifications that car
not be learned, that must be inborn—taste, imagination,
daring—all devoted to bringing out your innate appreciation
of jewels. I see it in your work, Pietra, in the way you
settings bring out the beauty of the gems. It's as if . . . you
are making love to them.''

Though she had to suppress an urge to roll her eyes at
Scappa's corny exaggeration, she was not immune to the part
of his pitch that made sense. If he wanted someone to set a

unique tone for a bold new enterprise, there was some logic
in turning to a designer rather than a manager. It *was* flattering
to be chosen—if it was indeed true that she was his first
choice. Scappa was known to be a difficult man whose taste
sometimes catered to the low end of the market rather than
the highest. It was understandable that he might seek advice
to upgrade his operation, yet there were many people who
would turn down the opportunity.

Should she? Taking it on would mean veering sharply away
from the independent success she had achieved.

And it would mean making a full commitment to business,
rather than to the chance of recovering her relationship with
Luke Sanford. But had that been anything more than an idle
dream?

"Give me time to think it over," she responded at last.

"There is a limit to how much time I can wait," Scappa
said.

"Just a day," Pete said. There was no point in delaying
longer: The choices were clear.

"Very well," Scappa said. If there was one thing he had
always done well, he thought, it was to recognize the weak-
nesses of character as well as the strengths. Looking at Pietra
D'Angeli, this niece who was unaware of their kinship, he
could see that she was more than intrigued; she had an appetite
for challenge.

To sharpen that appetite, Antonio took Pete after breakfast
to have a look at his newest store on the Passeig de
Gracia—the reason he had chosen Barcelona for their meeting place. Pete could see at once that Scappa had selected
a prime location, a lovely wide boulevard overarched with
linden trees and lined with other luxury stores and crowded
sidewalk cafes. The store itself was a little modern and flamboyant for Pete's taste—too much rose-colored marble,
smoked glass, and shiny brass projecting none of the inbred
elegance of Dufort & Ivères—but there was no doubt that
Scappa hadn't spared the pesetas in making it truly *luxe*. If
she worked with him, she would probably not have to argue
over a budget, a fact worth knowing.

"Diamonds are here," he said as he led her through the

main floor. "Colored stones over there. In the back we have
a boutique with less expensive pieces—gold lockets and
chains, jade pendants, engraved money clips, belt buckles
and the like, the things that will bring people with less to
spend into the store. I know there are some jewelers who
would limit the amount of inexpensive merchandise they
carry. But I believe if we can please a young boy buying a
locket for his first sweetheart, he will come back in ten years
to buy a diamond for his bride, and ten years after that we'll
sell him rubies for his mistress."

Pete wouldn't have put it in such crass terms, but she
endorsed the idea of a store that did not lock out everyone
but the super rich.

Scappa guided her on through the fine silver and gold
department, the section where antiquarian pieces would be
sold, the private salons.

"*É bellissima, eh?*" he remarked proudly when the tour
was complete.

Pete smiled, and replied in the language he seemed to have
unconsciously slipped into. "*Ma forse non bella come l'uno
qual' giorno a New York.*" While she had yet to take on the
job, she wasn't beyond teasing Scappa with fantasies of what
she might someday create for him.

At her response, Scappa was momentarily silent. Then he
said quietly, "Your Italian is admirable, Signorina. Where
did you learn?"

"My father is Italian, from Milano."

"Of course—with your name I should have realized. Milano, I hear, is a most beautiful city. Unfortunately, I have
never been able to spend much time there."

"A natural place to put one of your stores," Pete remarked.

Scappa nodded slowly.

Pete noticed that her host appeared suddenly distracted.
Though his eyes were on her, his mind seemed to be
elsewhere—as if, perhaps, from the corner of his eye he had
spotted something suspicious or dangerous happening in his
domain—a shoplifter, a customer who might actually be a
jewel thief casing a robbery. Pete looked around but saw
nothing out of the ordinary.

And then Scappa abruptly recovered his ebullience. "Well, there are a great many wonderful sights to see in Barcelona. While you consider your decision, why don't I escort you . . . ?"

"No, thank you, Signor Scappa. If I'm going to decide quickly, I think I ought to fly home." It was only there, Pete thought, that she could be in touch with all the deciding factors.

Scappa accompanied her obligingly to the hotel while Pete collected her bag, then rode with her to the airport in his rented limousine. Though Pete told him he needn't wait until she boarded, Scappa remained attentive and solicitous, buying her coffee in an airport cafeteria.

As they waited for the flight announcement, he asked about her personal life, her family, even her father. Pete took his curiosity as evidence of a softer side to his character, and she moderated her opinion of how difficult it might be for them to work together.

When the announcement came that the flight was boarding, he walked with her to the gate.

"One more thing, Signore," Pete said just before she went through. "It's about your daughter . . ."

Scappa stiffened. "Signorina, I'd rather not discuss—"

"Hear me out, please. I'm not Andrea's friend, frankly, but I admire her ability. I know you've been estranged, but this is an obvious opportunity to patch it up. Andrea knows the New York market, and she's had experience in exactly the areas where I'm an amateur. Has it occurred to you to offer her the job? I wouldn't want to be in the middle when there's a chance of bringing you back together."

An impulsive answer almost rose to Scappa's lips, a damning refusal to deal with his daughter. But then he forced an agreeable smile. If he had not already perceived that Pietra D'Angeli was a young woman of exceptional decency and integrity, her question left no doubt. It was best, he decided, to smooth over her concerns without further arousing sympathies for Andrea.

"I've tried several times to effect a reconciliation with my daughter," he lied. "She has ignored my overtures." He opened his hands, miming helpless surrender. "Furthermore, I don't want to be seen as driving a wedge between her and the man she loves . . ."

Pete nodded. Probably there was no way that Andrea could go back to work for her father without ending her personal relationship with Marcel.

She shook hands with Antonio Scappa. "I'll call you tomorrow with my decision, Signore. *Arrivederci.*"

He seemed unaware of the cordial gesture intended by her use of Italian. "Farewell, Miss D'Angeli," he said.

Watching her walk away, Scappa made a bet with himself about the decision Pietra D'Angeli would make. As he crossed the terminal to arrange for his own return to Geneva, he congratulated himself on all that he had accomplished at one stroke. By employing Pietra in a time-consuming effort, he could lead her away from continuing the search for La Colomba's jewels. Even if she did go on probing, it would be easier for him to know her activities and get an early warning. Beyond protecting himself, furthermore, he felt confident that he had made a shrewd business decision. He had not been idly flattering Pietra D'Angeli when he made his pitch; he believed she was uniquely qualified to help Tesori –New York succeed.

What a joke that would be on his poor foolish brother, thought Antonio. Already Stefano had "given" so much to enrich him; now Stefano's daughter would be helping to make him even richer. *Meraviglioso!* Antonio Scappa couldn't help laughing out loud. For good measure, the whole delicious venture would no doubt make his worthless daughter green with envy.

Gazing down at the cottony sea of clouds below, Pete mused on her predicament. Up in the air—that's exactly what she was. The more she mulled Scappa's offer, the more she thought the job had come at just the right moment in her life. It would mean learning some new ropes, but she knew the jewelry business—knew what the customers wanted. And Scappa was a shrewd, tough man, hungry for a crowning

uccess. If he was ready to take a chance on her, she ought
o be ready to take a chance on herself.

But what about taking a chance on Luke? Suppose she
ent to him now . . . and the spark was still there for both
f them. Suppose they could make a life together. Would she
hoose being with him over everything else, *instead* of every-
ing else?

Not yet. The prospect of testing herself in a new arena was
o exciting.

But was Luke ready, perhaps, to adjust his life to fit into
ers? Having been critical of her for designing to please the
ealthy few, would he be any more tolerant of her desire to
un a store that catered to them?

Never. Luke's distaste for her career had not come from
ld-fashioned male chauvinism. It had been a matter of prin-
iple, of his ingrained reaction against her devotion to some-
hing that existed mainly to delight the wealthy. She could
ot fight that, Pete realized. For better or worse, Luke's
rinciples—his dislike of hypocrisy and idleness and his de-
ermination to be of use to society—were a part of him, a
art of what she had loved.

If they were ever to be together again, it could only be
ecause they were ready, in their own time, to accept each
ther fully. Love would have to be a victory for both, not a
urrender of either one.

To speak to Luke before she made her decision about
esori, Pete decided, made no sense. She was not asking
ermission, not offering a sacrifice. She was following a
ream that had been set with her heart even before she had
et Luke, being guided by a destiny that was as much La
olomba's as it was her own.

Chapter 5

In the extensive reading she had done about jewels over the years, Pete had come across a story about a Turkish pasha afflicted with insomnia who had been able to lull himself to sleep only by dipping his hand in a bucketful of cabochon emeralds at his bedside, and running his fingers through the softly rounded gems. It was not an apocryphal tale from *The Arabian Nights*: The bucket with its priceless contents stood today in Topkapi, the museum in Istanbul that had once been the palace of the Ottoman sultans.

As Pete considered the approach she wanted to apply to the new store, the story of the emeralds supplied the inspiration. The essential appeal of jewels, she realized, was in the fantasies they conjured—as the coveted adornment of queens and kings, the most magical objects evolved from the substances of the earth, the most highly valued material expression of a man's passionate desire for a woman, and even the eccentric means to calm the nerves of an all-powerful man. At Tesori, Pete decided, fantasy would be emphasized. She would create a jewelry store where even a golden bucket of emeralds could be sold.

After meeting with several architects, she settled on

young man named Brent Lowell to design the store. Nine years out of the Yale School of Architecture, Lowell had already made his name in the specialized area of store design. An attractive, athletic-looking man with dark brown eyes and pale blond hair, he was a native of Kansas and a workaholic with no life other than his work. He and Pete cooperated well together, without any conflict of egos. He worked hard to achieve the concepts she outlined—to create an atmosphere that would combine elements of, as she put it, "a temple, a library for a sophisticate, and the boudoir of a great courtesan." The latter notion had, of course, not been incidental. From hearing her father speak about his one unforgettable night in the presence of La Colomba and her jewels, Pete conceived the idea of recreating something of the atmosphere that had cast such a lifelong enchantment. She began drawing her father out more on the details of her grandmother's villa, incorporating some of them into the ambience of the store design.

As plans were made, Pete was delighted to discover that Antonio Scappa interfered in nothing. He provided the money to pay all the bills and called every month to ask about progress. But, once assured that Pete was devoting herself to business, he left her alone. He even ignored Pete's urgings to fly to New York for the week of special previews before the opening.

Thus, a year to the day after she had flown to Barcelona, when Tesori–New York finally opened its doors on a corner of Fifth Avenue only three blocks from Dufort & Ivères, it fulfilled a vision that was exclusively Pete's. The walls were a combination of fine wood paneling, tapestries, still-life paintings, and sconces where candles flickered. Instead of carpet or polished marble for the floor, Pete had chosen a paving of unfinished black granite—a suggestion of a cathedral rather than a palace—in which naturally ingrained mica gave off a fine sparkle from the overhead lighting. Scattered around the interior space were display cases she had designed with Lowell's help—not mere transparent rectangular boxes, but each one constructed so that dozens of shelves were set behind faceted glass, making each case resemble an enormous

gem or, with non-symmetrical metal structure, a huge abstrac
suggesting a bracelet or ring.

Unlike other jewelry stores, where everything was strictly
departmentalized, at Tesori the full range of available item
was distributed throughout, creating a sense that visitors were
not merely entering a store, but a vast hideaway of treasure
accumulated by a king . . . or a pirate. To eliminate con
fusion, the Tesori sales staff, distinct in silver-gray suits with
midnight blue shirts, roamed the floor, ready to lead potentia
customers to whatever item they were seeking.

Finally, Tesori was filled with a variety of offerings tha
accentuated the aura of fantasy attached to jewels. The bucke
of emeralds was one, displayed in its own case, labeled with
a sign that whimsically identified it as an ''insomnia cure'
—and explained why—beside a silver engraved price tag
indicating ''$999,999.99.'' There were a dozen other such
''follies'' on sale, all equally frivolous, equally expensive
and derived from other fabled uses for jewels. A large dia
mond on a platinum stand was to be used for making wishe
and foreseeing the future, as it had been by ancient India
rajahs. A sapphire-studded ivory wand was explained as hav
ing powers to cure any ailment, the use to which its prototype
had been put by Viking warriors. A golden crown set with
a single large pigeon-blood ruby was presented as endowing
its wearer with infallible wisdom in all matters, a concei
based on the lore of Persian kings. To display these and othe
treasures required substantial additional security measures
but Pete never doubted it would be justified by the volume
of store traffic they would create.

Her expectations were surpassed. From the day of its open
ing, Tesori drew crowds. Of course, only a minority wer
buyers. But even wealthy prospects who ordinarily favore
the discreet, stolid environment of the old-fashioned jeweler
were drawn in by curiosity . . . only to find their sense o
fantasy awakened by the atmosphere and their appetites ex
cited by the designs and settings of the more practical offer
ings.

Tesori did not dislodge either Cartier or Dufort & Ivère

s the first choice of dowagers, but Pete had always known
hat would be a lost battle. The clientele she wanted, and
von, was the more daring and adventurous, the people in-
erested in something slightly newer and offbeat—the gen-
rations of today and tomorrow, not of yesterday.

They came . . . and they bought. In its first month of
operation, Tesori–New York had the highest rate of sales
ncome per square foot of any jeweler in the world. A bil-
ionaire real estate developer who was an insomniac even
ought the bucket of emeralds—and wrote Pete later to say
hat it worked!

On the last Saturday afternoon in September more than a
ear after the store's opening, Pete and Brent Lowell strolled
ack to the store from a lunch they'd had around the corner
t La Côte Basque. In the first sixteen months of operation,
raffic in and out of Tesori had become so unexpectedly large
hat there was often congestion around the entrance, and Pete
vanted to install another set of doors. The conversation at
anch had focused on the design problem, but there had been
few pleasant detours into personal matters.

During the intense period of design and construction, when
hey had often found themselves working late, discussing fine
oints of the building plans over a midnight sandwich, Pete
nd the architect had drifted into a romance of convenience.
n retrospect, it was obvious to Pete that, at a time when she
vas too busy to reestablish the connection with Luke Sanford,
passing affair was the most effective way to stop his ghost
om haunting her heart. It had continued for a time after the
tore opened, but as Lowell got caught up in other jobs their
ffair had ended with neither of them bitter or disappointed.
ete and the architect remained friends—she had even told
im about Luke—and she had called on him without hesi-
ation to discuss other design matters. When she purchased
cooperative penthouse apartment, lower down on Fifth Av-
nue, nearer the store, he designed and supervised a stunning
novation. Now she relied on Lowell to make the design
djustment in Tesori's bottleneck entrance. At lunch, he made

one or two passing remarks that indicated he might like to revive their liaison, but she ignored them and he seemed to have gotten the message and accepted it.

Arriving near the store, they stood off to one side, watching the flow of people. As they discussed different possibilities for handling it more efficiently, Pete caught sight of two familiar faces among the ingoing customers. Andrea and Marcel.

She hadn't had any contact with either of them during the time Tesori had been in the planning stages, nor had they attended any of the previews of the store arranged for the press, fashion notables, and colleagues in the jewelry business. Pete had taken no offense. Given the situation between Antonio and his daughter, Pete could understand that Andrea would feel an undying resentment toward her for taking the job and might never want to set foot in Tesori. As for Marcel, he certainly wouldn't want to show any kind of interest that might fan the flames of Andrea's jealousy. He had finally acknowledged her importance to Dufort & Ivères by making her president of the firm, and kicking himself up to the position of chairman.

Whatever their reasons for staying away in the past, it was apparent that their curiosity had finally become uncontrollable. Here they were, sneaking in with the crowds—incognito, as it were. Pete smiled to herself with satisfaction.

"Brent, I should get back inside," she said, and gave the architect a kiss on the cheek. "Try to get to those drawings in the next week. I'm available as soon as they're ready."

"Not as available as I'd like," he said as Pete started away.

"Hey," she stopped to reply, "let's not muddy the water again. We had something very nice together, but if it had any more substance than a soap bubble, it wouldn't have popped so easily the moment we came down to earth. I'll settle for the memories—and if that's going to make it hard for you to work with me, then I can get someone else."

"Not necessary, Pete. I just thought . . . if you'd managed to snuff out that other flame you've been carrying . . . well, we could keep each other company."

She smiled. "I like your company, Brent. I'm ready for more of it anytime—over a lunch table or a drawing table."

He nodded and gave her a little salute as they parted.

Inside, Pete scanned until she spotted Andrea and Marcel browsing, their heads together as they made comments on the wares and the decor. As she observed their intimacy, she felt a slight stab of envy at the way they had surmounted so many obstacles to survive as a couple.

Pete walked over. "Let me hear it," she said to announce herself. "It's too late to change, but I might learn something for next time."

They turned to her with expressions that seemed genuinely welcoming. "Don't change a thing, Pete," Andrea said. "But you don't need us to tell you it's fabulous. Your sales figures do that."

"And would Claude approve?" Pete asked, with a twinkling glance at Marcel.

"Probably not," Marcel said, "though I can't say for sure. But if *cher Papa* were alive now, probably I would discover that he was not always right about the business."

"Not *all* of us can be," Andrea said teasingly.

Pete noticed that Andrea's brassy ostentatious style had moderated to something much softer. Her hair was toned down and worn longer, her suit was a classic red Valentino rather than mix-and-match pieces worn to dazzle. Having achieved the recognition that in the past she'd had to claw to get, perhaps she no longer had to be a tigress.

"I'm sorry you didn't get here a lot sooner," Pete said amiably. "Even if we're competitors, I think we can still keep up an acquaintance."

"But we've been here many times," Marcel said. "You've missed us in the crowds, no doubt, but we stroll through often to see what you're doing with display and selection."

"When we steal ideas," Andrea said, "we want to steal from the best."

Without being too mawkish about it, Andrea clearly meant to bestow a compliment. There was an opening, Pete felt, to put all the hostilities behind them. She hesitated a second,

reluctant to say anything that might open old wounds. Ye
there were aspects of this tough but shrewd Swiss woma
that Pete had always admired, and she was intrigued by th
possibility of friendship.

"You know," Pete said, "before I accepted this job from
Antonio, I told him he ought to be offering it to you . . ."

"Oh?" Andrea responded with a wry lilt. "And what di
my dear father say?"

Pete looked between her and Marcel. "That he didn't wan
to come between you two."

Andrea tossed her head back and laughed. "The old bas
tard. As if that would have stopped him."

"Well, I think he was more discouraged by the fact tha
you didn't seem interested in working for him."

"Didn't seem—" Andrea appeared suddenly puzzled, al
most stunned. "I would have loved to have had the chanc
to do what you did," she said. "I don't resent you for it
Pete. But I wouldn't have minded at all—"

"He told me he'd made overtures and you ignored them.'

Andrea was silent a moment. She looked more vulnerabl
than at any time since Pete had met her. "He never tried t
talk to me," she said quietly, "probably never will. If I knov
my father, Pete, he took a special delight in giving the jol
to someone else, and in knowing I'd see this store create
practically before my eyes, an opportunity that might hav
been mine." Abruptly, she clamped her mouth shut, refusin
to reveal any more of her hurt and disappointment.

Pete shook her head sympathetically. "If I'd known—"

"Then it's best you didn't," Andrea said, recovering he
bright, confident tone. "Because I don't think I'd have don
this as well as you have." She slipped her arm through Mar
cel's. "And I might have walked away from something much
better—where I still have a chance for advancement."

Marcel looked at her with a show of feigned alarm. "Ol
no, *petite*, you're not thinking now of forcing me out of th
business altogether!"

"You know what I mean," Andrea said very softly
Though it was obviously a private joke.

They left and Pete went to her office. She sat awhile think

ng about the lie Scappa had told when offering her the job. Would it have made any difference if she'd known that Andrea was never considered? To be honest, Pete admitted to herself, probably not. If the rift between father and daughter was irreparable, she neither had to blame herself nor pay any penalty for it.

Yet it disturbed her that Scappa had not been honest and open with her. So far she had noticed no irregularities in their business dealings; in view of the fact that they were equal partners in the store, he had been surprisingly unmeddlesome. But knowing about his lie damaged the trust Pete had felt until now. She would have to be careful with Antonio Scappa, Pete thought. There could be other lies she didn't know about . . and lies yet to be told.

On a rainy Tuesday morning two weeks later, while Pete was on the phone in her office, Jess barged in, her hair straggly and her clothes dripping wet. Lottie, who had been elevated to the position of Executive Assistant, still occupied a desk guarding Pete's door and knew that Jess was one of the few people to whom her boss was always available.

From a quick look across her desk, Pete could see that Jess was excited rather than frantically upset, so she spent a minute to wind up her conversation with a travel agent. She had recently decided that, like the great jewelers of the past, she might try to select stones at the source, rather than dealing with wholesalers. Accordingly, she was planning to fly to the Far East in a few weeks to visit sapphire mines in Burma and Ceylon, the ruby mines at Chanthaburi in Thailand, and the opal mines at Coober Pedy in Australia.

The instant she said good-bye to the travel agent, Jess erupted. "Guess what!"

Pete studied the glowing expression on Jess's face and realized she knew exactly what news Jess must have run to tell her. But she didn't want to spoil the pleasure of Jess saying it. "You hit the Lotto . . . you're a finalist for Miss America . . . Fernando won the America's Cup . . ."

"Wrong, wrong, wrong again," Jess declared, laughing. "I give up."

"I'm pregnant!"

Exactly as Pete had guessed. Jumping up to run aroun'
the desk, she hugged Jess tightly. "I'm thrilled for you. How
did Fernando take it?"

"He doesn't know yet. I ran straight here from my doctor'
office at Sixty-third and Fifth." Jess paused. "Nando wi'
be glad, though. He's got to be, doesn't he?"

Pete thought the question had a plaintive tone, as if Jes
was worried. "Of course, he'll be glad," she assured Jess
"But not because it's an obligation. He'll be glad becaus'
he loves you, and he'll love a child that comes from both o'
you."

Jess nodded, but she had become subdued. Pete suspecte'
that there had been no discussion between Jess and her hus
band about having a child, no plans made. "Don't wait t'
tell him," Pete urged. "Let him share the excitement. Some
times it takes men a little while longer to get used to what i
means, the changes . . . but he'll come around."

The smile started to creep back into Jess's expression. "I
doesn't have to change anything, does it? That's all Fernand'
cares about—that nothing will change."

"I wouldn't promise him that," Pete advised lightly. "Bu
let him know the changes will be good ones."

Jess seemed excited again as they made plans to have lunc'
in the next few days, and then she left Pete's office to fin'
Fernando and break the news.

As she left, Lottie entered. "I hope you don't mind that
let her break in," she said as she dropped the morning mai'
on Pete's desk, already opened and sorted.

"Have I ever? And there's no way you could have mad'
her wait outside today. She just learned she's having a baby.'

"How wonderful!" Lottie said. "And while you're in th'
mood for surprises, have a look at this." She reached int'
the stack of mail and extracted a thick, fancy vellum envelope
which she handed to Pete.

From inside, Pete withdrew the engraved wedding invi
tation announcing that Andrea Scappa would be married t'
Marcel Ivères at the groom's family château in the Loir'
Valley on an October Sunday three weeks hence.

Pete also found a few words scribbled in ink on a separate card. "Please come. He's told me how you sent him back to me. And if it's not too late for us to be married, then it's not too late for you and me to be friends. A."

Of course, she would go. In fact, she could arrange her travel plans to fly on to Asia directly from France.

Pete smiled as she sat down again at her desk. She understood now what the private joke had been: This was Andrea's "chance for advancement."

Suddenly a wave of melancholy passed through her. Jess would be having her baby. Andrea would have confirmed her claim to Marcel. Pete was happy for them.

Yet she could not help feeling her own emptiness as the mirror of their fulfillment. All she could look forward to was being alone on a journey to find gems—so gloriously beautiful, yet lifeless.

Chapter 6

The French certainly do know how to put on a show, Pet
thought as she watched the crowd spilling through the ground
of the Château d'Ivères in the Loire Valley not far from Tours
The family of Marcel Ivères might occupy only a very minc
niche in a deposed aristocracy, nevertheless he had manage
to garner a respectable number of dukes, barons, and counts
some related by blood or marriage, many others his custom
ers. Add dozens of members of the worldwide jewelry com
munity, toss in large numbers of family, friends, an
colleagues down from Paris and across the sea from Nev
York, and spice the mix with the entire population of th
little village of Sanpeur, where the chalet was located, an
you had the makings of a very lively party indeed.

Such was the wedding of Marcel Claude Christophe Ivère
to Andrea Giulietta Scappa on October 12, 1988.

Drama and whimsy were the keynote of the day. For thi
day at least, Andrea had reverted to her old revolutionar
style. Not for her the usual virginal white miles of silk an
lace. Instead, she wore a long, slender tube of cerise satin
cinched at the waist, bustled and pouffed, with leg-o-mutto
sleeves and showing enough cleavage to accentuate the rub

nd diamond pendant Marcel had bought her as a wedding
ift. Her hair was teased and fluffed into a mound of gold
'ina Turner would have been proud to claim, topped with a
ot of pink and red feathers attached to a wisp of veil so tiny
was clearly a parody of the usual bridal finery.

Pete thought she looked absolutely smashing.

Following French law, the happy couple was first married
a civil ceremony in the village hall. The mayor, intoning
e formal words of the Napoleonic Code with great solemnity
nd looking every bit the part in his red, white, and blue
ash, pronounced them man and wife. The couple then re-
aired back to the château in an *attelage*, an open carriage,
rough the seventeenth-century gatehouse dripping with
limbing roses and up the long gravel drive past rows of
najestic chestnut trees to the château's private chapel for the
eligious ceremony.

As much as possible, Pete had avoided weddings since Jess
nd Fernando's. Whenever she saw a bride and groom, Pete
ouldn't help remembering that awful argument with Luke,
e night her hopes for a future with him had died.

Yet she was glad to be here at the Château d'Ivères. Rather
nan solemn or somber, this wedding was clearly meant to
e *fun*.

The assembled company gathered on the lawns and under
striped marquee where a hundred-meter-long table groaned
nder what seemed to Pete like every cold delicacy known
› Frenchmen plus light, fresh sparkling wine from Marcel's
wn vineyards.

Pete, who knew only a few people there, watched the
pectacle as she roamed about the lawns, along the paths of
he rose garden, between the hedges of the herb garden.
Iundreds of hands and acres of colored silken skirts fluttered
n the soft autumn air, and the Babel of half a dozen languages
nixed in a linguistic stew.

As she lingered not far from the tent where dancing had
ust begun, Pete saw René Vaugillande, the man who had
een unable to help her—or who had chosen not to help
er—at Drouot in Paris. She made straight for him. She had
› try one more time.

"Monsieur Vaugillande, how nice to see you again," sh
said, intercepting him as he headed toward one of the bar
where champagne was being poured like tap water. Pete wa
doubly thankful that she'd stopped in Paris on the way to th
wedding and bought the wide-shouldered jade green wra
dress with its kicky skirt and the huge flowered-challis shaw
from St. Laurent. With her coal black hair caught up by gol
ruby-set combs, she knew she was a show-stopper. She gav
the Frenchman a megawatt smile. He responded with a courtl
bow but frowned slightly, obviously not all that pleased t
see her.

"I'm so glad to have another chance to talk to you," Pet
went on. "That afternoon a couple of years ago in your office
I'm afraid we were both, well, a bit distracted."

"Were we? I don't recall."

"Yes, otherwise I'm sure I would have been able to mak
you understand how important my request was."

"Mademoiselle D'Angeli, you've had my letters. Yo
know my position. Now, please. We are here to celebrate—"

Pete persisted. "Did I tell you, Monsieur, that the sapphir
necklace Mrs. Fisk Haines bought from you once belonge
to my grandmother? For personal reasons, which cannot pos
sibly hurt Drouot, I must find out who sold it to her."

"Mademoiselle D'Angeli," he said, his voice stern, "a
I told you, I *have* contacted the gentleman in question, an
he doesn't wish his name to be made public. Now, we ar
here to honor our friends on their wedding day and to en
joy ourselves, not to conduct business. If you should lik
to dance, I would be honored; if not . . ." He held out
hand.

Suddenly she lost her patience. "Why are you stonewallin
me, Monsieur Vaugillande?"

"Stonewalling? I don't understand—"

A deep voice from behind her cut in. "An American idiom
It means refusing to help and refusing to admit you won't."

Pete spun around to see a Japanese man in his mid-fortie
leaning against the bar with a glass of Scotch in his hand
She thought he must look out of place in Tokyo because h
was tall, at least six feet, with broad shoulders, a narrow

aist and hips, long slender legs. His tailored suit appeared
o be Savile Row, his English echoed vaguely of Oxford, and
is smile seemed American in its warmth. The aura of power
nd self-confidence about him was palpable.

"Mr. Kiyosaki!" said Vaugillande, his voice filled with
n oily warmth, "I did not know you would be here today."

"Marcel Ivères is a good friend as well as a good cus-
omer."

"But of course," said Vaugillande. "As for the lady . . ."
Ie turned to Pete.

The Japanese cut him off by offering his hand. "Hiroshi
Kiyosaki," he introduced himself.

She shook his hand. The name had registered. "The Pearl
rince," she said. "I've heard of you. I'm—"

"Pietra D'Angeli. I've done more than hear of *you*, I've
een your picture . . . and I have long admired your work."
Ie turned back to Vaugillande. "Really, Monsieur Vaugil-
ande, I always thought Frenchmen were supposed to be gal-
ant, but I couldn't help overhearing that you've been churlish
nd disagreeable to this most beautiful woman."

"I certainly did not mean to offend the lady. I merely told
er—"

"I know what you told her." The tall Japanese turned back
o Pete, taking her in from top to toe and obviously admiring
he view. "This information you are seeking, it seems to be
xtremely important to you . . ."

"Vital," Pete confirmed.

He stared a moment more, nodded slightly, then turned
ack to the Frenchman. "Vaugillande, about those Renais-
ance pieces I'm considering selling . . ."

The Frenchman's eyes lit up. "We are very anxious to
andle the sale for you, Mr. Kiyosaki. I can assure you Drouot
vill get you the best possible prices."

"I've just been talking to Richardson, from Christie's.
They have made a rather attractive offer."

"We'll better it," Vaugillande said quickly.

"And if my price is that you assist Miss D'Angeli in finding
ut what she needs to know?"

Vaugillande paused. "We have promised the gentleman in

question confidentiality, Monsieur, something we conside
sacred.''

Kiyosaki sipped his Scotch. "Perhaps the gentleman i
question could be persuaded.''

Kiyosaki had not once raised his voice or even lifted a
eyebrow, but Pete felt the presence of nicely sheathed claw
behind his words. And when the Frenchman bowed slightl
in acquiescence, she knew she was right.

"Perhaps so. I will see what I can do, Mr. Kiyosaki.''

"I shall be most appreciative. And since you will be bus
with that, Vaugillande, we will put off discussion of th
Renaissance sale until this other business is behind you. Yo
will let me know . . .''

There was a tone of dismissal in Kiyosaki's words that wa
not lost on the Frenchman. "Of course, Monsieur," he sai
curtly. With a terse ''*au revoir*'' to Pete, Vaugillande walke
away.

Kiyosaki turned to Pete. "My guess is that you will hav
the information you desire in a week, two at most.''

"That was marvelous," she said. "How can I thank you?'

"You can dance with me, Miss D'Angeli.'' A smile o
immense charm spread across his handsome face the colo
of polished maplewood.

"I would be delighted, Mr. Kiyosaki.''

"Hiro, please.''

"Pete," she said and took his hand.

An outdoor parquet floor had been laid down by a lon
reflecting pool. As they glided across the mirror-smooth sur
face to the accompaniment of one of Charles Aznavour's slow
ballads, Pete was able to closely examine Kiyosaki's face
eyes so dark they were almost a match for his silky midnigh
black hair, high cheekbones, a strong square jaw.

She reflected on what she had read or heard about the ma
known as the Pearl Prince. As a scrambling teenager in Tokyo
fifteen years after war's end, he had begun by gathering scra
and bartering it for increasing gain. In an economy just be
ginning to come into its own after total devastation, items o
pragmatic use were most appreciated, so pearls were stil

ndervalued. However, Kiyosaki made them the ultimate tar-
et of his trades. After acquiring a large stock, he opened a
mall pearl concession in the lobby of a less-than-luxurious
'okyo hotel. Soon he opened others in better hotels. As Japan
ecovered and there began to be larger amounts of disposable
ncome for jewelry, his success gathered momentum, and he
ecame not only a seller but a supplier. Today, he was one
f the world's two most important dealers in cultured pearls.

"It's a shame we haven't met before," Kiyosaki said as
e maneuvered her effortlessly around the dance floor.

"I've bought your pearls for my store through your Amer-
:an dealers," Pete said. "But I'd heard the Prince himself
vas more involved with making his pearls than selling them."

"But as a designer you could have come to me directly—
o choose the ones that best suited your ideas."

"I don't use many pearls in my designs."

"Then that is something we must change. Perhaps I could
how you some of my best goods. They might inspire you."

"I'm sure they would," she said.

He was a confident dancer, and Pete enjoyed the feeling
f being led so effortlessly. As they circled the floor, Pete
earned some facts to add to his official biography. He had
een born the son of a noodle maker who had died when he
'as a boy, he lived alone, spending most of his time between
'okyo and an island where he raised his pearls; he loved to
avel, and—he added mischievously with a broad gleaming
mile—all his teeth were his own.

As he spun her around and she looked up at him, Pete
ouldn't help thinking how different he was from the image
he'd always had of his countrymen. Even the way he spoke,
'hich was not clipped and had only a faint accent.

He caught her appraising glance. "You are thinking," he
aid, "that I am not what you expect in a Japanese man."

Pete's eyes widened. "You're a mind-reader," she said.
'That's exactly what I was thinking."

Hiro laughed softly. "It's what every woman thinks when
he meets me," he replied. "Even the Japanese women."

Pete thought she detected a slightly disappointed edge to

his remark, as though that judgment of him made him fee
somewhat of an outcast. "Do you mind being different?"
she asked.

"Perhaps I did once. As a child I wanted, like all children
to be the same as everyone else. But it wasn't my fate. My
mother explained that it was because there was *gaijin* blood
in her family from a few generations back—one of Admiral
Peary's sailors, she always said. Eventually, I realized it was
an advantage to be different, and I came to value the rare
and different in all things. It's the reason I'm attracted to
pearls, the only jewel made by a living thing." His onyx
eyes glinted at Pete. "It's the reason that I could dance with
you all night."

His frank admission of attraction left Pete wordless. But
she was not annoyed, nor did she pull away as they danced.
She kept following as he spun her deftly across the floor.

The orchestra took a break, and he stayed beside her. As
they talked on, twilight began to fall across the chateau gar
dens.

"Tell me about this necklace you've been trying to get
Vaugillande to help you trace."

As she told him the whole story, describing La Colomba's
perfume bottle in detail and outlining her frustrating search
for the stolen jewel collection, he asked intelligent questions
and seemed genuinely interested in everything she said. She
found him easy to talk to.

"The use of the baroque pearl for the shoulders of the
figure sounds wonderful," he said. "Have you seen the Can
ning jewel?"

Pete knew he was referring to an exquisite jeweled figure
of a mythic Triton—half man, half fish—that belonged to
London's Victoria and Albert Museum. She had seen it once
on a buying trip.

"It's very much like that," she agreed, "even though my
grandmother's perfume bottle was made four centuries later.
I wish you could see it. It's a glorious piece of work. In fact
it was the perfume bottle that really inspired me to become
a jewelry designer."

"Then the rest of us should be thankful that this larcenous

ncle did not get away with *everything*. The world would be
a much poorer place without your beautiful designs. In fact,
think with your flair and taste, you and I could be very good
or each other. You could do wonderful things with my treasures. Pearls are the most sensuous of gems, you know.''

She smiled. His flirting was getting bolder, but still Pete
didn't mind. He really was a charming man and extraordi-
narily good looking.

''I must give pearls more thought,'' she said.

He hesitated a moment, holding her gaze with his intense
black eyes. ''I'm flying back to Tokyo in the morning. Why
don't you come with me? To see some of my stock and discuss
it further. I have a private jet. We could fly out together in
the morning.''

Disappointment flooded her. She would have loved to
spend more time with this dynamic and fascinating man. ''I'm
afraid I'm going to Thailand tomorrow, to Chanthaburi. I'm
buying rubies for my store.''

''I see. I am sorry. Another time then.'' He gave her a
smile that told her he'd be sure there was another time.

A loud crack sounded, and Pete jumped. It was dark now
and the fireworks had begun, lighting up the sky like a jewel
box full of colored gems exploding onto black velvet. Rubies
and emeralds and sapphires shot across the sky; tourmalines
and topazes, amethysts and aquamarines sparkled against the
blackness. A chain of diamonds came apart and drifted to
earth. More gems were hurled into the sky, trailing gold and
silver streamers as they fell.

Pete had always loved fireworks with a childish delight,
and as the explosions sounded and the colors sprayed down,
she found herself clutching Hiro's arm in her excitement. He
was smiling down at her when the last sparks fizzled to the
ground.

The wedding was over. Marcel, dashing in tweed, and
Andrea, looking cheeky in a short black leather skirt and
striped Apache sweater with a beret on her blond hair, climbed
into his Jaguar and roared away from the château in a cloud
of flying gravel. Just before they peeled off, Andrea picked
up her bouquet of vivid red blooms, scanned the crowd till

she found Pete, and threw it right at her. Pete had to catch
it in her hands or she would have caught it right on the nose.

Hiro walked Pete to her rental car, opened the door for her
and took her hand.

"There *will* be another time," he said. "My pearls demand
it."

The heat in Bangkok was blistering. It was, after all, about
places in Asia like Bangkok that Noël Coward wrote, "Mad
dogs and Englishmen sit out in the noonday sun." But Pete
wasn't about to stay in her air-conditioned room at the Oriental, the century-old hotel that had sheltered Joseph Conrad
and Somerset Maugham. She donned her lightest, thinnest
cotton shirt, khaki pants, and a broad-brimmed straw hat and
plunged into the vertical sunlight.

Though she had come to Thailand because it was the center
of today's ruby trade, Pete's appointment with a ruby dealer
in the Siam Center wasn't until after lunch, so she was free
meanwhile to wander the teeming streets. She felt an immediate affinity for this place with the name that means "City
of the Angels." Like D'Angeli. But if it really was their city,
the angels had a sense of humor. They'd filled it so densely
with color and sound, smell and movement that Pete hardly
knew where to look first.

Gaily painted and noisy three-wheeled *tuk-tuks* whisked
passengers through the snarled traffic, wending their way past
an overladen elephant and a water buffalo. Saffron-robed
monks and women in acid-colored silks swayed by. Burning
charcoal and smoldering incense mixed their heavy smells
with the scent of piles of fresh-cut orchids, cut-open tanger-
ines, and diesel buses. Horns honked and street vendors cried
their wares, almost but not quite overpowering the delicate
tinkle of wind chimes and the sing-song language of the
people in the streets.

She visited Wat Phra Keo, the Temple of the Emerald
Buddha. She stared into the vivid green of the giant carved
god, soaking up its peace for nearly an hour. Then, after a
mouth-searing lunch of chicken-in-coconut soup, curried cat-
fish, and mangosteens, she walked past a McDonald's and

hailed a taxi with a woven lotus flower necklace suspended from its mirror.

The gem dealer's office was blessedly icy with air conditioning. He laid a tray of unset rubies in front of her. She took them to a table by the window, where natural light streamed in, and studied them under a loupe.

"Too brown," she said, pushing away a three-carat brilliant cut. "Too purple," she said of another. A third was "nice and bright but badly cut." She went through the half dozen more stones in the tray.

"None of these will do, Mr. Toon. I thought I'd made myself clear, but perhaps you misunderstood. I'd like to see your finest goods—pure color, good brilliance, nice clean stones."

"Of course, Madame," said the dealer and went to get more.

She was neither surprised nor particularly annoyed. She encountered exactly this situation almost every time she dealt with someone for the first time. They assumed because she was a woman and relatively young she'd accept inferior stones either because she didn't know any better or because she would be too timid to object. She soon let them know they were wrong, and almost always got what she came for.

The next batch of stones was better, the third superb. She chose two three-carat stones, a rich vermilion with a slight violet tinge, both cushion-cut, and a six-carat oval that might serve as the centerpiece for a magnificent necklace.

"Wonderful, Mr. Toon," she said as she wrote him out a check.

"Yes, yes, Miss," he said, clearly pleased at the deal he'd made. "And tomorrow you will see the mines. It is all arranged."

The next morning a bouncy little plane carried her the one hundred twenty-five miles southwest to Chanthaburi. The plane came down on an earthen landing strip that was right on the edge of one of the world's largest ruby mining operations.

Chanthaburi was a dry, ocher-tinted place, hotter than hot. The same primitive methods were still used to take rubies

from the earth as had been used here a thousand years ago.
The mines were little more than holes dug into a vast plain
of hard flat ground, each one shaded from the overhead sun
by a woven bamboo awning supported on a frame of rickety
sticks. The only contrast of color to the dusty yellow of the
earth came from the bright cotton skirts and head wraps of
the people working the mines. No heavy equipment could be
used lest the fragile ruby crystals be damaged, so the digging
was done by hand—the hands of families of men, women,
and children.

In a hut at the center of the activity, a trade in freshly
mined rubies was conducted. Pete spent an hour dealing for
the best of the larger carat stones. An understanding was
reached whereby the stones would be delivered to customs
in Bangkok, and she would arrange payment after they were
consigned to a bonded exporter.

After concluding her purchases, Pete wanted to take a
closer look at the mines. A local guide steered her through
the maze of awnings to the edge of one of the holes where
a family was at work. She watched as the father went down
into the pit ten or fifteen feet deep and used his primitive
scraping equipment to cut away chunks of the yellow rock.
Then mother and children hoisted the stones up with pulleys
so the precious red crystals could be carefully prised out.

"You like try?" asked the father after Pete had been watching for a while.

She smiled and nodded. After removing her shoes, she
rolled up her sleeves and climbed carefully down the rickety
bamboo ladder. It took a minute for her eyes to adjust to the
light, then she began scraping carefully away at the rock as
the miner showed her, loading it into the baskets for hauling
up, breaking a fingernail but not caring. She kept it up about
half an hour before he pointed to something in her hand. She
looked down and saw a tiny crystal, red as blood, glinting
among the dust and gravel.

"I found one! Look, I found a ruby!" she cried, feeling
like a kid finding an egg left by the Easter bunny. Hot,
barefoot, and covered with ocher-colored dust, her hair tangled and streaming down the back of a cotton shirt that stuck

to her skin, she laughed. Although she had worked with jewels for years, it was the first time she had mined one for herself, seen it given forth as a gift of the earth. It was tiny, only about a quarter of a carat, but it was real.

Pete climbed out of the pit and handed it with great pride to the wife of the miner who had taken her down. These people needed every stone they could come up with to scrape a living out of the mine; she would not keep this one. It was the finding of it, seeing the red glint in the stone and freeing it, that had been the magic. She didn't need anything more.

She tried brushing her hands against her khaki pants, but they were as dusty as the rest of her, so she just blew her hair out of her eyes and stretched her back, looking down into the pit.

She heard silvery laughter behind her, but she didn't turn around. The miner's wife and daughters had been giggling behind their hands ever since she arrived. But when she felt a hand on her shoulder, she jumped, almost falling into the pit but for the strong hands that caught her.

"You're the color of a yellow pearl," said a voice in her ear, and she spun around to see Hiro Kiyosaki smiling at her.

Pete gaped at him in disbelief. "Hiro! What are you doing here?"

"You couldn't come to Tokyo, so I came to you. I plan to stay until your business is finished. *Then* you are coming to Tokyo."

She had planned to go on to see other mines, but sapphires and opals be damned! "I'm finished," she said, her teeth positively glowing in her dust-darkened face as she smiled.

Within two hours they were in his private jet with the South China Sea below them.

The plane's shower was hot and hard, just the way she liked it, and she emerged pink and warm. She put on an acid-green silk *cheongsam* she'd bought in Bangkok and joined Hiro in the cabin.

"Come, I have some treasures to show you," he said, beckoning her to a chair.

Laid out on a table were black velvet trays full of pearls.

But somehow the simple word pearl seemed too mundane for these giant globes and teardrops and knobs of glowing light. They were baroque pearls and they were huge.

"These are conch and abalone pearls," he said, "mostly from the Caribbean." He lifted an irregularly shaped chunk of iridescence as big as a baby's fist. "This one was found at Morro Bay, south of San Francisco—three hundred twenty-five carats. Worth about four million."

"It's glorious," said Pete, feeling the heft of it in her hand and running her thumb over the sleek surface.

"What would you do with it?"

She held it up to the light from the plane's window, moving it back and forth so it glowed. "Probably a pendant of some sort. No colored stones, no gold. Too distracting. A platinum setting, I think, delicate, with maybe a small diamond pattern of some sort at the top to balance the shape."

He nodded his approval. "These are South Sea pearls," he said, pulling out a tray of large, silvery black ones. "The warmth of the water gives them their unique color."

"These would be wonderful contrasted with good color sapphires and diamonds. Or maybe with black opals from Australia."

He pulled out more trays brimming with pearls such as she had never seen—freshwater pearls from the Mississippi River, black blister pearls as big as quarters, Tahitian pearls as green as jade. Delicate shades of pink, rose, yellow, cream, and deep blue-gray. She let her mind go and imagined fanciful settings for them, suggested gold for some, jade to set off others, a translucent enamel flower around one yellowish mabé pearl, an amethyst in a ring with another. It was a delicious novelty to be able to talk to an attractive man about her work in such a direct way, eliciting informed responses and curious questions.

"You do know your stuff," he finally said with a warm smile.

"I have a lot to learn about pearls."

His eyes locked with hers. "I am an excellent teacher."

She heard all the shades of meaning in his claim. "I'm sure you are," she said, and looked down at the pearls

rightened by the rising intensity of the feelings that overtook
er as long as his gaze held hers.

The plane glided over Yokohama Bay and landed in a
orner of Narita Airport just after dark.

"You can drop me at the Imperial," she said as his chauf-
eured Mercedes limousine picked them up beside the plane.
"If there's no room, I'll phone for something from there."

"No need for any hotel," Hiro said as he helped her into
he car. He rattled off instructions to the chauffeur in Japa-
ese.

Pete looked at him steadily as he seated himself beside
er. How much was she accepting if she stayed with him.
"Hiro, I don't think—"

"No need for thinking either," he cut in. "You will stay
vith me . . . because that's where the pearls are." He reached
ver and took her hand.

His hand was firm and smooth around hers. His ink-black
yes were piercing, his smile intimate and warm.

"Though perhaps," he added, "you didn't come to Tokyo
nly to see my pearls."

"No," she replied softly, accepting the depth of meaning
n her answer only as she said it. "Not just for the pearls."

Chapter 7

Hiro's house was an oasis of serenity and simplicity within the rushing glass and chrome city. They were met at the door by a tiny wrinkled woman in a kimono who bowed as she took their shoes and handed them *tabis* to wear instead.

"This is Toshi," said Hiro, and the old woman bowed again. "She will see that you are comfortable while you are here."

Pete smiled and bowed in return, and Hiro led her into the most peaceful space she could imagine—sand-colored walls, white *shoji* screens, black-bordered beige tatami mats soft and spongy beneath her feet, a white paper lantern hanging from the ceiling. An ink-wash painting of a flowering apple branch hung on one wall; in a corner a celadon vase held a long curve of pink-and-brown-flecked orchids. In the center of the room sat a low, black lacquered table, a rectangle of blue silk brocade in its center. That was all.

Pete took in a deep lungful of air. "I feel that I can breathe in this room."

"I'm glad. My office is as cluttered as any in the Western world, with computers and files and half-empty coffee cups and pearls sitting around in ashtrays, and I can never find a

554

pencil. It's the Oxford and New York and Hong Kong in me. But I need this, too. It is here that I am most Japanese.''

Pete tried to read the room, to understand the Japanese spirit he had described, and she fell in love with what she saw.

Toshi arrived with a tray and set out tea things on the table, bowed, and left as silently as she had come. Hiro poured the foamy green tea into tiny cups without handles and gave one to Pete. "Welcome to my home."

The tea was delicious, hot and faintly bitter with a sweet aftertaste. They drank in silence, and his polished-onyx eyes watched her as she watched him in return. It felt to Pete as though they were talking without saying anything.

When she was done, he took the cup from her hands. He reached up and pulled the combs from her hair, letting it spill over her shoulders and combing it gently with his fingers. She sat very still as he slid his hands through the thick, soft strands.

"Come," he said softly. "Our bath is ready."

He rose and pulled her to her feet. He slid open a *shoji* screen, led her down a short hall and into a room like a sauna, lined all in wood. The floor was also of slatted wood, and in the middle stood an enormous square wooden tub wreathed in steam.

Hiro turned her around, slid down the zipper of her *cheong-sam*, and let it fall to the floor. Her underthings were removed in a few seconds, and she stood naked in the rapidly thickening steam. He gazed at her, his eyes caressing her from top to toe, taking in every soft curve and jutting angle, every hair and hollow. "Sit," he said gently, and gestured to a low wooden stool.

The room, the man, the feeling he aroused in her all seemed unreal to Pete. She was in another world, totally foreign and very beautiful. There was nothing to do but simply let it wash over her.

From a copper-banded wooden bucket, Hiro ladled hot water over her shoulders then picked up a bar of soap and began slowly lathering her body. He soaped his hands till they were thick with foam and slid them down over her shoulders and under her arms. They circled her breasts, stopping to lift them lightly as though to test their weight, his thumbs lingering at the nipples, which rose to meet them. They slid down her rib cage to her stomach, drawing soap circles on the flat plain. More lather was stroked over her long, taut thighs, behind her knees, down to her ankles and her feet. Moving almost in slow motion, he soaped her arms and hands, her back, the line between her buttocks.

It was the most purely sensual thing Pete had ever felt.

When he was done, he rinsed off the soap with water from the bucket then helped her sink into the steaming wooden tub. When she sat, the water came almost to her chin. Quickly he stripped, offering her the sight of his tall, solid body, his broad, hairless chest, his skin almost exactly the color of the wooden tub. He soaped himself all over, rinsed, and lowered himself into the tub beside her, their toes touching.

The water was so hot Pete could hardly move in it. She felt the sweat break out on her upper lip and licked it away.

Then he grinned, breaking the magic spell he had created. "You are now an honorary Japanese," he said.

"I guess honorary will do for now."

"You don't have the right hair to be a true Japanese. Too curly. Here," he said, lifting the hair from her forehead, "and here." He reached under the water and brushed his fingers across the very top of her pubic curls, so delicately she barely felt it, though a muscle deep inside reacted nonetheless.

They leaned away from each other then, both smiling like contented cats, and began to talk—of people they both knew, of places they had been, of historic jewels they both admired. Professionally, they had much in common. They dissected the wedding, commenting on many of the people there, and she thanked him again for his intercession with René Vaugillande. Despite the air of sensuality, thick as the steam swirling about their heads, Pete felt completely at ease with him; he was the only other man she'd ever known who was as easy to talk to as Luke.

Finally, just as the water began to feel noticeably cooler, Hiro rose to his knees, pulled her up with him, and kissed

er. It was not a gentle kiss. It demanded her attention and
response, and it got it. Her mind had been waiting for it since
he'd walked into his house. Her body had been primed for
since he'd started washing her. Now her mouth opened
under his, his tongue slid inside her, and he pulled her close
until wet flesh met wet flesh.

She tasted his tongue and teeth and lips and ran her fingers
along the wet ridges of his spine and grasped his sides. He
held her tightly by the shoulders, exploring her whole mouth.
Then he released her.

He climbed out of the tub, opened an oversized white
towel, and wrapped it around her as she stepped out. With
brisk strokes, he dried her until her skin tingled and begged
for more when he stopped. He quickly dried himself, slid a
blue and white cotton kimono over her arms, and put one on
himself. Then he led her back to the tatami room.

The table had now been laid for dinner, and two chairs
had appeared, with wicker backs and silk-covered seats, bro-
cade-covered armrests, and no legs. The *shoji* screens had
been opened to show a courtyard garden, dark now but for
the glow from several stone lanterns. She could see a path
of smooth gray pebbles, the trunk of a tree, part of a bamboo
fence. Water dripped into a pool somewhere in the darkness.

Toshi appeared as soon as they sat down, the bell tucked
into her sash jingling softly as she moved to announce her
presence. Kneeling beside the table, she poured hot sake into
tiny conical cups, then brought forth dish after dish of things
Pete couldn't even hope to name.

"This is called *tororo-imo*," said Hiro, offering her some
julienned yellow vegetable. "It's sort of like a yam but not
sweet. And this is river eel."

Pete eyed the oily tidbit suspiciously, but when she tasted
it she found it rich and delicious, sweetened with a soy sauce
glaze.

Toshi set down a delicate porcelain bowl of miso soup
thick with buckwheat noodles, a black lacquer dish filled with
bamboo shoots wrapped around mustard-spiked seaweed, and
some fried broad beans. Finally she brought forth a red lacquered board loaded with *sashimi* arranged as precisely as a

sculpture. There was lobster and abalone sitting on their shells, a glistening red and white sea bream, deep red *magur* or bluefin tuna, and dojo, "a small fish that lives in the ric paddies," Hiro explained.

Toshi disappeared and they feasted and drank sake. He lifted balls of gummy rice with his chopsticks and fed them to her. And they talked some more.

It was two hours before they were finished. Then Hir helped her to her feet and led her into the garden.

The lantern light created shadows among the branches of the shrubs and reflected on the water of a rock-encircled pool He motioned her to a tiny wooden bridge that arched over the pond. In the middle of the bridge they stopped, listenin to the water falling one drop at a time from a bamboo dipper

"It's perfect," Pete whispered. She felt herself expan with the peace of it, filled with its simplicity, smoothed out unwrinkled, whole.

"As are you," he said and turned her toward him. Hi fine fingers unknotted the sash at her waist and her kimon fell open. He had already untied his own, so that when h held her close, their entire bodies caressed. He smelled of soap and *sake*.

"Come," he said, as he had already said so many time before. She was learning to love the word, for it alway seemed to presage another delightful surprise.

They went back inside, and though they had been in th garden less than ten minutes, all traces of their dinner ha vanished, the table had been removed, and in its place wa a thick futon made up with crisp white sheets, fluffy pillows and a blue and white quilt. The lights had been turned low Toshi was gone.

Watching each other, they removed their kimonos and san to their knees on the futon. Pete reached out to him, tracin on his body the movements his soapy hands had drawn o hers in the bath. His skin was smooth as silk, a little dew with sweat. His muscles were hard beneath it. From a nes of soft black hair, his penis rose toward her like a suppl tree. She cupped his balls, holding their weight in one hand He sucked in his breath but made no other sound.

He reached up for her face and pulled it close, then slid his hand down over the rise of her chin, down her neck to her collarbone. Her skin jumped at his touch. His tongue probed her mouth, seeming to search for her soul, and she returned the quest.

He pulled her down onto the futon's softness, kissed her everywhere. He kissed her toes and the soles of her feet, the backs of her ears, and the space between her fingers. He touched her in ways no Westerner had ever done, and she wondered if this was another of the secrets of the East. He whispered words she didn't understand, except that she did. And when she was ready—more than ready, nearly begging—he joined his black hair with hers, East and West, and began the rhythm that knew no boundaries.

It was slow and long and torturously sweet, building degree by degree to an undreamed of height until, when it finally came, her orgasm seemed to start in those toes he'd been kissing and shoot to every part of her body and out into the corners of the room.

When their breathing slowed again, he said, "You are perfect. I knew it from the moment I saw you talking to that stupid Frenchman at the wedding. I knew then that I would have you and you would be perfect."

And then they slept.

For the next four days, Hiro showed Pete Tokyo, streets bristling with cranes and scaffolding and holes in the ground as the city continued its relentless drive to build higher, bigger, newer—a city of neon and chrome, cement and glass. He took her to his ultramodern showrooms, where pearls of every size, shape, and color from every part of the world were sold. And he took her to the old quarter of Asakusa, through the winding back streets lined with small shops selling paper fans and umbrellas, ivory chopsticks, *happi* coats, baskets of rice crackers. He led her past the giant two-hundred-pound red paper lantern and between the thick red columns marking the entrance to the Temple of Sensoji, founded in the seventh century. Inside, the air was heavy with incense, vibrating with the clank of coins in the wooden collection box on the altar and the low voice of a chanting monk.

They went to the kabuki theater, and Pete was caught up in its pageantry even though she didn't understand a word. They took the Shinkansen, the Bullet Train, to Fujiyama, zipping along at one hundred thirty miles per hour, smooth and quiet. They climbed to the summit of the cone-shaped mountain, bowing at each of the dozens of other walkers they met along the way.

And at night, in the bath, in the garden, on the cool, firm futon, Hiro reminded Pete that while many things are different in Japan, one thing is exactly the same.

Time ceased to have much meaning for Pete. She couldn't seem to care that her secretary didn't know where she was, that she had commissions waiting to be finished, that her grandmother's jewels were out there somewhere in the world waiting for her to find them. For now, none of it seemed to matter. Only Hiro and the magic world he had created and enveloped her in mattered. She didn't know if she loved him—was it even possible in such a short time?—but that, too, didn't seem to matter. She knew she loved being with him, and she loved making love to him, and the thought of it ending was too painful to consider.

"Let me show you my garden," Hiro said on the morning of the fifth day.

"I thought you already did."

"This is another garden. Come."

That was getting to be Pete's favorite word. Whenever Hiro had some new delight to show her, he simply reached out his hand, smiled, and said, "Come." And when he made love to her, teasing her then backing off again until she was ready to scream for release, he always lay his mouth next to her ear at the best possible moment and whispered, "Come." And she did.

So she took his hand and followed wherever he chose to lead her. She knew it would be wonderful wherever it was.

She was surprised when he got in the car. She thought the garden would be nearby. She was even more surprised when he drove to the airport, put her in his jet, and took off. He

ouldn't tell her where they were going except to say "to
ay garden."

For two hours they soared over the white-capped Pacific.
inally he drew her to a window and pointed. Far, far below
ay a dot of green in the middle of the endless blue.

"My garden," he said and smiled.

The tiny island of Kapingoro in the Carolines was no more
aan a flyspeck on any map, a coral atoll encircling a lagoon
f deep transparent turquoise with a volcanic hump of green
n one side. It was here that Hiro created the pearls that had
uilt his fortune.

"I come three or four times a year for a month, sometimes
onger," Hiro explained. "It needs hands-on management
aat often to keep things running smoothly."

She grinned, watching the island grow bigger as they de-
cended. "It's a dark and lonely job, but somebody's got to
o it, right?"

"Well, it's true not everyone gets to work in paradise."

The rich, vibrant smell of frangipani blossoms suffused the
ir as Pete stepped onto the island. Views of the lagoon and
ae sea were on every side as they drove in a jeep to his
ouse, a white wooden plantation house surrounded by a
eranda, its columns draped with climbing white and purple
rchids.

After a lunch of broiled bonito and a salad of tropical fruit,
liro showed her over the entire operation. The tiny *Pinctada*
aartensii oysters and big black *Pinctada margaritifera* oys-
ors and several other varieties were set on rafts inside cages
nd lowered into the warm, shallow water of the lagoon.
Different varieties of oysters give different colored pearls,
nd bigger ones give bigger pearls," he explained.

He showed her the room where women gently prised open
ae shells and inserted the tiny irritant that would spur the
yster to patiently build up several layers of nacre to protect
self, producing a pearl. From three to seven years later,
earl divers fished out the oysters and the pearls were har-
ested for people like Pete to make into beautiful creations.

In the sorting and grading rooms, Pete was overwhelmed

by the sheer numbers of shimmering, luminous little globe of light, thousands of them in every shade and size.

"So many," she breathed.

"Have you ever heard of the Gaekwar of Baroda's pea carpet?" Hiro asked.

"You're kidding."

"No, early in this century, he had a carpet, six by ten fee made entirely of natural Oriental pearls. Natural, not cultured They were graded and blended so well that waves of colo —from pink to cream to silver to white—seemed to undula across it. I would like to have seen it."

"I should think so, though I'm still not sure I believe it."

"You'd be amazed what some of those maharajahs had.

She dipped her fingers in a bowl of pearls and stirred it a if it were a bowl of thick cream. Then she scooped up handful and studied them under the light.

"That glow you see on the surface, the iridescence, it' called lustre, or orient," Hiro said. "There are tiny space between the layers of nacre that let light refract between them That's what makes them shimmer." He picked up a larg creamy pearl and held it out for her. "Taste it," he said.

Pete hesitated only a moment before she put the pearl o her tongue and let it roll around. Since meeting Hiro, sh seemed to want to experience everything with all her sense as well as her mind. The pearl felt slightly gritty on he tongue.

"If you swallow it, you might live a long time," he said "Mikimoto, who perfected the technique of culturing pearl swallowed one every morning of his life from the age o twenty, and he lived well into his nineties."

Pete took the pearl out of her mouth. "I think I'll pass.

"Tomorrow, we'll go see the pearl beds," he said. "Bu right now, let us get acquainted with another bed."

She had no argument. Hiro in a bed beside her was be coming one of her favorite things in the world.

Pete was awakening as a sexual animal in a way she hadn known before. Sex with Luke had been wonderful, and sh had never stopped missing it. Because she'd loved him, sh had also loved everything he did to her and with her. Bu

ith Hiro it was different, more of an ongoing adventure of
ensual delights, reaching higher, going farther. He had freed
er to search for the very best in her sexual self. In a sense,
ete became someone she didn't know or even recognize,
et at the same time part of her thought she had become more
ully herself than ever before.

The next day Hiro handed her a *pareo*, the wraparound
arong-type skirt worn on the island. He had one on himself.
It's all you need,'' he said and so, trusting him, she walked
ut bare-breasted without compunction and without embar-
assment. Her long hair flew about in the light breeze, and
e sparkles of the water reflected in her eyes.

She watched as the *amas*, with their wooden tubs, dove
or the oysters. The water was so shallow they didn't need
o stay down more than a minute or so.

"Can I try it?" Pete asked.

He grinned and took her hand. "Come," he said.

The water was warm on her bare skin. It lifted her breasts
nd caressed her face. Following the lead of one of the *amas*,
he dove to an oyster bed, picked up several of the rough
hells, and returned to the surface to drop them in the floating
ub. Then she dove again.

"I love it," she cried as she broke the surface of the water
nd shook it from her hair. "Come down with me."

"Not now," he said. "But I'll dive with you later. At a
lace I know where no one ever goes."

She spent the morning diving for pearls. After lunch, Hiro
ut her in a catamaran and they sailed around the island
o a secluded cove. Flying fish skimmed low over the water
nd Hiro's muscles rippled in the sun as he worked the sails.
Vith snorkels and masks, they explored the reef. Yellow
nd black Picasso fish, orange parrot fish, and tiny white
rumpet fish played tag among the coral branches. A starfish
ndulated past. Sponges and sea anemones sat about doing
othing.

Beneath the water, time and space were suspended. Pete's
ong hair floated with the rhythm of the current, and it lifted
heir *pareos* so that it was as if they were wearing nothing
t all. Hiro swam over to her and, using his legs to tread

water, he reached out and stroked her body underwater, fee
ing the buoyancy the water gave to her breasts, caressing th
springy hair between her legs, going farther until he coul
feel inside her where she was warmer even than the wan
water.

Her hand reached under his *pareo* and took hold of him
pulled him close. Moving to shallower water so their fee
could touch bottom if necessary, he pulled off their mask
and snorkels so he could kiss her, a wet, salty, hungry kiss
Then he lifted her up and lowered her again, sliding her dow
onto his rigid penis. She wrapped her legs about him, wavin
her arms slowly through the water to keep them afloat, an
let the current set the rhythm. Their lovemaking was as el
emental as the tide, as basic as the water, as natural as th
sun overhead. They came with a sputter, arms thrashing, the
sank peacefully, letting the water close over them for a mo
ment as they held each other close.

Then they let the catamaran carry them home.

But Hiro was not through with her yet. "Don't shower,"
he said when they got back to the house. "I want to lick th
salt from your breasts." And he did.

One day followed another, sun and water and loving, con
versation and food and more loving. They made love on th
beach, on a straw mat under a coconut palm, on the cata
maran. They walked over every inch of his island. Soon Pet
was as brown as a chestnut, her hair glinting with blue-blac
highlights. "And no bikini line!" she told Hiro with a laugh
He gave her necklaces made of shells and sharks teeth an
flowers, and she wondered why anyone would prefer dia
monds and pearls.

"Just call me Eve," she said one morning as she picke
a mango from a tree. "This must be Eden."

Once, when Hiro had to helicopter to a neighboring islan
for a few hours and Pete was alone with time to think, sh
tried to analyze how she felt about him. And she found hersel
thinking about Luke. Every man she'd ever known, ever care
for, ever slept with since knowing him she had compared t
Luke, the only man she'd ever loved. Hiro was the first ma
who hadn't consistently come up short in the comparison

ad she finally met a man who could exorcise the memory
Luke Sanford?

Hiro returned and Luke was put out of her mind once more.
They joined in the natives' celebration of the Festival of
e Spring Moon, a night-long orgy of eating, dancing, story-
lling, more dancing. When it was over and they made love
the moonlight, lying on a palm leaf mat on the beach, she
arned he had set it all up, created the festival just for her
easure and got everyone on the island in on the act.

"What does it all mean?" she asked on the fifth day.

"I don't know. I'm making it up as we go along."

"Well, don't stop, okay?" For answer he kissed her.

They'd been there a week when Hiro said, "Stay with
.e." They were sitting on the terrace, watching a thunder-
orm far out on the horizon.

Slowly she turned to him. She had been waiting for the
ords, she realized, half eager for the chance—and half
reading the decision. This was paradise. But could she keep
forever?

"Stay with me." he repeated. "Here. Forever."

"Are you serious?"

"Do you remember where we met?"

"Of course. It was only two weeks ago. At Marcel and
ndrea's wedding."

"That's right. And what were you thinking at that wed-
ing?"

She thought a minute, then she remembered. She had been
inking about Luke, about how much she missed him. "I
as thinking about how happy Marcel and Andrea looked
nd about how ridiculously long it took them to make up
eir minds to finally *do it!*"

"Let's not take that long, Pete. Let's do it now."

"Do what?"

"Get married."

A part of her wanted to cry "Yes!," wanted this perfect
lyll to go on for all the tomorrows of her life.

But could anything so perfect last forever? When reality
egan to intrude, what would her days be like? Could she
ill make her life with Hiro?

"I need to think, Hiro."

He smiled. "Remember when I stopped you from thinkin[g] before? Was the result so bad? Do not think, Pete. Giv[e] yourself to what you feel."

"I'm not sure I know what I feel," she said. "That's th[e] trouble." She leaned down and gave him a kiss. "I'm goin[g] for a walk. When I come back you'll have my answer."

She walked on the beach for hours, letting the tide trick[le] in over her toes, feeling the wind carry her hair up behin[d] her or whip it into her face. Marry Hiro? Stay on this Eden[-] like island in the sun forever? She was tempted to say ye[s,] there was no doubt about it. She also had no doubt that sh[e] loved Hiroshi Kiyosaki. But did she love him enough[?] Enough to overcome the vast cultural differences that woul[d] loom larger with every year, enough to leave behind her wor[k] and her family and everything she'd built up over the years[?]

Perhaps because of her mother's illness, Pete was mor[e] aware than most—and more afraid of—the idea of a waste[d,] empty life. She had always wanted to fill herself up with a[s] many new experiences as possible—to do and see and kno[w] everything she possibly could, to not be afraid to reach u[p,] to stretch.

Was that really what had lured her into this idyll with th[e] most unusual and exotic man she had known? Was it simpl[y] a taste of something new and exotic, a deposit in her ban[k] of experience? Or was he a fantasy, an attempt to escape th[e] reality of the emotional barrenness of her life? Pete looke[d] up at the sky of brilliant blue above the island paradise. Wha[t] do you think, grandmother, her heart asked. Perhaps there i[s] simply more of you in me than I thought, more of the cou[r-] tesan. I sure as hell won't deny I've loved every minute spent in Hiro's world—and especially in his bed.

Maybe, like Bettina, Pete thought, I'm better at fantas[y] than reality. Luke was reality and look what happened to us[.] Poof, like the smoke from that volcano over there. So mayb[e] this is where I belong.

Or must she stay with the only real and lasting thing sh[e] had known—her work.

"I'm sorry, Hiro," she said when she finally went back
to the house. "I can't stay with you. It isn't my world."

"We make our own world, Pete."

"I know, and I've already made mine. But it's not with
you, not here. The past two weeks with you have been like
being in heaven. Magic happened to me here, and I learned
things about myself I never suspected, things I like. It's been
a fabulous fantasy, but the reality can't be kept on the shelf
forever. Sooner or later it will crash in on us whether we
want it to or not. I'd rather keep the fantasy perfect, just as
it is, with no chance it can ever become tarnished. I love
you, Hiro, and you have given me the greatest gift I could
ever receive, the gift of myself. Now I have to take that gift
away with me and use it to help me run the rest of my life.
I'd like to go tomorrow."

He lifted her face and poured his black eyes into her blue
ones. For a very long time he was silent. Then he said, "So
we still have tonight. Come."

In the silver gleam of the full moon, he made love to her
for the last time. He brought to the tatami room a wooden
bucket filled with perfect silver-blue pearls and poured them
slowly over her naked body. When he lay on top of her, the
pearls rolled down between her breasts, into the hollows of
her neck, into the creases of her groin. He raised himself
again and rolled them around the areolas of her breasts until
her nipples were as hard as little pearls themselves and she
came just from the touch of them as he was kissing her.

Then he rubbed a large one over and around the center of
her desire until she felt herself bursting again, falling into
fragments. He pushed two glossy black ones inside her and
left them there, then followed them in himself, driving them
home with each thrust until he erupted inside her, taking her
with him yet again, this one better than all the others.

At Narita Airport, as she waited to board her flight back
to New York, Pete picked up a telephone for the first time
in two weeks.

She had said her good-byes to Hiro on Kapingoro, where

he had stayed to accomplish the work he'd left undone durin the past two weeks—and so he wouldn't have to say good bye in the real world.

"This place has been frantic!" cried Lottie in a scoldin tone as soon as she heard Pete's voice. "I was ready to repo you missing to half the embassies in Asia. Where have yo been?"

"I told you I'd be away at least two weeks," Pete re sponded, deliberately leaving Lottie's question unanswered In fact, she decided, she would never reveal where she ha been for this brief span of time. It would remain her secre an untold dream.

Lottie didn't press. "You *didn't* say you wouldn't eve call in. You've never done that before. I have a pile c messages for you. Get a pencil."

"Yes, ma'am."

There were messages from suppliers, from Brent Lowell from a real-estate developer planning a new building in Lo Angeles who hoped to give tone to the project by persuadin Pete to install a new branch of Tesori, from a White Hous secretary to the First Lady, asking when Pete might be avail able to discuss a new piece. And there had been a call fro René Vaugillande of Drouot in Paris.

The only one Pete returned immediately was to Vaugil lande.

"I have the name you requested, Mademoiselle," he sai curtly as soon as she was put through.

After the call was completed, Pete stood by the phone fo a second. Then she left the area where she had been waitin to board her New York flight, and hurried back into th terminal.

She would not be returning home after all.

Chapter 8

The fourteenth Earl of Amberly lived in a pillared Georgian manor of awesome proportions that looked out over the rolling green hills of Dorset. As the taxi that had met her at the railroad station climbed a long drive toward the enormous ancestral home, Pete sensed that she was at long last on the verge of taking a giant step toward finding her own heritage.

Lord Amberly, Vaugillande had finally revealed, was the man who had consigned the sapphire-and-emerald necklace for auction in 1963. From what Pete knew of the habits of the aristocracy, it was highly improbable that the Earl had owned the necklace only a short time before parting with it. More likely was that he had owned it for many years. It was possible, therefore, that he had been the first buyer when it was offered for sale soon after the war, which would mean that whoever sold it to him would be a direct link to Vittorio D'Angeli.

Or Vittorio himself.

A butler of military bearing met Pete at the massive oak entrance doors and led her through a vast marbled hall to a comfortable, smoky, dark brown library where a man with

a lean angular face and iron gray hair was poring over a stam[
album at a desk by a sunlit window.

"M'lord," intoned the butler gravely, "Miss Pietra D'A[
geli."

As the Earl of Amberley maneuvered to turn toward Pet[
she became aware that he was in a wheelchair. She had bee[
told by Vaugillande, who remembered Pete's past suggestio[
that the man who consigned the necklace could be a wartim[
Fascist sympathizer—and delighted in proving how wron[
she had been—that Lord Amberley had flown for the RA[
in the Battle of Britain, had been shot down and serious[
wounded, and had thereafter become somewhat reclusiv[
Pete could see now that one of his legs had been amputate[
at the knee, and assumed the injury dated from the war.

"Good afternoon, Lord Amberley," she said. "Thank yo[
for receiving me."

"Well, well, Miss D'Angeli," he said heartily as he rolle[
toward her. "This necklace business certainly has broug[
you a long way on short notice."

Pete had telephoned from Tokyo only the day before yes[
terday to arrange the appointment. "I didn't want to wast[
any more time, sir."

"Quite. From what this fellow at Drouot tells me, you'v[
been on the hunt for years." Though elderly and confined [
the wheelchair, the English aristocrat managed neverthele[
to project a sense of strength. He sat with his back straig[
and kept his firm jaw held high. Pete felt an immediate sym[
pathy with him and was surprised that he had been so ob[
structive until now about her request.

"In fact," Pete said, probing for an explanation, "I aske[
him to put me in touch with you more than a year ago."

"I know. Shame, that. I'd have been quicker to help if I'[
understood the whole thing sooner. First time the fellow wro[
me, his letter was rather vague. Simply asked if I'd obje[
to releasing Drouot from an agreement to keep confidenti[
my connection to the article they'd auctioned. No reaso[
given. Saw no reason to say yes. Afraid I can be rather
testy chap at times." He gave her an apologetic smile an[

motioned her to a chair beside an exquisitely carved mahogany mantel. "Please sit down. Can I have Bannerman bring you anything?"

As she sat, Pete saw that the butler was still in attendance, silent as a statue.

"No, thank you."

With a small nod, Lord Amberley dismissed his servant. "Now. Tell me how I can be of help."

"I need to know everything you can remember about the circumstances surrounding your purchase of that necklace."

"Everything?" The aristocrat's thick gray eyebrows went up. "Tall order. Day I bought it goes back . . . let's see, pretty nearly forty years."

Pete pulled forward to the edge of her chair. As she had guessed, it hadn't been too long after the end of the war.

"I was spending a little more time up in London back in those days. I was in my club one day when a chap walked in off the street asking for me. Seemed respectable enough —perfect manners, didn't embarrass me to sit down with him and offer him a glass of something. He pulled the necklace out of his pocket, told me he wanted to sell, and said Reggie Remmington had put him on to me because I had a wife with a fondness for jewels. Well, I went for it at once. I had an eye for the real thing, and there was no doubt those stones were all aces. Solidest chap in the world, Reggie, and it was true enough about my Cassie—she did love her baubles." His eyes wandered upward to a place over the carved mantel.

Pete followed his gaze and saw a large oil portrait hanging on the wall above the fireplace. The subject of the portrait was a beautiful woman standing in a blue satin gown with a tiara in her dark hair, posed formally beside the very chair in which Pete now sat. Pete was about to look away from the portrait when another detail caught her eye: Around the woman's slender aristocratic neck was La Colomba's sapphire-and-emerald necklace.

"That's my Cassie," Lord Amberley said, his voice husky with emotion. "Necklace turned out to be far and away her favorite piece. That's why I put it up for sale after she died.

No sense locking it away, beautiful thing like that, and knew I'd never let anyone else wear it. Never married again anyway, as it happens.''

"The man who sold you the necklace," Pete said, anxiously bringing the Earl out of his reverie. "Did he tell you where he got it?"

"Let's see . . . said it was a family heirloom, hated to part with it and all that. Easy to see, though, that he needed the money. Good clothes but a bit on the shabby side, shoes worn around the heels, know what I mean? Lot of that going on back then, of course. The war and all. So many of these chaps coming over from the Continent who'd lost everything but what they could sew into a coat lining. I suppose it sounds silly now to have bought it the way I did, but it happened all the time then. Worked out well for both sides. They got the money they needed, and things could be bought for good value. Not like now, when every little trinket seems to go for millions.''

Pete's excitement was rising. Amberley had said the seller had come over from the Continent. "You mentioned that the man who came into your club was European. From which country?" she asked, and held her breath waiting for the answer.

"Don't recall exactly . . ."

Pete's heart sank.

But then Lord Amberley continued. "I'm not sure I asked."

"But he had an accent?"

"Oh yes."

"Italian?"

"No. More like . . . one of the north countries—Danish, Swiss, perhaps even German—though of course he wouldn't have admitted that, would he? Definitely not Italian, though. Had the Teutonic look, too, know what I mean? Blond hair. Then there was his name. Not one of those Italian things that sounds like raviolo or spaghetti. That part was English, in fact . . .''

"What was his name?" Pete asked impatiently.

Lord Amberley thought. "Don't recall the Christian name,

t the given name was Farmer. That stuck with me because
 sounded rather English, a bit at odds with everything else
out the chap."

Of course the name was probably an alias, Pete thought.
nd the hair could have been dyed, the accent feigned. But
mberley seemed to be a man who would intuitively have
iffed out a fake identity, just as he would have spotted a
ke gem. Probably Mr. Farmer was not Vittorio D'Angeli.
ut he could have been just one step removed.

"Lord Amberly, is there a chance you know where this
an Farmer went after he sold you the necklace? It's terribly
portant."

"Don't know where he went immediately, no. But as it
ppens I know where he ended up a few years later. Gave
e a bit of a start, I don't mind telling you."

"What do you mean?"

"Saw his picture in the papers. Chap had been arrested.
urned out to be a bit of a bad egg, after all. He went to
ison."

"Prison!"

"Yes. Of course I was afraid what it might mean for my
t. Thought the necklace might turn out to be stolen goods
ter all, so I had it pretty thoroughly checked out. But there
ere no reports of such a piece missing anywhere, no hint
 anything havey-cavey. I was more than a little relieved, I
n tell you. Cassie was so attached to her necklace by then."

Pete's mind raced. "Lord Amberly, I have to try to find
r. Farmer and speak to him. Do you happen to recall the
ison to which he was sent?" Even if he wasn't still there,
e thought, they might have records of an address.

"Wormwood Scrubs," Amberley replied. "But you'd
ed a medium to speak to him, dear girl. He died there."

This time the disappointment flooded in and she couldn't
sh it away. The chain was broken. "He can't be dead,"
e said in the soft, broken tones of a mourner, "not when
m so close."

"I say, are you all right, my dear? Would you like a brandy
ter all?"

She shook her head; she had to keep her mind clear. Think,

she commanded herself. There must still be a way to pic
up the thread.

Yet nothing occurred to her. Pete stood. "You've bee
very patient with me, Lord Amberly, and more than kind.
She offered her hand. "I can't thank you enough."

"Not at all, dear girl, not at all. You'd be welcome he
anytime. I haven't had so much lovely company since n
Cassie died . . ."

He accompanied her back through the great marbled ha
to the entrance, where the butler appeared to open the doo
Pete thanked the Earl again and was about to step outsic
when one more question occurred to her.

"When Mr. Farmer was sent to prison, Lord Amberle
what was his crime? Was it theft? You didn't say."

"Didn't I? No, it wasn't theft, Miss D'Angeli. Mr. Farm
was the engraver who made an unfortunately flawed set
plates for some homemade bank notes. The crime was cou
terfeiting."

As she sat in the compartment of the train traveling ba
to London, Pete considered the meaning of what she'd learne
from the Earl of Amberley.

Her larcenous Uncle Vittorio had only been able to wit
draw La Colomba's collection from the Swiss bank where
had been stored by presenting a perfectly forged replica
the top half of the perfume bottle held by her father—
counterfeit. Whoever had made it was obviously a superlati
craftsman—someone able to form metal to hold small pr
cious stones in place, someone capable of holding a bru
steady enough to add the delicate enameling—a man wl
might well possess the same ability required to craft a set
fine printing plates. Could the man who had forged the bott
be the counterfeiter?

Of course. The man who had made the jewel at Vittorio
direction had to be the same man who had sold it. Farm
was the key to finding La Colomba's jewels. Pete knew i

But Farmer was dead.

Despair descended on her as the vibrant autumn day passe

heeded outside the train window. To have come so far only
reach another dead end.

What could her next move possibly be? she wondered. She
as fresh out of ideas. She could scour the jewelry centers
Europe for any information about a forger named Farmer,
t it would be like jumping into the middle of the ocean in
arch of one of Hiro's pearls.

In any case, she couldn't spend any more time right now
nning around the world in search of a lost treasure. In her
ind, she heard Lottie's stern voice on the phone when she
d called to say she would be flying from Japan to England.
"You'd better get yourself home by the end of the week,
iss D. Because if you don't, you won't have a business for
e to help you run. And I like my job." The plump little
ay-haired secretary had turned into something of a kindly
artinet. Pete would have been lost without her.

She knew Lottie was right. She had been away from New
ork nearly a month, more than twice as long as she'd
anned. Now that she had left Hiro's arms and the powerful
rcle of his charm, she knew that it had been a chimera in
mparison to the solid rock of what she had felt—be honest,
te, *still felt*—for a different man. Hiro had been the bubbles
the champagne, or worse, the champagne itself—extrav-
ant and delicious to sip, intoxicating and heady, but ad-
ctive and perhaps ultimately destructive if it became a
ady diet.

Having made the decision to leave the Pearl King's dream
orld, she could no longer put off living fully in the world
e'd chosen.

Pushing her baggage cart across the international arrivals
rminal at JFK after clearing customs, Pete passed one of
e magazine kiosks. As her eye grazed across the front pages
the newspaper headlines, her mind flashed back once more
Hiro's island paradise. How refreshing it had been to forget
out disarmament talks and Washington scandals, brushfire
ars in the "third world," crime on the streets of the city.
only she could have—

A black wall slammed down against whatever pleasa
wishes had been running through her mind. Suddenly, s
was held transfixed by a picture on the front page of the *Da*
News. A woman's face in close-up, eyes closed as she l
on a bed or a stretcher with an intravenous feeding bot
hanging in the near background. The headline above the pi
ture read: LIVING DEATH.

The woman in the picture was Jess.

Even as Pete fumbled hastily for some coins and reach
for the newspaper, she noticed the picture on the front pa
of the *Post*: Fernando de Moratin entering a police station
handcuffs.

Grabbing up the second paper, too, Pete flipped it open
fiercely that the flimsy newsprint tore in her shaking hanc
She started to read, oblivious to the stream of travelers jostlii
her as they passed in and out of the terminal. Jess was
Lenox Hill Hospital in a coma, the result of an overdose
insulin. Pete's knees almost buckled as she read the next fa
Doctors feared that the brain had been sufficiently starved
oxygen to make the coma irreversible.

Barely able to take in the horror of what she was readin
she couldn't comprehend at first why Fernando had be
arrested. Her eyes raced faster down the column of words . .

> *Because Mrs. de Moratin was known to be a lifelong*
> *diabetic whose condition had to be closely moni-*
> *tored, foul play was not suspected originally. But*
> *Mrs. de Moratin's parents called for an investigation*
> *which led police to uncover evidence leading to her*
> *husband's arrest. Without revealing all the facts,*
> *Chief of Detectives John Terassi told reporters that*
> *police believe Mr. de Moratin injected his wife with*
> *a potentially lethal dose of insulin, and he is being*
> *held pending arraignment on a charge of attempted*
> *murder.*

Numb with shock, Pete shoved the newspaper into h
luggage cart and wheeled it hurriedly toward the termir
exit.

* * *

In a room brilliant with white light, Jess lay pale and completely still. Tubes and monitors of all sorts were attached to her body; electronic machines and breathing devices filled the air with beeping and whooshing noises. Sally Walsh sat beside her daughter, her usually impeccable presence now showing every day and more of her sixty-three years.

Pete stepped through the doorway, and Sally Walsh saw her.

"She'll wake up, Pete," said Jess's mother. "You know, she's been in coma before. She'll wake up."

Pete nodded passively for Sally's sake, but she knew the prognosis was bad. The doctors on the floor had informed her that Jess's insulin level had been off the charts when they brought her in, and this morning's EEG showed little brain activity.

"I've always been so afraid for her," Sally said softly. "All her life I've been afraid this would happen."

Is that why you kept your distance, Pete thought, why you cut her off from your love and never even touched her, so it would hurt less when it happened? But she didn't say the cruel words. What good could they possibly do now?

Looking at the immobile form of her dearest friend, Pete thought back to the last time they had been together, a lunch date at the Plaza's Palm Court—right before Pete left to attend Andrea's wedding. Jess had told Fernando about the baby by then, and she said he was as happy as she was . . .

Yet hadn't there been a dimming of her smile when Jess spoke about Fernando's reaction to the pregnancy? *He'll be glad . . . he's got to be, doesn't he?* A memory of that plaintive edge in Jess's voice came back to Pete.

Suppose Fernando had not been pleased. Could that conceivably have been the motive for murder?

As she pondered the causes, a question came unthinkingly from Pete's lips: "What about the baby?"

Sally Walsh said nothing, as though she hadn't heard.

Pete hesitated, but now she couldn't bear to go on wondering. "The child, Sally," Pete said a little louder. "Is . . . ?"

"Gone," Jess's mother said in a toneless murmur. "The took it last night."

Pete felt the words like a blow to the stomach. She walke around the end of the hospital bed and stood staring down a her friend's face.

Oh, Jess, Pete called to her silently, did I fail you as friend? Couldn't I have warned you?

Suddenly she was possessed by the memory of Jess's wed ding day and the fight with Luke that had caused the ruptur in their own romance. Luke had despised and distrusted Fer nando so much, and had minced no words about it, weddin or no wedding. Pete could hear his warning now: *Fernand as much as admitted he only married Jess for her money. . .* And she had shouted him down, criticized him for his lac of tolerance. Because Jess had so loved her dashing Spaniard Pete had tried to like him, to trust him, and she had defende him against Luke's judgment.

But Luke had been right. Dead right.

"Sally, why don't you take a break for a while, get a cu of coffee. I'll be here." Sally Walsh nodded and left th room.

Alone with Jess, Pete sat on the edge of the bed and too her hand. Impulsively, she began to speak, refusing to accep that Jess could not hear.

"Hell of a way to welcome me home, kid. I was lookin forward to so much with you . . . being a godmother . . and sharing . . ." Pete's voice died to a whisper. "Dam you, Jess, I can't afford to lose you. How many best friend do you think I have?" And then she erupted in a loud voic of anger. "What did he do to you, Jess? Why? Was he s afraid of losing even a little of the money that he would ki his wife? And his child?"

A young nurse stuck her head in the door. " 'Scuse m You Miss D'Angeli?" she queried in a hush. "Telephon for you. You'll have to take it out at the nurses' station . . ,

Pete released Jess's flaccid hand and placed it back on th sheets. Before leaving the room, she uttered one more phras a solemn vow: "He'll pay for it, Jess. I swear to you, he' pay."

Lifting the phone at the nurses' desk, Pete was prepared to speak to Lottie. Only her assistant knew she was flying home today and would have figured that she had headed straight for the hospital.

But the voice that replied to her "hello" wasn't Lottie's.

"I was sure you'd be there . . ."

Still, it was instantly familiar, and for a moment after hearing it Pete couldn't find a reply.

"Hey," he coaxed, "you still there?"

"Still here," she forced out, barely above a whisper.

"Thought it might help to hear from a friend," Luke offered sympathetically. "It's rough, I bet."

"Hell," she admitted. "But this does make it easier, hearing you."

"Any chance?" Luke asked.

Again she was silent, working out what he meant, so eager to think he was asking about *them*. But then she understood. "I don't think so," she said. "She's only being kept alive by machines."

Through a beat of silence she felt him reaching out to her across the thousands of miles of phone line between New York and California.

"I'm so sorry this had to happen, Pete. I know how much Jess means to you."

"It didn't *have* to happen, Luke. He did it to her. Do you remember what we argued about the day they were married?"

"Could I ever forget? I still ask myself sometimes if I wasn't a jerk to shoot my mouth off. If I hadn't, maybe you and I—"

"No, you were right. I didn't have the sense to listen to you, to be brave enough to talk to Jess . . ." For the first time since she'd heard the news, Pete lost total control of her emotions and began to sob. But not only for a friend who'd lost her life. She was crying at the same time for herself, and the loss of love.

"Pete . . . I can be there . . . if you want me. . . ."

"Want you? I've wanted you for so long." She could no longer rein in the feelings she'd harbored for so many years.

"Come, darling," she called across the miles. "Come. Don'
wait."

It was his turn for silence. Was he pulling back? Perhap
she'd misread an offer made out of kindness for a mirror o
her own intense feelings. "Luke . . . ?"

"I'm here. I just got lost for a second in thinking wha
terrible damn fools we've been. We should have been togethe
all along, and we've lost years because of pride, and fea
and—"

She broke in. "It's only time we've lost, thank God. No
each other. Now stop talking and start packing. I need yo
here."

"Give me 'til tomorrow. And Pete . . ."

"Yes?"

A pause. "Tell you when I get there."

She smiled and cradled the phone. She didn't have to b
told.

She went back to Jess's bedside. Her heart was burstin
with the mix of grief at the loss of a friend and joy at th
resurrection of love. The loss seemed all the more unbearabl
because it had provided the bridge to bring her and Luk
back together.

She was at the hospital the next afternoon, too. In th
morning she had been to the store and, as much as there wa
to be done after her absence, she had managed to get every
thing accomplished—or at least put it on hold for anothe
day. Without having made any arrangement with Luke, sh
knew he would look for her to be with Jess, just as he ha
known to call.

The sun had fallen low enough for a golden beam to sla
through the window when Luke walked in. He looked at Pet
and squinted slightly at the sun in his eyes. He appeared t
her exactly as she'd known he would—tan, fit, strong, an
just the least bit rough around the edges, a comfortable ma
to be with.

She got up from her chair at the bedside, walked acros
the room, and he took her into the circle of his arms. The
he stood beside her, his arm firmly around her, his chee

gainst her hair as they looked at Jess. For a long time neither
elt a need to speak.

At last, Luke said, "Let's go home."

It was as if he had never been away.

In the taxi to Pete's apartment, after Luke had consoled
er about Jess, they brought each other up to date. Robby
ad called Luke's attention to the story about Pete's success
rith Tesori in an issue of *People* several weeks before, so
e was aware that her career had undergone a change. Yet
e seemed nevertheless to have an appetite for hearing the
etails. It was a very different attitude than he had displayed
a the past about her involvement with jewels. But could it
.st beyond this "honeymoon" period? Pete wondered. Then
ae scolded herself. There should be no place for doubt now.

As if Luke had anticipated the need to reassure her, when
ete asked about his own business, he revealed that he was
a the midst of selling out to a larger company that would
so have a job for Robby. There was nothing to stop him
om moving east again.

"It'll take me a few weeks to complete the transaction.
ut then I'll be free to live here."

"You'd move back . . . ?"

"You can't run your store by long distance, can you?"

It seemed he was ready to make every concession.

As soon as the door of her apartment closed behind them,
.e hunger that had been building over all the time apart drove
em into each other's arms. She needed to feel his body
gainst hers, to hold him inside her, and she wasn't ashamed
» let him know. The time with Hiro had awakened her com-
etely to her own sensuality, and she felt it now as a gift
ae wanted to bring to Luke—the only man, she believed
ow, that she had ever loved completely, or ever would.

He answered her show of urgency with his own, and within
minute swept her up in his arms and carried her to the
edroom, where they undressed each other.

Desire raged through them, and they made love like two
ood-swollen streams coming together to form a river. The
parate currents crashed into each other with a churning,
rithing force, whipping up waves of sensation, eddies of

pleasure. After the long absence of his touch, Pete couldn'
feel him enough. She roamed over him with her mouth an
tongue, licking his skin, remembering his taste and thrillin
with the renewal of memory. They made love to each othe
with their mouths, until in whispered unison, they told eac
other they were ready to join, and she urged him insid
quickly.

When he thrust himself into her at last and she arched t
receive him to her depths, the two flooding currents mingle
in a single force, rushing onward, faster and faster until the
exploded together as if a huge wave had crested and the
crashed onto a primal shore.

"I love you, Pietra D'Angeli," he said as they lay togethe
and the streams of desire began to gather again. "I love yo
just as you are."

Chapter 9

While Jess lay in a state of limbo for month after month, stretching into a year and then beyond, a pall of sadness remained in Pete's life even though so much else had fallen into place.

After Luke spent half a year traveling back and forth to California to resolve the sale of his business, he settled back into New York. He had made a profit of more than a hundred million dollars on the sale of the company which, along with a share of his inherited fortune, he put into a new foundation devoted to a number of public causes, from saving the Amazon rain forest to furthering medical research. His direct involvement with these interests often took him on journeys to South America or Alaska, but when he came home to rest, it was with Pete. Most of the Grove Street house had been given over to offices for the Sanford Foundation, so he lived mainly at Pete's apartment, but since he still had eccentric work hours, he often went back to the house at night.

Tesori—New York continued to thrive. There were times when Pete's attention to the store conflicted with Luke's desire to be with her, yet he rarely complained, and he never

again made an issue of her involvement with a business tha
served mainly a privileged minority. Of course, Pete mad
a point of neutralizing this objection by taking a large pa
of the growing income she received as a full partner in th
store's profits and putting it into the foundation or makin
large donations to favorite social causes of her own.

As profits increased, Pete had begun to think of expandin
the American subsidiary of Tesori, but she found Antoni
Scappa surprisingly resistant.

"You are busy enough," he told her by phone. She coul
never get his agreement on a suggested new location in Bev
erly Hills or Chicago or even an expansion of the New Yor
space. It puzzled her, since he had continued to open mor
stores in Europe and had once spoken to her about overtakin
all his rivals. With a free hand, Pete thought, she coul
probably wipe out the competition. Eventually her confusio
became tinged with anger. After the success she had mad
from the start, she felt entitled to take her own operatio
further. On several occasions when Pete telephoned Genev
and mentioned planning a trip so they could meet again fac
to face, Scappa made excuses, told her he would be travelin
at the same time on business, or even that he was ill. It wa
clear he was avoiding her.

It would have been unbearably frustrating if she hadn
been able to take consolation from the extra time she coul
spend with Luke.

One other continuing disappointment was the failure t
make further headway in her search for the jewels of L
Colomba. After making the connection to the counterfeite
Pete had engaged a private detective in England to see wh;
other footprints the man might have left behind. By checkin
old news stories about the man whose full name was Geral
Farmer, then researching prison records, the English inve:
tigator had produced one piece of information that, at firs
sent Pete's hopes soaring. At Farmer's trial, one of the wi
nesses had been a young man identified in news reports ;
his son John. The same John Farmer was listed as an annu;
visitor to Wormwood Scrubs. After the prisoner's death,
was the man's son who had claimed his remains so that the

ould be returned to the city of his birth, which was given
s Amsterdam . . . in the Netherlands.

As soon as she had received that information, Pete rushed
o her grandfather. She was hopeful he would be able to
dredge up from his memory some knowledge of Mr. Farmer.

"He recreated half the perfume bottle, Opa, did it per-
ectly. He must have been a man of great skill—the kind of
man who would have made a reputation in the trade."

But Josef could only shake his head. "*Schatje*, forgive me,
ut I cannot remember hearing of anyone named Farmer who
vorked in the jewelry business. Not in Rotterdam, at
east . . ."

"He was from Amsterdam," Pete persisted. "How many
ike him could there have been in the whole of Holland before
he war? He must have been well known in the jewelry business . . ." At eighty, Josef seemed in excellent health, but
Pete wondered if his memory could be completely trusted.
'Think, Opa. Maybe one of your friends mentioned—"

"It's no use, Pete. You said yourself the name was prob-
bly false. Gerald Farmer is not a Dutch name. Your English
ord could have heard wrong. Or the name might have been
adapted from something else—Fermer, Frommer, Foerne—
here are scores of names like that in Holland . . ."

Pete kept the private detective at work. He made an ex-
ensive trip to the Netherlands, but he produced no answers.

It was winter when Fernando de Moratin was finally
rought to trial. The prosecution rested principally on evidence showing that Jess's husband had made secret purchases
of insulin apart from his wife's prescriptions and had told a
couple of disreputable drinking buddies that he had plans to
inherit his wife's money. Both Pete and Luke appeared as
witnesses for the prosecution to reinforce the case. Luke
testified about the venal remarks he had heard from Fernando
at the wedding, and Pete reported that Jess had learned she
was pregnant only a few weeks before the overdose. The jury
was led to understand in the D.A.'s summation that Fernando
feared a child would have diluted his claim to Jess's money.
For his crime, he was sentenced to eight years in jail.

It seemed too little to Pete. A lifetime had been stolen from Jess, who went on being sustained in a twilight existence by machines. But at least it was a kind of resolution, a part of the cloud had lifted.

On the evening that the trial ended, Pete returned home and went to the compact wall safe she had installed at the back of her clothes closet. It was still rare that she wore jewelry on her own time, but anytime she dressed for business she decked herself out with a representative piece from the store, and she kept a sizable number of pieces on hand. However, it wasn't jewelry she removed from the safe tonight.

Luke was sitting in the living room, scanning some project reports from the foundation, when she walked in and laid her half of the perfume bottle on the coffee table. It was the first time he had seen it.

His lips puckered in a whistle. "So that's it," he said, "the little piece of the puzzle that's kept you hopping and hunting for so many years. Beautiful."

"Beautiful but incomplete," Pete amended. "Which is exactly the way my life feels now." She sat beside him on the couch and slipped her arm through his. "There's so much that's right . . . but too much that's not done yet. I expected the feeling to go away once the trial was over, once I saw de Moratin punished. It can't bring Jess back, but there's been some justice, at least an attempt to balance the scales. That feels good. But it only makes me aware of what hasn't been done . . ."

He saw the way she was looking at the bottle. "Pete, that's the way the world is. Not everything gets wrapped up in a pretty ribbon. Some things have to stay incomplete. You have to accept it, get used to it."

"I can't. When I think about the half of that exquisite object that's missing, I remember it was stolen from me—from my father. And I can't help thinking of all the things that were robbed from us along with it. Hope, trust, peace of mind. It seems like nothing can be fair or right again until I find the man who did it and make him pay—make him give up what he had no right to take."

"It was so long ago, Pete. The odds are that your Uncle Vittorio is dead by now—the jewels dispersed."

She shook her head. "No," she said quietly, staring at the bottle. "I know he's not."

"Know?" Luke asked. "How can you know?"

She placed a fist over her stomach. "I feel it in here."

Luke studied her for a long moment. "Pete . . . while you had a chance of finding a real clue, it made sense to keep looking. But now, if you go on, it's just an obsession. And the trouble with obsessions is that you can't keep them in a little box. They keep growing, until they take over everything . . ."

She smiled at him. "Don't worry, I'm not going to let this get so big it comes between us. In fact, I've decided to try something I can do very easily, right here, and still put some heat on Signor Vittorio D'Angeli, no matter how far away he is." Pete picked up the incomplete bottle again.

Luke looked at her curiously.

"I'm going to stop hiding this away," Pete went on. "Tomorrow I'll bring it to the store and start planning a display, put it right at the center of all the treasures at Tesori . . ." Her excitement growing, Pete got up and began to pace as she spelled out the idea. "I'll tell the whole story, put it right out there as part of the exhibit. And I can offer a reward for information—a million dollars, or maybe twice that. It'll generate tremendous publicity—enough, I'm sure, to get picked up by the media around the world. And the idea fits right in with the theme of the store—only this is a treasure that's looking for its other half." She stopped pacing and turned to Luke. "Well, what do you think?"

After a second he replied, "I think you're right about the publicity—it'll double the crowds. But I think you're wrong about the obsession." He stood up and moved to grasp her arms lightly. "I've got a gut feeling of my own, Pete. It tells me we ought to be married, ought to be starting a family. That's treasure enough for me."

"If that's a proposal," she said, "I accept."

A funny look of surprise crossed his face. "I guess it was. But I don't like to think of myself getting left at the altar because you've suddenly traipsed off to track down one more dead-end clue to the end of the rainbow, still looking for your mythical pot of jewels."

"Fair enough. But a wedding should be preceded by an engagement, right? So that means I have a little time before I have to meet you at the altar. If I haven't found my 'pot of jewels' by then, I'll give up."

He hesitated, as though reluctant to bind her to terms she might regret later.

"I mean it," she assured him.

"I don't like long engagements," he said.

She laughed. "We've already waited too long. How about . . . three months?"

"Deal."

They shook hands. Then he kissed her, and a minute later they were making love on the couch.

The next morning she brought the section of perfume bottle with her to work. Wrapped in one of the silk-lined velvet pouches used for the store's best jewelry, she put it in her office safe.

During the day, Pete called a meeting of the window dressers and graphic artists who devoted their time to helping her concoct the displays for which Tesori had become famous. When they were all gathered around a table in the large private salon that also served as a conference room, she said, "I need the most eye-catching idea we've ever had to set off something unique, a treasure unlike anything else we've ever sold or tried to sell."

"What is it?" the display staff asked, almost in unison. Their eyes were already directed toward the velvet pouch, which Pete had left dramatically lying in front of her place at the table.

She opened the pouch and set the top half of the bottle before them, the upper torso that had been made in homage to La Colomba. There were gasps of appreciation.

Then Phil Rosston, the head window-dresser, spoke up. "It's fabulous, Pete. But I can't see exactly what it's used for. Is it a pin . . . a pendant . . . ?"

"Right now it can't be used for anything," she explained. "Because it's missing its other half."

The young men and women around the table turned puzzled glances to her, then to each other. "It may be tough to sell if it's not whole," said one.

Pete smiled. "I'm not selling this time. I'm buying."

She told them the purpose and significance of the exquisite object and what she hoped to achieve by using the store to attract attention to it. "I need maximum exposure," she concluded. "I need as many people as possible—wherever they are in the world—to see this, and know the story, and know that if they can give me the information I need, they can claim a small fortune."

"Why don't you just try to get that story into the newspapers," asked the young woman who assisted Phil.

"Because I don't want it to be just another human interest article that gets read one day and gets wrapped around the garbage the next. I want to keep this out in the open, day after day, while the crowds come. If it's going to be written about, okay, but let it be in papers and magazines all over the world. Give me a setting that's spectacular enough to get television exposure, too."

"That's a tall order, Pete."

"Remember the reward. That'll generate publicity, too. I'll give two million dollars to anyone who brings me the other half of the bottle and supplies information that leads me to Vittorio D'Angeli . . . or to his grave. Now get started," she told the display staff, "because I want to have this in front of the crowds by the beginning of next week."

There was a renewed chorus of complaint, but Pete didn't even listen. She adjourned the meeting and returned to her office to put the bottle back in the safe.

Lottie caught her at the door to report a couple of important calls. "One from your grandfather. He sounded like it was very urgent."

Pete was immediately stricken with worry. "Is he all right?" she asked anxiously.

"Seemed to be," Lottie said calmly. "Just excited. When

I told him you were in a meeting and could call back later he said he couldn't wait. He's on his way over.''

That kind of sudden action was rare for Opa. He lived his life these days the way he had cut his stones, with a great deal of deliberation—mornings lingering over his paper at the Gramercy Park apartment she maintained for him, afternoons and early evenings often spent at the Dutch Club, enjoying movies and dinners with friends he met there. He never seemed to be in a hurry. Yet now he had news that couldn't wait.

It struck Pete that he might have found a link to "Farmer," learned something from one of his Dutch friends.

"Don't keep him waiting a second when he arrives," Pete said. "I want to see him."

Lottie nodded, then told her the second call was from "Mrs. Ivères." The way she pronounced it, the name seemed to come with a blast of Arctic air.

Pete paused. "You'll have to forgive Andrea someday, Lottie. She's mellowed quite a lot since she was your boss.''

"She was never my boss," Lottie said frostily.

Pete smiled. "Right, I forgot. But if you see her here, be tolerant.''

"For you, Pete."

Back at her desk, Pete returned Andrea's call. There was no tension between them as they exchanged opening greetings and business small talk.

Then Andrea came to the point. "I thought we might get together, Pete. I'd like to discuss a business proposition with you.''

Even with all Pete's respect for Andrea, she couldn't see their styles meshing in business, yet she didn't want to discourage the cordial contact. "Any time," she said, and they set a date for Andrea to come to Pete's office at the end of the week.

Pete had just hung up when she saw Josef bustling into the reception area outside. She waved him in and stood to receive him. He looked excited indeed, his blue eyes dancing and his cheeks even rosier than usual.

"What's this all about, Opa? It gave me a start when I heard you were so anxious to reach me."

He pecked her on the cheek and said breathlessly, "Why wouldn't I be anxious? Who else should I call when I have such an emergency?"

"Emergency?"

"I must buy a diamond ring in a hurry."

So it wasn't fresh information about Farmer. But why was he talking about getting a ring in a hurry? Was it a throwback to some past event, the onset of senility?

"Opa, how can buying a diamond ring be an emergency? Sit down, catch your breath, and explain."

"I don't want to sit, and I don't need to catch my breath," he said. And then he broke into a merry grin. "But it's easy to explain. At my age, I don't feel I should waste a minute when I have decided to get engaged."

Pete's jaw dropped. "Engaged? Opa, you've got to be kidding."

"Do I?" His smile vanished, and his countenance grew very sober. "Do I look like I'm kidding?"

Pete stared at him. "Sit down, Opa, please. All this may make a lot of sense to you, but I need a chance to understand."

He settled into a chair. "It's very simple," he said in a patient tone that made Pete feel she was again a six-year-old learning about diamonds at his knee. "There's a woman I've known for some time, a widow named Mary Stone. We've spent a lot of time together since her husband died, and last night I decided I would ask her to marry me. She wanted to think about it overnight, but this morning she said yes. And here I am . . . to buy the ring."

Pete shook her head in bewilderment. "Opa . . . are you serious? Well, I can see you are, but I mean . . . it's a big step . . ."

Josef laughed. "Yes, it is, isn't it? But do you think I should wait and think about it?"

Pete opened her hands, helpless in the face of this extraordinary situation. "Well, I . . . I've never even met the woman."

"I'm not asking your permission, Pete. And Mary will not ask you for my hand."

"No. I didn't mean—"

"You will meet her," Josef assured her sweetly. "But she'll be away for a week, visiting her sister in Columbus, Ohio. It's because she was going to be away that I realized how much I cared for her. And I'm rushing to buy the ring before she leaves today because I know it will be a thrill for her to show it off while she's away."

As Pete continued to shake her head, speechless yet charmed, Josef got up and put his arm around her. "You know, I've been such a deliberate man all my life, walking around gems and examining them—'romancing' them from all angles before I struck. And then I did it wrong, perhaps, as often as right. It might have been better if I'd thought less." He shrugged. "Well, now I have found another gem to romance, and I will not think." He laughed again. "I will strike. Will you help me, *schatje*? I want to buy my bride the most beautiful ring in the world, but I need a discount . . ."

"You'll get the biggest I can give, Opa. Pick out anything you want and pay me a dollar—just for luck."

Josef argued about paying a fair price, but Pete insisted, and at last he headed out toward the selling floor.

"You really are a sly old fox," Pete remarked as he left. "All this time I thought you were going off to your beloved Dutch Club—"

"But I was. That's where Mrs. Stone and I met. She and her late husband were both Dutch. I knew him, too."

"Mary Stone doesn't sound at all like a Dutch name."

"Ah well, it's really Marijke van Steen. But when she and her husband first came to this country, there were lots of forms to fill out for jobs and what-not; and whenever they had to write their names down, none of the Americans could pronounce Marijke or Joop—that was his name. So they became Mary and Joe. And since they wanted to make a whole new start, they Americanized their last name too. Steen means stone in Dutch." Josef went off to choose his ring.

He had been gone almost five minutes before the lightning ⌐lization struck Pete and she raced out of her office.

Josef was poring over a tray of relatively modest two-carat ⌐itaires when Pete dashed up beside him, panting from her ⌐h down the stairs and through the store.

"What about Farmer, Opa?" she said, gulping the air into ⌐ lungs.

He looked at her blankly.

"You said Steen became Stone," she explained. "But ⌐at about Farmer? If a Dutchman went to England what ⌐uld he be changing his name from if it translated as ⌐mer?"

It was only a moment before Josef gave her the answer.

They arrived in Amsterdam the next day.

At first, Josef resisted making the trip. It was too rash and ⌐pulsive to head across the ocean on a midnight flight be⌐se they had a new key to try in a hundred new locks. ⌐ere wasn't a single name that might do for Farmer, nice ⌐ neat; there were several: Landman, Boerman, Keuter⌐r, Fokker, Pachter, or even some variation of one of these. ⌐vould be a daunting task to check them all.

But Pete played on his determination to be a new man. ⌐ we're on the scene, it'll be so much easier than trying to ⌐ it second-hand at a distance, Opa, especially with you ⌐re to translate." When he was still reluctant, she added, ⌐Ve'll only be gone a few days. You'll be home before Mary ⌐s back from Ohio. And you haven't been back to Holland ⌐ver forty years. Wouldn't you like to see your native land ⌐ last time before you 'settle down' into marriage?"

He'd been softening, but this last suggestion nearly stopped ⌐. He wasn't sure he wanted to confront the place where ⌐much that he had loved in the past had been taken from ⌐ or damaged beyond repair.

But Pete knew from the way he had always maintained his ⌐tch habits, read his Dutch newspapers, centered his life ⌐und the Dutch Club, that he missed his roots. Finally, she ⌐suaded him.

From the moment they stepped out of the taxi at Schip
Airport, Josef was at home. He hadn't wanted to rese
rooms at a big three-star hotel but at a small guesthouse
one of the *grachten*, the concentric rings of canals that g
the city the nickname "Venice of the North." After th
checked in, he couldn't wait to stroll through the city. Thou
she was impatient to begin their hunt, Pete indulged his ne
first.

"I was born here, you know," Josef said as they walk
past the Royal Palace on the Dam. "I didn't move to R
terdam until after I married your grandmother. She wan
to be near her family."

He showed Pete where he had lived in the old part of to
called the "Walletjes" because it was near the old city wa
The step-gabled brick canal house had changed little in
sixty-plus years since he'd left. But then, it hadn't chang
all that much since it was built in the seventeenth centu
The main difference now was the red light over the door a
the young woman in a teddy filing her nails in the fr
window and waiting for her next customer.

He showed her his school and the building where he f
learned to cut a diamond. They listened to a giant barrel or,
being played on a street corner, dropping a few guilders i
the brass tin the operator shook in time to the music, a
they took a boat trip through the canals while Josef poin
out more sights than the guide, every detail suddenly perfe
clear in his memory, though he hadn't been back in o
forty years.

"And now," he said when the boat docked, "before
find our Mr. Farmer, you must eat some *poffertjes*." He
her into a gaily painted building, and soon they were ser
plates heaped high with the little dollar-sized, thick panca
soaked with melted butter and coated with powdered sug

Josef pushed his empty plate away with a great sigh
satisfaction. "Well, if you are finished, perhaps we sho
do what we came for."

It took them only an hour at the central telephone excha
to cull out the full list of people to contact. Josef made a
of all the words for farmer and all the likely variations. T

me of the Dutch counterfeiter's son had been given as John
English, which limited the first rank of possibilities to
tings with a first initial J. or the names Johannes or Jan.
Then they started making calls, explaining that they were
•king for the son of a man who had died in England under
: name Gerald Farmer. It wasn't uncommon for the cos-
ppolitan citizens of Amsterdam to speak English, so Pete
d Josef each took half the list. Whenever she ran into
ficulty, Josef helped.

She had gone through more than three dozen names before
te dialed the number for Jan Boersma, who was listed as
: owner of an art gallery.

"Yes, yes, I speak English," the gallery owner said when
te began the conversation. After she gave the reason for
r call, there was a momentary pause, then Boersma ad-
tted that the man known as Gerald Farmer had been his
her. He agreed to meet with Josef and Pete at his gallery
t after closing time.

The Boersma Gallery occupied the ground floor of a grand
l building looking onto the Herengracht, the most elegant
the concentric canals. The proprietor opened the door to
:m and led them to a grouping of chairs at the rear of the
tangular open space hung with modern abstracts by young
known Dutch artists. Boersma was a spare, balding man
his early fifties who wore rimless glasses and moved with
elf-contained precision that bordered on prissiness.

After he reaffirmed that the man who had died in an English
son had been his father, Pete came quickly but tactfully
the point.

"Mijnheer Boersma, I understand your father was a great
ftsman."

"The best. There wasn't a gem he couldn't handle or a
ting he couldn't devise. My father knew everything there
s to know about the jeweler's art. It was only when he
ned to forging currency that he failed." He shook his head.
le was not an engraver."

Now Pete's heart was jumping with excitement. She
ched into her shoulder bag and pulled out the velvet pouch,

loosened the drawstrings, and slid out the top half of
Colomba's perfume bottle. "Could he have recreated som
thing like this?"

Boersma reached for the bottle, and Pete let him take
"He made this piece," the Dutchman said in a hush. "
else it's exact duplicate."

"*Bent U zeker*?" Josef asked, drawing on his Dutch
though it was necessary to ensure the truth.

"Of course I'm certain," Boersma replied, almost
fronted. He studied the bottle again and returned it to Pet
hand. "One does not forget such a sight. I was eleven wh
he began it, and my father worked on it for a long time
nearly two years, as I recall."

Pete leaned forward, her eyes bright. "Please, this is t
ribly important," she said. "Do you remember the man w
hired him to recreate the bottle."

"Oh yes. He was here a number of times while my fath
worked on it. I didn't like him at all, a pushy sort with
nasty temper. But my father could get no other work then
he said. "No one would hire him after the war."

"*Een collaborateur*," said Josef with a sneer.

"Yes, he was a collaborator," said Boersma, his vo
falling slightly. "But he truly believed the Nazis were t
best hope for Holland. Afterward, he had no choice but
work for the man who wanted this copied."

"His name," Pete asked quickly, "what was it?"

Boersma hesitated, for the first time unsure of a detail
his story. "You know, I don't think I ever heard his nam
My father simply called him 'the Italian.' "

It had to be Vittorio, Pete thought. It *had* to be. "Plea
think carefully, Mijnheer. You never heard any name . . .

After a thoughtful silence, he shook his head. "I'm sorry

Josef leaped in. "Where did he take the bottle, do y
know? When it was finished, did the Italian come to get
bottle, or did your father deliver it to him?"

"Oh, I do remember that. It was delivered to Lugano,
Switzerland. I remember because I got to ride on the tr
with him. That was quite a treat in those days. And fr

gano we went to Geneva, to a bank. Then we came home
ain, and a month or so later we left for England.''
That was all Jan Boersma knew. No matter how Pete
mped him, he couldn't tell her where Vittorio D'Angeli
s today.

It was dark when they left the gallery, and Josef took Pete
dinner at the Cafe Americain on the Leidseplein, a glorious
t Nouveau room where the infamous spy Mata Hari had
ld her wedding reception. But Pete was in no state to enjoy
beauty.

"It's over, Opa," she said, holding her wineglass tight but
t drinking. "He's covered his tracks too well. I can go to
gano, but I'll find nothing. No one will have heard of
ttorio D'Angeli, I just know it. And there's nowhere else
look.''

"I wish I could say you are wrong, *schatje*, but I have
thing else to suggest.''

While Pete picked at her dessert, Josef excused himself to
ake a telephone call. He was gone a very long time. Pete
agined he might be calling the woman whose name had
arked this final phase of a wild goose chase.

He was smiling when he came back, which told Pete that
e'd guessed right. "We can be home tomorrow, Opa, if
u're missing your bride-to-be. There's no reason to stay
w.''

"No reason for you, *schatje*," said Josef. "So I will take
u to the airport.''

"Take me . . . Opa—"

"Pete, I am not going back to New York with you. Now
t I'm home, I realize how much I've missed everything.''

"But what about Mary?''

Josef's happy expression grew brighter. "That was my
ll. She is leaving Columbus tomorrow and flying here to
et me. I want her to come and see if she feels as I do—
t we belong here. At home.''

"Belong? You want to *live* here, Opa?''

"Yes—to live where they know how to pronounce my

Mary's name. Marijke. Mar-eye-ka"—he said it slow "Don't you think it's more poetic?"

Pete could only regard her grandfather with amazeme After all his years of being a deliberate, sensible man, was discovering an entirely new self. Perhaps none of plans were cautious or safe, but that didn't mean they were sensible.

As disappointed as she was that their search had be fruitless, Pete suddenly burst out laughing. "You're we derful, Opa, really wonderful."

He smiled. "I am a dashing fellow, eh? Perhaps it is t that life begins at eighty."

The next morning, as Pete hugged her grandfather and on the plane back to New York, she felt reconciled to latest dead end in her search. Somehow La Colomba's jew seemed less important than they had yesterday.

Perhaps, she thought, she would even tell Luke that tl could shorten their own engagement.

Chapter 10

Andrea's suggestion for lunch had been La Grenouille, which was near both their stores. Pete almost proposed an alternative, thinking the role played by the restaurant in her brief flirtation with Marcel might be remembered by Andrea and create some awkward moments. But then she buried the thought. That kind of friction between them had been smoothed away by Andrea's marriage.

When Pete arrived at one o'clock sharp, Andrea was already waiting. Although she had toned down the extreme style of her youth, she still cut a striking figure in her electric-blue Claude Montana suit. Her hair had been toned down a shade or two, Pete noticed, and cut in a soft shoulder-length style. With the multi-colored Ungaro print dress she had worn today, Pete felt they made a good pair.

The mood was instantly amiable, with Andrea insisting on treating them both to champagne, showing none of the defensive edge that had been so common in the past. When she asked casually what Pete had been up to and that led to a mention of traveling with her grandfather and his decision to marry and migrate, Andrea provided an amused and sympathetic audience.

"Proof again that it's never too late," she said, raising h glass to Pete in an implicit toast to their own late-bloomir friendship. "As it happens," she added, "Marcel and I a also thinking of moving away. That's why I thought you a I might be able to do business."

The proposition unfolded. Marcel had never felt complete at home in America, Andrea began. He had come to Ne York originally because Claude sent him as his deputy, ar he had stayed because Claude died. Then Marcel had bee reluctant to go back to Paris, where his father cast an eve larger shadow. But he had become increasingly restless ar discontented in the jewelry business, until he was ready acknowledge that it was only the accident of birth that ha brought him into it.

"He's reached the point now where he's ready to tu everything over to me, which is what I've always wanted. Andrea looked thoughtfully into her glass. "The irony is tha without him there as part of it, I realized I wouldn't enjc going to work myself. I always liked the struggle betwee us, you see, the competition to show our best. Do you u derstand, Pete?"

"I think so."

"That's why we're going to close down the store."

"Close down?" Pete echoed in astonishment.

"Only in New York. Dufort and Ivères will continue Paris, where a cousin of Marcel's has taken over. But he a I will live in the country. Can you see me as Madame Ivère mistress of the family château?"

Pete understood now the change that was overtaking A drea. She was making herself over to take charge of th Château d'Ivères. "You'll be a success at whatever you do, Pete said, and meant it.

Andrea's eyes sparkled with a look that was at once mi chievous and ambitious. "You know, there's a vineyard the château," she said. "The wine's always been good, b not great, and they've never bothered to turn out more tha a few thousand bottles of the stuff annually since Napoleon time." She leaned closer to Pete, as though sharing a secr with a conspirator. "I'm going to set that place on its heel 'ete. Just give me five years and I'll have turned Château 'Ivères into another Château Mouton and be doing forty iillion in export.''

Pete laughed. "If anyone can do it . . ."

"But don't tell Marcel. He thinks I'm ready to settle into ie quiet country life and raise babies, not grapes."

"I'll carry your secret to the guillotine," Pete said. "But iy guess is Marcel won't be too surprised when you start to vheel and deal."

Andrea revealed finally what she wanted from Pete. "I iought you might be interested in buying all our inventory. 'he Paris store is already fully committed, and it's doubtful ve can dispose of very much before we close. Dufort has ever been able to move merchandise as fast as Tesori. I ever managed to budge D and I far enough from their fusty nage."

Pete considered the offer. She felt confident that she could egotiate a fair price, and by taking on enough inventory for whole additional store, she might be able to break the talemate with Antonio Scappa over opening another Amer- :an branch of Tesori. Pete had always thought she could do s well in Beverly Hills as in New York, if not better.

"I'll do it. Come back to my office after lunch. I'll check iy banks to make sure they'll cover the purchase, and we an sign a letter of agreement."

With business out of the way, they spent the rest of their me at the table in a rapid-fire exchange about all the things iat would have occupied two old friends—views about cur- :nt fashions and gossip about women they recognized at ibles around them.

When they arrived back at her office, Pete found the display taff waiting to show her several ideas for exhibiting the ottle. She told them to return in half an hour, after she had nished her business with Andrea.

"What's this special exhibit they were talking about?" .ndrea asked.

In the past Pete had not been friendly enough with .ndrea—or trusted her enough—to talk about the lost jewels f La Colomba. Even the trip to Amsterdam she had passed

off briefly as merely "a sentimental journey." But it occurre
to her now that the contacts Andrea had built up over th
years might yield the elusive connection to Vittorio.

While she launched into the story and an explanation f
the exhibit, Pete took the velvet pouch from the safe an
brought out her piece of the perfume bottle. "The other half,
she said at the conclusion of the story, "is with my missir
uncle—along with a forged replica of this . . . and a colle
tion of jewelry that, on today's market, might be worth an
where up to thirty or forty million dollars."

"An interesting story," Andrea said passively. "Now fo
give me for rushing you, Pete, but I have my own work
do. Could you confirm your financing and get the lett
ready . . . ?"

"Of course," Pete said. She put the bottle back in th
safe, moved to her desk, and placed a call to the store
primary bank.

Yet she couldn't help feeling surprised and vaguely di
appointed by Andrea's reaction. No one who had seen th
bottle had ever before given such an uninterested respons
—though, of course, Pete reflected, Andrea had other thing
on her mind. And as charming as she could be sometime
Andrea Scappa would always put her own selfish needs firs

Through the next couple of days and then the weeken
Pete concentrated on preparing for the bottle to go on displa
at the start of the following week. She didn't really expe
her idea to succeed in leading to a solution when so ma
years of searching had failed. Yet it would bring crowd
anyway, and earn publicity for the store. And—once it w
over—she would be able to say she had tried everything ar
relax into her marriage to Luke.

On Sunday evening, after she had spent all day at the clos
store in final preparation, Pete went home to Luke . . . ar
he gave her the engagement ring.

Only hours later the alarm shattered the night.

By mid-morning Monday, the police were beginning to fi
in some of the blanks. Without any doubt, they said, th

break-in had been handled by professionals, people who had great knowledge and experience of alarm systems in similar stores and the means to disable them. The essential proof that it had been an inside job lay in the one extremely valuable item that the thief or thieves had elected to steal: a rare but incomplete jeweled artifact that had been secreted in Pete's personal safe. The thief had to be someone who knew the bottle was there.

The suspect list included Lottie, the display staff, perhaps others in the store or outside it that these people had told. They were all brought in and questioned by the police.

"None of 'em strike me as suspicious," Pete was told by the detective in charge of the investigation. "They swear by you, Miss D'Angeli, and so far we haven't turned up even a whiff that any of 'em mixes with the kind of bad company who'd know how to do a smash-and-grab like this one. You think maybe there was some stranger who happened to pass by your office door when it was open and see you with that bottle? Or maybe you ordered a sandwich to eat at your desk, and a delivery boy got a look . . ."

Pete couldn't remember having the bottle out of the safe when any strangers were around.

It was only after the detective left her office that Pete recalled the lunch with Andrea—and her visit afterwards.

Almost as soon as she did, Pete tried to dismiss any suspicion. What motive would Andrea have had? She didn't need to steal any kind of jewel; she had a storeful of her own. Would she have coveted the bottle because it was rare and unique? But it was incomplete, imperfect . . .

Or had the act been pure malice—Andrea's friendship feigned to disguise a pathological hatred and jealousy she had never truly overcome?

No . . . her easy warmth had seemed too genuine.

The idea was absurd. Even if Andrea had wanted to take the bottle, how could she have managed it?

With professional help.

As the owner of a large jewelry store, Pete knew that circulars were sent around by police and insurance companies providing names, descriptions, and often photographs of men and women who had a record of jewel robbery so they could be spotted as soon as they appeared in any store. Using such lists, Andrea would have been able to make fairly quick contact with someone who could take the bottle.

Still, the question remained: Why?

Rather than go on nursing even a shadow of unfair suspicion, Pete grabbed up the phone and dialed the telephone number for D & I, never forgotten from her days as an employee.

"I'm sorry," Pete was told after she asked for Andrea, "Mrs. Ivères is out of the office."

"This is Pietra D'Angeli. Have her call me as soon as she gets in."

"She won't be back today, Miss D'Angeli. Mrs. Ivères is traveling on business."

Traveling. But what business would she be doing if she and Marcel had already made plans to close the store?

"Is Mr. Ivères in?" she asked quickly.

"Yes. I'll put you through."

When Marcel came on the line he was all charm and appreciation. Andrea had told him that Pete would be relieving them of their inventory.

"Marcel," Pete asked finally, "where's Andrea?"

"She had to go abroad."

"Without you?"

"She's gone to see her father, Pete. I wouldn't be welcome."

"I didn't think she was welcome, either . . ."

"She may not have an easy time with the old man, but she told me she felt a need to see him one more time—almost as if she had a premonition that he was going to die. She left quite suddenly."

Pete hesitated. "Marcel, there's been a robbery here. Something valuable was taken from my safe. And . . . I wanted to ask Andrea if she knows anything about it."

"Knows anything," Marcel echoed heavily. "What do you mean, Pete? How could she know . . . ?"

Again, the suspicion seemed suddenly absurd. Because

ndrea had visited her office a few days ago, did she deserve
be moved to the top of the list of suspects?

"Never mind, Marcel. I shouldn't have bothered you about
. When's Andrea coming back?"

"Tomorrow or the next day. It was just for a day or two,
he said."

Pete lowered the phone. Of course Andrea would be back.
Would a thief take something, run away, and then come back
face an investigation?

Coincidence, nothing more. The bottle had been taken.
ndrea had gone to see her father. Two events that had
othing to do with each other.

As Vittorio got older he slept less and less. For he *was*
Vittorio—it was *that* life he often relived when he lay awake
a bed, staring at the ceiling or casting an occasional glance
t the woman who slept beside him.

And because these days he felt less comfortable as Vittorio
an he did as Antonio, he rose earlier and earlier to begin
is day, to keep busy with the activities that for so long had
rovided his masquerade.

Vittorio was a failure, he had to admit, one of the losers
ho'd had to run for his life, leaving behind a reputation as
criminal, an accomplice of murderers.

But Antonio was a success. He'd never run from anyone.

A shroud of mist coming in off the lake was still hovering
ver the streets of Geneva as Antonio arrived at Tesori. He
fted the protective gates, turned off the alarm devices with
special key, unlocked the front door to let himself in, and
en locked the door behind him again. It was hours before
pening time. He would pass the time reviewing store re-
eipts, reports from agents in foreign cities who were looking
or new store sites, approving sketches of new pieces from
is workshops, and sometimes just puttering with the dis-
lays, rearranging them.

Occasionally, too, when he came to the store very early,
e went down to the large vault in the basement and opened
p one interior compartment to which he alone had the com-

bination. And there he would look at La Colomba's jewel
Except for the few pieces he had given Boersma, the colle‹
tion was still intact. Vittorio had needed to use the necklac
to pay Boersma for his work, but Antonio was not in such ‹
corner; he had only needed to use the collection itself ‹
collateral for the large loans that had built him a store an
bought him an inventory. A few pieces shown to sympathet‹
bank officials, that was all that had been required.

This morning Antonio didn't go down to the vault, hov
ever. In fact, he hadn't been to look at the collection for ‹
long time. He could take comfort in the fact that it was hi‹
but he had gotten little joy from it otherwise. His wife ha‹
never been able to wear it. He'd even been afraid in the en‹
to expose the jewelry to craftsmen, as would be required ‹
dismantle it and reset the gems.

Antonio went to his office to work. As he approached th‹
door, he saw a shaft of light falling through the open fram‹
A desk lamp left on last night, he assumed.

Turning into the office he saw that it was indeed the lam‹
at his desk.

But as he crossed the office, he saw something else th‹
stopped him dead in his tracks, as though he had seen a ghos‹
Lying smack at the center of the small arena of light projecte‹
by the lamp was the top half of the perfume bottle—the pa‹
he had forged.

What was it doing out of the vault?

The way the small half-figure of a woman lay under th‹
light it seemed somehow to be invested with life—as if ‹
was there to accuse him, a piece of the very soul of L‹
Colomba.

He hurried forward, his first impulse to seize it, hide ‹
away again.

At that moment she stepped out of the deep shadows in ‹
corner of the room into the gloomy edges of the lamplight‹
Antonio froze. It *was* her ghost.

"So it's true," she said. "Antonio Scappa is Vittori‹
D'Angeli—a thief, a war criminal, an insult to humar‹
ity . . ."

Now he saw the true outlines of the apparition. "You!‹

He spat out the word, then continued to the desk and grabbed up the bottle. With it safe in his hand, he whirled back to his daughter. "How did you get in here? How did you get this from the vault . . . ?"

Andrea spoke from the shadows. "Yes, I was always locked out, wasn't I? But you allowed Franco to have a set of keys. I went to him first. He was quite ready to help as soon as I told him why I was here . . . told him who our father is."

Antonio stared at Andrea as she advanced farther into the light. "As for that thing in your hand, I didn't have to get it out of your vault. I stole it from the safe of your niece in New York. You hear that, dear father? I stole it . . . I'm a thief, just like you." A grim ironic smile tilted her mouth.

Antonio took a deep breath. In his daughter's statement he heard redemption, not accusation. He understood now why she was here. "So you've found out," he said flatly. "Now what is it you want to keep your silence? A share of the store? Very well, you've shown you can manage, and it's getting too much for me, anyway."

Andrea shook her head slowly. "No, Papa"—she gave a mocking edge to the endearment—"that's not what I want, not at all."

"What, then?" Antonio demanded impatiently. "Tell me. You know I don't want to be exposed, you know I'll pay. So don't drag this out forever. Tell me and I'll pay, and we can get on with our lives."

Andrea stared at him, her expression mingling pity and fury. "I wish I had known sooner," she said softly. "I could have forgiven myself so much more easily for hating you."

"Tell me!" Antonio roared. "I don't give a shit what you think of me. You're here for blackmail, and I'm ready to pay. All right. Let's get our business done."

For another long moment, Andrea eyed him with contempt. How terrible it was to have such a man for a father, she thought. And then she realized that he was not her father, not really. He was a stranger, a man she'd never known—a man to whom she'd come only to do business.

"Very well," she said. "These are my terms . . ."

* * *

It came to her in the middle of the night. Not an alarm this time, but a realization, a searing truth that broke into her fitful sleep and sent Pete bolting up in bed as if from a nightmare.

Beside her, Luke woke, too. The light of a nearly full moon came through the penthouse windows, so he could see her nude body in sharp silhouette, even see the faint tremor that vibrated across her breasts. He reached out for her, his warm palm laid soothingly on the flat of her naked back. "What is it, darling?"

"Antonio," she said in a whisper, staring into the darkness. Then her voice rose. "It's Antonio. Andrea stole the bottle to take to him."

"Why would she?"

"Because she's like me . . . she never forgot."

Luke shook his head in confusion.

Pete turned to him fully. The story spilled out of her, how she had found the bottle when she was only a child, had been told then that it was a magical talisman, a piece of a fairy tale. "Andrea could have seen it, too, sometime long ago. She wouldn't have forgotten. Even if she didn't, there were other clues she must have put together. The way her father went after that necklace, or maybe things from her mother's side . . . Andrea must have realized her father was Vittorio. That's the only reason in the world it would have made sense for her to take the bottle."

"So," Luke said, "now you know where your uncle is . . . you know he must have the collection. What are you going to do?"

Pete thought. Could she make Antonio surrender La Colomba's jewels without the proof that he'd possessed them illegally, by means of forgery? Could she even challenge his identity? She could make claims, yes, but that's all they would be. How did she recover the proof now that it had been carried off to another country, locked away? There could be years of lawsuits.

And she was Antonio's *partner*. How would it look that she had taken his money to create an overwhelmingly suc-

sful enterprise—and then turned on him with a wild tale
upported by any evidence? It would become one of those
less controversies—a topic for an article in *People*, a
ure on "Sixty Minutes." A woman with an ax to grind,
spectable businessman defending himself.

I'm not sure what to do," she said. "But at least there's
e to decide. He isn't going anywhere."

That's right," Luke said. "There's time." Luke put his
s around her and gently pulled her down again. His ca-
es soothed her, made the biggest problems float out of
sciousness while feelings took over.

Maybe," she whispered, "it doesn't even matter. Once
uldn't live without jewels. But that was before you gave
all the fire and light I need."

le laughed softly as he brought himself over her, and they
ed.

Chapter 11

When the detectives came back the next day, Pete [told]
them that she had an idea now about who had been be[hind]
the robbery, but that she did not intend to press charges [so]
they could call off their investigation.

"I don't get it," their chief said. "You're just gonna [eat]
the loss?"

Pete smiled at his jargon. "It'll give me indigestion, L[ieu]-
tenant, but that's right. I'm going to eat it."

There was some consternation. The police didn't like [peo]-
ple who "played games," Pete was told, calling them o[ut to]
work on a case that then evaporated. But by five o'cloc[k in]
the afternoon, the situation was resolved. The store wa[s al]-
ready cleaned up, new windows had been put in, the al[arm]
systems had been fixed and reset, and the store was read[y to]
open again for business tomorrow.

Pete was on her way out when the phone rang.

"Hello, cousin," said the voice on the other end.

It took a second for Pete to recover. "Where are you[?"]

"At Kennedy Airport."

"And the bottle . . . ?"

"You'll see." She would be in the city in less than an ur, Andrea went on. She wanted to meet.

"I'll be home," Pete said.

"Fine. And, Pete . . . will you tell my uncle to be there, ?" Andrea hung up.

They were assembled in her living room by six o'clock, ke and Pete, her father and Anna. Maddy had been given night off. Steve couldn't stop pacing, on edge the whole ie as he talked about Vittorio, reliving his treachery, work- himself up with talk about taking action against his thiev- , brother now that he knew where to find him.

Another half hour went by and Andrea did not arrive.

"More game playing," Luke suggested.

"No," Pete said. "She'll be here."

The doorman rang up ten minutes later to announce Mr. d Mrs. Ivères.

When the bell rang and Pete went to open the door she v neither Marcel nor Andrea. Piled high and wide just side the door frame was a collection of large leather-bound es with gold fittings.

Andrea was off to one side. "They're all yours," she said. ours . . . and your father's. With my compliments and logies."

They were jewel boxes, Pete realized now. La Colomba's lection.

Having carried it to Pete's door, Andrea was prepared to and leave with Marcel, uncertain of Pete's feelings vard her.

But Pete summoned them both in. They were cousins, after And friends.

Over the champagne that Pete opened, Andrea described deal she'd struck with Vittorio. To save the reputation he built under a false name, and the business he'd started h stolen collateral, he was prepared to give up not only collection, but to surrender to Pete his share in the Amer- a branch of Tesori.

At first Steve said it wasn't good enough. Vittorio had to

answer, too, for the massacre of dozens of partisans i
village to which he had dispatched his murdering Nazi fath
in-law.

"That's between you and him, Papa," Pete said, "if
want to reopen such horrible wounds."

Steve looked at Anna, and she reached to take his ha
"Perhaps I can let it rest," he said. "Perhaps Vittorio wa
even responsible and I blamed him for that, too, only beca
. . . I needed someone to hold accountable."

They opened the boxes then, one after the other, until
room glittered with the multi-colored light of a thous
precious gems. Like children dressing up, the women t
on one piece after another, while the men gasped and
plauded and, finally, broke into giddy laughter at the
geous, priceless excess that surrounded them all. Seeing A
and Andrea decked out in certain pieces, Pete knew that
would bestow them as gifts, and share more of the collec
with Andrea. There were too many jewels for any one wor
to wear—any one but a woman like La Colomba.

By the light of a candle on her dressing table, Pete
looking at herself in the mirror, naked except for a l
necklace of perfect Golconda diamonds, the most fabul
piece of them all. She could sense the ghost of her gra
mother smiling over her shoulder—sense that past Pietra
ing within her. Certainly, Pete thought, the beaut
courtesan must have looked at her own reflection like
sometimes, dressed in nothing but her gems.

"Come to bed," Luke said.

Pete stood and walked toward him, the diamonds shoo
sparks of light as she moved. He reached up for her, and
lowered herself.

But before reclining, she paused to remove the neckl
There was no need for glittering adornments when she
in her lover's arms, there never would be.

La Colomba had known that, too, Pietra D'Angeli had
doubt as she lay down next to Luke. The light and the spa
and the precious beauty was part of their love, part of w
they would always make together.